THE COZY CORGI COZY MYSTERIES

COLLECTION THREE: BOOKS 7-9

MILDRED ABBOTT

Cover, Logo, Chapter Heading Designer: A.J. Corza - SeeingStatic.com

Main Editor: Desi Chapman

2nd Editor: Ann Attwood

3rd Editor: Corrine Harris

Recipe and photo provided by: Rolling Pin Bakery, Denver, Co. - RollingPinBakeshop.com

Visit Mildred's Webpage: MildredAbbott.com

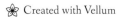 Created with Vellum

COZY CORGI COZY MYSTERIES
BOOKS 7-9

Quarrelsome Quartz
Wicked Wildlife
Malevolent Magic

CONTENTS

QUARRELSOME QUARTZ

WICKED WILDLIFE

MALEVOLENT MAGIC

for
Nancy Drew
Phryne Fisher
Julia South
and
Alastair Tyler

A Cozy Corgi Mystery

Quarrelsome Quartz

MILDRED ABBOTT

QUARRELSOME QUARTZ

Mildred Abbott

A pop sounded, drawing my attention to the glowing embers in the river rock fireplace. I'd lost track of time. I could've sworn the fire had been roaring pleasantly only moments ago.

Settling back into the sofa, I adjusted the book so the light from the dusty purple fabric of the antique lampshade filtered onto the page. The words seemed to swirl together, lists of precious stones and crystals correlating with chakras in the body and differing attributes. Black obsidian helped a person feel grounded. It was recommended they sleep with it in their pillow or clutched in their fist. I reread the suggestion, thinking I had misunderstood. Who would sleep with a rock in their pillow or in their hand?

I hadn't misread it.

How bizarre.

I moved on to rose quartz, a pretty pink crystal that assisted a person to connect with love.... I stopped right there. I wasn't sure if it meant romantic or self-love or something else, but I didn't need to know. After ending a relationship a few weeks before, love was the *last* thing I wanted to think about. Although, I supposed it hadn't really been a relationship, perhaps just the beginning of one, or the promise of one... something.

Good grief. That was exactly why I was skipping rose quartz. I didn't want to think about it, didn't want to spend any more time trying to figure it out. So I moved on again.

Clear quartz correlated with the seventh chakra and was apparently the master healer of the stone world. They even amplified the energy of other crystals while assisting a person to connect to their higher self, while also acting as a spiritual guide. I had to reread that too. A crystal could be a spiritual guide?

I had to shut my eyes and remind myself to keep an open mind. My mother was a strong believer in the power of the elements. And with the weeklong New Age conference, Estes Park was about to be filled to overflowing with people just like her. *Elemental Power* was written by the keynote speaker of the event, so I wanted to be prepared. But I figured I was wasting my time. None of this was sinking in to any useful degree.

A loud snort brought me back to the moment, and I reopened my eyes to peer through the two doorways that led to the front of the bookshop, where Watson rose from his nap. He stretched his tiny corgi legs in front of him while arching his knob of a tail in the air, and let out an exaggerated yawn. Finally, he gave a little shake, glanced out the large wall of windows at the growing night sky, and then leveled his stare on me.

I had no trouble reading his expression, and I offered him a glare of my own. "I know it's past dinnertime, but you had endless snacks today, as always. You'll survive, trust me; you're not even close to withering up and blowing away."

Watson trotted from the front room of the bookshop that held general fiction and new releases, through the following room made up of science fiction and fantasy novels, and joined me in the mystery room, which was my favorite location in the Cozy Corgi bookshop. He cast a judgmental glance at the fireplace, clearly thinking, not for the first time, that his mother was a crazy woman. Which considering I'd opened all the windows so I could light a fire in the middle of August, probably proved Watson correct. Finally, he plopped down in front of the Victorian sofa and chuffed.

Giving up on the quartz, I flipped through the rest of the pages, but nothing called out to me. Mixed in with all the precious stones and New Age artwork were photos of the author and artist, Aurora Birnbaum. She was beautiful in the expected, ethereal way. Most of the photos were of her modeling the gems in one fashion or another, but there were a few candid shots from her life as well—speaking to large crowds of people, trips to India, with her husband who drew a design on the ground as she stood nearby. These photos were just as prevalent as the ones featuring the crystals. While they seemed a bit indulgent, at least I'd be able to recognize Aurora if she came into the store, even if I wouldn't remember any of the elemental powers.

Watson chuffed again, more emphatically.

Instead of answering his demand for dinner, I held the book out to him. "What do you think? Would you take a hit out on me if I put a piece of black obsidian under your dog bed? It might help you feel more grounded."

He chuffed again.

"Yes. I agree. I should stick to fiction." With a sigh, I gave up, closed the book and stood. I'd return it to the New Age section I'd set up at the front of the shop to correspond with the conference, and wing it for any of the practitioners who might come in during their stay. I'd been doing the same thing with my mother and stepsisters, so I supposed, if it was good enough for family, it was good enough for tourists.

After gathering up my purse and slipping on Watson's leash, I paused to look around the store. I hadn't stayed after closing for quite a while. In the months of heavy tourist traffic, it had gotten easy to be caught in the pure business aspect of my dream bookshop. I needed an hour or two to connect with it again the way I had when it had first opened several months before. Sure enough, with the coziness of the fire in my favorite spot in the shop, and the warm aroma of the Cozy Corgi bakery overhead that now permeated every inch of the space, that little time worked its magic. Granted, it would've worked even better if I'd been reading a novel instead of something that felt like a strange kind of homework, but still...

Another admonishing chuff from Watson interrupted my wave of fondness for my little bookshop, and I acquiesced, extinguishing the fire, flicking off the lights, setting the alarm, and locking up after we exited the front door.

"All right, buddy. Let's head home; dinner is waiting. As are books with actual plots." We made it all of five feet before I halted at the shop next door. Dim light filled the darkened space, and I could just make out Zelda near the rear of the store. One hand was pressed to the back wall while the other rubbed her temples. Even from this distance, it was clear to see the weight of the world rested on her shoulders.

Knowing that Watson wasn't going to appreciate what was about to happen, I tapped on the window.

Zelda flinched and her long brunette hair whipped around her face as she jerked toward the window. Her wide blue eyes appeared clearly strained, despite the distance between us. She blinked, then visibly relaxed as she recognized me and hurried through the store to unlock and throw open the door. "Fred! What in the world? I thought you'd gone home hours ago."

"And I figured you'd still be at the conference."

"I should be." She sighed and nearly melted against the doorframe. "Tonight's just registration. It doesn't officially begin until tomorrow, but I'm already completely overwhelmed." Zelda cast her gaze back to the shop. "Every other year I've hit the ground running and was absolutely devastated by the time it was over, but I think with the added stress of owning Chakras... Well, it just changes things."

"I'm sure once you get past this week things will get better. It's a lot to take on with the conference happening and the official grand opening of Chakras all at once." Zelda and Verona had been transforming the old candy shop to the left of the Cozy Corgi into their version of a New Age mecca for months and had a soft opening a couple weeks before. At the beginning both of my stepsisters seemed over the moon with excitement. But as time went on, bickering between them increased, and Zelda seemed more drained by the day. I reached out and squeezed her shoulder. "I'm sorry that I've been so busy at the bookshop the past couple of days and haven't been able to come over to help. But I've got some time tonight if you'd like."

She smiled sweetly and patted my hand. "Like you haven't done enough over the months that we've been getting ready. But..." She released me and stepped back into the shop, making room. "Why don't you come in? We've made quite a few changes since you were in last. Dad and your mom have been miracle workers." Zelda chuckled. "As have your uncles. Even though it's not Percival's style, he and Gary definitely have a flair for decorating."

"I'd love to see what you've done." I walked in, but had to turn around as Watson's leash jerked me to a halt.

He sat in the doorway, glaring.

I couldn't help but laugh and patted my thigh. "Come on, grumpy pants. We won't be very long. You'll still get your dinner."

With the second tug on his leash, Watson complied, though his glower increased.

Zelda bent with a flourish and ruffled the fur between Watson's foxlike ears, earning a glower all her own. "We've got some dog treats in the back that will hold you over."

Watson perked up at his favorite word and gave a little hop.

"I thought that would work." Zelda straightened and gave me a wink before shutting the door and leading us through the shop. "I *also* have a little treat of the human variety, as long as you can keep a secret."

A sharp rap on the door, followed by Watson's yip, caused us both to flinch and whirl around. A large man stood shadowed, peering in with his hand pressed to the glass.

"Who in the world would be dropping by this time of..." Zelda squinted, then her shoulders impossibly tightened to an even greater degree. "Oh, it's Duke Riser." She spared me a glance as she hurried to the door. "He's the manager of the YMCA, where the conference is being held." Zelda flung it open. "What's wrong?"

Without waiting, he barged past, scanning the store. His gaze fell on me, then moved on with a shake of his head. "Is she here?"

"Who?" Zelda stood frozen by the door.

"Aurora." Disgust laced Duke's words. "She's supposed to lead a midnight..." he waffled his hands "...some event or other you New Agey people like for the people who paid for early registration. Her husband and assistant are there, but who cares about them? And they weren't any help at all." He continued to inspect Chakras like Aurora was hiding around every display.

"I haven't seen her at all, not even when I registered." Zelda started to shut the door, then paused. "Why did you think to check here?"

Duke finally stopped his inspection. "She and your sister were talking about your shop and I can't find Veronica either, so I figured they came here."

"Verona."

"Who?" Duke looked at Zelda as if she were speaking a different langue.

"My sister is Verona, not Veronica." At Duke's eye roll, Zelda managed a more patient response than I felt. "And I haven't seen either of them. I'm sure they'll show up. Verona is probably helping prepare stuff in Aurora's room. Did you check there?"

"Unlike the attendees of the Spirit, Health, and Heart Conference, I am *not* a moron. Of course I checked her room. I could smell sage seeping from under the door, though no one answered." Duke strode back to Chakras' front door. "The entire YMCA smells like burnt sage and we haven't even gotten through the first night." He halted by Zelda. "If you see Aurora, tell her that if she thinks the organizers of this batty conference are done with her, she's going to be bowled over by me. I'll sue her and the entire Spirit, Health, and Heart Conference for breach of contract. And to get the place fumigated while I'm at it."

Without another word, he turned and stormed off into the night.

The three of us stared through the empty doorway for several moments before Zelda shut and locked it with a sigh. "I don't think I can take any more. I can't even blame Duke at this point. I want to just crawl into a hole and hide."

Watson whimpered pitifully.

"Oh, right." Zelda chuckled softly, and her voice lightened somewhat. "I promised you a treat, didn't I. Promised all of us a treat. Well, now I need it more than ever." She motioned for me to follow. "Come on then."

"I should say no. I'll use commiserating with your stress as an excuse, though. Katie did a run-through of the quiches for your opening tomorrow, and I think I ate my own weight from the constant sampling. But that's just one thing Watson and I have in common; neither one of us can turn down a treat." As I repeated the euphoric word, Watson renewed his hopping as we followed Zelda through Chakras.

The only illumination was the innumerable fairy lights covering the hardwood ceiling, which created a soft glow over the space. In the soothing, dim light, I didn't notice any changes since I'd been in the last time. I was still pleasantly surprised at how the store had come together. I'd expected the shop to be a huge mishmash of incomparable items—random, brassy, and scattered, rather like the twins themselves. Despite Chakras displaying the true essence of Zelda and Verona, the store was utterly charming, even if I didn't know what half the things were. It fit in with the feel of the town perfectly. I supposed I shouldn't have been surprised; Estes Park had its heyday in the 1960s. Though a lot of the residents of the little Colorado mountain town had plenty of money, there was still an undercurrent of those naturalistic, flower-child days of the past. Chakras captured that whimsy with wind chimes, brass gongs, statues of fairies and mermaids, crystals and jewelry, and pleasingly displayed clothing that looked like it was designed for yuppies who preferred tie-dye to ball gowns.

Passing through a doorway of silver beads, Zelda flipped on the light and led us into a small break room with a compact kitchenette. She opened the cabinets and pulled a plastic bag from beside a row of jarred granola, then withdrew a large dried strip of jerky. "It's buffalo and especially for dogs. Paulie special ordered it for us. We're going to have monthly pet yoga sessions, so we thought it might come in handy."

Clearly expecting one of his favorite dog biscuit treats, Watson sniffed the withered-looking strip cautiously, then his chocolate eyes widened and he snatched it from Zelda so quickly she nearly lost a finger.

"Good grief, Watson. No need to be ungracious."

Watson didn't attempt to make amends for his rudeness, only stared pleadingly at me and gave another tug of his leash. I complied, and he trotted back through the beads into the store to devour his new treasure in private.

I turned back to Zelda. "I don't know whether to thank you or be angry at you. It looks like Watson's going to have another favorite treat, and I can't imagine special-ordered buffalo jerky is cheap."

"You can afford it. The bookshop is doing wonderfully." Zelda waved me off and turned toward the freezer, shoving aside several items until she finally turned back around with two pint-sized cartons in her hands. "Here you go." She thrust one at me before going to a drawer and retrieving two spoons.

I studied the label that read Frozen Tofu Delight and

then gave a scowl at Zelda that Watson would've been proud of. "I think you and I have different definitions of what constitutes a treat." Only then did I notice the specific flavor and nearly gagged. "Red bean and avocado? You must've lied before. You *are* angry at me for not helping the past couple of days. But trying to kill me seems a little extreme."

Zelda handed me a spoon and laughed. "Just try it."

Suddenly I longed for the days when I'd been an only child. Sure, there were times when I'd wished for a brother or sister, but there'd not been any moments like this, and no matter how much I'd grown to care about Zelda and Verona, I wasn't sure any love was worth red beans and avocado. Even so, I removed the lid and glanced down, determined to at least give it the old college try.

To my surprise, it didn't look half bad. In fact, it seemed rather... familiar.

In between bites, Zelda smirked at me from where she was leaning against the counter. "Go ahead. Try it."

I dug my spoon in and lifted up a small cluster with brown speckles that didn't resemble red beans or avocados. No sooner did the morsel touch my tongue than I pointed the spoon at Zelda. "Cookie dough!" I dug another bite, bigger that time and got a different chunk of heaven. I didn't bother to swallow before speaking. "I would know this anywhere. This is Ben & Jerry's Half Baked, cookie dough and brownie batter."

"Can't be. That's *not* what the carton says." Zelda grinned wickedly and took another heaping spoonful.

I'd caught Zelda at the ice cream parlor a while ago, sneaking behind Verona's back, so I knew that she didn't stick to the no-processed-sugar rule that the twins claimed to live by. "You're brazen to keep this here! What if Verona gets hungry for—" I had to check the label "—Frozen Tofu Delight?"

"She won't. She doesn't really like any of the flavors, but she absolutely detests the red bean and avocado. This is as safe as if it were invisible." She took another bite and sighed, her eyes rolling back in her head. "And trust me, I've more than earned it."

"Well, you're brave, I'll give you that. And thank you for not making me try anything flavored with red beans and avocado." We ate in silence for a few moments, each relishing the sheer ice cream perfection. Part of me hated to spoil such a treat, but it seemed that Zelda needed to vent. I'd never filled that role for her, or Verona, for that matter, though we'd been in the same family for over six years, but I supposed there was no time like the present to try on a deeper sisterly role. "I've noticed things between you and Verona have been a little tense lately. I bet that will get better as you guys settle into a routine and everything." As soon as the words left my mouth, I worried that it sounded like I was trying to gossip about Verona.

Zelda didn't seem to notice, or at least she didn't mind. "You can say that again. It's like I don't know my own sister. She's always been a little more..." She waggled a spoonful of ice cream in the air. "Dogmatic, I suppose. But she's downright controlling at the moment. Ever since we decided to open Chakras." Zelda winced and then backpedaled. "That's not really fair. She's been a little more intense ever since we decided to open the store, but it hasn't really been until the past few days that she's gone into full-blown controlling." Once Zelda started to talk, it was clear that she truly had needed to vent, as the words seemed to pour out of her. "I know it's just the conference and having Aurora and Wolf Birnbaum lead some of their sessions here at the store, but I'm not sure how much more I can take. Don't get me wrong. I was nearly beside myself when Aurora agreed to take such an interest in Chakras, but I didn't know it would be like this. I've always looked up to her—not as much as Verona does, but quite a bit. But the reality is different from what I expected." Zelda glanced around as if she too expected to see Aurora Birnbaum lurking around the corner and lowered her voice. "For someone who's so in touch with a deeper level of spiritualism and awareness, the woman is rather awful. Duke's not the most pleasant of men, but, like I said, if he's been dealing with Aurora, I can't blame him."

The whole family had heard of little else for weeks besides Zelda and Verona's excitement about Aurora and Wolf headlining the conference and incorporating Chakras into a daily event. That had been why I'd special ordered a few of the Birnbaums' books for the Cozy Corgi. I hadn't met them in person yet. With my history in publishing, however, it wouldn't be the first time I'd met someone famous in a book genre who didn't quite live up to the persona they had crafted for public consumption. "I'm guessing she's a little more businesswoman than spiritual leader?"

Zelda winced and took several moments before she responded. "It's not my place to comment on someone else's beliefs or spiritualism. And I shouldn't discount what she claims. They've built a huge career and helped multitudes of people." She lifted the half-eaten pint of Ben & Jerry's like she held a whiskey bottle. "Like I have any room to judge. I'm not exactly as I present either, am I? And yet here I am, complaining about Verona while eating this behind her back."

I didn't really see the correlation between sneaking ice cream and the New Age guru treating those around her in a horrible manner, but I'd never quite understood the dynamic between Zelda and Verona. I'd simply chalked it up to a twin thing.

Zelda shook her shoulders and tossed back her long brunette hair. "Enough of that. I'll do an extra-long meditation this evening before I go to bed, another one in the morning, and then throw myself into the conference. I'll get grounded and have a new perspective."

"Black obsidian is good if a person is wanting to be grounded. I believe you're supposed to sleep with it in your pillowcase."

The look Zelda gave me made me wonder if I'd sprouted feathers. "You're more like your mother than I realized."

Feeling like a phony, I shrugged. "I was reading one of Aurora's books before I came over. I can't actually say I understood much of it."

Zelda chuckled and relaxed. "Honestly, it makes me feel better that you don't. I thought I'd stumbled through a portal into a different dimension." She walked away from the counter, carrying her ice cream as she headed toward the beaded doorway. "Come on. Enough of my complaining. Let me show you what we've been working on. I think it's the highlight of Chakras."

Mimicking her example, I helped myself to some more ice cream and followed her into the shop. We turned instantly to another beaded doorway, though this one was strung with nearly transparent jagged crystals. I held a strand as we slipped inside. "Are these clear quartz?"

Zelda gave an approving nod. "You're a quick study, Winifred Page. Not that I'm surprised." She flicked the switch beside the door and more dim fairy lights came on overhead.

Across the room, Watson sat up straight in obvious surprise, what little remained of the large piece of buffalo jerky clenched in his mouth.

Zelda laughed at his clear annoyance at being disturbed. "It seems Watson approves of the room."

Clutching the jerky, Watson lifted his nose in the air and trotted past us to find more privacy.

"Those treats might actually be worth what you pay for them. Typically anything I give that dog lasts a matter of ten seconds, tops. That's rather amazing." Before I could inquire exactly how much the jerky cost, Zelda flicked another switch and I all but forgot about premium jerky for dogs. Stones and crystals of every color had been mixed throughout the river rock that covered the walls. Each of them had been backlit and glowed with ethereal beauty. On the far side of the room, a narrow fall of water trickled over the stones into a small, shallow pool. "Zelda..." I continued to spin slowly, unable to take it all in. "This is... I don't know how to describe it. It's unreal."

"I'm glad you like it."

"Like it?" I leveled my gaze on her. "It's like I just stepped into Narnia or something."

She let out a pleased laugh. "We think so too. This is the room that we'll rent out for special events, like the ones Aurora and Wolf will do this week. Different healing and yoga sessions, guided meditation. It will also be where we'll have one of the massage therapists from Pinecone Manor come down a few times a week."

Everywhere I looked, there was one more tiny detail that I'd missed—a streak of moss growing over some of the stones, small flowering plants scattered here and there, clusters of crystal pendants dangled from the ceiling on thin silver chains. Shoving all the individual things together should have been too much, way too much. But somehow, it wasn't. "This is quite literally perfect. I'm blown away."

Zelda visibly relaxed even more. "I'm so glad you think so. I know you've never said it, and you're kind enough you never would, but I figured you were nervous having Verona and me on one side of the bookshop, and probably doubly worried since our husbands are working on opening the store on the other side of you, but we really do want this to be a place that you're proud of."

Words were stolen from me for a moment. I *had* been worried. Even so, I'd not expected Zelda to be concerned with it. The store was theirs, they could do whatever they wanted. I was touched that I'd even been a consideration. "Zelda... you don't need to think twice about that. But even if you did, you definitely don't now. The whole thing is stunning. But please don't worry about me. Make it what you want."

She was only a couple of inches shorter than my five feet ten frame, and thin and wispy in comparison, but easily threw her arm over my shoulder and gave me a quick squeeze. "We're family. Of course your opinion matters. Especially considering how angry some people in town are that we're opening a New Age shop. I don't want that to affect you."

None of us had expected there to be any resistance to the shop. Estes wasn't exactly narrow-minded. "The church is still bugging you?"

She nodded. "Yes. Just today there was a note shoved under the—"

Tinkling chimes sounded, cutting her off.

From the main room, Watson let out a muffled bark as if he still had his mouth full, and then Verona's voice cut through the space. "Zelda? Are you here?"

Though she flinched in surprise, as Zelda raised her voice, she retained some of the ease that had returned as we'd spoken. "Back in the crystal room, with Fred."

"Oh! Good!" The tap of Verona's footsteps over the hardwood floor grew louder as she neared, though they paused as she greeted Watson. Another second or so, she parted the crystals hanging over the door and entered. A nervous expression covered her face that Zelda had demonstrated only moments before. "Do you like it?"

"Yes. I was just telling Zelda. It's complete perfection. So much so it would almost make me consider coming to one of your crystal healing thingamabobs." As soon as the words left my lips, I realized they weren't true. "Or massage. I will definitely schedule a massage."

Verona beamed. Once more, her expression matched her twin. They were completely identical, the only difference between them was Verona's long blonde hair compared to Zelda's brown. "I'm so glad. So very glad." Her demeanor shifted instantly and her blue eyes hardened as she turned to Zelda. "I can't believe you left opening night early when Aurora and Wolf were right there."

Zelda's ease vanished. "I'm sorry. I just needed to get away."

"Well, Aurora noticed. How do you think that looks?" Verona took a couple steps closer to her sister. Though I knew neither of them had an ounce of violence in their bodies, her posture was aggressive, as was her tone. "I'll tell you how it looks. It looks like we're not committed, that this is just a store or a hobby to us, not a lifestyle. She could change her mind in a moment and decide to do their events at the conference space instead of here. I wouldn't blame her."

"*You* might want to be concerned about our reputation

with *Duke*, since he's local. He was in here a while ago looking for you and Aurora." Zelda tilted her chin. "And as far as she's concerned, I suggest you be careful, Verona. Maybe what will make Aurora change her mind is if she hears you talk about this place as if you're worried about profit and exposure as opposed to fostering a *lifestyle*."

Verona gasped. Feeling awkward, I was about to step through the crystals and give the twins their space, when Verona gasped again and snatched the carton out of Zelda's hand. "What is this?"

"Nothing." Zelda reached for it, but Verona pivoted and stepped out of reach. "It's... just... Tofu Delight."

Tilting the carton toward one of the glowing crystals on the wall, Verona's eyes narrowed, she dug in a finger, retrieved a small mound and popped it into her mouth. She straightened to a rigid pole instantly and spit the bite back in. "Ice cream." She took a step back, glaring at Zelda with a mix of horror and betrayal. "Sugar." She held up the carton to read the fake name, then shoved it back at Zelda before whirling around and storming away.

"Here, Fred, hold these while I make some room." Mom dumped a handful of silver necklaces with purple crystals hanging from them into my hands and began rearranging the other jewelry on the display. "I made these several months ago after I got in a huge shipment of amethysts, then put them away for safekeeping. Of course, I spent the past several weeks searching for the safe place. Barry found them this morning under the vacon in the deep freezer when he went to make breakfast."

"You put them in the deep freezer?" I attempted to untangle the silver strands, then paused. "Wait a minute— what's vacon?" As soon as the words left my mouth, I remembered who we were talking about. "Hold on, don't answer that. It's vegan bacon, isn't it?"

Mom stood back from the display and nodded, though I wasn't sure if it was at me or if she was satisfied with her rearranging. One by one, she took the necklaces from me and situated them in the newly cleared section. "I don't remember putting them in the freezer, but it worked. There they were, safe and sound, happy as could be."

"I didn't know there was such a demand for amethyst that it would require a hiding place." I tried to keep the teasing tone out of my voice. I knew how important Mom's jewelry making was to her.

"At one point in history, amethyst was valued as highly as diamonds." Katie, my best friend and owner of the bakery above the bookshop appeared from nowhere, holding a platter of mini quiches. "It was also known as the jewel of the gods." She started to say more, doubtlessly some further, random trivia about the purple rock, but glanced down as Watson emerged from his hiding place from under my broomstick skirt and swatted her foot with his paw. "Oh no, buddy. No quiche for you, too much dairy."

"He doesn't need it anyway. Zelda's already given him two huge portions of buffalo jerky." Feeling slightly guilty for rubbing it in Watson's face, I snagged one of the quiches and popped it into my mouth. "I'll be glad when this is over. I think I've gained ten pounds over the last week from your quiches alone."

She grinned, her round cheeks flushing in pleasure. "You're not the only one putting on quiche weight. I've gone through more than three hundred of these little guys today."

"I'm not surprised. The girls are having a really amazing turnout." Mom took the last amethyst necklace from me and hung it with the others. "It's so sweet of them to give me my own spot in their store for my jewelry."

"I just have to say, I love your hair." A small, yet powerfully built, stunningly beautiful woman stepped between Mom and Katie and reached out with her right hand, lightly fingering the beaded coil Mom had woven through the one remaining strand of auburn in her long silver hair. "This is beautiful."

"Oh, thank you, dear." Mom beamed and returned the

gesture, touching the green crystals woven into the blonde dreadlocks. "And this is lovely. Aventurine?"

"Yes! It enhances intelligence." She cast her wide teal blue gaze at Watson, then gave a giddy wave to me, then Katie. "Hi there. I actually came over to snag one of these little pies from you." She plucked one of the quiches off the tray Katie held.

"Help yourself." Katie didn't correct her on what the pies actually were but gave her a once-over. "I have to say, you're adorable. Rather like a New Age Barbie. One with muscle tone."

She clapped her hands in delight, which caused a waterfall of quiche crumbs much to Watson's satisfaction. "Thank you. That's such a sweet thing to say." She stuck out her tiny hand. "I'm Tabitha, Aurora's assistant and her personal yoga and Pilates instructor."

As we did a round of introductions, I had to bite my cheek to keep from laughing. Katie's description was spot on. Tabitha had the body, face, and cheery personality of a life-sized Barbie, all dressed in a skintight, tie-dyed wrap that left little to the imagination.

"I also love your shoes, dear." Mom glanced down to where Watson was snorting at the blue-and-gold tie-dyed stilettos. "I think you might be standing on some quiche."

With a giggle, Tabitha lifted a foot and made room for Watson to snag the morsel. "Thank you, again. They're gorgeous, right? They were a gift from Aurora." Confusion crossed her features and she glanced across the store to where the New Age guru chatted with a small group of people. "She gave them to me yesterday. First gift I've gotten in the three years I've worked for her." She twisted her ankle to show off the shoes. "But they're Kamala. I looked them up online. They cost over a thousand dollars a pair!"

Katie nearly choked.

Gracious as always, Mom patted Tabitha's shoulder. "They really are stunning. You must be quite the assistant."

"Most of the time, I don't think so." Her confusion deepened and then vanished without a trace as she snagged two more quiches. "Wolf's demonstration is starting in a few minutes. I'm going to take these to him, if you don't mind. He works sooooo hard." With another giggle and wave, made awkward by crumbling quiches, Tabitha headed back toward the crystal room, Watson scampering happily in her crumb-filled wake.

We watched her go, then Katie eyed Mom and lowered her voice to a teasing tone. "What did she say those stones in her hair were for again?"

"Intelligence, dear. Aventurine helps with—" Mom's eyes widened and she swatted at Katie with a laugh. "Oh, stop it. You're awful."

As they chatted, I looked around Chakras. The place was packed. There were a few locals I recognized, but most were people I'd never seen before. I assumed the vast majority were from the conference. It was a very good thing, for many reasons. Simply for the success of the event and the shop, but even more than that, it was keeping the twins occupied. I'd witnessed many spats between Verona and Zelda, but I'd never seen anything like this. The coldness between them was palpable. Verona seemed furious, and Zelda was clearly humiliated. I was still kicking myself for not acting quicker the night before. It hadn't even entered my mind that the two of us had been standing there eating ice cream when Verona walked in.

Maybe the complete success of the grand opening would ease the tension between them.

Katie nudged my shoulder, bringing me back to the moment. "I'll catch you later. I'm going to go make the rounds again."

"You don't have to play waitress. It's enough that you're catering the event." I snagged another quiche from the tray, despite my sentiments.

Katie shrugged, followed my lead and snatched up a quiche of her own, and only chewed for a couple of moments before speaking. "It's kind of fun. Plus, all the walking counts as exercise, or close enough. And it's not like Ben and Nick need me at the Cozy Corgi. They can handle things on their own, and everyone's over here anyway." She leaned in, lowering her voice just enough to only be heard by Mom and myself. "Everyone's raving about the quiches, except for the headliner herself. Kind of surprised me. She was so nice to everyone else, but when I offered her some, she looked at me as if I was trying to give her sewage. Wanted to know if all the ingredients were *certified* organic." She winked. "I told her I got up early this morning and milked the cow myself and turned it into cheese. She didn't seem to find that humorous."

Mom swatted at Katie a second time. "You are too much. No wonder I adore you."

"The feeling is mutual, Phyllis." Katie straightened and returned to normal volume before spinning and heading away. "And great job on the crystals. They're going to be a smash hit."

As we watched her go, Watson returned, slipped under the hem of my skirt to avoid the crowd of people walking by, and rested his head on the toe of my boot.

Mom gave me a meaningful stare. "You know I don't

like to be negative, but I have to agree with Katie. There's something a little..." She shook her head but didn't finish the thought.

"What?" It really was rare for my mom to say anything bad about anyone. Or even to start to, in this case.

She sighed, giving in. "Just the way she treats Verona and Zelda. And"—she held up a hand—"I know they're off because of that ice cream incident last night, though I'm glad the cat's out of the bag finally on *that* little issue, but still... When Aurora is talking to the other people in the shop, she has this kind, gentle, almost ethereal tone, but as soon as one of the twins comes up to her, she becomes condescending and demanding. Almost"—she winced —"arrogant."

At that moment, Aurora Birnbaum let out a bell-like laugh as she departed from her group of admirers. Ethereal was a good descriptor for the woman. Though I assumed she was in her midfifties, she had an ageless quality—tall, willowy, and graceful. Soft chestnut hair was fixed on her head in a loose bun and long tendrils floated around her face. At first glance, the way she held her chin had looked like the mannerism of a gracious deity as she wove through the customers in the shop, pausing here and there to whisper and chat. But, after hearing Mom and Katie's take on the woman, I couldn't help but now interpret it as elitist. Apparently feeling my attention, her soft gray eyes flicked to me and held my gaze. After a moment, she smiled slightly and looked away once more.

I turned toward Mom. "They live in Estes during the summer, right? Then spend the rest of the year in Sedona. Haven't you met her before?"

Mom shook her head. "I've seen Aurora and her husband, Wolf, from a distance a few times while Barry and

I were out to dinner or something, but no. I've never been introduced. The twins have met her before, but I think they're having a different experience this time, from what I can tell. It's kind of like what your dad used to say about certain preachers or politicians. Sometimes when good people get in positions of power, they let it go to their heads. I know Barry met Wolf at a farmers' market a couple of summers back. He felt like the man was genuine and—" She sucked in a breath as her eyes went wide. "Barry! I completely forgot. With the truck in the shop, we only have the Volkswagen, and he was getting ready when I left. I told him I was just gonna drop these off and come right back to get him." She patted her thighs. "I must've left my purse and phone in the van." She got on tiptoe and gave me a quick peck on the cheek. "I'll be back in a little bit, dear. Sorry." And with that, she was gone.

I pulled my cell from the pocket of my skirt, but there was no missed call from Barry. Doubtlessly, he was patiently waiting at home. He was used to Mom's forgetfulness, and he was so easygoing there was a good chance he'd not even noticed.

Without Mom or Katie by my side, I felt a little awkward just standing there. Honestly, I was a little out of place. In the bookshop, I'd have endless topics of conversation, but here, I wasn't exactly sure how to approach people. I didn't mind the aspects of the New Age shop or the lifestyle the twins embraced or the more hippie, flower-child sensibilities Mom and my stepfather had, but beyond that, I was at a loss. I knew others found it odd that I could lose myself in a series of books and feel as close to the characters as I did to flesh-and-blood friends. Still, I was afraid if I tried to converse about some of the items in the store, I'd accidentally offend someone.

A soft smattering of applause issued from behind the wall of clear quartz that led into the crystal room. Taking the distraction, I nudged Watson lightly, waited for him to emerge from his hiding space below my skirt, and the two of us headed over. I might not have understood most of the things that were happening at Chakras or the conference, but that didn't mean I wasn't curious.

I pulled the curtain of crystals aside enough so Watson and I could slip inside. There were only a few people in the beautifully glowing space. Tabitha stood in the corner of the room, at the rear of the group, hands clasped at her breasts and staring in blatant adoration at the man in the center, sitting cross-legged directly in front of the trickling water feature. In many ways, Wolf Birnbaum matched his wife. Long and lanky and dressed in a similar fashion, the kind that on the surface portrayed casual and simple, but after a moment's inspection revealed it to be designer and expensive. He was attractive, like Aurora, although different. She was soft, glowing, and had that natural beauty that only money could buy. Wolf was weathered and rugged, but he too had a softness about him.

Watson and I had barely stepped more than a few feet into the room when Wolf clapped his hands, causing Watson to flinch.

"Sorry about that, little one." Wolf's voice was soft as well. "I didn't know we had a dog in our presence, a corgi no less." His gaze flicked up to me. "Animals are a true gift from the universe."

I wasn't exactly sure how to respond to that. "Well, he is pretty special to me."

"What do you call him?"

"Watson." As I spoke his name, Watson looked up at

me, but then he returned his attention to Wolf, who patted the floor in front of him.

"Come here, Watson." Wolf smiled gently at Watson and patted the floor again, and with his other hand retrieved a large deck of cards that sat beside him. He fanned them out in front of him with a smooth motion. "Let's give you a tarot reading."

It was my turn to flinch. I'd heard of tarot cards, but I wasn't entirely sure what they did. I assumed it was something like fortune-telling. "Oh no. Why don't you do that for someone else? Watson's a little bit of a grump. I doubt—"

Words fell away as Watson left my side, sauntered toward Wolf, and plopped down in front of the fanned-out cards.

Well... What in the world?

Watson wasn't jumping for joy like he did with a few select people, a *very* few select people, but he seemed intrigued nonetheless.

Wolf's gaze rose to mine. "You can join him if you would like."

Being curious was one thing, experiencing tarot firsthand wasn't something I wanted to do. But neither did I want to be rude at Verona and Zelda's big event. I crossed the space and knelt beside Watson. Maybe I just needed to understand it. That was how my brain worked, facts and puzzle pieces clicking together to form reality. Without thinking, I reached out and pulled out one of the cards to inspect. As I turned it over, another card slid free, and I realized I was holding two of them. I cocked my head as I inspected, blown away. "These are stunning. Absolutely beautiful."

"Thank you. Aurora believes that art is a gift from the

creator. A way to mimic our higher power, creating a shadow of what's already been created if you will."

I didn't look at Wolf as he spoke, I was too captivated by the cards. Both because of their intricate beauty and marveling that such creations could come from someone as abrasive as Aurora. One was a painting of two small mice on the edge of a stone basin filled with water, their tails entwined in a beautiful spiral, and surrounded by a golden yellow field of wheat. The other was painted in rich oil tones and portrayed a unicorn. It glowed white in the center of a dark, lush forest, and at its hooves was a small round pool of water.

Wolf snatched the cards from my hand. He studied them for a heartbeat, then gave an approving sound as he smiled at me. "The mice are the two of cups, the unicorn is the high priestess."

I nodded, once more trying to figure out the correct response. Finally I had to admit I wasn't going to find it. "Okay."

He chuckled. "Not a believer in all of this, are you?"

I shook my head. "Sorry. The cards really are lovely, though."

"No need to be sorry." Wolf laid the cards out, one at a time as he explained. "The two of cups represents a partnership, it indicates that you are one of those parts. It could be romantic or friendship. Whatever the case, it's a source of happiness for you, and the other party is one on whom you can count on at every turn." He motioned toward the unicorn card. "The high priestess is a sign of good judgment. And can often mean that, for you, intuition may be more valuable than intelligence at times."

A chill trickled down my spine.

"Do those make sense for you?"

"I... um... I guess so." They most definitely did. Over my months in Estes, I'd had to learn to trust my instincts or my gut, as my detective father had called it, over and over again. As far as partnerships and relationships I could trust? Well... I had more of those in Estes Park than I'd ever had in my life. With family, friends, with my furry companion seated by my side.

Wolf didn't wait for any more response and refocused on Watson. "Your turn. Pick a card."

Watson simply stared at Wolf and narrowed his eyes in his grumpy fashion. After another moment, Watson peered up at me with that look that clearly stated, *Good grief, can we go home and get a snack already?* Then, impatient as always, he collapsed on his forepaws and lowered his head to the floor with an exasperated huff.

At the puff of air, one of the cards moved. Wolf, who'd been silent during the small exchange, retrieved it and turned the card over, then laid it out for both of us to inspect. I leaned forward to do just that, while Watson ignored it entirely.

The card was equally as beautiful as the others. A snowy owl, its wings spread, each feather containing such minute detail I nearly wanted to stroke them. The longest feathers on either side morphed into long, glistening swords. The owl hovered over the background of a starry black night with the liquid moon directly above its head.

"Well, well. You two are quite the pair." Wolf smiled at me and then focused on Watson. "This is the knight of cups. It tells us that strength is not the only source of victory, but also cleverness and savviness of mind." He reached out to pat Watson on the head.

True to form, Watson pulled back after only a second of contact. He'd gotten better at allowing himself to be petted at the bookshop, but he still did so begrudgingly. There were only a few people who'd managed to steal his heart. Still, he didn't seem overly irritated by Wolf. There was no growl or annoyed groans. Just retaining his boundaries in pure Watson fashion.

"Truly, the two of you are fascinating." For his part, Wolf didn't seem the least bit offended and smiled at me once more. "It was the start of a very good draw, a positive one. Would you like to keep going?"

I shook my head before I could even think of manners or remind myself that this was Verona and Zelda's big opening and that I needed to play along. I managed to come up with an excuse quickly enough. "No. But thank you. My... sisters own the shop. I should let the guests have their turns." Before he could reply, I stood and stepped away, Watson following at my heels. I offered a brief glance over my shoulder and a wave as we passed back through the crystals. "Thank you."

Pausing for just a second outside the crystal room, I gave a little shake of my body. I knew I was being ridiculous. They were just cards, he was just a man, just like the sky-blue necklace of celestine crystal my mom had given me that hung around my neck was just that—stone and metal. But still. The reading had felt... revealing somehow. But it most definitely wasn't clear-cut fact and didn't click into place like puzzle pieces.

I was going to let the twins keep their New Age conferences. I'd stick to books, and Watson, I was certain, would stick with treats.

Speaking of books, I decided that was exactly what I needed. We'd go back over to the Cozy Corgi, and if Ben and Nick didn't have customers they needed help with, I'd curl up on the sofa in front of the fire and get lost in a book while Watson curled up in a sunbeam from the front window and got carried away in dreams.

We started to walk through the shop, but it was crowded enough it was slow going. A man was informing a large crowd directly in front of the main door about events at the conference later that evening, while Katie meandered between the people, still peddling her mini quiches.

Whether I was being silly or not, I didn't want to wait or barge my way through, so instead, I went the other direction, and led Watson toward the back door. I'd barely cracked it open when a voice reached my ears. "I'm sorry I offended you. Of course we'll shut down the store tomorrow." It was one of the twins, though I couldn't distinguish which. "We'll put an announcement on the front door so everyone will meet you at the Samson statue."

"Trust me, Verona. A sign won't be needed. Everyone will want to be at the ceremony. They won't be trying to bang down the doors of *your quaint* shop." Though the belittling tone was completely different from what I'd heard from her as she spoke to the guests in Chakras, Aurora Birnbaum's voice was instantly recognizable. "I must say, I'm surprised at you, putting profits over enlightenment. When Wolf and I agreed to do special events here, we believed we were doing so for kindred spirits. Not souls who saw spiritual enlightenment purely for financial betterment."

"We don't. *I* don't." Verona sounded panicked, and close to tears. "In fact, we'll close the store the entire week except for your and Wolf's special events. The rest of the time, we'll close down while the conference is in town."

Watson's hackles rose in what I recognized as a protective stance. He might not be as crazy about Verona as he was for her father, but he clearly counted her as family and part of his pack.

Before he could start to growl or move forward, I gave a gentle restraining tug on his leash. Verona wouldn't want to be observed in such a situation. Slowly, I began to back away, trying to close the door softly enough that nothing would be heard.

Aurora's voice reached me before the door click closed. "I think that's a wise decision, Verona. After all, I know you're not as all tie-dye and healing auras as you like to portray. As I've already demonstrated to you, it wouldn't take much for me to share your not-so-little secret."

THREE

"You know, I think Watson and I will stay here. It's been a long day."

Katie sent me a puzzled glance from where she was wiping up the marble countertop of the Cozy Corgi bakery. "Why in the world would you do that? We closed down early so we could attend. It's not like anyone's going to be shopping. I'm pretty sure the entire town is going to be there, tourists and residents alike."

I settled my gaze on Watson who was scurrying happily back and forth along the base of the counter devouring the crumbs as Katie cleaned. "I know. Still... it sounds nice to curl up and read a book. In fact, it sounds even better to do that at home. Maybe I'll even go to bed early."

"Fred." Katie paused, planting her hands on the counter and leveling her stare at me. "What's going on? It's not like you to miss a big event in the town."

No, it really wasn't. Nor was it like me to be evasive where Katie was concerned. But I hadn't shared with her the exchange I'd overheard between Verona and Aurora the day before, or talked about the uncomfortable stress between the twins. Not that Katie and I were above gossiping with each other, but when it involved my family, it felt like a sort of betrayal of Verona and Zelda's privacy.

"Is this what's getting to you?" Ben lifted a flyer as he entered the bakery from the stairs and headed our direction. "Saw you looking at it earlier."

Katie snatched it out of his hands as he drew nearer, glanced at it, then rolled her eyes. "Oh, good grief." She thrust it back at him. "One of those Looney Tunes came up here passing those out earlier today. I told them to mind their own business."

Nick paused from wrapping up the few remaining pastries and grinned at his brother. "She did. You should've seen her. It was hilarious. Katie told that lady to let people live their lives however they wanted and then suggested that she might be less inclined to barge into people's business if she were happier and ate more pastries."

Katie nodded. "I sure did. Gave her a free lemon bar. Although I think it's going to take more than one dose of heavenly butter and sugar to change that lady's disposition and the others of her ilk."

Ben chuckled along as he slid the flyer on the table where I was sitting and bent to lavish affection on Watson while he gave me a knowing expression.

Though the twins had only worked at the Cozy Corgi for a matter of months, and both were quiet and reserved, the two of us had gotten to know each other through our love of books and storytelling, and Ben was developing an uncanny knack at reading me. Although the same was true for me as well.

My life seemed encompassed by twins. Zelda and Verona, their husbands Jonah and Noah, and now Ben and Nick, all three *identical*. At first, I'd not been able to tell Ben and Nick apart save for the scar on Ben's bottom lip and a similar scar on Nick's right eyebrow. But now, I barely needed to glance at the brothers to distinguish between them. There was just a different feel to them. Even if there wasn't, Ben was one of the few people who Watson deemed worthy of hero worship, so there was that constant clue.

I didn't bother glancing at the flyer. Ben was right. I'd looked at it several times throughout the day. It was from the same church that had been a thorn in Verona and Zelda's side over the past several weeks leading up to the opening of Chakras. The flyer was condemning the conference, Chakras, and the ceremony that was happening in less than an hour.

Katie studied me in my silence, her eyes narrowing. "It is bugging you, isn't it?"

I shrugged, then began to fold the flyer into little squares as I spoke, deciding to be honest. "Mom's crystals and Zelda and Verona's New Age shop is one thing... But something about the Birnbaums is throwing me off. It was like Wolf could see into Watson and me during the card reading yesterday."

"Nah, that's just the tricks of the trade. They say things that are broad enough that they can fit for anybody." Katie waved me off. "Either way, it's not like you to not be curious."

"I was, but I think my curiosity was satiated, at least as far as the Birnbaums are concerned. And the ceremony at the elk statue is their thing, it's outside of the Spirit, Health, and Heart Conference events."

"I still love that their acronym for that thing is SHH. It's like they're telling the whole world to be quiet." Though Katie started to laugh, she cut it off abruptly as her eyes widened in realization. "Although, I suppose that's exactly what they're trying to do. There's a huge focus on meditation from what I understand. Maybe they *are* telling us to be quiet. As far as the event today, it's big for the town." She refocused on me again and pointed at her T-shirt. Typically she wore shirts with fun or snarky designs, but this one showed a massive bull elk lifting its head in a bugle with the words *Never Forget, Samson, 1995* beneath. "Even after all these years, Estes Park is still mourning him. For crying out loud, I wasn't even here and I feel like I missed something wonderful by never knowing him."

"Well, even that... a séance at the statue of a dead elk seems a little far-fetched." I held up the folded flyer.

"It isn't a séance," Nick whispered from where he was still putting away the pastries. His cheeks burned bright as if he were surprised by his own daring.

Ben took over from his twin. "It's just a ceremony, connecting to the power of nature and animals." He scraped a long strand of dark hair behind his ear as his eyes narrowed. "Although I don't understand why it's being held at his statue instead of where Samson was killed, but I guess it's just the more recognizable place. In our heritage, it was a belief that all physical features and elements are spiritually alive. So much so that they have a power that helps control the world and impacts fate." He glanced at his brother, who was blushing in an entirely different way. "There've been plenty of people who've compared us to demons and Satanists because of that."

I wanted to kick myself. Though it wasn't a constant topic of conversation, Ben had spoken a few times about some of the cultural beliefs and traditions of the Ute tribe. Most often, our conversations revolved around a character in a book he was writing based on one of the Ute legends, so it was easy for me to look at it from a literary standpoint as opposed to something that impacted daily life. And I knew the twins had faced discrimination over their short lives. I didn't want to add to that.

"Well…" I rose, making a show of walking to the trash and throwing away the folded-up flyer. "When you put it that way, it sounds like something a little too wonderful to be missed."

Sure enough, the entire town was present. The massive bronze statue of Samson was at the intersection of Highway 7 and Highway 36, and the police had shut down all roads in a quarter-mile radius. They stood guard at the road-blocks, and several of them were scattered among the crowd.

Watson, Katie, the twins, and I had to park the car a long way away and walk. The crowds spread out over the roads, grassy medians, and sloped yards of businesses and homes. Despite the innumerable people, there was a somber stillness over the crowd.

Katie elbowed me gently and pointed toward the spot a few feet away from the base of the statue. "There's Leo."

Right on cue, Leo Lopez turned his handsome face toward us, smiled, and waved for us to join him.

"Come on." Katie took the lead, starting to squeeze her way through the edge of the crowd to head toward the vortex.

Watson slowed, eyeing the surrounding horde of feet.

I bent and scooped up Watson, putting his forepaws over my shoulder and cradling his fluffy corgi butt in my arms like a big toddler. "Sorry sweetheart, better humiliated than squished."

He grunted, cast a murderous glare in my direction, but

didn't squirm, which told me he wasn't entirely opposed to the situation.

Ben patted his head encouragingly from over my shoulder.

I had to reposition Watson before he slipped. "Okay, I keep threatening, but it's diet time."

Within a few minutes, the five of us had meandered through the crowds and reached Leo. He was wearing his green park ranger uniform. I hadn't seen him in it in ages. It brought to mind the first time Watson and I had met him as we'd entered the national park.

Leo gave Katie a quick hug hello and attempted to do the same for me, but Watson began to thrash in his excitement and managed to reposition himself into Leo's arms as he lathered Leo's face with doggy kisses. Leo laughed while squeezing his eyes shut to avoid Watson's tongue. "Good to see you too, buddy."

Across the way, on the other side of the statue, I noticed Duke Riser at the edge of the crowd, his arms crossed, as he glowered. His face was flushed, in what I assumed to be anger.

Near him, were Mom, Barry, my uncles, Percival and Gary, and the twins' families. Zelda caught my gaze and smiled appreciatively.

It was good that we'd come. This may not have been an event for Chakras, but it was one more communication of support to my stepsisters.

I started to suggest that our little group join them, but Aurora and Wolf Birnbaum started to make their way up toward the statue.

Leo put Watson safely on the ground and leaned in, whispering loud enough so he included Ben and Nick with Katie and me. "Glad you guys could make it. I know it's kind of a strange event, but it's important. This town responds to any mention of Samson, but it's been long enough that some of the fervor around it has passed, and poaching is starting to go through the roof again this season. This might help get more awareness. Not to mention, the huge donation the Birnbaums are making to the national park."

"I read that the guy who killed Samson was planning on selling his—"

Katie didn't get to finish sharing her knowledge as Aurora raised her hands. "Welcome everyone! I'm so glad you made time in your day to help us honor this legendary creature." She laid one of her delicate hands on Samson's bronze flank. Though I didn't have any fond feelings for the woman after Katie's experience with her and with how Aurora had treated Verona, I couldn't deny that she made quite the impression. The gentle summer breeze played with the tendrils of hair that fell around her face and fluttered her long, flowing tunic in a way that made her resemble a mythical nymph. I could see the appeal that drew people to her. "Before we get started, my husband will lead us in a grounding meditation." Aurora kept her place front and center beside Samson.

"You may close your eyes or keep them open, let your mind still, and focus on your breathing." Wolf moved closer but didn't touch the statue.

Tabitha followed a few steps behind but stopped far enough back that she didn't crowd the Birnbaums. Her gaze flicked cautiously at Aurora then settled on Wolf.

He wasn't as loud as Aurora, his warm voice barely carrying over the quiet crowd. "Feel the earth beneath your feet, the power, the life. Sense the richness of the soil, the twisting and spreading roots of trees and plants offering a base of foundation, a source of sustenance. Let yourself become one with this force, for you are made of the same elements." As Wolf spoke, there were long pauses between words, in a way that in nearly any other situation I would've found annoying and pretentious, but somehow it all seemed soothing. "Feel the breeze, the gentle caress of air, the life-giving oxygen. Experience its dance over your skin, listen as it whispers in your ears. Focus on your breath. Breathe in. Breathe out."

His pause was long enough that I opened my eyes. Wolf's were shut and there was a peaceful expression over his face. Glancing around revealed that most people's expressions matched Wolf's. Many had their eyes shut, but others kept their gaze focused on the statue of the slain elk.

Wolf started to speak again, but I let his words fade away. It was a beautiful moment, in the way that all time outdoors around Estes Park was beautiful. Surrounded on all sides by mountains, the tallest peaks retaining the last vestiges of snow that had yet to melt. The sky above a soft blue behind thick cotton clouds that filtered the sunlight to gentle rays.

Back in Kansas City, Charlotte, my old best friend and ex-business partner who'd set up the publishing company with me, had joined the yoga and meditation craze several years before. I'd attended a few classes with her. I'd never gotten comfortable in yoga. Charlotte had been lithe and graceful. Me? Not so much. Those classes had been little more than sweaty torture. The meditation ones, however, though they took time to get used to, had been rather lovely. And it helped quite a bit during the aftermath of the death of my father and my divorce. I'd fallen out of practice over the years but in some ways, it was a similar sensation as to when I lost myself inside a good book. As Wolf's tone took on a quality that said the session was coming to a close, I decided it might be time to incorporate some of that back into my life.

The crowd shifted at the end of the meditation, a few whispers here and there, but mostly remained still. Considering the vast crowd, it was rather remarkable. Wolf moved back a couple of yards behind the statue to stand beside Tabitha, and all focus returned to Aurora.

With one hand still on Samson's flank, she lifted her other skyward and tilted her chin in a manner that I was unable to see as anything other than arrogance. I felt like Dorothy having seen the man behind the curtain where Aurora was concerned. "This is the spot of great power. Where a beloved beast of your town was slain."

Beside me, Leo flinched, and I glanced over. He was studying Aurora, his brows furrowed. On his other side, Katie had a similar expression. It was common knowledge that Samson had been killed at the grounds of the YMCA, where he'd spent much of his time and been the equivalent of a thousand-pound pet. It was an odd and obvious mistake.

From the quiet murmur that rustled through the crowd, we weren't the only ones to notice.

I glanced at Wolf, whose eyes were wide as he glanced toward Duke Riser, an expression of panic growing. He'd clearly realized the blunder. He started to take a step toward Aurora, but paused when Tabitha placed a hand on his arm.

Aurora continued to speak, seemingly unaware of the reactions she prompted. "Beyond that, this is also a sacred location of the Native American tribes who lived here in ancient days." She lifted her other hand. "This is doubly hallowed ground, and it is upon those traditions that we call." That time I looked toward the Pacheco twins. Ben and Nick stared at each other with matching shocked expressions that simultaneously held flickers of anger.

Maybe more attuned to Ben than I realized, a low rumble emanated from Watson, and he shuffled closer against my feet.

Wolf slid his arm from Tabitha's grip and began to approach Aurora as she spoke. He had nearly reached her when there was a commotion on the other side of the crowd.

"Sacrilege! Evil!" a female voice boomed out, cutting off Aurora's speech. "This sorceress is full of lies and deception." At the commotion, the crowds parted and a group of around ten people emerged, led by a woman who held a Bible in front of her, which was pointed toward the Birnbaums. "These are servants of Satan and should be cast out from our town."

Aurora didn't miss a beat. "You need to leave. You have no right to be here." She stepped forward, and again, despite my dislike of her, she had quite the presence.

The woman shook the Bible toward Aurora again. "You have no authority over us. You are the spreader of lies, of evil. Full of deceit and darkness."

A man next to her stepped forward also pointing the Bible at the Birnbaums. "You speak of goodness, of making the world a better place, yet you would use the power of God's creation for your own glory. For your own profit."

"Again I tell you, you have no right to be here. This event is sanctioned by the town. We have the permits, the permission, and the authority." Aurora took another step, and for the first time I noticed her body tremble, though it looked to be more in anger than fear. Wolf put a hand on her shoulder, stopping her from moving forward.

"*You* have no authority! All you have—"

"Be still. All of you." Sergeant Branson Wexler emerged from the crowd, a hand on his holstered sidearm. Though I recognized several other police officers, I hadn't noticed him. I hadn't seen him in weeks. Only a couple of times since I'd ended our relationship. Even in the midst of the drama, his bright green gaze flicked to me, held for a moment, narrowed as it turned to Leo, then refocused on the small group with the Bibles. "As I've told you multiple times over the past few days, this event was approved. We gave you the chance to petition for the right to protest, and you didn't respond."

"We are under the authority of God and his rapture. We are not bound by your laws." The woman stepped toward Branson, undeterred. "Especially when you let such vile sin happen in your midst."

"There is no evil here." Wolf released Aurora's shoulder and stepped around her, and though he kept his voice calm, it carried effortlessly. "We believe your faith to be just as valid as ours. And we only seek to do good. We do not do this for profit. Nor for our glory, as you say."

"Not for profit?" The Bible woman sneered. "With all the money you're making? The two of you charge thousands for a single appearance."

Branson stepped between the two of them. "I said—"

"The vast majority of that is given to a wide array of charities." To my surprise, and to Branson's from the look he gave, Wolf spoke, louder this time, and he changed from addressing the woman to focusing on the crowd. "This is not about money; this is not about power for power's sake. It is about connecting to the earth, to the creator, about bettering lives. Yes, there is money involved. That is of man's creation, and has to be used as such, but the Birn- baum Foundation donates over eighty-five percent of our profits from every event to charity." He scanned the crowd, and his gaze fell on Leo and he pointed to us. "Everything raised this week goes to your own National Park Service and is there to help strengthen the efforts"—his gesture shifted to the elk's statue—"to fight the poaching epidemic."

Branson turned to him, lowering his voice and taking on a beseeching quality. "You're only making this worse. Let me handle it."

"Lies!" Another of the small group of protesters screamed and threw a Bible. It hit Aurora directly in the forehead and she dropped like a stone.

Tabitha screamed and rushed toward Wolf.

"Liars, thieves! Demons!" More Bibles flew, hitting Aurora where she lay, as well as Wolf and Branson.

Cries and screams went up from the crowd. Again Branson's hand moved to his sidepiece, but he traded it for his walkie-talkie and called for backup.

It hadn't been needed. Though the episode only lasted a matter of seconds, at the commotion, many of the other police officers had already made their way over and began securing the scene and restraining those of the group who continued to try to get to where Wolf knelt on the ground, cradling Aurora in his arms as blood trickled down her face.

The following morning found Watson and me heading into the Cozy Corgi a good hour and a half earlier than typical. Though Watson had slept beside the bed, snoring the entire night through, I'd had little luck getting any rest.

We'd all dispersed after the incident at Samson's statue, too shell-shocked to truly take it all in. I found myself needing some normality. Everything felt off. I figured having a few rounds of dirty chais and freshly baked croissants while gabbing with Katie would get me back on track.

Typically, when Katie or Nick came in early in the morning to start the day's baking, they only flicked on a few of the lights in the bookshop so they could make their way to the stairs. To my surprise, as we walked in, all the lights were on and the shop was ready.

Though I'd intended to go directly to the bakery, I'd barely shut the door before Watson gave a little hop of joy and scurried away. Unless Leo or Barry had broken in, there was only one explanation.

Sure enough, as I followed Watson into the mystery room, I found Ben sitting on the antique sofa and setting aside a book so he could greet his corgi worshiper. He glanced up at me as he patted Watson, a blush rising to his cheeks. "I hope you don't mind. I know this is your spot. I'm not trying to steal it."

"Don't be silly. I'm glad you're making yourself at home." I walked over and motioned toward the other side. "Mind if I join you?"

He shook his head and scooted the book closer to him, making room.

With a chuff, Watson popped up, propped both of his forepaws on Ben's knee and nudged his arm, desperate to get both hands on him again.

Ben obliged and gave a contented sigh. "I really love Cinnamon, she's a great cat, but I do wish Nick's and my apartment allowed dogs. There's just something magical about them."

"I agree with you." I reached out to brush Watson's fur alongside Ben for a second and then leaned back, inspecting the book Ben had been reading. Though it wasn't what I'd expected, I wasn't exactly surprised to see one of Aurora Birnbaum's books that we'd ordered. "I doubt you're thinking of joining the fan club?"

"Not hardly." Ben gave a wide-eyed expression that held a healthy dose of cynicism, then cringed. "Not that she deserved what happened to her yesterday."

"No, no one deserves that. But it could've been much worse. They could've been throwing rocks. They're a lot harder than Bibles."

He snickered. "Which is kind of funny since that actually would have been more biblical."

I gaped at him for a heartbeat and then burst out into a laugh. He was so quiet, but every once in a while, he'd give a zinger. "I suppose you're right. But either way, all she's going to have is a bruise followed by a scab from the cut."

Aurora had still been refusing to go to the hospital when we'd left.

Even as he smiled and continued to pet Watson, Ben's expression grew sullen.

It looked like our emotions were in sync. "I imagine you had trouble sleeping last night and that's why you're here early?"

He nodded. "Yeah, I came in with Nick, thought there might be some comfort in being here."

At the mention of his twin, I suddenly became aware of the soft clatter of dishes drifting down from upstairs alongside the heavenly aromas that Katie and Nick were creating. My stomach rumbled in response.

Ben cocked an eyebrow. "Hungry?"

Apparently my stomach had rumbled louder than I realized. "I am. I'll get something in a moment." I transferred the book he'd been reading onto my lap. "I think what's bothering me the most is that it didn't feel like Estes Park yesterday. Maybe that sounds silly, considering that we've had a few murders recently—"

Ben chuckled but didn't offer commentary as he sat back on the sofa as well, keeping one hand on Watson.

"Okay, maybe more than a few." I couldn't help but chuckle along before growing serious again. "But still, Estes is a lovely place, and the vast majority of the people are lovely people. Ones who accept others, even if their belief or way of life is different."

Again he gave me a look but kept his thoughts to himself.

"Maybe not for you? I know some people have given you a hard time because of your Native American heritage."

Ben considered, then shook his head. "No, you're right. Sure, I've had teasing and a few people say things every once in a while, but yesterday was different. And it didn't feel right. It didn't feel like home."

"Exactly." I nodded and sighed. "That's exactly it. I came here for the very same reason you did. What happened yesterday was ugly, and I needed this place. To remind myself that one ugly moment doesn't change the town I love."

"Yeah."

We sat in silence for a while, the only noise was the pleasant sounds of Katie and Nick, and a contented groan from Watson occasionally. Finally, I started to slide the book off my lap and go grab the caffeine and pastries but paused, studying Aurora Birnbaum's name on the cover. After a second, I studied Ben. "Funny that you would pick this book if you were hoping to feel normal."

He shrugged. "I was just trying to understand. Yesterday just didn't make sense." Ben rushed ahead. "Before the whole Bible-throwing scene, that is. The location of Samson's statue holds absolutely no meaning to the Ute tribe. None. Aurora made it sound like a spiritual vortex or something. And it isn't."

"Well, she also seemed to think that was where Samson had been killed. I'm not sure how she hadn't done her research."

"That's just it." Ben reached over and tapped the book. "There's a huge section about different Native American beliefs and legends in this book, some of them from the Ute tribe specifically." He took the book and flipped through a few pages to a beautifully vivid picture of a Native American man with long black hair standing regally next to a coyote. The rich, detailed style matched that of the tarot cards. "This is Wolf and Coyote, remember?"

I nodded. Ben was writing a book where Coyote, the

trickster of the Ute deities, was a modern-day thief who solved murders.

"The details are perfect," Ben turned the page to the script. "As is everything that's written about them. Completely factual and rather insightful, if I'm being honest."

That was interesting. "Maybe Aurora didn't write it." Suddenly I recalled how Wolf had looked nearly as surprised as I'd felt at Aurora's blunder.

Ben beat me to it before I could offer my theory. "She wrote it and created the art, but if you look at the author notes in the back, she thanks Wolf for his research and beta reading."

Yep, that matched what I'd noticed. "I suppose that makes sense, then. Wolf does the research and makes sure everything in the books is correct, and Aurora just forgot." Something about that didn't feel right.

"Maybe so." From Ben's expression, it seemed like he had the same instinct.

Even though we were discussing the very things that had kept me from sleep the night before, just talking them over with Ben while surrounded by my beloved bookshop helped me feel more at ease, and I decided to give in to my rumbling stomach and stood. "I think it's time for a dirty chai and an almond croissant, or two. Want me to bring you down anything?"

Ben shook his head. "No, thank you. I already—"

"Zelda! Stop!"

Though Verona's cry was muffled, Ben and I both looked to the front window in time to see Zelda storm past, her brown hair trailing behind her like a cape from her speed.

A heartbeat later, Verona rushed past as well.

Zelda responded, and though both of their voices were raised, I couldn't make out the meaning.

After a few seconds of the argument continuing, I grimaced toward Ben and attempted humor. "Excuse me, I think I need to see if I can act as an intermediary before we have another murder. Or at least get them to go inside their shop so there'll be fewer witnesses."

Though he gave the appropriate chuckled response, Ben remained serious. "Do you need help? I can come with you." The offer was kind, but he clearly hoped I'd say no.

And I did. "No, it will be fine. They're not really going to kill each other." I was ninety-nine percent sure that was true. "I'll be right back."

Ben stood as well and headed toward the stairs to the bakery. "I'll have your dirty chai ready for you when you come back."

I waved my thanks—he really was a sweet young man— and hurried toward the door. To my surprise, when I got there, I discovered Watson hurrying along at my feet. I'd assumed he'd go with Ben. Feeling bolstered by his presence, I threw open the door and hurried to where the twins stood arguing in front of Chakras. "Guys!"

They both halted instantly, their identical faces whipping in unison to me.

"I don't want to intrude, but it sounds like things aren't going very well. Can I help? We can all go to the bakery. There's coffee and freshly baked pastries." I reached out, giving both of their arms what I hoped was a supportive squeeze. "Or we can go inside your shop if that's more comfortable."

"That's just it!" Zelda jerked her arm free and thrust it in the air. "It's not even our shop anymore. Verona gave it away!"

"Oh, for crying out loud! Stop being so dramatic." Verona ripped her arm free as well. "I didn't give our store away."

"You did too. At least for the rest of the week. You didn't even ask me." Zelda's cheeks were bright with fury, but a tear rolled down her cheek. "Not that I would've said yes to that horrible woman." She leaned forward, angling so she could yell to the middle of the street. "Aurora Birnbaum is a fake and an evil human being!"

"Will you shut up!" Verona suddenly sounded more panicked than angry, which surprised me.

I motioned toward the front door, which had the key dangling from the doorknob. "Let's go in. Come on." Reaching between them, I twisted the handle and pushed the door open. To my relief, both of them followed me inside. After a second, so did Watson. I shut the door, relocked it, and wished the large windows had curtains we could draw.

"She gave that horrid woman Chakras for the whole week. The entire week!" Zelda was on me in a heartbeat, yelling full in my face, though her anger wasn't directed at me. "We don't get to operate our business at all. It's hers."

Verona turned on me as well, though her voice was more pleading than angry. "The SHH Conference severed their ties with her yesterday. They won't let her be part of the events. And Duke Riser isn't allowing her to use the YMCA for any of her own events, so she needed a place. She asked, and it... was the kind thing to do."

"Kind!" Once more Zelda turned on her sister. "Stupid, you mean! Weak! Absolutely certifiably insane!"

"Kindness is not weakness," Verona yelled back, her anger returning. "You should have seen Aurora—she was devastated."

I was distracted from the screaming by Watson's sudden change in posture. He'd been several yards away, wincing at the noise, but was abruptly at full alert, ears pointed and his nose sniffing the air.

A chill ran down my spine. By this point, I knew that stance. I'd seen it a couple of times now, and it always meant the same thing. "Guys. Hush."

They kept yelling.

"Verona! Zelda!" I swatted at them, not trying to make contact but to simply get their attention. "Shut up!"

I'd never spoken to them in such a way, and they both went silent, gaping at me.

I pointed at Watson. "Someone's dead."

"What!" they both screeched simultaneously.

I gestured to Watson again, this time my words were a whisper as I turned to follow him as he lowered his head and began to creep farther into the shop. "Someone's dead."

They didn't speak, and I didn't look back to see if they were following us.

Vaguely, I was aware that the layout of the store had been altered somewhat. The paths between the sections were wider and a large space had been completely cleared near the middle.

Watson patted beyond that, but I knew where he was headed before he reached the destination. Maybe gut instinct or maybe it was the only thing that made sense. As he arrived at the doorway of crystals, he looked back at me.

As I was right behind him, I slipped my hand through the ropes of quartz, and we slipped inside.

On the far side of the room, directly in front of the water feature, Aurora Birnbaum hung lifelessly from a rope tied around one of the beams. Something gleamed at her neck and over her chest.

Watson whimpered, and I took another step forward, narrowing my eyes.

Quartz. Clear quartz, the master healer of all the crystals. Sparkling prism after sparkling prism hung from tangled silver chains like an obscene, garish necklace that sparkled in the dim illumination of the fairy lights.

There was a clattering of more crystals behind me as Verona and Zelda entered the room and began to scream.

"Seriously, what is it with you?" Officer Green folded her muscular arms and leaned against the doorway that led into the crystal room as she narrowed her pale blue eyes. "Do you meet people and set some internal clock ticking so they drop dead at a certain moment so you can discover them?"

"Susan—" I caught myself at her hardened expression. "*Officer Green*, are we really going to go down this road again? You can't possibly think that I murdered Aurora Birnbaum."

"Lord, I wish." Susan rolled her eyes and let out a long-suffering sigh. "Of course I don't. You don't have it in you to be serial killer. You're simply not that interesting. But you might want to do one of those ancestry tests. The only explanation is that you're descended from the Grim Reaper. Should I be worried? We've known each other for months now—is my time about to run out?"

I couldn't help myself. I duplicated her tone. "Lord, I wish."

Susan nearly caught her smirk in time—nearly—before her expression hardened. "I don't think threatening an officer of the law is probably such a great idea for you right now, Winifred Page. I might decide to take you in for questioning after all. Luckily for you, we've got an apparent suicide on our hands, which brings us back to it simply being Mrs. Birnbaum's bad luck to have interacted with you and set off the ticking clock to her demise."

"Suicide?" I flinched and glanced through the crystals to where other police officers were making notes on the scene.

"Here we go. As you give me your statement, do you think you can leave out the conspiracy theories this time?" Susan pulled her notepad out of her pocket and made a show of clicking her pen. "This is for *official* purposes, after all." Her smirk returned. "Did you forget that I've already talked to your cuckoo stepsisters?"

"What is that supposed to mean?"

Her gaze flicked over my shoulder to where I knew Verona and Zelda were sitting behind Chakras' counter. "Well... if you really want to go for the murder angle, I've got my two prime suspects right over there. They were at each other's throats halfway through the interview, both furious about the queen of the cuckoo birds hanging in there." She thumbed over her shoulder. "One of them... the brunette one, even admitted that she was screaming about how horrible Aurora Birnbaum was in the middle of the street before you three came in this morning."

Watson had been napping on top of a braided tie-dyed rug, but at the change in Susan's tone, he trotted over and plopped down at my feet.

"Pardon me, before you *four* came in this morning." Susan glared down at him. "Take your little threatening stare elsewhere, fleabag."

A low rumble sounded in his chest.

Ignoring him, she looked back up at me. "Don't get me wrong. While they might be slightly more interesting than you, I think between the two of them, the twins have about half of your brainpower, so I don't really see them being capable of murder. But if you're going to look for drama where there isn't any, I'll happily oblige."

"If that's really what you think, I'm not sure you're the one to talk about brainpower." In the hour since discovering Aurora's body, an overwhelming exhaustion had settled over me. That burned away with Susan's words, and I leaned closer, my voice a mix of whispered hiss and growl. "The woman hanging in there was beaten with Bibles yesterday in the middle of town. You think that's a coincidence?"

"Blaming the church now? *That's* brazen." Susan bugged her eyes exaggeratedly. "But as for Aurora, I would imagine that was a pretty humiliating experience. She's a well-known personality—granted only in these scatter-brained New Age circles, but still. Enough so she made the national news last night. The whole country saw her humiliation. She wouldn't be the first who couldn't handle such embarrassment."

"I think you're grasping at straws, Susan. Maybe you need a break."

At Branson's voice over my shoulder, both Susan and I stiffened.

She addressed Branson as I turned to face him. "I thought you were leaving on one of your little trips this morning."

"Change of plans." He didn't bother looking at her. "You doing okay, Fred?"

Before I could think of how to answer that question, Susan did it for me. "In case you hadn't noticed, Sergeant Wexler, your ex-girlfriend here has seen more than her share of dead bodies. She's not exactly the faint-of-heart type."

Despite myself, I cast a glance her way in surprise. I could've sworn that sounded like a compliment.

Branson motioned to the crystal room. "Why don't you go help Officers Jackson and Lin."

Susan stiffened. "Chief Briggs made it very clear about *her*"—she gestured her head at me—"getting involved in any more cases. I know you're his little lap dog and he thinks you hung the moon, but even you aren't above his orders. This is *my* case. Back off."

"Actually, it's mine now." Branson slipped an arm over my shoulder. At our feet, Watson growled but was ignored. "But go ahead, Susan. Run off and tattle."

Susan let out a growl of her own, looked like she was going to argue, and then stormed through the doorway of crystals.

I watched her disappear into the room, surprised. The two of them had never been overly fond of each other, and I'd constantly been an issue between them, but the exchange was more aggressive than I'd witnessed before.

Suddenly I realized I was standing there with Branson's arm over my shoulder, and I stepped away.

He cleared his throat. "Sorry about that. Didn't mean to make it awkward."

I wasn't sure if he was apologizing for the interaction with Susan or because of his intimate gesture. From the wounded expression that flashed over his face, my guess was the latter. However, I decided to pretend it had to do with Susan. Much less awkward. "Susan and I are used to each other by now. We've disagreed before, I'm sure we will again."

"No doubt." He eased somewhat and smiled before

angling his attention at the twins, who were speaking to another officer again. "They doing okay? Susan is right about one thing—you're used to finding dead bodies... They aren't."

"Shaken up but managing." I started to move away, then realized Watson had situated himself between us and was sitting on my boots, partially buried under my skirt. I reached down and patted his head soothingly. "Good boy, buddy. Everything's okay. Relax."

His wary brown eyes looked up at me questioningly, and after another couple of strokes, he seems satiated and wandered off, casting a glance over his shoulder every now and again as if to make certain we knew he was watching.

"I think I've burned my bridges with that one." There was regret in Branson's voice as he turned from observing Watson and refocused on me. "And with you."

That was true enough, but I didn't want to discuss it, not then, nor any other time. "Surely you don't believe this was an actual suicide?"

His handsome face twitched slightly, and for a moment, I thought he was going to push the point. Then, thankfully, he followed my lead. "I can't say. I haven't even seen her body yet, Fred. And of course, there won't be an official determination until there's been an autopsy."

I started to point out all the reasons why Aurora's death obviously wasn't a suicide, and then realized I was falling into old patterns. In more ways than one. Things were over between Branson and me. It was both how it needed to be and how I wanted it. While maybe we could keep up a friendship, this was neither the time nor the place. And beyond that, I needed to remember I owned a bookshop. Despite the fact I enjoyed solving murders for a variety of reasons, I needed to sit this one out. If for no other purpose than to allow more space between Branson and me. Not to mention, though it chafed, I had no doubt that my involvement would inspire Susan to make life difficult for the twins. They were going through enough.

"Well then, I guess we'll have to wait for the autopsy." I motioned toward Verona and Zelda. "If you don't need anything else from me, I'll check on them." Without waiting for a response, I started to head over.

"Fred."

At Branson's plaintive tone, I paused and glanced back.

"Susan was right. Chief Briggs is adamant that you not look into this."

Once more I felt my hackles rise. Here we were again, being told what I could or couldn't do. Branson knew *exactly* the effect that had on me. But again, this wasn't the time nor the place. "I didn't say I was going to. And for the final time, I don't need you telling me—"

"No!" He sounded panicked and reached for me but dropped his hand before he made contact and lowered his voice. "No. Sorry. You misunderstood. What I was trying to say is that Chief Briggs doesn't want you to look into this, or any other cases, but I won't stand in your way." His bright green eyes held on to mine, clearly attempting to put so much more meaning into his statement than the words themselves. "If I can help in any way, I will."

I studied him for second. Obviously it was his attempt at reparations, probably trying to build the road back to romance, but was it also something more? "Do you know something? Are you telling me that I *should* be looking into this?"

The confusion in his gaze was answer enough, then he seemed to understand and he shook his head. "No. I'm not.

I truly don't know anything about it. I'm just saying... I'm on your side."

I couldn't figure out how to answer that, so I didn't, and instead I pointed back at the twins. "I'm going to go check on my sisters."

I hovered a respectful distance away as Verona and Zelda finished up with another police officer, and then joined them behind the counter. Verona was sheet white, her eyes hard and strained. Zelda's were bloodshot and puffy, and she grasped my hands as I came nearer. "Fred, do you think I'm in trouble? It was so stupid of me this morning. Yelling that out there for the whole world to hear. I just never thought she would—" She let out a little sob and then tried again. "It's just too much. I was barely coming to terms with the reality of Aurora being so different from what we expected, so much worse, and now she's done this. And people will think..."

Anxiety flitted through me. I hadn't noticed whether Susan approached the twins while I'd been speaking to Branson. "Did the officers mention that to you? Are they threatening to say you had something to do with this?"

She shook her head, a fresh wave of tears. "No. But I was so mad that she took our store for the week, that..."

"Shut up!" Verona hissed and smacked Zelda's arm. "They'll hear you. And then we'll get questioned all over again."

Surely I was misunderstanding Verona's meaning. In case I wasn't, I glanced around and lowered my voice. "You *did* tell them that you gave Aurora the store for the duration of the conference, right?"

"Fred! Not here!" Verona hissed at me as well.

Once more, my temper spiked, and I let out a hiss of my own. "You *didn't?* Are you crazy?"

Zelda jumped in. "I tried to tell her that we needed to be as honest as—"

"I said shut up." Verona smacked her sister again and looked at me imploringly. "I told them that Aurora had a key to the place, which is true—she's had it from the very beginning."

"Yes, but—"

Verona wheeled on Zelda. "I swear, Zelda, if you don't shut up—"

"Is there a problem here?" I nearly groaned in dismay and rage at the sound of Susan's voice as she approached. "Something the police should know about?"

I glared at the twins, trying to communicate to let me handle it. The *what* I was trying to handle, I wasn't really sure. As I turned around, I decided the first thing to take care of was managing my temper. Between the fury Susan always sparked within me, the drama around Branson, and whatever insanity was happening between the twins, I was nearing my wit's end.

"I thought I told you I was handling things, Susan." Branson approached, and though I hated to admit it, I was relieved.

Susan glared between Branson and me. "Didn't you two break up? Isn't that why you've been mooning around like some pathetic teenager for the past few weeks?"

In an extremely rare event, Branson blushed in embarrassment, but it transitioned to anger quickly enough. "Keep it up, Green, I'll have your badge."

"Better men than you have tried, Wexler." She stepped toward him, forgetting me and the twins. "Briggs has a boss too, you know."

Before Branson could reply, Watson trotted up, directly between them and dropped something at my feet.

As I bent and picked it up, all eyes were on me. "What in the world?" It was a high-heeled shoe. A stiletto of the type that would've spelled out certain death for me if I'd ever attempted to wear it. An embossed silver flower glistened on the inside of the sole. Instantly, I realized my mistake in touching it. The shoe was covered in the same design as the high priestess tarot card—the unicorn on either side of the heel, the rich colors out of the forest making up the rest of the design.

Susan pulled out a cloth and snatched it from my hands, then glared at Branson. "Perfect. Even after she dumps you, your girlfriend and her little rodent of a dog can contaminate evidence."

Branson's face darkened in a renewed flush of embarrassment and anger.

"Wonder where he found this. Aurora was only wearing one of them." Susan scowled at Watson, then the shoe before letting out a mocking laugh. "If this doesn't show the woman was a fake, I don't know what would. Preaching about finding balance and being one with the earth, and all that junk, while all the time spending a fortune on designer shoes."

"Having good taste in shoes and fashion doesn't negate a person's devotion to enlightenment."

We all turned slowly to stare at Verona.

She, too, blushed but lifted her chin defiantly. "Well... it doesn't."

Susan withdrew an evidence bag and dropped the high-heel inside, then offered another of her scowls at Branson. "You know what, I changed my mind. You deal with the escapees from the insane asylum."

SIX

"I will love you forever if you can get a large dirty chai in my hands in the next five seconds, preferably with twenty shots of espresso." I nearly collapsed against the bakery counter, my hands accidentally making a loud smack on the marble. "And please tell me you have some more of that quiche, and not the little bite-size ones, I'm talking an entire pie."

"Good Lord, Fred. You nearly scared me to death." Katie whipped around from where she'd been sliding the tray of something into the oven, a hand clutched over her heart. She shut the oven door, and then she grinned at me. "First off, I'm devastated to think that your love for me is conditionally based on my expediency in crafting the perfect dirty chai. Secondly, I'm willing to bet that twenty shots of espresso is a recipe for a heart attack." Her face fell somewhat. "And I'm sorry to say I'm all out of the quiches, both the bite-size and the regular."

It was my turn to clutch at my chest, and I was only slightly teasing. "You're killing me. The past few hours have been..." I shut my eyes, trying to block out the memory, and then refocused on the pastry case. "You know what, that's fine. Just give me two of everything."

Katie leaned against the counter, still grinning. "Eating our feelings, are we? The twins aren't taking it very well?"

After the police told us we could go, I'd driven Verona and Zelda out to Mom and Barry's. They were arguing and fighting so much that even Barry's typically easygoing and happy nature hadn't made a dent in the squabbling. "You have no idea. You would think that Zelda secretly eating ice cream and Verona handing over the keys to the shop to Aurora were invitations to start World War III."

"Well, they are a little high-strung, and someone did just die in their brand-new shop. They might deserve some slack."

"Easy for you to say, you were just here dealing with tourists." I made a show of looking down at my empty hands. "Speaking of, if this is the customer service we give around here, we're not going to keep busy for very long."

Katie rolled her eyes and chuckled. "One dirty chai coming right up, madam. Although I'm cutting you off at three shots of espresso." She hopped up so she could lean over the counter and then looked at me in confusion. "Where's Watson?"

I motioned downstairs. "Having a love fest with Ben, of course."

Right on cue, the clattering of claws sounded from the top of the stairs, and Watson rounded into the bakery, prancing along, a big tongue-lolling smile on his face.

I scratched his head in greeting. "Probably shouldn't let people see you so happy on the same day as a murder. I'm pretty sure it's rude. Even if you did get to see Barry and Ben all in a matter of hours."

"So you do think it's murder?" Katie looked over from the espresso machine. We'd only exchanged a couple of text messages since discovering Aurora hanging in the crystal room.

"Well, of course it's murder," someone bellowed from the top of the stairs, and we looked over to find Anna Hanson walking toward us. She gestured down the steps and gave a winded sigh. "Those things get steeper every day. You should install an escalator. If I wanted exercise, I'd go to a gym, not a bakery."

Suddenly Watson's smile made even more sense. While Anna wasn't one of his favorite people, she came with snacks.

Anna always reminded me of Mrs. Claus—round, with rosy cheeks and fluffy white hair. I peered over her shoulder, waiting for her Mr. Claus. I thought maybe he was struggling with the steps as well, but after a few moments, it didn't look like he was coming. "Where's Carl?"

She gave a dismissive wave at the windows of the bakery toward the shop she and her husband owned across the street. "I told him to man the fort. I wasn't waiting to get the scoop." She gave me a reprimanding finger shake. "*Not* like the last murder. You barely found time to come talk to us at all." Before I could think of anything to say, she turned on Katie. "While I'm here, I'd like one of your red velvet brownies. Oh, and Carl demanded an apple turnover as payment for me getting to come and get the scoop without him. So if you'd get that to go, that'd be great." Anna considered for a total of three seconds. "Actually, while you're at it, throw in a cherry turnover for me. I won't mention the red velvet brownie."

Just as she started to look back at me, Watson gave a plaintive little chuff.

"Oh, I'm so sorry, sweetheart." Anna swiped across the counter, smacking Katie's arm as she so often did with her husband. "Get Watson one of his favorite treats. I can't believe I forgot to bring them over, though I suppose that would be silly, since I buy them from you in the first place. But I could see his little heart breaking when I greeted him downstairs empty-handed."

And we had confirmation on Watson's ridiculous grin. Barry, Ben, *and* an overabundance of his favorite all-natural dog bone treats.

Katie didn't bother looking at me for permission, knowing that when Anna Hanson demanded something, you didn't take the time to question.

With the large dog bone clinched possessively in his teeth, Watson trotted happily over to the window, and plopped down under his favorite table in the bakery and was utterly in heaven.

Once Anna had her red velvet brownie, she refocused on me, this time pointing at me with a fork instead of her finger. "Spill it. Who are your suspects? My guess is that church group." She stuffed a bite of the brownie into her mouth, but didn't give me time to respond. "I don't think I've ever been madder at Carl in my life. We were on our way to that... well, whatever it was at the Samson statue last night, and he started getting stomach cramps. We had to turn around and go home. I told him he's not supposed to eat dairy after eating popcorn. At least not for an hour. It always does horrible things to him, but did he listen? No!" This time she pointed the fork at Katie before taking another bite and continuing. "I can't believe we missed the show. Thankfully we saw it on the news, but it's not like seeing it firsthand. Stupid Carl." Her eyes narrowed, and she pointed again at Katie. "You know what, put in a second cherry turnover. He'll have one and can watch me eat two of them for payment." She sniffed. "Now, let's stay on topic, shall we? It sounds like you are skeptical about Aurora being murdered. Why? I thought you were smarter than that."

If I hadn't known Katie so well, I would've missed that she was struggling not to snicker. "Honestly, I haven't gotten any details yet. All I've heard was that she hung herself. But—"

"Oh, please. Like there's any question." Anna waved her off and looked back at me. She was in rare form. "You know better. *You* found her. That, in and of itself, means it had to be murder. Plus, Aurora would never kill herself."

I decided to jump over the assumption that just because I found a dead body implied that it always had to be murder. It was a little too similar to Susan Green's accusations. "Did you know Aurora?"

"Of course I knew Aurora." Anna nodded then, surprisingly looking like she was trying to choose her words carefully. "I can't say she was the nicest woman in the world. She had a tendency of treating Carl and I like *the help*, but she used Cabin and Hearth to completely furnish her and Wolf's summer home when they updated it a few years ago. Spent a fortune. An absolute *fortune*."

Katie handed me the dirty chai and winked. "I added a fourth shot, considering." She eyed Anna. "She spent a fortune on home decor, huh? That would go along with that group's accusation last night of the Birnbaum's misusing their financial resources."

I took a sip of the dirty chai and felt a wave of relief wash over me, then considered Katie's words. I'd been so caught up with the twins I'd not had a chance to really think about anything beyond the moment. "Do we know if that's true? Leo said they were making a huge contribution to the National Park Service."

"So is *that* what you're thinking? Wolf killed Aurora? For the money?" Anna squinted skeptically but then nodded. "I bet you're right. It's always the husband. Always. Plus, he was very nice. Although I only met him once, Aurora did all the shopping. Wolf returned a few things later, which I didn't love, but he had a very different attitude than his wife." She pointed to me again with the fork before taking her final bite of the red velvet brownie. "Yes, you're right. Has to be him. It's always the nice ones."

Despite myself, I chuckled, but knew I needed to be clear, otherwise within half an hour it would spread across Estes Park that Winifred Page said that Wolf Birnbaum murdered his wife. "I don't actually think any such thing, Anna. In fact, I don't have a list of suspects at all."

She balked and pursed her lips in a sour expression. "What is this? I thought last time you were overwhelmed with trying to help Paulie and you simply overlooked Carl and me. But now this? Claiming you don't have suspects?" Her eyes narrowed as her tone dipped. "What did Carl do? Why are you angry?"

For a second, I thought she was kidding, then realized she truly looked hurt. "Anna." I reached out and touched her forearm lightly. "I'm not upset with you *or* Carl. Not at all. I adore you." That was true. In many ways, they'd taken a while to get used to, but despite their gossipy and flighty manner, they were good, kind people. "I'm not telling you who I suspect, because I don't have anyone. There is no list of suspects. I'm sure the police have it under control."

She eyed me warily. "But you do think it was a murder?"

I hesitated but didn't see the point in lying. "It doesn't make sense for it to be a suicide. Granted, I didn't know

Aurora, but her being pelted with Bibles the night before seems like too large a coincidence."

Anna nodded in satisfaction. "So the Estes Valley Church is your suspect."

I started to ask if Anna knew any of the people specifically involved in the Bible throwing but caught myself. "No, I don't suspect them. I don't suspect anybody. Like I said, the police have this one."

I flinched when I noticed Katie's skeptical expression was identical to Anna's. "You think it's a murder, and you're *not* going to look into it? Did Branson tell you to back off again?" Before I could reply, she shook her head, brown ringlets quivering. "No, of course he didn't. Then you'd *definitely* be investigating."

"It's almost irritating that you know me so well." I took another sip of the dirty chai. Now that I was away from the twins and not in crisis mode, I had to admit I did have a pull to figure it out. "Branson actually said the exact opposite. He offered to help me in any way possible."

"Well, of course he did. He's desperate to get you back. As he should." Anna nodded sagely and then offered her own pat on my forearm. "Don't think you don't deserve him just because he's gorgeous. You're very... pretty too."

That time, Katie did snicker.

Anna transferred the pat to Katie's arm. "And you as well, dear. I must say you two know how to work the system. Don't get me wrong, you're pretty, I suppose, but let's be honest. That park ranger of yours is several steps ahead." Katie flinched, but Anna didn't seem to notice. "I wish I'd had whatever secret the two of you possess. Maybe I could've ended up with Robert Redford or something as opposed to Carl. Although Carl is a sweetheart." She patted her expansive belly. "Even if he has let himself go."

Katie and I exchanged glances. Clearly unsure if we were supposed to be insulted or find the whole thing hilarious. Probably a little of both. I couldn't help but take note that other people had noticed it seemed that Katie and Leo were together. After a few months of wondering, I'd been about to decide they weren't, but maybe I was wrong.

Anna grabbed the bag of turnovers off the counter, bringing me back to the moment, and then she focused on me again. "I am relieved to hear that you're not angry with Carl and me. I don't know what this ridiculousness is that you're not investigating, but whenever you come to your senses, you already have your answer. It's Wolf. It's always the husband, and it's always the nice one. So if you put those together, he's your man. The nice husband." She waved at Watson who was lost to dreams and then started to walk away before pausing again. "Or the church group. People who throw Bibles are most definitely one small jump away from committing murder." She took another step and then let out an excited cry of glee. "Oh, I've got it. They teamed up. Wolf *and* the Estes Valley Church. They united forces to take down Aurora." With a nod, she finally made it to the top of the stairs and walked away, muttering about how she was going to miss all the money Aurora spent on home furnishings.

Katie bugged her eyes out at me. "Okay, after that, I'm with you. I'll make us both twenty-shot dirty chais."

SEVEN

Even after a full night's sleep, my brain seemed foggy. Regardless, I was determined to have life return to normal. I made a quick breakfast for Watson and me, and the three of us—the third being my thermos of coffee and life-giving caffeine—took our newly cemented habit of walking through the woods outside of my cabin. Though it was barely August, the mornings were already a touch brisker and whispered that it wouldn't be too many more weeks before the verdant green of the aspen leaves shimmered into gold.

Watson wasn't overly prone to chasing the small animals we came across or barking at wildlife, so the chipmunks and mountain jays weren't startled away. The thick groves of pines and spruce we passed brought to mind the high priestess card of the tarot deck. The beautiful unicorn in her magical forest. Wolf had said drawing that card indicated good judgment and strong intuition. I didn't put any stock into tarot cards or crystals per se, but he hadn't been wrong. Both of those were qualities my father had in spades, qualities that had made him a stellar detective. Qualities that he'd passed on to me.

Was it judgment and intuition that instantly told me

Aurora Birnbaum hadn't killed herself? Was it simply because of the events of the past several months that I saw a dead body and instantly assumed murder? My gut told me it was the first option.

So why wasn't I diving in headfirst? It had been nearly twenty-four hours since discovering her body, and I hadn't done anything more than alternate between checking on the twins and taking space from them. Branson had assumed I was going to investigate, as did Katie and Anna. As did the whole town of Estes Park, probably.

Part of me wanted to, in that nagging, taunting way that temptation uses. Those thoughts that flickered through, wanting to know the answer of who and why. Not only the why of her death, but the why of locating it at Chakras. Even so, something was holding me back.

As Watson and I walked through the woods, I marveled at that nearly as much as the beauty of the mountains towering over the tops of the trees. Was this another side of my intuition and judgment urging me to sit this one out? To let the "professionals" handle it?

Or was it something else?

Despite being surrounded by the beauty of the unicorn's forest, no clarity came my way, no insight to why I was feeling strangely about it.

As we finally stepped out of the woods and headed back toward the front porch of the cabin, I paused and glanced back to the line of trees, imagining I could see a glistening white mythical beast watching me from within. I'd drawn the high priestess card, the very image that had been on Aurora's stilettos when she died.

I didn't know what that meant. Nor did I believe that a card could tell me about my personality, even if they were qualities I already believed were true. However, I also didn't believe in coincidence.

After Watson and I had a second breakfast at the Cozy Corgi bakery, I sipped the dirty chai Katie made me while I turned the Open sign over for the store and glanced out the window. Across the street, Carl Hanson was doing the exact same thing for Cabin and Hearth. We gave each other a wave in greeting, and I was about to turn around lest he motion for me to come over since he'd missed getting to tell me his theories the day before, when my gaze fell on Paws, the pet shop next door.

Then it hit.

I supposed it should have been obvious, though the realization brought along a wave of embarrassment, so maybe that's why I'd struggled to recognize my hesitation. "Ben?" I turned around to find him looking at me from the cash register, eyes wide. Suddenly I realized I'd sounded a touch panicked and readjusted my tone. "Sorry, didn't mean to startle you. Do you mind if I go see Paulie for a few minutes?"

"Of course not." Ben's intelligent dark brown eyes narrowed. "Do you think he know something about this murder too?"

It looked like Ben assumed I was going to investigate as well. I guess the only one who'd been uncertain about it was me. "No. I don't think so." But... maybe...

Watson had already been napping in the sunshine but rushed toward me as I started to step outside.

"I'm going to go see Flotsam and Jetsam. You sure you want to come?"

At the names, Watson paused and glowered.

Goodness, I adored my grumpy little man. "You don't have to."

After another moment, he passed through the door, joining me.

"Well. It really is love, isn't it?" I stooped enough to brush my fingers over the tip of his ears and then the two of us hurried across the street.

Carl was still in the window and hope lit his face when he saw us heading in his direction. With a touch of guilt, I shook my head and pointed toward the pet shop. Clear dejection crossed his features.

The second we stepped into Paws, wild barking emanated from the back, setting off the typical chain reaction of squawking birds and the high-pitched squeal of hamsters racing on their wheels. I was certain it was my imagination, but every time, it seemed even the bubbles in the fish tanks increased their ferocity.

The insane corgi brothers, Flotsam and Jetsam, emerged from one of the aisles, scampering and tumbling over each other in their frantic ways.

They were nearly to us when Watson growled, low, soft, and long.

Flotsam and Jetsam stopped less than a foot away, both issuing pathetic whimpers.

After a second, as if proving his point, Watson closed the distance, offering a reserved, yet affectionate, sniff for each. Unable to contain themselves, each of them licked his face and ears during this process, but when he walked past them, they didn't give in to chaos. The two corgis had an extended stay with us the month before, and the three dogs had finally come to an agreement of how things were meant to be. It seemed like that was going to last.

After Watson passed, I knelt and held out my arms.

"Okay, boys." And with that, Flotsam and Jetsam lost their minds, both plowing into me with pure unadulterated abandon. Within a second, the three of us were nothing more than a cloud of dog hair, and I was surprised at my genuine affection for the two. I guess what they say about forming lasting bonds while going through trauma together was true.

"Fred!" Paulie emerged from somewhere in the back, only slightly visible through the layer of dog hair in the air between us. "I wondered if you were going to stop by today."

Only more proof that I was the one late to the party.

I finished with an intense rub on the corgis' sides before I stood up. They scampered over to Watson, and after getting as close to him as possible without touching, began to wrestle. Watson simply stared at them in judgment of their undignified behavior. But if I knew my corgi, and I did, I sensed affection, or at least amusement.

"Sorry I haven't been in since you got back into town a couple of days ago." I crossed the remaining distance and gave Paulie a brief hug. "Family was good? Did you feel okay going back home for a while?"

"Family was good." Paulie gave a little shrug and smiled. "It's wonderful to have them back in my life. But it was also confirmation of what I'd believed. I already am home. My friends are here, the shop. My *life* is here."

I squeezed his hand before letting him go. "I'm glad of that." And *there* was something I wouldn't have dreamed of meaning when we'd met all those months ago. I had found the rather mousy man to be annoying and off-puttingly intense. But he'd become a friend, even before I'd discovered he had his reasons.

"Thanks, Fred. That means the world to me." He

glanced down at the dogs, and his smile increased further. "It's nice to see Watson playing with the boys, finally."

I decided not to suggest that Watson sniffing Flotsam and Jetsam as they continued to wrestle didn't actually qualify as playing. After all, for Watson, it was close. "Yeah, they bonded while they were houseguests. I'm glad."

"I'm sure you're not here to talk about corgi relations." Paulie grinned back up at me. "And I'm betting it has something to do with what happened at Chakras yesterday."

"Am I that obvious?"

He shrugged. "Well, the sun rises, and the sun sets. Winifred Page does what Winifred Page does." His smile broadened again. "And we're all better off for it."

I hoped that was true. At least for Paulie, I knew it was. And since he'd already dived right in, I decided to follow his lead. "Do you have any customers yet this morning?" I glanced back through the small aisles of pet supplies. I hadn't noticed anyone, but it paid to be careful.

"No, we're alone." Paulie suddenly sounded nervous. "You don't suspect that I had something to do—"

"No! Of course not!" Once more I grabbed his hand and gave a reassuring squeeze. "Not even a little."

He deflated a bit in relief. "Okay, good. I'm glad."

"But..."

His brown eyes flicked up to mine once more.

My heart rate increased as I forced myself to ask. I wasn't sure what kind of response I wanted. "You said, before... you said there were things about Estes Park you couldn't tell me. Secrets. But you also said you'd tell me if there was something I needed to know."

He caught on quickly. "I don't know anything about Aurora Birnbaum's death, Fred. Nothing at all. And that's the truth."

Though he was a friend, I couldn't keep from studying his eyes, seeing if there was even a hint of a lie. To his credit, he neither looked away nor seemed offended. And I only found sincerity there. Both relief and disappointment cut through me. "So... as far as you know... this doesn't have anything to do with my father's death?"

Paulie flinched, and this time he took my hand. "Fred, I didn't know my situation had anything to do with your father's death. I really didn't. If I had, I..." He considered. "Well, I'm pretty sure I would've told you. I like to think I would have."

That time, the disappointment overshadowed the relief. I hadn't realized until I'd glanced at the pet shop, but some part of me feared that somehow Aurora's death in my step-sisters' shop had something to do with how my father had died. One of the men involved in his murder had been in Estes the month before and hurt Paulie. Though things had never been crystal clear in my father's death, there'd been closure. Now, all these years later, to discover that there were loose ends left me feeling off-balance, and for some reason, slightly afraid of what I might discover.

It looked like Aurora Birnbaum wasn't going to offer any answers in that area.

Paulie gave my hand another squeeze. "Sorry."

I shook my head and started to say it was okay, but surprise emotion tightened around my throat, so I simply nodded. On cue, Watson pressed himself against my leg, and I smiled down at him.

And then, as if there really were a script that everyone had seen but me, the front door of the pet shop opened, and Paulie and I looked over. A chill washed down my spine.

Flotsam and Jetsam rushed the newcomer, barking in unbridled joy at new hands to pet them.

At my feet, Watson let out a growl that didn't hold the slightest hint of joy.

"If either one of these monsters gets slobber on my shoes, Mr. Bezor, I'll have them put down."

"Boys!" Paulie clapped his hands loudly. Watson let out a commanding bark of his own.

Flotsam and Jetsam stopped in their tracks, both of their heads drooping and their nubs of tails doing their best to retreat between their legs.

With a smirk, Chief Briggs crossed his arms and leveled his stare on me. "I stopped by your little bookshop so you and I could have a chat, and one of the Pacheco kids said you were over here." He glanced dangerously at Paulie, then returned to me once more. "Imagine that."

I'd only met the man once, officially, at Paulie's bedside in the hospital, though we'd seen each other from afar a couple of times since. He made his disdain of me very clear. Though he was part of the reason Paulie had stayed safe, I felt the need to get the police chief away from the pet shop. "Would you like to go somewhere and chat?"

His smirk only increased, but before he could speak, Watson growled again.

I knelt, just long enough to rest a reassuring hand on Watson's head.

The growling stopped.

Though I could see the thoughts in Chief Briggs' eyes, he surprised me by not offering any threats in Watson's direction. "No. It's probably appropriate to have this conversation here with"—he flicked a dismissive hand at Paulie —"him. Although it would be even better if I could round up the rest of your Scooby gang and get this over with all at once."

It took me a second to catch on, but when I did, I

couldn't keep the amusement out of my tone. "Scooby gang?"

"The baker, the park ranger, the pet shop owner, and the bookkeep... and the mutt." He rolled his eyes. "Your stepfather even has the van for it."

Despite my dislike of the man, and the clash of emotions I'd experienced only moments before, I couldn't help but laugh. He wasn't exactly that far off. "You know, I think I like that."

"You would." His smirk thinned to a narrow, hard line. "I was coming to let you know that I expect you to stay out of this investigation. It seems my sergeant has a hard time convincing you of that on his own, so I thought I'd step in. Make it a little clearer."

"Why would I investigate a suicide?" I couldn't help myself.

The smirk was back but filled with venom. "You're obnoxious, Winifred Page. You're a busybody, arrogant, disrespectful, and entitled. You are, however, not an idiot."

Though he stayed silent, Paulie drew himself up a little taller beside me as if offering his protection.

With Susan, though we'd taken an instant dislike to each other, her feelings toward me made sense, at least after learning of some of her problems with my family, and then our ongoing bickering. But with Briggs, it was more than dislike. The man hated me, it was clear, and he didn't attempt to mask it, which in some ways I appreciated. But I didn't understand it. This was only our second interaction, and if I was reading him correctly, if I dropped dead that instant, he would dance with joy on my grave.

The other thing I realized, though I hated to admit it, even to myself, was that he scared me.

I took a step forward. "You're right, I'm not an idiot. I

also know that I've not broken any laws, not a one, so if I want to look into Aurora's death, as long as I do it in the same way as I have before, there's nothing you can do about it."

He moved forward as well. Watson growled but stayed by my side. Chief Briggs didn't even spare him a glance. "I don't think you want to try me, little girl."

"Excuse me?" *Little girl?* Rage filtered in, mingling with the fear, which only made the anger hotter.

"No, madam, I will *not* excuse you. This is my town." He jabbed the thumb into his chest and then pointed at me with his forefinger. "Not yours. This is *my* town. I've tolerated you long enough and will keep it safe, and I will not have you continuing to harass everyone who lives here."

The laugh that burst from me sounded half-crazed, and I hadn't been aware that it was coming from me. "Keep it safe? How safe was Aurora Birnbaum?"

"She's not one of mine." He shrugged, making it very clear how unconcerned he was. "And neither are you."

Despite my anger, the fear returned, though I did my best not to let it show. I wasn't sure if I succeeded or not. "Is that a threat?"

"Of course not." He scoffed and took a step back. "But it's so very typical that's what you would think. Always see yourself as more important than you really are." He pointed at Paulie next. "Don't be led down dangerous paths by this one, Mr. Bezor. You avoided one shark; don't dive into an infestation."

EIGHT

By the time midafternoon rolled around, I had to admit it would've been more productive for me to have started snooping around. I'd been utterly useless at the bookshop, leaving Ben to handle the tourists. My body was there, wandering from room to room, straightening books on the shelves and smiling absentmindedly at customers, but my mind was a million miles away.

I believed Paulie. Aurora's death didn't have anything to do with my father's murder all those years before. It was stupid to think it would be connected. Kinda. I would've thought the same about the drama around Paulie the month before, however. But Paulie wasn't lying. He'd been sincere. Still... just because he wasn't aware of the connection didn't mean there wasn't one. He hadn't seen the link between his situation and my father. Maybe simply wasn't aware of the connection this time either.

Chief Briggs showing up only strengthened the possibility. He and Branson had been adamant that I stay as far away as possible when Paulie had been hurt. Having the police chief act in a similar way now made me believe there had to be some connection. Or... the man simply hated me on a visceral level.

One thing was clear, and it might be the only thing that was—it was time to quit pretending I wasn't going to look into Aurora Birnbaum's death. Whether it had something to do with my father or not. It seemed everyone assumed any time death occurred, Winifred Page was going to snoop around. And maybe, though I'd pretended not to be aware, I felt the same. I'd not been able to quit thinking about Aurora's death even though I hadn't started asking questions. So... whether looking into what happened at Chakras would shed light on my father's situation or not, I was going to see what I could discover. The question was: Where to start?

I suppose that wasn't much of a question. Anna had offered two suspects, and though I didn't think they were in cahoots like she seemed to think, the spouse always had to be a possibility, no matter how mild-mannered Wolf seemed to be. The church group had to be a possibility as well. It seemed a small leap from being willing to stone someone in public with Bibles to committing murder. Though I doubted it was an entire group effort, all it took was one fanatic.

Deciding I'd rather begin with a crazy religious group as opposed to a potentially mourning or murderous husband, I went up to the bakery and dug through the trash.

"Fred, there's not any more calories if you get the pastries fresh out of the case." Katie sounded like she was barely keeping herself from laughing.

"I'm not looking for pastries." Still digging, I glanced over at her just in time to hear the little click and she snapped a picture with her cell phone. "Really?"

She laughed, then gave an innocent shrug. "Never know when a photo like this will come in handy. There might be a cause to blackmail you one day." She lowered the phone and gestured over her shoulder toward the counter.

"I just finished a fresh batch of quiches. They'll be cool enough to slice in about five minutes."

"I'm not here for pastries, I'll..." My stomach rumbled, and I straightened. "Actually, that sounds great. Thank you. But I'm looking for that flyer, the one that church group sent out about the ceremony at the Samson statue."

She smiled knowingly. "I take it you've given in and decided to investigate."

"It seems silly to fight it at this point."

"Obviously. But I hate to tell you you're off to a bad start if you can't remember when our trash day is. That flyer is long gone. But..." She winked and tapped her temple "I bet you were trying to recall which group was responsible. They're the Holy Rapture Fellowship, connected with the Estes Valley Church. Though I couldn't tell you if they're one and the same or simply using the same facilities."

I studied Katie, my hand on my hip, and felt a smile grow across my face. I shouldn't have been surprised, not in the least. "You were already snooping?"

"Well... Anna got me thinking yesterday." She shrugged. "And I figured it was only a matter of time before you jumped in headfirst."

"You're right. This is me jumping. Sounds like my first stop is Estes Valley Church. At least I can quit digging in the trash."

"Sadly, you look rather cute digging in the trash." Katie winked. "Who's the second stop? Tabitha?"

"No, I was thinking Wo—" I halted. "Tabitha?"

Katie nodded. "Yeah. Surely you noticed New Age Barbie was kookoo for cocoa puffs for Wolf."

I had actually. How had I not considered her since? "Now there's a thought. She made it sound like Aurora treated her as badly as everyone else."

"Well, except for the gift of expensive shoes, yes." Katie shrugged. "I'm thinking Tabitha would do it more to get the competition out of the way for Wolf's affection. Or maybe she and Wolf were having an affair and Aurora found out."

It was a good thought. "You're no more just a baker than I'm just a bookseller."

"Well, duh. We're magnificent." She gave an exaggerated bow.

Laughing, I tried picturing the bubbly and rather flighty Tabitha murdering Aurora. "Hard to see such a small woman managing to get Aurora to hang herself."

"Did you forget her muscles?" Katie bugged out her eyes. "She looks like a dreadlocked Barbie, but has the arms of a GI Joe."

Tabitha had said she was Aurora's personal yoga and Pilates instructor. While Tabitha killing Aurora made quite the mental picture, I surprisingly could visualize it fairly easily. "Okay, then adding Tabitha to the list." I dusted off my broomstick skirt as I moved from the trash can, even though none of the garbage had gotten on it, then remembered Katie's words. "But, the church first. Right after a slice of quiche. Did you do the asparagus and Swiss?"

"I agree with your priorities, and of course I did, but I also did a bacon and Gruyère." Katie winked again. "Personally, since you're launching yourself off on an investigation, I think you need to keep your energy up. That could require a slice of each, don't you think?"

My stomach rumbled once more, this time in joyful anticipation, and I crossed to the sink to wash my hands. "Just when I don't think it's possible, I fall a little more in love with you every day."

She chuckled. "You're a smart woman, Fred."

"That she is."

Katie and I both looked over to find Branson waiting at the counter.

He leveled his stare at me. "Mind if I join you for a slice of quiche, or two?"

Before I could reply, Watson trotted over, apparently having abandoned his nap in the afternoon sunlight from the bookstore windows and followed Branson up. He looked expectantly up at me and then Katie.

I couldn't think of an appropriate response to Branson, but thankfully, Katie jumped to the rescue. She pointed to one of the empty tables by the wall of windows overlooking Elkhorn Avenue. "Why don't you two have a seat. I'll bring the quiche over to you when it's ready." She knelt partially toward Watson, though didn't pet him. "And one of your favorite all-natural dog bone treats, to boot."

As I followed Branson, I wasn't entirely certain if I should be thankful for Katie coming to the rescue or not. After my interaction with Chief Briggs earlier that morning, there was little chance I'd be able to keep my temper in check. Deciding to cut to the chase, the minute we sat at the table and Watson took his place under my chair, I opted for the direct approach. "I already had a visit from the chief. He made the police station's stand very clear. If you're here to reiterate it or give some new threats, I'd rather just skip it. You're more than welcome to have as much quiche as you'd like."

Branson stiffened and leaned forward, his bright green eyes hardening, as well as his tone. "Chief Briggs threatened you?"

"He—" I cut off what I was going to say, long enough to study Branson. "You didn't know we spoke this morning?"

"Yes. I knew." His expression didn't soften. "That's why I'm here. But I wasn't aware he threatened you."

"I doubt he'd put it like that. But he didn't leave me guessing as to whether my involvement would be welcome or not." I needed to tread carefully, but decided to push, just a little. "He also didn't pretend that Aurora committed suicide."

"The autopsy isn't finished, of course. But that's already clear. She was most definitely murdered." He started to lean back but then resumed his more intense position. "*How* did he threaten you?"

I opted to ignore that question, though it was obvious Branson hadn't been aware of how direct Chief Briggs had been, and it was also apparent Branson wasn't okay with it. "*How* was it clear that Aurora didn't kill herself?"

For a second, he looked like he was going to argue or push the point. Then he relaxed and kept his voice low, quiet enough that the few tourists seated around couldn't hear. "The bruising around her neck, under her noose and crystal necklaces, was consistent with strangulation. There's a chance that there was an altercation where she was strangled but lived and hung herself later, but that's preposterous."

"Who are you looking at? Her husband or—" I had to replay Katie's words. "—the Holy Rapture Fellowship?" I decided not to mention Tabitha, hoping that Branson would free flow with his own theories.

He didn't miss a beat. "Both, of course. Those are the obvious suspects. The husband always is, and that little group didn't exactly keep their hatred of the two of them secret." There was another beat of a pause. "Plus, it's not like there weren't a plethora of people who had problems with Aurora, so it's not a short list." If he was thinking of Tabitha, he didn't specify.

At the thought, another option came to me. Duke Riser

had been livid, both at Chakras and at the event at the Samson statue. Plus he and the leaders of the conference refused to let Aurora remain at the event.

Branson was right, the list of possibilities was anything but short.

"Here you go, a slice of plain quiche for you." Katie plopped a plate in front of Branson and then slid one in front of me with a double portion, cutting off my speculations. "And asparagus with Swiss, with a side of bacon and Gruyère for you." She pulled a large dog biscuit shaped like a bone out of her pocket and presented it to Watson with a flourish. "And for you, your highness."

To my surprise, Watson didn't hurry off to his favorite table, but remained settled under my chair as he began to snack.

Apparently feeling similar to Watson, Katie gave me a meaningful look. "You good?"

My heart warmed at the devotion of my furry sidekick and my best friend. "With fresh-baked quiche, how could I be anything but?"

"Okay, then. You know where to find me." She turned and headed back behind the bakery counter.

"It seems I've made an enemy." Branson sounded sad. "I hope you don't feel the same way."

I thought I preferred threats to the dangerous ground of talking about our past relationship. Instead of replying, I took a bite of quiche, drew some comfort from the perfect blend of cheese and smoky bacon, and avoided the question altogether. "What is this? Your boss threatens me this morning, tells me to stay out of it. And here you are, giving me behind-the-scenes details of Aurora's death and letting me know two of your suspects."

He paused with a forkful of quiche halfway to his lips.

"As previously stated a few moments before, you're a smart woman, Fred. You deduced instantly that Aurora wasn't responsible for her own death, and clearly the husband and the threatening group that attacked her mere hours before she died are the first place to look." Branson's gaze softened once more, and he took on a tone that returned us to dangerous territory. "And I have a lot to make up for. Like I told you earlier, I'm not going to stand in your way. I was wrong with how I handled the situation with Paulie. I'm not going to do that again."

I appreciated the gesture, and though it brought just a touch of doubt, just a touch of longing that maybe things truly had changed and we could see where things would lead between us again, it was too little, too late. I wasn't going to go back down that road, even if it was tempting. "I don't think that's going to go over very well with your boss."

"I don't care." Branson shrugged, but again, the intensity in his eyes betrayed his casualness.

I refocused on the quiche, on the sound of Watson crunching beneath me, on the sight of the tourists wandering over the sidewalks below. On anything that might give me time to figure out how to get out of this conversation, short of standing and walking away.

We ate in silence for a little while, the hum of conversations around us, the clatter of dishes as people ate, and the sounds of Katie and Nick baking away, easing some of the strain between us.

Branson erased that after a matter of minutes. "I couldn't help but notice Leo was with you the other night, during the... whatever it was at the elk statue." Though he clearly tried to sound nonchalant, there was just a hint of accusal and hurt.

"Leo?" I stared at him, partially thrown off by the

abrupt change, and simply astounded we were going there at all.

He met my gaze for a few seconds as he nodded, and then his glance darted away. "Yeah. Leo. He was with you. I wondered... Maybe he's why... or part of the reason why..."

A flash of embarrassment cut through me for some reason, which, thankfully, ushered on a spike of anger. "He's my friend. He and Katie and I hang out all the time. And Paulie. We're just—" No, I wasn't going to do this. I wasn't going to justify. There was no reason to. "What are you doing?"

Instead of answering, he gestured at me with his fork. "You're still wearing the corgi earrings he gave you." There was a touch of anger in his words now as well, though it seemed to be more filled with hurt. "You're not wearing the corgi necklace that I gave you..."

I pulled at the pendant around my neck. "No, I'm wearing this crystal my *mom* asked me to wear. I can't..." I shook my head in frustration. I'd just told myself we weren't going to do this, that there was no reason to justify, and there I was getting ready to do exactly that. Enough of that. I appreciated that Branson wasn't going to stand in my way, that he was willing to provide more details into what happened to Aurora, but enough of it. I wasn't going to play this game. "Branson, listen, we—"

"Stop it! You can't do this!" A scream from outside cut me off, and even before I stood to look through the windows at the sidewalk directly below, I recognized the voice as one of the twins. "I demand you let her go right now!"

From the angle, I couldn't see what was happening.

Clearly, Watson recognized the voice as well, and though he didn't have a strong adoration for the twins like he did their father, he obviously counted them his family. He scampered halfway across the bakery, then looked back at me, telling me to get a move on.

I did, without sparing Branson a second glance. I rushed across the bakery, and by the time I reached the stairs I caught up with Watson, and we hurried down them together. I heard Katie's voice not far behind as she followed.

We hurried through the bookshop, and Watson and I joined Zelda on the sidewalk as she screamed at Officer Green, who was loading Verona into a police cruiser.

"Zelda, get ahold of yourself." Verona glared at her sister as she slid into the backseat. Her voice was calm in comparison, and though shame covered her features, she sounded resigned.

"Get ahold of myself?" Zelda only bellowed louder and let out a cry of rage as Susan shut the door, cutting off whatever Verona was getting ready to say. "Why, you—"

Watson let out a bark, and I grabbed Zelda's arm, yanking her back in just enough time to keep her swatted slap from making contact with Susan.

Susan turned her pale blue eyes on Zelda, and though her tone was angry, there was also enjoyment there. "Please, Zelda. Give me a reason to bring you in too."

"Susan!" Branson stepped around us. "What do you think you're doing?"

The air of enjoyment gave way to pure unadulterated pleasure as Susan lifted her chin to her superior. "Just following through on your boss's orders. If you have a problem with doing *actual* police work, talk to the chief."

Katie's hand gripped my arm, forming a chain between Zelda, me, and herself. Maybe I'd been about to attempt to slap Susan as well and Katie had stopped me. Who knew? The red haze of rage was causing things to blur.

With a final glare at Branson, Susan walked around the cruiser and got in. Then, with a little wave, pulled away.

"What happened?" I turned to Zelda, who was suddenly crying.

She gestured toward the retreating police car, and though tears streamed down her face, her voice was nothing but fury and confusion. "She just showed up. Verona and I were trying to put the shop back together, and in walked Susan Green, saying that she had a warrant for Verona's arrest. That she could come down willingly, but that she hoped Verona would choose the hard way."

Branson grabbed Zelda's other arm, though it didn't seem aggressive. "Why? What reason did Susan say?"

"She... she..." Zelda shook her head at Branson and started sucking in breaths, sounding close to hyperventilation.

"Zelda!" I gave her arm a little shake. "This won't help. Tell us what happened."

She steadied as she refocused on me. "Duke Riser said he saw Verona meet with Aurora here." She ripped her arm free from Branson to gesture at Chakras. "Said he saw the two of them meet here in the middle of the night, and then Aurora was dead the next morning." Zelda shook her head again, this time confusion overtaking her anger. "It doesn't make sense. Verona never mentioned it. I didn't know she came back into town at all, let alone met with Aurora."

It didn't make sense, but there was Duke again. "Maybe he's making it up. He was furious with Aurora and seemed that way to Verona as well."

"No. Verona didn't admit it, but she didn't deny it

either." Zelda's voice lowered to a whisper, but she didn't pull her gaze away from mine. "I know her. Duke's not lying. She did it. Verona met Aurora here. I could tell. I could tell..."

NINE

With his nose poking through the railings, Watson glared at the chaos from the loft overhead, his head resting on a fuzzy lion, one of Leaf's stuffed animals. I couldn't blame him. With the eleven of us crammed into Zelda's living room, we were as loud as a herd of elephants. Plus, it had to be a terrifying experience, trying to dodge twenty-two feet walking around.

I was tempted to join him, and from the overwhelmed look on Katie's face, was willing to bet she felt the same way. After nearly an hour, the family didn't seem any closer to calming down. Zelda was beside herself, constantly crying. Her husband, Noah, and my mother, squeezed on either side of her on the couch, were unable to stop her flow of tears. My uncles were nearby, Gary's large ex-football player frame filling up an overstuffed armchair, while Percival paced back and forth behind him, gesturing wildly with his lanky arms every time a new thought hit him.

My nieces and nephews were gathered around the peninsula that divided the kitchen from the open-concept living room. Verona's boys, Ocean and Leaf, both had red puffy eyes, but their tears had dried up long ago. Zelda's daughters, Britney and Christina stayed near them, offering their cousins support. The four of them were handling the hours after Verona's arrest better than the adults.

"Noah, I really think you should go into town." Zelda sniffed and grabbed her husband's thigh as she turned toward him. "You need to demand something be done."

"Sweetheart, they're doing everything they can. There's nothing more I can do." Noah had explained that multiple times and simply sounded exhausted.

"He's right. Your father and Jonah got Gerald Jackson to represent Verona. It'll take him a while, but Gerald will get it done." Percival stopped his pacing to level his stare at Zelda. "They're probably on their way here now. We just don't know it because you guys don't live anywhere sensible and want to live like it's the 1800s again."

"Percival, don't start. Glen Haven is a charming place to live." Mom gave her older brother a withering stare while she patted Zelda's thigh.

"Sure, if you want to pretend like you're in the pages of *Little House on the Prairie*." As if proving a point, Percival pulled out his cell phone and lifted it into the air. "Not a bar, not a single, solitary bar." He pointed to the phone on the wall. "And I can't blame them if they don't want to use a landline. Being retro is one thing, but that monstrosity is most definitely *not* chic"

Glen Haven was only seven miles down the twisting road from Estes Park, nestled in a narrow valley between the mountains. While most of the houses there were log cabin versions of mansions, there was no cell reception, and the quality of the landlines in both of the twins' side-by-side homes was little more than static.

"You'll see, Gerald will get Verona out on bail any minute." Gary smiled at Zelda as he gestured for his husband to put his phone away.

"Bail?" Zelda sounded close to a breakdown. "She shouldn't have to post bail. She should just be free. Verona wouldn't hurt anyone. She shouldn't even need Gerald."

Katie and I exchanged glances, neither of us had an ounce of faith in my stepfather's favorite lawyer.

Mom noticed and cocked her eyebrow in a subtle warning. Though she was careful what she said, I knew she had similar concerns. She patted Zelda's thigh again. "You really have no guesses about why Verona would meet Aurora in the middle of the night?"

"No!" Zelda let out a fresh wail. "For the thousandth time, she didn't tell me she was doing it. I can't believe my own sister was keeping secrets from me."

"Now you know how Mom felt." Fifteen-year-old Ocean looked over from the dining room table with the disdain only a teenager could manage. "She was devastated when she found out about your sugar addiction." Beside him, his nine-year-old brother nodded along enthusiastically.

"I don't have a sugar addiction!" Zelda stood, hurried over to the table, and laid a hand on both of her daughters' shoulders. "Tell them, Britney, Christina. I don't have a hoard of sugar hidden away here at the house, do I?" Christina, who was also nine nodded hesitantly, her eyes wide, while teenaged Britney shrugged. "Well, you do have several king-size Snicker bars in the freezer."

"Oh, for crying out loud!" Once more, Percival threw up his arms. "None of this has anything to do with sugar. Although with as batty as that Aurora Birnbaum woman was, that actually wouldn't be too surprising."

"Percival!" Mom sucked in a shocked gasp, though I marveled that anything Percival said could ever surprise her at this point. "She *just* died. Don't say such things."

"Oh, my dear, sweet, innocent little sister." Despite being in his seventies, Percival cast Mom an expression that rivaled the teenagers. "The woman was doing a séance for a *dead elk*. She was a wackadoo."

"I don't think it was a séance." Noah scrunched up his nose in a puzzled expression and glanced over at Zelda. "Was she trying to contact Samson's spirit? That doesn't make any sense. It's not like he could say anything. He was an elk. It's not even mating season, so he wouldn't even bugle."

Percival clapped his hands before Zelda replied. "Exactly! Thank you, Noah! Exactly my point." He squinted. "Well, kinda. Regardless, the woman was a wackadoo."

Beside me, Katie snickered but covered it up quickly with a cough.

"Either way"—Gary cast a reprimanding glare over his shoulder at Percival—"Verona wouldn't have hurt Aurora, or anyone for that matter. Whether they were *wackadoo* or not."

"Of course she wouldn't have." Mom nodded sagely. "It doesn't matter that we don't know why she met with Aurora that night. We know Verona. There's no doubt that she's innocent."

"If she's innocent, then why did she agree to give Aurora and Wolf the store for the entire week when they were kicked out of the conference? She didn't even ask me." Zelda had barely finished her outburst before her eyes went wide and she covered her mouth. "I'm not saying she hurt Aurora, of course. Not at all."

"We know that, darling." Noah patted Zelda's recently vacated spot on the couch. "You're just emotional right now, which makes sense. We know you didn't mean it like that."

Percival rolled his eyes and focused on me. "We need to quit worrying about Verona. Gerald will fix that situation soon enough. What's more important is to figure out who killed Aurora. That will clear all speculation around Verona's name and put an end to several other things as well."

All gazes focused on me and a few heads nodded. Once more, everyone assumed I was going to jump in and investigate.

"I know you guys have faith in Gerald, but—" Suddenly, something struck me as strange about Percival's words, and I returned his stare. "What did you mean that finding out who killed Aurora will put an end to several other things as well? What other things?"

Percival's eyes widened, and he paled slightly. He almost looked embarrassed, which was an expression I didn't ever see on my flamboyant uncle. He exchanged a quick glance with Gary and then shook his head. "Nothing. I mean, obviously, anytime a murderer is apprehended... it stops... whatever other bad things they were planning on doing. Who can say?"

The family altered their focus to him, all of us thrown off by his unusual response.

"Percival." Mom cocked her head, and though she was the younger sibling, her tone took on a mothering timbre. "What's going on?"

He lifted his chin defiantly. "Nothing. Like I said. You simply want to catch a murderer before they do something else. Like... murdering again... or something."

Still we studied him.

At last, Gary sighed. "We may as well tell them."

Percival stiffened and glared at his husband.

The two of them exchanged a silent argument, the type that only couples of decades could accomplish.

Percival's shoulders slumped in defeat and he raised his hands in surrender. "Fine. Go ahead."

Gary repositioned in the armchair to face the rest of the family. "We suspect that church group, the Holy Rapture Fellowship, of being behind Aurora's death."

"The ones that threw the Bibles?"

Gary nodded at Mom and continued, and his normally low, soft voice became barely audible. "They've been harassing us for the past several weeks, sending"—he shrugged—"hate mail, basically, to the antique shop. Not exactly threatening Percival and me, but... close."

"Why would they threaten you? What did you do?" Britney sounded completely baffled, and from the expressions of the other three of the younger generation, they were all on the same page. The rest of us didn't require an explanation.

It was Mom who finally spoke and the pain of her voice was tinged with just a hint of anger. "Why didn't you tell us?"

Again, Gary and Percival exchanged glances, then shrugged in unison. Percival shook his head sadly before replying. "We thought it would pass. Estes has always treated us kindly. Even back in the day when we weren't safe in other places, we were in our little mountain town." He shrugged again and looked at Mom. "I know part of that is because you and I grew up here, but still..."

When his words faded away, Gary took over. "It reminds me of when I was growing up, back home. Everyone telling me gays were nothing more than sinners who were going to hell, and *deserved* to go to hell. It's why I stayed in the closet until after I retired from playing football."

Britney and Ocean both let out understanding gasps and looked utterly disgusted.

Despite the situation, I couldn't help but feel warmed at their response. It was beautiful that they couldn't imagine hating someone simply because of who that someone loved.

The whole room fell into silence for several seconds, and then we all jerked in shock and surprise when Watson let out a sharp bark from above us and then scrambled down the stairs, only pausing to grab the stuffed lion and bring it down with him.

With a pained wince, Percival cast an accusing glare at Watson. "Speaking of hate crimes…"

Though his bark had been startling, it hadn't been one of anger or warning. Watson came to a stop at the door and pranced about as if the world's largest dog treat was waiting on the other side.

"Looks like Barry's arriving." As I spoke Barry's name, Watson looked back at me and gave a little whimper through the stuffed animal. "Which means, hopefully, the rest of them are too."

Zelda hurried to Watson's side, but before she reached the door, it flung open and Verona marched in, followed by her husband, Jonah, the rotund and harried Gerald Jackson, and finally Barry.

I'd never seen my stepfather look so exhausted, even when he'd been falsely arrested for murder months ago. His skin was ashen against his purple-and-blue tie-dyed shirt, and he actually walked halfway across the room before noticing Watson circling desperately between his feet. A small smile cracked his lips, and he knelt to pat Watson with a sigh. "Nice to see you too, buddy. Cute little friend you got there."

Behind them, another reunion was happening as Ocean and Leaf were gathered into Verona's arms. Both boys sniffled, and for a second it looked as if Verona was going to join in on the tears. Though she held them tenderly and kissed each of their foreheads before releasing them, she shook the emotion away.

"I'm so glad you're okay." Zelda approached her sister, clearly getting ready to hug, but then stopped short. "*Are* you okay?"

"Of course I am." Verona's tone was suddenly harsh. "Please don't be dramatic about it."

"Dramatic?" Zelda sounded stung. The hurt gave way to anger. "Why would I be dramatic? *You're* the one being dramatic. Giving our store away for a week to that woman without even asking me." Her voice rose as she spoke. "Having midnight meetings with her right before she's killed? You... going around in secret, and now you're going to tell *me* not to be dramatic?"

"Apparently, I wasted my breath." Verona's tone was cutting, and though they'd been at each other's throats more than ever since getting Chakras up and running, I'd never heard such dismissive coldness from either one of them. "And *you're* hardly one to talk about secrets, Zelda Pearson." She walked past before Zelda could respond and attempted a smile at the rest of the room. "Thank you all for your support. I'm sorry to have been the source of drama. It means the world that you're here. Really. But... please go home. I'm beyond tired."

We all stared at her.

With a final stroke on Watson's head, Barry stood, and

his voice was gentle. "Verona, whatever's going on, we're your family. We love you."

"Dad, please don't start again. Not now."

She started to walk toward the other room, but Jonah grabbed her hand. "Baby, if we just—"

"We already covered this at the police station. Leave it alone." She jerked her hand away and gestured toward Gerald Jackson. "He got me out, and he'll make sure I stay that way."

"Well..." Gerald winced. "Like we discussed, if you won't even tell me why—"

"If you can't do your job, then just say so." Verona cut him off with a glare.

From the glances that were exchanged around the room, I wasn't the only one feeling like I was observing a stranger. She and Zelda sniped from time to time, but neither was anything but pleasant and lovely to everyone else.

Verona blushed slightly and seemed to realize how she was coming across. She attempted a smile in my direction. "You're on it, right? I'm sure you've already got a huge list of suspects. As soon as you figure out which one did it, none of this will even matter."

The entire room looked at me. "There's... a few possibilities."

Her eyes widened in surprise, and her tone conveyed disappointment. "A *few?*"

"Well, if you have any details, like everyone said, that would help." I braced to be the next recipient of her anger.

Sure enough, her gaze hardened once more. "Don't start, Fred. I've made my stance very clear. What Aurora and I talked about that night was *our* business, and no one else's." Verona glared around the room, meeting everyone's eyes before leveling back on me. "I did *not* kill her. I did *not* hurt her. Yes, I will admit that she went from someone I admired with every ounce of my being to someone I absolutely hated, but I didn't hurt her nor would I have."

"I didn't think you did. None of us thought that." Though I sounded placating, I meant the words completely. Several others nodded, but Verona kept her eyes on me. I decided to push a little. "But still, if you know something, it would help—"

"That was between Aurora and me." Verona crossed the room, halting only at Watson's growl. She glanced down at him with a flash of surprise, and when she looked back up, some of the anger had faded. "Sorry. I know this isn't your fault. And I'm not at my best."

"It's okay." I decided to go another route. "If you can't tell me why you guys met, can you point me in a direction? Should I look at Wolf, Tabitha, that church group, or—"

"I don't know. *Obviously,* if I knew who killed her, I would tell you." She shrugged and then seemed to deflate. She claimed the spot on the sofa that Zelda had occupied before, and when she spoke to me again, she sounded completely used up. "I really don't know. Maybe the church group. They've been making life a nightmare for us at the store, as you know." Another shrug. "I can't imagine Wolf being behind it. He seemed to really love her, and even if he didn't, Aurora was the cash cow of their business, so does it make sense that he'd cut off the source?"

Aurora was the cash cow? I supposed that wasn't exactly news. She'd definitely been the one in charge, but they seemed to be a partnership.

Before I could ask about that, Verona sat forward, new energy in her voice. "What about Rocky Castle?"

There were a couple of groans from other people. Though Gerald Jackson made an agreeing murmur.

"I'm sorry, I don't know who that is?"

Instead of answering me, despite how Verona had treated Zelda before, she looked to her twin for assistance. And as ever, received it.

"Rocky operates Rocky Road Tours." Zelda pointed to the far side of the room as if gesturing outside. "He lives down the way, right at the turnoff to our road. You've probably noticed the big vans and trucks in the yard?"

With that detail, it clicked into place. Though I'd never met the man, I had noticed the junkyard worth of vehicles every time I'd visited the twins in Glen Haven. Rocky Road Tours was painted on the side of a couple of them. "I have. How is he connected to the Birnbaums?"

This time, Zelda pointed to the other side of the house. "Aurora and Wolf's summerhouse is farther up the road, near the top of the mountains. Rocky used to lead his Bigfoot hunts up there before they bought the house. They refused to let him lead his tours there anymore. He still did it a few times, but they sued him."

Gerald cleared his throat. "In my defense, they have high-powered city lawyers. And Rocky didn't help himself by offering a free Bigfoot hunt to the judge."

Barry patted his shoulder. "Wasn't your fault, old man. Don't let it get you down."

Verona jumped in again. "I'm not saying he killed her, but he's a good place to start." Her voice rose in excited desperation. "Really, Fred, you could just take out darts, fling them at random, and get a bullseye. It turns out that anyone who got to know the *real* Aurora Birnbaum couldn't stand her." She cast an accusing glare at Zelda, but refocused on me before another war could break out. "She was horrible and a fake. And while I didn't wish her any harm, and I hate that she had the nerve to get murdered in my store, she had it coming."

"Verona!"

She ignored Zelda's admonition standing up once more. Though we were surrounded by the rest of our family and all of them could hear, Verona lowered her tone so her words were directed only at me. "Thank you for looking into it. I feel better with you trying to clear my name. But..." She pointed a finger directly at me, eliciting another growl from Watson; this time she ignored it. "Don't snoop into me. My life is *my* life. And I won't have that vile woman ruin it just because she died."

I simply stared at her, completely taken aback.

Verona shook her finger. "Are we clear, Winifred?"

"Verona..." I couldn't keep the hurt out of my tone.

"Sweetheart, I think you should stop. You're tired. Clearly delirious." Barry cast an apologetic glance at me as he spoke to Verona with a placating tone and attempted to put his arm over her shoulders.

She shook him off and thrust her finger at me again. "If you can't keep your nose out of my business, then just let the police handle it." With that, she turned and stormed off into one of the bedrooms, leaving everyone speechless in her wake.

It was a good thing I didn't return from Glen Haven until late in the evening. Late enough that there was nothing to do besides go home and go to bed. If it had been even an hour or so earlier, I would've let my temper get the best of me.

By the time morning arrived, I'd cooled somewhat, but I still decided that though there were a plethora of possible suspects, there was only one option of where to begin. Not only did they seem likely, I needed to confront their hate. I waited until a little after ten before gathering up an assortment of Katie's finest offerings and heading out to the Estes Valley Church.

As I walked up the winding cobblestone path to the front door, I felt my temperature rise again, to the point that I regretted bringing the pastries. I'd figured they might make what was surely going to be a tense conversation a little more productive. For once, I was going to go with my mother's old adage of catching more flies with honey, but now that the moment was upon me, I was ready to fight, not offer the best baked goods Estes had to offer. Maybe some overly dry scones, not Katie's delicacies.

Watson, on the other hand, was in an exceptionally

good mood. He quite literally pranced along beside me as if playing the part of Little Bo Peep's sheep instead of my grumpy little corgi. The only explanation was getting to spend the previous night with Barry, followed by the morning with Ben, and topped off with Katie making a fresh batch of his favorite dog treats.

He was almost cute enough to calm my increasing rage —almost.

I was tempted to take the box of pastries back to my Mini Cooper but figured I was nearly there and that would just waste time. The smarter option might have been to sit down right where I was and eat them all myself. The sugar high would probably keep me from somehow making the situation worse.

Instead of eating a corgi's weight in baked goods, I paused, knelt, and held out my hand. Proving just how good of a mood he was in, Watson trotted over without any other direction and nuzzled me affectionately. I needed to get myself together. Yes, my anger was justified. It had been bad enough knowing the Holy Rapture Fellowship had been giving the twins a hard time for their shop, but discovering how they'd been treating my uncles was more than I could handle. And if that's all this little meeting was about, I wouldn't care how I came across or what I said. But there was a very real chance that they were behind Aurora's murder. Clearing Verona's name was more important than giving them a piece of my mind. Besides, if they were guilty, and I proved it, that would be more than enough payback.

Petting Watson worked like a charm, lowering my heart rate and grounding me in the moment. Despite my anger at the church, the building itself was rather soothing. It resembled a tiny log-cabin version of a castle from where it nestled amidst the trees. Utterly charming and, as in most things in Estes Park, pure storybook quality.

With a final pat on Watson's head, I stood, and we finished making our way to the arched front door.

Now that I was there, I realized that despite having the evening to calm myself down, I hadn't really thought the situation through. I hadn't called or made an appointment. It wasn't like it was Sunday and I could interrupt the middle of a service. Nor was it like one of the businesses downtown; it wouldn't be open tourist hours.

Hoping for the best, I tapped on the old wood planks. The door was thick and solid. I doubted anyone could hear. I rapped again, harder that time. Hard enough it kind of hurt my knuckles. Even so, I still didn't get the feeling that the knock carried.

After several moments of waiting, and Watson staring up at me with an expression of *what's the holdup*, I tried the door, expecting to be thwarted.

It opened with a creak, just like it really was an old castle. Unlike me, Watson didn't hesitate and waddled right inside. I followed his lead and shut the door behind me. There was no vestibule or entrance like I'd expected. Watson and I found ourselves in the center of a long, narrow sanctuary that was just as beautiful inside as out. The log walls towered high above us and reached the steep arch at the pinnacle. Long wooden benches made up either side, forming an aisle down the center. A score of narrow stained glass windows, depicting scenes from Christ's life, cast colorful prisms throughout the space. In the front there was an altar of rock and wood, and behind that, a similarly designed pulpit. A large cross fashioned from timbers and rusty metal hung just below a round stained glass window at the base of the peaked ceiling.

I wasn't sure what I was expecting, but not this. It didn't seem like a place where hatred was spewed. Not just because it was beautiful, but the feel in and of itself. It reminded me of something... though I couldn't quite place it.

Watson scurried around, sniffing curiously here and there before settling at the end of the altar, finding the perfect place to nap—right in a pool of gold-and-blue light streaming in from one of the stained glass windows.

And then it hit me. It reminded me of my bookshop, at least the feel of it.

No, I most definitely had not expected that.

If anything, that threw me off even more and made me a touch angrier. How anyone could spend time in a place that was the spiritual equivalent of my bookshop and make their ultimate purpose hurting other people's lives, was incomprehensible.

It seemed I was wasting my time, though. No one was present. While I couldn't imagine leaving the church unlocked with no one to protect it, there wasn't exactly a place for anyone to hide either. I was about to tell Watson to abandon his nap when another creak sounded, causing both of us to jump.

Behind the altar, a door began to open from the log wall. There was no frame around, and it blended in seamlessly. It really was a little like a castle, complete with secret doors and everything. Despite myself, I couldn't help but be further charmed by the place.

The man who stepped through was nearly a foot shorter than me, probably barely five foot flat, and I guessed him being around three hundred pounds. The purple robes he wore floated around him in a way that brought to mind Violet Beauregarde after chewing her three-course gum. A book was open in front of his face, and I could only make out the top of his bald head.

Watson let out a yip.

The man, in turn, let out a high-pitched yelp and dropped the book as he clutched at his chest.

From his round, wizened face, white in shock, it was clear he was at least eighty years old, if a day.

I tossed the box of pastries on the front pew and rushed toward him as he clutched his chest, figuring I'd accidentally murdered an old man. An old *preacher*, if the robes were any indication. "It's okay. It's just me and my dog. I'm so sorry. I'm so, so sorry."

Still clutching at his chest, the man looked at me as if I were the Grim Reaper himself, but then his expression softened when he glanced at Watson. Releasing the grip on his robes, he patted over his heart and gave a chuckle. "Oh my goodness! You two scared the ever-loving beans out of me."

I stopped within arm's length of him. "I am sorry. We really weren't trying to scare you."

"Well, if you had been, you'd have succeeded." Another chuckle and another pat on his chest. "And if you weren't, you succeeded anyway."

"Do you need to—" I motioned toward the altar, then adjusted my aim toward the front row of benches... er... pews "—sit?"

He waved me off. "Goodness, no. Don't you worry yourself about me. My ticker is as strong as it ever was." He winked. "It's thanks to all those marathons I run."

I started to respond, and then I had no idea how to.

The preacher laughed harder and clutched at his chest again. "I'm just kidding. Even the Lord and Savior couldn't get me to run a marathon, and he works miracles."

I started to smile, and then realized I was being

charmed by him as surely as I'd been by the church building itself and remembered why I was there. He could be as charming as he wanted, that didn't make him a kind person.

Turning from me, he placed a hand on his robe-covered knee and bent slightly, not that it made much of a difference, and held out his other toward Watson. "And who are you, cuteness?"

Continuing in his good mood, Watson pranced over and sniffed the man's hand. Though he didn't offer a lick or anything quite so lavish, he allowed himself to be petted before heading back to his stained glass sunshine nap.

With a groan, the man straightened again and refocused on me, his eyes narrowing. "Why, I know who you are. You're Winifred Page. You moved to town last winter and opened a bookshop." He gestured toward Watson. "The corgi something or other."

"Yes. The Cozy Corgi." Despite my flickering anger, I felt a moment's shame at doing such a poor job of introducing myself. "People call me Fred, and he's Watson."

He waved a pudgy hand at Watson, who was already fast asleep, and then turned back to me. "I'm Stuart Davis. I'm the pastor here." Though his smile was bright, it dimmed suddenly as his eyes narrowed. "Oh... I think I know why you're here. I've heard you do a little bit more than run a bookshop." Without waiting for an answer, he attempted to bend to pick up his fallen book.

I couldn't help myself and snagged it for him.

"Thank you, dear." He reached for it. "More proof that the good Lord didn't call me to run marathons."

I started to hand the book to him but paused as I noticed the cover, then gaped at him. "You're reading *The Moving Finger*."

"Very true. And not for the first time." Pastor Davis tilted his head. "Are you a fan of Agatha Christie?"

I couldn't bring myself to answer, I was so shocked. "*You're* a fan of Agatha Christie?"

"Oh yes. I have everything she ever wrote, all first editions." He winced toward the decorative cross on the wall. "Though I shouldn't sound quite so pompous about that. Pride being a sin and all."

I stared at the book. It was the final insult. This man loved mystery novels? It was bad enough that the church was charming and felt cozy like a place of peace. Bad enough that the preacher seemed good-natured, kind, and rather humorous. But add all that together with him being an avid fan of Agatha Christie, and I simply could not accept that he was behind harassing my uncles.

And then it clicked. There was only one reason it felt so wrong.

I handed the book back to him and met his eyes. "The Holy Rapture Fellowship isn't part of your church, is it?"

He sighed as he accepted the novel. "Yep. That's why I thought you were here." He started to motion behind him, toward the secret door and then glanced at Watson. "I was going to invite you back to my office, but he looks too comfortable." He pointed to the front pew. "How about we chat here?"

The pew groaned in protest as the two of us sat, but seemed sturdy enough.

Pastor Davis looked at me with sad eyes. "Unfortunately, the Holy Rapture Fellowship *is* associated with the Estes Valley Church."

Again that flash of anger, but I shoved it away before I said something regrettable as I replayed his words. "Unfortunately?"

"Yes. Most unfortunately." He laid the Agatha Christie book aside and picked up a Bible that lay between us. "*This* is not a weapon. It is the greatest love story ever told." He clutched it to his chest, and there were tears sparkling behind his eyes. "The Bible is *not* a weapon."

"So... the Holy Rapture Fellowship is part of your church, but..." The pieces were coming together forming. "You don't condone what they did at the Samson statue, personally?"

Still clutching the Bible, he sighed. "Let me clarify. The members of the Holy Rapture Fellowship are part of my congregation, but they are not sanctioned by the church or our denomination. While I do not condone, I must confess that I am responsible, as they are part of my flock."

That made a little more sense. "In other words, you're not preaching from the pulpit to stone people with Bibles?"

"Goodness, no!" He looked affronted.

That meshed with the feeling I got from him, but I wanted to be clear just how much he was denouncing. "What about harassing storeowners because you don't approve of what they sell?"

"Your sisters' shop." He sighed again, shook his head. "I can't say I'm comfortable with the premise of some of the New Age beliefs and practices, but no, I don't approve of harassing storeowners."

Though before I voiced my next question I told myself to stay calm, I didn't succeed and anger seeped into my tone. "What about harassing loving, married couples who've been together for decades?"

Pastor Davis looked confused. "Winifred, I can honestly say I don't know what you..." His words fell away as his eyes widened. "No... surely not..."

Strangely, I felt inclined to rescue him, but I didn't.

"Are you telling me that Percival Oswald and his husband are being harassed?"

I nodded. "You didn't know?"

Pure anger washed over his cheerful features. "I most definitely did not. I've known Percival since he was a young man. And Phyllis since she was a girl. Your grandparents, Marty and Marion, were members of this church when I arrived to be pastor. It was my first assignment, and I've never left. I'm very fond of your family. Even though your grandparents were the last to attend."

I believed him. Still, I needed to double-check or alleviate some of my anger, I didn't know nor did I care which. "So you truly didn't know that the Holy Rapture Fellowship, which you admit is part of this church, is telling my uncles they need to prepare for the fires of hell?"

He grasped my hand and met my gaze. "I can assure you, I most definitely did not. Furthermore, I'm quite fond of your uncles. I must admit I get a kick out of seeing Percival wander around town every winter in that purple fur coat of his."

My heart warmed at the visual, and I couldn't hold back a little laugh. "According to him, it's a *boysenberry* fur coat, not purple."

He chuckled, but the laughter didn't reach his eyes. "I will go down to their shop and personally apologize. As well as to your sisters." He let go of my hand and sat back. "I am at fault. I've let warnings and reprimands go on too long without taking action. It is not how I do things, not how we as a denomination do things, but I will make an exception. The members of this Holy Rapture Fellowship, as they like to call themselves, will be kicked out of church until they repent."

The last part was all well and good, but all I really cared

about was the reparations with my uncles. The very fact that they'd kept it a secret, when they constantly gossiped and chattered on about everything else, only showed how deep their pain went. "Thank you. That will mean a lot to Percival and Gary."

He shook his head. "Do not thank me. I should've acted sooner."

I couldn't disagree there, though I still didn't quite understand. "If you don't approve of what this group is teaching, how is it part of your church?" My phone buzzed in the pocket of my skirt, but I ignored it.

He stiffened slightly, and I could see the debate behind his eyes. Loyalty to his congregation or transparency with me. I was surprised at what he chose.

"Sandy and Paul Anderson moved to town a few months ago. I'm afraid they're from a rather fanatic denomination." He sniffed and wiped away the moisture from his eyes with the back of his hand. "Unfortunately, as such extremism often does, their teachings have been shiny, new, and alluring to some. In a sick way, they offer membership to a very exclusive and elitist club, and a few members of my flock have joined them."

"Why haven't you kicked them out before?" Though I decided I genuinely liked the pastor, I didn't feel overly guilty for the accusation in my tone.

"Fear, I'm afraid." He winced. "Actually, that's not entirely true either. Though I do regret not acting sooner, I will insist that my hesitation came from a good place. I'd hoped to be able to change their hearts from within. When you forbid something, it often gives it more power, and they've made it very clear that if I push them too far, they would look into starting their own church. The last thing I wanted was to see my congregation split." He lifted his chin defiantly. "But as the good book says, it is better to cut off your own hand lest it cause you to sin. I need to cut out the infection before it tarnishes everyone within these hallowed walls."

Sandy and Paul Anderson. Probably the first two to throw their Bibles. It looked like I knew my second stop. "Do you know where the Anderson live? I'd like to talk to them."

"I do. But of course I can't give out their personal information." His expression changed again, and he leaned forward slightly. "Right... for a moment there, I forgot that you're more than a bookseller." His eyes widened in horror and once more, he grasped at his chest. "You don't think... that woman, the New Age woman, the one who died..." He snapped his fingers repetitively. "Aurora. You don't think..."

It was my turn to lean forward. "I don't know. You know Sandy and Paul, and the others involved in the fellowship. What do you think?" Again my phone buzzed, and I ignored it once more.

Pastor Davis shook his head again, violently at first, but then it slowed and his expression shifted from one of disbelief to repulsion. "I... I don't know. I want to say that wouldn't be possible, and I don't think it is. But..."

That was quite a but. Not for the first time, with the color drained from his face and his skin clammy, I worried I was putting too much strain on his heart. "Are you okay? I didn't mean to distress you."

He nodded but didn't look convincing. "Clearly I needed to be distressed. I should've acted so, so much sooner." He grabbed my hand again. "I'm so sorry that my lack of action has harmed your family."

Pastor Davis's sincerity and regret was nearly tangible, and it endeared the man to me permanently. "Thank you.

And thank you for taking the time to talk to Percival and Gary."

"I will. This afternoon. I'll go to their antique shop this afternoon."

Though it probably wasn't an act of kindness where the health of his heart was concerned, I responded to my need to care for him in the only way I knew how, and reached behind me to get the discarded bakery box. "Before you visit them, I think this conversation requires a little pick-me-up." I opened the lid and revealed the large assortment of pastries.

Not missing a beat, at the first crinkle of cardboard, Watson sprang from his nap like a lion hearing an antelope in the Serengeti and rushed toward us expectantly.

Pastor Davis chuckled and ruffled Watson's fur between his ears. "Looks like you've got a dog after my own heart."

After buckling up when Watson and I returned to the Mini Cooper, I checked my cell. I'd missed four calls from Zelda. Before I could call her back, the phone rang again, and her face flashed over the screen. I jumped, startled, but managed not to drop the phone.

From the corner of my eye, I noticed Watson cast a judgmental glance my way. I pretended not to notice and hit Accept.

Zelda launched in before I could say as much as a hello. "Hey, you okay? What's going on? I called you about a hundred times over the last hour. Where have you been?"

"I just talked to—"

"Never mind!" Zelda rushed ahead, her voice breathy with excitement. "I have the best news, although I'm sure you've already heard. You're always on top of everything. I'm surprised you didn't call us. Wait..." Her tone turned quizzical. "Why didn't you call us? We should have been your first stop. Where were you again?"

I had to blink and shake my head, Zelda's frantic pace was nearly making me feel dizzy. "Zelda! Breathe. What news? I haven't heard anything that would interest you."

"Really? Branson didn't tell you they've arrested Wolf?"

"Branson and I aren't dating anymore. You know that."

"Fred, it's just a glitch. You two will figure it out." Zelda was bright once more. "And even though you're on a break, I still expected him to fill you in."

"We're not on a break. Not like that." I started the Mini Cooper and began to pull out of the church parking lot and then hit the brakes, earning another glare from Watson. "Wait, what? Wolf was arrested?"

"Yes!" She puffed out an exasperated breath. "That's what I've been trying to tell you, if you'd answer your phone. Wolf was arrested early this morning."

"*Wolf* killed Aurora?"

"Well, obviously." The exasperation left Zelda's tone. "It's over, Fred. It's all over. We can get back to business as normal, and maybe Verona will start acting like herself again."

It was all over. To my surprise, there was no flicker of disappointment. Maybe I'd prided myself in solving murders quicker than the police in the past, but it didn't matter. I was very much with Zelda on this aspect. I just wanted it over. After checking that the road was clear, I stepped on the gas and pulled into the street. My next thought nearly had me hitting the brakes again, though I didn't. "Why?"

"Why what?"

"Why did Wolf kill his wife?"

"Well, obviously..." Zelda paused for a heartbeat. "I have no idea. Who knows? Probably because she was a truly horrible woman. That's awful to say, but she was. So different than we thought she'd be. Those few days with her were a nightmare. I can't imagine being married to her."

I continued driving, heading back toward downtown, having to pause frequently with the summer traffic. I supposed she had a point. Aurora Birnbaum hadn't been the warmest of personalities. But Verona had said herself that Aurora was the cash cow for Wolf—killing her would put an end to their career, and the money.

"Fred? Are you still there?"

"Yes, sorry. Just trying to make sense of it."

"Don't worry about it. You can let that part go. I'm sure the police have it all under control." It was nice to hear Zelda sound like her typical, cheerful self once more after being stressed and dark for so many days. "Where are you? Come down to Chakras. We're all meeting here and going out to lunch to celebrate."

"Actually, I was going to go talk to Sandy and Paul Anderson, as soon as I can find their address."

"Who?"

Traffic came to a complete standstill as a large herd of elk meandered at a snail's pace across the road. "The leaders of the Holy Rapture Fellowship, apparently. I just left a meeting with the pastor from Estes Valley Church. He was a very nice man and is completely devastated that people in his congregation have been harassing you and Verona, and Percival and Gary. He's going to come down and apologize to you all personally."

"That's good of him. It'll be nice to have that over with, though, really, the Rapture crazies are little more than a nuisance in comparison to what we've already been through. But now you don't need to bother with them. I'm assuming you thought they might have something to do with Aurora's death?"

"Maybe. I—"

"See, there you go, now you can rest easy. It's all handled and done. Besides, going to see them now would only stir the hornets' nest and probably make them start bothering us even more." Some of her impatience returned. "Hurry down to Chakras. Everyone else will be here in just a few minutes. Verona wants to go to Habanero's for Mexican, but I was hoping for burgers from Penelope's. I'm gonna let her win this one. Obviously."

For whatever reason, I hated to let it go.

I pondered that for a second. What was that reason? I truly didn't have any feelings about the police solving it quicker than me. Even so, I still wanted to speak to Sandy and Paul. But why?

Maybe just to get out my anger at them for how they treated my family?

"Fred? Are you coming?"

Zelda brought me back to the moment. "Yes. Yes, of course. I wouldn't miss it." I needed to let it go, at least for now. Zelda was probably right. I was certain I'd lose my temper with such people and end up making matters worse. Perhaps Pastor Davis could handle them and finally put a stop to it. "I'll be right there. Although I'm stuck behind a herd of elk, so it may take me a few minutes."

"Great. See you soon." She was gone with a click.

"Well, that was abrupt." I turned to Watson and scratched his head as he followed the progress of the slowly meandering elk. "Looks like we can go back to selling books and napping in the sunshine."

Watson cast me a quick glance with his version of a raised eyebrow and then refocused on the elk.

"I can tell you're very upset about it." I chuckled, but once more wondered at myself. I wasn't upset about it being over, but there were still a lot of unanswered questions.

As the final few elk made their way across the street and traffic was preparing to move, I noticed a familiar large, broken-down Army Jeep at the gas station. It had been among the junkyard of vehicles as I'd turned into Glen Haven. If I hadn't been already certain, the chipped yellow paint on the side reading Rocky Road Tours clarified.

On impulse, I veered off the road and turned into the gas station. Surely I wouldn't be too late for lunch. I pulled up beside the Jeep, facing the opposite direction so Watson's window was next to the Jeep's passenger side.

After hopping out of the Mini Cooper and darting around the back toward the Jeep, I suddenly realized I had no idea what I was hoping to accomplish with this. Maybe an unexplained attempt to hold on to this case... *not* that it was a case.

I needed to let this go.

"I know you!" A gruff voice stopped me in my tracks from where I turned to get back into my car.

I looked over to find a huge giant of a man walking around the front of the Jeep, his massive ginger hair and beard glowing vibrant red in the sunshine.

"You do?"

"Sure do." His burly facial features scrunched in consideration. "You're that book lady with the man's name." He bypassed me and headed toward the passenger door of the Mini Cooper. "This fat little thing must be the corgi you go all over town with." As he bent to stick his hand through the open window, he made my little car look the size of a Hot Wheel. "I just love animals. Even short, chubby ones that are more of an overgrown hamster than a dog."

From the rear window, I could see Watson make a hasty retreat to the other side of the car.

The giant gave a displeased rumble, tried again, and when Watson growled, he pulled his hand from the window and glared at me. "He's a rude little rat, isn't he?"

My hackles rose. This had most definitely been a

mistake. No matter that Aurora Birnbaum had been elitist and rude, and Wolf was apparently a murderer, I could hardly blame them for having conflict with this man.

Once more, I started to head back to the driver's door. "Well, nice to meet you. I should get going."

"Hold on now, you're the one who pulled up within inches of my Jeep here, obviously wanting something." He thumbed at the yellow lettering on the side of his vehicle. "You wanting to book a tour?"

"No. Thank you. I—"

His sky-blue eyes widened. "I know. You probably want me to come give a talk at your bookshop. About Colorado history or some such." He shrugged. "I'm not much of a reader myself, but I know these mountains like the back of my hand." His eyes widened further. "Nah, you want me to give a talk about Bigfoot, don't ya? Sell some of those books you got."

Despite my better judgment, and even knowing that curiosity killed the cat, I had to take the bait. "That wasn't what I was thinking, actually. But I did have a question about your Bigfoot tours."

There was only the briefest flash of disappointment over his face before he turned serious. "I don't do those til the fall, typically around Halloween, but that's just because tourists are stupid. Sasquatch doesn't care about holidays; he wanders the mountains all year long. But no sense offering a tour when I'm only going to get one or two takers during months like this. Halloween? The Bigfoot van is filled to overflowing."

"Thank you, I'll keep that in mind." I was going to require a double shot in my dirty chai to recover from the energy zap from talking to this man. "At this point, I'm not needing to book any tour myself. I simply wanted to ask you about a rumor I heard."

Before I could continue, he bristled and puffed himself up to an even larger height. It was rare that a person, even a man, made me feel small physically, but he was achieving it. "I don't know what rumors you heard, woman, but you best keep your nose out of my business."

I bristled right back. *Woman?* In *that* tone?

Stuffing my reaction away, I attempted to keep my tone neutral. Reprimanding him wouldn't help me get any information, needed or not. "I've no interest in sticking my nose in your business. I'd simply heard that the Birnbaums were trying to impede your livelihood."

"Impede?" Confusion sounded, and then his eyes widened once more "Oh! Sure. Hurt my business. Well, you heard right. Those rich, arrogant pieces of trash think they're better than me. I've been giving tours on that land for over twenty years. Then they come along and build their mansion right up there at the top. Like that gives them permission to tell everyone else what to do with the rest of the mountain. Not only hurting my bottom line, but also made it harder to catch sight of a Sasquatch. Luckily, they're just here in the summers." He chuckled, and for the first time, looked truly happy. "'Course, with that uppity woman dead, I bet her pansy of a husband isn't going to *hang* around too long."

The man made my skin crawl to the point that I was tempted to go home and take a shower before I met the others for lunch. But still, might as well see it through. "I take it you haven't heard about Wolf?"

He leaned his arm against the Mini Cooper, causing the whole thing to shift forward, his voice lowering in excitement. "What? Somebody string him up too?"

Yes, completely repulsive. "He was arrested this morning."

"Arrested?" The man flinched, causing the Mini Cooper to shift again. Watson growled from inside, but he didn't notice. "For what? Murder? Killing that wife of his?"

I shrugged.

He laughed, hard. "That's the dumbest thing I ever heard. That loser wouldn't pull off a tick for fear of killing it. Don't have the stones for it. Plus, he wouldn't kill his wife without her permission first. Ran around her like a lovesick puppy. Didn't make a single move without her permission." He straightened once more, and the Mini Cooper rolled back to its original position. "A disgrace, let me tell you, a man acting that way. Why, if I had a wife and she talked to me the way—"

"So who do *you* think killed Aurora Birnbaum?" I asked the question more to shut him up and to keep from hearing what he would do, as opposed to him actually offering any insight.

"No idea." He shrugged and gave another laugh. "Can promise you it wasn't Wolf. Talk about a man with the wrong name. He's about as far from a wolf as you can get. Shoulda been named Poodle"—he flicked a large hand toward Watson—"or Corgi, or something. Although, if he did do it, I'll shake his hand. Getting rid of that wife of his did the world a favor."

And with that, I was done. No information was worth putting up with him. "Well, I'm supposed to meet my family for lunch. I should get going."

He stepped toward me, moving quickly.

Though I prided myself in not being easily intimidated, I couldn't keep from stepping back.

"No reason to rush off so fast." He came forward

another step but paused within an arm's length of me. "I don't think I properly introduced myself. I'm Rocky Castle."

I blinked, thrown off. "Okay." I couldn't make myself say *nice to meet you* or any other pleasantry.

Rocky gave me a quick once-over. "I've heard about you, but never seen you in person. I like the looks of ya. Would be a good match. Both made of solid stock. We'd have a brood of strong redheaded boys, you and me."

I gaped at him, and even if I had known what to say, forming words wouldn't have been possible from the gorge that rose in my throat. Instead of trying, I walked over to the driver's side door and threw it open. Watson scurried to the other side, making room as if he were as desperate to leave the situation as I was.

"Where you going?" Rocky's voice followed me, but I didn't look back. "You didn't even give me your name."

I slid in, shut the door and started the car, before looking back at him as I shifted into Drive and pressed the gas. "No, I didn't."

To my surprise, he grinned in delight. "A redhead with fire. I like that. I'll look you up. Guy's name, right? George? Charlie?"

Despite the gorgeous August weather, I rolled up the windows to cut off his voice as Watson and I drove away.

"My wife is going to be so mad that she missed this. But it's her own fault that her hair appointments take so long." Marcus Gonzales clapped his hands excitedly as he approached our tables at Habanero's—we had two of them, the eight adults at one, the four kids nearby. He looked down at Barry's steaming plate of cheese enchiladas and gave an apologetic wince as he pulled out his cell phone. "I hate to do this since you all were just served, but I didn't know you were here. Do you mind if I get some pictures?"

"Absolutely. I never turn down a photo opportunity." Barry grinned up at Marcus as he wiped tortilla chip crumbs off his tie-dyed tank top. "How would you like me?"

Marcus looked flummoxed but finally gave a shrug. "Well, I was actually meaning a photo with Miss Verona"—he pointed at Zelda—"but a group shot would be fine."

From her place beside Zelda, Verona stiffened. "Why do you want a picture with me?"

Marcus's eyes narrowed as he looked back and forth between the twins and then realized his mistake. "It's not every day we have an accused murderer in the restaurant. I'd like to have your picture hanging on the wall with the other celebrities that have come in."

Verona grimaced. "I'm not a celebrity. And I'm not a murderer."

"Oh, I know." Marcus sounded disappointed. "That's why I said *accused*. But still, very exciting. That's the closest we've gotten in here."

"Now that's just silly, Marcus." Barry scooted his brightly painted chair back and stood. "Estes Park has had a whole rash of murders lately. I'm certain plenty of those murderers have eaten in here." He refocused on our two tables and gestured for us to join him. "Well, come on. We don't want to disappoint the man. Or let our food get cold."

"Dad, I really don't think—"

Barry cut off Verona. "We're here to celebrate. Might as well document it with photographic proof." He turned back to Marcus. "Sorry we don't have the entire family here. Percival and Gary are down in Denver at an estate sale. They obviously didn't know in advance that Wolf was going to be arrested today and clear Verona's name."

Marcus brightened once more. "Wolf was arrested for the murder?"

Barry nodded. "Just this morning. You didn't hear?"

He shook his head. "No, but you're right. He has eaten in here." His smile broadened, then faded quickly. "But I didn't get a picture with him."

"Well, you're getting a good one now. So perk up." Barry patted Marcus's shoulder, then gestured toward the wall with a painted rainforest motif. "All right everyone— Phyllis, girls, kids, let's look pretty."

Mom and the younger two kids hurried over cheerfully, while the rest of us cast begrudging glances at each other.

As we started to arrange ourselves, Barry angled back at the table. "Katie get over here."

She looked uncertain. "He just wanted the family."

"Actually, he just wanted Verona." Zelda sounded a touch jealous.

Barry ignored her and waved Katie over. "How many times do we have to tell you, darling, you *are* family."

Looking just as happy as my mother, Leaf, and Christina, Katie hopped up and hurriedly squeezed between Jonah and me.

"Come here, buddy." Barry scooped Watson up from where he'd been sitting at my feet and held him in his arms like a baby as he took his place beside Mom. "Got to have you front and center."

If I'd had tried such a move, Watson would've thrashed about to the point that he would've fallen from my arms, but with Barry, he just wiggled happily and lathered his face with kisses.

Marcus raised one hand over his head, snapping his fingers as if we were kindergartners having a class photo. "All right everyone, say murder!"

"Murder!" Mom and Barry chirped out the word as if they were wishing someone Merry Christmas.

"Good grief. Someone kill me now," Verona muttered through a clenched-toothed smile.

"I don't think that's a good thing to say around here anymore." Zelda elbowed her twin.

A couple more clicks, and Marcus was satisfied. As we headed back toward our table, he pulled me to the side, stood on his tiptoes so he could wrap his arm over my shoulder, and held his phone in selfie mode. "I don't know why I haven't thought of this before. You're quite the celebrity. You deserve a spot on the wall."

Before I could object, our image was captured. Habanero's was Katie and Leo's and my main hangout, but after this, I wasn't sure if I'd ever be able to darken its doors again.

"Hold on! I was squinting." Marcus leaned his head toward mine and snapped another photo. "Perfect. Maybe one day there will be a murder here and you and your little sidekick can solve it. Wouldn't that be exciting?" He released my neck and then sucked in a gasp. "Your sidekick. I need a photo with him."

"He's not the greatest lover of photos. And if things keep going like they have been, chances are you'll get your wish." Barry came to the rescue, once more patting Marcus's arm, and his tone grew conspiratorial. "While I have your attention, I've been meaning to talk to you about adding some more vegetarian options to the menu. Do you have a second?"

The two of them wandered off, Watson trailing behind Barry, as everyone else resettled around the tables.

"So much for a celebration lunch." Verona raked a hand through her long blonde hair and sighed. "I thought this would be over with Wolf in jail." She shook her head. "I still can't believe he killed her. It doesn't make any sense. The business will go nowhere without her."

"Don't worry. Something else will happen soon, and you'll be old news." Zelda managed to make the words sound sweet, kinda.

"Has anyone heard if they've mentioned a motive?" Katie glanced at me and then around the table after I shook my head.

"I don't care about the motive, just glad it's done." Verona broke a piece of her specially ordered baked tortilla shell off her taco salad. "I simply want to reopen Chakras tomorrow and enjoy the shop. School starts next week, and then tourist season will begin to die down, so things will slowly go back to normal."

There were four groans from the kids' table.

"I don't know." Zelda sniffed. "Can things really ever be back to normal now that we know there're secrets between us?"

Daggers flashed from Verona's blue eyes. "Really? You're *still* on that? Do I need to remind you of ice cream and Lord knows what else you've been lying about?"

Zelda's cheeks burned, and she shook her head.

"I think we've had enough of stone throwing." Noah gave a meaningful look at his twin.

Jonah nodded and ran a soothing hand up and down Verona's forearm. "I agree. And it's normal for people to have secrets. Even twins. I'm sure Noah and I do." Across the table, Noah looked skeptical, but Jonah continued. "We all have stupid skeletons in the closet. It doesn't mean we don't love and trust each other."

Something in the inflection of Jonah's words gave me pause. He knew Verona's secret. For some reason, that surprised me. Maybe it shouldn't have as he was her husband, but it shocked me that Verona would tell him and not Zelda. I shoved the thought from my mind. I didn't need to be curious about any secrets. I didn't even need to concern myself with Wolf's motives. It was done. Even the fringe religious group drama was done, or at least on its way out, if Pastor Davis was able to pull his weight.

"Great news!" Barry's cheerful voice drew all our attention to him as he and Watson headed back toward us. "Marcus has agreed to create a vegetarian section of the menu. And not just with cheese, but with tofu tacos, tempeh tortas, and chickenless chicken chimichangas!"

As one, the entire table stiffened at the three police officers following Barry and Watson.

Barry's smile faltered. "Goodness, why do you all look so worried? That's great news." At Watson's growl, Barry turned and saw what the rest of us had noticed.

Chief Briggs cast a quick warning glance my way as he stepped up to the table. To his right, Susan Green's smirk confirmed that things most definitely weren't over. As did Officer Jackson's devastated expression from where he flanked the other side of Rusty Briggs.

"Verona Pearson"—Chief Briggs walked directly toward the twins, but didn't confuse the two—"you're under arrest for the murder of Aurora Birnbaum."

The entire table erupted into chaos. And when Verona was led out in handcuffs a few minutes later, Marcus Gonzalez scurried around, gleefully snapping pictures with his cell phone.

"I'm beginning to feel extremely incompetent. I can't find anything substantial. There are a few articles about how Aurora was more of a diva than she pretended to be, but those are few and far between and didn't get much traction." From her place on the couch, Katie scowled at the computer perched on her lap. "This would go a lot quicker if Leo was here. Maybe a fresh set of eyes and perspective. We can call Paulie, see if he wants to join, maybe Athena."

"No, I don't want to bug anyone yet. It feels like there's not enough to go on to really get things moving." I was seated on the floor at the other end of the couch, computer on my lap, and Watson pressed against my thigh, asleep.

The rest of the day had been a complete whirlwind. Verona's arrest was so unexpected that for a few hours, it seemed like the family just wandered around in shock, unsure what to do. The only people they were letting speak to Verona were Jonah and Gerald Jackson.

Jonah reported that Verona was stressed and angry, but otherwise okay. Meanwhile, Gerald Jackson was hardly any use at all, spouting out random and obscure laws he thought he could use to get her free, in between drinking bottle after bottle of homemade kombucha.

All evening, Katie and I had been scouring the internet for any leads that could give us a new angle to clear Verona's name. We'd looked at Rocky Castle but found nothing. Though my gut told me he had absolutely nothing to do with it, despite being beyond repulsive. Even looking into the Holy Rapture Fellowship hadn't revealed much, other than Sandy and Paul Anderson having ties to the Sovereign Citizens. But there was no connection between that group and Aurora or Wolf. We'd found several photos of Tabitha in articles related to the Birnbaums, but not even a mention of her last name.

Everything was a dead end. Everything.

Though Katie hadn't meant bringing in other people as a change of subject, I latched on to the topic, my brain needing to focus somewhere else for a while. "Leo said there was more poaching today?"

Katie made an affirmative hum but didn't look up from her computer. "Yeah, bighorn sheep. Third one this month."

"And no leads?"

"No. Nothing at all. It just doesn't make any sense. I'm betting the police suspect an affair."

"An affair?" I blanched, causing Watson to let out an annoyed groan in his sleep. "What do affairs have to do with poaching?"

"Why would affairs have anything to do with poaching?" Katie looked up at me, her brows knitted, and then she chuckled. "Oh, you were still talking about Leo. Sorry. I was back to Verona. There's something strange, obviously. I mean, I don't get how Verona is arrested and Wolf is still in jail. I know it looks like Tabitha is head over heels for Wolf, but that doesn't mean he feels the same way." Katie's tone turned cautious. "Perhaps he has feelings for someone else. For Verona... Maybe if the police suspect an affair, they think the two of them teamed up to get rid of Aurora."

Now that was an angle. "I know Verona apparently has some secrets that she doesn't want anyone to know, but Jonah is right; we all have skeletons. However, I don't see an affair being one of hers. I can't imagine her doing that to Jonah. She loves her family, completely."

Katie shook her head. "Of course not, I didn't mean to suggest... I just meant maybe that's what the police are thinking." She sounded more apologetic than convinced.

I couldn't blame her. If it was anyone else that theory would make sense, but not with Verona. My gut rejected that even more than the idea of Rocky Castle being involved. But maybe that was just because she was family and I didn't want to consider.

"I have found a few reports of Duke Riser's temper." Clearly attempting to change the subject, Katie rushed ahead. "Not only complaints from other conferences he's overseen, but from employees and guests of—"

A soft knock sounded on the door, causing Watson to leap and rush toward it barking.

Katie and I both flinched, more from Watson's reaction than the knock at the door. She glanced over from her computer. "Who in the world do you think that can be at this time of night?"

I used the seat of the couch to help push myself to a

standing position, my knees popping from sitting on the floor so long. "I have an idea. I've been expecting to hear from him since Verona was arrested."

"Branson."

"Yeah." I nodded at her as I headed toward the door. "Didn't you find it odd that he wasn't there today?"

"I did, actually." Katie slid the computer off her lap and looked like she was about to get up. "I'll give you two some space."

"Don't you dare. Stay right where you are." I gave her a meaningful look before joining Watson at the door. I glanced through the peephole before opening the door wide. "Hi."

Branson smiled hesitantly, as if he expected the door to be slammed in his face. "Hey." When I didn't shut him off, he glanced down at Watson, who sat but let out a low continual grumble in his chest. "I'm still never going to hurt your mama, little man."

I stood back from the door and gestured toward the living room. "Come on in."

With a relieved nod, Branson entered, then halted when he noticed Katie. "Sorry. Didn't realize you had company. Good to see you, Katie."

She offered a tiny wave. "You too."

The only thing thicker in the air than Watson's annoyance was the awkwardness. And nothing cut awkwardness better than being direct. "I imagine you're here to talk about Verona?"

"I am." Again his gaze flicked to Katie. "Can you and I speak on the porch, Fred?"

I hesitated, considering, then shook my head, deciding to stay strong. "Whatever you have to say can be said in front of Katie. She's trustworthy. And you know anything you tell me I'll tell her anyway, so why add a step?"

"No!" He reached toward me, then let his hand fall as he looked back and forth between Katie and me as he spoke. "No. I wasn't meaning that. I trust Katie. I just..."

Yeah, that's what I'd thought. Once more I opted for bluntness, even if it meant losing out on receiving his help. "You know that I want to hear whatever you have to say. Especially if it's going to help Verona, but if it comes with strings between you and me, I'm not interested."

He blinked, clearly stung. For a moment I thought he was going to turn around and leave, pride too wounded to allow himself to stay. Then, with a sigh, he crossed the room and sat down in the overstuffed armchair. "No strings. But since you'll tell Katie everything anyway, I'll make this abundantly clear. I'm not giving up. I'm not going to harass or demand or manipulate, but I'm hoping you'll change your mind, and if me proving that I'm on your side assists in that endeavor, then so be it."

"Branson... It's not going to..." With another shake of my head, I cut off the response and crossed the room as well, and this time sat on the opposite end of the couch, with Watson at attention by my feet. I'd already made myself perfectly clear, my mind was made up, and I didn't need to reiterate. From this point on, whatever help Branson gave, I would accept, especially when it might help my family. It wasn't like I was manipulating or leading him on. He was a grown-up who could make his own choices. "Well then, what do you have? To be honest, we're completely baffled. None of this is making sense."

Branson smiled his handsome smile and sounded encouraged. "That's because it doesn't make sense. Probably not even with the details I'm going to give you."

Katie and I both leaned forward as one, but it was Katie who spoke. "Why are Verona and Wolf both under arrest? Do you suspect an affair?"

"An affair?" He chuckled and shook his head. "No. Definitely not. Very separate issues, actually. Wolf..." His words fell away, and he leveled his green gaze on me. "I need to make it clear, Fred, I'm breaking the law for you, here. In a very big way. The things I'm going to tell you cannot be repeated or be known they've come from me. Use them however you need to figure things out, but you *did not* hear them from me."

Despite my earlier thoughts, I had to clarify one more time. "As long as you offer them without strings, I agree. Otherwise, keep your information."

The look that crossed his face cut my heart a little bit; I was tired of hurting him. "I love how strong you are." Before I could respond, he shifted toward Katie. "That goes for you too."

"That's sweet of you, Sergeant Wexler. I'm flattered that you love how strong I am. Thank you for noticing." From her smirk, it was clear she was intentionally being obtuse. And from the chuckle that she elicited from Branson, I was grateful.

"You know what I mean." He grinned at her. "You didn't hear this from me?"

She raised her right hand and formed her fingers in the Vulcan salute. "Scouts honor."

After another chuckle, he grew serious, and Branson's eyes met mine one more time. "Wolf isn't in jail for Aurora's murder but for a long laundry list of other reasons. Embezzlement, charity fraud, and tax evasion to name a few."

The accusations the Holy Rapture Fellowship shouted

before they started throwing Bibles came back to me. "The Birnbaum Foundation was a front?"

"Not completely confirmed yet, but at least partially, yes. It appears they do quite a bit of charitable work, but not nearly as much as they claim. From what's been uncovered so far, at least eighty percent of the donations and profits that were meant to go to the charities fell right back into the Birnbaums' pockets."

Katie let out a low whistle of awe. "How awful. It's amazing how low some will go to steal money from kind-hearted people. I don't understand how they can lie about such good things. It's just like that breast cancer charity, the Boobies Rock one. It was nothing but a..." She caught herself, slipping into her trivia mode. "Never mind. Beside the point."

Despite the severity of the situation, a wave of affection coursed through me for my best friend. I let it linger for a second before turning back to the information Branson had just given us. Definitely revelatory, but not overly shocking. A lot of charities were scams, and three minutes with Aurora revealed that she wasn't who she claimed to be. "How does that tie with Verona?"

"At this point"—Branson shrugged—"it doesn't."

"Then, what?" I exchanged a look with Katie before returning to Branson. "You've met Verona. She and Zelda are a little eccentric, sure, but they aren't killers. This is too familiar with what happened to Barry not even a year ago. It's just another scapegoat situation."

"It's funny that you mention Barry, because that's exactly where we are again." He paused for breath but continued before I could push. "We found correspondence between Aurora and Verona as we searched the emails. Aurora was blackmailing Verona."

"Blackmailing? You've got to be..." It clicked, making complete sense, so much so I felt foolish for not having recognized the signs before. Verona being overly defensive, demanding privacy, letting Aurora walk all over her, giving her free run of Chakras without including Zelda in that decision. Meeting Aurora in the middle of the night. I still didn't believe Verona would kill Aurora, no matter what, but the motive made sense. "What was Aurora hanging over Verona's head? What secret could be big enough to kill over?"

"That's just it, we don't know. The emails are vague, clear about the threat Aurora was using of exposing Verona, but never specific." He raised his brows expectantly. "I hoped you would have some idea."

The next morning I headed down to the police station where Verona was being held. It was early enough I skipped Watson's and my morning walk through the woods, even skipped caffeine, then left him behind in the cabin. There were very few things that were worth the cold shoulder I was certain to get from Watson after such a stunt, but I hoped this would be.

As he had promised, Branson met me at the door of the police station and walked me past the front desk with a wave—not bothering to sign me in—past an ancient poster of a cat hanging by one paw from a branch, and down the narrow hallway. He paused outside a narrow door. "Again, I need to remind you to be quick. It's not like this will be kept a secret, but the quicker you get it over with, the less chance this whole thing has of exploding."

As I had the night before, I was tempted to reiterate that this couldn't come with strings or any form of expectation. But it was too late for that. I'd already made that clear and wasn't turning down the chance to talk to Verona. "Got it. Thank you for doing this."

"Don't thank me yet." He smirked. "Verona nearly took

my head off when I told her I was arranging for you to see her."

"She did?" I had to admit, that stung.

Branson nodded. "Yeah. Sorry." Concern filled his voice, but he opened the door, and let me pass before shutting me in.

Verona sat at the same metal table where my mother and I had talked to Barry when he'd been arrested under suspicion of murder. A sense of déjà vu probably would've washed over me if not for the very un-Barry-like glower on Verona's face. Her complexion was sallow and next to the orange jumpsuit, her blonde hair was a sickly green. "I appreciate you coming, Fred, and I know your heart is in the right place, but please, just turn around and go home."

Though she spoke through gritted teeth, she'd said please, so I took it as a good sign and sat down across from her. "I know you didn't do this—"

"Fred, I said leave it alone."

I barely caught it, but it was there—the tremble of fear behind her anger, and it made me wonder. "You didn't hurt Aurora, did you?"

She flinched back, sounding thoroughly offended. "Of course I didn't."

"Then why are you doing this? What are you hiding?"

Verona's lips moved silently, and she glanced toward the two-way mirror and shook her head.

I reached across the table and took her hand; she didn't pull it away. "Branson gave me his word that he wasn't going to listen in or even watch. Whatever it is, you can tell me."

She seemed to consider for a second, then shook her head again. "No. I can't. I won't."

"Verona, what in the world is bad enough that you're

willing to risk going to jail for murder in order to keep it a secret?" Despite my efforts to hold back, frustration seeped into my tone.

She did pull her hand away then. "That won't happen. I'm innocent. I didn't kill Aurora, didn't even think about it after discovering what a horrible woman she was. I'm surprised the thought didn't cross my mind, even in jest."

"Innocent people go to jail all the time, Verona. And you're playing the part of a fool if you can prove you didn't do it and keep that proof to yourself." My anger was getting the better of me, but I simply couldn't believe how stubborn she was being.

"Even if I told you, it wouldn't prove I didn't kill her. I don't have proof of that. I met her at Chakras that night, shortly before she was killed. That's true. How can I prove that I didn't do something when I was there?"

"You can let me figure that part out. But I need to know why she was blackmailing you."

"Blackmail?" Her blue eyes flashed icy toward the two-way mirror. "I can't believe Branson told you." She shifted the glare to me. "I thought the two of you weren't together anymore."

"We're not. He's trying to help you."

"Sure." Verona sneered. "*That's* what he's trying to do. I'm sure he's so concerned about me."

"Verona, that isn't the point." I should've taken some time to prepare some persuasive arguments before coming. I hadn't expected her to put up any protest after being charged with murder if I already knew about the blackmail. "Can we please stop this and you just let me help you?"

"Telling you won't help. If my secret got out, it would ruin me. Completely and utterly ruin me. Why else do you think I let that horrible woman blackmail me? Why else would you think I'd turn over Zelda's and my shop to her, even for a week? No one can know."

I couldn't imagine how horrible the secret must have been. Maybe as bad as murder itself... Then I remembered Jonah's expression during lunch the day before. "Your husband knows."

She flinched again and shook her head. "No... No. He doesn't."

You didn't have to be intuitive at all to be able to tell she was lying. "Yes, he does. So if one person can know and your future not unravel, why can't I?"

"He's my *husband*," she hissed as she leaned forward, both hands pressed flat on the table. "And don't you dare pull him into this, Winifred Page. Again, I know your heart is in the right place, and you can snoop everywhere else, but if your family asks you to stay out of it, then stay out of it."

Maybe I'd been foolish. I should've gone around her from the very beginning. I stood. "Fine, have it your way."

I was nearly to the door when she called out, "Fred, don't you dare talk to Jonah. Don't. You. Dare."

I didn't look back, simply stepped out into the hall and shut the door behind me.

Branson was waiting. "I know that look, things didn't go how you wanted."

"You can say that again." I knew I shouldn't ask him for any more favors, knew I might regret it, but I couldn't stop myself. "Can you keep her from making a phone call for half an hour?" I thought of Watson back at the cabin and of caffeine. "Actually, for an hour?"

He narrowed his gaze. "Sure. I take it you've got a plan?"

"Not so much a plan as simply remembering that there's

more than one way to skin a cat." I shuddered. "I don't know why I said that. I've always hated that expression."

Within half an hour, a thoroughly offended Watson sat in the passenger seat of the Mini Cooper staring determinedly away from me out of the window, and I held a gargantuan thermos of coffee. It wasn't as good as Katie's dirty chai, but it would do. We were halfway to Glen Haven when Branson called. I waited until we were around one of the sharper bends before hitting Accept on the phone. "You weren't able to keep her from calling?"

"No, she still hasn't called anyone, though she keeps demanding to call her husband, so I'm assuming that's where you're headed." Branson didn't wait for a response before continuing. "That's not why I called. Thought you might want the latest update."

A thread of stress moved through me. "This isn't going to be good, is it?"

"I doubt it impacts Verona at all, but like I said, figured you'd want the update. You always said everything was a puzzle piece, even if it didn't fit into the right puzzle."

I didn't remember saying that exact expression, but I did think of things as puzzle pieces. It was bittersweet how well he knew me.

Thankfully, he kept going. "Wolf is out on bail."

"Oh." I sat with that for a moment as I focused on the road. "That's not too surprising, actually. I'm sure he's got a high-powered lawyer, at least a much better one than Verona has with Gerald Jackson."

He sniggered on the other end of the phone. "That's not saying much, but from the evidence presented, even Gerald Jackson could've pulled this one off. Unless there's some deception somewhere, Wolf didn't know about any of the embezzlement or charity fraud. He's innocent."

"Okay, then. Well, that fits with the things I've heard about him, and even my brief interaction with him. He seems like a genuinely sincere man." I hoped Branson was right that this development didn't affect Verona, but it probably did, somehow.

Branson wasn't finished "He's also having a memorial for Aurora this afternoon. Back at the Samson statue."

That I definitely didn't see coming. "Are you serious? So soon? And at the Samson statue? Again?"

"Yeah. It all happened since you left." His voice lowered to a whisper, and I wondered where he was in the police station. "Chief Briggs has already approved the permit for the event. I'm willing to bet there's a sizable donation to the town somewhere in there."

I considered. "Okay, thank you for letting me know. Looks like I have plans this afternoon."

"See you there." Branson hung up before I could respond.

Crud. If those three words didn't imply strings I didn't know what did.

That worry was for a different time, and I cast it aside as I turned onto the road that led to Glen Haven. I slowed as I passed the junkyard equivalent of Rocky Castle's house and stared at the rather hideous bus covered in brown fur. I suppose, if nothing else, the people who paid for his tours could count the bus itself as a Bigfoot sighting if they didn't see anything interesting in the woods.

I stepped on the gas and hurried on, in case Rocky was home and noticed me. I drove past Zelda's and pulled up to Verona's house next door, and parked. After I opened the passenger door for Watson, he paused as if debating whether I was worthy enough to open doors for him.

"I'm sorry I left you at home this morning. Trust me, I didn't have any fun without you." I glanced around to see if anyone was watching me grovel to my dog.

From the other yard, Gerald Jackson stared at me wide-eyed.

I'd forgotten Gerald was a neighbor with the twins.

Gerald gave a twinkling finger wave with one hand as he sipped from his kombucha jar with the other. "Don't you worry, Fred. I'll get your sister out of jail in no time. I'm on the case." He took another sip. "It may just take me a few days."

I forced a smile and raised my voice. "Thanks, Gerald. We have all the faith in the world in you." That was true for the men in my family at least, so I supposed it wasn't an out-and-out lie. I turned back to Watson as I lowered my voice. "There, Mission Humiliation accomplished. Will your highness exit now?"

With his nose raised in the air, Watson hopped out and pranced smugly toward Verona's front door.

Jonah answered almost the instant I pressed the doorbell. His eyes widened when he saw me, confirming he hadn't checked before opening the door. "Fred."

"I already know you're home, Jonah. Too late to close it and pretend otherwise." Before he could react, Watson and I stepped past him.

"What? I would never..." Jonah's words faded away with a sigh, and he closed the door. "Can I get you anything to drink?"

I realized I'd left my half-finished thermos in the Mini Cooper. "I don't suppose you have coffee?"

"Be right back."

As Jonah fetched the coffee, Watson trundled back up to the loft and returned a few seconds later with Leaf's toy lion in his mouth, hopped up into one of the armchairs, and settled into a nap, his head resting on the lion's overly stuffed belly.

Jonah was back in a moment, handed me a coffee, and motioned toward the living room. He grinned when he noticed Watson. "Goodness. He really is the cutest little thing."

"Thank goodness for that. It distracts from his entitled attitude." Though I constantly teased about Watson's disposition, his stubborn, entitled attitude was one of the things that endeared him to me. I settled down on the couch next to Watson's chair, and Jonah sat on the opposite side. Suddenly, I realized how quiet the house was. "Ocean and Leaf aren't here?"

"No." Jonah took a sip of coffee and then rubbed his temples. "Zelda and Noah are taking them with Britney and Christina to the rainbow slides and then the adventure park. They needed some distraction, and I was hoping to get some rest before going to visit Verona."

I wasn't sure if not having the kids there would make things easier or more difficult. Ultimately, it didn't matter. It was what it was. I decided to be as direct and blunt as possible. Both to hopefully throw him off guard a little and because I wasn't sure how much longer Branson would keep Verona from calling home.

"I just spoke to Branson. Wolf is out on bail and organizing a memorial ceremony for Aurora this afternoon."

"He's *already* out?" Jonah sounded offended but then gave a tired shrug. "Well, I guess that makes sense. He wasn't in jail for murder. Verona didn't think he killed Aurora anyway."

"Who do you think did?"

Another shrug, this one wearier than the first. "I have no idea. I didn't interact with Aurora much, or Wolf, for that matter. I knew she wasn't living up to Verona and Zelda's expectations, but I had no idea she was blackmailing Verona."

I only had to study him for half a moment to see he was being honest. "But you know *why* she was blackmailing Verona."

He shook his head; it seemed he only had the energy for half a lie. "Yeah, I do." The words were barely more than an exhausted whisper. He straightened, and his tone grew firm. "And I'm sure that's why you're here. You're welcome to stay as long as you want, you're family, and I love you, but there's no reason to ask. I'm not going to tell you."

"It might get Verona out of jail."

"I know. But I promised her." Again the tiredness washed over him, as if the little bits of strength he'd shown were the last little grains he possessed.

Maybe that would serve me well. "Jonah, we're talking about Verona's freedom. Don't you think that's a little more important than a promise?"

"It's not that I don't trust your ability, Fred. I do. Believe me. I do. But she's innocent. Maybe she'll have to stay in there a little longer, but she's innocent, so it will all come out in the wash, as they say." He lifted the coffee to his lips, more like he was trying to hide than take a drink.

"There are plenty of innocent people in jail, Jonah." Though it hadn't worked with Verona, I thought I'd try again. "And every second in there, the more rumors and talk go around town, labeling your wife a murderer."

"That's just it!" He threw his hands wide, almost

spilling his coffee. "Verona won't say, won't let me say, because the truth would ruin her reputation."

I gaped at him. "Are you serious? The secret is worse than *murder*? It would hurt her reputation worse than being called a murderer?"

"I... No, it's..." He shook his head and once more began to rub his temples. "She thinks so. Yes."

I jumped on it. "But you don't agree."

Still rubbing, he shook his head. "No, I don't."

I scooted nearer on the couch and put my hand on his knee. "Tell me. Let's help her. She'll forgive you once she's free."

He laughed and looked at me again. "No, she won't. If I tell you, she will *never* forgive me."

I heard the truth in those words as well and lost all hope of cracking his shell. Withdrawing my hand, I settled back into my spot in the sofa and tried to think of another angle, though there wasn't going to be one.

We sat in gloomy silence for a while, only broken up by Watson's soft snores.

I finished my coffee and decided to leave Jonah alone and head to the Cozy Corgi, get a dirty chai, finally have breakfast, and brainstorm with Katie and the Pacheco twins —Good Lord, so many twins. Just as I was getting ready to stand, Watson let out a garbled snort in his sleep and snuggled closer to the stuffed lion.

Jonah sucked in a gasp.

I looked at him, started to speak, but he held up his finger.

"Hold on. Let me think." Jonah's eyes narrowed as he studied Watson, the fingers of his free hand started to drum on the arm of the sofa. After a few more moments, he began to whisper to himself.

For the first time since we arrived, I could feel an electric energy surging off him, wiping away all his tired features. It took all my willpower to keep silent.

After a bit, Jonah downed what remained of his coffee and sprang to his feet. "I'll be right back." True to his word, he barely left before he reemerged once more, crossed the room, and handed me a silver key. "Here you go."

I studied it. The key was small and thin and had the letters RMS pressed above the hole on one side and the number 365 on the other. It looked like it could be easily bent. "What is it?"

Jonah didn't answer, not directly, and began to pace, the excitement still continuing to build in his voice. "Okay, I think I got it. I can't tell you. I swore I wouldn't *tell* you, and I promise you if I did Verona would leave me in a second, but I'm just giving you a key. I'm not telling you anything, not exactly."

"You're not telling me anything at all. What's this—"

"Shhh!" He shushed me with his hand and continued to pace. "If I give you clues, then it's not exactly like I'm telling you. You have to figure it out."

It seemed like he was speaking more to himself than me, so I remained silent.

He muttered a few more things that were unintelligible and then halted to face me. "Don't you think? That's not me telling if I give you clues. She won't be mad." He winced. "Okay, yes she will. She'll be furious. *If* she finds out, but... not like she would be if I told you directly. I think..."

It seemed like a game of dangerous semantics to me, but I for sure wasn't going to say that. "Yeah. That... makes sense."

"Does it?" Jonah's shoulders slumped, his determination clearly slipping away.

"It's our only chance, Jonah. I won't tell her you gave me the clues, whatever the clues are. I'll figure them out, and it will save Verona. *And* her reputation. She won't be angry about that." Those were two promises I couldn't swear to keep, but whatever. He seemed to be considering, so I pushed on. "What's the first one?"

He winced again and shook his head.

My temper spiked. "For crying out loud, Jonah, what's the first one?"

He flinched, then lifted a trembling hand and pointed at Watson.

"Watson?" I stared at my sleeping pup, wondering how in the world he could be involved. "*Watson's* the clue?"

"No. Not Watson." Jonah pointed again.

Not Watson. The armchair? The stuffed animal? "The stuffed animal. That's the clue?"

"Yes." Then he shook his head. "Well, no, not exactly, but yes." He pointed at it again.

It didn't matter how angry Verona was going to be. If this continued another second, I was going to murder the man myself. I studied Watson and his lion sleeping buddy again, then looked back at Jonah. "The lion?"

He beamed. "Yes. Exactly."

Despite my frustration at him, a little thrill went through me at figuring out his clue, and I looked from the stuffed toy lion to the key. "What in the world do that lion and this key have to do with each other?"

"One more clue." Jonah looked toward the ceiling as he thought and then grew excited again. "I told you the clue yesterday. Or, told Verona, actually." He snapped his fingers several times as he pointed at me. "Everyone has skeletons in their closet."

That was a clue to tell me that Verona *didn't* kill someone? I looked to the key between us. "This key is going to help me discover a skeleton?" I glanced toward Watson. "Someone killed by a lion?"

He rolled his eyes like it was the stupidest thing he'd ever heard. It was a good thing he tried again that instant or he would've truly been a dead man. "Everyone has skeletons in their *closet*." He practically spat as he said the last word.

"Closet. That's the clue, not skeleton."

Jonah nodded, returned to the edge of the sofa, and collapsed back in exhaustion.

I still wanted to throttle him. "You're telling me my clues are a lion, a closet, and a key?"

"Yes."

"Jonah, for crying out loud, you gotta give me more than that. Unless you're wanting me to try to get into Narnia." I clenched my fist around the key and then softened my grip afraid I'd bend the stupid thing. "A closet and the key together make sense, but what in the world does a lion have to do with anything?"

"I've already told you more than I should, Winifred. You're smart. You'll figure it out." He jumped as the phone rang.

I knew who it would be, and I wasn't sure if Verona had just saved her husband from a furious corgi mama murdering him or if she'd kept me from beating the clues out of him.

When Jonah answered the phone and heard Verona's voice, his eyes grew wide, and the guilt was clear in his greeting. He waved frantically at me toward the front door, as if wiping away sin.

I patted Watson awake.

He glared at me and closed his eyes once more.

I patted him again.

This time, still glaring, he stood on the cushion, made a show of stretching as if he were a cat, and then hopped down to the floor, carrying the lion with him. I nearly insisted on leaving the lion behind, but then decided it wasn't worth the power struggle. Plus, maybe it would get me back in his good graces quicker. And perhaps there was a chance if the stuffed animal was with us, I'd figure out what in the world the lion had to do with Aurora's murder.

Katie cast a quick glare over her shoulder as a large man shoved past her through the crowd before looking over at Leo and me. "Are either of you experiencing déjà vu?"

I stepped nearer to her in order to avoid my own collision with a tourist. "If you mean, do I feel a sense of impending doom, then, yes."

"I think we'd be fools to not feel both of those things." Leo nodded to where Wolf was speaking to Chief Briggs and Branson in front of the statue. "This didn't go so well the first time, after all."

"Oh yes, that too." I grinned at my friends. "I think my sense of impending doom is more around leaving Watson alone at the house for the second time in a single day. He might not have opposable thumbs, but there is a pretty good chance he's figured out how to use my laptop and is searching Google, as we speak, for step-by-step instructions on how to booby-trap the house." Though Watson had looked fairly put out to be left behind once more, I hoped his new lion would offer some damage control. I was going to have to ask Leaf how important his stuffed animal was to him. Maybe the nine-year-old would like the idea of his lion and Watson being BFFs.

"After what happened last time, you could hardly bring him. What if things go worse this time around? There're too many feet to properly protect him." Leo motioned toward the protesters who paced behind the police-sanctioned picket line. Around fifteen of them were on the other side of the road by the river, each holding handmade signs, and all of them chanting various choruses of protests in unison.

"You don't really think it's going to turn dangerous, do you?" Katie sounded more excited at that prospect than concerned. "After all, I think every member of the police force is here, and we know where the members of the Holy Rapture Fellowship are, so there shouldn't be any surprises."

"Right... because *that's* how Estes works." Unlike Katie, I didn't feel any excitement around it, but neither could I talk myself into skipping Wolf's ceremony—my curiosity was too great. Plus, maybe something there would click with the ridiculous clues Jonah had given me.

"That's rarely how many protests work. There's always a chance tensions will explode." As Leo spoke, he too scanned the crowd, his eyes narrowed, and his wide shoulders tensed. "Can't you feel the difference in this one? Everyone is *expecting* something to happen."

He was right—the electricity going through the crowd was palpable. Above, as if mimicking the turmoil below, gray clouds gathered overhead, preparing for the typical afternoon rain showers. As in the first ceremony, most of the faces in the crowd I didn't recognize. There were many tourists, and though I didn't spot Duke Riser anywhere, I was certain most of the attendees of the SHH Conference were there, probably looking to bookend their week's events with the matching drama to the one that started the whole thing.

Across the way, Anna and Carl were in deep conversation with Athena and Paulie. As if feeling my gaze, Paulie looked my way and gave a frantically happy little wave before turning back to the others. It seemed he had the same inclination as myself, as his corgis, Flotsam and Jetsam, were nowhere to be seen. Narrowing my gaze a little further, I noticed the absence of Pearl, Athena's little teacup poodle, who was normally sticking her head out of Athena's purse.

The dogs weren't the only ones not in attendance. Ben and Nick had decided to stay at the Cozy Corgi. I had the impression one ceremony that insulted their heritage had been enough. My family had also opted to miss the festivities, as they were focused on the kids, Jonah, and trying to assist Gerald Jackson with Verona's case.

"What do you think the holdup is?" Katie's whisper pulled me back from looking at the crowd. "They seem to be arguing."

I followed her gaze to Branson, Briggs, and Wolf. Sure enough, the tension between the three men matched the growing rumble in the crowd and the clouds. Upon further inspection, however, that wasn't quite right. As Wolf laid a hand on either man's arms, I realized it was Briggs and Branson who were arguing.

That didn't bode well.

"That's how it's been, lately. Those two have always presented a united front. The only thing they seem to agree on anymore is that I have no idea what I'm talking about when it comes to poachers." Frustration filled Leo's voice and turned apologetic when he looked my way. "Sorry. I try not to say anything bad about Branson. I know you two are... were"—he winced—"are close. I'm just a little more frustrated than normal with the increase of incidents over the past several weeks."

"You don't need to be sorry." I laid a hand on his shoulder, then pulled it away quickly. "I... ah... didn't realize you've been holding back. I knew the poaching had gotten worse. I wasn't aware that the tension between you and the police had escalated as well."

"Par for the course." Leo shrugged. "But it does add insult to injury that we keep gathering at the statue of the most beloved elk in Estes Park, who was a poaching victim, and we can't seem to get anything done."

Katie leaned in to whisper again, though with the rumble of the crowd and the overarching shouts of the protesters, I wasn't sure why she bothered. "A mountain lion was killed early this morning."

I gaped at her and then turned to Leo. "Another one?"

He nodded, his lips hardening to a thin line.

It truly was becoming an epidemic. Poaching within the national park was something I'd been aware of since the moment we arrived in the town and Watson had found a dead owl in a freezer, but it seemed to be getting worse—bighorn sheep, elk, bears, mountain lions... I froze at the thought. Mountain lions.

Lion... Jonah had said one of the clues was a lion. Maybe it wasn't a lion of the cowardly lion variety that Watson's borrowed stuffed animal represented, but the Colorado mountain lion type.

Though, I didn't seem to offer much help either. What connection could Verona possibly have to mountain lions? No matter what her secret was I was certain she wasn't connected to poaching. She wasn't a vegetarian like her father, but both twins were avid supporters of animal-rights.

"Did we miss the show?"

I turned to find Percival with Gary right behind him,

attempting to squeeze his large frame through the press of the crowd. "You came!"

The five of us exchanged a quick round of hugs as Percival responded. "For ulterior motives, I must confess." He nodded toward the line of protesters. "This may not be about us, but I want to make sure that we make it clear we're not hiding."

Katie giggled and smiled in adoration at Percival. "I don't think anyone could accuse you of that. But you look wonderful."

"Thank you, Katie dear, but the word is *fabulous*." Percival adjusted his rainbow sequined suit jacket. "I look *fabulous*."

"Pretty sure I just look uncomfortable." Gary gave me a wink and gestured toward the fuzzy pink fedora crammed on his head. "Your uncle forced me to wear this—it's back from his glory days and a couple of sizes too small for me."

Before I could tell him he looked dashing, Percival let out a squawk. "*Back* from my glory days? *These* are my glory days, I'll have you know. Right now. I've never been more fabulous in my life."

Leo chuckled. "I have to agree with you, Percival. Although I would say fabulous and brave. Showing up to this thing wearing a rainbow jacket and fuzzy pink hats sends a clear message to the crazies."

Percival waved him off. "Oh, please. This is nothing. *They* are nothing. We've protested against a lot scarier than the likes of the Holy Rapture Fellowship." He scoffed. "Like they're going to scare us off with a few flyers and poorly rhyming chants."

Though he spoke to Katie, Leo, and me, Gary cast an affectionate gaze on Percival. "And this is nothing. You should've seen what he forced us to wear during the protest of '93. That was really something to—"

"Attention! Attention!" Chief Briggs' voice cut through the crowd, silencing everyone instantly, even the protesters quieted. "Let me make this abundantly clear. This event *will* go smoothly. There *will* be law, order, and respect, or there *will* be consequences." Though he cast a glance toward the Holy Rapture Fellowship by the river, he let his steely gaze wander over the crowd. "This is a moment of remembrance and respect. Whether you are a citizen of this town or not, you *will* act accordingly. If not, every single one of my officers here is more than capable of helping you comply."

Complete silence reigned as he shut his mouth and continued to glare. The rumble in the clouds above seemed to throw their support behind Chief Briggs' threat.

I didn't care for the man, but I had to admit he cast an impressive figure.

After a few moments, Wolf stepped around him and took his place so the spread of Samson's antlers crowned him. The contrast between the two was striking. Both were large, strong men, but Wolf, despite his name, had an air of gentility and softness to him. The same was true for his voice when he began to speak, and as before, it struggled to carry through the August afternoon. "Thank you for coming to the ceremony of love, remembrance, and healing."

"You are a false prophet. You offer no healing. Only a path to fire!" A woman's shrill voice cut through the crowd. I couldn't pinpoint which of the protesters had cried out, but I was willing to bet it was Sandy Anderson.

Chief Briggs began to step forward, his face flushed in anger, but Wolf stretched out a hand and shook his head. To my surprise, Chief Briggs returned to his place beside Branson.

As Wolf started to speak again, more of the Holy Rapture Fellowship began to chant, but still his voice carried. "We are here to remember my lovely and caring wife. To honor the life and passion of Aurora Birnbaum."

I glanced behind Wolf and the statue, looking for Tabitha near the edge of the crowd. Sure enough, there she was, her gaze trained on Wolf's back and wringing her hands like she too expected something bad to happen.

"For some of you, Aurora was a stranger, but to others she was a neighbor and friend, and to many, many more, to those here and across the nation and the world, she was a spiritual leader who offered guidance, hope, and peace."

The protesters called out louder at that, but Wolf simply waited until their volume decreased slightly.

He lifted his chin and his gaze skyward as he spoke. "In all things on this earth, there is a cycle, and in all things there is a perfect imperfection, and before we can honor Aurora's legacy, such imperfections must be addressed. The mission of the Birnbaum Foundation has always been one of charity, giving back to better enrich our world, both through the environment and in social and economic issues. It has come to light that those who have been entrusted to handle such matters have fallen into the temptation of greed." He looked from the heavens toward the protesters. "A thing we can *all* agree leads to destruction." There was a silent pause between the group and Wolf.

I marveled at that, at him, at the entire situation. The whole thing was odd and yet somewhat otherworldly. Maybe it was just a strange set of circumstances and events combined with the majesty of the mountains and valley, of the billowing clouds overhead. But... maybe it was more...

"Since this has come to light, I have taken things into my own hands, and the untrustworthy individuals are no longer part of our organization. Not only will things get back on track, but the Birnbaum Foundation will remedy every wrong and unfulfilled promise." He raised a hand and pressed it to the side of Samson's massive neck. "Both to honor Aurora's memory and her devotion, and to better our world. That has already started with a huge donation to the Rocky Mountain National Park and will continue on an ongoing basis in an effort to fight against poaching and the harming of the innocent souls of nature."

I glanced at Leo, and he nodded at me, confirming it as fact.

"And now, please join me in honoring my wife's life and her passing." The chanting protests increased in volume once more, but Wolf only bent and picked up a large straight wooden staff that had been placed at the base of Samson's statue. Wolf stepped out a couple of feet to a wide stretch of open earth that was free of rocks and plants. He began dragging the tip of the staff through the dirt as he spoke, emotion thick in his voice. "While we... *I* will miss Aurora Birnbaum with every fiber of my being for every second of every day that I walk over the surface of the earth, though her absence will be felt by the countless souls who were touched by her guidance, who were brought into a closer relationship with our higher power, whose eyes and hearts were opened to the mystical beauty of the nature and the world around us, let the period of mourning be finite. But let us grieve, only for a little while, that Aurora's human body is no longer with us, that we can no longer hear her voice or feel her loving touch."

With the exception of the chanting protesters, every member of the crowd was captivated by his heartfelt words.

There seemed a hypnotic quality to them, and I found myself slightly fuzzy, almost as if I were floating or something as I listened to him. The sensation was heightened by the entrancing swirling patterns he made in the dirt. Circles and whirls formed a continuous flow, creating looping fractals in a pattern that seemed to whisper some secret that was just out of reach.

"The essence of Aurora is all around, in the earth, and the wind, the clouds above." With his right hand, he continued the staff's journey through the dirt as he lifted his left hand toward the sky. "She is in every element, just as every element is in each of us. Therefore, she is not gone, nor are the lessons of love and compassion that she taught, nor are the qualities of justice, enlightenment, and spiritualism that she embodied and dedicated her life to offering to other people."

"You are a false prophet! You are of the devil!" That time, I put a face to the voice as a woman I figured to be Sandy Anderson broke free from the others and rushed past the picket line.

Beside me, I felt Percival stiffen, and I reached for his hand.

Though he took it, there was no tremble or weakness in his grip. Even so, it was clear how much the Holy Rapture Fellowship's presence, and the effects of their harassment, were taking a toll on him.

A faint click of static caught my attention. Chief Briggs lifted a walkie-talkie to his lips, but I couldn't make out what he said.

Sandy rushed across the street but stopped at the edge of the crowd. This time, there was no Bible in her hand to throw. To my relief, there was no stone either. "You spread lies. Dangerous, evil lies. And you, and all who believe your words, will be judged. You will—" Her words were cut off as Susan Green, Officer Jackson, and another police officer surrounded her, forming their own barricade between her and the crowd. As one, they walked toward her, giving Sandy no choice but to step back to the barricade or be enfolded by them. After a few moments, even as she retreated, she began to call out again.

Tabitha had moved closer to Wolf. He put a reassuring hand on her arm, but ignored the protestors, as if the scene weren't happening and there were no disruption at all. "It's in that vein, in following Aurora's example of love and justice, that I speak for one of the souls who still embody her earthly form. Verona Pearson has been jailed for ending Aurora's life."

Behind him, Chief Briggs stiffened and started toward Wolf. Branson shot out a hand, grabbing him at the elbow. Though Briggs shook Branson off with a jerk, he scanned the crowd and remained where he was.

Wolf continued, either not noticing or unconcerned at the disruption at his back. "Both Verona and her twin opened their arms and their shop to Aurora and me, to our work, and in that way, took part in our mission of peace. While I seek justice for the loss of Aurora's presence at my side on this journey over Earth's surface, it only adds insult to Aurora's death to cause an innocent to suffer."

Katie and I exchanged shocked glances. Of all the things I'd anticipated, a cry for Verona's release hadn't been one of them.

Wolf paused and closed his eyes as he lowered his hand behind him to rest on Samson's statue, and his other never stopped its looping pattern in the dirt. "We will all leave behind these marvelous and fallible human forms and one day join Aurora and the others who have gone on before us

to become part of the earth, wind, and stars. In the meantime, let us remember the words and the example Aurora
gave us. Let us be good and filled with love."

Katie leaned into me, tilting her head so her whisper
was for me alone. "Wolf is clearly a good man who sees the
best in everyone, but apparently, he never tried to serve
Aurora a bacon and Gruyère quiche. Otherwise, this little
memorial would have a different theme than being filled
with love and kindness."

I glanced down and almost chuckled at the skeptical
expression on my best friend's face. "If you make me laugh
right now, I'm going to kick you."

She shrugged. "I'm just saying—who treats a person like
poo on their shoe when they offer them Gruyère cheese?
Not the same woman Wolf is describing, I'll promise
you that."

"Perhaps—" Percival leaned in, proving that Katie's
whisper hadn't been as private as I'd thought "—Aurora was
just lactose intolerant. Tummy cramps make anyone
cranky."

Katie snorted out a laugh.

"Stop it, you two." I elbowed her and gave Percival the
evil eye as I tried to remain serious. "You're evil."

"Duh, my darling niece." He gestured with his chin
toward the protesters. "If you ever forget that, all you need
to do is ask Sandy Anderson over there and all her Holy
Roller followers."

Within another five minutes, the ceremony was over,
and Wolf walked away, protected on either side by Branson
and Chief Briggs. Despite his unusual ways and his lack of
clarity around his deceased wife, a wave of gratitude
washed over me. He'd used the moment in front of everyone
to try and clear Verona's name, to put his support behind

her when he didn't have to do anything. In fact, he could've done the exact opposite. It spoke highly of Verona that she'd made such an impression on Wolf.

The protesters' volume increased, distracting me, but there were no further outbursts, no threats, and the crowd dispersed in an easy and organized manner.

If I wasn't wrong, I got the sense the attendees were disappointed in that fact. As if most of them were hoping for more of a show than to honor Aurora's memory. I was relieved, though disappointed, there'd been nothing to help point a finger in the direction of Aurora's actual killer.

The Holy Rapture Fellowship's chants never decreased in volume as the crowds thinned, drawing my attention once more.

Maybe killers, plural, was the correct term.

To my surprise, Watson was almost cordial when I picked him up from the house. I'd arrived to find him in his dog bed in the bedroom, snuggled up with his new toy lion and his stuffed yellow duck, which had been his previous favorite. It seemed he wasn't going to choose between the two. A lion and a duck, what a strange combination. Though, for Watson, somehow it made sense. And though he didn't offer the cold shoulder as I expected, he didn't go so far as to allow me to snap a photo of him in such a compromising position.

I managed to squeeze in just enough hours before closing at the Cozy Corgi to remember that I owned a book-shop. Even so, no books were sold, at least not by me. Instead, Watson slept in the afternoon sunshine, and I went back and forth from the bakery to the bookshop, listening to the various gossipy conversations and theories surrounding Aurora's death, Verona's involvement, and the outspoken behavior of the Holy Rapture Fellowship.

By the time I locked up for the evening, I'd gotten Sandy Anderson and her husband's address. I told myself I was going to give myself time to cool down after seeing Percival's reaction to the group earlier that afternoon. I decided I'd spend the evening researching both the Holy Rapture Fellowship and anything to do with lions and closets. I also decided that if I thought it necessary to speak to Sandy directly, I would go with Katie or Leo. Maybe even Branson. Instead as I drove toward my cabin with just Watson curled up with his two fuzzy friends in the passenger seat, I found myself heading to the Anderson home.

I'd just drive by, see what kind of house they lived in.

See if one of them was outside doing yard work or getting their mail. If they were, I'd just slow and wave, see if I got any sort of reaction.

Maybe, better yet, see if any of their neighbors were out in their yards. See if any of them felt like telling tales on the Anderson family.

Their neighborhood was one of the few in Estes Park that looked like a Midwestern suburb, complete with cul-de-sacs and identical houses in varying shades of cream, taupe, and beige. With the exception of a couple of kids tossing a ball in one of the front yards, no one was outside as dusk began to fall.

As I promised myself, I found the house number that matched their address and paused. I was simply inspecting, just getting details, one never knew what could turn out to be useful.

There didn't seem to be anything special about the house, no indicator that hateful people lived inside. Nothing stood out, nothing at all.

At the moment when I should have stepped on the gas and zoomed out of the cul-de-sac, I slipped the Mini Cooper into Park and turned off the engine.

Watson sat up, clearly expecting that we were home,

and glanced around at the unfamiliar setting quizzically before turning to me.

"This is your chance, Watson. Talk me out of it. I have no business going alone to talk to the people who are harassing my uncles and my stepsisters." I leveled my gaze on his chocolate brown eyes. "It would be stupid to go into the home of the ones who might've killed Aurora Birnbaum. Definitely not by myself, right?"

Watson blinked and one of his quirky eyebrows lifted. We stared at each other, and then he blinked again.

"You're right, as long as *you* go with me, I'm not alone." I reached over the console and scratched his side. "You're very persuasive."

His gaze narrowed, either telling me he was not amused or that we both knew I was neither convincing him nor myself that my justifications were valid.

I opened the car door and stuck a foot out before turning back to him. "You probably want to leave your friends in the car because if you take them in, they might get left behind if we have to make a run for it."

Watson abandoned the lion and the duck and hopped gracefully onto the sidewalk in front of the Anderson's home. He was so accommodating that I almost wondered if he truly was giving his sanctioned approval.

As we walked side by side up the sidewalk that led to their front door, painted a pale peach, I decided this wasn't such a bad idea after all. Watson was a fairly good judge of character. Granted, it was hardly a definitive test as he either disliked or barely tolerated most people, but none of the ones he'd fawned over had turned out to be murderers, so perhaps Sandy would answer the door, Watson would go hog-wild with joy, and I would know she was innocent.

Before I could change my mind, I rang the doorbell. At

least, I told myself it was before I could change my mind. I knew that wasn't a real possibility. I was too curious and too stubborn. I'd set the plan into motion… no, that wasn't quite right… I didn't actually have a plan. I'd set the ball rolling and didn't have it in me to turn back. That was more apt.

After several moments of standing on the front door stoop, Watson whined and then gave an impatient chuff.

I rang the bell again. Maybe they weren't home. They'd had a big day, after all. I imagined preparing signs for a protest, picketing events, yelling and chanting, and having a minor run in with the police was exhausting. Who knew, they might have a tradition around it, after such a day, they might require massages or a night out at the movies.

Now that was a thought. They could be gone for quite some time.

I eyed the front door. I could jiggle the handle, just to see if it was unlocked. It wasn't exactly breaking and entering if the door was unlocked, right? Especially if that jiggling revealed the door to be partially open, even if that jiggle involved a slight twist?

Watson chuffed again, and I realized I was reaching toward the door handle.

I yanked my hand back. What in the world had gotten into me? The daughter of a policeman distorting semantics to justify breaking and entering into someone's home. It didn't matter how horribly they treated my family; that didn't justify me breaking the law.

I focused on Watson. "Thanks, you're a grumpy little conscience, but I'm glad for you." I was, too, even if my disappointment increased as we turned around and headed back to the car.

"Hello, there. Sorry, I was in the middle of making dinner—my hands were covered with flour." I'd not heard the door open but recognized Sandy's voice instantly, even though it was a conversational tone and not shouting threats and insults. "Can I help you with—" Her words fell away as I turned to face her.

This was the part where I reprimanded myself. I was better than this, smarter than this. Never, ever go into any situation without a plan. If I'd paused to consider, even for a moment, I would've realized that, obviously, Sandy would recognize me. She knew the rest of my family. Most people around town, if not all, knew of the lady who owned the bookshop, her dog, and that she had a penchant for looking into murders. Plan or not, there was no way to play this off. I forced a friendly smile, one that I didn't feel, onto my face. "No need to be sorry. I'm the one coming unannounced and interrupting your dinner preparations. I was, ah... just hoping we could... talk."

Her gaze flicked skeptically to Watson, then back to me. "You want to talk?"

Though she would've recognized me either way, if I'd taken the time to plan, I could've at least had some premise of an excuse for my arrival. I was far from being on top of my game, so I went with the truth; it was easier. "I've heard quite a bit about the Holy Rapture Fellowship. I have some questions."

"Questions?" Her expression changed, softened some-what. "You want to know more about the fellowship?"

There was a clear spark of excited hope in her voice. Though unexpected, I latched on to it. "Yes, very much."

She smiled and held up a finger. "One second." She leaned back, angling her face inside the house and raised her voice, managing to yell without sounding like she did at the protests. "Paul! I hate to bother you, could you come here, dear?"

It was only a matter of moments before the door opened wider and Paul Anderson stood beside his wife. He gave me a similar expression to Sandy's when she first opened the door.

"She..." Sandy glanced my way. "Your name is Winifred, correct?"

I nearly told her most people called me Fred, then simply nodded.

Satisfied, Sandy turned back to her husband. "Winifred has some interest about the fellowship."

"Really?" Once more, Paul matched his wife as his expression shifted. "That's wonderful." He stood aside. "Come on in, and welcome to our home. Your dog is welcome too, as long as he is housebroken."

Watson chuffed again, clearly insulted.

Paul didn't wait for a response but turned and disappeared inside the house. I followed, reprimanding myself even as I did so. Not only should the policeman's daughter know better than to try to justify breaking and entering, but even more so, to never, ever go alone into the home of people who might be murderers.

Sandy shut the door behind Watson and me the moment we'd stepped in and bent to pat his head. "Who's your little friend?"

Watson backed away. He didn't growl, but intense dislike radiated from him.

Sandy jerked her hand back.

"Watson. He's a little... grumpy. He's had a long day." I attempted an apologetic smile.

"Yes, we all have." She motioned through an arched doorway that led to a large living room, where Paul was already seated in a leather recliner. "Come on in. May I get you any refreshments?"

Refreshments? Considering my family, I most definitely hadn't expected that sort of hospitality. "No, thank you. But I appreciate it."

"I'll take an iced tea, Sandy." Paul lifted his chin at his wife and then gestured toward the couch nearest his recliner. "Have a seat, Winifred."

Sandy took off before I'd even managed a step. I glanced over my shoulder to see her disappear into the kitchen, then I moved into the living room to face Paul.

He made quite the impression, sitting there in his worn, leather recliner. Like the king of his castle. But the rest of the castle didn't seem to match him. Doubtlessly, Sandy had been in charge of the decorating. Everything was ruffled or frilled, floral or covered in a blue-and-white checkered pattern. Paul stretched out a hand toward Watson. "Come."

Watson stiffened. Though there was still no growl, his hackles rose.

Paul thrust his hand again, and when Watson didn't comply, looked up at me. "I thought you said he was trained."

"I said he was housebroken, and he is. But he's also stubborn and has his own personality." While Watson's reaction to Sandy and Paul didn't indicate the two of them were murderers, it didn't mean I couldn't strike them from my list.

With a judgmental glare, Paul leaned back into the recliner and folded his hands. "Sandy said you have interest in the Holy Rapture Fellowship. Are you considering joining?"

I nearly laughed at him. After the way they'd treated my uncles and stepsisters, he thought I would join? It took a second before I felt I could answer in a way that wouldn't slam communication shut. "Not exactly. But I do have questions about your... organization."

"Of a theological nature?"

I considered. "Yes. I suppose you could put it that way."

He gave a nod of approval. "Very good. I respect that." Before he could continue, Sandy entered the living room, carrying a tray containing a glass of ice, a pitcher of tea, and a sugar jar. She placed it on the side table next to Paul, poured a glass, then stood aside.

He took a sip, considered the sugar jar, then nodded. "Good enough. Thank you, Sandy." He gestured to the other end of the sofa. "Join us."

With a nod, Sandy left his side and sat opposite me. I did my best to study them without staring. I'd imagined speaking to Sandy, not Paul. Clearly I'd misjudged the relationship.

"Now—" Paul took another sip of tea and placed it on the tray before refocusing on me "—what sort of theological questions do you have about our fellowship?"

I'd attended church a few times during the holidays when we had driven to Estes to visit my grandparents, but hardly enough that I had sufficient background knowledge to conjure a convincing question. After a brief attempt to formulate something, I gave up. "Honestly, I'm curious how your religious beliefs give you the right to harass innocent people who don't believe the same as you."

From the corner of my eye, I noticed Sandy flinch, but Paul didn't miss a beat, only leaning forward slightly as his tone darkened. "So you came into our home to make accusations and cast judgment." He glanced at Sandy before looking back at me. "Just like the rest of this town. What gives you the right to come into our home and behave in such a manner, despite your clearly sinful ways?"

How could he ask me that? "Do you know who I am?"

He waved me off. "You sell books."

"Yes, I do." I leaned forward, matching his position. "I'm also the stepsister to Verona and Zelda Pearson, and the niece of Percival and Gary."

"Oh." Dawning lit his eyes. "So you are one of the corrupted. Still, there is hope for you yet. There is forgiveness in repentance." Paul leaned back in his chair as if suddenly relaxed. "It won't be easy for you, having been raised in this sinful town. Raised around the corrosive abominations that are your uncles."

"Are you serious?" I knew it was ridiculous to be shocked or appalled. I was speaking to the same people who had thrown Bibles at Aurora, who harassed my uncles and stepsisters. But it was an ugly part of human nature that allowed people to do such things from afar. I hadn't expected it up close and personal in their living room.

"Deadly serious. Those raised among darkness have to fight harder to shake off the shackles." Paul reached for his glass of tea but spoke before taking another sip. "Take your stepsisters, for example, brought up under the influence of your corrupt uncles, they turned to witchcraft and dark magic."

"Witchcraft?" I nearly laughed. "Verona and Zelda aren't witches, as if such things even exist. And furthermore, they weren't raised here." Though utterly ridiculous, I felt compelled to defend them against this man and to punch as many holes as possible into his preconceived notions. I should've known better. I did. I did know better, not that it did a lick of good. "They were adults before they even discovered who their father was, before they joined my family or moved to this town."

"Ah, so they are bastards." Sympathy crossed his face.

"Still, that's not their fault, but the result of sin nevertheless. Corruption comes in all forms." He turned to Sandy. "What more proof do you need? This place attracts the depraved. You escaped, and though it speaks highly of your pure soul that you wanted to come back and offer a better way, there is none to be had for the people here."

I should've gotten up and left, but I couldn't make myself. "And as far as me, I wasn't corrupted by anyone. I didn't even grow up here, so you can't blame the town." I paused, his words replaying even as I spoke, and I turned to Sandy. "You came back here? You're from Estes?"

She opened her mouth, but Paul answered for her. "Sandy grew up in Lyons, though close enough to this place. She made her escape and found her salvation."

"I have such fond memories of this area." Sandy flinched as if she'd spoken out of turn and glanced toward Paul. He nodded, she continued. That interaction confirmed that I'd been wrong. Sandy may be more outspoken in public, but it was Paul who was in charge. I had a feeling that aspect was part of their theological beliefs as well. "I hoped to be able to save this place. Lyons, originally, but as we drove through, we noticed the pot shop, and I knew it was too late. But here... for Estes, there was still hope..."

Paul's gaze drilled holes into Sandy as he gestured toward me. "And now? Are you convinced? Are you ready to shake the dust from our feet? My indulgence of this fantasy of yours has come to an end. The word is very clear on what we must do. After yet another day where no one listens to our warnings except for the few who are already beginning to waver, surely listening to this woman is the final straw."

"I suppose." Sandy nodded, and sank back into the sofa, looking utterly defeated.

My skin prickled. "What do you mean? What do you think the word is telling you that you must do?"

"Think?" Paul whipped back to me, leaning forward so quickly, he caused Watson to growl at my feet. Paul ignored him. "I don't think the Bible is telling us what we must do; I know it. It's perfectly clear in black-and-white. We are to shake the dust from our feet."

I blinked, trying to make something of that repeated phrase. "What does that mean? More of what you've done to Percival and Gary? What you've done to Verona and Zelda? What you did to Aurora? Did you take care of Aurora's sin forever? Is that dusting off your feet?"

A grin spread over his face, and he laughed. "For owning a bookshop, Winifred, you're very poorly read on the only book that matters."

"Surely the Bible doesn't tell you to murder those who don't believe like you."

His glare was so cold it sent ice down my spine, and he didn't answer for a long time. Finally he shrugged. "We are leaving this town, shaking the dust from our feet and never looking back. We've tried. Sandy has tried. We hoped and prayed Estes Park would go the same way as Nineveh at Jonah's teachings. Instead, it will suffer the same fate of Sodom and Gomorrah."

Jonah? Hearing Paul say my brother-in-law's name threw me off, but I caught up quickly enough. Jonah and the whale, from the Bible. Though I didn't know how it connected to Nineveh, but I knew all too well what happened to Sodom and Gomorrah. Even realizing our time was done, I tried one more tactic, just to see. "Did you kill Aurora? Did you cleanse her soul that way?"

Again he stared, long and cold. "Aurora's soul was too dark to be cleansed. Just like her husband, your uncles and sisters." He shook his head, almost in what looked like regret. "As is yours."

"You're wrong." I stood, giving him a glare of my own before turning to Sandy. "God doesn't operate in hate. He doesn't want you to be controlled."

She flinched and with a quick glance at Paul, stood. "I'll see you out now. I'm sorry you've refused to see the light. I truly am, for all of you."

The entire conversation with the Andersons left me feeling so disgusted I went home, made dinner, curled up with a book, and did my best to block out anything resembling the reality of life. I simply needed to escape for a while. After half an hour or so, I managed to get swept away in the world of *Anne of Green Gables*, a frequent comforting reread.

By the time sunrise arrived in a blaze of pink and gold, I was ready to go again. So ready, that once more I skipped Watson's and my walk through the woods and the two of us headed downtown. Dirty chai, pastries, and talking over the ins and outs of the past few days with Katie was exactly what the doctor ordered.

As Watson—with his stuffed lion firmly grasped in his jaws—and I walked toward the front door of the Cozy Corgi, we found Zelda standing as if in a trance in front of the door of Chakras. I hesitated to touch her, remembering from somewhere that it was dangerous to wake sleepwalkers. A ridiculous thought, like she'd sleepwalked all the way from Glen Haven. "Zelda?"

Sure enough, she flinched violently at the touch on her shoulder and whipped toward me, eyes wide and unfocused. "Oh, Fred." She swallowed and blinked. "I..." As her words fell away she shook her head.

"Are you okay?"

"Yes, I thought I'd spend some time at the store, see if I could find some normality somewhere. I wanted to..." She sniffed, shook her head, and a tear made its way down her cheek. "No. I'm not okay."

I slid my hand down her arm to take hers. "Come on, this calls for some of Katie's baking."

Within five minutes, with Nick happily buzzing around in the bakery's kitchen in the background, Zelda, Katie, and I settled in at Watson's favorite table by the windows overlooking Elkhorn Avenue. We each had extra-dirty chais, and Katie had laid out an assortment of pastries that was better suited for a party of ten as opposed to three. Watson settled in below with his lion and his morning dog bone treat.

"Maybe it's silly to ask, but what's wrong?" Zelda's tears had dried, and I'd waited until she had drunk a little of her dirty chai and eaten half of her bear claw before deciding to push the issue. "I mean, clearly there's a lot wrong at the moment, but is there something new?"

Zelda kept her focus on the pastry. "I'm just... lost. I don't know what to do, what to think."

Katie made soothing circles over Zelda's back. "It's hard when the whole town is talking about you. Trust me, I know. It will pass. Things will get better. Everything will return to normal. Verona will get out of jail, and you two can get back to enjoying your new shop."

"No, it's not that. I mean it's kind of that. But not really." She forced a smile at Katie, then looked at me, eyes pleading. "I've never had a time where I couldn't talk to Verona. *Ever*. Not even for a day." A sad chuckle escaped.

"Outside of sleeping, I think the longest we've ever made it is a couple of hours without seeing or phoning each other. I'm sure that sounds pathetic or something."

Suffocating is what it sounded like, but I'd been an only child, so I couldn't fathom how twins felt. But if that were true, no wonder Zelda was struggling so much. "I can't believe they're not letting you talk to her. Branson got me in to see Verona. I can… contact him, see if he'll force the issue." I needed to be careful. No matter how clear I was with him, if I kept asking for favors, he would assume there were strings involved.

"No, the police aren't keeping me from seeing her." Tears began again. "*Verona* won't see me. She's refusing to let me visit, won't talk to me on the phone, nothing."

Katie and I exchanged glances. I was willing to bet she was having the same thoughts as me.

That behavior sounded like guilt, shame. Maybe Verona wasn't as innocent as I'd thought.

"I know she's angry, she has a right to be. I betrayed her."

Katie shifted in her chair to better face Zelda. "How in the world did you betray Verona?"

"The ice cream." Zelda sounded hysterical, and like the reason should've been obvious. "All of my little cheats. All my little secrets. The ice cream, drinking soda when she's not looking. Listening to pop music in the car—"

"Wait a minute, Verona doesn't know you listen to pop music?" Katie gaped at her. "I always assumed Britney and Christina were named after… well… Britney and Christina. You don't get much more pop than those two."

"They are!" Zelda's tears increased, and she covered her eyes. "I told Verona they're names that were important to Noah, and he went along with it."

If Verona wasn't in jail, and Zelda so genuinely heart-broken, I probably would've died laughing from the sheer ridiculousness of it. Once more, from the expression Katie cast my way, she was having a similar experience. And if the curve of her lips was any indication, she was closer to giving in to the laughter than I was. "Zelda. Look at me."

After a second, she did, dabbing at her eyes with a napkin.

"Obviously, you know Verona better than me, but there's no way she's refusing to see you simply because she found out you ate ice cream."

"Yes, there is." She blew her nose on the napkin, which earned me another look from Katie, and then she spoke, clearly trying to regain some control. "You don't understand what it's like with us. Things are wonderful now. We have our husbands, our children, our father." She reached across the table and took my hand. "You and your mom are part of our family." With her other she took Katie's. "And you, friends who are like family. Life is wonderful. But it wasn't always that way." She pulled her hands back and began to twist the napkin as she spoke. "Verona and I only had each other growing up. It was always just the two of us. Mom meant well, I suppose—we weren't abused or anything—but we were always more of an afterthought."

I'd heard the twins talk about their mom from time to time, and I knew things weren't good between the three of them, but I never felt comfortable enough to push for details.

After a sniff, Zelda kept going. "Mom was always obsessed with her new husband, or a new boyfriend, or her new group of friends." Zelda fluttered her hands. "Every-thing was always new. Whatever was shiny or in style or popular, that's what she was drawn to. Money went to fashion and hair and makeup. Men and trips. Verona and I didn't starve, but we weren't exactly well cared for either. Sometimes Mom would leave for a day or two—she'd tell us in advance and make sure there was food in the fridge or whatever, but it was really just the two of us."

Katie's hand returned to Zelda's back. "Goodness, I had no idea."

Zelda shrugged as if all of it was nothing more than minutiae. "We're fine. We always were. And that is because of Verona. She was always the stronger one, the leader. It was in sixth grade when Verona discovered meditation and New Age practices. I just went along for the ride. Gradually it became more and more part of her life, almost an obsession. One that offered strength and comfort when there was hardly any to be found elsewhere. It helped me too. But Verona was always a little more staunch than me. It helped us deal with being little more than a nuisance to our mother and having been abandoned by our father."

She smiled at me, and the tears that started to flow changed in nature. "When we discovered Barry was our dad and that he'd never known of our existence, it was the most wonderful day of our lives. Not only had he not known about us, but he wanted a relationship with us. He loved us instantly. Even though we were already grown, it changed everything." She laughed, glanced out the window, and made a sweeping gesture of the town. "And then meeting him and moving here, having Barry be *Barry*—he was a different version of us, of Verona. With his vegan, hippie ways, it was like it made sense that Verona and I had fallen into this lifestyle on our own. A matter of genetics. Of nature over nurture. It was a connection between the three of us, roots that we'd longed for our entire lives." Her smile faltered again. "And I've betrayed that."

Over my months in Estes, I'd gotten closer and closer to my stepfather. Before then, I had always liked him, but kept him at arm's distance until I moved to be near Mom. I'd grown to genuinely love and care for him, but hearing Zelda speak of him so, took him to a whole new level. No wonder Watson worshiped the ground Barry walked on.

Suddenly I became aware of Katie's gaze drilling into me. When I looked up at her, she cocked an eyebrow.

I didn't need words to read her mind. I knew what she was thinking. Zelda was hurting, blaming herself for all that was happening. We could alleviate that, somewhat. By doing so, we'd be betraying Verona, as well.

The choice was easy.

"You're not responsible, Zelda." She looked up at me and started to protest, but I cut her off. "Verona's not talking to you because of her *own* secrets, not yours. Because *she's* embarrassed and ashamed."

Zelda leaned back from the table, offended. "Fred! That's a horrible thing to say. I know Verona has a secret, but it's not going to be anything so horrible as—"

"No." Katie jumped in. "Fred's right. Aurora was black-mailing Verona for something. And whatever it was is bad enough that Verona is willing to be charged with murder to keep anyone from finding out."

Though Zelda shook her head, she looked back and forth between Katie and me. "Really?"

"Yes. Jonah knows as well, but he's too afraid to tell." I stood up from the table. "Hold on, I'll be right back." I hurried downstairs and dug the key out of my purse. Ben had come in and started getting the bookshop ready to open. We exchanged quick pleasantries, but I was back at the table in a matter of minutes. I handed the little silver key to Zelda. "Jonah gave me this. He wouldn't tell me what was going on, but he gave me a couple of clues. This key." I motioned toward Watson napping below us, his head resting on the stuffed animal. "A lion. And he mentioned skeletons in a closet. He said the closet is the clue."

Zelda's brows furrowed. "Are you serious? *Jonah* knows? She told him and not me?"

Katie blinked, clearly surprised at the reaction. "Well, he *is* her husband."

"I'm her *twin*. That's a whole different level of..." Zelda shook her head and straightened her shoulders. "Whatever. I deserve it. I was keeping secrets from her." She looked at me expectantly. "What does it mean?"

"I don't know. I have no idea." I pointed to the three letters on the top of the key. "Do those look familiar to you? RMS? Do you know someone with those initials?"

"I don't think so. The number 365 doesn't mean anything to me either." She studied the key, turning it over and over in her hands, tracing the letters with her fingertip. "There's a key, and it has something to do with a lion and a closet. None of that rings a bell. I haven't heard Verona ever mention a lion, I don't think. And as for closets..." She shrugged. "We're always in and out of each other's closets, borrowing clothes and such. She can't be hiding anything in those."

"Maybe she found Jimmy Hoffa's twin."

Zelda and I both turned as one to Katie, though it was Zelda who spoke. "Jimmy Hoffa had a twin?"

"No. Sorry." Katie chuckled and shook her head. "Bad time for a joke. I was just thinking of skeletons in closets. They say Jimmy Hoffa's bones were discovered in a rolled-up rug in the back of a storage locker, believe it or not." She grimaced. "I was just kidding about Jimmy Hoffa's twin.

Maybe if Verona had found that, she was holding onto it for the money. Bad joke. Sorry, again."

Zelda rolled her eyes and returned to staring at the key. "RMS. I can't think of anyone with those initials. Can you, Fred?"

I barely heard her, instead, kept staring at Katie. "They found Jimmy Hoffa's bones in a storage locker?" That sounded familiar, some random piece of trivia I'd heard in the past?

"Well, it's just an urban myth really. Though plenty of people swear to it." She smiled sheepishly. "Just more of my useless, random trivia for you. I'll try to focus on the matter at hand. I—" Her brown eyes widened a second later and she snatched the key from Zelda's grip. "Storage locker. This could be to a storage locker."

"You read my mind." I sat back down in my chair, the realization making my knees weak. That's what it was. I could feel it. In a way, it was so completely and utterly obvious. "Storage locker number 365."

"A storage locker? Verona has a storage locker?" Zelda studied the key. "So maybe those aren't somebody's initials, but wherever the locker is."

Katie smiled over at her. "Brilliant." She slammed the key on the table and scooped up her phone.

Watson let out a startled yelp at the noise, and darted from underneath the table, turning to glare at us.

"Sorry, buddy. I got overly excited." Katie gave him an apologetic glance before turning back to the phone. "Go get a treat from Nick as an apology."

Watson's eyes brightened at the word *treat*, and he glanced back at the kitchen. To my surprise, he darted back under the table, snagged his stuffed lion, and took it with him as he waddled over to demand payment from Nick.

Katie let out an exasperated sigh. "Googling storage locker and those initials only brings up about ten billion options, and none of them helpful. But it's a place to begin."

I started to turn back to them, but continued to watch Watson as he dropped the lion at the edge of the counter as Nick offered him another large all-natural dog bone treat.

Lion. It was the only clue left. We had the key, and we knew it was to a storage locker. We were so close. So close. "What in the world could a lion have to do with this?"

"Maybe Verona has a lion caged in a locker some-where." Katie chuckled as she continued her search. "Hope-fully it's a dead one, for our sake. If not, were going to be in trouble when we open it up."

"That's ridiculous. Verona would never harm an animal. Much less keep one caged up in some storage lock-er." Zelda's tone became defensive. "Verona and I have even protested circuses and zoos. Keeping those magnificent, wild animals in cages is nothing more than depraved."

Katie spared Zelda a withering look. "I was kidding. I don't actually think your sister has a lion in a locker."

"Wait a minute, Zelda, what did you say?" I could feel the answer, it was right there. I just couldn't touch it.

She shook her head, looking abashed. "Never mind. I was being ridiculous. Of course Katie wasn't saying that. I'm just exhausted and on edge."

"No. Not that. What did you say about keeping animals in circuses and zoos?"

Zelda shrugged. "That it was bad?"

"Depraved. She said it was depraved." Katie looked at me quizzically. "You're about to figure it out, aren't you?"

"Depraved... Why does that word sound so...?" At the rush of anger that coursed through me, I knew, and I addressed Zelda and Katie together. "I went to see Sandy and Paul Anderson last night. It turned out Paul's the ringleader of that whole thing, not Sandy, though she's just as involved. He called Percival and Gary, the entirety of Estes Park, *depraved.*" Katie and Zelda's expressions both turned to disgust, but I kept going. "They came here to save or enlighten or whatever, everyone in the area because Sandy is from here. From Lyons, specifically." I grinned at the light dawning in Katie's eyes and tapped the table. "Lyons. The storage locker is in Lyons."

In less than a minute, Katie had pulled up the contact information for Rocky Mountain Storage, twenty-one and a half miles away in Lyons, Colorado.

Within half an hour, the three of us and Watson had left the Cozy Corgi in the capable hands of Ben and Nick and driven to Lyons. We spent the time traveling down the curving canyon highway speculating what Verona would stash away in a storage unit that would make her willing to suffer murder charges. We couldn't come up with one feasible possibility other than an actual dead body.

The crowded Mini Cooper buzzed with a mix of excitement and anticipation. One last hurdle to jump and we'd finally have some answers.

I slowed as we passed The Green Munchie, a marijuana dispensary, just inside of the town's city limits. It looked just as bright and modern as it had the November before.

Katie squeezed my shoulder from her spot in the backseat with Watson. "I think about Eddie from time to time too. He was such a nice guy. What happened to him was a tragedy."

"Yeah. It really was." I was ashamed to say that with the exception of a week or two that followed those events, Eddie had faded from my mind. His was the second murdered body I'd ever seen in my life, in the first pot shop I'd ever been in, and he'd faded away before Christmas had even rolled around. In my defense, he hadn't been the last dead body I'd discovered, but still. He'd been a surprisingly sweet man, and I had never gotten a clear answer from Branson on who had killed him.

Shaking it off as best I could, I hit the gas once more, and within two blocks, we pulled up in front of Rocky Mountain Storage. I turned to Zelda in the passenger seat. "You sure you want to do this?"

She'd already been gripping the handle, and she scowled at me. "We went through the plan. I'm supposed to pretend like I'm Verona and tell him I lost the key to the main gate. You're not the only one who can be sneaky, Fred."

"I meant, are you sure you want to break into Verona's storage unit. You don't have to. If you're afraid it will damage your relationship further, Katie and I can do it alone."

"Oh." She grimaced in an abashed manner. "Sorry. Still on edge. Didn't mean to bite your head off. And yes, I'm sure. No matter what's in there, no matter what's going on between us right now, we'll be fine, Verona and me. Maybe even stronger than ever. After all, we've been twins for forty-seven years. That should count for something." With a wink, she was gone.

"You know..." Katie's voice was thoughtful. "The twins are so pretty and glowy. That yoga thing must really do a body good. I always forget that they're nearly a decade older than you."

"Hey!" I twisted to glare at her. "Thanks a lot."

Her eyes widened, and she mouthed silently for a few moments and then gave up and snickered. "Sorry. I guess that sounded bad."

"You think?" I couldn't quite manage to keep my own grin at bay. She wasn't wrong. Verona and Zelda were both beautiful in that wispy sort of way I could never be. I'd made my peace a long time ago with never having a magazine-model's body. I twisted some more, giving me enough room to swat at Katie. "Besides, the extra ten pounds or so I've put on since moving to Estes is entirely your fault."

She gave the most exaggerated bow that she could from her cramped, seat-belted position. "And you're welcome."

With Watson staring at us like we were insane, we both chuckled and turned to watch Zelda pretend to be her twin.

She stood at the counter, talking to an older gentleman. She kept tossing her head back and laughing and twirling strands of her hair.

"Does Verona whip her hair back and forth like that?"

I cast a glance at Katie. "Does anyone other than a high school cheerleader whip their hair back and forth like that?"

Katie cringed, then shrugged. "Maybe Zelda is just nervous."

"Clearly." If this worked, it was going to be a miracle. "I'm a bit nervous about it myself. I don't think we're going to find a skeleton in Verona's storage unit, but who knows what else it could be."

"Maybe hoard of diamonds and gold, like a dragon's lair." Katie shrugged at my skeptical expression. "Or maybe just cash. We don't think she was having an affair, so money seems to be the biggest motivator for stuff like this. Maybe she was embezzling it."

"From whom?"

Another shrug. "No idea." Katie cocked a brow. "Although, I was thinking about the embezzlement from the Birnbaum Foundation. What if Tabitha—" Before she could continue, Zelda got back into the car in record speed, despite Katie's and my criticism of her acting skills.

She pointed us to the main gate. "That was kind of fun."

"You think he believed you?"

That question earned me another scowl. "I got the key, right? I simply told him that I left my driver's license at home by accident, probably in the same place I lost the key to the main gate. They had Verona's picture on file, so I said I'd recently dyed my hair brunette, and of course I knew her address, birth date, and Social Security number."

"Nice work!" I decided not to mention the hair tossing. If nothing else, when this was all over, I was willing to bet Katie would be able to reenact the whole thing and have everyone in stitches.

Once we were through the main gate, it only took a few moments to find unit 365. The four of us scrambled out of the Mini Cooper. Katie stretched, and let out a groan as her back popped audibly. "Why in the world did we take your car?"

I shrugged. We'd been in such a hurry to go it hadn't even been a thought. I'd led the way, and we'd all crammed inside. "I'll let you drive on the way back. I'll take the backseat."

"With those long legs of yours? Even I'm not that mean."

"Focus, you two." Zelda stood at the padlock and didn't look over as she reprimanded us. Her hands trembled as she slipped the key inside and twisted. With a click, it fell open, and she slid it free. "Well, here we go."

I helped her bend down and lift the pine-green garage door, and then the three of us stood at the entrance, staring inside.

"Well, unless Verona chopped her victims into little

bread-box-sized portions, there aren't any dead bodies in there." Katie almost sounded disappointed.

Watson trotted in ahead of us and began sniffing around.

The entirety of the storage unit was filled with racks surrounding the three walls of the inside, with two more in the center. Each one had three rows of shelving, and every single available space was filled with identical-sized boxes.

"They almost look like"—Zelda touched the nearest one when she entered—"shoeboxes."

"Yes, they do." I followed her in, Katie at my side. "There are a lot of things that can fit in shoeboxes, though. Paperwork, photos, jewelry..."

Zelda continued to study the box. "No, she wouldn't have jewelry. She owns some, but not much."

"Good grief." Katie scooped up one of the boxes and held it toward Zelda and me. "We don't have to speculate anymore. We're here. Who wants to do the honors?"

I looked toward Zelda. Verona was her twin; she should have the right, if she wanted it.

She reached toward the box but pulled back her hand with a shake of her head. "No, I can't. Fred, you do it. Please."

"Okay." As I stepped forward and put my hand on the lid, I had to admit that I was a little afraid. I was certain Verona hadn't killed Aurora, but I hoped whatever black-mailable secrets were in the boxes wouldn't tear our family apart. As if I were ripping off a Band-Aid, I pulled off the lid in one smooth flick of my wrist and peered inside. "What in the world?"

"What? What is it?"

I turned to Zelda, wondering why she needed clarification, to find she'd covered her eyes with her hands.

"Shoes, Zelda. They're just shoes."

She cracked her fingers slightly and peered through, then let her hands fall. "Shoes?"

Balancing the box with one hand, Katie removed the stilettos and shoved them on top of another box and began to pat around inside the empty one. "There doesn't seem to be a false bottom or anything." She held it up toward the fluorescent lighting overhead. "No writing or secret messages."

I took another box from the shelf and opened it. "These are shoes too."

The three of us exchanged bewildered stares, and then, as one, we each began yanking boxes off shelves and tossing the lids away. Before long, there was a growing pile of open boxes on the floor, each with a different pair of high-heeled shoes inside.

"There must be over three hundred pairs of shoes in here." Katie stood with her hands on her hips, staring at the pile, as Watson sniffed quizzically at each box.

Zelda hurried to the other side of the storage unit to begin opening those boxes. "These are all shoes as well."

I studied the pile. They were all similar. Each different versions of high-heeled shoes, most with the exact same silhouette, just in various colors, designs, and materials. They were beautiful, I supposed. I was more of a cowboy boot kind of girl, and a stiletto was little more than a torture device, but they looked expensive. "This doesn't make any sense. We must be missing something. Verona wouldn't be in jail for murder because of a secret stash of shoes. Aurora wouldn't have been able to blackmail her for these."

"No kidding." Katie held up a strappy pair encrusted with glittering black stones. "Having exquisite taste is hardly an embarrassment."

"Yes, it is." Zelda gaped at us as if she couldn't believe we didn't understand. "Look at all of these. I can't imagine how much they cost, how much time and money has gone into collecting them."

"Well, that's a little judgmental." Katie gestured at the expanse of shoeboxes. "Sure, maybe Verona has a bit of a hoarder situation going on, but that's still not as bad as murder."

I thought I understood. "Your mom, right? The things you said about your mom." As I spoke, Zelda started to nod. "These shoes are ones your mother would like, things that were more important than the two of you."

"Yeah." Zelda pulled another box off a shelf and flipped open the lid, revealing a deep red stiletto with gold stitching. "These represent everything Verona's stood against her entire life. I don't blame her for not wanting anyone to know. She'd be utterly humiliated. And how would that look, the owner of Chakras having this sort of secret?"

Watson nudged the lid off one of the boxes that had fallen down in our haste, sniffed inside and then trotted away. Doubtlessly, he was experiencing disappointment after disappointment, with each box being filled with shoes instead of delicious treats.

I started to reply to Zelda but did a double take at the newly revealed pair of shoes. "Wait a minute. I've seen these." I walked over, bent down, and pulled out the left stiletto. "These were the ones that Aurora was wearing when she was killed." I struggled to believe it, but there was no possible way it was any other design. The white unicorn was on either side of the heel, and the rest of the shoe was covered in the rich colors and textures of forest and the swirling fractal pattern of stars in the sky. "This is the high priestess card from one of Aurora's tarot collections."

"That's too big to be a coincidence. And you weren't kidding about these being expensive shoes." Katie snatched the stiletto from me and pointed at the pink satin sole. "I didn't bother looking inside any of them. These are Kamala shoes." She twisted it so the silvery embossed flower caught the light. "They're right up there with Jimmy Choos, Manolo Blahniks, and Louboutins. They came on the scene about ten years ago and have been keeping up with the best of them ever since."

"It's like I don't even know my best friend. I had no idea you were so in touch with fashion." I gestured toward her T-shirt embossed with a chipmunk stuffing its cheeks with circus peanuts.

"I'm not!" She rolled her eyes at me and tapped her head. "Trivia, remember."

This time, Zelda snatched the shoe, her face going pale as she stared at the flower.

"What is it?" Katie reached for Zelda. "You look like you're about to faint."

She stared at the flower and then up at us. "It's so much worse than we thought."

"Worse than hoarding shoes?" I was careful to keep my voice neutral. I understood where she was coming from, given their history, but I still had a hard time accepting a storage room full of high heels was worse than being accused of murder.

"Kamala is the Hindi name for the lotus flower. Verona has one tattooed on her back." She tapped the flower as Katie had moments before. "*This* exact lotus."

"Wow. That's devotion to a brand."

Zelda shook her head at Katie. "No. You said this line is around ten years old, right? Verona got the tattoo in college.

Besides her hair, it's the only physical feature that sets us apart."

Katie gave Zelda a puzzled expression, but I thought I understood. "You think Verona doesn't collect Kamala shoes... she *designs* them."

"Yeah. I do." Zelda's gaze traveled from the shoe in her hand to the piles on the floor to the scores and scores of unopened boxes filling the shelves, her expression flickering back and forth from amazement to disbelief to irritation. "And she had the nerve to be mad about ice cream?"

Katie put a soothing hand on Zelda's shoulder, but focused on me, cutting to the point as was her fashion. "All that makes sense, in a weird... totally weird way, but why would Aurora's high priestess card be on one of Kamala's shoes?"

"That's a good question." The anger continued to grow behind Zelda's eyes. "But I can guarantee you it has something to do with Aurora blackmailing and taking control of our shop." She held the shoe to her chest. "And I can also guarantee that my sister is going to talk to us this afternoon, whether she wants to or not."

EIGHTEEN

Verona stood, both hands clenched into fists on top of the table in the police questioning room. "Fred, I'm not sure how to make myself any clearer, but I told you to keep your nose out of it. And Zelda, I'm not ready to—"

"What?" Zelda crossed the small space in two strides and slammed the stiletto right between Verona's fists. "You're not ready to what, exactly? Stop punishing me for ice cream?"

Verona gaped at the shoe, as if she were staring deep into the soul of the unicorn on the heel. Her arms started to tremble, and she sank back down into the chair.

Behind me, having once more pulled strings, Branson closed the door and left the three of us alone. I followed Zelda and put what I hoped was a calming hand on her shoulder. "Let's sit."

Though it took several moments, Zelda finally followed my lead and sat across from her twin. "Well...?"

Verona continued to stare at the shoe. "Who told you?"

Zelda smacked the metal table with her open palm, causing the stiletto to fall over. "Are you kidding me? *That's* what you have to say?"

Apparently my hand wasn't all that calming, so I

squeezed. "No one told us, per se. We just followed the clues." I was certain she'd know that Jonah told us soon enough, but I didn't want to be the one to enlighten her on that detail. "What matters is that we know. Unless there's another reason Aurora was blackmailing you?"

Still not looking at us, Verona shook her head.

"Good. Now it's out in the open, we can tell the police and hopefully get things in order and you can leave."

Verona's blue eyes flashed up at me, horror-stricken. "Are you insane?" Her gaze flicked to the door and back. "Do they already know? Did you tell Branson?"

I shook my head. "No, but he saw the shoe. I imagine he's smart enough to put two and two together, or at least connect some of the dots. The only other person who knows is Katie. And Watson. They're back at the Cozy Corgi."

She rolled her eyes. "The *only* one I'm okay with knowing about any of this is Watson. You two included."

"How could you?" Zelda's whisper was soft and so very, very dark. "How could you, Verona? After all this time..."

"I know." The defensiveness left Verona's voice, and her shoulders slumped. "I didn't mean for all this to happen. I know that sounds insane, a person doesn't just fall into designing shoes, but... I did. And I know it's embarrassing. Shallow and materialistic."

"Not that!" Zelda snatched the shoe up off the table, looked like she was going to throw it across the room, then slowly placed it back down once more. "I don't care about the stupid shoes. You lied to me, for years. And you've made me feel..." her voice broke and for the second time that day, tears began to fall "...like a fraud next to you so many times. That I could never measure up to your level of enlightenment."

Verona flinched and her lips went slack.

"You made it where I felt so horribly guilty about sneaking ice cream and listening to the *music of the masses*, a million different ways that I knew I didn't measure up to you. And the whole time..." She smacked the table again, "*The whole time*... Verona, you were running a dynasty of a *shoe* company. You have this whole other life."

If I could have managed in an unobtrusive way, I would've snuck out of the room; the moment felt too personal. As it was, I sat frozen in place.

"I know." Verona reached across the table and took Zelda's hand. For a second it looked like Zelda was going to pull away, but she didn't. "I know. I just felt so guilty, so embarrassed. And I didn't want you to think less of me."

Zelda scoffed. "So you made me think less of myself?"

"No! I never—" She blinked rapidly and then finally nodded. "I guess that is what I was doing. That part wasn't intentional. I swear."

They were silent for a while but kept their hands clasped. Eventually, Zelda picked up the stiletto again. "Why?"

Verona's cheeks went scarlet, and she seemed unable to meet either of our eyes. "I love them. I love shoes. I hate to admit it, but I do."

"I've *never* seen you wear any like this." Zelda huffed out a frustrated breath. "It doesn't even make sense. We're always together."

"I *don't* wear them, only when I visit the storage unit. And I design them at night, at times when I can't sleep. It's almost... meditative." She shrugged. "As far as the company goes, all I do is design them. Other people handle everything else. I don't bother with any of the details."

"Well... you're better at keeping your double life a secret than I am at eating ice cream."

Verona chuckled out a laugh at that. "I'm sorry. Will you forgive me?"

"No. Not yet." Zelda finally moved her hand. "But I will, I think. Sometime."

More silence fell, long enough it seemed the twins had gone as far as they could. Still feeling like I was infringing on their privacy, I tried to refocus the conversation. "How did Aurora find out about your shoes?"

It took a few seconds for Verona to answer, as if she were struggling to transition from confessing to Zelda. "Honestly, I've never understood that. I contacted her a few years ago, just letting her know I was a fan, thanking her for how much her books and inspirational messages had touched me and changed my life." She motioned back and forth between her and Zelda. "*Our* lives."

When Zelda didn't give a reaction, Verona continued. "Then one day, I got an email from her, telling me that she knew about me being behind Kamala. She asked if I would make a pair exclusively for her. That's where those came from. She sent me her print of the high priestess, and I adjusted it to fit." She pointed toward the unicorn. "There were only two pairs ever made. The one for her, and this one."

"Is that when the blackmail started?"

"No. The shoe design was years ago." She sank back into her chair and gave a confused shake of her head. "It was part of why I was so excited to get to work alongside her when she enrolled for headlining the conference. She was the one person who knew my secret, and she'd kept it. Didn't judge me." Verona sent an apologetic grimace toward Zelda, who didn't respond. "But I guess I wasn't the only one with a secret. The entirety of that woman was a secret, nothing but lies. She was nothing but belittling, mean, and threatening. Nothing like she presented."

It took all my willpower not to question why Verona allowed herself to be mistreated because she had a successful shoe line. Though both the twins had explained, it simply was beyond my understanding. But the last thing Verona needed was to feel more judgment from me. "So what happened the night you met her at Chakras?"

Verona shrugged. "Nothing more than I've already said, really. The conference had kicked her out because of what happened at the Samson statue, so she demanded I give her the store for the rest of the week. That's all. I gave her the keys and left. What else was I going to do?"

"Was she demanding money?"

Confusion flitted over Verona's features. "Why would she demand money?"

That seemed obvious to me, money typically went along with blackmail. "From what Katie says, it sounds like your company probably makes a fortune."

"We do. Well... *Kamala* does. I don't."

"You don't?" Zelda leaned forward.

"No, of course not." Verona turned a beseeching gaze onto Zelda. "You know I don't care about being rich or anything like that. All my profits are filtered into charities, mostly for environmental organizations."

Zelda let out a relieved sigh and reached for Verona's hand again. "So you are still you."

For the first time, Verona smiled.

Something tickled at the back of my mind, but I couldn't quite place it. "Then you have a secret company that gives large amounts of money to charities. Whereas the Birnbaum Foundation was anything but secret, but wasn't giving to causes like they said."

Verona considered. "Yeah. I guess so."

Even though I wasn't certain where the bunny trail was leading, I went with it. "Was Tabitha there that night when Aurora demanded your shop?"

"Tabitha?" She laughed darkly. "Goodness no."

"What about Wolf?"

"*No!*" Her answer was emphatic. "He didn't know. He was leading an all-night meditation retreat in the forest. Tabitha was probably there as well. The conference was allowing him to do one more evening, since so many people had signed up and everything had happened so last minute. Aurora made it very clear that Wolf didn't know what she was demanding from me. He wasn't like her. Wolf was the same in private as he seemed in front of everyone else. I don't know why he stayed with her. He's the real thing; she was the fake."

Again, that description matched my impression of Wolf. It matched everyone's impressions of Wolf. Just because one member of a marriage was rotten didn't mean the other was —maybe it wasn't fair for me to judge Wolf based on his wife, but it did make me wonder. "Do you think Aurora knew that the money from the Birnbaum Foundation wasn't going to where it was promised?"

Verona didn't miss a beat. "I don't know, but it wouldn't surprise me."

The answer was there, so close I could feel it whispering right behind my ears. I just needed to sit with it.

That could come later. At the moment, I needed to focus on my family. I held Verona's gaze. "All right, let's call Branson in here, and we'll fill him in. Gerald Jackson too, I suppose. Let's get you out of here."

Panic crossed her face. "Absolutely not. I've already made that clear. No one else needs to know." She flashed a quick smile at Zelda before looking back at me. "In all honesty, I'm relieved that you two know, finally. And I trust Katie. But no one else. No one."

"For crying out loud, Verona. They're just shoes! Who cares if people know you design shoes?"

At her insulted expression I realized my judgments had slipped out. "I don't expect you to understand. Whether you do or not, it's not your call." She grew stony as she had before. "And what difference does it make? It doesn't prove anything. It doesn't give me an alibi for when she was killed. It only clarifies motive."

"But the truth is..." Words faded away as I realized she was completely right. Her actions and secrecy made sense now, at least from Verona's way of thinking, but it didn't help. She was right, too, that if anything, it made it worse. "Sorry. I'm sorry, Verona. I can't say it completely makes sense to me, but it doesn't have to. You're right. Whether I understand or not, it isn't my call. And you're also right that it doesn't help that much."

Her shoulders slumped once more, and her gaze softened. "So you won't tell?"

"No. I won't tell. I promise." I reached across the table and took Verona's hand. "I promise this too. I'm going to figure this out and get you out of here."

"*We're* going to figure this out." Zelda slipped her free hand into mine so the three of us were linked, and for the first time, truly for the first time, I felt like I had sisters.

"There's nothing that I can find on Aurora." Katie didn't bother looking over at Leo or me as she continued to clack away on the laptop from her place on my sofa. "Honestly, considering how she was rather inept at not being condescending to those she considered beneath her, there's hardly any gossip about her. It's nearly all flattering or benign stories about her work in the New Age movement and environmental issues. Even the reviews on the classes she leads around healing crystals, tarot cards, and meditation are stellar."

"Maybe her poor attitude has been a recent development." Leo managed to keep his laptop balanced on his lap from his spot on the floor as he reached across to take another slice of pizza from the box with one hand and continuously pet Watson with his other. "She's been in the limelight for a couple of decades. It could've just been wearing her down."

Watson nudged Leo's palm with his nose and received a bit of the sausage topping. It wouldn't matter if he got an extra bite of food or not, either way, Watson was in heaven.

The three of us had dinner together frequently, and the night had already been planned. We were supposed to go to

Habanero's as normal, but switched to bringing a pizza back to my house to make it a night of research. Frequently, Paulie, and sometimes Athena, joined us, but I was glad it was just the three of us. Though two more brains would've helped, we would've had to talk in code as I wasn't comfortable sharing Verona's secret with that many people. But with Leo, I didn't think twice.

I snagged another slice of pizza for myself, and though Watson's gaze followed my movements, he didn't leave Leo's side. "I've found some complaints about the Birnbaum Foundation. Things that would indicate their financials weren't exactly on the up and up, but I had to really dig. They were very deep. And what little I found was rather generic and inconclusive."

"Maybe that's a recent development too." Leo spoke with his mouth full.

"Chew your food, rudeness." Katie winked at him, then grew serious. "And I think you might be a little too innocent in your train of thought. I'm betting she had a really great publicist, an expensive one, who managed what was printed about her, and maybe even one of those firms, or whatever they are, that scour the internet for bad stories and either bury or get rid of them."

"That feels right." I clicked to a new website that showed Aurora and Wolf in front of their home in Taos. Though beautiful and bigger than average, it wasn't one of those lavish compounds that it seemed so many televangelists lived in, nothing that would indicate they were stealing millions from their foundation. "But I don't know if how Aurora treated people was the reason she was murdered. It would make more sense that the misdirected money would be more of a motive. Money is often a motive."

Still petting Watson, Leo studied me. "You don't think so, though."

I shrugged. "I'm not sure. Maybe it's part of it, but it feels personal. She was strangled, and then hung up with a ton of quartz around her neck. I don't think it was supposed to convince anyone it was suicide. At least, not really. It feels personal."

"Maybe she was blackmailing someone else besides Verona."

Leo considered Katie's words and then shook his head. "That seems like a rather strong coincidence, don't you think? Surely she wasn't blackmailing someone else in Estes Park."

"Well, remember that the conference was here. And she'd just been kicked out of that conference." Katie's eyes widened. "What if she wasn't kicked out because of the disaster that happened at the Samson ceremony but because she was blackmailing one of the organizers? Or Duke Riser."

It could work. Almost. "Probably a little overkill. If one of the organizers killed her, surely they wouldn't have made a show of kicking her out of the conference. That would seem to point fingers right back at them. Maybe the same for Duke."

"You're right." Her face fell. "So if the crystals were personal, what kind of message do you think they were meant to send?"

"I don't know. No matter how much I've heard about them I can never retain their qualities. Too bad Mom isn't here, she could rattle off all the supposed powers of every crystal there is. Hold on." With a few strokes, I pulled up a list on the internet of healing crystals and gemstones. "Clear quartz are associated with the seventh chakra." I referenced the image of a figure with their legs crisscrossed and their arms resting on their knees. "It's also called the crown chakra. It is the highest spiritual center."

Leo let out an approving hum. "That's a little on the nose, considering she was seen as a spiritual leader."

"Not to mention Aurora acted as if she always wore a crown."

"No kidding." Chuckling, I kept reading. "Clear quartz are the healers of the stone world and amplify the energy of other crystals while assisting a person to connect to their higher self and act as a spiritual guide." I recalled reading that before, it all felt familiar. I scanned through again and then looked back up at Katie and Leo. "That's on the nose too. I don't know if Aurora considered herself a healer or not, but she was a spiritual guide."

"From that description, it kinda sounds like clear quartz is the equivalent of the ring to rule them all."

"Oh, Leo. I love that you're such a geek." Katie chuckled. "But you're not wrong."

"No, you're not. And that only makes it feel more personal. And indicates that whoever murdered Aurora knew enough about the aspects of the crystals to make a point. Whoever it was chose clear quartz intentionally—they took every necklace from Mom's display of that variety and left all the others. Both the crystals and killing Aurora was personal. *Very* personal."

"Wolf..." Katie's words were barely a whisper, and a dawning light came into her eyes.

"You read my mind."

Leo looked back and forth between the two of us. "Wolf? Are you serious? He's a genuinely good guy." He quit patting Watson as he stared, and earned another nudge with Watson's nose. "Oh, sorry, buddy." He looked back at us again. "Don't forget, like we said, there was a whole conference of people who probably knew that stuff about quartz."

"That's true." Katie's brows knitted. "Plus, what would Wolf's motive be? Granted, I can't imagine being married to Aurora, but they'd been together for a long, long time. What was the final straw? Why now? Why here?"

"Good questions. And I don't know. Maybe I'm wrong." I wasn't wrong. I'd been close to thinking of Wolf earlier in the day with Zelda and Verona, but it hadn't clicked. In a way, it felt like I'd been close to considering him several times. The very fact that he was kind and appeared to have a genuinely gentle heart had kept me from it. "Something tells me it's him. Even if I don't have a motive yet."

Leo studied me for a moment, then shrugged. "Well, if your gut is telling you it's Wolf, that's more than enough proof for me."

"Yep." Katie nodded. "Me too. So, Wolf. Let's refocus our attention there."

I marveled at them, touched by their faith in me. I hoped it wasn't misplaced. "Guys, just because my gut says something doesn't mean—"

"Yes, it does." Katie shook her finger. "Don't waste time with all that. Let's just get to it. This won't be easy. I can think of more reasons he *didn't* do it off the top of my head than any possible motive."

"Same here." Leo sighed. "So we've got our work cut out for us."

Deciding to just accept their trust, I turned back to the computer. Even if I was wrong, with the three of us all traveling down the same path, we could at least disprove my theory quicker that way. I kept rereading the page I had open about the clear quartz. For some reason, I felt like the answer was there, though I couldn't put my finger on it.

Surely Aurora wasn't killed because of anything directly related to crystals. I read the passage enough that the words started to blur and mean even less than they had to begin with. "Actually"—I turned to my friends, hoping they would offer some clarity—"why don't we start with all those reasons that Wolf didn't do it. Maybe that will narrow it down."

"Well, for one, he was just a nice guy. A thousand times nicer than Aurora. He didn't eat any of the quiches that day either, but he didn't treat me like I was some servant in his way like she did."

Leo piped in as well. "The day after Aurora died..." He cocked his head, considering. "No, I guess it would have been the day she died, Wolf came to the National Park's main office and cleared up the donation issue. He was a wreck. Couldn't even get through it without breaking down over Aurora's death, but still he was there, making sure things were right."

"*That* day?" Katie gaped at him. "His wife just died, and he was worried about donations?"

"Well, when you put it like that, it does sound rather odd." Leo winced. "But if you were there, it didn't feel that weird. It was like a compulsion. Like he needed to do something. He talked about her the whole time. I got the sense that he was doing it to honor her, *for* her, you know?"

"Or..." I considered if I was being cold or jaded, then decided it didn't matter. "He was acting out of a guilty conscience."

Leo's eyes widened. "That could be..."

Katie chimed in. "I was about to add his memorial for Aurora in *the how he was a good guy* column, but I suppose that would be true as well. He gave her such a beautiful eulogy, or whatever they call what he did, out of the guilt of killing her."

"And..." Leo leaned forward, once more forgetting to pet Watson, and didn't even seem to notice when Watson nuzzled him again. "And I can't believe I'm using this as proof against him, but it would also explain why he used that ceremony to speak out for Verona. Because he didn't want an innocent person in jail for Aurora's murder when he was the one who did it."

"Wow." Katie blinked and almost sounded dazed. "So we're going with that Wolf killed his wife, but is also a good guy."

They continued their back-and-forth, but I tuned them out. Something else clicked when Katie mentioned Aurora's memorial ceremony. It replayed in my memory. Wolf talking so sweetly and full of admiration for Aurora as he drew patterns on the ground. How he spoke up for Verona. How he paused calmly as the Holy Rapture Fellowship chanted and protested him and his entire belief system.

The patterns. My brain returned to the patterns he drew in the dirt. The swirls and spiraling fractals. I'd seen them before.

I'd seen them since.

Sucking in a breath, my fingers flew over the keys, pulling up Aurora's unicorn painting of the high priestess.

"You found it, didn't you?" Katie set aside her laptop and walked toward me. A second later, Leo stood and joined her, flanking me on either side, looking over my shoulder. Watson scurried after him, plopping down on the edge of Leo's foot.

"I found *something*." My fingers traced the pattern of the stars that hung over the darkly painted forest. "See these fractals? They're exactly like the ones Wolf drew in the dirt in front of Samson's statue." No sooner had I traced them in the stars than I noticed the pattern repeating elsewhere. "And here, in the trees themselves, the way the branches are done, different shades of greens and browns."

"And here too." Leo reached over and pointed at the unicorn. "Barely visible freckles on her flank."

Katie leaned forward issuing the sound of awe. "You're right. That's crazy. But what does is it mean?"

"It means..." What did it mean? "Aurora painted the images, right? So isn't it a little strange that those very same patterns are what Wolf drew in the dirt?"

We were all quiet for a moment, each studying the high priestess painting.

Leo whispered as if we'd entered some sacred place. "I suppose Wolf could have been drawing them as a way to honor her. Maybe those themes repeated in all her work."

With a couple more keystrokes, I pulled up the entire collection of images from the tarot card set Wolf had used for Watson. The fractals were everywhere, on every card. Some glaringly obvious and others as subtle as the ones on the unicorn's flank.

"I'm not saying Wolf didn't do it, but maybe this fractal thingy—" Katie tapped the screen, her fingers tracing the pattern in the painting of wheat blowing in the wind "—is kinda like the quartz. Maybe it has a specific meaning that most people in their belief are familiar with. Maybe it's not specific to Wolf or Aurora. Perhaps other people, those from the conference let's say, who were at Aurora's memorial recognized what Wolf was drawing in the dirt.

"Drawing in the dirt. That's it." I sat up straighter in excitement. "I saw that before. In that book. The one in my shop. I can go get it real quick." I started to stand and then remembered we had technology literally sitting in my lap and sank back into the armchair. "Wait, I can just upload it to the Kindle app. What was it called..." I closed my eyes, trying to remember the book I'd read before all this had begun, the one with the exhaustive list of crystals and their powers. Powers! "*Elemental Power*. That's it!"

In a matter of moments, I'd purchased the book and it was uploaded to the app. I scrolled through quickly, recalling that the image was near the back. Then I was there. I tapped the screen again. "Look, right there. That's him drawing in the dirt, with Aurora standing beside him."

Leaning in closer, Katie read the caption beneath. "This was the day I met Wolf in Santa Fe. The day our higher power brought us together and changed our destinies."

"So drawing in the dirt has always been a thing Wolf does. But we can't see what he's drawing. It may not be those fractals." Leo looked at me. Though his tone was questioning, he didn't sound skeptical. "Even if it is, what are you thinking?"

"I don't know how we prove it, but what if..." I played my newly forming theory out for a few seconds before I spoke. "What if the reason all this doesn't seem to match Aurora is because it never did. What if Wolf is the one behind it all—the spiritualism, the art, the teachings. What if he is the one who truly believes it and wants to teach it, and Aurora's just the face of the Birnbaum Foundation."

"Why would they do that? Why would Wolf need her?" Unlike Leo, Katie did sound skeptical. "You're thinking it's just because he needed a woman? That when it comes to New Age spiritual teachings, people are going to believe it more coming from a woman than a man?"

"I don't know. I hadn't really gotten that far." I considered again, thinking of Wolf's warm tone, barely able to carry over the crowds. "Perhaps he didn't possess the stage presence, star power, or whatever it was that Aurora had. Maybe he had the knowledge, belief, and the artistic talent to do it, but not everything else."

"And Aurora had the rest." Katie seemed more convinced.

"But why pretend like it was all Aurora? They worked together. Why couldn't they each take equal credit?"

"Spoken like a genuine good guy." Katie reached around me to pat Leo's shoulder. "Maybe you didn't see Aurora for who she truly was. She definitely wasn't wanting to share the limelight."

"I agree." It was right. Definitely right.

"So... what?" Leo squinted, inspecting the black-and-white picture of the much younger Aurora and Wolf. "He finally got tired of Aurora taking all the credit?"

Katie jumped in, not really answering Leo. "Even if that's true, how do we prove it?"

"I have an idea." Again, the plan formed even as I spoke. "But it won't be the three of us. It'll be Zelda. And..." I let out a heavy sigh. "It won't work unless Wolf is actually the good guy we think he is."

"Remember, everything you can possibly tie back to Verona, do it. I don't think we can go too over the top with this."

Zelda cast me a narrow-eyed stare from where she adjusted the brightness of the fairy lights overhead, lowering them to a soft glow. "I think I've got it, Fred. Though we don't practice the tarot readings personally anymore, Verona went through a phase of doing them constantly in college. Trust me, I've got them memorized. I can make whatever he draws work. And since Verona's freedom might very well rest on this playing out like you hope, it won't even be that much of a long shot for me."

A thin wave of panic washed over me with that comment, but I pushed it away. "I can't think like that. Even if we can't get Wolf to admit that he killed Aurora, that doesn't change Verona's innocence. I have to trust that whether the killer is caught or not, we'll get Verona back." I knew that wasn't always the case. There were plenty of innocent people in jail, but Verona wouldn't be one of them. She just wouldn't. And while my gut told me Wolf was the killer, there were no guarantees.

Zelda adjusted her necklace as she crossed Chakras, centering the large clear quartz pendant between her breasts. We'd borrowed it from Mom; the quartz was half the size of my fist—more of a paperweight than a piece of jewelry—and wrapped in a silver coil. "I still think it would be better to do this in the crystal room where he did the readings before."

"That's also where he killed his wife. I doubt we can get him to darken the door of that room."

"But it's so pretty, with the waterfall and the crystals in the ceiling and walls." Zelda sighed at my expression. "Fine. But it feels rather anticlimactic to do a tarot reading next to the cash register."

I kind of agreed. "You have that pretty silver-and-green tie-dyed shawl over the counter. That adds some mystical flair, right?"

She cocked an eyebrow. "Mystical flair?"

I shrugged. "Best I could do."

Before we could rehash more of the plans, there was a soft knock at the front door of the shop.

Barking, Watson rushed with a clatter through the doorway of quartz from the crystal room where he'd been snacking on the expensive dog jerky.

Wolf's large frame was silhouetted against the soft sunset light filling the main street of downtown until he stepped in when Zelda opened the door. His smile was friendly when he entered, as always. His gaze flicked from Zelda, held on her quartz pendant, then moved to me, and then to the crystal room, where, unless I was reading it wrong, it lingered for a few moments too long.

"Thank you so much for agreeing to come down here this evening." Zelda shut the door and locked it before turning back to Wolf. "Making this time for me when you're in the middle of your own loss means the world."

"It was the least I could do." Another smile for Zelda,

which continued as he nodded to me in greeting and then knelt to pet Watson. "Good to see you again, Mr. Corgi Worgi."

Though he quit barking, Watson only allowed Wolf to pet him for a second or two before pulling away and taking his place beside me.

"Has an old soul." Wolf studied Watson for a few more seconds, and then his gaze flicked to mine. "As do you, actually."

"I've been told that before, about both of us." I'd heard it all my life, even as a kid. And more than one person had said similar about Watson. "Probably just because we can both be so grumpy and stubborn."

With a chuckle he turned to Zelda. "Where would you like to do this?"

Again, maybe I was reading into things, but I thought I picked up on the tremble in his words, as if he feared she might say the crystal room. Perhaps we should've done it there.

Zelda pointed to the counter. "Right over there. I've already got the cards arranged into their major and minor stacks."

"That will be perfect." Sure enough, some of Wolf's tension seemed to leave. He walked to the counter and took his place behind it so he was facing out toward the store and then addressed me. "Since I'm teaching you how to do this, Fred, why don't you come stand beside me? Zelda can be on the other side."

The three of us took our positions and Watson settled several feet away, underneath a row of tie-dyed T-shirts that I imagined reminded him of Barry.

The dim fairy lights were the only illumination in the store. Zelda had turned on music in the background, soft flute playing with the sound of birds chirping overhead. She lit a large candle next to the cash register, and an incense stick on the other side. The scent of balsam fir completed the ambience. I couldn't decide if the effect was more magical feeling or spooky.

"Perfect." Wolf looked at me. "Are you ready?"

I forced a smile. "As I'll ever be."

He chuckled again. "The tarot makes you nervous. I noticed that before."

I was glad he was chalking my unease up to that. "I'll try to keep an open mind; anything to help Zelda."

He addressed her next. "I have to admit, I'm surprised you need me to help teach the tarot. I would assume you know it backward and forward."

"In one way I do. At least as far as the cards' meanings, but I'm simply not comfortable doing it for myself. Verona has always done it for me. Always." Zelda's voice broke. "And with how it looks now, with her being falsely imprisoned and the police not having any suspects, well..." She motioned toward me as her voice faded away, overcome. She was good, better than I'd feared.

Wolf cleared his throat. "That makes sense. And I assure you, I'll keep speaking out for Verona's innocence. This isn't what Aurora would've wanted."

Zelda nodded her thanks and then made a show of adjusting her hair so she could pull the necklace over her head. She handed the massive clear quartz to Wolf. "Here, to neutralize the energy and vibrations."

He flinched when he took the quartz from her hand. Nothing drastic, but it was noticeable. Enough that it gave me another surge of confidence that Zelda and I could pull this off. He laid it between the two stacks of cards, paused for a moment with his hands hovering over the piles, and pulled the shorter one toward himself before looking at me. "The first step is to establish the archetype for the reading, from the major arcana." He began shuffling the stack.

"Okay." I nodded and then jotted down a line in the notepad I had placed by the cash register.

Wolf smirked, though it seemed more affectionate than judgmental. "You seem the type to take notes on a lesson." He turned the card over, and his face paled. On top of the deck sat the unicorn, surrounded by her dark forest and the fractals of stars overhead. "This..." His voice was strained. "This was always Aurora's favorite of my—" he cleared his throat again "—of the deck. The high priestess." His gaze flicked to me and back to the card. "This showed before in your presence. The high priestess represents—"

"Good judgment," Zelda broke in. "And good intuition." She sniffed dramatically. "Goodness, it's already started. I can feel Verona here. In many ways she was the high priestess in my life. She was the one with discernment. I don't know what I'll do if—" She reached across and laid her hand on top of Wolf's, both of them enclosing the high priestess card as she took a steadying breath.

Zelda was definitely much better than I'd anticipated. Especially after her show at the storage unit with the flipping of the hair.

Wolf patted her hand with his free one, taking a steadying breath of his own before pulling away and returning to teacher mode. He reached for the other deck and began shuffling the cards. "All right, Fred, the next step is to shuffle the minor arcana cards eight times. And then we split them into three smaller piles."

I jotted down the instructions as he continued shuffling, then arranging the piles in front of Zelda.

"This first stack represents the physical realm. Since

this is Zelda's reading, it might symbolize what's going on for her in this present moment in her daily life." He turned it over, and flinched. This card was another unicorn. It stood in the middle of a crystal lake, its long spiral horn pointing to the fractal stars. "The... ah... Queen of Cups. She—"

"Sensitive and affectionate nature." Zelda cut in again. "Oh, Wolf. Its really like Verona is here. She's the more sensitive between the two of us. Part of why she was better at guiding tarot readings."

"Okay, next." Again he cleared his throat. Though I hadn't ever seen a tarot reading, I got the sense that he was rushing. I couldn't blame him. If I hadn't seen him shuffling the cards himself, I would've thought it was a setup. Well... it was a setup, but there was no way Zelda or I could arrange the cards to be the high priestess followed by another unicorn. "The second of the minor cards deals with the mental realm. This could represent what's heavy on Zelda's mind or might be something that's holding her back." He flipped it over and froze.

So did Zelda. So did I. The two of us cast questioning glances at each other, then refocused on Wolf.

"The... the Queen of Swords." Wolf's voice truly trembled now. The card depicted a unicorn plunging its horn into the heart of a dragon. The flames issuing from its open jaws repeated the fractal pattern. "The... a queen..."

"Indicates being sharp-witted..." Zelda's voice trembled as well, and I got the sense none of it was for show. "It can also mean someone who's perceptive." Her blue gaze latched on to mine as she fell silent.

I glanced at Wolf to make sure he wasn't watching us, but he was glued to the unicorn card. I bugged my eyes out at Zelda, hoping she got the message to get on with it, to remember her role.

She did. "Verona is so much more perceptive than me. She was always keeping me from being taken advantage of. If she isn't set free, I don't know how I'll function."

She didn't quite pull it off, not as believably as she had before, but it didn't matter. I got the feeling that Wolf barely heard her.

"This represents the spiritual realm." When he reached for the third stack, he was speaking to himself, quiet and rushed. "It could be a message from a spirit. It could be..." His words evaporated as his trembling fingers turned over the card, then they returned with a soft curse.

The fourth unicorn card of the night was revealed. In this one, the fractal was found in the unicorn's glistening white mane flowing in the breeze as she dipped her horn to touch the wound of the wolf kneeling at her feet.

He didn't offer any explanation. Zelda didn't try to tie it back to Verona. I didn't write anything down.

The three of us stared at the unicorns.

After a short while, Wolf picked up the final stack and flipped through. But we didn't speak, I had no doubt what he was doing. Making sure the deck hadn't been quite literally stacked. It hadn't. There were no more unicorn cards in the pile. Convinced, he set it back on the table and traced the figure of the unicorn and wolf with his finger. His words were barely audible over the soft flutes and chirp of birds in the background. "Aurora was my world when I painted this. She opened the entire universe to me. Made me come alive. She healed wounds I didn't even know I had." A tear slid down his cheek.

The pain he felt was so tangible that for one insane

second, I nearly stopped myself from pressing onward. Then I thought of Verona. *"You* painted the cards, Wolf?"

He nodded absentmindedly, then froze and looked up at us with wide eyes. "No. I meant..." He shook his head, and his shoulders slumped. "Yeah. I did."

Wolf looked even more broken than he had before, and already older. But I swung the hammer again. "You were behind all of it, weren't you? You did the painting." Though there was no proof, I decided to bet everything on my instinct. "You wrote the books, all of them. You crafted the lessons. You did everything."

He just nodded, more tears flowing.

"You were the soul of it all, weren't you, Wolf? Aurora was just the face, the marketing tool."

"No." He shook his head, but the tears didn't stop. "Aurora and I met at the perfect time. There was a fresh wave in the New Age movement, people were growing more open, willing to see beyond their narrow-minded view and government-approved religions. *I* was the marketing tool. My paintings, my writings. She just took them and made something. She made them into a movement, a force to change the world. She was the face of it, yes, but she used all of me to make it happen. In ways that I never would've been able to."

I couldn't tell if he sounded more in awe or resentful. Maybe both.

One more swing. Just one. "Is that why you killed her? Because she took all of your work, all of your passion, and then took all the credit?"

"No. Not at all. That's not why—" His eyes widened even further as he stopped himself just in time. Then he looked directly at Zelda and placed his hand over hers once more. "I'm so sorry. I'm so, so sorry. I'll fix this."

Zelda gaped at him, but didn't speak.

He released her, then turned back to me. "I killed Aurora because I learned the truth. I'd had my suspicions, but I hadn't been sure. Not until the ceremony at the Samson statue. Not until that crazed religious group made accusations about us stealing money."

I barely found words myself. I'd bet everything on guilting him into confessing, but now that it was happening, it was rather hard to believe. Although, I supposed I'd bet on Wolf as much as I had on Zelda and me, that despite him killing Aurora, the core of him was a good man, as hard as that was to comprehend. "Tell us what happened. It's obvious you need to, that you want to. It's wearing you down already. You didn't plan on killing her, did you?"

"No." His tears continued to fall, and his voice trembled. After a second, Wolf took my hand and squeezed hard, and seemed to find some strength. "I was leading an all-night meditation group that evening. We would do a session together, then split up for two hours, and then return to do another group session. The accusations had been driving me crazy all afternoon, the thought that we were using the money for personal gain instead of bettering the world... When I was out in the woods, I couldn't meditate, couldn't connect to my higher power, to the earth. I was consumed. As I sent the rest on their individual sessions, I went back to our room to confront Aurora. As I approached, I saw her leaving. It was nearly midnight, she wasn't a night owl by any means, so it was strange. I followed."

His tears slowed. Though he kept hold of my hand, he looked at Zelda. "She met your sister, and though I didn't hear their exchange, once Verona left, I came in here. Confronted Aurora."

He refocused on me. "I'd fallen out of love with Aurora years and years ago. Knew that she didn't have the same passion that I did. But we'd built this empire together, and we were helping people, like I said, more than I ever could have done on my own, so for that I was grateful. For that, I loved her. I would always love her." Pain swept over him followed by a fresh flash of anger. "She threw it all in my face. Said that she'd never loved me. Though that hurt, it wasn't too surprising. I'd suspected that for a long time. Then she made fun of it all. Of *all* of it. My beliefs, the conference, all the people attending, everyone who looked to us for spiritual guidance and help, for a better way. She admitted nearly all the money from the Birnbaum Foundation was diverted away from charities." Wolf's face contorted. "Bragged about it, actually. She thought it was a brilliant scam."

Tears started again. "I have no memory of strangling her. None. One minute she was going on and on about how stupid it was, how stupid the people were, how stupid *I* was, and the next she was lying on the floor with my hands around her throat. But I was still so mad. Still so, so mad."

He quit talking, so I decided to press just a little further. "You hung her in the crystal room. You didn't really try to make it look like suicide, did you?"

"No." He gestured toward Mom's display of crystal jewelry. "I took all the quartz from there and wrapped them around her after I hung her up." His voice broke again, and sadness seeped in once more. "Clear quartz is the master healer. I'm still not sure if I did that in hopes of healing her spirit, or as a final insult."

When he stopped talking, the three of us just stood there in silence, only the sound of flutes and birds drifting between us, joined by Watson's occasional snores from underneath the tie-dyed T-shirts.

I hadn't grieved for Aurora the entire time. She hadn't deserved to die, but I'd seen enough death in my months in Estes, and plenty of it before as a detective's daughter to know that people just died, either by natural or foul means. But for Wolf, I hurt. My reaction surprised me, considering.

Judging from the tears pouring down Zelda's cheeks, she felt the same. "Wolf?"

Sniffing, he looked at her.

"Will you admit this to the police? Will you set my sister free?"

He nodded, then collapsed to his knees and fully fell to pieces.

"Oh my sweet, beautiful heaven." Pastor Davis laid a hand reverently over his heart, closed his eyes in ecstasy, and popped the remainder of the bite-sized quiche in his mouth. "What kind of cheese did you say this was?"

Katie beamed at the praise and held the tray closer to him so he could snag another one. "Gruyère. It pairs perfectly with bacon."

"Now that's the gospel truth." With a wink her way, he popped in another, proving that it truly was bite-sized. "Have you considered"—crumbs flew as he spoke, and Stuart brushed at his lips—"a combination of brie, mustard seed, and smoked duck?"

"No! But I am now." Katie's eyes went wide. "Granted, that would be a little daring for most, but I'm betting it would be pure perfection. You're a genius, Pastor Davis."

Watson paced between them, craning his head up, looking back and forth in a desperate search for falling crumbs.

Stuart patted his expansive belly. "There's more where that came from. I'm willing to bet fig, pear, and ricotta quiche would be rather inspired as well."

"Seriously, where have you been my entire life?" Katie's

attention darted from the pastor, across Chakras, to where one of the customers waved to get her attention. "Unfortunately, I need to make the rounds again, but you simply *must* come to the Cozy Corgi bakery sometime. You and I need to sit down and have a brainstorming session. We might just have a whole line of Preacher Davis Pastries for those with refined and daring palates." She wrinkled her nose. "No, that doesn't sound right. Father Davis Pastries, that's better. I know you're not Catholic, but we'll just fudge a little bit."

"I'd be delighted, my dear." Stuart patted Katie's shoulder affectionately and swiped another of the quiches before she walked away.

Watson darted after her, doing his part to make sure the twins wouldn't have to clean up any food off the floor at the end of the night.

The pastor gave me another one of his winks as he devoured the quiche. "This one has asparagus. Gotta keep a balanced diet."

"With Katie as my best friend and business partner, I've given up all pretense of a balanced diet." I smiled at him affectionately. I'd become fond of the pastor at our first meeting, but he'd since endeared himself to me as he'd stopped by Victorian Antlers to visit with my uncles on multiple occasions, making an obvious show of support. And here he was again, at the grand reopening of Chakras.

In the three weeks since Wolf turned himself in, a few changes had occurred. September arrived, bringing the touch of fall to the air. Kids and teachers had gone back to school, which decreased the tourist population. Verona and Zelda had used the time to do some small renovations on the shop, and they felt it best to let the drama die down before continuing the business.

"I have to say, your sisters have a beautiful shop." He gestured toward the doorway of quartz that led into the crystal room. "That space in there is straight out of a fairy-tale. It rather inspires me to try to do something similar in the church. A little room for prayer and reflection."

"I'm sure that would be lovely." I wasn't certain if it was my business, since I wasn't one of his parishioners, but I was curious. "How is everything going at Estes Valley Church? Are things returning to normal since Sandy and Paul moved?"

"Slowly, they are, yes. Those who joined the Holy Rapture Fellowship have returned to the fold." He released a heavy sigh, and for the first time, some of his humor gave way to seriousness. "However, once a person has truly looked into their darkness, and seen how cruelly they can treat others, it changes things. Still, in my experience, those who have the most compassionate love to share, most often have had to weather those dark nights of the soul. There's beauty in that."

Uncertain how to respond, I simply nodded.

Pastor Davis took my arm in a firm grip and held my gaze. "And you, Winifred? I know you have a reputation for solving murders and being so much more than just a book-seller, but I get the sense that something about this partic-ular situation still weighs heavy on you."

Again, he momentarily stole away my words. Though we'd had limited interaction, he seemed capable of looking into my soul. The strangest aspect of that was I found it comforting rather than unsettling. "It does. It's hard to see a man like Wolf, someone I think is truly good at heart and only wanted to help the world, give in to such a dark act. And I've been reminded how even those I love dearly have their own secrets and fears. Nothing I didn't know, but just a reminder." I clutched the celestine crystal Mom had given me that hung around my neck, and recalled the tarot reading, the unexplained appearance of the four unicorns. "I tend to be fairly black-and-white in my thinking, as far as how the world works. Things can be explained if you dig deep enough, find the right clues. Unlike most members of my family, I like to think that a pretty rock is just a pretty rock. But there are times lately when I'm not so sure."

He studied Chakras for a few moments before looking at me again. "Personally, I can't say I buy into many of the beliefs represented here, but God is a god of mystery." He looked meaningfully at the sky-blue stone in my hand. "I'm with you. That's just a pretty blue rock. However, a god of mystery created it." He shrugged and smiled. "So who am I to say what marvelous qualities he gave it. He made us extremely special, after all. Why not a pretty blue rock, too?" Another grin, then he released my shoulder with a gentle pat and scanned the shop one more time. "I'm going to find that sweet friend of yours and get reacquainted with her talents. My tummy is rumbling."

At the end of the day, with the sunset filling Chakras with a soft warm glow, only Mom, Barry, the twins, and their families remained. Barry sat on the floor, lavishing affection on Watson to such an extent that the pink-and-white tie-dye of his T-shirt was barely visible beneath all the corgi hair. He smiled at me. "You are a marvel, Winifred Page. I can never thank you enough for what you did for my daughter."

"Barry, don't. You've already thanked me, and I told you then, there was no reason to. Verona was innocent. She didn't need me to prove that."

He shook his head. "It doesn't matter whether she

needed it or not. You proved it nonetheless. And even more than that, more than the outcome, you showed your love for my girls, your devotion." I was used to Barry keeping things light and fun, but tears filled his eyes as he spoke. "Honestly, I try not to think about what their lives were like as they were growing up, thinking they had a father who hadn't wanted them, knowing they only had each other to depend on. I do my best not to be angry about the time I lost with them. That time was threatened again, and you stopped it. You gave it back to me." He offered Watson a final pat and stood, then wrapped me in his arms, covering us both in dog hair. "I will never be able to thank you enough. And I love you. Not just because of all you do for me and our family, but simply because you're Winfred." He pulled back slightly and met my eyes. "I'll never replace your father, I'll never try to, but know that I consider you just as much my daughter as the twins."

The truth of his words wrapped around me as surely as his arms did, and they meant everything. Though I couldn't say I counted him as a father, he was no less family to me because of it. "I love you too, Barry."

"Now that makes my heart happy." Mom smiled happily as she joined us, followed close behind by the twins and their families.

"We come bearing gifts." Zelda glowed as she ate from her pint of Ben & Jerry's. "Our way of saying thank you for helping all this happen." She gestured to Chakras. "But also simply for being our sister."

Good grief! The emotional punches just kept coming, and though each was dear and sweet, that was exactly what they felt like. Punches of love to the gut that kept stealing my breath and words.

"The question is, do you want to start with your gift?"

Verona held up a large present, wrapped in metallic paper, then looked to where Leaf held a gift bag. "Or Watson's?"

At his name, Watson gave a little hop, probably expecting a treat.

I cleared my throat and took a second to make sure my emotions were in check. "Well, no presents were necessary, but that's an easy choice. We gotta keep his highness happy, after all."

"Great!" Leaf hurried forward and knelt in front of Watson. After untying the ribbon, he pulled the gift bag open, and angled it so Watson could see.

Watson hopped again, gave a bark, and shoved his head inside the bag, wiggling his furry butt furiously. Seconds later, he popped back out, with a matching stuffed lion to the one we'd returned to Leaf.

"Now he's got his own Chester." Leaf rubbed Watson's head, then considered. "But I guess he can name it whatever he wants now."

Not bothering to say thank you, Watson waddled away carrying the brand-new Chester across the store, and then disappeared through the doorway of quartz into his favorite room to take a nap with his lion by the trickling waterfall.

I smiled down at Leaf. "That was very sweet of you, thank you. And thanks for letting Watson borrow Chester in the first place, not that he bothered to ask before he stole it."

"My turn." Verona stepped up and handed me the gift.

I nearly dropped it. "Dear Lord! What's in this thing? It probably weighs twenty pounds."

She, Zelda, and Mom exchanged knowing glances that made me nervous. "Just our way of saying thank you. For setting me free. Both literally and figuratively." Verona gave a meaningful look toward the renovated wall of Chakras, which now displayed every one of her shoes. "I have to say. Coming out as the face of Kamala was the scariest thing I've ever done. Much scarier than being arrested for murder, but I couldn't have done it without you." She reached for Zelda's hand. "Or you."

"Donating all the profits solely to fight the poaching in the national park is good for business. And your brand, *our* brand, but..." Zelda shook her pint of Ben & Jerry's. "I'm just glad I can have ice cream in public."

"Oh, good grief." Verona rolled her eyes, then gestured toward the present. "Well, go ahead."

Considering the source of the present, I was a little nervous about what was inside. As heavy as it was, I had to lay it on the floor and kneel. I made a show of ripping off the paper, knowing it would please them, then opened the lid. My gasp was part shock and part horror. I hoped that last part didn't show.

"I know you don't like stilettos, so I tried my hand at cowboy boots." Verona sounded worried. "Zelda and your mom picked out the crystals, and I designed them."

Zelda managed to speak over her mouthful of Half-Baked ice cream. "Clear quartz, for obvious reasons."

"Celestine for calming and balance. And to match your necklace." Mom knelt beside me and pointed out each of the stones. "Amethyst for inner strength, and green fluorite for clarity."

I stared down at the crystal-encrusted boots. After the initial shock passed, I had to admit that Verona had done the impossible. She managed to mix the clear quartz, sky-blue celestine, deep purple amethyst, and seafoam green fluorite in a beautiful and somewhat organic fashion. Still, the end result was much more suited to a country music star hoping to crossover to a pop career. "Thank you... They..." I searched for a way to describe them, and came up lacking. Instead, I met my sisters' and mother's gazes one by one. "I can't believe you did this for me. So much work, time, and thought went into these. I'll treasure them forever." Even if I never wore them, that much was true.

Verona gave a happy sigh, and when Zelda spoke, her eyes twinkled over her ice cream, giving me the sense she could read my thoughts. "Well, put them on."

Feeling like I was rising to a challenge, I pulled free of my own boots and lifted the crystal ones from the box. Taking a breath as if they might be made of dynamite, I slid my feet inside and took a few hesitant steps, which was harder than I expected. "Okay, seriously, do these things actually weigh twenty pounds?"

Mom reached up and patted my shoulder. "You're beautiful, tall, and strong, Fred. It takes a special woman to pull these off, and they look perfect on you."

I was glad Watson had retreated to the crystal room, otherwise I was certain I'd see judgment in his corgi eyes. That or he'd roll on his back and get lost to a barking laughter.

"Not only are they beautiful, Winifred." Barry tucked his thumbs into his baggy tie-dyed yoga pants as he inspected the boots and nodded seriously. "But the next time you're investigating a murder, if someone comes after you, those will work as a weapon. Probably better than a can of Mace."

"Dad!" Verona swatted at Barry. "Crystals are not a weapon!"

I wasn't so sure about that.

A Cozy Corgi Mystery

Wicked Wildlife

MILDRED ABBOTT

WICKED WILDLIFE

Mildred Abbott

Under the muted pastels of sunset, a high-pitched wail cut through the crisp air. Beside me, Watson issued a low grumble from his chest and stuffed his muzzle between my thigh and the picnic blanket. I scratched him on the top of his head, then tickled one of his foxlike ears. "If you're trying to block out the noise, you might want to bury these, not your nose."

Watson sat up with a chuff, cast me an annoyed expression, and waddled over to his favorite national park ranger. Well... actually one of his favorite people in the world in general. I doubted the park ranger aspect mattered to my grumpy little corgi.

"Here, is this what you need?" Leo Lopez took the tips of Watson's ears and gently folded the tips down.

Watson only looked up at him in adoration.

"If I tried that, he'd give me the cold shoulder for a week." I gestured toward the red bandanna tied around Watson's neck. "Of course, you get away with dressing him up as well. So what else is new?"

Leo simply grinned.

Another high-pitched wail made Watson wince again,

and Katie, my best friend and business partner, elbowed me in the side before pointing. "Look!"

Leo and I both followed her gesture. The three of us—four, counting Watson—were spread out over a blanket on the far side of a meadow in Rocky Mountain National Park. Though no sun remained, the edges of the rugged snow-tipped Colorado mountains glistened with a soft dusty pink that transitioned to purple and then a deep blue, revealing the first few stars of the evening twinkling high above. A movement caught my attention at the base of the mountains. A bull elk stepped from the shadows of the pine forest and into the clearing, then lifted his head. The pink hue of sunset illuminated his crown of antlers, and a cloud of fog seemed to billow from his mouth as he elicited yet a third wail.

"I find it beautiful now, but the first time I heard it, I thought someone was getting murdered." Katie paused until the elk finished its cry. "Did you know what makes the elk's bugling sounds so strange is that they're actually whistling through their nose and roaring through their mouth at the same time?" She started to nod in satisfaction, then narrowed her gaze at Leo. "Of course *you* already knew that, Smokey Bear. Why do I even bother with animal trivia when you're around?"

He winked at her. "I can feign shock and surprise if you'd like me to."

"Oh, shut up." Katie chuckled and reached across me toward Leo. "Give me your mug. I'll fill up your hot chocolate. That is if Watson will allow you to free one of his ears for a second."

"Watson nearly went into hysterics when the bugling started last month. We were dead asleep, and then suddenly a couple of those ultrasonic wails happened right outside the bedroom. Pretty sure he thought we were going to be eaten alive." I chuckled at the memory of Watson, wide-eyed and pounding his tiny forepaws on the side of my bed, demanding that I wake up and take care of things. "The bugling season was over by the time we moved up here last year, so he'd never experienced it before. Honestly, it startled me as well. I hadn't heard it since I'd visited Estes Park as a kid."

The elk bugled again, silencing us. In truth, the sound was rather creepy—like a scream, whistle, and guttural groan, creating some otherworldly song—but also hauntingly beautiful. Especially combined with our majestic surroundings. Possibly it was my imagination, but there seemed to be a sadness in the tone. Maybe it was because I knew it was one of the last of the season. October only had one more day and like the few remaining gold leaves on the aspen trees, this would be one of the last elk calls until next autumn.

The three of us sat on our picnic blanket, huddled in sweaters and under other blankets against the growing chill, a hint of snow in the air. There'd been a slight lull in the tourist traffic between high summer, kids returning to school, and the couple of weeks surrounding the elk fest which took over Estes Park to celebrate the bugling season. Katie and I had been so busy at the Cozy Corgi Bookshop and Bakery that we had very few moments like this to relax and revel in the astoundingly beautiful place we called home and be with friends who were family.

As the elk disappeared back into the shadows of the forest, Leo glanced at me once more, his hand never stopping its caress over Watson's back. "I hadn't even realized. You and Watson have been in Estes Park a year now."

"Almost." I nodded. "We moved here last November."

That was a marvel as well. I looked between him and Katie, remembering the moment I'd met each of them. Katie, behind the candy counter of Sinful Bites, offering me chocolate, her smile wide and her hair frizzy. I should've known in that moment we'd be best friends. And then Watson and I meeting Leo as we'd entered the national park for the first time. I'd barely been able to string an intelligible sentence together at the sight of his ridiculously handsome face. A wave of gratitude swept over me, and I reached out from my place between them, patting each one on the knee. "I'm so glad Watson and I made the choice to move to Estes. I knew I wanted to be closer to family and open the bookshop, but I never dreamed I'd find..." My throat constricted taking away my words.

"Ahhh..." Katie wrapped an arm over my shoulders and pulled me close. "We love you too, you big sap." Despite her giggle, I caught the hint of emotion in her words as well.

Leo scooted closer so he could follow her gesture, putting his arm over Katie's and my shoulders and squishing Watson between his and my legs. Watson didn't even grumble. "It's true. We do. Honestly, I loved living here, loved my job, but I didn't really feel connected before you, hadn't quite been able to call it home. Then Winifred Page and her sidekick Watson showed up, and everything just clicked into place. Turns out you're the glue."

There was no chance I'd be able to speak after that.

"Glue?" Katie leaned forward so she could look around me. "Let's not call Fred glue. How about... icing? She's the icing that holds..." She shook her head. "No, that doesn't work." She slapped my thigh with her other hand. "Ice cream! She's the ice cream that holds the ice cream sandwich together." She grinned, then scowled, clearly dissatisfied.

Leo considered. "How about she's the binding that holds the book together."

"Now *that's* good. Perfect for our little bookseller." I could feel Katie pat Leo's arm over my shoulder. "Although, she could also be..." She snapped her fingers rapidly. "What's that envelope called in the Clue game? You know, the one where you put the cards of murderer, the weapon, and the room."

"I think it's called an envelope," Leo answered smugly.

"Well, whatever," Katie responded with another scowl, before looking at me. "That's another part you didn't antici-pate when you moved to Estes, huh? That you'd become the resident Nancy Drew."

"You can say that again." Though I hadn't expected to discover such amazing friends, that aspect was much less surprising than the bevy of murders I'd stumbled across over the past year.

"Speaking of, it's been a little over a month since—"

"Don't you dare say it!" I smacked my hand over Leo's mouth with a laugh before he could finish that statement. "There's no reason to jinx anything."

He muttered something behind my hand and made a show of waggling his eyebrows.

Katie giggled and scooted away so it was easier to face us. "He has a point, Fred. Tomorrow is Halloween. It'd be a perfect night for murder."

Leo repositioned once more, so the three of us were spread out over the blanket again. "That may be true for most places, but Halloween in Estes is about the least scary thing I've ever seen. If there was any night to count on not getting murdered, I think Halloween is the one."

Watson remained at my side, lifting his head to make

sure Leo was near but then drifting off again almost instantly.

"I like that answer." I pointed to Leo. "Let's go with that. I'm looking forward to tomorrow night's celebration. A bunch of cute kids and pets in Halloween costumes wandering around downtown. It'll be fun. No murders needed."

"I agree." Katie shimmied happily. "Plus I have a new recipe I'm going to try out on everyone tomorrow. Can't have another murder take away from that." She considered. "Come to think of it, it's amazing how many of my recipes get overshadowed by murder."

"Katie, my dear, I've not seen a murder yet that can overshadow your baking." Leo smiled warmly at Katie, and for the millionth time I wondered if something much more than friendship was going on between my two best friends.

Katie shimmied again. "You know what, I can't disagree with you there." She grew serious. "Are you going to be able to make it down tomorrow?"

Leo shrugged. "I'm not really sure. Hopefully." He gestured toward the forest. "Depends on what happens."

I looked between them. "Why, what happened?"

Katie sucked in a breath, aghast. "Oh! I forgot to tell you." She gestured toward Leo but answered for him. "There was another poaching incident yesterday."

I turned from Katie to gape at Leo. "Seriously? How many is that this month?"

"Six. Another elk this time." All levity from the moments before fled his tone, and his expression became hard and angry, making him look more like a man in his early thirties than he normally did. "And the police are doing the bare minimum possible and say that it's because of our incompetence." He winced in way of apology at me.

"You know I try not to say anything bad about Wexler, but... it's getting old."

Despite ending things with Sergeant Wexler months ago, I felt my cheeks heat at the mention of him. "I don't blame you. And I know you and Branson have never seen eye to eye on the poaching."

With a sigh, Leo shook his head, his anger transitioning to annoyance. "Of course, there're a few rangers who think it's just part of the job, that there's only so much we can do, so I can't put all the blame on the police force."

"At least you're not alone now. That new ranger..." Katie snapped her fingers again.

"Nadiya," Leo provided.

"Right!" Katie pointed at him like he'd just won a trivia game. "You said Nadiya is really taking it on as a cause, so you're not quite as alone in the fight like before."

"That's true. She is. But still..." He sighed and shook his head. "Sorry. I don't mean to ruin a good night. We haven't been able to do this in a while. No reason to make it depressing."

We were quiet for a minute, only the gentle breeze cutting through the branches and Watson's soft snores breaking the silence, until Katie giggled again.

Leo and I both gave her quizzical glances, which only made her giggle harder.

"I'm sorry! I really am. It's just that... It's awful that we were joking around about murderers a few seconds ago but then got all serious around the animals getting killed." She held up a hand toward Leo. "*Not* that poaching should be a laughing matter."

She had a point.

"You're right." Leo shrugged. "But there's something, for me at least, that gets to me about animals. Maybe it's because I'm a park ranger, but... animals don't ask for any of this. They're just going about their lives. We're the ones who intrude, the ones who hurt them. Granted, I'm not saying hunting is bad when done responsibly, *and* I'm not saying humans deserve to be murdered either, but...." He wrinkled his nose. "I don't know... people as a species get into all this drama and twists and turns and lies and secrets and all that jazz that goes behind murder a lot of the time. Animals don't do that."

"Tell that to Bambi."

I flinched and looked over at Katie at her unexpected comment, unable to hold back a laugh. "What?"

"Bambi." Katie looked between Leo and me as if the explanation should've been obvious. "When the bear ate Bambi's mother. Just saying, I don't think Bambi would've made a distinction between human drama and the bear being hungry. Either way his mother died."

"Katie, what weird non-Disney version of that film have you seen? A *hunter* killed Bambi's mom."

Katie narrowed her eyes at Leo, then looked to me for confirmation.

I nodded. "That's true."

"Really?" Katie tapped her chin. "Wonder what movie I'm thinking of? Maybe *Cujo*."

"*That* was about a killer dog, and most definitely *not* Disney. It was based on a book by Stephen King." I laughed again. "I have to say I'm surprised. After all this time, I never would've expected it. I thought the trivia queen knew everything. It seems you have an unusual gap in the movie knowledge category." Although, Katie had experienced a rather unusual childhood, so that might be an explanation.

His mood brightening, Leo stage-whispered in my direction. "Quick, let's go to your house, dig out Trivial

Pursuit, and beat the trivia master while she's having an off night."

"None of that." Unamused, Katie straightened. "So movies aren't my strong point. I'd say that's a good thing. There're much more important things to do in life than stare at a screen all day."

I couldn't help myself. "Don't your frequent binges into the wormhole that is the Google search engine require a screen?"

Katie practically sputtered. "That's different! That's... educational!"

Leo and I both laughed and then laughed harder as Katie scowled. Between us, Watson gave an annoyed huff.

Leaning toward Katie, I grabbed her hand. "Oh, sweetie. We're just giving you a hard time. Honestly, I'm glad to know there's one area where you have a few gaps. I was starting to wonder if you were human at all, that maybe the government had installed some high-powered encyclopedic software in your brain and..." A light in the distance caught my attention, and I refocused on the forest, close to where the elk had bugled.

There was nothing there. I must've been seeing things.

Then another quick flash. I pointed toward it. "Look. There's something down there. Besides the animals, I mean. I could've sworn I just saw a flashlight."

Leo stiffened instantly and looked toward the forest.

Several moments passed, the night once more undisturbed by anything other than Watson's snores.

Just as I was about to decide I'd been wrong, it flashed again.

"Leo," Katie whispered. "Your poacher."

Leo sprang up, startling Watson awake, and started to rush back up the hill toward where we'd parked. "I left the walkie-talkie in the truck." He'd nearly reached the ranger vehicle when a gunshot sounded.

All four of us, Watson included, turned toward the sound in the dark forest.

Then Leo tore past us, nearly leaping over the blanket in his haste. Springing up, Watson was instantly on Leo's heels, and the two of them raced across the meadow.

Katie and I sat dumbfounded for a couple of heartbeats, then looked at each other. As one, we stood and began to follow.

"Leo! Stop!" Katie called after him as we ran.

Whether he heard and ignored her, or Katie's voice was lost over the crash of underbrush beneath our feet, I wasn't sure. Either way, he kept going.

The toe of my cowboy boot snagged on something and I stumbled. Katie reached out a hand, steadying me before I fell, and then we were off again.

By the time Katie and I were halfway across the meadow, Leo and Watson had disappeared into the darkness of the trees. Somewhere in the back of my mind, a voice yelled for me to calm down, to *slow* down. To take just a moment to figure out the right plan, because this wasn't it. Clearly. Whoever was in the forest had a gun. The most dangerous thing Leo, Katie, and I had was a corgi. And while Watson could turn being grumpy into an Olympic sport, he was hardly deadly.

Even so, nothing broke through the adrenaline of the moment and our crazed rush toward the trees or the pounding of the heartbeats and footfalls thudding in my ears.

Katie and I paused at the edge of the woods, unclear where Leo and Watson had gone. The only thing I could hear for a few moments was our combined panting breaths.

After a few seconds, Katie pointed off toward the left. "There!"

With the gesture, I heard Leo and Watson crashing through the underbrush.

Katie and I took off again in their direction. For the first time, fear trickled in, past the adrenaline and the excitement of catching Leo's poacher. Because that's what it was—excitement. Fear for Leo and Watson eclipsed all of that, and the voice in the back of my head grew louder, scream-ing, *Gun! You're all running toward a person with a gun!*

Well, there was nothing to do about it then. I wasn't about to leave Leo or Watson alone. It didn't matter if I had no clue what I was going to do once I reached them. I continued our flight through the forest, still trying to think of options.

Pausing a couple more times to judge the sound of Leo and Watson's trajectory, Katie and I followed and came to a screeching halt as we discovered them in another clearing, this one barely more than five feet wide.

Leo knelt over the prone body of the bighorn sheep, a bullet wound in its side.

Watson nudged the sheep's nose with his own.

Leo looked up at us, his expression a mixture of grief and fury. "The poacher heard us coming, obviously, and ran."

Katie took a step forward. "The sheep, is it...?"

Leo looked down at the animal, running a hand lovingly over the curve of one of its twisting horns. "Dead. Whoever the guy is, he's a good shot at least. It was quick."

Watson whimpered and looked back at me.

Kate and I walked over, and I knelt beside them, putting my hand on Watson's back. "I don't think we should stay here. We need to—"

Sound broke through the night from far into the forest. All of us went rigid and looked into the darkness. It could have been the poacher, the elk, anything.

Leo stood, angling toward the noise.

I shot out my hand and grabbed his wrist. "Leo, no."

"Fred I've got to—" He started to jerk his arm away but stopped, his gaze flicking from me to Watson and to Katie. After a moment, his shoulders slumped. "I'm sorry. This was stupid. I shouldn't have... put you all in danger." With a nearly longing glance back toward the woods, Leo motioned the way we'd come. "Let's get out of here. I doubt the poacher is coming back. I'm sure he's not, but... whatever. Let's get to the truck, and I'll make the call."

"Oh my goodness, Fred! I thought Watson wouldn't wear
outfits." Paulie gaped at my feet as he approached Katie's
and my table outside of the Cozy Corgi. "Although, I'm not
sure a bandanna qualifies as an outfit per se."

"I think it does. He's a cowboy." I decided not to let
Paulie in on the secret that I hadn't taken off the bandanna
since Leo had put it on Watson the night before.

"Then he needs a hat. I have one at Paws that should
fit." Paulie gestured toward his pet shop across the street as
his two corgis surged forward to greet Watson.

Watson let out the tiniest of growls, and the pair
managed to calmly lick and sniff him, as calm as I'd ever
seen them in any case.

"Feel free if you want to lose a hand." I smiled up at
Paulie as I knelt to pet Flotsam and Jetsam. Considering
they were two of the most obnoxious dogs in the entire
world, Watson and I had both grown rather fond of them. I
paused as I took in their long green costumes that had a row
of black felt running down their spines making it look like a
mohawk. As they wriggled in their barely contained excitement at seeing Watson, their fabric tails wagged behind
them. "They probably don't know what to do with them-

selves, since they're not used to having tails. What are they? Some sort of dinosaur or..." My words trailed off as the answer was obvious. "They are their namesakes. Flotsam and Jetsam, the eels from *The Little Mermaid*."

"Yep!" When I looked up, Paulie beamed, and only then did I notice his face was painted red, which highlighted his yellowed teeth. He leaned forward with a stage whisper. "I actually used these costumes two years ago, but they're just too cute to let go to waste."

"Can I pet your dogs?" A little girl dressed like a chipmunk didn't wait for a reply and reached for the corgis. Watson took shelter beneath my skirt while Flotsam and Jetsam lost control and bounced all over her.

The little girl's parents glared at me as if it was my fault.

Paulie didn't even notice. "That's my good boys. Show that little chipmunk how much you love her."

Within another couple of seconds, the father scooped up his daughter in his arms, and they hurried off toward another table.

Still oblivious, Paulie shifted his grin back to me. "I think this is my favorite night of the year in Estes." He gestured around the downtown. "All the store owners out in front of their shops, with the local families and some tourists wandering about, all eating and happy. It's almost like Christmas."

I snorted out a laugh, feeling a wave of affection for my odd friend. "Yes, Halloween is *just* like Christmas."

"Now that's a weird thing to say." Katie emerged from the front door of the Cozy Corgi with a tray of bakery items and plopped them on the table in front of me. "If Christmas is like Halloween, then you're doing one or both of them wrong." She grinned at Paulie, gave him a once-over, inspected the eel-corgis, and caught on instantly. "Very literal interpretation, Paulie." She pointed at his red-painted face. "Sebastian the crab?"

His smile broadened even further. "You got it. I tried to talk Athena into dressing up like the little mermaid for me, but she wasn't going for it." His brown eyes went wide. "Athena! Oh, shoot! I left her manning my booth. I was supposed to get us some hot apple cider." He pointed all the way down toward the other block. "That's what they're serving at the toy store. I better go." He waved to Katie and me. "See you guys later! Come on, boys." He hurried off, dragging his two corgis behind him on their leashes as they attempted to jump on every person they passed.

"He's a hot mess, that one." Katie smiled after him, her voice communicating the same affection I felt for him, before turning her attention back to the food. "Here, try these. They just came out of the oven."

I did. On one side of the tray, there were buttery, golden brown bread balls, and on the other, bruschetta. I picked up one of the warm toasts piled with tomatoes, capers, and olives. The beautiful tang of garlic combined with the salty flavors overwhelmed me, and I glared at Katie, talking with my mouth full. "I hate you. I have no choice but to eat ten of these tonight." I took a second bite, finishing it off. "*At least* ten."

"Those are good. I have to admit." She beamed. "It's a new bread recipe I'm trying. The dough is infused with garlic." She pointed to the balls. "These are the same recipe, but there's mozzarella and pizza sauce inside. Better than candy for all our trick-or-treaters."

I snagged one. *Homemade pizza balls! I love my life.*

"This is wonderful." Katie sighed as she inspected the downtown. "It just feels like this big, happy family." She chuckled. "Maybe that's what you meant by saying Halloween is just like Christmas."

I didn't correct her, instead taking in the sights and sounds around us. Despite the drama of the poaching incident from the night before, a peaceful feeling enveloped me.

Orange lights were strung over the two-block length of the downtown, creating a cheerful glow over the streets that had been shut down for the occasion. The shops, fashioned in a mixed typical 1960s mountain style and log cabin façades, were charming on a normal day, but with all the storeowners dressed up and handing out candy, toys, and souvenirs to the meandering hordes of trick-or-treaters, I couldn't help but feel that Estes Park had outdone itself. I supposed it hadn't, since it was a yearly event.

Judging from the ornate costumes that ranged from little children dressed up like animals to adults looking like they just came from a cosplay convention dressed as superheroes and comic book characters, I decided I needed to put a lot more thought into my outfit for next year. I'd donned a black broomstick skirt, black blouse, and black pointed hat and called myself a witch. Next to Katie, who'd dressed as Rainbow Brite, I appeared downright lazy.

"You look rather marvelous, if I haven't told you already."

"Thank you!" She tugged on the wig's blonde ponytail and gave a twirl. "Though I need to choose more wisely next year. I'm a little cold. I thought with these rainbow puff sleeves I'd be warm, but—" She gestured toward the blue miniskirt. "—brrr."

"At least the rainbow UGG boots you're wearing are toasty, I bet."

She started to reply, but then a fresh wave of trick-or-treaters and their parents swamped our table and began devouring the tray of bruschetta and pizza balls before moving on to the assortment of pumpkin scones and chocolate cupcakes, which were decorated on top with either fondant books or marzipan corgi heads. Katie had surpassed herself with the baking. I didn't know how she managed at all, but I was glad she did. The only thing I had to do all day was oversee the bookshop. Though, that had been enough. Katie and I had given the twin brothers who worked for us the day off to go to Denver, and with the influx of tourists for Halloween, we'd stayed rather busy.

"I say, don't these just look delicious!" Two large pumpkins walked up to our table, and the one with the female voice began shoveling scones and pizza balls into a large trick-or-treat bag. It took me a moment to recognize their faces, which had been painted orange and were peering from the cutout of the matching billowing fabric.

"Anna and Carl! Well, don't you two look completely adorable." I wasn't really sure *adorable* was the right word. Anna and Carl Hanson owned a high-end home décor shop across the street, and neither of them were petite on a normal day, but with both dressed as large round pumpkins, they were taking up nearly half the sidewalk and forcing a small group of ghosts and skeletons to give them a wide berth.

"Thank you, darling. We do, don't we? And you look..." Anna's gaze traveled over my witch outfit, and she was clearly unimpressed. Instead of finishing her statement, she focused on Katie and tilted her head in confusion. She probably wasn't familiar with the 1980s cartoon icon of Rainbow Brite. Giving up, she waved her hands in the air. "Where's my favorite little guy in the world?"

On cue, Watson emerged from under my skirt, knowing exactly what Anna Hanson had in mind.

"Oh my goodness, a scarf! You're the cutest little Frenchman in the whole entire universe, aren't you?" With a cry of pleasure, Anna started to bend down to pet him, but wasn't quite able to pull it off, given the round structure of her costume. Grimacing, she swatted at her husband and missed. "Carl, get Watson his treat."

Carl pulled his hand inside his pumpkin costume, rustled things around, and a few moments later pulled out a large dog bone that they'd bought from Katie a couple of days before. Knowing his role, he handed it to Anna. "Here you go. But I don't think he's a Frenchman, not with the pattern on the red. I think he's a cowboy."

"No one asked you for unsolicited input, Carl." She swiped the dog bone, made a second attempt to bend toward Watson, then ended up tossing it to him instead.

Showing atypical athletic skill, Watson caught it in midair, made a chuff that I hoped was his version of *thank you*, and disappeared under my skirt again.

Anna let out a satisfied sigh. "Sweet little thing." After a second, her smile faded as her gaze darted toward the windows of the shop to the right of the Cozy Corgi. "It's one thing for your brothers-in-law to be taking this long to open up their store, but the least they could have done was decorate for the occasion."

I nearly pointed out that the paper they'd covered the windows with was black so that sort of counted, but didn't. "They keep putting it off. You know Jonah and Noah—they get close to making a decision and then change it and have to alter the whole layout of the shop. It's been a couple of weeks since we've been allowed in to even help. I swear they're making mazes and trapdoors in that place." Despite meaning it as a joke, I wouldn't have been very surprised if that was exactly what they were doing.

Anna cast her scowl to the other side of the Cozy Corgi where my twin stepsisters were handing out crystal necklaces in small velvet bags in front of their new age shop, Chakras. "At least Verona and Zelda are making a go of it. Though I find their tie-dyed scarecrow window display utterly garish. It makes my eyes tired from staring at it across the street all day."

"Well, that'll teach you to stare, won't it?"

All four of us stiffened at Katie's comment, and from Katie's surprised expression, she'd clearly not meant to say the sentiment out loud. After a second, she cleared her throat and lifted what remained of the tray of garlicky bits of heaven. "Here. Take more of these. It's a new recipe. Let me know what you think. Your expert input of flavor is invaluable."

"Don't mind if I do!" Carl reached out and plucked up a bruschetta.

Slower to be persuaded, Anna gave Katie a narrowed-eyed stare for a couple more moments before leaning in, but not bothering to whisper. "I've been hoping to come over all day. But we've just been too busy. Rumor has it you were with Leo last night when the newest poaching incident happened." She leaned closer yet, and instead of growing quieter, got louder. "*And* rumor has it you were mere feet away from the *murderer* himself." Her volume spiked on the word murderer, clearly finding it delicious.

"I don't know if a poacher is considered a murderer or not." It seemed Katie couldn't help herself. Once more her eyes widened, and she held up the tray a little higher. "Here you go, take some more."

"A poacher is most *definitely* a murderer and should be

treated as such." A sultry voice drew all our attention away from the food. An absolutely gorgeous woman with straight dark hair past her shoulders and flawless brown skin, stood a few feet away in a skintight pink bodysuit. She pushed her thin wire-rimmed glasses higher on her nose. "An eye for an eye is what I say."

We gaped at her, but I wasn't sure if it was because of her looks, her revealing outfit, or the fury in her tone.

"Goodness, breathe, darling, breathe." An equally gorgeous, though much taller, redheaded woman in a matching pink bodysuit nudged the first woman with her elbow. "There are no poachers here now." She smiled over at me. "Good to see you, Winifred. It's been a while. You never come in. You never visit." She smirked. "One would think you didn't approve of me."

On the other side of her, Anna sniffed and quite literally lifted her nose in the air. "Can't imagine why."

Delilah Johnson was the owner of Old Tyme Photography, the shop that dressed tourists up in old-fashioned clothes and transferred their image onto tintype pictures. At forty-two, she was only a little older than me, my exact height, probably the same weight, but whereas I was full-featured and curvy, Delilah was pure sizzling centerfold. Nor did she bother downplaying the rumors of her being somewhat of a man-eater, whether the man was married or not.

At the sound of her voice, Watson popped his head from underneath my skirt once more.

Delilah knelt in one smooth, serpentine swivel and stroked Watson's head. "Well, Watson! Hello there, my handsome man."

Though he wasn't insanely head over heels in love with

Delilah like he was with Leo, Watson pressed into Delilah's touch, and let out a satisfied groan.

I couldn't figure out my feelings for the woman. I didn't approve of her affairs with married men, and I found her somewhat abrasive. But on the other hand, maybe it was none of my business, and she'd taken what was easily my favorite photo of Watson and me. Not to mention that Watson liked her, and that went a long, long way.

"What if someone hurt your dog? Wouldn't you want that evil person to be treated like a murderer?" The other woman looked between Katie and me and gestured toward Watson. "Surely you would want justice for him. Why should a wild animal have any less value?"

In my periphery, I noticed Katie, Anna, and Carl bristle at the idea of Watson being harmed. I did as well and felt my temperature rise. Though it wasn't explosive, my temper had been known to make me say things I later regretted, so I bit my tongue, trying to figure out what to say.

"Really, Nadiya!" Delilah gave a final stroke to Watson's head and stood. "You sound utterly unhinged. Don't say such horrible things about Watson, even in theory." And there she went, ever swinging the pendulum of how I felt for Delilah Johnson.

"I'm just saying that—"

"Nadiya!" Katie breathed out her name, just loud enough to draw all our attention. She blushed as our small group looked at her. After a moment she stuck out her hand. "You're Nadiya Hameed? The new park ranger who works with Leo, right?"

Though it took a second in coming, a friendly smile finally crossed Nadiya's face, making her even more beautiful as she shook hands. "I am. You must be Katie"—her dark gaze flicked to me—"and Fred. I've heard a lot about you. All wonderful things, of course."

Without realizing it was happening, I was shaking Nadiya's hand. "Nice to... ah... meet you." *This* was Leo's new park ranger?

I glanced at Katie, trying to judge her reaction to the stunning woman. If there was any spark of jealousy or worry about Leo and Nadiya working together, I couldn't see it. Maybe that meant there was nothing going on between my friends after all. That... or Katie was too well-adjusted to let it bother her.

"I do want to thank both of you for trying to help Leo last night. That's very brave of you to go after a poacher like that." As Nadiya released my hand, she pulled my attention back to her as her tone grew darker. "I only wish I would've been there. I should be in the park with him right now instead of—"

"No, no." Delilah shook a finger. "You promised Halloween to me, no work. Not tonight."

"Plus, I'd say it's lucky for the poacher you weren't." Carl nodded at Nadiya, clearly impressed with her ferocity, and his gaze traveled over the two women. "What are you supposed to be, exactly?"

Delilah turned and shook her hourglass rump in Carl's direction, a long pink tail waggling, which bopped Watson on the nose. It was enough to make him disappear once more. "We're the Pink Panthers, obviously. It's a new club I've started, but we don't normally take the dress code quite so literally." She turned back around with a wink.

Before he could respond, Anna snagged his hand. "Come on, Carl. We need to get back to our table. The tourists have probably robbed us clean." She dragged him back across the street without bothering with goodbyes.

Delilah chuckled as she watched them go, clearly enjoying the reaction she'd gotten. "That was fun."

And... with that, the sour taste was back in my mouth.

Nadiya rolled her eyes "And you call me unhinged." There was humor in her tone as she refocused on Katie and me. "Seriously, thank you. The world needs more people like you, willing to throw themselves in the line of fire to save our animal kindred."

"You're welcome, but, honestly, I think we were more trying to make sure Leo and Watson stayed safe." I didn't want a bighorn sheep to be killed any more than the next person, but neither was I going to throw myself in front of a bullet for one.

Katie shot me a glare that clearly told me to shut up. Delilah chuckled. "I really do like you, Fred. Your bluntness has its charms." She leaned back, looking over her shoulder before gesturing across the street in front of her shop to the three women manning the Old Tyme Photography table— each one of them in a matching skintight pink bodysuit. To my surprise, not all of them had the bodies of Barbie dolls or 1950s pinups. "You should consider joining our group. You'd make a wonderful Pink Panther." Her deep blue eyes glanced apologetically to Katie. "I'm not sure about you, Katie. Sorry. You're very sweet, but maybe a little too sweet. A Pink Panther needs some edge."

For the second time in a matter of moments, Katie bristled.

"Pink isn't really my color, Delilah." I couldn't keep the disdain out of my voice. "And I'd rather take the place of the bighorn sheep than wear a bodysuit." Realizing how that sounded, I gave an apologetic grimace toward Nadiya.

Delilah only chuckled. "See? There you go again." She shrugged. "Oh well. The bodysuit is just for Halloween, but pink is most definitely mandatory." She bent, stuck her hand under the hem of my skirt, and patted Watson. "See you later, handsome."

With that, she turned and walked away. With a dirty look—not that I could blame her after my bighorn sheep comment—Nadiya followed, her long pink tail sashaying in her wake.

"That woman has a serious problem," Katie fumed. "And is completely obsessed. Her softball team is called the Cougars, and now she's got a... I don't know... a *sorority* called Pink Panthers? She needs psychiatric help." Katie snagged a pizza ball and popped it in her mouth but didn't bother to stop speaking. "She also needs a few more pastries to take her down a peg or two. Although with her luck, it would probably only make her more *voluptuous* or whatever." She miraculously managed to convey a gagging noise without spraying any crumbs.

"Still, from the way Leo talks about Nadiya, it sounds like he's pretty impressed with her skills." I studied Katie for some sign, some reaction that would tell me if my suspicions were founded.

"Oh, what does he know? He likes Delilah too." She waved me off. "What man wouldn't?"

From what I could tell, Katie didn't seem to have any feelings about that at all. Maybe I'd been wrong.

Or... maybe I was the one who had feelings around Leo working alongside a woman like Nadiya Hameed.

And that thought made me want to take the place of the bighorn sheep as well. Good Lord! What in the world was wrong with me?

"Thanks for helping me carry everything up. It would've taken twice as long by myself." Katie popped another pizza ball in her mouth, then plucked a second off the tray and tossed it to Watson before leaning against the bakery counter.

For the second time in as many hours, Watson gave a surprisingly agile leap, snagged the morsel, and scampered off to sit under his favorite table in the bakery over by the corner window.

"Katie, we're business partners. You don't have to thank me for helping you pick up. And even if we weren't, you're my friend." I mimicked her stance from the other side of the counter so we were face-to-face. "Not to mention that you're going to be back here in a matter of hours." I glanced over her shoulder at the mess of pans in the kitchen. We'd spent the last fifteen minutes carrying supplies and leftover food from the sidewalk, through the bookstore, and up to the bakery, but we hadn't started washing anything. "You sure you don't want to clean up?"

"Goodness no. Nick is coming in before school tomorrow to help me clean up and get the baking going for the day. I'm ready for that boy to graduate in December.

Still so unfair that after all of his teacher's biases he still has to repeat this final semester." She groaned and sank a little bit closer to the countertop. "You know, I think I might just sleep here."

I patted her shoulder and straightened. "So you'll be complaining about having a crick in your neck all day tomorrow? No, thank you. Get yourself home and grab some sleep. I'd say the first Halloween of the Cozy Corgi was a success, and even if I never see another pink panther bodysuit again, it will be too soon."

"Success indeed! No murders!" Katie pushed herself into an upright position once more and dusted off the wrinkled shiny fabric of her outfit. "I'm going to agree with you about the Pink Panthers, though. I was so pleased with my Rainbow Brite idea, but next to them I just felt like an overgrown five-year-old." She grimaced and glanced at the tray of food once more and shoved an entire bruschetta into her mouth. "There. That makes me feel much better." Crumbs flying as she spoke, she held one out to me. "Take your medicine."

Laughing, I followed her advice, and at the savory butter-and-garlic tang, I did feel better.

After flicking a few switches and plunging the bakery into darkness, Katie, Watson, and I headed back into the bookshop.

"Actually, you know what?" Katie glanced over at me as we reached the bottom of the stairs but didn't wait for a response. "I don't feel bad at all about how many samples I had this evening or the ones I'm going to have to help me wake up in just a few hours. With as many trips up and down the steps as we've taken, we might as well have run a marathon."

"I don't know if your logic is sound, but I'm going to go

with it." We'd left the overhead lights of the main level on the dimmest setting the whole night, so the warm wood tones of the floor and bookshelves glowed softly, soothingly. After the chaos of the evening, despite bordering on exhaustion, spending a few minutes alone in the Cozy Corgi sounded like a little bit of heaven. I paused at the door as Katie turned to lock up. "You know, I think Watson and I will hang out here for little bit."

Katie cocked an eyebrow. "You okay?"

"Yeah. I am." I bent down, ruffled Watsons fur, then motioned him back inside. "I think it's the whole 'coming up on a year' thing or whatever. I'm just feeling nostalgic, and grateful. Going to curl up in the mystery room and enjoy the reality of living my dream."

In a rare somber moment, Katie raised her hand and patted my cheek softly. "You do that. I'm so glad you are here. Not only because I got to open my dream bakery a lot sooner than I would've, but because you are my best friend and have made my life so much better." She offered Watson a similar gesture. "And you too, my hungry little fuzzball."

I locked the door after Katie left and paused, simply looking at the beautiful reality of my dream. The Cozy Corgi was so much better than I'd imagined, and I knew firsthand just how rare that event was in life. From the bakery upstairs and its myriad of heavenly smells and flavors permeating the air, to the picture-perfect bookshop that resembled a house with the main room in the center and smaller ones around the perimeter. It was a little slice of heaven, *my* slice of heaven. At my feet, Watson whimpered, staring longingly at the door. It seemed he was not having a sentimental moment and was ready to get home to his bed.

"Sorry, buddy. You're going to have to indulge your mama for a little bit."

Even though the lights were dim, with the large picture windows on either side of the door. I felt exposed to the night, so I flicked the switch and plunged us into darkness once more. With the moonlight and streetlamps, there was enough reflected glow to help me easily find my way to my favorite spot in the bookshop. I considered lighting a fire in the corner river rock fireplace of the mystery room, but didn't plan on being there very long. Instead, I flicked on the standing lamp, pulled a book at random off a shelf, and settled on the antique sofa.

Though his judgmental glare communicated that he was unhappy with this development, Watson acquiesced, trotted over and curled up by one of the carved feet of the sofa, and instantly fell asleep.

Without the fire, the light from the dusty purple portobello lampshade barely offered enough illumination to see the words on the page. It didn't matter. Much of the pleasure was simply sitting with the book, being surrounded by its fellows, feeling the pages beneath my fingertips and the comforting weight of it settled on my lap.

Even so, I scanned the lines through squinted eyes, none of it really sinking in as my mind wandered and my body grew heavy. When Watson's loud snores grew softer as he sank deeper into his doggy dreams, I began to be lulled to sleep as well. After closing the book, I reached up, pulled the tasseled string to turn off the lamp, and then rested my head on the puffy, recently reupholstered arm of the sofa and joined Watson in dreamland.

I woke, disoriented, not entirely sure where I was or even when it was. Not entirely certain why I'd woken at all.

There was a low rumble in the dark at my feet. Watson.

It came back to me in less than a matter of heartbeats. I was on the sofa in the bookshop and must've dozed off for a few minutes.

Watson let loose another rumble, a touch louder that time, nearly a growl.

I leaned toward him. "Watson, what's gotten—" A noise in the dark cut off my whisper and caused gooseflesh to break out over my arms.

For all I knew, it was the foundation of the old bookshop settling.

Even as the option flitted through my mind, some instinct told me differently. Sliding silently to the floor, I pulled Watson into my lap and wrapped my fingers gently over his muzzle.

Watson rumbled again.

I tightened my grip, not enough to hurt, just to communicate what I was afraid to say. Maybe he felt what I did, because despite hating being held or picked up, he didn't struggle. Though I could feel the rumble where my hand was pressed against his chest, he stayed silent.

There was another creak, faint enough that I couldn't tell where it came from—by the front door or above us in the bakery. Then another and another, followed by the unmistakable sound of a doorknob turning.

My overactive imagination went wild, picturing scenes from old horror movies I'd watched and moments from haunted-house books I'd read. From our spot on the floor at the edge of the sofa, I didn't have a great view of the rest of the shop. But my eyes had adjusted, and I could see clearly, thanks to the light filtering in through the windows. Nothing moved. No monster or villain was creeping toward us over the floors.

Watson's heartbeat against my hand brought me back to

the moment, told me to quit being an idiot. Just as I decided to stand, to take action, there was a creak of a door followed by footsteps. Then a whisper.

"Yep. They're gone. The place is dark." Even as the voice spoke, it grew louder; though high-pitched, it was clearly male and unfamiliar. Enough so, between the voice and the sound of the doorknob, I now knew where it was coming from. I'd changed all the hardware in the shop except for the old brass knobs to the bathroom, the storage room, and the door that led to what had once been a crawl space but now was nearly big enough to qualify as a basement, filled with boxes of books and supplies for the Cozy Corgi. All three old handles were in the back of the store by the rear exit.

"Took them long enough." The second voice was deeper, softer. "'Course they probably left twenty minutes ago. I told you I heard them lock up."

I felt the rumbling growl build in Watson's chest again, and I gave another squeeze. He stopped.

"That's all we need. Running into the women who own this place." There was the sound of a door closing and the twist of a door handle, followed by a quiet curse and a grunt, then a click.

That settled it. They'd been in the basement. That door never shut easily and required a push for the latch to catch.

"I told you we should've waited until the whole thing was done. But oh no, you *had* to come in while everybody was still doing that stupid trick-or-treating business outside. Couldn't wait for a sensible time."

"And I was right, wasn't I?" The higher voice spoke again. "Nobody noticed—they were busy. How was I supposed to know the whole thing was almost over?"

My blood chilled at the implication. They'd been down

there while Katie and I made trip after trip to the bakery. Though why it mattered, I wasn't sure. Either way they were there right then. I tried to think what to do. Being woken up in the dark left me feeling completely unsettled. Much different than if I'd opened the door and walked in on the two men. Not being able to see them, not knowing how big they were, if they were armed had me at a loss.

Maybe they'd just empty the cash register and leave. There wasn't much to steal in a bookshop and a bakery. I couldn't imagine there was high demand in the black market for the newest Nora Roberts book or a day-old cinnamon roll.

"What are you doing?" The man with the deeper voice sounded annoyed and a little farther away. "Let's get out of here."

"You going to give up? Just like that?" Higher Voice took on an apologetic and whiny quality. "I know I should've waited, but we've got time now. Nobody is here."

As the deeper voice started to speak, his footsteps creaked over the hardwood floor, and to my relief continued to sound farther away. Probably heading toward the back-door. "There's no reason to look. All of Sid's supplies down-stairs were gone. Just like I told you they'd be."

I jolted. *Sid? What in the world?* Sid had run a taxi-dermy business, Heads and Tails, in the building before I turned it into a bookshop. Below, he'd operated a grow house filled with marijuana plants.

"Maybe they moved them upstairs." The footsteps came closer, but I hoped he was walking toward the staircase.

"You're an idiot. A complete idiot. Obviously they got rid of everything." This time the other man's footsteps came toward the mystery room. "You're a complete screwup, Jim. I don't know why I bother with you. You lost the bighorn sheep last night and got us trapped in that storage room for an hour tonight. I'm about done with you. You're going to end up getting us killed, just like Sid and Eddie."

"What did you want me to do last night? I had no idea there was anybody around. Should I have shot that guy and his fat little dog? *Over a sheep?* I'm not a murderer, Max." For the first time, the higher-voiced man sounded irritated instead of pitiful. "There's a line, and I'm not going to cross it."

"Then you'll be the one who ends up dead." Again the footsteps came closer.

I was utterly frozen—both in terror and from shock. Sid, Eddie, the sheep. These two men were the poachers, in *my* shop, mere feet from me, and murderers or not, they were dangerous. And it sounded like only one of them had a problem with becoming a murderer.

"I say we check upstairs, maybe some of the plants are there. If so, this whole thing won't be a complete loss. Sid had enough to make a small fortune if we sold them to the right place."

"It's a *bakery*, Jim. You saw the women that own this place. Did either of them look like the type to stuff pot leaves inside a croissant or something. No! More like the 'stay at home with a book and pie on a Saturday night' type." As he spoke, his footsteps drew nearer until finally large work boots came into view, followed by the rest of the deeper-voice man as he stood between the doorway to the mystery room and the front counter.

With my heart pounding, I pulled Watson closer to my chest, praying he didn't growl.

Though his rumbling never stopped against my hand, he didn't make a noise. But at my movement, I must have stroked him, causing a small cloud of corgi fur to float up and tickle my nose.

I had to bite the inside of my cheek to keep from sneezing or trying to blow it away with my breath.

The man matched his voice. He was huge, like two football players smashed into one. And from what the moonlight revealed of his profile, his nose looked like it had been smashed on several occasions, his jawline heavy and straight.

I prayed he wouldn't turn toward us. That was all it would take—if he just looked over his right shoulder, he'd see Watson and me cowering in the dark.

That wasn't how this was going down. I wasn't going to cower, wasn't going to be a victim.

Just as I started to release Watson and spring forward to catch the man off guard, he turned the other way and headed toward the counter. "Let's get the money and go." He paused at the cash register, looked toward the stairs and raised his voice. "*Now*, Jim. If you go upstairs, I'm leaving you. If you weren't my brother, I'd have left you already after your constant screwups."

The other man cursed, but I could hear his will deflating as he spoke. "Fine. I'll get the money. Then we'll check out the Green Munchies. It's still in business."

"Are you insane? You want to take produce from their store when Eddie isn't there? You really do have a death wish." The mountain of a man turned back to the cash register and opened it, then gave an approving laugh. "Not a complete waste of a night."

I'd not even thought about the cash register when Katie and I packed up. We'd done a couple thousand dollars' worth in cash that day but hadn't had time to run to the bank between closing hours and getting ready for the Halloween fest.

I couldn't care less. They could take it all, as long as they left.

Sid, Eddie, the Green Munchies? I thought my whole world was about to crumble. Or explode.

When the larger man slammed the cash register shut, Watson growled, bringing me fully back to the moment. I clinched my hands tight enough to cause him to squirm.

The man didn't look over. Watson's growl must've been much louder to my ears than in reality. Even so, I didn't loosen my grip. Every moment made it clearer than ever that any noise would've gotten us both killed.

A few more curses and grumbles and threats were exchanged between the men. A few seconds or minutes later—I wasn't sure—and they headed toward the back once more, and I heard the door click open, then shut.

We were alone.

Even so, I held Watson tight, straining my ears. After several more moments of silence, I released his muzzle and crushed him to me, burying my face in his fur in relief, gratitude, and terror.

Whimpering, Watson lavished my face with kisses.

I only gave in to the impulse for a few seconds before springing to my feet and rushing to where I'd left my purse under the counter. I yanked out my cell phone and dialed 911 as I hurried to the back door to make sure it was locked.

If someone had told me there would come a time when I saw Susan Green's face and would want to break into tears of relief and throw my arms around her, I would've said they were insane. But when I unlocked the front door of the Cozy Corgi for Officer Green that was exactly what I felt. I stood back, giving her room to enter. "I'm so glad you're here. Thank you for coming."

Susan halted with one foot through the door, looking at me with a mixture of shock and repulsion. "Wow, you must really be in a state."

Even her grumpy response didn't lessen my inclination to give her a hug. Still, I refrained, waiting for her to come the rest of the way inside, and then shut and dead-bolted the door behind her.

Susan took out a notepad and pen before pausing to glare down at Watson, who offered his own glare in return and added a low rumble to boot. "Your ever present sidekick is... still ever present I see." She sniffed. "Oh, goody."

Even her disdain of Watson couldn't lessen my relief. "Their names were Jim and Max. They're brothers. And they were the poachers that killed the bighorn sheep. Or...

one of them was at least. I'm not really sure about that." I launched in without preamble. The words gushing forth like a waterfall. I would've kept going if Susan didn't cut me off.

"Slow down. We'll get to the report part. On your call you said two men had broken into your shop, but you didn't realize it until you woke and they were coming up from your lower-level storeroom?"

"Yes, I already told that to dispatch when I called." There wasn't time for this. "I think they're heading to Lyons, to the Green Munchies. They said—"

"*I* said to slow down." She narrowed her eyes at me again. "What do you mean exactly that you didn't realize they were here until you woke? You were sleeping at your bookshop?"

I shot a quick gesture back toward the mystery room. "I was reading for a few minutes after Katie and I finished cleaning up from Halloween. I fell asleep."

She *tsked*. "Well... *that's* quite the exciting life you're living." She cocked her head. "I gotta give it to you, Winifred, you're playing the game with more skill than I would've anticipated. Did you even attempt to call him first?"

"Call wh—" I realized who before the word had even left my lips, but Susan jumped all over it.

"Don't play dumb. Your *boyfriend*. Obviously."

"Sergeant Wexler and I haven't dated in months, Susan. You know that." After feeling powerless during the break-in, it was almost a relief to feel my temper rise. "I didn't call *you,* for that matter either. You're simply the one dispatch sent over, or you saw that I was the one calling and decided to come over to make a stressful situation worse."

She smiled at that, like she was winning some sort of

competition. "So you didn't even shoot him a text. Like I said. You're playing it well. Got him eating out of your hands."

"That doesn't even make sense. I had a break-in at my store, and I called the police. It's a *thing*—it's what people do. It's not some ploy to get Branson's attention. Or to have him eating out of my hands. We haven't dated in months. I'm not even sure if I'd call it dating or—" I had to shake my head to stop myself from talking. This was absolutely none of her business.

She studied me. "I almost believe you. I would, too, if it weren't working so well. I admit, most of the time, I'd enjoy seeing an arrogant man like Branson mooning over you from afar, but it's really just pathetic knowing that you're going to get exactly what you want. All while one minute playing the hapless victim, then the next acting like you're too good for him." She let out a dark chuckle. "Which, maybe you are. And that says something when I can't decide which one of you is more of a cliché."

Leave it to Susan Green to make me feel entirely like myself again, even if it was the version that had to replay my mother's words in my head to keep from saying things I might not truly regret later. I lowered my voice to keep better control. "Are you insinuating that I'm making all this up for attention?"

She started to speak, and I could see her lips forming a *yes*, but then she hesitated before letting out a long sigh. "No. No, I guess not. I definitely have your number, and while I don't like that particular number, I don't believe you'd lie about something like this, not even to jerk Branson around for your own enjoyment." She relaxed a little. "Sorry. Let's focus on the matter at hand."

I felt like I was the one being jerked around, getting

insulted and apologized to in the same breath. But none of that mattered. None of it.

Before I could think of how to respond, Susan launched in again, her tone calm and professional. "All right, you said both when you called and now that you think the two intruders were the poachers. How do you..." Her pale blue eyes darted down to Watson, then back up to me. "Wait a minute. Did you check to make sure that they were gone?"

"I heard them leave. I locked the door behind them as soon as I called the police."

She rolled her eyes. "So the answer is *no*, you didn't. And here you keep pretending you're better than the professionals." She pulled her gun, and Watson growled. She shot him a glare. "Don't tempt me, fleabag."

"Susan, there's no reason to—"

She shot me a matching glare.

"Fine. *Officer* Green, there's no reason to search. They're gone." I started to take a step toward her but decided to stay where I was. I doubted Susan would actually shoot me, but I figured it was wise for neither one of us to have a loaded firearm in our hands around the other. Why push it? "Like I said, I think they're on their way to Lyons. We're just wasting time."

"Protocol, Ms. Page. Protocol." She lifted her chin. "Stay here while I secure the scene."

Maybe she was doing it for protocol—though she was several minutes too late—or maybe she was simply taking every opportunity to needle me further. I couldn't tell. Either way, I decided not to fight as she searched room to room and disappeared into the back.

I knelt and petted Watson with one hand as I fingered my cell phone with the other. Part of me wanted to call

Katie, get her down here to have a friendly face. But it wasn't like she could do anything, and she needed her sleep. Same was true with my mom and stepfather.

As much as I hated to admit it, the real temptation was to call Branson. And not, like Susan suggested, to *jerk him back and forth*, but because I had no doubt he would take me seriously. He would've made sure I was safe and then headed down to Lyons to try to catch the intruders. At least I figured. There were times he was hot and cold, one minute telling me I did a better job at solving murders than some members of the police force, and the next telling me to keep my nose in my own business. But I didn't think there was a chance he would do that with this, not with what happened.

Part of me wished I'd gone ahead and called him to begin with. Then I wouldn't have been stuck with Susan. I supposed I could still call him, at least text. Try to convince him to not drop by the shop but head directly to Lyons. But as I considered it, Susan's taunts echoed in my head, and I let them get the best of me. I put the phone away.

"We can add anal-retentive to your list of irritating idio-syncrasies." Susan's voice sounded from the back, followed by a muttered curse as she struggled to get the door to the lower level closed. She rolled her eyes at me again from across the store as she emerged and headed toward the steps to the bakery. "You have your boxes of books and supplies labeled and alphabetized. Was that another fun Saturday evening for you?"

When I didn't respond, Susan slowed, almost looked disappointed, and then continued, gun still drawn, up the steps into the bakery.

Watson started to follow her, but I grabbed the edge of the red bandanna, and held him in place. "Oh no you don't.

I know you're protective of where all your carbs come from, but we're not giving her a reason, not when she's got a gun in her hand."

He offered me a glare that rivaled the ones Susan had been doling out, but plopped back down with a grunt.

As Susan searched, thanks to her bringing in a sense of normality, no matter how irritating, I replayed some of the finer points of the intruders' conversation. Not only were they Leo's poachers, or at least two of them, but they had some connection to Sid and Eddie—which made absolutely no sense at all.

As I continued to stroke Watson, I realized it did, at least somewhat. Though Sid had already been murdered when I moved to Estes, thanks to Watson discovering a dead owl in the freezer in the back of the Cozy Corgi, it was revealed that he had been involved in poaching, or at least in the trafficking of poached animals. But Eddie... I couldn't imagine him hurting a fly. The young manager of the pot shop in the nearby town of Lyons had been a complete sweetheart. And the second in a long line of dead bodies I'd discovered since moving to town.

"All clear." Susan arrived at the base of the steps and headed back in our direction. I'd been so caught up in thought, I'd not even noticed her coming down the stairs. "Are you sure you didn't just hear things? There's no sign anyone was here at all, other than the money you claim was stolen. No footprints, nothing out of place. They didn't even take time to rearrange your alphabetized organizational system. Katie might have taken the money to deposit it in the morning, or, who knows, buy a cake from somewhere else. Maybe it was all a dream and you thought—"

A knock at the door caused me to jump and Watson to yelp, revealing we were both still on edge.

Proving that she wasn't, Susan simply steadied her stance and readied her firearm as she looked past Watson and me toward the front door. She lowered her weapon instantly and let out a curse that was almost too low to hear.

As I turned toward the sound, I mentally agreed with Susan's nasty word choice.

Moving quicker than me, Susan made it to the front door, unlocked it, and threw it open. "Chief Briggs. There was no need for dispatch to wake you up in the middle of the night. I have this well under control."

As the large man entered, he cast Susan a dismissive glance and headed my way. "You claim the poachers were in your store this evening, Ms. Page?"

Watson growled again at his approach, a little more threat in the sound than the one he offered Susan.

I tightened my grip on his bandanna.

To my surprise, the chief didn't make any comment about impounding Watson. Nor did he sneer when he spoke to me. The two of us had only had a couple of interactions, but whereas Susan disdained me, seemed to relish in making my temperature rise, it was clear that Chief Briggs hated the very air I breathed, though I wasn't entirely sure what I'd ever done to earn that—outside of solving more murders in the past year than his police force.

I took just a second to make sure my tone matched the professionalism I heard in his. "Yes. They were talking about it. Referenced both the bighorn sheep and Leo and Watson's interruption—though of course they weren't named by name."

"Seems like a coincidence, doesn't it? You just happened to be present during that incident, and the two poachers show up at your bookshop two nights later?" A little of his professionalism cracked, letting some of his clear dislike seep through. "In my experience, poachers and book thieves are rarely the same individuals."

I should've called Branson. No matter if things were complicated between us personally, no matter that I was never entirely sure if he was going to be supportive or belittling, he never offered the contempt that Briggs and Green often did.

It was too late for that.

"From what I gathered, they came here planning to get marijuana plants or the supplies that were used in the grow house. It was my impression they'd hoped there were some left or that they'd not been discovered. I don't know. They mentioned Sid by name, but maybe they weren't clear on how long he's been dead." I managed to not sound the least bit irritated, and I considered that a win.

Chief Briggs balked, and for the first time in any of our interactions, he sounded interested. "Sid? Now there's a blast from the past." From his expression, it looked like the thought of the man left Briggs with a sour taste. Good to know I wasn't the only one who could cause that expression. "I'd hoped to never hear that man's name again."

At least he wasn't accusing me of lying or making it up. Though it was probably pointless after all the time that had passed, I figured I might as well push my luck and see if he'd believe me a second time. "The two of them also talked about Eddie and the Green Munchies. One of them wanted to head there to see if they could get... some produce, I believe, is how he termed it. The other didn't think that was a good idea, but... if they did, maybe you could catch them."

Another balk. "Eddie..." He took a step forward, causing Watson to growl again, but Chief Briggs didn't seem to notice. His eyes narrowed, and though he sounded skeptical, it seemed more out of disbelief than accusation. "You think these two men knew Sid and Eddie?"

"I didn't exactly have a conversation with them, Chief Briggs, but that's how it sounded. Or at least knew of them." As I spoke, the exact nature of what the larger man had said came back to me. I'd been so distracted by the mere mention of their names that I hadn't caught the implication. "I got the impression that he believed the same person killed Sid and Eddie, but... we all know who poisoned Sid. She didn't kill Eddie. *He* was shot, and that was never her style."

I hadn't really meant to say my thoughts out loud, and I braced myself for some new bit of scorn from Briggs for insinuating that I understood anything at all. To my surprise, there was no condescension as he spoke. "That is bizarre."

Susan must've felt the same surprise as I did. She looked at him in wonder. Not for the first time, I felt a little bit of sympathy for her. Briggs barely treated her with more respect than he did me, and she had to work with him day after day. After a second, she looked my way and attempted to join in. "You said you got their names, didn't you, Fred?"

"Good grief, Green, I'm trying to think... Why don't you..." Chief Briggs's snarl toward Susan broke off, and he whipped toward me. "You got their names?" His voice rose. "Holy Lord, woman, why didn't you lead with that?"

I gripped Watson's bandanna tighter for good measure as I reminded myself, at that moment, the most important thing was catching Leo's poachers and making sure the two men wouldn't come back here. "There was a big guy named Max, huge, actually. And then another one named Jim—I didn't get to see him. And one of them, Max, I think, referenced them being brothers."

Chief Briggs straightened and looked a little scary. "Max and Jim." His low rumble of words seemed more like he was talking to himself than either of us. "I was right, most definitely a blast from the past." He met my gaze, and once more, I was caught off guard by his return to professionalism. "Good job, Ms. Page. It makes sense now. Haven't heard hide nor hair of those two idiots in a long, long time. I'd hoped they'd flung themselves off a cliff by now." He lifted his walkie-talkie to his lips and gave a directive for dispatch to contact Sergeant Wexler to head to the Green Munchies.

Once more, Susan looked as shocked as I felt. "Sir, if you need someone to—"

He cut her off with a glower and looked back at me. "I trust I can count on your discretion, at least for a couple of hours, before you call in your Scooby Gang and give them all the details?"

As I'd observed Chief Briggs, another part of my awareness was trying to fit the puzzle pieces together. "I still don't understand why they think the same person killed Sid and Eddie. It doesn't make any—"

"Max and Jim are two of the dumbest human pieces of —" He shook his head as if catching himself, and then glared again. "For the billionth time, Ms. Page, leave the murders to the cops. You'll only embarrass yourself." As if noticing Watson was there for the first time, Chief Briggs sneered down at him before turning and snapping his fingers at Susan. "*Clearly* things are under control here, *Officer* Green. Please go pretend to do something useful and not waste the taxpayers' money on your salary." He stormed away into the night, leaving the front door open behind him.

A glance at Susan revealed her cheeks were red with fury and maybe embarrassment.

I couldn't help myself. "Susan, don't let him—"

"Don't—" She swiped angrily in my direction but didn't look at me. She too left the Cozy Corgi.

FIVE

I gave up pretending to sleep a little after 4:00 a.m.

Watson, woken midsnore, glared through accusing eyes the second my foot hit the floorboard. Despite his grumpy feelings about being woken up, he popped out of bed and debated which of his stuffed animal bedfellows to bring. He snagged the yellow duck, made it a couple of feet, then rushed back and traded it for the fuzzy lion, before giving me an impatient chuff in his demand for breakfast.

"You're ridiculous." I ruffled his fur before heading to the kitchen.

I fried bacon and brewed a pot of coffee. For a moment, I considered taking it all to the front porch and letting my mind wander there as I stared into the dark forest that surrounded my little cabin. That notion scattered the second I opened the front door. Thick dark clouds covered the sky, obliterating the moon and stars, and there was the bite of snow in the air. Instead I settled in at the seafoam-green kitchen table. The coffeepot was in reach that way anyway. After a couple of slices of bacon, Watson plodded away, and within a few moments, his soft snores drifted back into the kitchen.

A million different scenarios of *what-ifs* played through

my mind, just like they had when I'd lain in bed, staring at the ceiling. Somehow, with crispy bacon and hot coffee, they were a little less terrifying, but didn't fully evaporate either.

If Watson had barked or growled any louder than he had... If I'd sneezed as his fur wafted up to tickle my nose... If I'd gasped... If the larger man had looked to his right instead of his left...

Maybe the results would be the same. Maybe we would've startled each other, and they'd have run off. But from the sound of his voice—from *Max's* voice, I was never going to forget his name—I had a feeling he wasn't the type to turn and run. His brother Jim, maybe.

I didn't think they'd be back. Couldn't come up with a reason why they would. They hadn't found what they were looking for. Surely they had enough proof that all of Sid's pot plants and drug paraphernalia had been discarded.

By the third cup of coffee, my mind traveled other bunny trails. For whatever reason, clearly Max had thought Sid's and Eddie's deaths were connected, and that if he and his brother tried to do anything at the pot shop in Lyons, they would meet the same fate.

It didn't make any sense. I knew who'd killed Sid, and she was in prison. As far as Eddie, I never met the person who killed him, but I'd seen the reports. His murder had been solved as well. And it most definitely had not been connected to Sid.

Unless I was wrong.

I stared at the yellow-and-green tie-dyed curtains covered in pink flamingos that hung over the window above the kitchen sink. The blurry, swirly pattern seemed to fit my frame of mind, despite the injection of caffeine. I was thinking crazy; I had to be. I wasn't wrong with what I knew.

"I was *there*. Well, I wasn't actually present when Sid was killed, but I was the one who heard the confession from his killer." I met the gaze of one of the pink flamingos.

It didn't respond.

"Maybe I'm being silly even considering what Max said. Clearly the two of them didn't know what they were doing. They were wrong about what they'd find in the Cozy Corgi, after all."

None of the flamboyant flock of flamingos said anything. "Who knows? Maybe I didn't even hear their conversation correctly. I was rather in a panic, and my heart was beating loud enough to wake the dead. In fact—" I suddenly realized I was talking to the flamingos on my curtains. It was one thing to talk things over with Watson; it was another to bounce ideas off flamingos, especially when those flamingos were nothing more than tacky material picked out by my stepfather. I stood up. "Well, if that's not a sign that I need to talk to a living person, I don't know what is. If you'll excuse me, I'm going to—" For crying out loud. I was *still* talking to the ridiculous flamingos.

I waved them off and didn't bother filling them in on my plans. Katie and Nick would've been at the bakery for a while already by that time. I'd go there. Have a second breakfast, more caffeine, and talk things over with the two of them. Maybe I'd help them prepare for the day. Although with my baking skills I'd probably only slow them down.

It was a little after five by the time Watson and I hopped into my Mini Cooper and headed into town. If anything, the clouds had gotten heavier in the past hour; snow was definitely in the forecast. And though sunrise was less than three hours away, the morning was as dark as midnight.

As I came to the intersection of highways 36 and 34, I saw a figure walking her dog under the streetlamp across the way. She was just on the other side of what was commonly known as *Sheep Island*. In a decorative portion of the intersection, a large bronze bighorn ram stood proudly at the top of a rock outcropping, and below him, surrounded by landscaped flowers and shrubbery was a bronze mother ewe and their little lamb.

Though Athena was bundled up against the cold, she was easily recognizable. I pulled the Mini Cooper into the nearby parking lot of a doughnut shop, snapped on Watson's leash, and caught up with Athena Rose within half a block.

Her white teacup poodle, Pearl, noticed us first and gave a happy yip.

Watson answered with one of his own and scurried to meet her. I wasn't sure if he would put it quite so formally, but the two most definitely had a crush on each other.

Athena's eyes narrowed and then widened in pleased surprise. "Well, Winifred Page, what in tarnation are you doing out at this ungodly hour?"

"I can ask the same of you." I gave her a firm hug, and when she pulled back, I noticed a tightness in her smile and strain over her dark face. "Are you okay?"

She lifted a gloved hand to her cheek. "Apparently I don't look it."

I couldn't help but laugh. "Athena, it's *five* in the morning, and you look more glamorous walking your dog than I would if I'd had a team of stylists working on me for hours." There was only one woman I knew who would have her face fully painted, false eyelashes attached, and look ready to step onto the cover of *Vogue* at that hour in the morning.

She laughed along, but the sound didn't quite ring true. "I appreciate you saying that."

I noticed she didn't disagree with the sentiment. She was kind, but she was honest.

She bent and patted Watson. "Hello there, cute stuff. I was just thinking Pearl and I needed to come visit you soon."

Watson gave a quick lick to her gloved hand but refocused on nuzzling Pearl.

"I just saw Pearl's cute pink boots. She's almost as stylish as you."

"*Almost*, but she opted not to wear her tiara this morning." Athena straightened, and a little twinkle returned to her eyes. "I noticed from across the street that Watson actually dressed up last night. Sorry I didn't come over and say hello, but I was tired. I just came down long enough to give Paulie a break. I didn't even bring Pearl with me."

"He wore a bandanna. I don't know if that qualifies as a costume or not. The only reason he wore it was because Leo managed to get it on him." I reached for Athena's arm and gave it a gentle squeeze. "What's going on?"

She waved me off and started walking. I fell into step beside her, the two dogs trailing a few feet behind. "It's Odessa."

Apparently she was going to tell me after all. It took me half a second to remember who Odessa was. "Your granddaughter, the one who sings on Broadway?"

She nodded. "Yes. She's changing. Hardening somehow. I know it's a rough life. The expectations from producers and fellow actors and all the critics reviewing everything she does. Hard for any woman, but doubly so for a woman of color, especially one as beautiful as she is." Athena went silent for several steps, then shook her head. "She's not sounding like herself when I talk to her."

I wasn't sure how to respond. "You think maybe you might need to go visit?"

She smiled at me but didn't pause in her pace. "That was my first inclination, yes. But it's hard to know which mistakes to let you young ones make and when to try to rescue."

I doubted Odessa and I were anywhere near the same age, but I didn't make a comment about that. "If you're worried, maybe it would help you to see her."

Another smile, and this time Athena paused. "You're a darling, Fred, but it's clear you don't have grandchildren." She chuckled. "Obviously. But the point remains. Part of the parental role is trying to figure out when to stay away." She blinked rapidly, those long lashes fluttering, maybe even helping to drive away the tears. She shook her head, and her voice took on its more typical firm quality. "And you? You're not the type to go joyriding in the wee hours of the morning."

"No, not hardly." For a moment I considered turning things back to Odessa, wanting to make sure that I was a good friend, but decided that it seemed Athena was ready to move on.

I filled her in on the events of the night before, her sharp eyes grew shrewd during the retelling, after I spent several moments convincing her I was truly all right. "I can't say that Sid's passing was too big of a loss for this world, but the way he died seemed clear enough. And I have no question that we have the full story on that one. It made sense and went with the pattern. And I agree with you, I don't see how his death would be connected to that poor boy in

Lyons." She paused again, considering. "Although they were both doing illegal drug trafficking. It sounds like it was rather on the small scale, but... that can't be discounted."

"But that had nothing to do with why Sid died."

"True." Athena started walking again, and we were getting close to the intersection once more where we'd started. "I'm inclined to think your other theory is correct. Those two hooligans that broke into your shop last night don't sound like the sharpest tools in the shed. I can't imagine they'd return."

And that brought us to the notion I'd had the moment I'd seen Athena walking under the streetlight. "I'm sure you're right, but..."

Shrewd indeed, when she turned narrow eyes to me once more, the streetlamp caught the playful glint. "You'd like me to use my resources at the paper to do some digging?"

Athena was the obituary writer at the *Chipmunk Chronicles*, and I figured there might be some answers in the archives there somewhere or through databases we couldn't access. "If you have time, either about Eddie or Sid. Maybe even Max and Jim. I know we don't have a last name, but I bet between you searching at the *Chipmunk* and me getting the Scooby Gang on it, we might find something."

"I'm not fond of Chief Briggs, but him labeling Katie, Leo, Paulie, and you the Scooby Gang was one of his more brilliant and apt moments." She chuckled. Though there was no traffic, we both paused at one of the green spaces, *Sheep Island,* between the stoplights and waited for the walk sign. "Honestly, it sounds like just the distraction I need. Count me in."

Watson growled and suddenly pulled at his leash.

I looked back at him. "What in the world, Watson?"

"Pearl! Stop that." Athena turned as well and started to scoop the little growling poodle into her arms. Before she did, she glanced to the side, gasped, and straightened with a jolt.

I followed to where she and the dogs were looking. I didn't notice it at first. In the dark of the night and the shadow cast by the large bronze ram and the jutting cropping of rock, it looked like nothing more than a mound of earth at the base of the statue of the mother and baby. Until I noticed a sliver of light illuminate a pale hand splayed palm up.

Now that I had seen it, despite the shadows, the picture became clear. I followed up the arm, which led to a large body equally splayed out over the flowers. There were drag marks through the plants that led to massive work boots. One of the broad shoulders lay at an angle, resting against the base of the rock with the head tilted back on another jut of stone like it was a pillow. The man's eyes were closed as if in sleep. But the bullet hole between his brows stripped away any illusion of dreams or pillows.

Beside me, Athena muttered a soft prayer and a curse.

Almost on instinct, I stepped forward, trying to get a better look.

Athena grabbed my wrist and brought me to a pause. Even so, she leaned forward as well. "Who is it?" Her voice didn't shake or even have a hint of panic. "I don't recognize him. A tourist?"

I started to say that I didn't know who he was either, but then there was something familiar about him. Shifting slightly, I got a different angle and realized I did indeed know him. The flattened nose that had clearly been broken multiple times. The work boots.

Though he was clearly no longer a threat, at the recognition, remembered fear from a few hours before coursed through me. When I spoke, I could hear the tremble in my words. "Max. That's Max."

"Who is—" Before she finished, Athena let out an understanding sigh. "Oh."

"Yeah." The two of us stared, and when Watson got close enough to nudge his nose on the man's boot, I realized my grip had gone slack on his leash and I pulled him back. "Watson, no."

He obeyed and trotted back to me. As he did, Pearl stopped pulling on her leash and settled in beside him.

I glanced around, looking for Jim—not that I would recognize the other intruder, but I figured if there was another body, it would be self-explanatory. I didn't see one. Finally, I turned to Athena. "Would you mind calling the police this time? Technically you saw it first. That way it won't increase the body count that I keep stumbling over."

SIX

Katie and the Pacheco twins greeted Watson and me as we walked into the Cozy Corgi. It was still early enough that we had half an hour before opening.

Watson, who'd been in a sullen, irritated mood after an exorbitant amount of chaotic time with the police, bounced at the sight of Ben, gave a happy bark, and rushed toward one of his favorite humans. In response, Ben knelt, tucked a strand of shoulder-length black hair behind his ears, and greeted Watson with open arms. "Hi, my friend." He pressed a kiss to Watson's nose and kept stroking him as he smiled up at me, his tone warm and little more than a whisper. "Good to see you too."

Beside him, his even quieter twin brother, Nick, nodded and gave a wave.

Katie mimicked Watson and hurried my way, throwing her arms around me. "Are you okay?" She squeezed so tight I couldn't answer, and then let go only to grip my arms just as firm. She glared up into my face, her voice transitioning from worried to angry. "Obviously you're okay. Why in the world did you not call me last night?"

"Last night?" I blinked, that wasn't what I'd expected. "I

figured you'd heard about what Athena and I found this morning."

She gave me a shake. "I did! I *also* heard that the body belonged to some horrid man who broke in here last night, and that he was the poacher who killed the sheep when we were with Leo the night before!" Another shake. "And again, why didn't you call me? He must've been here when I left you. You could've been—"

"I'm okay." Warmed by her concern, I laughed and twisted free. "Honestly, the only physical harm I've experienced is the bruising that's going to occur on my arms from your fingers digging in."

Her cheeks blushed, and she tilted her chin in the air. "Serves you right."

"And I'm sorry I didn't call. I knew you'd be back in here in the blink of an eye, and you needed your sleep. Besides, there was nothing you could do. It was over. I was on my way in here this morning to talk things over with you and Nick when I saw Athena walking and we found the body of one of the intruders." I glanced over Katie's shoulder where Ben was still lavishing Watson with attention. "Why are you here so early?"

"I came in with Nick." He lifted one hand and made a circle gesture encompassing the shop. "I thought we agreed that we would decorate after Halloween was over."

Watson head-butted his knee, demanding both Ben's hands be on him.

Ben chuckled and obliged.

I glanced at the Cozy Corgi, surprised I hadn't noticed the change despite getting accosted the second I walked in. "Ben, wow! How in the world did you do so much? You completely transformed the place."

There was the typical fall and Thanksgiving décor all

over the shop—assortments of pumpkins and dried gourds and large stalks of corn, revealing multicolored kernels within their husks, arranged artfully at the ends of shelves. Colorful turkey cutouts placed here and there. Yellow, orange, and brown streamers draped artfully over the counter in the center of the shop. And amid all of that, were posters and framed art depicting the Ute deities of Wolf, who was the creator, and Coyote, his younger trickster brother. There were illustrations and descriptions of both the sun and bear dances and a large beaded circle depicting the Ute symbol. A couple of mannequin busts were on stands—one displaying fringed buckskin decorated with deer teeth and the other wearing jewelry of seeds and juniper berries and turquoise with bear claws below a headdress of feathers and more beadwork.

Katie and I had been midpreparation with our plans for decorating for Thanksgiving when we wondered how that would make Ben and Nick feel, especially considering some of the discrimination they'd experienced as Native Americans from select people in town. The twins instantly volunteered to bring in some items they'd collected over the years.

I was blown away. "Ben, Nick, this... is amazing. Absolutely beautiful. Thank you for—"

"Later! Good grief!" Katie went shrill, which was very atypical of her. "Are you sure you're okay?"

"Yes! I'm fine. Watson and I both are. I was scared more than anything." I walked around her and headed past the twins and Watson to shove my purse under the counter. "I was coming in to talk to you about some of the things I overheard the intruders say last night, but then, as you heard, we found one of their bodies."

"At the sheep statues." Nick spoke, but it wasn't a question.

I answered anyway. "Yes." I considered the time. "Shouldn't you be getting to school? We don't want to give them any reason to cause you more problems."

He grinned. "I'll be fine as long as I leave in the next ten minutes."

Katie joined me at the counter, and when she spoke, she sounded more like herself. "It didn't hit me until right now, hearing Nick say that. The poacher who killed the bighorn sheep was found dead at the statue of the *bighorn sheep*?"

I opened my mouth to reply and halted. "Yeah... I... hadn't thought of that, either."

"It sounds like you've been a little busy." Ben gave me another smile but turned his attention back to Watson. "Both of you."

"That's true, we have, but..." I refocused on Katie. "That's interesting. Although, I'm not entirely sure I got the impression, from what the brothers were saying..." I rushed to clarify at Katie's puzzled expression. "The intruders were brothers—Max and Jim. Max is the dead one, but like I was saying, I got the impression that Jim was the one who killed the sheep. At least Max was blaming him for leaving it behind and not taking care of Leo and Watson."

Katie's eyes went wide as she gripped the counter. "Taking care of Leo and Watson?"

I shrugged. "I don't know if that's too big a shock. I mean, we were all thinking it. Running into the woods toward a person who'd just killed an animal. We heard the gunshot."

"I know..." She shivered. "But still, it was just confirmed."

The front door of the bookstore was flung open—apparently I'd forgotten to lock it when I entered.

"Fred!" My tiny mother practically flew across the floor,

rushed around the counter, and like Katie only a few minutes before, threw her arms around me. "You're okay! I've been calling and calling. When you didn't answer—"

"I told you she was fine, dear. Fred can handle herself. Plus, none of the gossip said she was hurt." My stepfather, Barry, entered the Cozy Corgi and shut the door behind him.

Watson let out another happy yip, gave another hop, and rushed toward Barry, another of his favorite people. If only Leo would enter, he could have his perfect trifecta. He made it halfway to Barry before skidding to a halt and looking back at Ben, clearly torn. He whimpered and trembled.

Laughing, Barry closed the distance, put one hand on his head and used his other to motion toward Ben. "Join us before Watson has a heart attack. He's been through too much the way it is."

Ben had already been on his way, and Watson was lost to pure heaven. The three of them managed to stir up an impressive cloud of dog hair in the process.

Mom spoke again, and for the second time that morning, I got scolded. "Why didn't you answer? I was worried sick all the way here."

"I didn't know you called. I guess I shoved my cell in my purse in all the chaos and never got it back out. I'm sorry." I shook my head, laughing, and pointed between her and Katie. "You know, you two have a funny way of showing that you love me. I survived a break-in last night and discovered a body this morning, and *I'm* the one getting in trouble."

"You are just like your father." Mom *tsked* and shook her head. "A magnet for danger." She paused to glare at my chest. "Are you wearing your necklace?"

I pulled it out and held up between us the sky-blue crystal of celestine Mom had made me a few months before. "You asked me to always wear it, so I do."

"Good, now take it off." She held out her hand.

Knowing better than to question, I did as she asked.

Her fingers barely closed around it before she started toward the door. "I'm going over to Chakras. I have a key. Although Verona and Zelda should be there any minute. Celestine is good for calming, balance, and remembering dreams, but you need something stronger, clearly. I should have insisted on it from the beginning. I'll be right back."

Barry grinned after her as she hurried out of the shop and then smiled over at me from where he and Ben still knelt on either side of Watson. "Seems like you're doing just fine with the celestine to me, but who knows? Maybe you'll do even better with something else." His watery blue eyes warmed as he inspected me. "Sure you're okay, darling?"

"I am. Just shaken, but apparently not enough, judging from everyone's reactions." Truth be told, though it probably shouldn't be thought, I was less shaken than I'd been all through the night. I hadn't really thought that the intruders would come back, but the one who'd scared me was now no longer a threat. I wouldn't go so far as to say I was glad he was dead, but of all the dead bodies I'd discovered, his was the first one that had brought a sense of relief. "What I really need, Katie, is a dirty chai and as many pastries as you can fit on a platter." I grinned at her. "In the last twelve hours, I've had two rather unpleasant interactions with both Susan Green and Chief Briggs. Caffeine and sugary carbs won't fix it, but they'll sure help."

"No Branson?" Katie cocked an eyebrow.

I shook my head. Maybe he'd called. His message might be waiting in the cell alongside my mother's.

· · ·

When Nick left for school, the rest of us headed up to the bakery. We were seated around the table, sharing an assortment of Katie and Nick's creations and I'd only had my second sip of dirty chai when the first of the morning's customers came up the stairs in search of both nourishment and gossip.

It was going to be a morning. Actually, it was going to be a day. With most of the tourists gone from the Halloween festivities of the night before, there wouldn't be many books sold, but with the events of the night before and the morning, every last local and their dog would be in for the latest. And from the completely restocked pastry cases, it looked like Katie was more than prepared.

Before too long, with Ben manning the bookshop below and Katie filling bakery and coffee orders, Mom came up the steps followed by Verona and Zelda, my stepsisters. The three of them hurried to the table where Barry and I still sat and took the seats that Anna and Carl had just vacated.

"Here. The girls gave their input." Mom thrust my necklace back at me. It still had the larger sky-blue crystal in the center, but it was now bookended by a shiny black stone and a shimmering blue-green one that resembled the color of a peacock feather. "The black tourmaline was my idea. It repels lower harmful frequencies. The girls..." She grimaced. "Well, Verona, decided on the labradorite."

"It shields against psychic attacks and ill wishes." Verona tapped the peacock-hued crystal. "You never know."

Zelda crossed her arms, sounding somewhat putout. "I wanted rose quartz. There's no better defense against darkness than love. Plus I think the pink would have been a good addition to the necklace."

Mom gave a soothing pat to Zelda's shoulder. "I know dear. But Fred's been very clear about anything to do with love and relationships. This necklace is about protection." She fluttered her fingers at me. "Put it on."

I did, Barry lending a hand by holding my long auburn hair out of the way but accidentally getting it entangled in the dangling earrings of silver corgis. After all was put to rights, he dusted some croissant crumbs from his tie-dyed shirt and made Watson very happy from his place under the table.

Sure enough, the steady stream of customers didn't stop for five solid hours, transitioning from breakfast to midmorning snack, lunch, and beyond. Each one wanted details about the break-in and the discovery of Max's body. By the time all the pastries were devoured, Nick had returned from his half day at school and helped Katie start afresh. For the billionth time, I wondered how the two of us had managed the few months without the twins. They were godsends, both of them.

Things had started to slow down, and I was getting ready to head back to the bookshop when Leo, in his park ranger uniform, appeared at the top of the steps, his brown eyes panicked and searching the space before they landed on me.

Watson noticed Leo when he was halfway across the bakery and rushed toward him. For the first time I could remember, Leo merely dipped slightly, just enough to brush his fingertips down Watson's back, but didn't so much as pause.

More than anything else, that made my adrenaline kick in. I stood as he reached me. "What's wrong?"

"The police. They just—" He shook his head, a crease forming between his brows as he leveled his gaze on me. "Sorry, first things first. I shouldn't take for granted just because you're tough that you're okay." He gripped my arms as Katie had earlier, but his touch was gentle, and he didn't shake. "*Are* you okay?"

For whatever reason, the way he asked, or the tender care in his eyes, I felt some of my strength crumble. The feeling surprised me. As did the tears that threatened to burn right behind my eyes. Maybe I wasn't as unaffected as I thought. Feeling ridiculous, I blinked the emotion away. "I am. Thank you. Watson and I were safe last night too." I shrugged and forced a laugh. "Well... as you're aware, it was hardly my first time seeing a dead body."

"I know, but just because you've gone through it a couple of times doesn't mean it doesn't take its toll." A smile played his lips. "I'm glad you're okay."

Katie appeared beside us. "Leo, are you all right?"

He grinned over at her. "I was just asking the same of Fred." He gave my arms a soft squeeze and let me go, and then his gaze turned hard and worried again as he glanced around. "Is there someplace we can talk in private? I know it's going to spread through the gossip chain like wildfire within the next half an hour, but I don't want it to come from me."

Katie groaned. "Something else happened?"

He nodded, then looked at me expectantly.

I considered. We could go to the storeroom, but it would be rather cramped, or the storage space underneath the bookshop, but after the events of the night before I didn't really want to be down there for any reason.

Katie came to the rescue and pointed through the bakery. "Let's go to the back of the kitchen. We'll be mostly out of view, and with the noise of the mixers, dish-washers and such, we won't be overheard. If Nick happens to hear something, he's not the type to spread it around."

"Good enough." Leo gave a nod, and he and I followed Katie.

I paused at the edge of the bakery and knelt toward Watson, who was staring at Leo with hurt in his eyes. "Sorry, buddy, I need you to stay here for a little bit." Though I didn't do a perfect job of keeping him out of the kitchen portion of the bakery, I at least needed to do so when we had a room full of customers. Although, since they were all locals, they had no illusions about Watson not being the king of the Cozy Corgi—the bookshop *and* the bakery.

Leo knelt beside me, finally taking Watson's face in his hands and rubbing his cheeks with his thumbs. "Sorry, little man. I wasn't trying to ignore you."

Watson whimpered and his knob of a tail wagged, causing his whole fuzzy butt to shimmy in happiness.

Despite whatever was going on, Leo's affection was clear in his patient tone. "I'll come down and see you in a bit, but for now, go be with Ben."

Watson's little brows rose.

"Good idea." I patted Leo's arm and then Watson's head before pointing toward the stairs. "Ben, Watson. Go to Ben."

I nearly laughed at the war that clearly waged behind Watson's honey-brown eyes, the pull of desire between two of his dear loves. Finally, once Leo pulled his hands away, Watson took a few steps backward, then with a huff, whirled and took off through the bakery and down the steps.

Leo chuckled, but by the time he stood, his expression was serious again.

We joined Katie, who was already in the back of the kitchen with her hands on her hips. "What happened? More poaching?"

"No." Leo shook his head, and though his gaze darted between Katie and me, it focused longer on me. "The police just arrested Nadiya for that man's murder. She didn't do it. The police are adamant about it, and as ever, Branson and the chief won't listen to me."

A check through the voicemails revealed that Branson hadn't called or texted. Apparently he'd been busy. I didn't need further explanation from Leo, and I sighed. "You want me to look into it."

He started to nod, then paused. "Only if it's not going to upset you or put you at risk. I know you've got to be shaken after last night. And from what I've heard, there were two intruders, so there's still one out there."

Katie answered for me. "Of course she'll look into it, and it's not like she won't have you and me helping her." She grinned my way. "Plus, I think I just saw a delivery of a magically protective necklace."

I didn't have to consider. Leo was clearly upset. There was nothing he or Katie could request that I wouldn't do. Besides, at this point, even I couldn't pretend that it took much of a motive for me to try to solve a murder. "Of course I will, you know that."

Katie nodded in approval, then turned a questioning gaze on Leo. "Are you sure Nadiya *didn't* have anything to do with it? He was a poacher after all, and she seemed pretty emphatic last night about what she thought should happen to poachers."

While I didn't necessarily disagree with her, I was a

little surprised Katie would verbalize the thought. Though I tried, I couldn't read if it was a genuine concern or if Katie had decided she didn't quite care for Nadiya Hameed.

Leo also surprised me with his resigned sigh. "I admit, it looks bad. Nadiya is... passionate in her animal advocacy, and if she'd caught him in the act of killing an animal"—he grimaced—"well... maybe, but that wasn't the case here. She insists she didn't do it. I believe her. She's become a good friend, and she is one of the best park rangers I've ever seen, one we've needed for a long time." He held my gaze once more. "I hate to ask it of you, but—"

"Stop it. Anything for you, or you." I grinned to Katie. "There's no request that's too big between us. Besides, we all know I like solving murders just as much as settling down with a good book."

"I wouldn't go that far." Katie winked.

Though I didn't say so, I kinda thought I enjoyed solving a murder even more.

Leo and Katie came to my cabin after closing the Cozy
Corgi. By late afternoon, the ominous clouds that had been
threatening all day let loose, and within an hour Estes Park
was transformed into a winter wonderland. Though the
snowstorm slowed, there didn't appear to be any sign of it
stopping.

Katie and Leo made tomato soup while I worked on
grilled cheeses, and then we spent the next couple of hours
going back and forth between Leo filling us in about Nadiya
and attempting to uncover anything we could about Max
and Jim.

Katie and I curled up together on the couch, poring over
our laptops while Leo took a similar position by the roaring
fire, searching his computer while never ceasing to stroke
Watson.

On the one hand, between the friendship and the fire, it
was a pleasant evening with the beautiful snow drifting
down on the other side of the windows. On the other, it was
frustrating. We couldn't find anything about the poachers.
Nothing. There'd still not been a solitary word from Branson, and I wasn't about to call and ask for details anymore.

Even getting Leo's perspective on Nadiya wasn't overly

helpful. He painted a picture of a passionate and devoted park ranger, one who tirelessly wrote to political leaders requesting stricter animal protection laws and was active in animal-rights marches.

By the time they left, the snow was a couple of inches thick, and it didn't feel like we were any closer to figuring out who the poachers were, if there was any possible connection to the Green Munchies in Lyons, or helping Nadiya.

Deciding that my brain had reached its fill between the stress of the night before, the lack of sleep, and the nonstop events of the day, I slipped into my flannel nightgown, picked up the newest Dean Koontz novel I'd started right before Halloween, and settled into the armchair in front of the fire with Watson at my feet. I was willing to bet I'd make it a total of four pages before falling asleep. Maybe by the light of a new day, with a rested brain and body, I'd have an idea of where to begin.

I made it two and a half pages before a growl rumbled from Watson and he trotted toward the front door. An arrow of fear shot through me, my first notion being that Max's brother had come to get his revenge. I shoved that aside. It was a ridiculous thought born of exhaustion. Jim didn't know I'd been hiding in the mystery room while he and his brother discussed poaching and stole the contents of the cash register. And as far as revenge, I wasn't the one who'd killed Max.

Refusing to give in to fear, I set the book aside, stood, and nearly caught up with Watson by the time a knock sounded. Even then, despite myself, my adrenaline spiked. Again, ridiculous. If the ludicrous happened and Jim was at the door, he would hardly knock. He'd just kick it in.

Although from what I'd overheard, that sounded more like his brother's style.

I peered through the peephole and was met with darkness. For a second I thought whoever was there was covering the peephole with their hand, but then I realized I'd not turned on the front porch light. Leaning over I did so and looked back once more.

Relief washed over me at the sight of Branson Wexler's handsome face, but it was quickly followed by a different sort of anxiety.

For a couple of seconds, I considered not answering, pretending not to be home. I was exhausted and on edge. I'd either say something to him I'd regret or allow myself to feel things for him I had no business feeling.

Another knock.

Watson growled.

"Fred?" Branson's voice was muffled. "If you wanted to pretend you weren't home, you shouldn't have turned on the porch light."

"I might have installed one of those motion sensitive ones." I couldn't help myself.

"My bad, that must be what it is." His warm chuckle issued through the door. "I'll come back when you're home."

Joining in his laughter, I released locks and opened the door.

He smiled at me and glanced down when Watson growled again. "For the billionth time, little man, your mom is safe with me. Always."

Watson gave a final rumble, a chuff, and then turned around and sauntered back toward the fire as if tossing his front paws in the air in surrender.

Branson focused on me once more as he motioned

through the door. "May I come in? That is, if you're sure that you're home."

I rolled my eyes and stood back, giving him room. "Come on in."

He started to, then paused, stamped the snow from his boots onto the welcome mat, dusted off his jacket, and then entered. By the time I turned around from locking the door, he'd removed his jacket and scarf. He wasn't in uniform, but wearing dark-wash jeans and a deep green sweater that brought out the brighter hue in his eyes.

He started to say something, sniffed, and glanced toward the kitchen. "Tomato soup and grilled cheese?"

I nodded. "You know me, it's snowing outside, so I've got to have my tomato soup and grilled cheese."

He hesitated, looking nervous, which was always a strange expression on his strong face. "Got any leftovers?"

A sudden pang of loss settled over me, and the year folded in on itself to a night so similar to this one. The first time Branson had been in my home we'd shared an identical meal.

I knew I should tell him no, see why he had come, and then send him on his way. Maybe it was the exhaustion, or feeling sentimental due to the extreme swing of emotions the past day had brought. Whatever it was, I sighed and headed into the kitchen. "I'll warm up the soup and make some fresh grilled cheeses."

"You don't have to go to any trouble."

There was my out, if I needed one. I didn't take it. "And deprive Watson of yet another unhealthy snack? I wouldn't be that cruel." I'd already had two grilled cheese sandwiches with Katie and Leo. The last thing I needed was another one. Perhaps that wasn't true, as I suddenly needed one desperately.

I retrieved the pot of soup out of the fridge and swiped up the frying pan that had been air-drying on the towel by the sink.

Branson stood by the stove. "May I help you with anything?"

The question caused another ache, and I turned to look at him, partially frozen in place. I wasn't sure if those had been his exact words or not the year before, but the sentiment had been the same, and that had caused my heart to skip a beat, even more than his movie-star good looks. My ex-husband had been the kind to not do so much as lift a finger, only demand and criticize. He hadn't started out that way, but after years of marriage, I realized I had been the proverbial toad in the pot, never noticing just how hot the water had become.

Branson's brows knitted. "Sorry, did I say something wrong?"

"No." Mentally I gave myself shake. "Sorry. I appreciate the offer. It's been a long day, more than a long day. I'm just tired and..." I blinked, feeling a little exposed, but despite how things had ended between us, what Branson said to Watson had been true. I was always safe with him. "I'm a little overly emotional."

For the billionth time, he proved he was not my ex-husband. "Anyone would be after the time you've had. Hiding during a robbery last night and then finding yet another body this morning."

"Heard about that, did you?" The moment needed lightening. "Funny, I thought I'd managed to keep it a secret." I found my movement once again and put the frying pan on the stovetop. At the sound, Watson rushed into the kitchen and took sentinel by the stove, waiting for any morsel to accidentally fall onto the floor.

"Well..." Branson winked. "As secrets go in Estes, it was a pretty well-kept one. Luckily, I'm a policeman, so I have the inside scoop. That and the whole town might be talking about it."

I gave a pretend wince. "Oh, right. There was that." I motioned toward the table. "Thanks for the offer, but go ahead and have a seat. Grilled cheeses are a one-man job." I didn't give him a chance to respond before I kept going. "Did you just get back into town?" I nearly clarified that I was referencing the night of the break-in, since he'd clearly been in town at some point as he'd refused to listen to Leo's concerns.

Branson hadn't moved from his spot beside the stove and tilted his head quizzically at me. "No. I wasn't out of town."

I'd started to head toward the refrigerator to get the cheese that I'd forgotten when I retrieved the pot of soup, but I froze, looking back at him. "You weren't? You were in Estes last night and early this morning?"

"Yeah, why?" His confused expression softened, and his shoulders slumped. "Oh, because I didn't come to the Cozy Corgi last night or to the crime scene this morning."

Branson had been in town.

Hurt trickled in, closely followed by anger. Anger at myself for feeling hurt. Branson often disappeared for a day or two on overnight trips in his role as sergeant, and I'd just assumed that was where he'd been. It was the only reason he ever missed an occasion when I called the police. I had no right to be hurt by the fact that he didn't come this time. None at all.

"Fred, I'm sorry..." He reached for me.

"No." I held up a hand, but in what I hoped wasn't an unkind way. "You have no reason to be sorry. You're only respecting my wishes. So... thank you." Strangely, saying those words helped both alleviate the feeling of hurt and the guilt around it. Things were exactly how they should be. Except for Branson being in my kitchen and me making him a late-night snack.

He hesitated, then gave one of his bright smiles, though it seemed slightly forced, and finally crossed the kitchen and plopped down at the table. "You know, I honestly forgot I didn't tell you this. When the edict was passed down, I considered giving you advanced warning but then figured from what you said, you wouldn't want me to. As much as I went back and forth trying to decide, I think I truly forgot that I didn't tell you."

I tried to decipher that for the correct meaning and failed. Finally I just laughed. "*What*?"

"I guess that wasn't very clear, was it?" Branson gave a laugh of his own, then darkened somewhat. "My... superior has forbidden me from being part of any investigation where you are even slightly involved, or answering any calls you make." His gaze rose and locked on to mine. "I was here last night and this morning, but I wasn't allowed to take part or to help."

"Chief Briggs said to..." The surprise that had risen faded instantly, and I propped my hip against the oven door, the cheese slices still in my hands. "Of course he did." I thought back to his and Susan's interaction at the Cozy Corgi. "Was the opposite decree passed down to Susan?"

He nodded.

"Is that punishment for me or her?"

He winced a little. "Both. I believe."

Strangely, the knowledge infused a sense of kinship for Officer Green. Unsure how to respond, I decided not to, and turned back to the stove to start in on the grilled cheeses.

Watson began to whimper in anticipation as soon as the smell of melting butter filled the kitchen.

As I prepared Branson's and my sandwiches, I put mayonnaise on mine the way I liked it and left his plain. I paused with the mayonnaise-covered knife in midair, staring at the bread slices. I didn't have to ask him how he liked his grilled cheese. I already knew. And again that sense of loss.

It had been a mistake. I shouldn't have been making sandwiches for him, not when I was exhausted and emotional and on edge. Not when I was prone to only see the wonderful and charming parts of Branson, when I was tempted to overlook the other aspects. True, he'd never been as dismissive or commanding as my ex-husband, but he'd gotten close. And ultimately it didn't matter if those times had been because of commands he'd gotten from a superior or not. We'd crossed this bridge. It wasn't fair to me to be tempted to walk back across it just because of the moment we were in. Nor was it fair to him.

I'd make it fast.

After the sandwiches were sizzling on the frying pan, I returned things to business as I stirred the warming tomato soup. I made certain my voice was going to be neutral when I spoke, not cold, but not overly familiar either. "So, did you come here to just check in? Just make sure that I'm safe on your off-time so you're not breaking orders?"

"Yes, partly."

Partly. Despite my best effort I turned to him in surprise.

"That is most definitely the main reason I'm here." Branson's tone shifted to neutral as well. "We had several calls from Leo Lopez this afternoon, and I have no doubt he's requested for you to get involved in trying to clear Nadiya Hameed's name. I thought I would come out here to circumvent that."

And there we were. I bristled. "Let me get this straight. You came here to check on me, which is appreciated. I'm fine. Thank you." I still attempted to keep a neutral tone, though I figured I wouldn't be able to pull it off. "But you're also here, not in uniform, on your off-time, and when you've been given explicit instructions to stay away from me as far as police business is concerned, to tell me to keep my nose out of it?"

He opened his mouth, and I saw a flash of anger behind his eyes, but then it was gone as he laughed. "I've made that mistake more than once, and it should have only taken me one time to realize it wasn't going to work."

"Does that mean you're not—" A faint burning scent reached my nose, and I paused to flip the sandwiches before looking back at him. "Does that mean you're not here to tell me to keep my nose out of it?"

"Would it do any good?" Though his eyes crinkled playfully, the humor didn't quite reach his voice.

"You know the answer to that."

"Yes, I do." He leaned back in the chair, stretching out his legs and accidentally bumping the sole of his boot against Watson's flank. "Sorry, little buddy."

Watson answered with a glare, shuffled closer to the oven, and looked up at me expectantly.

I tore off a corner of a fresh slice of bread and tossed it to him before looking over at Branson, probably giving him an identical expression to the one Watson had just given me.

He didn't need any more prompting. "I know you're going to look into Nadiya. Both because Leo will want you to and simply because you're Winifred Page—that's... what you do." He must've realized the exasperated sound in his tone as he raised both his hands in surrender. "And you do it well. Anyone who says otherwise is either an idiot or a liar. You're smart, capable, and insightful."

I took a moment to plate the sandwiches, ladle two bowls of tomato soup, and place them on the table. "But...?" I sat down across from him, and as was typical with Branson, I had the sensation I was both sitting down to a meal with a friend—someone who was extremely important to me—and yet sitting down with an adversary. "There's a *but* coming."

Proving the second sensation correct, Branson continued. "But... you'll be wasting your time on this one. There is no doubt that Nadiya is guilty. I know Leo believes differently." He rolled his eyes. "Trust me, I've gotten more than an earful today. I know he means well. He's proven that over the countless, and I do mean *countless*, calls and complaints he's made about poaching in the park."

I'd started to take a bite of the grilled cheese but didn't. "And he was right, just like with Sid being involved in the poaching. Leo tried to tell you that Sid was part of it, but none of you would listen."

Again he offered the hands of surrender. "And I've admitted, and will admit again, that he was right and we were wrong. But in our defense, he had absolutely no shred of proof. None. Not until you came along with that owl feather."

I leaned across, and even as I did so, I wasn't sure why I was trying so desperately to convince him. "But that's just my point. It's always been my point. I can look into things in a different way than you can, without breaking any laws. You could never have found that feather without a search warrant—I could. If Leo believes Nadiya is innocent, then she is. And I'll help prove it. Maybe in ways that you're not able to. We both know I don't need your permission, and since you're not allowed to be talking to me about it anyway, this is all beside the point."

"It isn't beside the point." Branson matched my position but leaned forward a little farther and placed a hand on my forearm. "There are no missing pieces to this, Fred. Nadiya is guilty. She did this." His gaze darkened, just for a flash. "And part of me, the man I am when I'm not in uniform, is glad that she did."

I flinched.

"I am. I admit it." His thumb made a solitary caress over my skin. "I have no doubt that you were in danger last night, none. This man, Max, was a threat to you. Chances are high you wouldn't have been in jeopardy from him again, but..." He shrugged. "Who knows? But now, thanks to Nadiya, that's no longer a possibility. And from everything that's known about Jim, you're not in danger from him either." He released my arm and sat back. "But when I'm in uniform, I have to admit that Nadiya took the law into her own hands in a very violent and deadly way."

I couldn't figure out how to answer that, overwhelmed by what he'd just admitted. I tore off a bit of my grilled cheese and handed it to Watson, partly to give myself a moment to think. Finally I looked back at Branson, deciding to just skip completely over the "he was glad Max was dead" part. "But what if Leo's right? He has been before, and he knows her, apparently very well. If he's convinced she's innocent, that she wouldn't kill someone, then I believe him. I've never gotten in the police's way before. I've never broken any laws. I won't this time either. But it's not going to hurt you or the police force if I... do my thing."

"It might hurt you."

"I thought you weren't going to tell me to keep my nose out of it."

Brandon flinched, but then he shrugged. "You might've noticed that Chief Briggs is fed up with your involvement. And he's not going to hurt you, obviously, but if you slip up, even a little, and do something outside the lines, he's going to bring the full weight of the law against you."

"And what does that say about him?"

He'd taken a bite of grilled cheese and chewed it before speaking. "You're the daughter of a detective, Fred. Don't pretend to be ignorant. Just because the chief doesn't want a civilian butting their nose into every murder that happens doesn't make him a bad man. Would your father have welcomed a layperson barging into his investigations?"

I started to argue the points but couldn't. So I didn't try. "That doesn't change the fact that you have—*may* have—an innocent woman in custody for murder. And from what Leo said, you're not letting anyone speak to her. No one can get her side."

"Just because Leo doesn't get a chance to talk to Nadiya doesn't mean squat." Branson thumped the tabletop with his forefinger and caused Watson to let out a startled yip below. "He's not her lawyer, he's not her husband, he's not family—he's nothing to her besides a coworker and a friend. He has no legal standing. I promise you that Nadiya is getting every right to which she is entitled. She'll have legal representation, the whole nine yards. Just because Leo doesn't get what *he* wants doesn't mean there's a conspiracy."

Even at the best of times, with his tone my rage would've boiled, but in my exhausted state, it took every single ounce of willpower to bite my tongue. Because somewhere in there, beneath that tone that sounded like my ex-husband, I knew he was right. In every single thing.

Branson cocked his head, and his volume lowered. "Sorry if I sounded harsh, but I need you to wake up."

I'd started to soften at the beginning of his apology and then had to grip the edge of the table to keep from losing my temper. I managed to speak through gritted teeth. "You need me to *wake up*?" That time Branson started to speak, but I cut him off. "What you said is true. Leo doesn't have any legal right to see Nadiya or get her side of things. But you also have to admit that it would hardly be the first time someone in this town has been set up for murder, or that the police department has gotten the wrong person in a cell." It was my turn to punch the table with my finger, and Watson let out yet another yip, but I couldn't bring myself to comfort him. "You also have to admit, that if it wasn't for me sticking my nose into things where it didn't belong and refusing to butt out, some of those people would still be in jail. So why should I trust that that isn't true with Nadiya this time?"

Branson opened his mouth several times and closed it. Each time an array of emotions flickered over his face, shifting from anger to hurt to frustration to resignation. Finally, leaving the rest of his food uneaten, he stood. "This was a mistake on my part. I'm sorry. I should've listened to my chief. But..." When he met my gaze, though his eyes were hard, there was sorrow there. "I can't protect you anymore, Fred. While you're technically right, you haven't broken any laws, Chief Briggs is well within his right to expect you to let the police do their jobs." He turned and was nearly to the kitchen door before he looked back at me. "Here's my final overreach for you. Even though I shouldn't even give you these details, I hope that it will convince you to stay out of it. We found the murder weapon in the cab of Nadiya's truck."

"Maybe someone planted it. It's obvious that—"

He cut me off with a growl and a swipe of his hand. "She was *in* the truck at the time. Caught by the police in Lyons, not us. There was blood in the bed of the truck, which I'm sure will come back as a positive match for Max's. There were drag marks and mud in the bed well. And that's just a few of the details. I won't even get into Nadiya's past and what else she's done. Mainly because it would be breaking the law to tell you, but also because it's none of your business." His expression softened once more. "I hate that this is where we are. I hoped... I hope..." He shook his head. "I have always told you, you'll always be safe with me. But... I can't protect you anymore, not when you're too stubborn to let me. Being a detective's daughter won't protect you from the law."

He didn't wait for a reply, not that I would've been able to come up with one, before he retrieved his scarf and jacket and walked out of my house.

By late morning, the snow had started again, not in thick torrents as it had the day before, but in large fluffy flakes that drifted lazily outside the windows. During the summer, I had played the part of a crazy person by lighting the fire in the mystery room and having the windows open so it wouldn't get too hot. Now it was cold enough that both fireplaces in the Cozy Corgi were roaring, and I was snuggled on the sofa under the antique lamp in my favorite room, of course. Unfortunately, though I'd assumed the position, I held no new or well-loved book in my hands, but instead was searching away on the computer perched on my lap.

In frustration, I looked up from the screen. I'd been searching the internet for too long; maybe I needed a break. I peered into the main room, where Ben leaned against the front counter and scribbled in a notebook. Doubtlessly, he was mapping out plot points for a series of mystery novels he hoped to write that revolved around an incarnation of the Ute deity, Coyote. It was rare for him to turn to the notebook. Even in lulls between customers, Ben always found some chore to do—straightening books on shelves, rearranging the Cozy Corgi merchandise section, or simply cleaning. It pleased me to see him taking a moment to himself.

Having had the fill of gossip the day before, after the bakery's morning rush had passed, there'd not been many people in. Which worked for me. I'd planned on making headway on Nadiya's case, but... I just wasn't.

Maybe feeling my attention, Watson looked up from where he'd been curled at Ben's feet. He cocked his head in that inquisitive way of his, got up, gave an exaggerated stretch with his nubbed tail of a rump in the air, then plodded toward me.

Ben glanced down at the movement, his gaze following Watson's path, then offered me one of his shy smiles before returning to his notebook.

Watson looked at me expectantly when he reached the edge of the sofa.

"I don't have any t-r-e-a-t-s, if that's what you're hoping for." Watson was a smart old soul. If I wasn't careful, he'd learn the spelling of his favorite word, but as we hadn't crossed that bridge yet, the letters didn't elicit any frantic exuberance. Shifting the computer slightly so I could bend, I stroked his head.

Watson pressed his cheek into my palm.

My heart melted a little. "How do you do that? You're such a grumpy little thing, but you always know when my mind or soul is heavy, don't you?"

He twisted slightly so I had no choice but to scratch down his spine.

I chuckled. "I guess you get something out of it too, though, don't you?" With a final pat, I repositioned myself back on the sofa. I expected Watson to return to Ben's side, but to my surprise, he waddled a few steps closer to the fire, plopped down with a contented sigh, and cast me an unusually adoring glance before he closed his eyes.

Katie came down the steps, catching my attention just as I was about to return to the computer screen. She crossed the room to Ben, gave him a baked item, then headed directly to me, not needing to look around—I was a creature of habit, after all.

She handed me a twisted knot of bread as she sat down beside me. "Here, I tried a new variation once the breakfast rush stopped. These just came out of the oven." She laughed when Watson raised his head and whimpered. After tearing off a small section of her own roll, she tossed it to him.

He caught it, chewed, then lowered his head once more and fell back to sleep.

I shook my head at his laziness. "He really does think he's king of the world, doesn't he?"

"Isn't he?" Katie motioned toward the roll. "Well, try it. I'm pretty pleased and considering adding it as a staple as one of our savory selections. Do you think the horseradish is too much?"

"As if anything you do is ever too much." I motioned toward her sweater, which depicted a turkey wearing a Santa hat. "Except for your clothing choices. We just decorated for Thanksgiving yesterday, and you're already moving on to Christmas."

"Technically it's the holiday season—they all blend together. And as long as it's got a turkey on it, I think it's fair game. And don't get me started on the drab, baby-poo color palette of your wardrobe." She motioned to the roll again. "Well?"

I took a bite of it and instantly rolled my eyes back in my head as a groan escaped. Katie could say whatever she wanted about my wardrobe as long as she kept feeding me these. The sharp sting of the horseradish blended perfectly with Katie's new obsession of the bread with garlic in the dough. The sharp cheddar she'd folded inside was still melty, and the meat was crispy.

"I thought the black-forest ham gave it a little extra bite, as well as more salt to combine with the cheese, which goes well with the creaminess of the horseradish. The subtle underflavor of the garlic ties it all together." She took her own bite and nodded before talking with her mouth full. "I don't think the horseradish is too much. It burns your nose just a touch."

Following her lead, I took another bite, larger that time, and didn't bother swallowing. "I don't know about the burn, but this thing is heaven. At this rate, I'm okay if you use this garlicky bread for everything else you create from this point on."

She laughed again. "I'll use it as the crust on the next batch of lemon bars and see if you still say that."

I shuddered at the thought. Although, if anyone could pull it off, it would be Katie.

We polished off the rest of our rolls before she spoke again, this time concern lacing her words. "Are you hurting about Branson?"

I'd slept in that morning, trying to recoup from my exhaustion and only had a few moments before opening to fill Katie in on the events of the previous night.

"No." I reconsidered. "Maybe a little, at least in the back of my mind. We wouldn't have worked out. I have no doubt of that. I'm glad I didn't allow things to go further. It wouldn't have been fair to either of us, but I did hope we'd settle into friendship. But... I don't think that's going to happen. At least not with the strain of Chief Briggs's vendetta against me."

Katie let out a growl that almost resembled Watson's. "What is that about anyway? Talk about unfounded bias."

I shrugged but didn't reply. Branson had been right. Though my father would've handled things with more respect and in a smoother manner than Chief Briggs, I had no doubt he would've felt the same about a civilian doing what I was doing. Granted, I also knew he would've seen me as the exception, but that would have been because I was his daughter and he had faith in me. Chief Briggs had no such ties.

Though it had played around the periphery of my thoughts and emotions all morning, talking about it brought Branson front and center, which wasn't helpful or fun, so I shoved it back. "He's not who I've been thinking about this morning." I angled the computer so Katie could see the screen. "Since we couldn't dig up anything about our poacher brothers last night, I figured I'd start with Nadiya, try to discover a lead that would help clear her name." I sighed. "I'm finding just the opposite."

Katie's brown eyes widened as she straightened and scooted closer. "Really? What have you found?"

"Nothing that links her to the poachers, obviously, but quite a few things that make me think she might be capable of what Branson said. Just a scroll through her Facebook page was quite enlightening." I slid my finger over the track pad of the laptop, slow enough that Katie could read the comments on Nadiya's social media posts.

"Wow!" Katie lowered to a whisper as her eyes skimmed the screen. "Leo wasn't kidding about her being passionate. Granted, a lot of these aren't things she wrote herself, just memes that she's shared from other pages."

True enough. "Maybe so, but if she's sharing them, they obviously match how she feels." I scrolled a little further until I found a post from a couple of weeks before. "Check this one out."

The image was a cartoon of an elephant and rhinoceros sitting in high-backed armchairs in front of a fireplace. On the walls around them were the mounted heads of humans, each wearing a variety of hunters' hats. Above the image, Nadiya had typed, *If only every poacher could get what they deserved. How I'd love to visit a room like this.*

Katie grimaced. "Wow. That's..." She cocked her head, reminding me of Watson only moments before. "Although, if it weren't for the murder yesterday, would you really think twice about this? It doesn't seem that out of character for a park ranger to feel this way."

"Maybe so." I'd considered that as well. "If it was just one or two, but, Katie"—I met her gaze—"this goes on for months and months, posts like these. It's not just once when she was angry or something. Almost all of her social media accounts follow this line of shares and comments."

"Sure, but like I said, she's a park ranger, and..." Katie shook her head and let out a heavy sigh. "But I can't see Leo posting things like this. Maybe a comic like that every once in a while, but never with the hate and the tone of the comments that she's demonstrating. And we both know how angry and passionate Leo can get about poaching."

I nodded. "That's where I'm coming from as well. And..." I clicked on another tab. "Look at all the groups she belongs to. All of them are animal-rights groups, which isn't bad, obviously, but a lot of them are extremist." I judged Katie's expression before clicking one more tab. "And then there's this."

Katie read for several moments before she let out

another sigh and leaned back against the couch. "That's public record?"

I nodded again. "Yeah. And it came up pretty quickly, so chances are there's more." I'd found three separate arrests on Nadiya's record. Two charges of assault. "She wasn't convicted on any of them, but... they're there, *multiple* charges. And that suggests a pattern."

Katie blinked, suddenly looking tired. "Still, we're talking murder here."

"Patterns escalate. Most people don't just wake up and decide to kill someone out of the blue."

"You know that's not how it always works." She sounded skeptical. "We've seen it ourselves enough lately— crimes of passion where someone wasn't planning on murdering someone. They just... do, or whatever."

"That's not what it was with Max." Though it hadn't shaken me, I could picture Athena and me discovering his body perfectly. "He was shot right between the eyes, and his body was specifically taken to the statues of the sheep. It was intentional."

Katie was unusually silent for a moment, then shrugged. "I can't argue with that. It doesn't mean Nadiya is guilty, but..."

"There's one more thing." I clicked on the final tab, which opened to a link on Nadiya's Twitter feed.

Katie leaned forward once more and then groaned. She looked at the picture of the beautiful woman holding up a blue ribbon in one hand and a rifle in the other. "She's a master marksman."

"Yep. Seems kind of strange to me that someone so against hunting would be skilled with the gun."

"For self-defense?" The false hope in Katie's tone was clear.

I tapped the blue ribbon. "That's not what this says to me."

"No. Me neither."

"It all adds up to a pretty incriminating picture." I shut the laptop, feeling sick. "All abstract and nothing definitive, obviously. But when you put it together with what Branson told me last night, that she was arrested *in* her truck, *with* the murder weapon, and blood and mud that looked like drag marks in her truck bed, it would've been negligent for the police *not* to charge her with Max's murder."

"No kidding." Just as she was about to sink farther into the sofa, Katie straightened once more, her eyes brightening. "But from what you've said, that Max guy was huge. Nadiya is built like a cheerleader. You saw her in that pink panther getup. How in the world could she drag a man that size?"

And again, I'd thought the same thing. "Cheerleaders are strong, and I bet most park rangers are too." Then I went a step further. "And... maybe... she didn't do it by herself. Though if she was caught driving away from dropping off Max's body at Sheep Island, you'd think whoever helped would still be with her."

Katie gaped at me.

"What?" I saw accusation in her eyes.

"The way you're talking. It sounds like you've decided that Leo is wrong, that Nadiya did kill Max."

"No, I haven't. I..." I paused, considering. "Maybe I have." Clearly I did. Though I'd not let myself solidify that thought. But it would explain the sick feeling in my gut.

I waited for Katie to argue, to offer some other explanation, but she didn't. Finally she gestured toward the closed computer. "Do you think Leo knows all of this?"

"I was wondering about that. It's hard to imagine that

he does and for him not to bring any of it up last night." I hated the way I was thinking. "Unless he was trying to protect Nadiya."

Katie shook her head instantly, her curls flying. "No way. If Leo thought she did this, he wouldn't cover for her. *And*, he respects you, *believes* in you. If he knew all of this, there's no way he'd ask you to investigate. I mean"—she gestured at the computer again—"you found this in a matter of minutes. He knows you're not an idiot." Some of her dogmatism faded, leaving her sad. "He's going to be devastated."

"Are they together... romantically?" I hadn't really planned on asking, but the answer would affect things.

Katie's brows furrowed. "Who?"

"Leo and Nadiya?" I tried to keep the *isn't that obvious* out of my tone and failed.

"No. Absolutely not." Again with the headshake and then once more with the shoulder slump. "I mean... I did consider it the other night when I met Nadiya for the first time. The way she looks, she'd be hard for any man to ignore. And she and Leo have the whole love-of-nature thing in common. But... no, I don't think he's looking at anyone else like that."

Anyone else? That was as close as Katie had ever gotten to confirming my suspicions that there was something going on between the two of them. I put my hand on her knee. "Are you sure you're not just seeing what you want to see?"

She looked at me, puzzled. "Surely you don't think Leo had anything to do with this."

I flinched. "No, of course not. I mean..." It was time to rip off the Band-Aid. I'd been wondering for months, been getting mixed signals and clues from both of them. Might as well get all cards on the table. "It's okay, you don't have to hide it anymore. I know you and Leo are together, that you've been trying to keep it under wraps, probably not wanting me to feel like the third wheel. So it makes sense you may not want to think he has ulterior motives as far as Nadiya is concerned, but I think we have to..." My words trailed off at the expression of utter bafflement on her face.

"What are you talking about? Leo and I aren't together." Katie shuddered. "Gross. I love him, but he's my brother. Well... *like* a brother, obviously. But we've never..." She shuddered again. "Gross!"

There was no doubt that Katie was being completely honest, and I just stared at her. I'd been so sure. Well, no, I hadn't been, but there'd been moments. "Katie, Leo calls you all these endearments—sweetie, honey, all that kind of stuff. The way he looks at you, and he rubs your shoulders or touches your arm. He only does that with you, not with me. You're special."

She rolled her eyes. "And you're an idiot."

I flinched again. "What?"

"He's only had eyes for you since the moment he met you. You know that."

"No. He..." Why was I denying it? Leo had made it very clear he had feelings for me when we met. I'd had them for him. "Katie, that was months ago. And it ended nearly a year ago. As soon as it looked like Branson and I were... whatever we were doing..."

"Exactly." This time, Katie grabbed my knee. "You know Leo—he was doing the gentlemanly thing. He expressed interest—you said you wanted friendship. So... that's what he gave you."

I sat there dumbfounded. Though, in truth, I was only partially dumbfounded. Just like there had been moments that I'd observed with him and Katie—though he never called me any sweet names or touched me in the way he did Katie—there'd still been moments... where I felt something between us, some tension, something... I'd shoved it away, ignored it.

Katie released my knee but gave it a couple of pats before she pulled her hand away. "I really thought you knew."

I didn't answer. I couldn't.

She leaned a little closer, tilting her head so her hair fell in a short curtain around her shoulders. "Do you also not know that *you* have feelings for *him*?"

"Katie, I do not. I..." Couldn't finish that statement either, it seemed. Maybe I did. There was no *maybe* about it; I knew I did. But I'd been shoving those away and ignoring them with a passion that rivaled Nadiya's social media posts.

Katie stretched out her hand and tapped one of the earrings that were made up of a chain of silver corgis Leo had given me on the opening night of the bookshop. "You never take these off."

Dear Lord, I really was an idiot.

Branson had pointed out the same thing about the earrings months ago. But I'd told him, and myself, that it was because Leo was a friend and because I loved corgis. All of which was true. But there was more to it than that.

I met Katie's gaze, and she chuckled and smiled sadly. "Oh, Fred. How many bodies have you stumbled across? And I don't think I've ever seen you look quite as terrified as you do right now."

It was a true statement. So very, very true. "I... I don't know what to do with any of this."

She shrugged. "Who says you have to do anything with it? At least right now."

"But, Leo…"

"Leo's fine." She smiled. "He's head over heels for you, but he's fine. He's sweet and kind, but he's also strong. And while maybe he's not pursuing anyone else, he's also not putting his life on pause for you either." She shrugged. "That's part of why I was wondering if maybe he was moving on when I saw Nadiya. I don't think he is, but… I suppose there's a chance."

I most definitely did not know what to do with *that*.

So I shoved it away as well. As always, I focused on what I did much better than feelings and romantic relationships. "First things first. Nadiya. Gotta figure her out."

Though Katie clucked her tongue and shook her head, her voice brightened. "Of course." She gave a little chuckle and stood, waking Watson in the process. "Where are you going to start?"

Leo was probably the best place to begin, but pushing the other matter aside or not, I wasn't quite ready to cross that bridge. So I'd start with second best. "Delilah." I stood and smoothed out my skirt. "However, I think I'm going to require fortification in the way of another one of those heavenly rolls you just made, and another dirty chai." I turned to Watson. "Come on, buddy. Delilah loves you, so *we've* got work to do. I'll even give you a treat in prepayment."

Though he'd been blinking heavy eyes, at his favorite word, he brightened, gave a little happy yip, a hop, and hurried over to the base of the stairs, prancing back and forth as he turned toward Katie and me, clearly wondering why we were moving so slowly.

NINE

After a second of Katie's heaven-filled garlic rolls and a dirty chai, I left the Cozy Corgi. With Watson at my side, I reminded myself that I was well-slept, well-fed, well-caffeinated and accompanied by my not-so-secret-weapon of fur, grump, and cuteness. I might have some personal qualms with Delilah Johnson, but they were just that —*personal*. They shouldn't interfere if she could possibly help me clear an innocent woman from murder charges. Or... interfere in getting facts that might help Leo accept that his friend and coworker—or secret crush, *whatever* she was to him—was guilty.

Bundled in my jacket, scarf, and positive self-talk, we crossed to the other side of Elkhorn Avenue. I'd anticipated seeing Anna and Carl Hanson in the window of Cabin and Hearth, always ready and waiting for gossip to enter their front door, but instead, noticed Jetsam sitting behind the glass door of Paws, staring at us forlornly. I gave the redheaded corgi a finger wave and kept going.

Within four steps, I was pulled to an abrupt halt by Watson's leash. I looked back only to find him straining to get to Jetsam.

The sight was enough to make me wonder if I'd overdosed on caffeine and was seeing things. I dismissed the notion quickly. It was impossible to have too much caffeine. Clearly I'd simply not had enough.

Watson gave another tug and pulled me closer to the pet shop. To my utter amazement, when I followed him, Watson pressed his nose against the glass. Jetsam mimicked his gesture.

"You actually want to go in there?" I thought I was pretty good at understanding what Watson desired at all times, but I had to be misreading things. True, he and Paulie's two crazy corgis had formed... not a friendship, more an understanding that led to mutual respect, but never in a million years would I have believed Watson might initiate contact.

Watson glanced back at me with a pitiful whimper, then turned around with another tug. Clearly he wanted to keep me guessing.

"Okay, then." I shrugged and headed toward the door. "Remember you brought this on yourself."

When we walked into Paws, Jetsam not only didn't go insane at the sight of Watson, he barely moved. I had to lift my skirt to keep from tripping as I stepped over him. And while there was the ever present bubbling of aquariums, squawk of birds, and whirl of hamster wheels, there was no onslaught of barking from the back, no rush of Flotsam hurrying through the shop to meet us.

When I noticed Pearl wandering over from a couple of feet away, I decided she was the reason Watson had demanded we stop in. However, after a quick greeting to her, Watson pressed his nose to Jetsam's just as he had through the window and then nearly bowled me over when he gave the other corgi a lick.

"Oh, hey, Winifred." I'd been so distracted by the dogs,

I'd not even bothered to look toward the counter, where Paulie gave me a weak smile and sounded nearly as forlorn as Jetsam looked. Athena was with him behind the counter, and if I wasn't mistaken, was just pulling back from an embrace.

I gave another quick glance toward the dogs. With Pearl nuzzled against him, Watson had laid down beside Jetsam, their backs pressed together. Baffled, I released my hold on his leash and turned back to my friends. "Hi. Sorry to interrupt. We were walking by and Watson practically demanded we stop in."

"Did he?" Paulie's voice shook, and a tear rolled down his cheek. "He must've known."

Athena lifted a hand and rubbed his back.

The only possibility slammed into me. Paulie clearly upset, Jetsam heartbroken, and Watson acting in a very un-Watson-like manner. Even so, I took a final glance around the shop, hoping to be proven wrong. But no chubby, tricolored corgi emerged. I almost couldn't bring myself to ask. "Is Flotsam...?" No, I *couldn't* bring myself to ask if he was dead. I just couldn't.

Paulie nodded, started to speak, then sucked in a breath and got lost to tears.

Athena shifted so her arm went all the way around him and pulled Paulie into her side as she spoke softly to me. "Flotsam got really sick this morning, apparently. He's at the vet. Paulie called me a little while ago, and I came right down."

It wasn't what I'd expected to hear, so it took a moment to process. "He's sick?"

Paulie's bloodshot brown eyes flashed up at me.

I realized I'd sound relieved and adjusted my tone as I hurried forward. "Paulie, I'm so sorry. I know how horrible it is when one of our babies is sick." I reached over the counter and placed my hand on his, rubbing him as Athena continued to hold him tight. "What's wrong with him?"

Paulie shook his head, and though he slammed his eyes shut, a fresh wave of tears began.

Athena cast him a hesitant glance, then refocused on me. "They're not sure. From what Paulie says, it sounds like it was really sudden. They're wondering if he got into something poisonous or"—she cast another look at Paulie, and her tone became questioning—"if he might've had a stroke?" When Paulie nodded, she continued, "Sounds like Flotsam has to stay at the clinic for tests to be run and remain under observation until he's stable."

Paulie nodded again in confirmation.

Most of my relief faded at the dire news, and with a grateful look back at Watson, who was still cuddled up with Jetsam and Pearl, I released Paulie's hand so I could make my way around the counter and wrap him in a hug as well.

Paulie broke, sobbing and shaking, and my heart broke right along with him. His corgis might still drive me the tiniest bit insane, but I'd grown fond of them, and Paulie had become a dear friend. I knew he loved his boys as much as I loved Watson. Athena and I exchanged sorrowful glances. Though they didn't fall, tears glistened on her long dark lashes.

I didn't know how much time passed, but we stayed that way until Paulie calmed and his breathing returned to normal. Finally, once more under control, he gave himself a shake and cleared his throat. "I shouldn't break down like this. I need to believe that things are going to be fine. I'm just so..." His trembling fingers reached out and grasped the edge of the counter for support, but he didn't finish speaking.

Athena had resumed rubbing Paulie's back, and though she addressed me, her gaze remained on him. "I was about to contact you earlier, Fred, when I got Paulie's call." When he gave a small nod, Athena focused on me. "I haven't been able to find anything revolutionary about Sid or Eddie, at least nothing that wasn't already public knowledge. In fact, there's not a single report or article that connects the two of them. Which, we know that they were. You said yourself that their relationship had soured when Sid changed their agreement on the drug distribution. So you already know more than what I could find."

"I was afraid of that." I too glanced at Paulie, making sure he was okay to talk about other things. His tears had stopped, so I took that as a good sign. Maybe puzzling over other things would distract him. "We've not been able to find anything either. Although, since you and I found Max's body, I switched to researching him and his brother instead of Sid and Eddie. But I'm not having any luck there either."

Athena's gaze turned shrewd. "Well, that's what's interesting." She grimaced. "Not interesting, so much as *frustrating*. I've been looking into them as well, of course. It's been a day and a half since you and I discovered his body. That's why I was going to contact you a little bit ago, because the police finally released his last name. They claimed they were having trouble getting in contact with the nearest kin to give notice of death. Someone other than his brother, obviously. But I don't believe it took that long."

"I'm afraid that's my fault." I felt a flicker of my temper ignite, which was preferable to the sorrow and worry over Flotsam. "It's hardly a secret that Susan and Chief Briggs don't appreciate me looking into murders." *And occasionally Branson*—I kept that thought to myself. "It seems that

Briggs has decided to make things as difficult as possible for me to do so."

I started to fill them in on Branson's and my conversation, but it felt too personal in a way. And considering Paulie's state, also a bit inappropriate.

"As you know, Chief Briggs considers Paulie part of my *Scooby Gang*, as he calls us." I glanced at Paulie, hoping for a flicker of a smile. He'd been so lonely and desperate for friends, I'd hoped the reference would bring him a bit of happiness. He only winced. "He knows how close you and Paulie are, Athena, so I would imagine he assumes anything you know, I will know."

She nodded. "I guarantee that you're right." She shrugged. "Although, I can't let you take *all* the credit. You know firsthand that I've historically not had the best relationship with a few of the higher-powered members of the town council. Chief Briggs is most definitely in their pocket, and vice versa. There's never been any love lost between him and me."

"With the vacancies that have opened up recently, I hope that will be changing." Two members of the town council had been murdered a few months ago.

"Dream on." Athena waved me off. "Anyway, Max's last name is Weasel. So Max and Jim Weasel."

I cocked an eyebrow. "Weasel?"

She chuckled. "Yep, can't make these things up. But I've not had the chance to see what I can find out about them. I quite literally just got the call right before I came down here."

"Well... it's a place to start." And more than I had before.

I was tempted to bring up Nadiya, see if either of them had any interactions with her and be able to share something that might be enlightening, ask Athena to do some deeper research on her as well, but it seemed rather cold to keep going when Paulie was rightfully so upset. Chances were low he'd had much interaction with Nadiya. I knew Delilah found Paulie rather repulsive, and if Nadiya was part of her new Pink Panthers club, I figured she would feel similarly. I could always call Athena later to see if she'd mind adding another name to her research.

When I became aware that we'd been quiet for an awkwardly long time, I glanced at three curled-up dogs and decided I'd done all I could do. I pulled Paulie into another quick hug. "I'm so sorry, sweetie. Let me know the minute you have an update. I'm sure Flotsam will be back to his crazy self in no time."

Paulie choked out a wet-sounding laugh and nodded into my shoulder.

"In the meantime, let me know if you need anything, you hear? Anything at all."

Another nod, and then he released me.

Before I stepped away, I gave Athena's hand a squeeze, and she nodded.

When I picked up Watson's leash and he nuzzled Pearl goodbye and gave a goodbye lick to Jetsam, I felt tears threaten once more.

My thoughts were still on Paulie and Flotsam as Watson and I walked the short distance to Old Tyme Photography. The thought of one of Paulie's dogs being sick made me hurt for my friend, but also made me fear for Watson. The concept of loss and knowing that a solitary day could make such an impactful change on a life had been driven home years ago by my father's murder, but it was a fact that I did my best to ignore as much as possible. I assumed most people did as well. If we kept that front and center, who would be able to function?

I blamed those heavy thoughts for both causing me to bump into someone when I entered the photography shop and for not recognizing the woman instantly. I didn't get a chance to apologize before Delilah's voice drew my attention.

The stunning redhead was behind an old-fashioned camera at the far end of the narrow shop, with a family of four—consisting of a mother, father, toddler daughter, and infant son—all dressed in black-and-white striped prison garb and standing behind a false wall of bars. Delilah turned from the camera and waved. "Watson, darling! I'm so thrilled you came to see me." She lifted her blue eyes to me, and I caught a playful glint. "And you too, Fred. Please don't leave—let me wrap up here. I've been meaning to talk to you." The glint faded slightly. "Although, there appears to be a line for the pleasure of my presence."

Unsure what to say, I just gave a little wave back.

Delilah returned her attention to the family. "Now remember, you're in the slammer. You're supposed to look serious and depressed." She took on a flirtatious tone. "And, Mr. Porter, the camera loves you, but if you can't quit giggling, you're going to ruin the shoot."

"Please keep your filthy animal away. I'd rather it not urinate on my shoe."

At the sneer from the woman beside me, I glanced down at Watson, who was merely sniffing the hem of the woman's skirt. I pulled his leash just a touch tighter. "Watson is house-trained. I promise you he won't..." My words fell away as I looked up into the thin face of Ethel Beaker. We'd not had any interaction before, but she'd inserted herself in the top slot of the town council after her husband had been killed, and her daughter-in-law and I had never seen eye to eye. I cleared my throat. "Sorry that I bumped into you. I was a little distracted."

"I noticed." She sidestepped farther and lifted her nose in the air.

A tense silence fell between us. I should've counted that as a blessing, as it was certainly preferable to anything Ethel would have to say to me. But being who I was, my tongue seemed to work on its own accord, more concerned about filling the void than common sense. "How's Carla and..." I drew a complete blank on Carla's husband and baby's names. "I haven't seen her in months, not since..." For as much as my tongue wanted to talk, it was doing a rather remarkable job of not finishing a thought. Though, that was probably wise.

Ethel cocked a severely shaped eyebrow. "Since she shut down her coffee shop in shame? The location of my husband's death?" She sniffed. "Since then?"

I felt my cheeks burn, and I wished that Watson would prove me wrong and urinate on her shoe, or mine, or anything that would provide distraction. "Yes... since... around that time, yes." And then, by some supernatural power of awkwardness given to all booklovers, I kept going. "I've noticed that there's no For Sale sign or anything in the windows of Black Bear Roaster. Is Carla hoping to reopen?"

Ethel's other eyebrow came up to the higher level of the first. If I wasn't wrong, she almost looked impressed with my ability to stick my foot in my mouth. "Worried about competition?"

"No. No, of course not. It's just..." I realized how that sounded. And though it was true, at least in terms of bakery items—there was no competition between the prepackaged stuff Carla had served and the carby bits of heaven Katie crafted—I bit my tongue, finally, and refocused on Watson.

He was smirking. Although he might've simply had a spot of flatulence, I wasn't really sure, but I was willing to bet he was smirking.

And, *dear Lord*, was Delilah ever going to get done with the photo shoot?

I thought that Ethel Beaker and I were done talking, that we'd reached an implied agreement to keep things unspoken. But she suddenly shifted toward me once more, leaning her elaborately dressed elbow on the glass countertop. "And you, Winifred? How are you finding our little town? Business going well?"

Her tone had taken on a friendly, conversational quality

that elicited fear. Unable to find the trap, or a way out, I answered honestly. "I'm loving it. Estes Park is the most beautiful place in the world, and I'm surrounded by wonderful people and a store full of books... not to mention pastries. What more could a girl want?"

Ethel's smile grew. "From what I've observed, it seems pretty clear what you're after."

"Oh?" I'd already been certain I was wading into quicksand, but if there'd been any doubt, that rushed it away. I truly couldn't fathom where she was leading, outside of the looking into murders.

She nodded. "I've heard through the rumor mill that you're a divorcée."

Okay, definitely not about murders. I simply nodded.

Ethel leaned forward slightly, as if getting ready to gossip with a girlfriend. "I can't blame you for looking for a replacement. Estes Park has its share of eligible, handsome bachelors." Her gaze flicked toward Delilah. "And I suppose some that are neither eligible nor bachelors, but still."

I swallowed, wished I could think of a way to stop wherever this was leading, but the only thing that came to mind was turning tail and running as fast as I could to the door. Pride, stupidly, held me in place.

"Interesting thing is, you—" When she looked back at me, her gaze traveled slowly down my body and back up, leaving no question that she found me lacking "—caught the crown jewel. The man every woman in town had been longing for and throwing themselves after, to be quite honest."

Branson. *That's* where we were going. "I wasn't trying to catch anything, Ms. Beaker."

Her smile turned wicked. "Come now, we both know better. What I can't understand is why in the world a woman like you"—she gave yet another flick down my body —"would risk playing such a dangerous game with a man so completely out of her league." She chuckled. "But then again... it's working, isn't it? You've got our dashing sergeant wrapped around your finger. No one gave you enough credit. You're just as much of a manipulating temptress as this jezebel over here." Without looking away, she cocked her head toward Delilah.

I was almost relieved at the place we'd landed. It allowed my indignation to ignite my temper. "I can assure you, none of what you're saying is factual, nor... is it any of your business."

The second the words left my lips, I realized my mistake. I'd given her exactly what she wanted.

Ethel leaned in for the kill, her voice cold and filled with disgust. "You think you're so much better than everyone else, don't you? Let me tell you something, *you're not*. And one day, hopefully sooner rather than later, Sergeant Wexler will wake up and realize that he's a much higher caliber of person than you are. You're arrogant, abrasive, entitled, and nothing more than a joke. The whole town has watched you yank a good man back and forth as you've dragged his affection through the mud. And soon he'll wake up and realize that he can do so, *so* much better than the likes of you."

"Let me guess, that someone better would be *you*?" From out of nowhere, Delilah appeared between us on the other side of the counter and smiled sweetly at Ethel. "Darling, if Winifred is out of Branson's league, then you are on a completely different planet. And..." She leaned forward, mimicking the position Ethel had taken only moments before, and when she gave her version of the wicked smile, she made it clear that she was the master between the two of them. "Talk about robbing the cradle. I know you must spend a small fortune on moisturizer, but just between us girls, it's not *that* good."

"You sleazy, hateful..." Ethel bristled and drew herself up to her full height before glancing over at the tourist family who were changing their children back into their normal clothes. When she spoke again, she was under control. "I won't take much of your time, Miss Johnson. I simply came here to tell you that if you insist on continuing gang behavior, it will be brought up at the town council and ordinances will have to be passed. Ones with financial or licensure consequences, or both."

Delilah started to retort, then blinked. "I have no idea what you're talking about. Gang behavior?"

"I'm surrounded by imbeciles." Ethel pointed to a pink silk jacket that was thrown over a chair a few feet away. White embroidery over the back read *Pink Panthers*, and just the topmost portion of a similarly embroidered panther head was visible. "You and your gang of hussies, roaming the streets of our town all wearing the same outfit of your exclusive club? That looks like gang behavior to me."

Delilah looked from Ethel to the jacket, then back again. Her expression revealed utter bewilderment, then shock, and then she threw back her head and laughed. Finally she looked back at Ethel. "What's the matter, you old witch? Jealous your application into the club got rejected?"

"As if I'd ever—"

She pointed to the door. "Get out of my shop." All humor left Delilah's eyes and tone. If I'd ever wondered if Delilah was capable of murder, all doubts fled. "You have three seconds before I throw you out myself."

To my surprise, Ethel moved instantly, but her tone

didn't waver as she gave a dark hiss. "Remember, you've made your choice. You'll have to live with the consequences. Might want to check your mail for an official notification."

"Do that, please! I've been wanting to throw some money at a lawyer." She waved at Ethel's retreating form, and then with a smile as sweet as candy, she turned back to the tourists who were staring wide-eyed from their pace at the counter. "And that's why you'll see the signs that say don't feed the wildlife. They can turn rabid and try to take over the town."

The family chuckled awkwardly, paid for their order, and agreed to come back in a couple of hours to pick up their tintype photograph souvenirs.

Finally, Delilah looked at me, and when she did, all pretense left her features and voice. She almost sounded as if we were friends when she spoke. "What did you do to her? I figured she worshiped the ground you walked on. Didn't you solve her husband's murder?"

"I did. Yes. But..." I shrugged. "I assumed she hated me because of Carla. I had no idea she had feelings about Branson."

Delilah waved me off with a laugh. "Oh please, it's no secret that Ethel hates her daughter-in-law more than she could possibly hate you. And as far as Branson"—she shrugged—"I don't really know what that's about. I can't imagine she actually has any designs on ensnaring him for herself, but she isn't wrong. After all the women who've tried to capture Branson's affections, it's a scandal that you're the one who succeeded. And even more so that you know how to play him like a fiddle." She cast a similar appraising glance over me as Ethel had before, but there was no disgust or judgment behind her eyes. If anything, she seemed impressed. "I say, go you! Woman power!" She shook her fist in the air with a laugh.

Though it was a completely different reaction, it was the same interpretation. "I am *not* trying to play him like a fiddle. Nor am I trying to jerk him around. I don't understand why people keep insinuating that. We've gone on some dates. That's all. That's what dating is, to decide if you're compatible, decide if you're meant to be together and make a good team. Sometimes that's clear instantly, and others, like... with us... it takes a while to figure out."

When Delilah smiled, there was no teasing or any of her normal edge. "That's actually how it is with you, isn't it?" She didn't wait for a response and patted my hand. "I knew I liked you. You're real. And while we're very different people, you and me, we have a couple things in common. We're blunt, and we're smart. And we don't pretend to be anything other than what we are." She pointed her thumb over at the jacket. "Any chance you'd like to be a Pink Panther?"

I nearly choked. "Are you serious?"

She nodded. "Very."

Despite myself, some middle school part of me was flattered. I'd just been invited to sit at the cool girls' table. It only took a moment to remember my qualms with Delilah Johnson. "That's kind of you. But no. Thank you. As I'm sure you've noticed, I have my hands full right now."

She surprised me a second time when I noticed a flash of genuine hurt in her beautiful blue eyes. "I don't meet your standards, yes, I know." She sloughed off whatever hurt she felt as easily as I imagined she made the men she wanted fall at her feet. "But that's okay. You meet mine in a lot of ways." As if putting on battle armor, she walked over, lifted the jacket off the chair, and slipped into it, before walking around the counter and kneeling in front of Watson. "Sorry, hot stuff. Wasn't trying to ignore you."

As before, Watson didn't lose his mind over her but seemed to thoroughly enjoy her attention without the promise of a treat.

I couldn't help myself. "So that jacket isn't part of the Halloween costume. Your group actually wears them all the time?"

Without taking her attention off Watson, she nodded. "We do. I'm surprised you haven't seen us wearing them around town. I was always obsessed with the movie *Grease* and wanted to be a Pink Lady. This is my version. Personally, I think it's better. Panthers are sexy."

I couldn't figure her out, and I discovered I rather enjoyed that aspect of Delilah. Despite my personal judgments of how she chose to engage in her affairs, her quite literal affairs, I found myself liking the woman. "Well, I didn't know about the jackets, but I did know about your group, and that's why I'm here, because Nadiya was one of you, right?"

"*Was?*" Delilah looked up, stroked Watson another couple of seconds, and then stood. "Nadiya *is* a Pink Panther. She's not dead. And she's why I wanted to come see you, obviously. I figured Leo was going to ask you to look into Nadiya's innocence. And honestly, as much as it seems you enjoy showing the police that you can outsmart them, I figured it wouldn't take much, if any, convincing." She leaned against the counter as Ethel had before but without the feeling she was laying a trap.

"I'm not trying to show the police that I—"

"None of that. It wasn't an insult." She cut me off and gave me a meaningful stare. "I'm sure that your main reason is because you wanted to clear several people important to you. But don't pretend that you don't enjoy getting the job done. Especially when we all know that certain members of the police force and the town council don't like you sticking your nose in the middle of things."

As much as I wanted to deny her accusation, I couldn't. It was true. And from her tone, it wasn't really an accusation. "Okay, then, I am looking into Nadiya, but everything I've found about her makes her look guilty. Honestly, it seems like the police are on the right track."

Delilah scowled, and an offended quality entered her husky voice. "Why? Because she's passionate about animal rights? Because she's been in the police's face about all the poaching in the few months that she's been here?"

"No. It's because..." I was about to list the litany of reasons I'd found on the internet and to tell her the things Branson had confided to me about the night Nadiya was arrested, then thought better of it. "*You* wanted to see me, Delilah. Was it only to ask me to look into it? You said yourself, you already figured I was. So why did you really want to see me? Do you have any proof of Nadiya's innocence? You were with her that night, you and all the Pink Ladies were going around for Halloween, right? Can you or one of your group be her alibi?"

Her defensiveness fell away, and she shook her head in defeat. "No. We all split up after." For the second time, she touched my hand. Just when I thought she was about to pull away, she slipped her fingers around and held on. "What I said before was true. I do like you. I think you're smart, and I think you're honest. And I truly believe you're trying to help people, even if you do get a kick out of outsmarting the cops." Her lips twitched into what started to be a smile, but then she grew serious once more. "I'm sure of what you found on the internet. I know Nadiya's past. I know what she's passionate about. I know all the reasons she looks guilty. And I don't have one solitary thing to give you to say that she isn't. I wish to God I did. I'd be giving it to you, to the police, to whoever. But I don't."

That wasn't what I was expecting. Not at all. "Nothing? Then why did you want to see me?"

"Because I'm scared. For that very reason, the fact that I can't give you anything scares me. It's true Nadiya's only been here a short while, but she's become a very dear and trusted friend. She's become family to me, and the Pink Panthers are all the family she has. If you knew her, you'd love her."

Maybe she was right. Judging from the way Leo felt about her, it seemed to be an effect Nadiya had on people. Some of Delilah's words rang in my mind. "What do you mean the Pink Panthers are all the family she has?" Now that she mentioned it, I realized I'd not seen a single family connection on social media.

Delilah balked as if caught off guard, but hardened instantly. "That's Nadiya's business and has nothing to do with this."

"Maybe you're wrong. Anything you tell me might lead me to proving her innocence."

"It won't." She relaxed somewhat. "Listen, Fred, I just need to know that you're not going to give up. No matter what else you uncover about her or whatever *proof* you think you find that she did this, just keep looking. And if you need my help, I will do anything—*anything*. I'd be doing it now if I could think of something." She gave a sad laugh and shrugged once more. "Well, I guess I am. This is the only thing I thought of—begging you. She's innocent. I'd bet my life on it. But I also know that if you don't prove it, she'll go to jail for murder. When even her friends can't offer anything to clear her name, I don't know how I can rightly expect the police to think anything different than what they already do, especially when they already had a grudge against her to begin with." She was squeezing my hand so hard it nearly hurt. "But they're wrong, Fred. I swear to you. They are."

ELEVEN

Watson curled up in the passenger seat of the Mini Cooper as we drove out of downtown Estes Park. And though I didn't mention Leo's name, Watson must've been able to sense him, as he sat up straighter the closer we got to the national park. By the time the tollbooths, which resembled tiny narrow log cabins, at the entrance to Rocky Mountain National Park came into view, Watson had both forepaws perched on the passenger door and craned his head to see through the windshield.

"Your mamma might be stressed, but you're having a great couple of days, aren't you? Just an endless string of people you adore." Though I rolled my eyes at him, it was just for show. I loved how happy Watson was in Estes, despite his unrequested role of being the bookshop's mascot and therefore getting petted by strangers much more than he would choose if left to his own devices.

His eyes, wild with excitement, rolled my way, then back as they refocused on the tall silhouette in the tollbooth as we pulled up. Before I had the chance to come to a complete stop, Watson threw himself across my lap and shoved his nose through the crack in the window as I lowered it.

"Well, Watson Charles Page, when did you learn to drive?" Leo leaned out of the tollbooth window, and the two of them met in the space between, Leo's hands stirring up a cloud of fur and Watson whimpering, licking, and trembling all over.

The easy use of Watson's full name threw me off, and I used Leo's distraction to inspect him for a moment, thinking of what Katie had declared about Leo's feelings for me. I knew he adored Watson, but the fact that he remembered I'd given Watson my father's name, Charles, seemed a good bit of confirmation. I must've mentioned it in passing, though I didn't recall. But Leo had held on to the detail.

"What brings you two out?" Still lavishing attention on Watson, Leo glanced my way, his gaze hopeful. "Do you have news? Find something?"

Wishing I could've rewarded that optimism, I shook my head. "Just the opposite, sorry to say. I thought I'd talk to you in person if you have a few minutes."

Sure enough, his expression fell but didn't become unfriendly, and with the final scratch on Watson's cheek, he smiled, then motioned across the row of tollbooths toward the wide meadow at the base of the mountain. "My shift ends in ten minutes, and there's been nobody but those guys for the past few hours. Tourist season is officially over."

"The same is true at the bookshop. There wasn't..." My words trailed away as I followed his gesture. Though I'd grown up visiting Estes Park as a kid to spend time with my grandparents and extended family, and even after living in the town for a year, Estes Park still stole my breath away. Either end of the snowy meadow was filled with two clearly distinct herds of elk, each with massive bulls with crowns of antlers the king would be jealous over, guarding his large harem. And in the middle, a group of twenty or thirty bighorn sheep. So different from the life I'd lived in Kansas City. It was no wonder Leo was so passionate about the animals, or Nadiya for that matter.

Despite being held captive by the beauty, I sensed Leo's gaze on me and looked over to find that his smile had transitioned to something soft and wistful. "Spectacular, right?"

"Yeah, it really is."

That time he motioned in the other direction toward the ranger station, which was an actual log cabin that sat a little ways back from the tollbooths. "Meet you over there?"

"You bet." Watson didn't leave my lap until I pulled away from the tollbooth and Leo was no longer beside the window. As if offended, he whirled, bumping the steering wheel, and then leaped to the passenger seat. Once parked, I snapped Watson's leash onto his collar, and we exited the car. Though there were only a few yards to walk to the cabin, because of the risk of mountain lions, I'd learned not to take chances without a leash, unless we were in the middle of downtown. Although, mountain lions had been known to wander along Elkhorn Avenue from time to time as well.

Leo held open the door to the ranger station for Watson and me, and we entered. It was a small main room made up of a table and couch on one side and a computer desk in front of a large picture window looking out over the park entrance on the other. When I'd been in before, Leo had sat at the computer researching an owl feather I'd brought in. This time he motioned toward the sofa. As we sat, it gave a warning squeak. "Excuse the accommodations. We don't exactly have the budget to turn this place into the Ritz or anything." Leo's smile seemed forced, and he clutched his hands together as he propped his elbows on his knees.

I decided to dive right in. "The couch is fine. I don't

want to take too much of your time. I don't know what your plans are. I just thought I'd talk to you in person. See if you could give me some sort of lead, because everything I'm finding, Leo, only makes Nadiya seem more and more guilty."

"She isn't." He flinched, as if his biting tone surprised him as much as it had me. He instantly shook his head and apologized. "I'm sorry. I know it's not your fault. None of this is. And I'm not upset with you. If anything, I'm upset with myself. I've been trying to think of something, but I have no idea where to begin. But no matter what you found, she's innocent."

I believed Katie was right in what she said Leo felt for me, though I'd shoved the obvious away for a plethora of reasons, but with his defense of Nadiya, I was willing to bet I wasn't the only one he held feelings for. "Are you sure, Leo? Sometimes people have a whole separate life than what they present. I don't want you to be hurt at the end of this."

Though he tightened his lips, he didn't snap again. "I am sure. She's become a good friend, Fred. Beyond that, I just have that gut feeling, like the one you describe sometimes. I simply know, with everything in me, that she didn't do this."

"Okay then." I wasn't sure what else to say.

"You don't... have that feeling?" Again his tone took on that hopeful quality.

And again, I had to kill it. I shook my head. "No. I don't." As his shoulders slumped, I rushed ahead, for all the good it would do. "But I don't have a gut sense that she is guilty either." I left out what logic was telling me.

"That's something, I suppose."

Watson had been sniffing around the corners of the

room and came over to plop between Leo's feet. Automatically, Leo began stroking him.

Maybe the distraction of Watson would help as I laid out what I'd discovered so far. "I did quite a bit of research on Nadiya this morning. Do you want me to tell you what I found out, or since she's your friend, do you feel like that would be violating her privacy or something if you knew?"

"She's in jail for murder. I doubt she's too worried about privacy." His lips curved into a bit of a sneer before slipping away again. "Not that I can ask her, since the police still won't let me see her."

I imagined he'd been calling nonstop all day, probably hoping to wear them down, just like he'd hoped to convince them about the poaching. I started to suggest giving them some space, but then decided it wasn't my place to do so, and clearly I wasn't doing such a great job of navigating the police either. I let it pass and focused on why I'd come. "Okay, then, here it is. From what I found online, Nadiya is a member of several animal-rights groups and—"

"So am I! That doesn't mean—" Leo's voice rose, not in aggression, just in self-defense.

"Hold on." I held up a hand. "I'm not accusing you, and I'm not saying that animal-rights activism is wrong."

"I know. Sorry." He took a deep breath and let it out with a sigh. "Please continue. I'll remember that you're just the messenger and you're doing me a favor, doing Nadiya a favor. You can't help what you find out."

"I'm not so sure, especially at this point, whether I'd say I'm doing Nadiya any favors. From everything I've found, I'd call it a pretty open-and-shut case. At this point, I'm only looking into it for you. Because your gut tells you she's innocent." When he nodded, I continued. "Like I was saying, some of those animal-rights groups are the run-of-the-mill kind of organization, but others are fairly extremist. Even so, that in and of itself may not be that big of a deal, but it's a substantial puzzle piece. She's also a master marksman—I found photos with her holding first-place ribbons from shooting competitions. And there's nothing wrong with that, either. I'm not saying there is." I felt the need to say it all as quickly as possible. Leo's brows rose, but he didn't interrupt. "Just because she knows how to shoot and owns a gun doesn't mean she's a murderer. But it does fit with them finding her with the gun in the truck, and she would have the skill to shoot Max in the manner in which he was killed."

Leo looked like he was about to argue again, so I paused. After a moment he simply nodded.

I leaned forward, lowering my voice as if I was breaking bad news. Which, I suppose I was. I figured there was a good chance Leo had already known about the other details if he was as good a friend with Nadiya as he'd said, but she might not have shared the darker details of her past. "There have been no convictions, from what I can find, but Nadiya has had a few charges brought against her, including assault." I paused to judge his reaction, but he didn't give any. "Again, she wasn't convicted, but it seems to indicate that she has a propensity toward violence."

Leo only sighed again, gave Watson a final scratch on the head, and leaned back, sinking into the broken-down sofa.

I studied him, surprised. "You already knew all of this, didn't you?"

He nodded.

I wasn't sure if I'd ever been irritated with Leo before, but I was in that moment. "Then why didn't you tell me? That took me a few hours on the computer today. Not that I wouldn't have looked into it anyway, but if you know things, you need to be upfront with me."

He winced, looking abashed. "Sorry, again. I wasn't trying to hide it from you. I just wanted you to go into it with an unbiased opinion. Although I suppose that's stupid as I knew you'd find all that easily enough." Another wince. "I guess I was afraid if you knew, you'd say it was a waste of time. And it's not. Even with all that you just shared, I know that she's innocent."

Though my irritation didn't vanish, it hurt a bit to know that Leo would think I'd turn him down for any reason. "I don't know if it's going to be a waste of time or not. It sure looks like it, but if you're convinced, that's all I need. Katie too. You know we'll keep looking until we find something that either clears her name or..."

"Makes me accept that she did it?" He looked at me with a cocked brow.

I just nodded.

"Fair enough." He smiled and sounded a little more like his normal self. "I think that's all I know. Have you found anything else?"

I started to say *no*, but then changed my mind. "Do you follow Nadiya on social media? Like Facebook, Twitter, and such?"

He shrugged. "We're friends on there, but as you know, I don't spend much time on any of that junk."

"Okay then, tell me if you're aware of some of the feelings she expresses here." I pulled out my cell and tapped a couple of the social media icons, went to her profiles, and then handed the phone to Leo.

He took a few minutes, tapping back and forth between the various screens and scrolling to read her posts from the past. From the color draining from his face, I knew the

answer before he finally spoke. "I haven't seen these. And
—" He cleared his throat "—while Nadiya is very passionate, *very*, when we talk about it, she's never actually said
things such as this about people meeting the same end as
poached animals and such." He tapped a few more times,
then shook his head before returning the phone. "But...
that's kind of real-life, right? People say things online,
drastic things, that they would never say out loud."

"That's true. But I think a lot of people would argue
that the things people put on social media, even the ones
they wouldn't say out loud, reveal how they truly feel,
what's in their hearts and souls." I put the phone away and
softened my voice once more. "The thing I didn't find on
social media was any connection to her family. Delilah
mentioned that the Pink Panthers were the only family
Nadiya has."

"That's basically true." Leo nodded openly. "She's
estranged from her family."

I considered. "To the point that they wouldn't even
come to town when she's been arrested?"

"I doubt they know. Nadiya wouldn't want them
contacted." He shook his head sadly. "Sorry, Fred. I know
where you're going to go next, but it's not my story to tell.
It's Nadiya's."

"It might help her. You said yourself privacy isn't a
concern given the circumstance."

From Leo's expression it was clear he was debating, and
for a couple seconds I thought he was going to break. He
didn't and shook his head again. "Sorry. It wouldn't help,
and if you knew her story, I know you, of all people, would
sympathize and have her back."

Clearly arguing was pointless. I'd just have to trust that
Leo knew what he was talking about. Leo and Delilah.

Instead, I moved on to another issue that had been bothering me. "The thing that makes the least sense about this
whole thing, regardless of how Nadiya feels about poaching,
guns, and all of that, is the timing."

Leo's eyes grew hopeful once more.

"Hardly any time passed between the Cozy Corgi being
broken into and Max's murder. How did that happen? And
how would Nadiya know that he was a poacher?"

He groaned and his face fell once more. "That's easy.
Nadiya listens to police scanners. She would've heard when
dispatch communicated the break-in. If one of the police
mentioned the suspects name and description and
connected him to the sheep, then..." He finished with
a shrug.

Good grief, everything pointed to Nadiya Hameed.
Everything. "Leo, this is looking pretty cut-and-dried."

Somehow his large, muscled frame seemed to shrink,
trying to disappear in the sunken couch cushions. "I can't
accept that she would do this, Fred. I'm not wrong
about her."

I only considered for a moment. "Okay. We'll keep looking." Another thought had hit me driving up to the national
park, one that I was surprised hadn't occurred to Katie and
me as we'd gone over the things we'd found about Nadiya.
"I was wondering... I haven't researched how strict guide-
lines are being a park ranger, but I'm a little surprised with
her past that she got a position, especially here. I know
Rocky Mountain Park is one of the most coveted spots.
Maybe since she hasn't been convicted, her potential legal
trouble wasn't considered?"

He gave me a sheepish expression. "One of the higher-
ups in the National Park Service is a good friend of hers. He
pulled some strings."

Another hit! "Oh, Leo." I mimicked his expression and sank back into the couch. "This doesn't look good."

Leo just nodded.

Giving up on receiving attention, Watson wandered off, sniffing around the edges of the cabin again, and finally settling in to watch a chipmunk peering at him from the windowsill.

We sat in silence for quite a while, heaviness settling between us.

After a bit, I realized Leo was staring at a small row of lockers on the far side of the room. "What are you thinking?"

"I'm thinking I can't talk to Nadiya, can't get her side of things, so maybe we use her stuff, see if any of it will speak for her." As Leo spoke, he stood and walked toward the lockers. "Maybe we'll find something, who knows what, that might clear her name. We could check here and maybe her apartment."

That seemed like a long shot to me. If anything, that was the opposite of how it worked. You searched for hidden things to prove someone was guilty, or to find clues on what they were hiding, not prove their innocence. But I didn't have any other suggestions, and I couldn't bear to take more hope away from Leo. "You have a key to her locker?" I got up and crossed the room.

Watson left the chipmunk to its own devices and followed me.

Leo gave another sheepish expression, though this was accompanied by grin. "I know how to pick a lock, Fred."

"You do?" That didn't match my version of the Leo Lopez I knew.

He gave a nod and then turned back to the locker and got to work, offering no further explanation.

"*Should* you pick a lock?" My words echoed back to me from the night before, telling Branson I'd never broken the law.

He chuckled as he tinkered. "Don't act like you haven't snuck into places where you weren't supposed to be."

He had a point. Though, each of those times I'd walked the line of the law, if not the letter. Until now.

In less than a minute, the lock clicked, and we opened the rusty metal door with a squeak. Leo took a deep breath, as if he was getting ready to dive underwater, and began to sift through Nadiya's things.

There was nothing. At least nothing of interest. It was a jacket, a couple of scarves, gloves, a flashlight, a few snack items, and an extra pair of shoes, but nothing that proclaimed innocence or guilt.

"I guess that was a waste of time as well." Leo sighed and started to put the boots back but froze when the metal floorboard shifted under the weight of the boots. He leaned forward, inspecting. "I think there's something under here." That spark of hope sounded again.

I stepped nearer, looking over his shoulder as he pulled the thin piece of metal up. "I take it yours doesn't have a hidden compartment?"

"I don't know if it's so much of a hidden compartment as simply a loose bottom. With as old as everything is, I imagine if I lifted up mine, I'd be able to put something underneath it as well. I just never thought of—" He'd been moving slowly, clearly being careful not to cut himself on the rusty metal, but then he froze.

There, underneath the bottom portion of the locker, lying on the dusty hardwood floor, lay a gun.

We both stared at it, and for the billionth time that day,

as far as Nadiya was concerned, my heart sank again. "Good grief, how many guns does she have?"

"This doesn't mean..." Leo shook his head. When he spoke again, it was clear he was trying to convince himself as much as me. "It's just a gun, and nothing we didn't already know. The poacher was shot. Nadiya owns guns, legally I'm sure, since she's a master marksman. We... *already* knew she owned guns."

"But we didn't know she was hiding them in random places." I hadn't meant to say that out loud, and I rushed ahead, trying to fix it, not that it helped. "This doesn't prove she did anything wrong. Obviously she didn't shoot him with this gun. Even if it's illegal for her to have a gun *here,* the police already found the murder weapon in the cab of her truck with her." No... that didn't help at all.

There was a slam of a car door, which caused Watson to yelp and Leo and me both to flinch. Straightening, I looked out one of the windows and saw an older woman walking away from a run-down pickup truck.

Leo stood, then let out a curse. "Etta, crap!" He dropped to his knees and started shoving everything back into Nadiya's locker as fast as he could. "She's not on the schedule till tomorrow."

Katie and I had heard about Etta Squire many times over the months during our frequent dinners at Habanero's. She was another park ranger and liked to claim she'd been on staff since the mountains themselves were formed. Leo often said she was as lazy as a bear hibernating and as grumpy as a grizzly who'd just lost his dinner. It said a lot about the woman as Leo wasn't one to complain about people.

He'd just managed to click the lock back into place and

practically flung himself across the room when Etta opened the door.

"What are you still doing here, Leo? I thought you were off twenty minutes ago. You know I'm not going to approve overtime if..." Her bloodshot eyes widened when she saw me, then narrowed as her gaze flicked to Watson. "Oh. You two." She didn't bother with introductions, though. Apparently she knew who Watson and I were and clearly wasn't pleased by our presence.

"I'm not trying to get overtime, Etta. Fred and I were just... talking." Though Leo managed to make his voice sound completely normal at being caught breaking into Nadiya's locker, the same couldn't be said for the flush that rose to his cheeks.

"This isn't a—" Etta cut off her own words with a long, painful-sounding smokers cough and then sucked in a wheezing breath before refocusing on Leo. "This is a ranger station, *Mr. Lopez*, not a brothel. You need to keep your girl-friend elsewhere." She sneered down at Watson. "And her dog."

Watson didn't growl but once more made me believe he understood a great deal of what was said as he plopped down in front of her and lifted his muzzle defiantly.

If Leo had been red-faced before, it was nothing compared to the crimson that stained his cheeks then. "Fred's not my... we're not... Why are you here?"

"My fool sister is sick and needed me to pick up kibble for her nasty mutt. So I thought while I was out, I'd..." I could swear a blush rose to Etta's weathered cheeks as she motioned out the window toward the large bag of dog food in the back of her truck and then toward the computer. "That's not your business, boy." She finished with a snap in her tone. "Are you done here? I'm not approving overtime, and I need my privacy."

"Sure, Etta." Leo crossed to the computer desk and picked up our jackets, which we'd discarded over the chair. "We'll get out of your way. Have a good night. See you tomorrow."

Etta mumbled something low on the enthusiasm level, sneezed, and then began to hack again.

Despite the depression I thought Leo was slipping into about Nadiya when we'd found the gun, his eyes twinkled as he whispered to me after we closed the door. "Etta doesn't have a computer at her house, so she comes here to answer messages on her dating site."

I nearly choked and glanced back at the door as if I could see her through it, then goggled at Leo. "*Dating* site?"

He chuckled. "She doesn't think we know. But we know." His grin faded as his tone turned serious. "Don't give up yet, okay?"

For half a heartbeat, I nearly argued, told Leo that it might serve him better if he could start to come to terms with how things were. But I knew how I would be if I was convinced of someone's innocence when no one else was. I'd turn over every stone, multiple times if I had to, until I either cleared their name or found something to irrevocably prove I'd been wrong. "I won't. How about I call Katie, and the three of us can spend another night on the computer and brainstorming. Maybe we'll hit on an idea that will help me start fresh tomorrow."

TWELVE

The following morning brought Watson even more happiness, to such an extent that Carl Hanson noticed the change in my cantankerous pup as he waddled across Cabin and Hearth—the large all-natural dog bone treat Anna had just given him clutched in his smiling maw. "He was grinning when he came in here. Did you notice, Anna?"

She nodded, staring at Watson's retreating fluffy backside. "I did. He was practically chipper." When he finally squeezed beneath a log four-poster bed and out of sight, she looked at me with suspicion. "Did you put him on one of those doggy antidepressants? It's not natural seeing him quite so giddy."

I agreed. "No. I didn't. He's just had an abundance of people he loves lately. For the second night in a row, Leo and Katie came over for dinner and hung out. Between seeing Barry a couple of days ago, constantly getting to be with Ben in the bookshop, and a sudden abundance of Leo time, I think Watson believes he's in heaven." I barely caught my mistake in time. "And seeing you two so much, of course. Halloween night and now... today."

Anna's smile had just started to falter but slid back into place. I figured she knew, deep down, that Watson used her for treats, but whatever delusion made them both happy, I was good with. Still, the concerned look didn't leave her expression. "That's nice, but I do think I prefer him a little grumpy. Something about it makes him more charming."

"You're just saying that because then he matches your disposition more." Carl's eyes went wide, and his mouth fell open after he finished his statement.

It was all I could do to keep from laughing. Clearly, he'd experienced one of the most challenging aspects of my own personality—thinking some thought in your head but accidentally blurting it out in the open.

Instinctively, Carl sidestepped, clearly expecting one of Anna's frequent swats.

To both of our surprises, she merely cast him a glare, dusted off her gingham skirt as if brushing away the insult, and turned to me. "You're here because of that Nadiya girl, aren't you? Trying to clear her name."

I'd long ago quit pretending I didn't come into Cabin and Hearth to take advantage of Anna and Carl's skill at gossip. "I know she's relatively new in town, but I thought maybe the two of you would have some insight."

With a tilt of her chin, Anna took a deep breath, which showcased her ample bosoms, and nodded decisively. "She is guilty as sin, *that* I can promise you. And I use that word intentionally."

I was a little taken aback. "Really? I thought you'd have a whole range of possibilities."

"Why would I, when it's as obvious as the pimple on Carl's nose? Guilty, guilty, guilty." She dusted her hands off and relaxed somewhat, as if the case were closed.

For his part, Carl ducked his head as his cheeks went scarlet. He did have a rather unfortunate large spot of acne right at the tip of his round nose. He grumbled something, but I couldn't catch it.

It seemed Anna did, as she cast him a glare. "Don't you disagree with me, Carl Hanson. You're just taken in by her wily ways." Anna looked back and forth between the two of us now. "Anyone hanging out with that Delilah woman is guilty, you can mark my word. Running around town in those horrid pink jackets, flaunting their... wares." She reached out, finally swatting Carl's arm, having to lean over to reach. "You can't take a man's opinion on the matter. They're weak when it comes to such issues." Another swat.

Though rather abrasive, I typically found their bickering rather charming and humorous. At the moment, I was beginning to feel sorry for Carl. "I know Delilah has a... reputation, and so maybe her friends get some of that by default, but I hardly think that is akin to murder."

Anna shook her finger at me. Despite myself, I flinched, expecting to get swatted next. "Besides, it's silly you're trying to help her anyway. You decided Branson wasn't good enough for you. Clearly Nadiya has her sights on your park ranger. The two have been seen all over town together. If you lose that handsome man, what other prospect do you have?"

"Anna!" Carl hissed in admonition before taking another step away.

I appreciated the gesture and gave Anna a glare of my own. "I did *not* decide Branson wasn't good enough for me. That's never been the issue. I'm tired of people saying that. We're just not a good..." I shook my head. "I'm not explaining this. It's no one's business. And as far as Leo's concerned, he and I are just friends. And I don't think I'm too good for him either. It's just..." I fluttered my hands in the air, frustrated with myself. "Good grief, that's no one's business either. And I don't need any *prospects*. That's not why I'm in Estes. I wasn't looking for a husband. I came to open a bookshop."

When Anna reached for my arm, I flinched again, but she wasn't trying to swat me. Instead, she patted soothingly. "Breathe, Fred. I'm sorry. I should have known that was such a touchy subject for a woman your age." Her ministrations became patronizing, though I figured she meant well. "Of course you don't need a man. You're a strong, independent woman, right?"

From across the store, Watson poked his head out from under the bed, probably hearing my raised voice. After a couple of moments of inspection, he disappeared once more. Whether because he decided I was fine, or determined that he wasn't going to get another all-natural dog bone treat anytime soon, I wasn't sure.

I made certain my tone was back under control before I spoke. I was just so sick of everyone having an opinion about my love life, or lack thereof. Although I should have expected it. When my ex-husband had his affairs, it was amazing to me how many people looked down on me in judgment as if I hadn't done my part in keeping his wandering eye in check. "I actually didn't come here about Nadiya to begin with." My voice still sounded a little tight, so I took another breath before continuing. "I'm looking into the angle of Max and Jim Weasel—they're the poachers, and Max was the dead body." Being the masters of gossip that they were, I was certain they already knew that, but still. "Katie, Leo, and I researched them for hours last night. Even so, we didn't even get close to finding all that was on them. It was hard to know where to begin. They have a rap sheet so long, I think you could unroll it down Elkhorn Avenue and still have paper to spare." Having their last name had been the key. It'd been frustrating to see just how much legal trouble they'd been in and that they'd still been roaming free. "Theft, drug trafficking, assault—you name it, it was there. Well, *except* poaching, strangely."

Anna shook her head and sounded apologetic. "Never met them. Don't know a thing about them." Tentatively, she reached out and patted my arm once more, again an apology, probably for prying into my love life or because she didn't know anything about the Weasel brothers.

Beside her, Carl shook his head in agreement.

That surprised me as well. "Really? From what I overheard when they broke into my shop, it sounded like they had rather long business dealings with Sid and Eddie."

"Eddie?" Anna wrinkled her nose. "I don't recall an Eddie."

Carl opened his mouth to say something, then closed it quickly, his eyes wide once more.

I kept my gaze on him as I answered. "He ran the Green Munchies, the dispensary in Lyons."

"Heavens to Betsy, Fred! Why in the world would we know a scumbag like that?" Anna scoffed. "I'm aware the wacky weed is legal across the state now, but I don't approve. I'm just glad we live in a town that doesn't allow it to be sold."

From Carl's pained silence, I was willing to bet he felt differently and had probably partaken in either Sid's or Eddie's products behind Anna's back.

Anna didn't notice, and she continued, "As far as Sid is concerned, he mostly stayed in that nasty little taxidermy shop of his and kept to himself. I can promise you, we didn't run in the same circles." She smiled sweetly at me. "You're a blessing, Winifred Page. You transformed that horrible place into the most charming bookshop in the entire world.

It was depressing having to look across the street and see dead animals in the windows of Heads and Tails. Just revolting. Now, thanks to you, and Katie of course"—her gaze flicked toward the four-poster—"and wonderful Watson, it's a delight to be located across from you."

"Thank you." To my surprise, I remembered enough social graces to return the compliment. "And I feel the same. Your store is absolutely lovely."

Anna preened. "*And*, we help you solve murders."

I couldn't help but laugh. "Yes. There's that too."

There was a chime as someone entered behind us, but Anna kept going. "*Exactly*. So take my word for it—this time, there's nothing for you to solve. That woman is guilty."

"What woman?" Paulie stepped up beside me.

I jumped a little in surprise, then pulled him into a quick hug. "Paulie, hi! How are you? I was planning on coming into Paws after I left here. How's Flotsam?"

I could see the answer all over his face as we parted. His eyes were even more bloodshot and swollen than the day before. He looked as if he hadn't stopped crying since I'd seen him last. He just shook his head. "Not good. Flotsam's still..." His voice trembled and faded.

"Still at the vet?" Carl took on a sympathetic tone and rubbed Paulie's back.

Paulie nodded.

"It's just a matter of time, that's all." Anna's tone matched her husband's. "You mark my words. That little guy is too crazy to be sick for long. He and that other one will be bouncing around together, getting into mischief, and driving the entire downtown nuts once more. I promise you."

Paulie managed a weak smile. "Thanks." His gaze flickered to me, and he sounded apologetic. "I should've waited.

I would've if I'd known you were planning on coming to see me. But I noticed you heading in here. As soon as my customers left, I came over."

"I'm glad you did. Is there something I can do? Do you need me to watch Jetsam or—"

I was interrupted by Watson shoving between Paulie's and my legs. He pressed his forehead against Paulie's shin. Once more, my little hero proved he understood more than people gave him credit for.

Paulie sank to his knees and wrapped his arms around Watson's neck and cried.

Watson didn't pull away or whimper.

Carl leaned down, continuing to rub circles over Paulie's back.

After a couple of uncomfortable minutes, Paulie's sobs lessened, and Watson shot me a *get me out of this* expression.

I touched Paulie's shoulder. "Is there any improvement?"

Paulie shook his head after ruffling Watson's fur a final time and stood. "No. He is..." Paulie's voice broke again, and he cleared his throat with a headshake. "Sorry. I can't talk about him without breaking."

"It's okay." I wanted to hug him again, try to fix it, but knew that there was no way I could and that a hug would probably cause him to lose control once more. "You said you were coming to see me. Is there something I can do?"

Another headshake. "No. I just know that you're looking into Nadiya, of course. And thought I'd tell you what I... overheard at"—his words became a squeak—"the vets."

"You just take your time, sweet man." Though Anna's voice was still warm and caring, her eyes glistened like she was about to get a delicious tidbit. "You say what you need to say."

Paulie nodded and stared at Watson as he spoke. "While I was there this morning, Susan Green was in the next room, and I heard her and the vet talking."

"Why in the world was Susan at the vet?" It was one of those moments where my thoughts spewed from my mouth.

"Her pet is sick." Paulie looked over at me, startled, as if it should've been obvious.

"Susan has a pet? *Susan Green* takes care of another living creature?" There was no way that could be true.

"Yeah. She has an albino python name Dexter." Paulie's voice cleared somewhat, evidently the distraction helped. "He's a cute little thing."

Ahhh... that made sense. Susan with a snake, one named after a serial killer no less. *That* I could believe.

"Oh... cute." Anna shuddered and nudged him on. "You, ah... said you overheard something."

"Right." Paulie cleared his throat again. "Right. She was talking about Nadiya. Apparently, they had to put her in solitary confinement because she hurt her cellmate."

"What!" Anna's voice rose, not in shock or horror, but confirming that she indeed was experiencing the equivalence of a five-star dessert.

Odd... I wouldn't picture Susan for one to spread official gossip. Maybe not so odd, actually. I'd been almost certain a couple of different times Susan had let slip a few details of the cases I was involved in one way or another. Maybe she despised Nadiya as much as me.

Paulie didn't require any prodding. "I guess there was a mouse in their cell, and her roommate, or whatever, killed it. Nadiya went ballistic."

And again, with context, it made sense from all I'd gathered about Nadiya.

Anna bugged her eyes and gave me a nod, clearly relaying *I told you so.*

Paulie kept going. "I also heard Susan say that since moving here, Nadiya had sent a couple of strongly worded letters to the police department, saying that if they didn't take action against the poaching situation she'd take matters into her own hands."

That also fit the picture that had been forming of Nadiya Hameed.

This was going to devastate Leo.

And it seemed that Branson truly was done feeding me any information. That surprised me somewhat. Especially considering it supported his position on Estes Park's new ranger.

I could just imagine what Anna would say about *that* thought as well.

Feeling like I was wasting time, after leaving Cabin and Hearth, I led Watson across the street and down the two blocks toward my uncles' antique shop. On the way, I passed the toyshop where old Duncan Diamond was perched precariously on a stepladder as he hung Christmas lights on the inside of the large picture window. Noticing Watson and me, he gave a little wave, nearly fell, caught himself, and then laughed before finishing the wave.

Just as I was considering going in to help him, his son Dolan appeared from somewhere in the back, didn't notice Watson or me, and began scolding his father. By the time we passed, the two had changed places on the stepladder.

The little intrusion into their family moment took away the sensation of wasting time. Percival and Gary were slightly better at gossip than Anna and Carl, but even if they didn't have any insight or revelations, perhaps that was exactly what I needed. A family moment. Plus, though they'd called a couple of times since the break-in, we kept missing each other.

When Watson and I stepped into Victorian Antlers, I stopped dead in my tracks as Barbra Streisand's version of "I'll Be Home for Christmas" blasted so loudly I was surprised the antique vases weren't shattering. At my feet, Watson whimpered.

Just as I was deciding this was going to count as another time my uncles and I missed each other, Percival emerged from behind a huge armoire placed in the middle of the store. He tossed a string of silver garland over the top as he hollered toward the back. "I'm not saying it's impossible, Barry! I'm saying it will be expensive."

Someone spoke from out of view, but over Barbra, I couldn't make out who it was. Watson's reaction clarified for me as he instantly went on full alert and rushed forward, straining at the end of his leash.

Barry, apparently.

Knowing there was no backing out at that point, I released Watson's leash, and he tore off through the antique shop, hurtling past Percival and taking the corner at such a speed that the leash whipped around and flicked Percival's calves, causing him to let out a high-pitched screech.

"Rats! Gary! Call the exterminator. We've got rats!" Percival shuddered and did a little jig, which as he hadn't released the tinsel, pulled it down on top of him from the armoire. In all his flailing about, he twisted my direction and paused when he saw me, though he didn't lower his hands from the air. His eyes narrowed, and he glanced down at the floor just to be sure. Though Watson was nowhere to be seen, Percival put two and two together. He raised his voice once more. "Never mind! Not rats! Just a furry tub of grumble and attitude." As he headed my way, he finally lowered his hands enough to stretch them out and wrap me in an embrace. "Fred, darling! Lovely to see you as always. I'm so glad you're okay after all the excitement in your world, although I know you're used to it by this point." He released me before planting two air kisses on my cheeks.

"It's good to see you too. I'm sorry it's taken so long..." I realized I was shouting and pointed up toward the speakers on the ceiling. "Kind of loud, isn't it?"

"It's Barbra, darling. She's a diva. She can be as loud as she wants." Percival adjusted the tangle of tinsel around his shoulders like a feather boa before taking my hand to lead me through the shop. His husband, Gary, came into view as he stood behind a computer at the main counter. In front, Barry, in matching tie-dyed T-shirt and yoga pants—both of lime green and neon green—lavished attention on Watson. Despite his claim, when he released my hand, Percival walked over to the stereo behind the counter and lowered the volume.

Gary left his place behind the computer and headed to greet me with another hug as well. "I suppose I have you to thank for finally lowering the volume. I love Barbra, but goodness, lady, get home for Christmas already."

"Hi, sweetheart!" Barry waved at me, but knew better than to leave Watson lacking for attention so soon.

I waved back but still focused on the ringing in my ears. "I just saw the toyshop decorating for Christmas as well. Is the Cozy Corgi behind if we're not stringing up lights and tinsel?"

"No, Fred, it's just—"

"Absolutely," Percival cut off his husband. "It's the holiday *season*! They all blend together."

Well... that was a vote on Katie's perspective, I supposed.

Gary rolled his eyes as he patted my arm. "No. You're not late. Plus, we saw your Thanksgiving decorations when we tried to catch you the other day. Festive *and* inclusive. I quite approve."

I followed him back to the counter, and joined the

others as Gary took his spot behind the computer once more. "Despite the volume, I couldn't help overhearing. *What's* going to be expensive?"

The three of them exchanged hesitant glances.

Though curious, I held up my hands. "Never mind. You're allowed to have your secrets."

Barry lifted one hand from Watson's head to wave me off, but returned it quickly after a nose nudge. "No, you can know. You're good at secrets. At least better at keeping them than these two, so what harm could be done?" Leaving his hands firmly on Watson that time, he nodded toward my uncles.

Percival looked affronted. "We can keep secrets."

"*I*"—Gary leaned slightly around the computer—"can keep secrets. *You* just hold on to them until the time is the most beneficial for you to elicit the biggest reaction."

Percival shook his head, opened his mouth to argue, then paused to consider. "Actually, yes. That's factual."

I chuckled and felt a little warmth sink in despite the walk in the cold November day. Time with family was most definitely what I needed, answers or no.

Giving in, Barry shifted from his kneeling position to sitting spread out over the floor with Watson between his legs. "It's too hard for my old knees to do that for very long." He grinned up at me. "As far as your question, your uncles are helping me hunt for an anniversary present for your mother."

"We are *attempting*," Percival clarified. "There are no promises of success. There is no map with an X marking the spot on an antique treasure hunt."

I felt a moment of panic, thinking I'd forgotten their anniversary, then remembered we'd just celebrated. "Your anniversary is in September. You're a little late with the gift." I shook my head the second the words left my lips. "No. You're not. You got Mom a trip to Scotland. A cave tour of all the healing crystals." She had been over the moon.

Barry nodded. "This is for *next* year. And this one's going to take some hard work."

"Hard work that *we're* doing." Percival clarified again, "And there are no guarantees." He leveled a stare at Barry before looking at me. "You may not remember, but Mom and Dad's... er... your grandparents' cabin... er... well, your cabin now, I suppose, was broken into when you were a little girl. Mom had a small jewelry box with several pieces of heirloom jewelry that had been handed down through our family."

I hadn't thought about that in years. "I do remember. Mom was really upset." It stuck in my mind because Mom had never been one to cry about material things, but she'd been nearly inconsolable for several days after the call about the break-in. I knew part of it was worry over her parents being robbed, but it had also been about the jewelry.

Barry continued the story from his place on the floor. "Phyllis's favorite piece was her mother's cameo brooch. Well, her great-great-great grandmother's cameo brooch." A wistful smile crossed his face as he traveled back in years. "She wore it at her high school graduation."

My eyes burned with just a hint of tears at Barry's expression, and the gesture. Not for the first time, I was nearly overcome with gratitude that my mother had gotten to experience two such different men who'd loved her so completely.

"We're going to try to find the very one, hoping that it's changed hands a few times, and maybe someone's trying to get rid of it on eBay or through an estate sale. If nothing else, maybe we can find one similar." Though he spoke to me, Gary smiled down in affection at Barry. "It's a very sweet gesture."

"I'll say!" Percival had moved on to pulling more tinsel out of a large box of Christmas decorations. "My sister is a lucky woman, nabbing herself such a romantic. It's been a long time since *I've* gotten such an elaborate declaration of love."

Gary's facial features as they transitioned from affection toward Barry to annoyed frustration at Percival was nearly laughable. "I got you tickets to another one of Cher's farewell tours last year. In New York!"

Percival sniffed. "True. But you didn't spring for the VIP backstage all-access tickets, did you?"

Gary leaned on the counter. "You're not legally allowed backstage at Cher's concerts anymore after the way you behaved during her *Believe* tour."

Another sniff. "True, but it's the thought that counts."

I did laugh then, and though it earned me a narrowed-eyed glare from Percival, Gary and Barry joined in. Even Watson let out a laughter-sounding chuff. Although maybe he was just trying to keep Barry's attention on himself.

For the next fifteen minutes or so, we talked about everything and nothing, a few family stories, talks of a new restaurant opening that my uncles had attended in Denver. How Percival had won the last monthly spades tournament he, Gary, Barry, and my mother played, one he swore up and down he'd achieved without cheating—much to the protests of Barry and Gary.

Finally the conversation turned to all the events surrounding the poaching and the break-in. "I think I'm wasting my time." It felt like a bit of a confession as I announced it. "Leo is so determined that Nadiya is innocent, and I'm afraid he's going to be utterly crushed when it's proven that she's not."

Barry was standing once more, with Watson asleep at his feet as he leaned against the counter. "You really think she killed that poacher? She seemed like such a sweet girl. Though, I only met her a time or two."

"Every single thing I find out about her says that she would be capable of it, yes." Even as I said the words, I felt like I was betraying Leo. "Honestly, if it weren't for how adamant Leo was about her innocence, I wouldn't be looking into it anymore. And at this point, I'm not even doing it because of him believing that she's innocent. I'm just doing it because..."

"Because it's Leo." Gary's deep voice was soft and a little too-knowing.

I nodded.

"Well, I think she's fabulous!" Percival declared with the smack of his hands, startling Watson awake. They exchanged glares before Percival refocused. "She's an easy scapegoat. She defies convention and refuses to be what everyone tells her she should be. So what if she takes a stand for what she believes in with poaching and rubs the police the wrong way?" He gestured between Gary and himself. "I've said it before, and I'll say it again. We've had to fight long and hard against the powers that be to gain equality. And I know plenty who said we should sit down, shut up, be respectful, and wait our turn." He shimmied his shoulders. "Not to mention, the woman's gorgeous and not afraid to flaunt it. Believe me, I understand." He laughed in a way that made it a mystery whether he was only partly kidding or not at all. "There's a lot of jealousy around that, especially when a woman like her, and the rest of that Pink Panther posse, have no problem parading it around."

"I don't think she's a suspect in Max's murder because she's beautiful." I winked at him. "But believe me, if anyone knows what it's like to be tortured because of how attractive they are, I know it's you."

Barry nodded as he ran a hand over his head. "It's true. Balding is beautiful." He winked, confirming he was in on the joke.

"I just left Cabin and Hearth, and Paulie came over. He overheard Susan Green talking about the threats Nadiya had made to the police about taking matters into her own hands. She has a couple of different assault charges, and has a fairly hostile social media presence. She's won multiple shooting competitions, and was arrested in a vehicle that had blood in the back of the truck, *and* the murder weapon beside her in the cab. It's hard to set up someone without their knowledge when they're sitting right next to the murder weapon as they drive."

When Gary spoke, his voice was soft once more, but this time more in apology. "She did come in here asking if we sold collectible antique guns." He grimaced. "Which, we don't."

I thrust my hand out toward him. "See! Granted, shopping for guns doesn't make her guilty, but it's one more piece in a very unappealing puzzle."

"What is your gut saying, Fred?" Barry's voice took on a fatherly tone he rarely used with me—I thought more out of respect for my own father than his feelings for me—but that I'd heard him use with the twins. "Your mother always said you inherited your father's gut. That, even when all the evidence points the other way, your gut instinct is always right."

"That's just it, I don't have a gut feeling this time. Not at all." At his words, I realized that had been part of my problem this whole time. Some sense of embarrassment or failure. That some irrational part of me thought I was proving I wasn't as much like my father as everyone, myself included, claimed.

Barry studied me. "You don't have a gut feeling that she's innocent, but do you have a gut feeling that she's guilty?"

I started to nod in affirmation, then hesitated, actually considering. Did I?

After a few moments, I shook my head, using the motion to test the accuracy of what I was about to say. "No. I don't. Not a gut feeling. Logic says that she's guilty. But I don't have a feeling about Nadiya Hameed one way or the other."

Barry nodded as if that settled it. "Well, then, you're not wasting your time. And you're not failing Leo. Though that wouldn't be true even if you had a gut feeling that she was guilty. But you don't. Therefore, you don't know for certain. That's all you're doing—trying to find out for certain."

That was true enough. "Everything I'm finding points to her. Nothing that takes away every shadow of doubt that she is the one who shot him between the eyes and arranged him on Sheep Island, but it's close." Very, very close. "Leo, Katie, and I were doing research into the poachers last night. They had dealings with Sid and also with Eddie at the Green Munchies. So there's got to be a lot of dangerous connections from that angle."

"Eddie was a sweetheart. There's no way he would've been involved in—" Barry's words trailed off as if remembering Eddie's fate, and his eyes widened. "Maybe *that's* your connection. Whoever killed Eddie is the one who killed Max."

"No. Eddie's case was closed. His killer is in jail." I'd

had that same thought, but with the case being settled, it was a dead end. "There's still a chance that it's someone in that world, for sure, but I can't find anyone, nobody at all. And without that, there are no more suspects other than Nadiya. She's the only one with any motive I can find. There's no one else that knew Max was around, or that he was the poacher."

"His brother did."

At his words, I turned to look at Percival and found him practically covered in tinsel as he tried to untangle the strands. His eyes widened at my expression. "What? Didn't you say that the other guy... whatever his name was, the one that broke in with him, was his brother?"

I nodded.

"Well, you said you felt Max was the leader between the two, that he kept threatening the other guy, belittling him? That could be motive."

"Yeah... but..." But what? I cocked my head as I stared at my uncle. "How have I not even considered that possibility?"

He shrugged. "Probably not listening to enough Barbra."

Watson gave a great shake as we entered the Cozy Corgi, flicking snow over the hardwood floor and the bottom portion of my skirt.

"Watson!" I gestured at the closed front door. "I just asked you to do that outside. For crying out loud!"

He peered up at me with his honey-chocolate eyes and gave an expression that brought to mind what I imagined he looked like as a puppy. Heartbreaker, no doubt. He dipped his head, snagged a larger portion of snow on his tongue with a giant lick and then looked up at me again.

I couldn't help but laugh. "You really are in a good mood, aren't you? If you're helping me clean"—I ruffled the fur between his foxlike ears—"you're forgiven."

With that, he trotted a few steps away, scanned the bookshop, his gaze lingering on his favorite napping spot in the ray of sunshine pouring through the front window, then tore across the shop and sprinted up the steps to the bakery.

Shaking my head at his disappearing backside, I headed to the counter to rip a sheet of paper towels. Either Ben was in the bakery, or Watson was hoping for a snack. Knowing Watson, probably both. After wiping up the snowy mess, I paused to inspect the shop as well. From the angle, I could just make out the glow of the fireplace near the back in the mystery room. And the flickering glow of the second fireplace on the other side of the shop. With all the Thanksgiving decorations and the Ute trappings, the Cozy Corgi was even more charming than usual. Still... it would be even better with Christmas lights strung here and there. Maybe I should give in to Katie and my uncles' insistence that the holidays really did all blend together. Plus, while I'd owned the bookshop last Christmas, it hadn't been opened. The most decorating I'd gotten to do was some homemade cutout snowflakes on the windows.

After removing my jacket and scarf, I opted to walk past the mystery room and the temptation of curling up on the antique sofa to get lost in a novel, and followed Watson upstairs. Sure enough, Watson had found Ben *and* treats.

Nick sat beside his twin on one of the overstuffed sofas Katie had intermingled among the antique tables in the open-concept bakery.

Katie was carrying over a small tray of what looked like a mix of chocolate pound cake and pumpkin gingerbread. She motioned for me to join them when she noticed me. "Nick just got in from finishing up his half day at school, so I figured we needed a snack. You're just in time."

"It's one of the things Watson and I have in common. We always know where the treats are." After all the conversations I'd had across the downtown that morning, I could use a pick-me-up. Salad or hummus or something would probably have been wiser, but I was more than happy to settle for sugar. I started to head behind the counter to make a dirty chai—Katie had attempted to teach me how to use the espresso machine—when I halted at the new decoration that sat on top of the gray-and-white striated marble countertop. A ceramic, cartoon-looking blue narwhal grinned almost psychotically beside the cash register. "Are we going for a nautical theme?"

Katie dropped one of her hands on her hip. "Are you kidding? That's *Mr. Narwhal*. He's a Christmas decoration."

Deciding to play along, I nodded. "Great. He's adorable. I didn't know putting the title of mister in front of animals suddenly made them a Christmas decoration."

Katie's face grew serious. "He's a character in the movie *Elf*, with Will Ferrell."

That explained it. "I've never seen that movie. I can't say I enjoy the Will Ferrell type of humor in most movies. But the narwhal is cute."

Katie missed a beat and then threw up her hands. "Well, it's been a nice run. Good being friends with you, Fred. I'll miss you and the bakery." She gave an exaggerated wave to the twins. "It's been lovely knowing you, boys. I'm packing up my toys and going home now."

I laughed as I fiddled with the espresso machine. "Someone's dramatic this afternoon."

"I just feel like the world shifted on its axis, and I'm completely off-kilter. I had no idea my best friend had such a deficit in her taste in cinematography. And to have never seen *Elf*." She hurried over to the espresso machine and bumped me out of the way with her hip. "Scoot over. You can't be trusted not to break things. Not with this new knowledge. Next thing you'll be telling me you don't like Adam Sandler movies."

I didn't answer.

Katie paused from her packing of the espresso grounds to give me a look. "You don't like Adam Sandler movies?"

I let my wince be answer enough.

Katie let out a disgusted sound. "Fine. You might want

to look away as I make your dirty chai. I'm going to poison you."

After the twins assured Katie that they liked both Will Ferrell and Adam Sandler movies, we settled down to heavenly snacks. I warmed up with the dirty chai as I filled them in on my conversations with Anna and Carl, Delilah, and my uncles.

"That Beaker woman is just horrible." Katie sounded utterly offended as she expertly arranged a portion of chocolate pound cake and pumpkin gingerbread on her fork. "As if it's any of her business who you date. Or don't date. Besides that, like she has any room to talk. Her husband was an absolutely wretched human being." She popped the food into her mouth and considered. "Which, I suppose means that she actually chose well—they were a perfect match."

Chuckling at her cattiness, I swatted at her. "Be nice."

Nick shook his head. "Katie's not wrong. Mr. Beaker was rather wretched. His wife isn't much better."

I'd forgotten for a moment how horribly Mr. Beaker had treated Nick when he worked at the Black Bear Roaster. "Well, either way, that wasn't quite the point of the story."

Some of the playfulness left Katie's voice. "Right. The point was even more circumstantial evidence against Nadiya."

I nodded. "It was. I'm not saying we should give up yet or anything, but I do think we should try to help prepare Leo for the worst-case scenario."

"I was just reading about this guy put in jail for murder." Even though it was just the four of us—five, counting Watson—Nick's voice was still little more than a whisper. "During the murder, they were at Disneyland. The murder happened several states away. He had tickets and pictures and everything to prove that he was on vacation, but they still put him in jail."

"I heard about that," Katie agreed. "But it was Disney World. Not Disneyland."

"Oh, right." Nick pushed a portion of the chocolate pound cake around with the edge of his fork as he spoke. "There was another guy convicted of murder because his DNA was under the fingernails of the murder victim. The police thought it had gotten there when the victim fought back. But the murder suspect was somewhere else entirely at the time. It turned out that there was a DNA transfer, which they didn't even know can happen."

Katie nodded enthusiastically. "Exactly! Fascinating stuff. The suspect touched something"—she shrugged —"like a carton of milk at the grocery store or something. Some of his DNA got left behind. Then soon-to-be murder victim wanders by, picks up that same carton of milk, maybe buys it and takes it home, and the first guy's DNA inadvertently gets transferred onto his hands when he's pouring himself a glass or whatever."

Ben and I exchanged baffled expressions as we darted looks back and forth between Katie and Nick as if we were at a tennis match.

"The opposite is true as well, though," Nick countered. "There was another guy convicted in the 1980s of murder, and it wasn't until twenty-some years later that he was cleared when DNA testing proved that he wasn't the killer."

I grabbed Katie's hand. "Oh my Lord, what have you done to this poor boy? You've introduced him to the dark, addictive world of getting lost in a Google wormhole, haven't you?"

She merely shrugged and looked smugly pleased with herself. "You can never have too much knowledge."

Ben chuckled and looked so content and relaxed, my heart warmed. I really was building quite the little family in Estes Park.

I lingered on that for a moment and then refocused on the matter at hand. "Knowledge or not, and as fascinating as those anecdotes may be, they don't really help us. They're the exact opposite of what's going on with Nadiya, who was arrested in her own truck, with the murder weapon, and what is safe to assume was the victim's blood in the back."

"Speaking of, I wonder if they've gotten the DNA of that blood back yet. If it matches Max's." Katie slid a careful glance my way. "No contact from Branson at all?"

I shook my head. "Nothing since he came to my house the night after Halloween. If I'm not mistaken, that's the last I'll hear from him unless we run into each other."

"Or you stumble on more dead bodies." She grinned at me.

"Yes. Or that." With my luck, it was only a matter of time. "Speaking of, Percival had a pretty good theory. He wondered about Max's brother, Jim, being the murderer."

Katie had just taken another bite of the pumpkin gingerbread, and the theory made her suck in a breath, causing her to choke. She pounded her chest for a second, grabbed a sip of my dirty chai, and then managed to breathe. "Goodness, sorry about that! However, that actually works with all that Leo, you, and I found out about the Weasel brothers the other night. The only thing they *hadn't* been convicted of was murder." Her brows knitted. "Although, from what we read, and from what you overheard when you were hiding, it sounds like Max was the one more likely to kill."

I started to agree, but Ben spoke before I could. "That

might be, but you can only get abused or tormented so long before you snap. Maybe the little brother had reached his limit."

Nick nodded along but didn't say anything.

Not for the first time, an ache rose in me as I studied the brothers. Though Nick continued to open up more and more as he grew more comfortable, there were times when his silence let me know there were many dark shadows in his and Ben's past he wasn't ready to share, maybe never would.

From Katie's expression, I could tell she was feeling something similar, but she pressed on before it got awkward for the twins. "Even if all that is true, it still leads us back to Nadiya being caught driving the truck, sitting next to the murder weapon. It wasn't like she was being carjacked at gunpoint or anything." Her brown gaze flicked at me. "And with what Paulie overheard, even though it's nothing we wouldn't have assumed anyway at this point, I don't really see any sliver of proof that makes us think that Jim is responsible for his brother's murder. But... we keep looking until Leo's convinced, one way or another."

"Agreed." I was about to turn the conversation back to Ethel Beaker and her war against the Pink Panthers, when the door to the bookshop chimed.

Ben started to get up.

"No, no. I'll get it." I stood, leaving a good portion of the pumpkin gingerbread but taking my dirty chai. "You managed the bookshop all morning. I'll pretend I work here for a few minutes." Giving him a wink, I headed toward the stairs and then looked back at Watson. "You are the mascot. Maybe you should make an appearance today as well?"

With a whimper, Watson glanced up and then over at

the table as if hoping for crumbs to rain down like a waterfall.

"Fine, Benedict Arnold. I'll be social on my own." With a final glance at the little group that filled my heart with joy, I walked down the steps into the space that did the exact same thing.

For a second, I didn't see who had come in, but then I found him wandering around in the children's book section. "Dr. Sallee! I haven't seen you in the shop in a while."

The vet grinned. "True. Sorry about that. Busy schedule and all." He paused in his pulling out of books from the shelves, looked toward my feet, and then scanned behind me. "Watson doing okay? Where is the little guy?"

I motioned upstairs. "With one of his favorite people in the world, and doubtlessly begging for snacks."

Dr. Sallee chuckled and shook his finger at me, probably only partially in jest. "I'm sure that makes him happy, but he could stand to lose a few pounds."

I patted my waist. "So could his mamma, so I can't say too much."

Dr. Sallee didn't offer comment on that, and true to his normal, he got right to business. "I actually need your help. My niece is turning eleven this weekend, and I'm at a loss on what to get her. All she does is play video games and spend countless hours on all those social media apps. Snaptweet and Instachirp."

"Snapchat, Instagram, and Twitter?" I gave him a wink. "My mother has a massive following on Instagram."

He shuddered. "Yes, those. And your mother is exponentially cooler than me, apparently." He pulled out another book, inspected the back cover. "Anyway, I'm sure the last thing she wants is books, but I'm trying to broaden her horizons. And I'm feeling a little out of my league here."

While mystery novels were my forte, I actually had quite an affection for children and teen literature. "Do you know any other interests she has besides electronics and social media? If not, I do have a couple of books that revolve around a character who is a gamer, and another where a fifth grader discovers that his principal is a spy when he hacks into the school's website."

"No, I'm afraid that would only encourage her addiction." He gave another shudder. "Kendra always has her head in the clouds. She likes anything fanciful—fairies, unicorns, mermaids. Anything with dragons." He snapped his fingers a couple of times. "She doesn't like aliens, though, or stuff to do with space."

"I have just the thing." As always, sharing the love of my favorite books brought a little thrill. I hurried over to a shelf behind Dr. Sallee and pulled out six thin books. "These were some of my favorites when I was younger. I must've read them fifty times." I held the stack of *The Secret of the Unicorn Queen* books out to him. "The series is out of print now, at least in this format, but I have four sets that I found on eBay. They're only slightly used, but I promise you, if she likes unicorns, she'll love these. It's about a girl who gets transported into this land of warrior women who ride unicorns, where she discovers that—"

"Is there anything about iPhones, social media, or how many likes she gets from her followers?" He stared at the stack with narrowed eyes.

"No. Remember, these were some of *my* favorite books when I was a kid. That was before the days of iPhones and social media."

"Perfect." He snapped the books from me. "I'll take them all."

I handed the books back to him in a Cozy Corgi bag

after he paid. "You'll have to let me know how she likes them. If they're a hit, I have a couple other series that she might enjoy."

"I'll do that. Thanks, Fred. You're a lifesaver."

He started to head for the door, and I decided to ask what I'd been trying not to. "How's Flotsam?"

Even as he turned to look at me, dread washed over me. I could imagine the pain Paulie was going through. And even thinking about it brought out my own issues around loss and death.

"Flotsam? As in Flotsam and Jetsam? Paulie's dog?"

"Yes." Strange that he had to ask. Those two corgis are about the most unforgettable animals a person could ever meet.

"Good, I suppose." He sounded confused. "Why? Is Flotsam sick?"

"Well, yeah, you—" Before I could finish the thought, I realized something was wrong. "I must be confused. You *don't* have Flotsam under your care right now?"

Dr. Sallee hesitated. "I... don't typically discuss other people's pets with someone not on their treatment plan. No offense, Fred." His brows creased. "*Should* I go speak to Paulie? Are you concerned about Flotsam's welfare?"

"No! No." I waved my hand as if to stop him, then lowered it to the counter, utterly confused. "I must've misunderstood something. I'm sorry."

He studied me. "Are you sure? I don't mind popping in."

"Like I said, I've misunderstood something. There's so much going on lately that my brain is just spinning."

He nodded, knowingly. "The poacher murder." He *tsked*. "I won't grieve the loss of such a person, but murder is never the right answer. Especially when committed by someone who was such an advocate for animals. She's not going to do them any good behind bars."

"No, she's not." I forced a smile. "Thanks for understanding. And please let me know what Kendra thinks about the books."

Dr. Sallee had barely disappeared around the block before I rushed out of the Cozy Corgi. I was halfway across the street before the cold registered against my skin, and I realized I'd not bothered with my scarf or coat. It wasn't until I threw open the front door to Paws and saw Jetsam curled up close to Pearl that I realized I'd left without Watson. I hadn't even gone upstairs to the bakery to tell Katie and the twins I was leaving.

Pearl hopped up hopefully, scurrying to me in search of Watson. Jetsam simply lifted his head, raised an eyebrow, then sank back to the floor.

"Sorry, guys. Watson's not with me today." Stooping to brush my fingertips along both of their heads, I stepped over Jetsam and headed toward the counter. There was no one to be seen, but I could hear voices slightly raised above the soft cacophony of fish bubbles, hamster wheels, and bird squawks.

Before I reached the door that led to the back room, Paulie stepped through and halted, his eyes wide. "Oh, Fred!" He glanced back at the door, as if hoping someone else were there. "I heard someone come in. I was just..." He thumbed over his shoulder as his words fell away.

Though it had only been a couple of hours since I'd seen him, I could've sworn he appeared thinner. He was gaunt and worn. Eyes still bloodshot and swollen. He looked sick. I reached for his shoulder. "What's going on, Paulie? You're not doing okay."

To my surprise, he flinched at my touch. Just slightly, but it was noticeable. His mouth moved wordlessly for a few seconds, and then he seemed to find words. "I'm sorry that I'm not handling Flotsam being sick very well. I admit. I'm a mess." His words took on an unusually defensive tone. "Not everyone can be as strong as you, Fred."

For a second, I felt guilty at his accusation, then swept that emotion away by remembering why I'd hurried over here so quickly to begin with. "That's actually why—"

Athena stepped into the pet shop from the back room as well. She too looked strained, possibly angry. "Hello, Winifred."

Yes, definitely angry. Her voice was tight and thin. I wondered what I'd done to make her mad, then recalled the raised voices I'd heard. She and Paulie, obviously. Maybe he was the object of her frustration, not me.

"Hi, Athena." I looked back and forth between the two, debating whether I would get more or less from Paulie with Athena present. "How's everything going?"

"Not good. As you know." Again Paulie sounded irritated.

Athena glanced at him in surprise and then looked at me. "I, ah... was planning on calling you. I—"

Paulie shot her a glare, and she caught herself.

When Athena didn't continue, I decided to prompt her. "Did you get more information? Find something about the Weasel brothers?"

As Paulie had done before, her lips moved wordlessly

before sound came. "No. I mean, yes. But nothing... just more of the same. An endless litany of petty crimes with a few major ones thrown in for good measure."

She was lying. At least I thought so. Maybe the two of them had been arguing, and she was just off because I'd interrupted. "Anything that would lead you to believe that Jim could murder his brother?"

Athena tilted her head. "Now there's a thought." She sounded like herself again, mostly. She considered for a few moments before continuing. "I can't say that I did. At least not overtly. But there's enough in the Weasel brothers' past to make it a strong possibility. I'd be inclined to believe it if Max had been the one to kill Jim as opposed to the other way around, but"—she shrugged—"maybe."

Paulie brightened. "That *is* a thought! You could be onto something, Fred."

I narrowed my gaze at him. "You sounded pretty convinced earlier that it was Nadiya."

He flushed, and then paled, his gaze darting around the pet shop. "From what I overheard Officer Green telling the vet, that's what I assumed. But it would sure be nice if it was Jim who was guilty instead of Nadiya. It's a good idea."

Strange. I glanced at Jetsam and then back at Paulie, feeling slightly guilty at trying to entrap my friend. "Have you got Flotsam back yet? Any news on how he's doing?"

He just shook his head, and though he still didn't meet my eyes, his filled with tears once more.

Something was definitely going on, with him *and* Athena, but I could tell his tears were real. He was worried sick over Flotsam. Still, I pushed. "How much longer does he have to stay for observation?"

"I'm not sure. They have to—" Paulie's voice caught

with emotion and he had to give himself a shake. "I'm not sure."

Athena stepped closer to Paulie and began to rub his back as she had the other day. As she did, she gave me an inquisitive glance.

Time to go in for the kill. "Dr. Sallee was just at the Cozy Corgi. He was looking for a birthday present for his niece."

"He was?" Paulie's brown eyes flashed up, wide and a bit afraid, confirming my suspicions.

"He didn't know anything about Flotsam being sick, Paulie." I took a step forward. Though I kept my voice firm, I tried to put as much tenderness in it as I could.

Athena leaned back, gaping at him. "Paulie?"

"I... I..." Paulie fluttered his hands, once more searching around the pet shop, then flinched as it seemed he discovered what he'd been looking for. "I never said anything about Dr. Sallee. Flotsam isn't at Estes Park Animal Clinic. I never said that either. He's... at a specialist in Denver. He's really, really sick. Worse than what they could handle up here."

Athena darted a look my way, then turned her furrowed browed expression on Paulie. Clearly, whatever was going on with Paulie, she wasn't aware of it.

I took Paulie's shoulder once more, felt him flinch again. "Paulie, you said you overheard Susan talking to Dr. Sallee about Nadiya."

"No. No, I didn't." He shook his head, somewhat frantically. "I said she was talking to the vet. I never specified Dr. Sallee. It was a vet in Denver." He nodded as if to himself and then finished in a whimper, "She was in Denver as well."

The story was so ludicrous that I almost felt sorry for

him. I *did* feel sorry for him. "Paulie, why are you lying to me?"

"To us," Athena clarified.

Paulie simply shook his head, tears streaming down his face.

Suddenly I knew. Not specifically, but I knew. "Paulie, look at me." I tightened my grip and waited until his tear-filled and bloodshot eyes rose to mine once more. "You told me before that there were things in Estes that I still didn't know about, that there were things you couldn't tell me."

He gave the most minute of nods.

Beside him, Athena's expression of shock returned. That surprised me a bit. They were so close, I figured he'd told her about our conversation.

I could ponder that later. "You told me that you would tell me if I was ever in danger."

"And I would." Though his voice trembled, there was truth. "If you are in danger, I would tell you." He looked at Athena. "Either of you."

"Paulie, are *you* in danger?"

He shrugged.

I knew the answer before I asked the next question. "Flotsam is in danger, isn't he?"

He froze, and though he didn't answer, didn't nod or shake his head, when he met my gaze again, the answer was evident in his eyes. "Please let this one go, Fred. You're not in danger. I'd tell you if you were. But... by you looking into this, you're putting people in danger, people you love."

"Paulie, if you tell Fred, if you tell us, we can help—"

He cut Athena off with a glare. "No. If I say anything more, then you're both in danger, and this is bigger than Fred can solve. Bigger than anyone can solve." He pulled his shoulder free from my grip and stepped away. "I need you both to leave. Please."

He headed toward the back room, and Athena rushed after him.

I watched them go, feeling slightly dazed, slightly nauseous.

A couple of hours later, I was on my way home with Watson in the passenger side of the Mini Cooper. Katie and Leo were coming over shortly to have another night of brainstorming. I had a feeling it was going to be a *very* late night of brainstorming.

As I turned onto the street that would wind past the very un-Estes Park-like subdivision and then lead back through the forest to my little cabin, I got a call from Athena. "Hey. You all right?"

"Hardly." She sounded exhausted. "I've been debating what to do ever since our conversation with Paulie. He made me promise I wouldn't tell you. Swore it would only make things worse. That it would put you, and possibly me, in danger. But I think it's better to face it head-on."

"I agree. It's always better to face things head-on." A tingle of fear entered, and though it probably showed just how crazy I was, an even bigger rush of excitement. "What is it?"

"It's why I was at Paulie's. As soon as I found it today when I was researching at the paper, I went to him. I planned on going to you next, but... well... you saw."

"I sure did." I wished she'd just blurt it out already. "What did you find?"

"Honestly, I didn't think it was much. Just a strange coincidence or connection. Until Paulie's reaction. Now I think it's much bigger than I feared. Do you remember the name Charles Franklin?"

I hit the brakes, sending Watson flying but managed to shoot my hand out to catch him just in time. He glared, but I didn't have it in me to apologize or try to soothe. My blood turned to ice. "Of course I remember Charles Franklin. Not only did he try to kill Paulie, but he was involved in the case my dad was investigating when he was murdered, remember? He was part of the Irons crime family in Kansas City."

"Oh, of course. I forgot that part. Sorry. There was so much happening when you mentioned it that I..." She paused.

"Don't worry about it." I hated to cut Athena off, but I needed to know. "What about Charles Franklin?"

"Like I said, it wasn't much. I just found an old article from a paper in Eureka Springs, Arkansas, about a drug bust. There was a list of suspects. Max and Jimmy Weasel were on there, as was Charles Franklin. I don't have anything other than that. Just proof that they knew each other, if the article was correct. I nearly passed it off as a coincidence, but..."

"Even if I believed in coincidences, which I don't, this wouldn't be one of them. Not when Paulie has been lying to us and is clearly terrified." Still, it didn't make any sense. Not at all. "But it's not like Franklin could be here. He was killed in Glen Haven."

"I know." Athena sounded baffled. "You think it's possible that Nadiya is related to him or something? That she came here for revenge?"

"I've seen photos of Charles, he didn't look Pakistani. But maybe he and Nadiya were involved romantically." It was a thought, but I dismissed it quickly. "Unless she went to a whole world of trouble to make a bunch of fake social media accounts over the last several years, I don't think she'd have anything to do with a man who's involved in poaching and animal trafficking." I'd nearly forgotten about Nadiya over the last couple of hours. "I'm not sure what the connection is to all of it yet, but even though I have no idea how it was managed with her in the truck, I'm about willing to bet that Leo was right. Nadiya is innocent."

SIXTEEN

"So let me recap, to make sure I've got it." Leo listed things off on his fingers. "Paulie was lying about his dog this entire time. Flotsam isn't at the vet, never has been. Which means what he claimed to overhear Susan say about Nadiya and her letters to the police wasn't true."

"We now know that the Weasel brothers have a connection to Charles Franklin." Katie jumped in, but as she spoke, Leo still kept track. "Which means two out of those three are dead. Charles and Max."

My skin tingled at the connection to the Irons family and the death of my father. "And all of this confirms, at least seems to, the theory that this is bigger than just poaching." I touched Leo's arm from across my kitchen table before he could object. "That's not downplaying poaching, just that there are a lot more spokes to this wheel. And that it connects to things far larger than simply what's happening in Estes and the national park."

"No, I don't disagree." Leo held the soupspoon in midair. "Poaching often goes along with other high-level, and often deadly, crimes. But I'm still having a hard time accepting that Nadiya was part of it."

"I don't think she was." For the first time since Max's

murder, my gut seemed to wake up at my declaration. I repeated the statement, testing the resolve. "I don't think she was. If Nadiya was connected to the Irons crime family, if that's who's behind all of this, then her legal issues as well as her social media activity doesn't make sense. They would need her to be squeaky clean to fly under the radar if she was acting to help them in some way. On the flipside, if she was part of them and they were trying to set her up by planting a fake social media trail, she would've caught on unless they adjusted all the social media going back *years* and her record all in one night, which doesn't sit right."

We fell into silence, each of us considering as we ate. Katie had brought over her homemade French onion soup and a new version of the bread with the garlic base, formed into round loaves. Once at the house, she hollowed out the inside of the bread to make bowls, ladled in the French onion soup, and covered each with a thick layer of Gruyere. As we sat down to brainstorm, she presented us with piping hot bowls of perfection covered in bubbling, golden brown cheese.

"I know I say this with everything you make—" I ripped off a part of the bread bowl and used it as a spoon to get a heaping portion of oniony goodness and stringy cheese "— but I think this is my favorite thing you've ever made."

Leo hummed his agreement.

Katie shrugged it off. "With as cold as it is outside, and the heaviness of all we've been dealing with, soup seemed the right way to go." Her eyes twinkled. "But, yes, I think I did find the magic combination for this bread recipe."

I peered down at Watson, who was enjoying his feast at Leo's feet. "It was also super nice of you to bring steak for Watson. Talk about lavish."

She shrugged again. "Well, dogs aren't supposed to have

garlic or onions or all that much cheese. Couldn't very well cook for us and leave the Scooby of our Scooby Gang hungry."

Leo chuckled but sounded strained.

"Chief Briggs always puts Paulie as our fourth Scooby Gang member." Though I knew she'd been attempting humor, it made me sad. "I'm really worried about him. He's clearly terrified for Flotsam, and maybe just in general as well."

"So if Flotsam isn't sick and with the vet, where is he?" As if the thought of the missing corgi was too much, Leo bent slightly so he could stroke Watson as he spoke.

"With Charles Franklin is my bet." As soon as the words left my lips, the gut feeling came back once more.

Katie looked at me as if I'd lost my mind. "Sweetie, Charles Franklin is dead."

"I know that." I rolled my eyes though I grinned at her. "I mean Flotsam is with him *figuratively*. Like we've said, there's no coincidence that Charles's name came up again. He tried to kill Paulie, and now Flotsam is gone, and Paulie is worried sick and lying to people that he loves."

Leo sat up straighter, excitement bright in his honey-brown eyes. "Max and Jim are revealed as active poachers and break into the Cozy Corgi looking for marijuana, and they have past ties to Charles Franklin. That may or may not mean they have ties to the Irons family. From what you've said, Fred, though you're not sure to what extent, Charles was involved in your father's death, or at least part of the organization of drug dealers your father was investigating that was also part of the Irons family."

"Exactly." I nodded as I tapped the table. Some of Leo's excitement was contagious, but the sense that this was connected to my father was more surreal than anything else.

Katie spoke, sounding as if she were puzzling it out through her words. "So... Charles Franklin has Flotsam, or at least whoever his group is now, has Flotsam." Still considering, she finished with a large spoonful of soup, a long trail of cheese bridging her lips and the bowl before she pulled it apart.

"Poor Flotsam." Leo nodded as he sobered. "It all kinda makes sense."

"Yeah. It does." My skin tingled.

"What if Chief Briggs has Flotsam?" Leo asked suddenly.

Katie and I both looked up at him.

"Hear me out." He rushed ahead before we could say anything. "Paulie has always been terrified of him."

"That's true, even when Briggs knew Paulie's secrets and was in charge of keeping him safe." My mind began spinning with the possibility. "I saw myself how Briggs bullies him. I didn't think much of it because"—I shrugged—"well, he does that to everyone."

Leo jumped right in, nodding. "The police have never been open to my complaints about poaching. That would make sense if Briggs is involved. If he was somehow the ringleader of it."

"Or maybe Charles Franklin was the ringleader," I pondered aloud, "and Chief Briggs took him out. I don't know. Either way, for whatever reason, maybe he's the one who killed Max." If Briggs really was involved that could mean Branson knew and was trying to keep me from digging too deep. Maybe he was working undercover, trying to gather evidence. Or... maybe he was in danger. Him and Susan.

"Why would Briggs kill Max?" Again it sounded like Katie was working things out in her own mind as opposed to actually asking questions, but she brought me back to the moment. Trying to figure out where Branson, or Susan for that matter, fit in it all was too much. "Max and Jim didn't seem like much more than incompetent lackeys."

"Maybe too incompetent." Leo let the spoon fall against the bread bowl and left it there as he propped his elbows on the table. "This actually makes sense, or at least more than anything else. If Chief Briggs is behind Max's death, it would've been easy for him to set up Nadiya."

From below us, Watson let out a long, loud, satisfied belch.

Katie smirked, then winced. "If we're right, then that means poor little Flotsam is with Chief Briggs. That's terrifying. I can imagine how he's being treated."

"No wonder Paulie is such a mess." I looked down at Watson, my heart aching. "Briggs looks at dogs as if he wants to squash them like bugs. I'd be beside myself if Watson was with him for more than two minutes."

"You don't think..." Katie stiffened, and when she started again, her voice was barely a whisper. "You don't think he hurt Flotsam? Killed him?"

The thought only had to play out for a couple of seconds before I shook my head. "No. At least I don't think Paulie believes so. If we're right, and it is Briggs, then he's using Flotsam to hold over Paulie's head, making him lie about Nadiya or whatever. Though I can't imagine him putting up with Flotsam for a second longer than he has to."

That time, Leo stiffened and sucked in a gasp.

Katie whirled on him. "What? I know that sound. You just had an idea."

"Hold on." Leo held up a finger as he squinted. "Let me think about this."

Katie and I exchanged glances, then focused on Leo as we waited.

As he thought, Leo shook his head several times and made a few grunting noises. When he finally met our gazes, there was a mix of determination and anger in his expression. "Briggs doesn't have Flotsam. Etta does."

"Who?" The word barely left her lips before Katie shook her head. "Oh! Etta Squire, your cranky old park ranger. That's a random theory."

"Maybe it is, but maybe... not." He considered a few more seconds and then tapped the table with his forefinger.

Watson let out a startled yelp, and Leo dipped his hand to pat Watson's head to soothe him, but kept going.

"She's always downplayed the poaching. Shrugged it off as just being part of the job, how the world works. That the rest of us were young and had on rose-colored glasses and thought we could change the world. She never stood in the way exactly, but... now that I look at it from this angle... close." His brown eyes went to me. "When we were at the station two days ago, I didn't think anything of it, but she was sneezing, and her eyes were bloodshot. She's allergic to dogs. And cats, for that matter. I thought maybe she just had a cold or something, but if she is part of this—"

"If she's part of this, then she could have been helping Chief Briggs from inside the park."

Leo glanced toward Katie at her interruption, then nodded and kept going. "Right. And if she's part of this, maybe she was in charge of taking care of Flotsam, and she's having an allergic reaction."

She had seemed pretty miserable. I'd chalked it up to a smoking habit based on her voice and her cough. A thrill shot through me at another memory. "She had a bag of dog food in the back of her truck, remember? She said it was for her... niece or someone."

A huge grin spread across his face. "Her sister. You're right, Fred. Even more proof."

Again, that feeling in my gut settled. It was relaxing. I hadn't realized how much I'd come to depend on that sensation. "We're on the right track. We may not have the details right, I don't know, but we're getting there. Finally."

"I know where she lives. I could swing by, see if I can hear Flotsam, or wait outside long enough to see if she lets him out to go to the bathroom." Leo started to stand.

Katie shot out her hand, holding him in place. "Hold on. Let's slow down a little bit. If this crazy theory is right, and some sinking part of me thinks it is, we're not just dealing with grumpy old Etta Squire. We're dealing with Briggs, a man we think may have killed or have had at least two people killed. Let's be as sure as we can before we go rushing into anything."

Though he looked like he wanted to argue, Leo sat back down after a few moments. "You're right. Of course, you're right. But how do we figure out if she has Flotsam without going there?"

"I can call Paulie." My heart was thundering away, some exhilarating mix of excitement and fear. "If we're right, and I put it to him point blank, I don't think he'd lie about it. Or if he does, I don't think he'd try very hard to cover it up."

"And if Briggs has his phone tapped or has him under surveillance?" Leo grimaced. "Maybe I'm sounding paranoid, but at this point..."

Katie practically popped up from the table. "Hold on, I'll be right back. She hurried into the living room and came back with her laptop, placed it on the table, and began tapping away before she'd even sat back down. "Let's see if Etta has a Facebook page."

Leo scoffed. "Etta hates people. Why would she have a Facebook page?"

"You said yourself she's pretty heavily involved in online dating."

Katie straightened, looking at Leo as if he was going to contradict my reminder. When he didn't, she swatted his arm. "For crying out loud! How have you left out that detail when you've described her to me?"

He grimaced again. "I try not to think about Etta dating, online or otherwise."

Katie rolled her eyes and turned her attention back to the computer, and almost instantly smiled in triumph. "She does have a profile. Now, we only need a couple more strokes of luck."

It was hard not to ask questions as Katie typed away, but when she was on a roll, it was best to just let her do her thing. After a few more seconds, she nodded and gave a happy shimmy but kept going without explanation. A few more keystrokes, and she fist-pumped the air. "Got her and luck *is* on our side!" She beamed at Leo and me. "Not only is Etta on Facebook, but she's connected to her sister, Sylvia. It seems Sylvia isn't the least bit concerned with online privacy. Under her profile on Facebook she has her address, birth date, employment, and her phone number. She might as well throw in her Social Security number for good measure." Katie leaned back in her chair so she could dig her cell out of the pocket of her jeans.

"What are you going to do?" Leo sounded wary.

She winked at him and she stood. "Just watch. And

cross your fingers. We need just a little bit more luck that she's similar to others in her age group and feels weird about letting calls go right to voicemail." She began tapping on her cell. "I'm just going to block my number..."

After a few more seconds, she held the phone to her ear and began to pace around the table. She had the volume up so loud that we could hear the ringing on the other side.

Leo, Watson, and I swiveled in our spots, watching as she slowly circled us.

There was a glitch in her step, and her face brightened. "Hello there. Have I reached the residence of Sylvia Bortz?" She began to pace again. "I have? Wonderful. May I speak to her, please?"

Leo and I gaped at each other. Katie's voice had taken on a British accent. Or, at least what was meant to be one. Leo smirked, and I had to look away to keep from laughing.

"Oh, this is she? Wonderful." Katie's footsteps sped up and Watson scooted under Leo's chair. "I hate to bother you on this fine evening, but I'm with the Charleston Dumb Friends League, and we're doing a survey." There was a protest on the other end of the line. "No, I'm not going to ask for donations. Please don't hang up. I promise it will only take a couple of seconds. We're just doing an... animal... census." There were some more words, but I didn't have time to make them out before Katie rushed on. "Our first question is, how many dogs do you have in your household currently?"

She halted again when the woman answered.

She looked over at us with wide eyes as she spoke to the phone. "Oh really? You don't have any of those disgusting mongrels at your residence you say?"

Something else unintelligible.

"Do you ever have one stay the night?"

The voice on the other line went shrill.

"Because... dogs have sleepovers too." Katie's cheeks turned crimson, and she hurried on as she picked at the fuzzy decal of a snail dueling a saltshaker embroidered on her sweatshirt. "Well, that marks you out of the running for finishing the survey. Sorry about that. And thank you for your time." Katie clicked a button on the phone and shook it in the air in triumph, her voice returning to its normal state of being. "No dog! And Sylvia sounds just as miserable as her sister." She flinched, looked at the screen of the cell, and then practically sank against the table. "Oh, thank goodness. For a second I thought I forgot to hang up."

Laughing, Leo patted her on the shoulder. "Brilliantly done."

Chuckling along, I echoed his sentiments. "Good job, Katie. I didn't know you could act as well as you could bake."

"I wouldn't go *that* far." Her eyes narrowed.

"And *I* didn't know you were part British."

Katie flinched as she looked at Leo. "Part British? I'm not. What made you think that?"

He studied her for a second as if to see if she was teasing. "You didn't mean to do a British accent?"

Her mouth fell open. "I *didn't* do a British accent!" She looked to me. "Did I?"

"You did." I laughed again. "Or at least something British adjacent."

Her cheeks flushed even brighter. "Oh. That's odd."

"And why the *Charleston* Dumb Friends League?" Leo was still laughing as he beamed at her.

"Did I say Charleston?"

We both nodded.

Katie waved her hands in the air. "I don't know. It's

called improv. I was just saying whatever came to my mind."

Tears were streaming down Leo's face as he lost himself in laughter. But he managed to gasp out a few words. "Says the woman who just told us we needed to slow down and that we don't want to go rushing into anything."

She narrowed her eyes at him, and smacked Leo on his shoulder. "Well, I got the job done, didn't I? We now know that Sylvia does not, in fact, have a dog, which means Etta is lying. It lends more credence to our theory."

Laughing as well, I soothed my hand up and down her arm. "You did amazing, Katie. You really did. I wish, however, that I'd recorded that for posterity."

"You're both awful, horrible human beings." She bent to pet Watson. "Except for you." She made her way around the table to plop back into her chair. "I think I want out of the Scooby Gang." Then she too began to chuckle.

Once the laughter died enough, things became serious again. I almost hated to ask the next question. "So what do we do with all this? There's a lot of what-ifs, but I'm not sure who we turn to. If Briggs is involved, it's not like we can call the police." And worry spiked over Branson.

"I think we could." Leo was still wiping tears from his cheeks, but was utterly earnest. "Susan has always been receptive anytime we made a complaint about poaching. I think she'd have our backs."

"Are you insane?" Katie's expression communicated that she clearly thought he was. "Susan might like *you*, but she hates Fred, and me by extension. Whether she's in on it or not, the second we call and report this, she'd run straight to Briggs." Without waiting for a reply, Katie turned to me. "I say we call Branson." She held up a hand before I could protest. "I know things are… awkward between the two of you. But if we can convince him, he'll help."

Leo made a sour face but didn't say anything.

"No. I'm not calling Branson." That time I held up a hand before Katie could protest. "And I'm not just being stubborn. It's not fair for me to keep pulling him into things, especially when were not really certain. With something like this even more so. We're talking about his supervisor. We're not sure what danger we might put him in. Especially if he doesn't believe me and says something to Briggs." Though I didn't pause in my explanation, my brain was rattling on. This would explain many things—why the chief hated me so much, why he demanded Branson shove me out of cases, especially this one. "I don't want to put him in that position, not yet. And I'm not sure about Susan. She and Briggs certainly don't have a good working relationship, but I'm not willing to bet that she hates him more than me. I don't think it's wise to risk finding out."

Though it looked like it took effort, Katie didn't argue. "Fine, then. How do we get more proof?"

"Back to my plan." Leo stood again. "I'll go to Etta's house, hang out, see if I can hear Flotsam or something." He glanced down at Watson. "He can come with me. From the way Flotsam responds to Watson, if they smell each other, I bet Flotsam would start barking inside."

"And again, I ask, are you insane?" Katie yanked him back down into his chair. "If we're right, and Etta is a part of this, and she sees you? And if we're right about Briggs? Then she calls him, he shows up, and you and Watson are the next bodies on Sheep Island."

He glowered but didn't disagree.

Truth be told, I was edging toward Leo's reasoning.

Now that it felt like we finally had movement, I wanted answers sooner rather than later. But Katie wasn't wrong.

Maybe a compromise... I leveled my gaze on Leo. "Do you know Etta's work schedule?"

He nodded. "Yeah. She's on tomorrow morning. I'm on tomorrow afternoon."

I looked at Katie. "Then tomorrow. We'll check it out tomorrow."

SEVENTEEN

"And I thought *my* cabin was out in the woods." I stared out the passenger side window of Leo's Jeep as he parked on the gravel driveway of Etta's tiny shamble of a house. It was so far back in the woods, at the end of a long narrow road, there was no sense in parking a distance away and trying to disguise that we were there. The most we'd attempted in terms of disguise was using Leo's Jeep instead of my too-easily recognizable volcanic-orange Mini Cooper.

"I wasn't kidding about her not being a people person." Leo shifted the Jeep into Park, turned off the engine, and unfastened his seat belt. "She wouldn't be getting any unsolicited visitors out here."

"That makes the perfect place to keep Flotsam, then." My heart was pounding so hard I wondered if Leo could hear it. I wasn't sure whether I hoped we'd find Flotsam and have our suspicions confirmed or not. I didn't really want to start back at square one, but the other possibility seemed too large to face.

We'd waited until half an hour after Etta was scheduled to go in for her shift at the park. We also decided it was smarter to have Katie stay behind. Both so she could be with

Ben at the Cozy Corgi and keep up appearances and so she would be able to bring in reinforcements, just in case.

Maybe saying *we* decided was a bit of a stretch. Katie pointed out that we could simply put a Closed sign on the Cozy Corgi, claiming that she and I both had food poisoning or something. She also argued that the only thing that could possibly go wrong was Etta herself being sick or finding some other reason to be home and that in such a case it would be better to have three against one as opposed to two against one. I worried that she wasn't going to forgive me for putting it to a vote.

I shoved that worry aside as I snapped on Watson's leash and we exited the jeep. It was the right decision, the smart decision. Plus, we needed to focus.

Leo inspected what remained of the crusty snow around Etta's house. "There are the tire tracks from her truck and footprints from it to the door, but I don't see any evidence of Flotsam anywhere."

"No, me neither." We'd come up with the semblance of a plan on the drive over, so Leo and I didn't have to discuss anything. We walked up to the front porch, and he knocked on the door. Since the truck wasn't there, we knew Etta wasn't home, but still, just in case.

No one answered.

Following our plan, we left the porch and began to walk around the house, checking for any signs of Flotsam. We both swore we weren't going to break in unless we found some evidence that he was there. I wasn't entirely sure either one of us planned on sticking to it, but we were going with the pretense anyway.

Watson sniffed along the ground curiously, weaving back and forth from the foundation of the house to the edge of the trees that surrounded the property only a couple of feet away—much like he did on our walks to the forest around my cabin. When we turned the corner to the back of Etta's house, Watson whimpered, seemed to catch a scent, and hurried forward.

"Leo, I think—"

"Yeah, I see." Leo hurried along beside us as Watson beelined to the back door, shoved his nose against the jamb, and then looked back at me with a bark.

"Do you smell Flotsam, buddy?"

He whimpered and barked again, clearly answering my question.

"That's enough answer for me."

"For me too, but if it wasn't..." Leo leaned his hand against the side of the cabin and lifted one of his feet. "Here's more proof."

I looked down to see that he'd stepped in something, and then noticed that same something in a few different spots around us. I pointed to a small patch of snow a few feet away. "And there's even more proof, as if we needed any."

Leo glanced at the corgi-sized pawprint in the dirty patch of snow, then met my gaze. "Between Watson, the poop, and that, I'm convinced Flotsam is here. Although I'm not sure why we don't hear him barking, so maybe *was here* is the correct phrase. But it's enough reason for me to think we were right. Are you sure you want to go through with this?"

I didn't even have to consider. "A hundred percent."

"Are you sure? Up until this point, you haven't actually broken any laws when you've been looking into the murders. Breaking and entering is definitely a—"

"Shut up, Leo." I gave him a wink and laughed, sounding fuller of bravado than I actually felt. "Besides, technically we broke that with Nadiya's locker, so put your lock-picking skills back to work."

He grinned but didn't argue anymore and focused on the doorknob.

Watson continued sniffing around the base of the door, whimpering, clawing at it every once in a while, like he was trying to dig beneath.

After only slightly longer than it had taken Leo at the locker, there was a click and with a satisfied nod, Leo turned the handle and opened the door.

No sooner had we stepped in than I heard the sound of claws, similar to what Watson had just been doing trying to get in.

Watson took off so fast that he jerked the leash from my hands as he tore through the small house. After a second, he barked.

Leo and I entered a decent-sized living room. I could see the front door on the other side, but the curtains were drawn and things were dim. Through the doorway on the right, there was a small kitchen. On the left, where Watson had disappeared, was a hallway. Leo and I followed and found Watson whimpering and clawing at another door.

Neither of us spoke, and just as my hand reached the doorknob I heard whimpering from the other side. "He's in there." The *why* he wasn't barking scared me to death. I tested the doorknob gently to see if it was locked, but it twisted easily enough that I pushed open the door.

Flotsam barreled through, crashing into Watson in a storm of whimpers and batting paws and wagging of nubbed tails.

For his part, Watson desperately licked Flotsam all over, as if he was a long-lost friend. Which, I suppose he was.

As I knelt, Flotsam's attention turned to me, and I reached for the tricolored corgi's head. "Oh, poor baby." He had on a muzzle, the cage so tight that he didn't have enough room to bark, though it didn't seem tight enough that it was causing him any pain. With a couple of quick snaps, I unleashed the muzzle at the back of his head and pulled it off.

Flotsam let out a bark and began completely bathing my face in corgi kisses. For the first time in our acquaintance, I didn't try to get him to stop and was a little surprised when I realized a couple of tears had escaped.

Leo knelt beside us, ruffling Flotsam's and Watson's fur and receiving his own wash of doggy kisses. "We're glad you're okay, you crazy thing."

Watson pranced about, proving that he was nearly as thrilled as Flotsam.

Leo looked at me over the bouncing dogs. "What do you think? Stick to the plan or take Flotsam and get out of here?"

Part of me must've thought we'd been wrong. That we wouldn't actually find Flotsam in Etta's cabin, because now that we had, I wanted to take him and run. But all that would accomplish was prove Etta's involvement. We needed to try to find some kind of proof of who she was working with. If we were right that Chief Briggs was part of this but didn't find proof, it would be easy enough for him to simply blame her. Unless Paulie would be brave enough, with Flotsam safe and sound, to say all that he knew. I didn't want to depend on that, though. "Stick to the plan. Where should we start?"

"Luckily, there's not much to look through." He glanced around, then gave a shrug. "I'm betting the bedroom. Something in a drawer. Although I'm not really certain what we'll find. It's not like she and Briggs are going to have some sort of formal contract."

The dogs' barking increased in their celebration.

"True, but there might be something. We'll know it if we see it." I reached out to stroke Watson. "All right, buddy, I know you're happy, but try to breathe. You'll call in the neighbors, even though there aren't any." As I spoke, I realized from the way he was glaring over my shoulder that I'd misinterpreted Watson's barking.

Leo and I followed his gaze at exactly the same moment, just as there was a click of the rifle that was aimed at us.

"Turns out it was a good day to forget my lunch." Etta sneered over the barrel of the gun, her eyes even more bloodshot than when I'd seen her last time.

Growling with a fury I wouldn't have thought possible of Flotsam, he rushed at her, fangs bared.

Just before he was out of reach, I managed to snag his collar and pull him back. I didn't know Etta Squire, but she had a gun in her hands, so she might shoot him, or at the very least kick him. Flotsam squirmed in my grip. Though he growled, he didn't attempt to snap at me.

As Watson's rumble joined in, Leo slipped his fingers inside Watson's collar as well.

"You've always been a pain, Leo." Etta glared at him and then at me. "Never interacted, but I've heard the same about you. Apparently the rumors are true." She let out a hacking cough, managed to keep the rifle steady on us, and didn't take her gaze away.

This wasn't good. I nearly laughed at the thought. Talk about an understatement. But it was true, nonetheless.

Granted, there were two of us, but she had a gun. For one crazy moment, I considered hurling Flotsam at her, letting him use his fangs however he wanted, while I dove for her legs. Some crazy unexpected move that might catch her off guard enough to get the gun free.

And Katie's voice from the night before, warning Leo to take things slow whispered in my ear and held me in place.

Etta could have shot us already. So I had to believe that wasn't her plan. And if that was the case, then there might be a better moment to do something risky.

As if reading my thoughts, Etta took a couple of steps back. "I don't want to shoot you. Either of you. But one stupid move and I will." Though there was no tremble in her raspy voice, the rifle wavered in her declaration.

"You're not a killer, Etta." Leo spoke softly beside me, and the barrel of the gun moved slightly in his direction.

"You don't know what I am." That time, her voice did tremble a bit.

Flotsam turned loose another round of barking and struggled in my arms once more, bringing the gun's focus back to us.

Leo started to stand.

"Don't even think about it!" Etta barked at him, swinging the rifle back to him and then returning it to Flotsam and me. "Put the muzzle back on that little demon."

I hesitated.

"Do it!" Etta shouted, which elicited a string of hacking and coughing. As she tried to get herself under control, she backed away several feet until she was in the center of the living room and far out of reach. "I'm sick of that mongrel. Don't tempt me. Put on the muzzle."

I did as she ordered, lowering my head to whisper apologies in Flotsam's big ears as he struggled to get free. Beside him, Watson licked his face through the metal cage. I was disheartened to see my fingers trembling as I fastened the clasps.

Leo's hand came to rest on my back, offering a bit of strength and reassurance.

Etta motioned toward the bathroom door with the rifle. "Put him back in there. Your fleabag too."

Maybe insanity took hold, but I started to argue, to demand that Watson stay with me, but then thought better of it. If he was out of sight, there would be less chance of her swinging the gun in his direction or kicking him, or a million other horrible possibilities that flitted through my mind.

I did as she said, having to push Flotsam through the bathroom door, and was grateful when Watson stayed without a power struggle, though he looked at me with judgment behind his fear-filled eyes. Shutting the two of them away in the bathroom nearly broke my heart.

"Now, get back on your knees, Fred."

I did as Etta commanded.

She glanced around the living room, the rifle trained on us. With Watson out of harm's way, I considered using her distraction and rushing down the narrow hallway and tackling her.

Again Leo's hand came to rest on my back.

Finally, taking another step back, Etta marked a path from where we were to the middle of the living room with the rifle. "Now both of you crawl in here. Hands and knees. When you get to the center, sit down."

We did as she demanded, exchanging glances as we crawled across the floor. Again, Leo must've been able to read my thoughts, my inclination to attack, as he gave a nearly imperceptible shake of his head.

"Good." Etta managed to keep the rifle aimed toward us with one hand, her shaky finger dangerously on the trigger, and pulled out her cell from her pocket with the other. "Now—"

Watson cut her off with a string of panicked and ferocious barks from the bathroom.

Etta flinched, and I thought for sure she was going to pull the trigger. "Shut that thing up or I will."

"Watson!" I practically screamed.

At the sound of my voice, Watson began to bark louder, more frantically.

No wonder, I sounded utterly terrified. Forcing some calm into my voice, I lowered the volume. "Watson! Be quiet."

He continued to bark.

"Come on, buddy." Leo called out soothingly. "Be quiet, Watson. No more barking."

He barked again, though the sound was hesitant.

"Watson!" I took the fear and the pleading from my voice as much as I could and infused a commanding tone I rarely used. "Be still!"

His barking trailed off into a pitiful whimper.

Etta nodded, tapped her phone, and lifted it to her ear. She was silent for a few moments as the call rang through. "Yeah. It's me. You'll never believe who showed at my place. The most irritating Smoky Bear you've ever seen and his truly annoying Nancy Drew."

She was silent for several more moments. Though I strained to hear, I couldn't make out what was said on the other end of the line.

Finally she nodded, slid the cell phone away, and brought her hand back up to steady the rifle once more.

I couldn't help but feel like we'd missed our chance.

She stared at us from the other side of the gun as she backed up a few more feet. "Sit on your hands too. No funny business."

Leo did as she asked.

I hesitated. Clearly whoever she'd called—I was willing to bet it was Chief Briggs—was on their way. Whenever he got here, the odds shifted from two against an older woman with a gun to two against an older woman with a gun, and a police chief with a gun who hated me with a passion. There might not be another moment to act.

"Fred." Leo didn't bother whispering, but his voice was soft and firm. "Don't."

The rifle trembled again in Etta's grip.

He risked sliding one of his hands out from underneath to touch mine. "Don't."

He was right. It might be the best odds we had, but they weren't odds at all. There was no way I could move from my seated position and make it across the living room before she shot one of us. If it had been just me, maybe I would've taken the chance. If it had been just me, I probably would've been shot already.

I sat on my hands.

As we waited, Etta didn't speak. Didn't rage, talk, or gloat. If anything, she looked sick to her stomach.

Leo must've noticed the same thing. "Etta, you don't have to do this. We've known each other for years. And I know you don't particularly like me, but—"

"Shut up, Leo." She coughed again.

"Etta." Leo's voice grew softer, calmer, more soothing. It didn't waver, and I didn't hear any fear. I had no idea how he did it. "It's not too late. Don't make things worse. You still have a choice. We can—"

Etta laughed. But it wasn't full of wicked glee, not at all like some comic book villain. It was dark and sad and angry. And when she spoke, her voice trembled. "You have no idea. I've told you countless times that your rose-colored glasses needed to break before you got yourself in trouble. You should've listened."

"Etta."

"I said shut up, Leo!" The tremble was gone.

A million different plans, each one crazier than the previous flitted through my mind as we sat there. Sweat began to roll down my back. My phone rang in the pocket of my skirt. If Etta heard the vibrations, she didn't let on. I felt it go to voicemail. Then a few seconds later, it began to ring again.

Katie. It had to be Katie.

Somehow I'd forgotten. And thank God we'd made a contingency plan even though it had felt pointless to do so.

She tried one more time and then quit calling. She would help. No doubt.

Several more minutes passed; I had no idea how long. Every once in a while I heard twin whimpers from the bathroom, but Watson didn't bark again, and Flotsam couldn't.

With the length of time, somehow the panic began to fade, but it spiked again as we heard the engine of a vehicle, the crunch of tire over snow and gravel. Then the engine died. The sound of car doors slamming was followed by footsteps on the porch.

Chief Briggs sauntered through the front door of Etta's cabin, looking smug. Even though we'd guessed at it, his presence brought back a spike of fear. But it was the figure behind Briggs that made my heart leap into my throat.

Branson.

Katie had called him; he was here to save the day. Those were my first thoughts, but they lasted less than a heartbeat. His gaze flicked over Leo and me and then landed on Etta. "Good grief, you crazy old woman, can't you do anything right?"

EIGHTEEN

"Give me the gun, Etta." Branson held out his hand as he walked toward her. "You're liable to blow us all to bits."

A spark of hope ignited in the darkness that washed over me when Branson walked in. He was taking the gun. We were going to be okay. He was undercover, playing a role. Maybe he had been the entire time. I just needed to give him a chance to turn the situation his way.

Etta practically shoved the rifle at Branson. "Take it! This is more than I ever wanted. I don't babysit dogs." She sneezed as if to prove her point and wiped her nose with the back of her arm. "I don't hold people at gunpoint. This isn't what I agreed to."

Beside me, Leo shifted.

"Quit complaining, Etta." Briggs rolled his eyes and dismissed her with bored disdain. He pulled his pistol from its holster and aimed it at us, his tone uninterested. "Don't try to be a hero, little park ranger."

I kept my gaze on the gun but felt Leo tense beside me and then settle back down.

With the rifle in his hands, Branson turned to face Chief Briggs. "What are you doing? There's no need for all of this. I guarantee you neither of them are armed."

I dared to glance at him, hoping to see some quick look my way, some secret message behind his eyes to tell me to be patient, that he had it under control. There was nothing, and his tone was just as bored as Briggs's.

The chief kept his pistol trained on Leo and me but gaped at Branson. "Are you kidding me with this? Do you think we're just going to sit here and lounge about in Etta's nasty little cabin and have tea?"

"I'm just saying there's no need to overreact. Neither of them is going to try anything stupid." Branson started to say something else, but Etta began sneezing again.

Briggs motioned from her to us. "Get yourself under control, Etta."

She glared at him through watery eyes but said nothing.

From the bathroom, Watson barked, and Flotsam joined in with high-pitched whimpering.

Chief Briggs cocked his head. "I thought you muzzled that thing." Etta didn't have a chance to respond before he looked at me. "Dear God, you brought your dog, didn't you?"

"Let Fred go." Still sitting on his hands, Leo shifted again, facing Briggs. "She doesn't have anything to do with this. She's not involved in the poaching. I'm the one who's—"

Briggs laughed. "You really are as original as cardboard, aren't you, Lopez? The whole *take me not her* thing?" He rolled his eyes. "Have you ever seen that work in any movie?"

I dared a glance in Leo's direction. Clearly he thought we were moments away from getting shot. Which... we were being held at gunpoint, but I couldn't accept that was how this was going to end. No way Branson would let it get that far. He'd blow his cover to save us. I had no doubt.

Leo remained focused on Briggs. "I don't know what deal you have with Etta, but I'll join in. What has she been doing for you? Helping the poachers get out of the park? Adjusting records, covering tracks? Whatever it is, count me in."

"Leo!" I hissed at him, partly in shock at what he was saying and also trying to get him to stop, to get him to give Branson a chance to figure this out.

He ignored me. "I guarantee you, I know the national park better than Etta. I'll make it worth your while. Just let Fred walk out of here, and I'll do whatever you tell me to do."

"Shut up, Leo." Branson sneered at him. "You're pathetic."

"*I'm* pathetic?" The placating tone vanished from Leo's voice. "*I'm* pathetic! You're the one wearing a badge, the one who put Fred in danger by lying to her this whole time!" Though I couldn't imagine how he managed, Leo sprang to his feet and charged at Branson. "If you even think—"

Chief Briggs swiveled the pistol in Leo's direction, and I lunged toward Leo to knock him out of the way.

Before Briggs could pull the trigger, Branson swung the rifle like a baseball bat, smashing Leo across the face with the handle.

The force of the impact caused Leo to spin backward. Unable to stop my forward motion, we collided, and he flipped over me, crashing to the floor with a groan.

Chief Briggs let out a loud guffaw of approval and clapped Branson on the back.

Spinning on my knees, I hurried to Leo. His nose was broken, and blood made its way down his face and onto the carpet. "Leo! Leo!" My hands roamed over his back and gripped his arm as he tried to push himself back up into a kneeling position. "Don't move. You're only going to hurt yourself more." I was vaguely aware of Watson barking like mad.

"Don't move, boy." Briggs's voice had gone cold. "The gun is trained on the back of your little girlfriend's head."

Leo froze and glared past me through an eye that was already beginning to swell shut. Then he met my gaze.

I just shook my head.

"Etta!" Branson's bark made me flinch. "Tie Leo up so he doesn't cause any more problems." There was a pause before Branson spoke again, his voice cold. "And gag him."

As Etta retrieved what she needed from a kitchen drawer and made her way over to Leo, I desperately tried to think through my options. There had to be something I could do to save us. There had to be. But not a single option came to mind. Trying to rush Briggs wouldn't work, clearly. The only thing I could see was to simply wait. Believe there would be some moment that I could take advantage of to get us out of this. Though I couldn't help but feel we'd already missed that moment when it had just been Etta and us. We should've gone for it then.

"You don't need to restrain Leo or gag him. He'll stay where he is." I kept one hand on Leo's back and turned to Briggs and Branson. Briggs did indeed have his pistol pointed right at my head, so I turned a beseeching gaze toward Branson. "Please."

There was no secret message in his green eyes, just coldness. "Sorry, Fred. It's not an option."

"It's okay, Fred." Leo's whisper was pained but firm behind me. "Let it happen." I heard the implied *save yourself*.

"You always were such an annoying little Boy Scout."

Etta kneeled beside Leo and began to tie his arms behind his back. "I told you. Certain things in life aren't able to be changed, but you wouldn't listen."

I couldn't believe I wasn't fighting, that I stayed at Leo's side while he was bound and gagged and rendered powerless. But I was as well. I could think of no move that wouldn't make things worse.

"When you're done with that one, tie up Ms. Page here, and make sure you gag her properly. I've wanted her to shut up from the minute she came into town." As Briggs spoke to Etta, he grinned wickedly at me over the gun.

"No!" Branson stepped forward, almost like he was going to step in between the gun and me, but he didn't. He turned to look at Briggs. "There's no reason to do that. She's not going to attack, she is no danger." He shot a look my way. "You'll do what you're told, right?"

I finally saw what I'd been looking for, the man I thought I knew, in those green eyes. He was there, and he was pleading with me silently. Relief washed over me, but I tried not to let it show. I hadn't been wrong. "Right. I'll do what you tell me to."

There was a spark of relief in Branson's gaze, as if he'd expected me to argue or not understand, but then he faced Briggs once more. "See?"

Briggs gaped at Branson. "Seriously, Wexler? Still?" He gestured at me with the gun. "What is it about this woman? I don't get it? There's a whole lot prettier options in town, and this one's strung you along for months. Had you playing the part of a fool, and here you are, still acting like her little dog." Before Branson could respond, Briggs raised his voice to a near scream. "And speaking of, somebody shut up that dog! Or I will!"

In my panic and the blood pounding in my ears, I'd barely registered Watson's whaling.

"Watson!" I let out a wail of my own, and there was no keeping the tremble out of my voice. "Mom is okay. Be quiet, baby."

He barked again, just as loud, but the feel of it shifted slightly, turning almost questioning.

"Good boy, Watson. No more barking. Be quiet!" For the first time since Etta had appeared, I felt tears streaming down my cheeks, heard the pleading desperation in my voice. What had we been thinking, bringing Watson?

I knew what we'd thought, what we'd planned. None of this was supposed to happen.

"Watson! Be quiet!"

He barked again and then faded off into a constant whine.

I looked back at Briggs and lowered my voice. "Please don't hurt him. He hasn't done anything wrong. He won't—"

"What are you going to promise me, Ms. Page? It was pointless for Leo to try, but at least he had the potential of something. What do you think *you* have?" Again the look in Briggs's eyes left no doubt that he hated me, though I still didn't understand why. "Free books? Pastries from that annoying friend of yours?" He sneered at Branson before looking back at me. "Maybe you think you have some strange effect on men." He laughed. "Apparently you do, considering you have that idiot park ranger and a man I consider one of the smartest, cleverest men alive in any *other* way, groveling at your feet. Let me make it clear, you have the exact opposite effect on me."

Branson shot out a hand and grabbed Brigg's arm as the chief took a step in my direction. "Briggs. Knock it off."

The chief whirled back on him. For just a second, he lowered the gun, but before I could even consider whether I should leap, he leveled it at Leo. He didn't even have to look away from Branson, as if he'd read my mind and knew exactly how to stop me without a glitch in his concentration.

With his free hand, he jabbed at Branson's chest. "How do you expect this to go down, Wexler? That we're going to sit here and have a conversation and come to an understanding? Do you really think there's some happy ending for you in this with that obnoxious woman?"

"I'm saying calm down. Fred has done everything you've asked." Branson dropped his grip from the chief's arm and softened his tone. "She's not fighting back. She's not going to try anything crazy."

I was certain that was directed as a command to me almost as much as reassurance to Briggs.

"Let's just slow down. We can figure this out."

"Really?" A smirk played over the chief's face. "How exactly are we going to figure this out? You think no matter what they promise that we can just walk out of here and things will go back to normal?"

Etta sneezed again from behind me but didn't even cause a glitch in their debate.

"What I think, is that if we act too quickly, or make a rash decision, this whole thing is over. How are you going to explain a dead park ranger and a dead..." Branson's voice had been steady up until right then, and it broke. He shook his head. "Everything you've built in this town would be for nothing. You brought me here because I'm good at this. Like you said, I'm one of the smartest men you know, so trust me. We need to be smart about this."

Briggs was silent for several moments. He looked back and forth between Branson and me, keeping his pistol trained on Leo. "What I think, is that no matter how this plays out, things in Estes are done. What I *know* is that you need to turn your brain on. Regardless of what comes next, these two know our part in this. And maybe you're not worried about that, but that's just because she has you under some sort of spell." He lifted his hand and tapped hard enough on Branson's temple to cause him to wince. "What delusion do you have in that head of yours? That somehow the two of you are going to skip away from this cabin to a happily ever after? She didn't even love you when she thought you were a knight in shining armor. You weren't good enough for her then. Why in the world do you think she'd accept you now?" He took a step from Branson and moved my way, shifting the barrel of the gun from Leo toward me.

Branson made a motion toward him but paused. Any move he made would end in my death.

Briggs knelt in front of me so we were eye to eye, and angled the gun toward my chest.

My tears over Watson had dried. I wasn't sure if he was barking again or not. Everything was static—the voices of Briggs and Branson loud and causing everything else to fade away. I tried to think. I could feel the clock ticking, feel it winding down. There wasn't going to be another moment.

I had to make a chance of my own. Somehow. Maybe... if Briggs got just a touch closer, I could somehow manage to use my legs to knock him off-balance while twisting my torso out of a bullet's trajectory.

Right, because I was a gymnast and lived in *The Matrix*.

Still, it was the only possible chance I saw. But he needed to get closer, just a little closer.

"Tell poor little Branson the truth, Winifred. You don't love him. You never did. You were just using him to help you play detective. Help you feel like you were Daddy's little girl." His smile was huge as he stared at me—like a shark. I could practically see him salivating over what was surely about to happen. "Tell him what you think of him now." Though he did nudge closer, he twisted the pistol slightly, centering it on my chest. "Even if there was a chance before, what about now, now that you know what he is?" He chuckled. "Maybe I'm giving you too much credit. Perhaps you have an effect on me after all and I'm making assumptions that you're smarter than you are." He shifted his weight, but still didn't move closer, his feet still out of reach of my legs. "Have you still not figured out that *Branson* killed Max? Not that you care about him. But what about all the others? What about our little traitor, Eddie? You liked that little rat, right?"

Despite my fear, I couldn't help but glance at Branson.

And I saw the truth in his eyes.

Briggs laughed again. "I see I was right. You are a moron. Couldn't even figure that out." He did scoot just a little closer then, just a touch. The gun was near enough that I could reach out and touch it. Maybe I could kick it?

"What do you think he was doing all those nights when he would just randomly disappear? A bunch of fishing trips? You're a detective's daughter—have you ever known a policeman to get that much vacation time?" His voice rose as he addressed Branson, but he didn't look away. "Ask her, Wexler. Ask her what she thinks of you now."

Branson didn't reply, though he came nearer.

I kept my gaze trained on Briggs's gun, waiting for it to get just a touch closer and I'd take my chance.

Briggs didn't look away from me. "Too much of a coward to ask, Wexler? That's okay. Once she's gone, you'll get back to normal. We can—"

The thunder of the rifle filled the little cabin.

One second Briggs was glaring into my eyes. The next, he was gone.

As if from a million miles away, Watson began his frenzied barking once more, Leo made a muffled scream, and Etta started to yell.

The chief's dead body came into focus, sprawled at my feet. I looked up at Branson just in time to see him swing the rifle past me, and another shot filled the cabin.

I screamed and whirled around, attempting to throw myself in front of Leo, though I was already too late. I grabbed him, meeting his wide, shocked eyes, his muffled words barely reaching my ears, and then saw Etta sprawled on the floor behind him.

It was probably a matter of seconds, but it felt like endless minutes as I stared at her, waiting for my brain to override the fear and make sense of the picture. Even so I had to scan down Leo's body before trusting that there was no wound, that he wasn't shot.

I turned back to Branson as he lowered the rifle. It paused in its arc, at the point it was aimed at Leo. Before I could say anything, plead or shout, before I could throw myself in front of Leo, the rifle lowered farther and pointed at the floor. Branson's eyes met mine.

NINETEEN

"I thought..." I tore my gaze away from Branson's eyes, glanced at the rifle aimed at the floor and then back up. "I thought you were going to..." I shook my head. I couldn't finish the sentence, didn't need to. Spinning on my knees, I started to peel back the duct tape of Leo's gag, but the blood coming from his broken nose gave me pause, bringing back the image of Branson hitting Leo in the face with the butt of the rifle.

Leo's wide brown eyes, filled with panic and anger, tried to warn me as did his muffled words.

"Don't, Fred." I froze at Branson's hard words and looked over my shoulder, some crazed part of me expecting to see the rifle pointed at me again. It wasn't, but Branson hadn't dropped it to the floor either. "Leave him tied."

Everything had happened so fast, and yet it felt like we'd been stuck in the cabin for weeks. A weird slow-motion whirlwind of drama, confusion, and panic. Even as I'd attempted to figure out how to survive—when to kick out at Chief Briggs, to determine if we'd missed our chance—the back of my mind had been shoving puzzle pieces together. Though I hated the picture it formed, it was the only one that made sense. "You weren't undercover with them? You weren't playing a role?"

He didn't budge. "You're smarter than that."

Yes, I was. Though apparently not smart enough, considering how long it'd taken me to figure it out. Not that I'd *figured* anything out. It'd been shoved in my face. Without looking at Briggs or Etta, I motioned behind me. "But if you're part of them... you just killed..."

He shrugged as if he had done nothing more than smash a spider. Despite that, for the first time since I'd met him, worry and fear appeared in those bright green eyes. His voice didn't betray those emotions. "Briggs was going to kill you."

So it was that simple. "Etta wasn't. She didn't even have a gun."

"No, she wasn't." He didn't give any other explanation.

"You're not going to...?"

Hurt flashed in his eyes, superimposing itself over the worry and fear. "I've always told you that you are safe with me."

Yes. He had.

I turned back to Leo, reaching for the duct tape covering his mouth.

"I said leave him tied!"

Watson began barking like crazy from the bathroom.

Promises of being safe or not, I flinched at Branson's shout of command. As I faced him once more, I repositioned myself so I was directly between him and Leo. "You're not going to hurt him."

Though it wasn't a question, Branson treated it as one. "No, I'm not." He sounded disappointed. "You and I need to talk. I'm not having his interference when we do."

Maybe my nerves were on the edge of breaking,

doubtlessly. Perhaps it was the combination of fear, relief, exhaustion, and adrenaline, I had no clue, but whatever it was, he sparked my anger and I laughed.

That time, *he* flinched.

"Are you kidding me? You sound just like you did when you would order me off a case. Has it ever worked for you? Have I *ever* listened when you bark orders at me?" I gestured at the rifle. "I'm untying Leo, and he needs medical attention. Did you forget hitting him in the face with that thing?"

"I most definitely haven't forgotten." Branson smirked as he took a step forward. "And me hitting him in the face was the only thing that saved his life. The only reason I did that was because I knew you wouldn't forgive me if he died."

That took my words away for a second until the muffled sounds of whatever Leo was trying to say brought me back to him. Once more, I turned and started to gently remove the tape.

Branson cursed. "He's fine, Fred! Give us a few minutes to talk. You and me. Without his stupid interference."

I didn't look back, just used the fingertips of my left hand to gently smooth out the bruising skin of Leo's cheek while trying to take off the tape as painlessly as I could with my right.

"Please, Fred."

There was a pleading in Branson's voice that almost made me pause, but I didn't.

"Just a few minutes before I have to—"

The crunch of tires pulling to an abrupt halt, accompanied by the sound of gravel and ice spraying against the small cabin, froze all three of us in place.

There was the slamming of doors and pounding footsteps.

I twisted toward the doorway.

Watson's barks were beginning to sound hoarse.

Branson lifted and aimed the rifle at the door and steadied his stance.

The door was flung open and Katie rushed in. "Fred!" She came to a screeching halt when she saw the barrel of the gun, but then she was shoved forward several stumbling steps as Paulie smashed into her. He too froze.

Every emotion I'd been feeling was echoed in Katie's eyes as she lifted her gaze from the barrel of the gun to Branson, then looked over to me, to Leo, and to the bodies on the floor, before finally back to Branson. I couldn't help but have a shot of pride for my best friend when she tilted her chin and anger filled her voice. "I called you to help. I called *you* to help her!" She took a step forward in her anger and paused. When she spoke again, her voice trembled slightly as it lowered in volume. "When Fred still wasn't answering her phone and you weren't answering yours, I went to Paulie. He told me... He told me that you..." Tangible disgust filled every part of her. "Even so, he said Fred would be safe with you. But here you are with—"

"I did help her. She's alive, isn't she?" I almost thought I heard guilt in Branson's voice.

"So now what?" Katie cocked an eyebrow at him. "You kill the rest of us and take her?"

Behind her, Paulie put a hand on Katie's shoulder as if telling her not to give Branson any ideas.

For several moments, Branson actually seemed to consider, but then he used the rifle to motion Katie and Paulie toward Leo and me. "Get over there with them. Kneel down."

Katie took another step forward. "You've got to be kidding me if you think I'm going to—"

"Do it!" Branson screamed in a tone I'd never dreamed would come from him—full of anger, fury.

They did, both of them. Paulie kneeled beside me, with Katie on the other side of Leo, her hand coming to rest on his back.

Branson nodded his approval before his eyes met mine once more and his expression softened for just a second. I could see he was saying something, trying to get me to understand, but I couldn't. His eyes hardened again. "Toss your cell phones to me. All of you. And keys."

Paulie complied instantly, pulling it out of his pocket and sliding it to Branson.

After a moment, Katie did the same with hers, her key ring as well.

I debated for a few seconds, maybe it was foolish, but I did believe I was safe with him. So much so that I thought I could pull out the cell phone, call the police, and he wouldn't hurt me. But he *was* the police. I wasn't so certain he wouldn't hurt one of the others to make me obey. I wouldn't have thought such a thing possible before, but... things had changed...

I slid the cell from the pocket of my skirt and noticed countless missed calls from Katie. I hadn't even felt them coming through after her first couple of tries. I tossed it toward Branson.

He motioned toward Leo. "His too."

Without waiting, Katie reached into the pocket of his jeans as Leo twisted and raised his hips to give her better access, and then his phone and keys joined the others at Branson's feet.

Branson kept the gun trained on us as he kneeled on

one knee to retrieve the cell phones, each one disappearing into various pockets. When he stood again, his eyes met mine once more. "Don't follow me."

He lowered the gun, turned, and walked toward the door, completely unconcerned that any of us would try to tackle him.

We didn't. All of us remained frozen exactly where we were as Watson's barks continued to fill the cabin.

Then Branson was gone, leaving the door open behind him and letting the bright cold day rush in. None of us moved a muscle until we heard the rumble of a car and its retreat as it drove away.

As one, Katie and I clicked into motion. Me working on the duct tape as Katie began untying Leo's wrists and legs.

Just as I pulled out the sock that had been stuffed into Leo's mouth, Watson crashed into me, nearly knocking me over. I caught myself in time to avoid landing on Leo and wrapped my arms around Watson, burying my face in his fur as he barked and licked and whimpered. "Oh, sweetie, I —" My throat constricted, cutting off my words as tears finally began to fall.

Paulie emerged from the hallway. Fat, fluffy Flotsam cradled in his arms like a baby, muzzle-free and lathering Paulie's face with kisses as he washed away the tears that streamed down his cheeks.

"It's okay, Fred. We're all okay." Leo was sitting up, and he wrapped an arm around my shoulders, pulling me to him. He did the same with Katie on the other side. "It's over."

Watson darted a quick lick over Leo's face, which made Leo wince, and then Watson returned to me.

I angled so I could see Leo's face. "You're hurt."

He shrugged. "I've broken my nose before. Though I'm

betting I have a nice old concussion, judging from the headache. Who knows, maybe a skull fracture." Another shrug like it wasn't a big deal, and then he grinned. "Better than the alternative."

Katie lifted her hand to his cheek but stopped before making contact. "Your teeth, they're chipped."

Sure enough, three of his top teeth had chipped, ruining his perfect smile. Again he shrugged. "We don't get paid a lot being park rangers, but we've got killer dental insurance." The humor left his eyes as he held mine. "Are you okay?"

"You were here. You know I'm okay. You took all the—"

"That's not what I meant." His brown gaze darted to the door and then back.

I simply nodded.

I wasn't sure if I was.

Paulie sat in front of us, Flotsam still in his lap, tears continuing to stream, though they seemed to have changed from those of relief to guilt. "I'm so sorry. I'm *so* sorry." He sounded close to hyperventilating. "I've hated lying to you, to all of you. But..."

Katie leaned forward and rubbed his knee. "They had Flotsam. We understand."

He nodded frantically and dipped his head to wipe his eyes as best he could on his arm, clearly unwilling to take either hand from Flotsam. "It's not just that." He sniffed and looked at me. "I've never been able to tell you everything. I've always known... but I couldn't..." He spoke between sobs and then seemed to give up.

More puzzle pieces fell into place, filling the gaps in Paulie's story once we'd finally figured out why he'd come to Estes, why he'd used a fake name. The ferocity Branson had displayed when I'd attempted to look into Paulie's past.

Paulie telling me there were still secrets in town, things he couldn't say, but that he'd tell me if I was in danger.

Watson had finally begun to calm, but I kept stroking him as I addressed Paulie. "Were you under Briggs and Branson's control before you got to Estes or after?"

"After." He choked out another sob. "I came here under police protection, to be safe, to start again, and then got here... only to find I wasn't safe at all."

Leo's hand joined Katie's on Paulie's knee. "You are now. You're safe now."

Paulie attempted a smile, almost succeeded.

The four of us sat there, dazed, cuddling and reassuring the two dogs, taking comfort from them, as we tried to come to grips with what had just happened.

Once more, time played the game where a couple of minutes felt like hours. But however much of it passed, the reality of our surroundings crowded in again—the little cabin, Etta, Chief Briggs.

"How do we get out of here? It's a long, long walk back into town." Katie kept her eyes averted from the bodies.

"I have the CB in the Jeep. I'll call for help." Leo stood, groaned in pain, and held his head.

"I can do it, Leo." Katie started to stand. "You shouldn't be moving."

He waved her off with a pained smile. "I'm fine."

I inspected Leo. He did seem fine. He would need to get checked out, but he seemed like himself. "The question is, who do we get help from? We can't call the police." I looked at Paulie. "Can we? Is it just Briggs and Branson? Or are there others?"

He shrugged. "Briggs and Branson were the only ones I had contact with. They were the ones who would tell me what they wanted me to do." He glanced at Etta. "I knew about her, but…" Paulie refocused on me. "I know there are more people involved in town, but I don't know who they are. I don't think anyone's as high up as Branson and Briggs, but I can't say."

"Seriously?" Leo had made it to the doorway and turned back. He had to grip the doorjamb at his swift movement. "Then who do we call? Maybe nobody. Maybe we walk back to town. Who knows who'd be listening if I use the CB. If none of the police can be trusted, then we could just end up with another rifle in our faces."

"Brent Jackson wouldn't be involved in this. I'd swear to it." I glanced at Katie for confirmation, and she nodded. "He nearly died protecting Katie and me."

"As far as I know, Briggs and Branson are the only police that were involved. They made certain to tell me never to talk to any of the other officers about anything. Not to call them for help, nothing." Paulie nodded at Leo. "I think we'll be okay with the police."

Another thought hit me. "So… Susan?"

Paulie almost smiled. "She definitely wasn't in on it. Briggs hated her."

"That makes sense. She was the only one who'd take me seriously when I called about the poaching."

As Leo continued toward the Jeep, I placed Watson on the floor, and we headed out after him.

Katie, Paulie, and Flotsam followed.

Within a few minutes, we were all huddled on the porch, under large packing blankets Leo kept in his Jeep. The cold was preferable to waiting inside the cabin.

Another few minutes passed before three police cars made their way up the gravel road. Susan Green and Brent Jackson exited the first one and walked toward us. Officer

Jackson's face was filled with concern and he went directly to our little group.

Susan marched right past us, eyes straight ahead, and walked into the cabin. At least that was her intention. She gasped, a sound I'd never heard Susan Green make and froze in the doorway. After surveying what lay inside, she looked back, and to my surprise, her eyes met mine. "Branson was one of them?"

I nodded.

After a second, she did as well. "Explains a lot."

The Cozy Corgi had never felt so good. There'd been the typical morning rush from the locals as they got their coffee, pastries, and gossip. As per normal, anytime that gossip was particularly juicy, the rush lasted nearly till noon.

From my spot at the counter of the bookshop, I watched Watson napping in his favorite spot, the radiant November light filtering through the window, warming him. Beyond him, huge, fluffy snowflakes drifted slowly across Elkhorn Avenue. Somewhere behind me, Ben laughed gently as he helped a young woman pick out a meditative coloring book. The soft chatter of voices and clatter of pans from Katie's bakery overhead drifted down along with the comforting aroma of yeast and sugar. The fireplaces crackled and popped, just barely audible over the piped-in music of the Mills Brothers "I'll Be Around."

After everything was said and done the night before, the four of us didn't want to part. After being cleared by the doctor, Leo and Katie helped me make dinner at my house, and Paulie brought the dogs. Before we knew it, Athena dropped by, as did my parents and my uncles. Long after everyone else left, Katie, Leo, and I curled up on the couch,

Watson snoring by the fire, and we slept through endless reruns of Katie's favorite, *The Great British Bake Off*.

Though it had been wonderful to be surrounded by people I loved in my own home and feeling safe, being in the Cozy Corgi was better. Working, returning to normal. Some part of me wanted to grieve over Branson's betrayal, wanted to scream in rage. Another part felt like the biggest fool in the world. And some other little portion whispered that somehow, somewhere, some part of me had known, had warned. I shoved all of that aside—it was too much to deal with at that moment. I knew it would come up at some point, but there was no reason to face it then.

Watson's paws twitched in his sleep, and I wondered what he was dreaming. I didn't think he was reliving any of the moments from the day before, the gentle smile on his muzzle seemed pleasant enough. Chances were he was having visions of a parfait of various offerings from Katie's baking, with a couple of his favorite all-natural dog bone treats in between every layer. I hoped.

I decided he had the right idea. Katie and Nick were happily baking away overhead, and Ben was helping the only customer in the bookshop, so it was the perfect time for me to curl up on the antique sofa in front of the fire in *my* favorite location. It didn't even matter which mystery I pulled off the shelves. I just needed the weight of a book in my hands and to get carried away on someone else's adventure.

I started to turn and head to the mystery room, when the front door opened and Delilah walked through, flanked by four women. All five were wearing their silk Pink Panther jackets. The woman to Delilah's left was Nadiya Hameed, and she held hands with the larger blonde beside her.

"Well, Winifred Page, looks like luck is on our side." Delilah practically slithered across the hardwood floor. "I was afraid you'd already found a new dead body and wouldn't be here."

Some of the ease I'd been feeling evaporated at the sight of Delilah's little club. It didn't matter that I'd be forty in less than a year, or that I was a strong, independent woman, as Anna had put it. I couldn't help but feel that nagging insecurity left over from middle school as I walked by the cool girls' table and prayed they wouldn't see me. Although, as I glanced at the larger blonde and then at a couple of the others, I had to admit the difference. Despite Delilah's and Nadiya's pinup beauty status, the group wasn't entirely made up of Barbie dolls. Not even close.

I reminded myself that I'd looked down the barrel of a gun the day before, and this was nothing compared to that. And I was most definitely *not* still in middle school. "No, no dead bodies today. Just lots of dirty chais and pastries."

"As it should be. You deserve it." Delilah's smile turned from teasing to casually friendly. As she reached the counter, I looked over the group's shoulders and saw Watson lift his head, inspect, and then sink back down with a tired sigh. "We all took the day off work to celebrate Nadiya's release, and we wanted to come down and say thank you."

Nadiya let go of the blonde's hand and adjusted her glasses as she walked around the counter. She hesitated, and I thought she was about to stick out her hand, but instead she practically flung herself my way and wrapped her arms around me, trapping my arms at my side. "I can't thank you enough." She trembled.

Feeling awkward, I glanced around for some sort of rescue as I attempted to pat Nadiya but only succeeded in patting my own thigh. Delilah caught my gaze, and I could tell she was about to chuckle. Finally Nadiya pulled away and looked up at me. "You don't have anything to thank me for, Nadiya. I didn't figure it out. Everything I uncovered made you look guilty, honestly. If it weren't for Leo, I would've given up and said that the police were right. That you are the one who killed Max."

"I wanted to." She laughed and took a step back but didn't return to the other side of the counter. "And I'm thankful for Leo. But I'm also thankful for you. You may not have figured it out, but you didn't give up, and because of that"—she shrugged—"things went down in a way that cleared my name."

"I'm glad it worked out as it should've." Again thoughts of Branson threatened in the back of my mind, and I shoved them away. It hurt. I didn't want to hurt, or be angry. "And I'm sorry that you were in jail for something you didn't do."

"I intended to." She pushed up her glasses again, and she shrugged once more and laughed. "Well, I wasn't actually going to *kill* either of the poachers, but I was going to hold them at gunpoint until the police arrived."

"So you were going after them that night?"

Nadiya nodded. "Yeah. I heard the call on the scanner, saying that your bookshop had been broken into by the poachers. That they suspected they were heading to the dispensary in Lyons. That's where I went. That's where Sergeant Wexler found me and arrested me."

She'd given them the perfect scapegoat. "Was it your gun beside you as they said?"

"No. Mine was in the glove compartment. I didn't even have a chance to get it out." A hardness came into her dark brown eyes, and some of the anger that was apparent on her social media accounts flitted into her voice. "It's ridiculous. I think Max Weasel got *exactly* what he deserved. But I didn't do it." A dark grin split her beautiful lips. "Who knows, maybe it's for the best. My time in solitary confinement for the past few days might make it where if I ever run into Max's nasty brother, I won't give him what he deserves. Maybe."

Solitary confinement. And again, it all made sense. No wonder Branson wouldn't let anyone talk to her.

"There's a lot more creative ways to get revenge on men than killing them, Nadiya. Stick with me—I'll teach you." Delilah pulled the focus back to her once more, and again when she smiled at me, there was genuine affection and not even a hint of humor. "You'd make a great Pink Panther, Fred. Maybe the color of the jacket wouldn't exactly go with your hair, but..." She tilted her head and squinted her blue eyes, "I think you could pull it off."

That junior high girl still inside me, whispering insecurities, did a happy dance and pumped her fists in the air. "Thank you, but the answer is still no. I'm more of a book club kinda gal."

A couple of hours later, Watson sprang up from his nearly unending nap when Mom and Barry came into the shop. With a happy bark, he scurried over, going so fast that he slid over the hardwood floor and crashed into Barry's legs. He did that so often, I was starting to think it was intentional.

Barry ripped off his jacket as if it was too much clothing, revealing his silver-and-teal tie-dyed tank top, and bent to greet Watson with adequate enthusiasm. "I wish everybody in the world was as happy to see me as you are, little man."

Mom patted Barry's head lovingly from where he knelt

and came to meet me as I walked in from where I'd been reading in the mystery room. She wrapped me up in another hug. I had a feeling I was going to be getting even more of those than normal from her for a while. "Fred." She whispered my name and just hung on.

Her hug didn't feel awkward. If anything, it threatened to make me think about all the things I didn't want to think of. Made me want to pull my tiny mother onto the couch in front of the fire and just talk and talk and talk until she magically fixed everything like I'd thought she was able to do when I was small. Instead I just stroked her long silver hair, my heart swelling at the remaining streak of auburn in the strands.

From the corner of my eye, I noticed Ben sneak up the steps to the bakery, probably giving us privacy.

After a moment, Barry followed, squeezing my shoulder as he passed, Watson right on his heels.

Then it was just me and Mom, and still she held on.

"Are you okay?" I didn't attempt to pull back to look at her, just kept stroking her hair. "You know I'm fine. We were together last night. I'm not in any danger."

She only nodded against my shoulder.

After a little while, she cleared her throat, and with a final squeeze stepped back. Tears brimmed in her eyes, but they didn't fall. "I don't think it really hit me at your house. Not really. Somewhere in the dead of night, I woke up in a complete panic. All of it crashing down right then."

"Mom." I took her hand. "You should've called me. You could've come over."

She shook her head. "No. You needed your sleep, your rest. And I had Barry." She touched my blouse, right over where the necklace she'd made hung beneath. "Plus I knew you were okay. The danger had passed."

I'd had my own panicked thought in the middle of the night. I'd woken cold on the couch, Katie and Leo both asleep at opposite ends, the never-ending baking show still playing on the television. It had taken a while to fall back to sleep. I told myself I wasn't going to bring it up to Mom for a good long while, but now that she was in front of me again, I couldn't help it. "It's another connection to the Irons family, Mom. *Here* in Estes. And Branson was part of it. I can't even take it all in. The fact that he's connected to Dad's murder, I—"

"It doesn't mean he's connected to your dad's murder. The organization is, but Branson and Briggs probably had nothing to do with Charles. The Irons crime family is huge, all over the nation. Your dad was just investigating that one small part of it." Her hands shot up suddenly to clasp both of my cheeks. "Don't go chasing the Irons family, Fred. Don't you dare."

The thought hadn't even entered my mind. Though it did then.

And Mom could see it. She gave a slight shake. "Don't you dare! You listen to me. I lost your father. I nearly lost you last night, *not* for the first time. It's hard enough knowing that you're looking into all these murders, that you've got enough of your father in you that you can't let it go. But I'm begging you. Focus on your life here. Don't go chasing danger."

"But they *are* here, Mom." Why couldn't I just be a good daughter and simply say yes to soothe her? "They are in Estes."

"*Were.*" Still she wouldn't let my face go. "They *were* in Estes. Briggs is dead, and Branson is gone. Please let that be enough."

I hadn't told her what Paulie said about there still being

connections in Estes Park, though he didn't know who they were. And I wasn't going to. Maybe I wasn't such a bad daughter after all. "Okay, Mom. Okay."

She studied my gaze as if looking for some deceit, then finally nodded and released my face. "Okay."

At that moment, the door opened again, and both of us looked around. Leo walked in, snow over the shoulders of his park ranger uniform. He smiled when he saw us, his chipped teeth looking out of place on his handsome face. "Guess who got promoted?"

"You did!" Mom's voice shot up happily as she clapped. I couldn't help but marvel at her a little bit. How quickly she'd stuffed it all away again. I never forgot how tough she was, not really. She might present as flighty and ever increasingly whimsical, but she had a core of steel every bit as strong as my father. "Well deserved, I'd say."

"*I'd say* it's more of a matter of protocol than anything else. They gave me Etta's position." He winked at my mom. "But thank you for the congratulations." He accepted a hug from her and then bugged his eyes out at me. "They *also* offered me her cabin, said I could live there rent-free. Apparently it's owned by the national park, which I didn't know."

I couldn't even pretend to hold back my shudder at the thought, but managed to come up with a positive response. "No rent. That's..." Okay, half a positive thought.

"Are you kidding? You couldn't pay me to live there. Not after yesterday." He glanced toward the stairs. "Katie here? I thought she'd get a kick out of it."

"Of course she is, baking away." I started to step aside so he could head up. "Actually, I could do with another dirty chai. Mom and I will join you. Maybe get some pastries while we're at it."

Mom grabbed my arm and gasped. "Leo, look!" She pointed to the front windows.

Leo and I both followed her gesture and gave little gasps of our own.

As one, the three of us crossed the store and stopped at the window. Outside, walking down the middle of the street in the dying light of day, between the streetlamps as they sputtered, as the snow drifted down, a ram walked ahead of his harem of ewes.

"Well, look at that," Leo whispered quietly, but even so, his wonder was clear.

It wasn't unusual to see elk and sheep walk through the downtown of Estes Park, even a bear or mountain lion wasn't overly newsworthy, but as the ram paused right in front of the Cozy Corgi, the snow gathering on his curling horns, and looked our way, there was no denying the moment was magic.

Masses of swirling stars filled the crystalline night sky over the white peaked mountains as the full moon illuminating the forest glistened off the freshly fallen snow covering the pines. Even the winding trail of footprints Watson and I left in our wake sparkled. The only sounds were the crunch of our feet cutting through the deep powder and Watson's easy breathing.

Over the past week, I'd taken to bookending our days. The morning walk through the woods that surrounded my cabin had become routine over the last few months, but once in town, even after hours spent surrounded by books, pastries, and friends, I discovered my soul needed some solitude to be able to settle down. The quiet companionship of my little grump in the winter forest helped.

Maybe it was strange that I wasn't experiencing flashbacks of the rifle pointed at my face, of being certain the end was near, but I wasn't. Perhaps that was because even in those moments where I saw no possible escape, some part of me simply hadn't accepted the inevitable. Though, it hadn't been inevitable.

No, it wasn't fear that kept trickling in. True to form, it was my anger that continued to boil. I'd read someplace that anger wasn't really a primary emotion, that it covered up what was real below it—either betrayal, loneliness, embarrassment, whatever.

It didn't really matter. I felt how I felt. And I couldn't help but admit I'd played the part of the fool. How had I not realized? It all seemed so obvious in retrospect.

Branson's random nights and days away that seemed to happen spur of the moment? He was out doing the bidding of the Irons family. Duh! Okay, maybe that wasn't exactly obvious. I would've had to be truly paranoid to have leapt to that conclusion, but still. His waffling support? One minute gung-ho on me looking into a murder and the next causing whiplash as he set his foot down and demanded I keep my nose in my own business. From that perspective, it was easy to see which ones he'd been involved in and which ones he hadn't. And that, I thought, was what made me feel like the biggest fool of all. Clearly he'd been involved in some of the murders I'd looked into, at least in some fashion, and I hadn't noticed.

And to think I just sloughed off Chief Briggs. He hadn't been off the mark. As a detective's daughter, I knew how the police force felt about civilians shoving their way into an investigation. His hatred of me seemed a little extreme, but I hadn't given it much more thought than that. Besides, Susan Green hated my guts, and Paulie still swore that she'd never been part of it. From her reaction at the cabin, I believed him.

And of course, that was all cerebral.

The other part, the one that was harder to consider and even harder to admit, was that I'd considered giving Branson Wexler my heart. I'd nearly fallen for him. Nearly chose to ignore the warning signs and the little whisper of that voice. Nearly let all those who told me I was being unreasonable and throwing away a good thing convince me.

I hadn't, ultimately. So that was something. But I wished I hadn't even come close.

Maybe I was being too hard on myself.

I stopped at the edge of the forest where the clearing opened to my little cabin. Watson plodded ahead a couple of yards before coming to the end of his leash and glaring back at me in irritation. I grinned at him but leaned against the tree. I took a few more seconds to give thanks for the life I'd built in Estes, the life I was building. It was going to look different than it had so far, but... that proved that it was a life.

Even though it was only the second week of November, Mom and Barry, assisted by Verona and Zelda, had come over a couple of nights before and helped me put up my Christmas tree. They said I needed some brightness. They'd been right.

From my spot against the tree outside, I had to admit that my grandparents' old cabin now looked like a Thomas Kincaid painting, surrounded by stars and snow-laden mountains and trees. Thick blankets of the stuff covered the roof and porch. I'd left the lights on, so the windows glowed warm and inviting, and the Christmas tree sparkled from within frosted windowpanes.

Not all aspects of my life were picture-perfect, but more than enough of them were. Within five minutes, I'd be in my nightclothes, curled up in front of the fire with a book and Watson snoring at my feet. And that would be enough.

Watson gave a little tug, and I answered with a roll of the eyes and then conceded. "Fine, Your Highness. Ruin a perfectly magical moment."

As we drew nearer to the porch, Watson began to pull harder at the leash and growled.

"Good grief, Watson. You're getting more demanding every day." I sped up. He had a point. Now that I was picturing a fire, I had to admit how cold it was outside.

I flung open the door to the cabin, pounded my snow boots on the mat, and was met with a pleasant wave of warmth.

Watson's growl increased, and I finally recognized the warning sound that had been there all the time.

Branson sat in the overstuffed armchair, his handsome features highlighted from his spot by the fireplace. Considering the seismic shift in my view of him, it threw me off how normal he looked in his dark-wash jeans and soft brown sweater.

He smiled. "I hope you don't mind. I helped myself. I thought the night called for a fire." He gestured at the little side table. "And hot chocolate. It won't be as good as what you make, but I did my best."

My heart raced, startled at finding him sitting, unannounced, in my home. Wounded by the familiarity. And then an image of the rifle barrel flashed in my mind. I took a step back before I realized what I was doing.

"You're safe, Fred." Branson didn't move, and he glanced down at a growling Watson. "I don't blame you for being angry, little one, but I've always told you, your mama is safe with me. She still is." Those bright green eyes flicked back to me. "Always will be."

"What are you doing here?" I remained in the doorway.

"I wanted to talk. I wanted to see you."

As if nothing had happened. I glanced behind me, looking for tracks that should have alerted me; there were none. Just departing and returning sets of Watson's and my own. He must've come in through the back. "You broke into my house."

Branson nodded. "Yes, that's true." He smiled, *he actually smiled*. It held a hint of humor and affection. "Don't worry, I didn't steal anything. I'm not a thief."

"No. Just a murderer." The words were out before I considered, but I had no desire to take them back.

His smile faltered, but the expression in his eyes remained calm, kind. "Yes. That's also true." He casually picked up one of the mugs of hot chocolate and took a sip. "Sadly, not as good as yours. Can we talk?"

I should have run, snatched up Watson, rushed to the Mini Cooper, and driven away as fast as possible while calling the police at the same time.

Instead I walked into the house, closed the door, unleashed Watson—who stayed by my side, growling—and removed my jacket, scarf, and snow boots. If I called the police, he'd be gone into the wind. They wouldn't have a chance. And I knew, without a shadow of a doubt, that I truly was safe with Branson. Plus, I wanted to talk to him too.

My heart still pounding like a twelve-piece band, I crossed the living room, accepted the hot chocolate, and then sat on the couch across from him. In a very un-Watson-like move, Watson leaped onto the couch and snuggled beside me, resting his head on my lap and keeping a wary gaze on Branson.

We sat in silence for several minutes, or maybe seconds, I had no idea. We sipped our hot chocolate. He was right, it wasn't as good as mine, but decent. After the first taste another warning went off, at how stupid I had to be drinking something he offered me. But again, I was safe with him. I just was, so I sipped again.

He shifted nervously. "You know, I'm not really sure where to begin now that we're here."

"You're associated with the Irons crime family, right?" Though I felt a bigger fool because of the romantic notions I'd had for him, those paled in comparison to my chief concern.

He grinned. "Okay, I guess we'll start there. And yes, I am."

"So does that mean you were..." I caught myself. I did know I was safe with him, but the man had lied to me from the moment I'd met him, so I narrowed my eyes and leaned forward slightly. "If I ask you questions, will you be honest with all of them?"

He didn't even hesitate. "Yes. You deserve that. If you ask something I'm not willing to or can't answer, then I'll say that. But I can promise you, I will never lie to you again."

Again... I nearly snorted in disgust but held it back. I started to repeat the question and then realized my emotions were about to get the best of me, so I took a couple more seconds, some slow breaths, and another sip or two of hot chocolate, then began again, my voice steady. "Were you involved with my father's murder?"

"No." Though Branson winced, he didn't hesitate then either. "I was already working for the Irons family at that time, but I've never been stationed in Missouri. I wasn't part of it. Honestly, I didn't even know about it. Sure, about the bust and how it affected... business, but I wasn't aware of the details or the players. Not until later."

I studied him, hard and long, and I believed him. A larger wave of relief than I would've expected washed over me. It only lasted for a second. "Did you know from the beginning, when you met me at the first murder in the Cozy Corgi? You knew who I was? Who my father was?"

"No." Branson held my gaze and leaned forward like he was going to stretch across the distance to take my hand. He didn't go that far, thankfully. "I didn't know, Fred. Not then."

Some of the relief came back, though I couldn't exactly say why it mattered. It wouldn't change what was. "When did you know?"

He shrugged. "I can't say. I don't remember the exact moment. But not too long after that."

"Before you asked me to dinner?" *Good grief!* Why was this so important?

"No, I didn't know then." Branson winced once more, then sighed. "I did know by the time we actually went to dinner at Pasta Thyme. But by then, I'd already fallen for you."

That stung, and then I realized why it did matter. "You went out with me, knowing that you were involved with my father's murder."

"Not directly, I wasn't." He was matter-of-fact.

I stared at him. I couldn't believe his reaction. He was part of the Irons crime family.

"*Charles Franklin* was involved in your dad's..." He cocked his head. "I just realized that he and your father both had the same first name. Strange." His tone returned to normal. "Anyway, Charles Franklin was involved in your dad's murder, though I don't know if he's the one who actually killed him."

I thought I knew where he was going, but I couldn't bring myself to prompt or urge him to stop.

"You know that we killed Franklin during a police shootout in Glen Haven after he went rogue and tried to hurt Paulie." His eyes held mine, maybe daring me to look away, or begging me to see the truth. "When I shot him, it was partly for you, for your father."

I stared at him, speechless for several moments. My emotions were so all over the place I couldn't come close to landing on one of them. "Am I supposed to thank you for that?"

My whisper must've sounded strange, as Watson looked up at me in concern.

Another gentle smile played on Branson's face, but he didn't respond.

More for something to do than anything, I took another sip of hot chocolate, and though I wasn't a big drinker, I wished he'd spiked it with something stronger. I couldn't take thinking about my father anymore. Branson had already said he didn't know who killed my dad. What did any of the rest matter? "Is what Briggs said true? You killed Eddie?"

He laughed softly, but it wasn't a mocking sound. "You had a strange soft spot for that weird little drug dealer."

Yes, I supposed I did, though that wasn't how I'd thought of him. He'd simply been a charming hipster who'd owned a dispensary, hero-worshiped my stepfather, and had been kind to Watson and me.

Branson didn't wait for more prompting. "Yeah, I did." He shrugged once more, and I had to marvel that as he spoke of murder, his tone was so casual. There was no hint of guilt or aggression. It was all matter-of-fact. "There was no other choice when it came to light he'd been going behind our back, selling produce to Sid at a cut-throat rate. He was the same as Owen, poaching those birds for his own profit behind our back." He shrugged. "As you know, someone else helped me out with that one, though unintentionally."

I'd guessed at the reason. It had been one of the things that had plagued me all week, the memory of telling Branson what I'd discovered about Eddie. When I'd told him, I'd thought Branson's anger had been about drugs filtering into his town, not that he wasn't the only source. I knew I wasn't responsible for Eddie's death, but... I'd helped ignite the fuse. I pushed on.

"So the person in jail..." My intellect caught up with my words. I'd never seen proof of an arrest for Eddie's murder. Branson had said it was solved and justice had been served. I'd simply believed him and moved on. "There's no one in jail for Eddie's murder, is there?"

He shook his head with a sad smile. "No."

Just another lie. I moved on. "And Max? Is his brother dead too?"

He sighed. "Fred"—he motioned toward the doorway —"you said it yourself, right there. I'm a murderer. Do you really want the list? It's a long one. I'll give it to you if you want. How much time do you have?"

I warred with attempting to shove everything I knew about the man to one picture. I believed the gentleness and kindness I'd seen in him, *felt* from him, was genuine, but so was this—that he could speak about ending people's lives with such little regard.

"Sorry if I'm upsetting you, Fred." He truly sounded like he meant it. "I promised you I'd be honest."

I took another sip of hot chocolate and stroked over Watson's back. I didn't need the list. It wouldn't do any good. That was what I needed to focus on. The past was done, the future? Not so much. "Who else in Estes is part of the Irons crime family?"

He shook his head, almost regretfully. "That's one of those that I'll have to answer with the disclaimer. I won't tell you that. And... to a large degree, can't. As you can imagine, most of it's on a need-to-know basis. For all I know, *you* could be working with them." He hurried on when I flinched. "I know you're not, but you see my point."

I didn't push. I knew he wouldn't tell me, but he'd confirmed what Paulie had said. They were still here, just cloaked. I'd known the organization was large from the few things Dad had mentioned when he'd been investigating them, but I'd assumed they'd been local to the Kansas City area. Clearly, they were much bigger than I'd figured. But... how big?

He kept going, not waiting for another question. "I don't know if it matters to you or not, but I'm no longer part of the Irons family."

That threw me off. "You're not?"

He gave a snort of a laugh that made it seem like he felt it should have been obvious. "No, Fred. I killed Briggs, and Etta." He shrugged again. "Granted, she wasn't a big deal, but Briggs was. I have a price on my head now."

That hadn't entered my thoughts all week. Not once. That he'd have a price to pay for sparing my life. As he stared at me, I wondered if I was supposed to thank him. I couldn't make myself. If he wanted me to feel guilty or indebted, I wasn't going to.

But then, when I thought of how it could've gone down, I did feel indebted. And when I met his eyes, I meant every word I said with *every* ounce of my being. "Thank you for that. For sparing Watson, Leo, Katie, and Paulie."

He cocked an eyebrow. "And yourself?"

For whatever reason, I couldn't respond to that.

Strangely, that seemed to please him as his smile broadened. "You're ever Winifred Page, aren't you?" He stood, setting his hot chocolate aside, then moved toward the couch.

Watson lifted his head, growled, and bared his fangs.

Branson held up his hands. "Always safe, little man. Remember?"

I laid a reassuring hand on Watson's back. Though he hid his fangs once more, the rumble never left his chest, nor did his head return to my lap. He stayed focused on Branson, who sat beside us on the couch.

"And that brings me to why I'm here. Why I wanted to see you again."

"What does? The fact that you displeased the Irons family?"

"No." Branson reached for my hand but pulled back, reconsidering. "Come with me. Please."

I gaped at him. I hadn't seen that coming.

Still his eyes met mine, but they shifted, allowing me to fully see into him. See the hope, to see the inevitable hurt he knew would come.

"I don't even know your real name." I'd done a search on him many times throughout the week, and only found enough to realize Branson Wexler never existed. "And you want me to go away with you?"

"Branson Wexler isn't my real name—you're right. But if you choose to go with me, I'll tell you." He rushed on before I could respond. "Watson can come too, of course. I would never ask you to leave him behind. My feelings for you weren't ever a lie. I think you know that. I love you. I didn't expect someone like you to show up. Honestly, I didn't even want anyone. I had no desire to fall in love, but..." Another shrug. "But I did."

The voice of that middle school girl in the back of my

mind joined with the refrain I'd heard from so many of the townspeople over the last several months. Asking me if I was crazy. How a woman like me could turn down a man like him. As they marveled, sometimes right to my face, about what was wrong with him that he could want me. As they threw metaphysical stones, telling me I thought too much of myself and that he deserved someone better. That cacophony shouted at me to ask why. Demand the list of reasons why in the world he loved me.

I shoved that aside. I was *not* a middle school child. And I'd heard all those voices before during my divorce—that somehow it had been my fault, that I needed to give him a second chance, and who was I to think I was good enough to say no.

Reaching over Watson, I took Branson's hand. "No."

Genuine pain flashed behind his eyes and then covered his face. He lifted my hand to his lips, pressed a kiss, and closed his eyes. When he lowered my hand and met my gaze once more, the pain and disappointment slid away behind his perfect exterior. "I knew you'd say that." His thumb smoothed over my knuckles. "You have a standing invitation, if you ever change your mind."

Strangely, affection for him flooded through me. For the friend I'd found in him in the beginning, and then the spark of heat that had ignited. "I won't change my mind. I don't want you to hold out hope for—"

"Let me take care of me, okay." He smiled gently, kissed my hand again, and released it before standing once more. "You're an amazing woman, Winifred Page. I regret any ounce of hurt I've caused you."

I had an impulse to stand, to pull him to me in a goodbye embrace. I didn't. But when I spoke, I held his gaze and allowed him to see into my eyes as he'd done to me. "Goodbye, Branson."

"See you later, Fred." He nodded at Watson. "I know I don't have to tell you, but take care of your mama." With that, he turned and left the way he'd snuck in.

There was a click of the back door. He even paused to relock it, which made me smile.

I knew the right thing to do was to call the police, let Officer Green, or Officer Jackson, or whoever answered the phone, know that a fugitive was making his way out of town. I wasn't even tempted to make that call. I wasn't sure if it was because I was certain they didn't have a chance of catching him, or if it was because I was grateful he had spared our lives. Or maybe... just because he was Branson.

Exhaustion swept over me, and for the first time in a week, it wasn't unpleasant.

I stood and finished what I'd planned on doing the entire time. I got into my nightgown, turned down the bed, dimmed the lights except for the Christmas tree, and moved what remained of my hot chocolate next to Branson's on the side table.

"I know you're going to hate me for this, but give your mamma a little gift, okay?" Without waiting for permission, I scooped Watson into my arms and settled myself in the armchair. I didn't have it in me to read, so I sat by the crackling fire, Watson heavy on my lap, only squirming occasionally, and I stared out past the twinkling Christmas tree to the snow that had begun to fall over the trees once more.

A Cozy Corgi Mystery

Malevolent Magic

MILDRED ABBOTT

MALEVOLENT MAGIC

Mildred Abbott

The Scroogiest of Ebenezer Scrooges wouldn't have a ghost of a chance remaining immune to the holiday spirit once they entered the toy store. With Christmas a little over two and a half weeks away, I began counting the days for it all to be over. Though I most definitely would not consider myself a Scrooge, in my defense, Halloween had barely sighed its dying breath before Estes Park began stringing lights and hanging tinsel. Those aspects only increased the charm of the Colorado mountain town, making it a beautiful Christmas village, but there are limited versions of Christmas carols a person can bear on endless loops after so many weeks.

Still, surrounded by the massive assortment of old-fashioned Christmas toys carved from wood or made of hand-painted metal that filled Bushy Evergreen's Workshop, the high-pitched voices of Alvin and the Chipmunks singing "The Christmas Song" nearly got me back into the mood—I was practically in the middle of Santa's toy factory, for crying out loud. The six-year-old girl who lived inside me couldn't help but be swept away by the wonderment and magic of it all.

A whimper at my feet drew my attention away from a

carved elk with the nose painted bright red to resemble his more famous reindeer cousin. Watson grimaced up at me through slitted eyes as if he was in pain. It seemed he held no enjoyment of Alvin and the Chipmunks. If he could, I had no doubt Watson would've curled his fox-like corgi ears to block out the noise.

I smiled at him and shook my head. "You are the definition of a drama queen."

He only continued to scowl. Maybe I was wrong. Watson was probably the Scroogiest of Ebenezer Scrooges, and he wasn't a convert.

We rounded the corner, past a pyramid of stuffed animals, and came into view of the counter, which was outlined in twinkling multicolored lights. Old Duncan Diamond, the carver of the wooden toys, and his son, Dolan, were huddled together in front of a computer screen. Both seemed heavy in concentration. So much so that at Watson's and my movement, Dolan glanced at us and then instantly returned to the computer before flinching and looking back up once more, clearly startled. He darted his gaze from me to Watson, then toward the front door and back. "Goodness! You two snuck in."

Duncan gave a little flinch of his own at Dolan's voice but smiled instantly when he saw us. "Didn't even hear the door chime." There was a flicker of sadness in his eyes, and I knew he was thinking of the year before, the loss and betrayal that had happened where Watson and I stood, but the look was gone in an instant and his smile returned. "To what do we owe the pleasure of a visit from Winifred Page and her corgi sidekick? I know your nephews and nieces are much too old for any of the toys I offer here at this point."

"Nice to see you both." I didn't try to argue and finished my path to the counter, letting a little slack loose in

Watson's leash so he could wander around if he wanted. "And there are two things, actually." I dug into my purse and pulled out a notepad. "Katie and I had an idea, and I'm making a quick jaunt around town to see if other store owners are interested."

Dolan gave an exaggerated shiver. "It's the coldest day we've had in weeks. If you're walking all over downtown in this weather, you're tougher than me." He shrugged good-naturedly. "Although, we already knew that."

Before I could respond, Duncan patted his son on the back. "But you're sweet, kind, and pure of heart." He refocused on me. "So what's this scheme you and the baker sent from the gods have come up with?"

The first time I met him, Duncan Diamond seemed so old and sad. Now, despite heavy wrinkles on his face, he was lighter, happier. That helped me remember the point of Christmas spirit even more than the beauty of the toy shop. "We thought we'd use the final rush of tourists for some good. We're putting together a coupon book for all the shops. The booklet will cost twenty-five dollars and will have discounts for all participating stores inside. All the profits will be split between the toy drive at the hospital, the women's shelter, and the animal rescue." Though Bushy Evergreen's Workshop was at least the tenth store I'd visited the past couple of hours, I felt heat rise to my cheeks. I hated asking for things, even when they weren't for me. "There's no pressure at all, but anything you'd be willing—"

"What do you think, Dad?" Dolan didn't even hesitate as he looked at Duncan. "Fifteen percent off all purchases, and a free stuffed animal for those over fifty dollars?"

Once more Duncan patted his son on the back. "See? Sweet, kind, pure of heart." Duncan nodded at me. "Put us down."

There was the sound of a door slamming in the back, and Dolan's rather plain face lit up into a thing of beauty as his wife emerged from more rows of toys, snow falling from her long raven hair while she unwrapped the bundle in her arms. She smiled brightly when she noticed us. "Fred, Watson. So good to see you!"

Dolan hurried to help her finish unwrapping the bundle, revealing a chubby baby girl with a mop of bright red curls who giggled as her daddy kissed her cheeks.

Daphne let out a sigh of relief and straightened, her back popping audibly. "Darby is barely five months old, but I swear it feels like I'm lugging around a preschooler." She started to laugh and then worry filled her beautiful eyes. "Is everything okay? Has someone been murdered?"

When I moved to Estes Park a little more than a year ago, I figured I'd be known around town as the owner of the Cozy Corgi Bookshop. And I was, but even more than a reputation for book-nerd status, my appearance had become associated with finding dead bodies. "No. Just here begging for money."

She relaxed in relief and began sloughing off the layers of scarf and jacket. "Thank goodness."

"You're hardly begging for money, Winifred." Duncan walked from behind the counter and scratched Watson between his ears. "But you did say you came for two reasons. What's the other? We'll help you in any way we can."

"Always." Daphne nodded her agreement with her father-in-law and looked at me in a sense of hero-worship, as she had on the rare occasions we ran into each other. Hardly something I felt I deserved.

"Well, Katie and I had a second idea as well. Next Thursday evening, we thought we'd throw a party at the

Cozy Corgi, just for residents of the town, before the Christmas tourism starts the next day. Nothing lavish, just Katie's baking and a time to chat and hang out. We thought we might make it a Christmas tradition."

"I've never had one sampling of Katie's baking that isn't lavish." Duncan gave a final pat on Watson's head and stood. "And it's a marvelous idea. For such a small town as we are, and everyone knowing everyone else's business, we should do more things where tourists and sales aren't the primary focus. We will be there."

By the time we left Bushy Evergreen's, though it wasn't quite five yet, dusk had fallen. The thousands of lights strung up with the silver tinsel that swept from streetlamp to streetlamp covered Elkhorn Avenue in a canopy of Christmas. Not for the first time, with the snow falling softly, I couldn't help but feel like we'd built our lives inside of a Christmas snow globe.

Estes Park was always beautiful, but with the Christmas lights and decorations, it was even more lovely than usual. I changed my mind—I didn't want it to be over in a couple of weeks, even if it meant the end to the background of carols everywhere we went.

Some of my Christmas cheer gave way to a rush of anxiety as I glanced across the street toward the frozen waterwheel, also outlined in twinkling white lights. Right behind it, nestled among the few stores along the wooden pathway that led up from the main sidewalk, the window of the magic shop got my attention. Even from across the street, it was easy to see that they took Christmas seriously. There were so many lights, it glowed like a beacon. Alakazam was the reason I'd chosen to only do one side of the street first. I wanted to put off going into the magic shop for as long as possible. But with it staring at me from across the street, I could practically feel it taunting me.

That was a problem for the following day. Without a look back, Watson and I returned the way we'd come. I'd show Katie all the shops who'd signed up for the Christmas coupon book. Maybe over a dirty chai...

As we neared the Cozy Corgi, my mother, laden with boxes in front of her face, slipped and slid as she attempted to open the door to my step-sisters' New Age shop. "Mom, hold on. Let me help." I picked up my speed.

With a startled squeak, Mom flinched, her left foot kicked out, making contact with the front door of Chakras, and the boxes tumbled, their contents spreading over the sidewalk in glistening arrays of red, green, and silver.

I arrived just in time to grip her by the arm before she joined her fallen necklaces. "Sorry! I was trying to help, not scare you to death."

She laughed and fluttered a hand in front of her chest. "That's all right dear. I think the jewelry and I were both destined to end up down there, so it's good you came along. I should've knocked on the door and waited for Zelda or Verona to let me in, but I was being stubborn." She smiled up at me tenderly and then refocused at her feet, pulling out of my grip to bend toward Watson. "And hello to you too, handsome."

Watson pressed into her touch, a simple acknowledgment that she was part of his pack.

I knelt to begin picking up the strands of crystals, stones, and beads. "I'm afraid these are a tangled mess."

With a chuckle, she gave a final pat to Watson and began to help. "Can't blame you for that either, Fred. Barry helped me carry them from the house and dropped them as well. He offered to help untangle them, but I figured the twins and I could do it once I got here. It looks like that was the correct call. Otherwise I'd have to do it all over again." She grabbed the jewelry by the fistful and stuffed it back into boxes, only making the tangled situation worse. "It serves me right. I chose to make the collection out of barite, zincite, and quartz more for their green, red, and clear colors than for the correct blend of physical and metaphysical attributes. It's what I get for putting commercialism of the holiday season over—"

"Good grief, you three, you're making an absolute mess." Zelda stood above us in the doorway.

"Actually, I would say barite's qualities of assisting with regeneration and relaxation are perfect for the holiday season." Verona, Zelda's identical twin, except for her long blonde hair compared to Zelda's brunette, peered over her shoulder. "Although, blending it with zincite's influence over creativity and sexuality is an interesting choice."

As the twins assisted by scooping up strands of gems, they began to bicker over the positive and negative attributes of Mom's Christmas jewelry collection. Within a matter of moments, we were inside Chakras and had deposited the tangled mess of jewelry in a huge heap on top of the counter.

Mom let out an exhausted groan. "Goodness. This is going to take hours."

"Actually..." Verona cast a conniving glance toward Zelda. "Just this morning, the kids were asking for new cell phones for Christmas. Both of them."

Zelda cocked an eyebrow. "Interesting timing. So were mine. Apparently they've been talking."

"Of course they have. Power in numbers." Verona gestured toward the daunting mass of jewelry. "I bet our four little elves could tackle this in no time in hopes we might be more amenable."

"Brilliant." Zelda grinned and patted Mom's shoulder. "Don't give it a second thought. All will be handled. And from the looks of things, they're absolutely beautiful. And regardless of their... *interesting* combination of attributes, I guarantee you there will be plenty of shoppers who will require such a focus of energy."

A year before, I never would have dreamed I'd be standing in the middle of my step-sisters' New Age shop talking about the powers of crystals as if it was the most normal thing in the world. It was bizarre, and... rather wonderful. I hadn't been in Chakras for over a week. The store was always beautiful with its mishmash of outlandish and unique merchandise and decor, but Verona and Zelda had gone all out for their first year being open for the holidays. Christmas lights covered every single available surface. But there were new additions hanging from the ceiling that nearly took my breath away. Large round spheres, the size of beach balls hung in differing heights from the ceiling. They glowed in a shifting silvery, grayish white, their shards making them look like an explosion of snowy stars. Without thinking I started to reach out to touch one.

"I wouldn't do that, Fred." Verona's tone had the hint of exasperation. "These are Jonah and Noah's latest creations. They're made from the same material they used for last year's garlands."

I yanked my hand back and turned to stare at the twins. "Are you serious? Your husbands made more deadly Christmas decorations?"

"Just for Chakras." Zelda shrugged, unconcerned.

"They're not going to mass market them or sell them or anything like that. There won't be any more lawsuits."

"Besides." Verona sounded a little more exasperated than her twin. "They keep going back and forth on what they're going to do with their shop. I don't think they're ever going to get it opened." She gestured toward the gleaming orbs. "These gave them a couple days of focus, which they needed."

"They are lovely." Mom eyed them skeptically. "Although... You may want to hang them a little higher. I can't reach them, but there's plenty of people Fred's height or taller who will be tempted."

"Oh! That reminds me!" Zelda turned to me, her long brown hair fanning out in an arc. "Verona and I were talking about the little coupon book thingy you and Katie are doing. In addition to the discount on all incense items, we thought we would also throw in a free energy consultation, no purchase required."

"Thank you. That would be lovely." I glanced back at my inventor brothers-in-law's beautiful but deadly creations. "You might want to include a free box of Band-Aids or something as well."

"Oh, Fred." Mom swatted at me but couldn't hold back a giggle at the twins' sour expressions.

Alakazam taunted me once more from down the street as I left Chakras. However, I was in such a pleasant mood after laughing with, and at, my mother and stepsisters, I decided to simply get it over with. Otherwise, I'd worry about it all evening, probably to the point that by the time I went in the following day, I'd end up sticking both feet in my mouth instead of only one.

"Come on. With any luck, he won't even be there." Right, because *that* was how my luck worked. A resigned sigh escaped as I walked Watson across the street and up the steps that lead past the frozen waterwheel.

Watson gave a happy shimmy as we pushed open the doors and walked into Alakazam. Despite the rather horrendous sound of bagpipes accosting our ears, without hesitating, he trotted toward the wizened fairy already making her way from around the counter.

As I stamped off the snow on the welcome mat, the squealing of the bagpipe melody revealed itself to be "Good King Wenceslas." Apparently there *was* a way to make endless Christmas carols more excruciating.

By the time I thought I was mostly snow-free, Watson had already received his anticipated dog treat from the fairy. He trotted off to the end of his leash to settle down at the base of an old fortune-teller coin machine, its flashing bulbs clashing with the Christmas lights and garlands strewn all over the tiny shop.

The old fairy placed one gnarled hand on the edge of the counter for support. "Happy solstice season, Fred. Such a lovely pleasure to see you and your furry companion once more."

"Thank you, Glinda. And a happy... solstice to you as well." I thought that was the first time I'd ever said those words, which was surprising considering my sisters.

Glinda smiled, pleased. Though I knew it was only a costume, the old woman had such a wise and earthy feel to her that if I let myself, I could almost believe she truly was a fairy. Unlike the bright red-and-green Christmas decorations around her, she was dressed in flowing gossamer strips of burgundy, brown, and gold. Though they didn't move, the moss-green wings at her back were nearly translucent, crusted with amber gems along the spines, and looked as if they'd been plucked from a giant, mythical moth. A ring of holly and dark red berries nestled in her tangled mass of wispy silver hair. "It's been a while since I've seen you. I was just about to close up, but I'm so happy you're here. Are you here to purchase a gift for someone, merely to visit, or do you require an audience with the wizard?"

The first time I met her, I would've sworn she simply took her role as assistant in the magic shop extremely seriously and that she was a devout believer in the method theory of acting. I couldn't quite figure the woman out, but I liked her, even if she did make me slightly uncomfortable. Though not nearly to the level as *the wizard*, as she referred to him. "I just wanted to drop in and let you know about a couple of things we're doing at the bookshop and bakery to see if you want to participate. I know it's right at closing time, but I won't take long."

"Don't give it a second thought. The wizard and I are going to be here much of the evening. There's more decorating to do." She waved me off with a fluttering gesture around the shop. "There's not much time left before the rush of holiday revelers."

Despite myself, I couldn't keep from looking around the store again. Alakazam was squeezed between two larger stores on either side, and as a result every one of its walls, each painted a different color—plum, crimson, marigold, and sapphire—was angled, making the place look like two triangles mashed together. Even with its crowded layout and being stuffed with costumes, framed posters of wizards, toys, magic items, and collectibles ranging from crystal balls to medieval swords, the place was lovely and remarkable. It was still hard for me to believe a man as gruff as Mark Green was responsible for such a magical place. It'd been packed before, but now with all the Christmas and holiday decorations, it was nearly overflowing. I couldn't fathom where they planned on doing more.

When Glinda chuckled, I got the sense that she truly could read my mind. "You'll have to come back in once it's done. I love this little place all the time, but this time of year it's at its best."

"It really does feel like stepping into a magical world. You and Mark do a wonderful job."

"Thank you. But that's because it *is* a magical world." Glinda leaned against the counter and motioned me closer. "Now, pray tell, what plans does the Cozy Corgi possess that require our assistance?"

I filled her in on the Christmas party we were having, and by the time I started to explain the coupon book,

Watson had finished his treat and joined us, looking longingly up at his favorite fairy and giving her his best puppy dog eyes.

"I can't speak for the wizard, but I will most definitely be in attendance. Thank you for your invitation." She reached down and ruffled Watson's fur. "It will be a pleasure to see you again in such a brief amount of time, little fellow." To my surprise, and most definitely to Watson's, she didn't offer him another treat. A person either had to be hardhearted or truly magical to be able to withstand the power of Watson's puppy dog eyes, and I couldn't believe Glinda was hardhearted. "As far as taking part in your charity, while I think it most definitely is a worthy cause, that's for the wizard to decide." She motioned over her shoulder toward a narrow door in the back. "Allow me to inquire. I'll return briefly."

"Oh no, no need to bother him." I started to back away. "Just give me a call in the next couple of days and let me know what you two have decided. There's no rush."

At that moment, the door in question creaked open and a large man wearing flowing purple robes outlined in swirling silver embroidery slipped through. He clutched a tiny white bunny lovingly at his chest. Mark Green's pale blue gaze locked on Watson, then rose to me. With every inch they traveled, his expression transitioned from relaxed to hard, to furious. "Why are *you* here? Come to accuse me of more murders?"

"I've never accused you of murder, Mark." That part was true. Though I had suspected his wife of murder.

"She comes with tidings of joy and goodwill." Glinda stepped between us. At five ten and large in frame, I wasn't a small woman, and Mark practically towered over me. In comparison to the two of us, Glinda truly was practically the size of a fairy. She placed a hand on Mark's forearm. "We're invited to a celebration at her establishment, and she was wondering if Alakazam would like to take part in raising money for local charities."

Mark's face didn't soften for a moment. "Really? Her family doesn't have enough money? Come to demand gold from the peasants?"

I had to bite my tongue to keep from saying the things I knew about Mark's financial situation. To do so would have been cruel. I wasn't a cruel person, not even close. But there was something about the Green siblings that brought that temptation out in me. It was rare that I had an interaction with Susan, Mark's police officer sister, that didn't leave me regretting my word choice.

Glinda handled it for me, and scratched the bunny's head as she had Watson's only moments before. "Some of the proceeds will go to the animal shelter. You could consider it a gift in Drake's honor."

Mark looked down at the bunny, and for the first time, he softened. "I suppose that would be nice."

I saw my chance for a positive interaction and leapt on it. "Your bunny is absolutely adorable."

He rewarded me with a smile, the first I'd ever gotten from him.

"And Drake is such a serious name for the little guy." The moment the words left my lips, I realized my mistake.

Sure enough, Mark returned to a scowl. "His full name is Mandrake. Drake is just a nickname."

"Mandrake..." The meaning clicked instantly, knowing Mark's obsession with magic and wizards. "As in the screaming plant from Harry Potter?"

His eyes widened. "You've read Harry Potter?"

"Many times. I love those books."

He cocked his head and studied me as if trying to determine if I was mocking him.

"Winifred owns a bookshop, Mark, as I'm certain you recall. I'm sure she's well versed in the magical world of Hogwarts." Glinda was clearly trying to soothe the way between Mark and myself and managed to do so effortlessly in a way that reminded me of my mother's peacemaker skills. She continued to scratch the bunny's head as she addressed me. "We discovered little Drake likes to scream when the moon is out."

Mark chuckled. Actually chuckled. "It took me three nights before I realized I simply needed to cover his cage with a blanket to put him to sleep." Another very un-Green-like chuckle. "Though why he requires that when the lights are already out, I have no idea." Laughter faded as he studied me again. "You truly like the Harry Potter books?"

"Very much. My favorite character is Professor McGonagall." I half sensed I'd somehow given the wrong answer and rushed ahead. "And my nephew, Leaf, is obsessed. I think he's hoping he'll get a trip to the theme park."

"Really?" He passed the bunny to Glinda and motioned for me to follow. "Check these out. We just got them in for the holiday season." He led me to the back of the store, close to the room he'd exited. There was a tall narrow display case filled with the most ornate snow globes I'd ever seen. The base of each one was a heavy pewter sculpture. He picked one up and handed it to me. "That's Hogwarts Castle inside."

I nearly dropped it as it was at least twice as heavy as what I'd expected. Watson had been at my feet and scurried back, knowing what a klutz his mother was. Luckily, I didn't accidentally squish my corgi nor destroy Mark's merchandise. Once I was certain the crisis had been averted I inspected the snow globe. Inside the glass a perfect replica of Hogwarts gleamed in gold and bronze.

"This is absolutely stunning. A perfect keepsake." I gave it a little shake, causing the silver snow to swirl. "Almost feels like you could get lost in there."

"I agree." Mark still sounded like he was trying to determine if I was leading up to some big punchline of a joke at his expense. He pointed out a couple of others. "We've also got the Shire from *Lord of the Rings* and Mr. Tumnus from Narnia. We have some less magical ones just for Christmas, like this one of Scrooge from *A Christmas Carol* and the nativity from the Bible."

I nearly told him I'd been thinking about Scrooge earlier but decided against it. On a whim, feeling like this was my one and only chance to turn the corner with Mark Green, I passed the globe back to him. "We'll take it. It'll be a perfect Christmas present for Leaf. I don't suppose you have one of *Beauty and the Beast*? My niece Christina is obsessed." As true as that might be, I doubted that a single one of my four nieces and nephews were hoping for a snow globe. Well... whatever.

"The company makes one, though it's not the Disney version. I can order it." Again he sounded skeptical.

"That would be perfect. Thank you."

Glinda had knelt beside Watson and smiled up at us. "Oh, that is wonderful. The children will love it. The globes truly are magical."

"And expensive." The tone I knew like the back of my hand from his sister filled Mark's voice. "Are you sure you want to spend that much money here?"

I'd been led into a trap. No doubt. I couldn't determine which way the snare tied, though—at the end that led to me spending more money than I'd intended or the insult of not buying anything. Chances were there was a noose at both ends. I opted to take a note out of my mother's playbook and go the more gracious of the routes. "Absolutely. They're perfect. I'll take this one now and order the *Beauty and the Beast* one. Does that work?"

Less than five minutes later, Watson and I walked back into the snow and headed toward the Cozy Corgi. He trotted along happily after having received a second treat, his puppy dog eyes finally working on Glinda. I, on the other hand, felt like I'd been sucker punched. Each snow globe was five hundred dollars. The price of one of them was more than I'd planned on spending on Christmas gifts altogether. Even though I was painfully a thousand dollars lighter than when I'd walked into Alakazam, I still felt like I'd chosen the lesser of the two evils. Although, knowing Mark's sister, I was certain Susan would find some way to turn this around and make it where I'd done something wrong.

More than anything, I hoped that Leaf and Christina wouldn't think this was going to become a yearly event. Then it hit me that I had another niece and nephew to buy gifts for, and that to be fair they should match. "Speed it up Watson. Mama needs a dirty chai quickly! And probably a lemon bar to boot."

Watson looked as happy as a kitten trapped in a yarn store filled with catnip, which was a typical state of being for him anytime my stepfather was around. He was currently on his back, in front of the bakery counter on the top floor of the Cozy Corgi, with legs splayed while Barry scratched him into ecstasy.

Never abandoning his "grandfatherly" duties, Barry's fingers danced through Watson's fur as he addressed Katie's assistant behind the counter. "Congratulations, Nick! It was a travesty that they held you back for a semester, but you've graduated. No more high school. No more school at all!" Barry's eyes widened. "Not that I'm suggesting you shouldn't go to college. Higher education and all that jazz."

"Thanks." Nick blushed as he mumbled. "But no more school. Ever."

"Don't say that. I guarantee you college will be easier than high school was. Plus, you don't have to go the traditional route, you could get a degree in culinary arts." Katie didn't pause in her work, handing a large tray of breakfast quiches to Nick before turning back to the oven.

"I'm learning everything I need to know here." From his expression, the thought of more school made him nauseous.

I couldn't blame him. High school had been hard enough for both of the Pacheco twins, but especially Nick. "No need to decide now. Just celebrate being done and then we can enjoy the holidays." I plucked up one of the bite-size quiches, ignoring how hot it was.

"And tonight, we celebrate *you!*" With a final pat on Watson's belly, Barry stood and beamed at Nick. "Well-deserved."

Again, Nick looked close to being sick. He didn't attempt to speak, just shook his head.

Katie paused long enough in her baking to nudge him on the shoulder. "Don't worry, we're not going to have you make any speeches tonight. It's a combination of celebrating your graduation and our new annual tradition of Christmas at the Cozy Corgi. People will simply give you their well wishes and move on."

It didn't seem like that was much comfort.

Barry switched directions, maybe trying to ease things for Nick a bit, as he refocused on Katie and me. "I have to say, I'm so proud of you two." He snagged one of the newly printed coupon books off the counter. "Look at the size of this thing. The tourists are going to eat these up and provide so much money for the charities."

In the past week the coupons really had come together. "That's simply due to the other shops' generosity. All Katie and I did was—"

"Nonsense. It wouldn't have happened if it weren't for the two of you." He waved me off. "Shows the true meaning of Christmas." He placed the coupon book back on the counter and sighed contentedly. "I love this time of year. So beautiful, but even more important is all the families returning home, people who grew up in Estes Park coming back to see their parents and grandparents. Bringing their new babies." He turned his beaming gaze on me. "And they'll all be here tonight. This was a wonderful idea, Fred. The town needed a reason to come together and celebrate, to be light. Especially considering all that happened with..." His voice trailed off, probably at my stiffening posture—I didn't want to think about Branson or the drama in the police department. Barry shifted gears and pointed at the quiches. "Katie, my dear, do you mind if I take six of these little bites of heaven? I'm on my way to visit Percival and Gary. We're to do a little planning around their anniversary party. We're thinking of renting out Baldpate Inn. And you know Percival, we're going to need sustenance."

Before he left, he gave Watson another scratch behind his ears and offered me a loving, yet all too knowing, smile of support.

Thankfully, within a matter of seconds, I was swept up in preparations for the celebration and the rest of the day sped by in a blur.

A strange sense of déjà vu combined with accomplishment washed over me as I stood behind the counter of the Cozy Corgi that evening. The bookstore was packed with people for our "Nick graduating from high school and holiday" combination celebration. It reminded me of the opening night nearly a year before.

Many of the same people were in attendance. Myrtle Bantam and the twelve members of her Feathered Friends Brigade—though the specific people of those twelve had altered somewhat—huddled in the nature section, each in their matching vests, sporting badges and various pins related to their ornithological achievements. My family had already arrived and were upstairs in the bakery, visiting other locals, though there were plenty of trays filled with Katie and Nick's delicacies scattered around different sections in the bookshop. Watson, of course, was in the bakery as well, tagging along wherever Barry went.

What a difference a year made. Last Christmas I'd been doing finishing touches to the hardwood floors and bookshelves, and the only decorations I'd bothered with had been hand-cut snowflakes affixed to the windows. There were nearly a hundred of those this year—mostly made by the Pacheco twins—but that was where the similarities ended. This year the Cozy Corgi Bookshop, as well as the bakery, was festooned with countless sparkling lights accompanying glistening emerald ribbon interwoven in garlands made of fresh pine branches. Five different Christmas trees filled the space, two in the bakery and three on the main level. When I heard Katie and the twins talking about five trees—*five!*—I'd insisted it would be too much. I'd been wrong. It was all just enough. One decoration more and we might've bordered on tacky, but this was a perfect wintery, Christmas wonderland.

Not for the first time, I was overwhelmed with how much better the reality of my dream little bookshop turned out compared to the fantasy. Not only beautiful, but filled with laughing and chatting people, devouring the world's most delectable pastries, meandering about, and flipping through books. And over it all was the smell of butter, cinnamon and cloves, the hot spiced apple cider brewing at various stations, and the woody aroma of fresh pine. I supposed it was the perfect wintery, *mountainy* Christmas wonderland.

There were two notable differences from the grand opening that had happened just a few weeks after the previous Christmas.

I touched the dangling silver corgi earrings as I thought of Leo Lopez. They'd been a gift from him on opening night. But as he'd recently been promoted to a supervisor's position as a national park ranger, he was required to be elsewhere that evening. But as he, Katie, and I hung out constantly, it was only a matter of a day or two since I'd seen him.

The other absence was a little more acute. Branson Wexler, the Estes Park police sergeant, had also been in attendance at the grand opening. Our first date had been on Christmas Eve. Our relationship—which had gone back and forth, to say the least—had ended in what I'd hoped would be friendship. But that illusion met its fiery conclusion just after Halloween. Despite finally realizing Branson's true identity, I couldn't keep a swell of loss from cutting through me. I'd never see him in my bookshop again.

"Fred, darling! Are you all right?" A rather sharp voice thankfully sliced through my memories and melancholy, bringing me back to the present, which was beautiful and more than enough. I looked across the counter to see Anna Hanson staring at me. Her husband, Carl, stood directly behind her. Both of their round faces peered out from underneath Santa Claus hats.

As the owners of the home furnishing shop across the street, and town royalty of the gossip variety, their concern brought a smile to my face. "I am. Just got lost to the past for a moment."

"Branson?" Anna reached across the counter and patted my hand. "Lamenting the one who got away?"

I felt my smile begin to falter, but I plastered it back in place and lied, at least partially. "No, just thinking of this time last Christmas when I was getting the bookshop ready to go. I remember wondering about how I'd decorate this

Christmas. Plus, tonight reminds me of the grand opening with everyone wandering about."

Carl, wearing his Feathered Friends Brigade vest and sporting his badge for the best bird caller, spoke with his mouth full, crumbs flying as he waved the partially eaten bite-size pastry at me. "Are these sweet potato empanadas? Katie has outdone herself!"

I nodded and latched on to the change of subject. "I have to agree with you. She really has." I leaned closer as if sharing a secret. "Katie and Nick have the full-sized pie versions upstairs. And for some reason, they're even better."

His eyes gleamed as he started to head in that direction, but Anna grabbed his arm. "Hold on, we'll get there. First things first." She looked over her shoulder and appeared to be searching for someone. "Billy!" She raised her voice to a level that caused both Carl and I to wince, as well as stop all the various conversations in the immediate area. "Billy!"

A short man I judged to be in his early- to mid-forties popped his head around the edge of a bookshelf. "Hold on, Mom. There's a book here about how to brew homemade beer."

Anna rolled her eyes. "*That's* the last thing you need. Get over here."

With a grimace, the man shoved the book back into place and headed over. I knew who he was before any introduction. He had the exact same body shape that Anna and Carl shared, and though he lacked Carl's glasses and fluffy white beard, he could've been a carbon copy.

Anna grabbed his shoulder and gave a squeeze, as if holding him in place. "Fred, this is our son, Billy. He got into town just a couple of days ago. He lives in Los Angeles."

Billy attempted a smile and a nod.

Anna nudged him. "Offer your hand, Billy." She let loose a long sigh in my direction. "A mother's training is never done."

His cheeks reddening, Billy stuck out his hand. "Hiya, nice to meet ya."

I could tell Anna was about to offer commentary on his chosen greeting, so I quickly took his hand. "Nice to meet you, Billy. I've heard wonderful things about you from your folks."

Over Billy's shoulder, Carl's eyes widened at my lie.

I'd known Anna and Carl had a son, but I'd never heard more about him than his name.

Anna patted Billy's shoulder again. "Good enough. I suppose." She looked at me again and this time practically crowed. "We're having the *whole* family in town for Christmas. The girls, Sarah and Betsy, will be here too. It'll be the first time the entire family is together for Christmas in several years." Her nose wrinkled. "Of course Betsy's husband will be here as well, but..." She shrugged, her smile returning. "The grandbaby will be too, and it's his very first Christmas."

Billy rolled his eyes, but Carl's expression matched Anna's—pure happiness at the mention of the grandchild.

"I'm glad for you all. This will be my second year home for Christmas with my extended family. It's made the holidays much better." Christmas in Estes was so different from those of my childhood when it had just been my father, mother, and myself in Kansas City. With the large family, including stepsisters and their husbands and children, I'd found the whole ordeal a little overwhelming the year before. But now that I was used to it, I was very much looking forward to the celebrations.

Anna nodded in absentminded agreement, her gaze flitting around the bookshop before she rose on tiptoe to peer behind the counter at my feet. "Where is he?"

I didn't need any explanation; Anna was completely obsessed with Watson.

I pointed above our heads. "Barry and the others are in the bakery, so of course Watson is acting as his shadow."

Anna scowled as if put out that Watson wasn't waiting for her with bated breath. "Well, I'm going to go steal him away. I brought his favorite all-natural dog treat bone. I know that Katie makes them by the scores, but still, it's from me, so I'm sure he'll find it special." Without waiting for a response, she grabbed Billy by the meat of his upper arm and began pulling him around the counter and toward the stairs up to the bakery. "Hurry up. You've simply got to meet Watson. He is the cutest dog who ever existed. A little grumpy, but"—she shrugged as she continued to yank him onward—"with the state of the world these days, who can blame him?"

Carl finished the last bit of the mini sweet potato empanada and smiled at me apologetically. "Sorry about Billy. He's..." I could see a million different words flash behind his eyes, and then he seemed to give up. "You say there's regular-sized sweet potato pies upstairs?"

"There are." I pointed toward one of the silver percolators warming at a nearby table. "Grab a cup of hot spiced apple cider, too. It's a heavenly combination."

"You're a jewel, Fred. Just a jewel." Carl hurried off to get himself a glass.

Absentmindedly, my gaze traveled after him until he finally disappeared upstairs. I'd grown to love the Hansons, though they'd taken a little getting used to. At the core of their gossipy, eccentric personalities, they had hearts of gold. That said, I couldn't help but send Billy a thought of sympathy. The couple was wonderful in smaller doses, but I couldn't fathom having them as parents. I imagined it was rather an intense experience. And probably why it had been a while since their last family Christmas as a unit.

Taking my own advice, I poured myself a glass of apple cider and meandered around the bookshop. The whole town really had shown up. The mix of friends, acquaintances, and people I'd only met once or twice came and went. Not only was Katie's baking a hit, but everyone was enthusiastic over the display of coupon books.

I was about to leave the bookshop in Ben's capable hands to join Watson, my family, and the Hansons in the bakery, when Glinda walked in. She had on a similar flowing gown to the one she had the week before, though this one was in muted tones of powder blue, silver, and brown, but the fairy wings were nowhere to be seen. Maybe she took them off when she left the shop, or perhaps they were just invisible. The thought made me smile. The next thought washed it away. A large group of people had come in with her. As I scanned their faces, I relaxed once more as I realized neither Mark nor Susan were among them.

Glinda paused to inspect the bookshop before she and her entourage headed straight toward me. "Fred! The Cozy Corgi is enchanting. Not that I expected any less." To my surprise, the tiny woman offered me a quick yet tender hug before pulling away.

"Thank you. Although it's several times bigger than Alakazam, we don't have nearly as many decorations."

"Well, that's true. Maybe next Solstice. Mark and I have been adding to them little bit by little bit every year. It takes a while." She stepped aside and gestured toward the people with her. "This is the Sweitzer family." She patted an older woman's hand who sat in a wheelchair. "Charlene here is my dearest and oldest friend. It wasn't until I mentioned this celebration a day or two ago that I learned that none of them have ever been in your bookshop. So we decided to make an event out of it."

Charlene gave a friendly if self-conscious smile. "It's very lovely. We should've come in before. It's just hard to—" One of the children of the group pushed another and bumped into Charlene's wheelchair cutting her off. A tired and extremely pregnant-looking woman grabbed the one who'd been shoved into the wheelchair. "Parker, knock it off. You need to be gentle around your grandmother."

"I didn't!" Parker sounded thoroughly offended. "Joseph pu—"

"I don't want to hear it." She gave me a smile. "Sorry. My four boys tend to be a handful. It's part of why we haven't been in here. It's like trying to corral a three-ring circus." She patted her extended belly. "I hear girls are easier. I pray that's true." She stuck out her hand. "I'm Sheila. My husband, Brian, couldn't make it. But the boys are Maxwell, Joseph, Parker, and Tate." She didn't bother to point them out by name, just lumped them into one big group before patting her belly once more. "This is Tiffany, or will be any day, Lord willing."

"So nice to meet you. I—"

One of the boys, I wasn't sure which, only that it wasn't Parker as it was a different one, was shoved into the wheelchair once more.

"Boys!" Sheila sounded close to tears.

I couldn't blame her. And I cast a quick prayer of thanks the only child I had was a grumpy, chubby corgi. Sure, there was a lot of dog care to contend with, but that wasn't so bad.

"Hey there." Like an angel of mercy, Ben Pacheco arrived from out of thin air and squatted down in front of the boys. "We've got an amazing section of kid books over here. An entire shelf devoted to nothing but superheroes." He cast a quick questioning glance up at me and then over at Sheila. "Mind if I show the boys around?"

"This is Ben. He works for me in the bookstore. His brother, Nick, is the one who just graduated high school and helps Katie out in the—"

Sheila waved me off. "Yes, I don't care who he is. Take them."

Ben chuckled and stood as he nodded across the store. "Come on, boys."

Both Sheila and Charlene let out audible sighs of relief, only Glinda joining in on Ben's laughter before motioning to the woman who was pushing the wheelchair. "This is Charlene's oldest, Connie."

The woman nodded but didn't offer her hand, which maintained a tight grip on the wheelchair's handle. "Nice to meet you. Great place."

Before I could reply, the man in the group stepped forward and thrust his hand out at me. "I'm Adam. It really is a spectacular bookshop. Granted, rather small compared to the one I frequent in Portland, but pretty good for this podunk town."

As I shook his hand, it took me a moment to replay his words. His tone had been so happy and cheerful that I barely caught the implied insult. "Well... we do what we can."

"Adam!" his mother and oldest sister hissed in unison, and Connie finished the thought. "You're being rude."

"What?" Adam sounded genuinely confused. "No, I'm not." The small man was wearing a gray pinstripe suit, and he adjusted his polka-dot bowtie in indignation. "I mean it. It's a cute place."

"Thank you." I repeated the sentiment, infusing as much sincerity as I could manage. Though I had been enjoying the night immensely, I was suddenly reminded that I was an introvert at heart, and desperately wanted to escape to an armchair, fire, and a good book, with Watson snoring at my feet.

Nonplussed, Adam puffed his chest and shoved his hands into his pockets. "You know, I've written a few books. I'd be happy to let you carry them in your store if you'd like."

Both of his sisters rolled their eyes, and his mother rested her elbow on the arm of her wheelchair so she could cover her eyes with her hand.

"That's a wonderful idea, Adam," Glinda jumped in cheerfully. "Winifred owned a publishing house before she opened the Cozy Corgi. I bet she could offer you some insight into finally getting your books accepted by a publisher."

The woman pushing the wheelchair smirked as Adam nearly sputtered in his indignation. "Rejection from a publisher is the sincerest form of flattery. It lets an author know they are doing their strongest work if it won't be readily accepted by the masses." Somehow his chest puffed up even farther, and though I was several inches taller than him, he managed to look down his nose at me. "Actually, now that I think about it, I don't know if my books would fit here. They're probably a little too highbrow and require a more elevated sense of taste than most people in this town possess."

Luckily I'd also been a college professor and been married to a narcissistic blowhard for several years, so I was well equipped at rolling with the punches, and rolled directly to any other topic than books. "Not a fan of Estes

Park? Maybe I misunderstood. I thought you were all from here."

"We are." Sheila, still rubbing her belly, was clearly trying to stop a collision from the speed of her words. "We all grew up here. Love it. It's just that—"

"It's just that I'm the only one with enough sense and talent to break free." Adam cast a quick glare over his family before turning back to me. "I hear there's a bakery upstairs. From the smell, it promises to be better than expected. After I get a bite to eat, I'll pull up my novels online and let you pick which one you'd like to read. I'll even autograph it for five dollars, which is quite a bit less than I normally charge."

Well equipped at rolling with the punches or not, I had no idea what to say to that.

It seemed words weren't required as Adam kept going. "You'd do a lot more business here if you changed the name. Seeing a dog on the shop sign outside doesn't really make a person want to eat at a bakery. It indicates dog hair. Anytime I open a new business, I turn to the classics for inspiration. For instance—"

"Twenty-five years and you haven't changed a bit, have you? Like you've opened any businesses."

We all turned toward the sneer of a voice.

I was surprised to see that it belonged to Billy Hanson. He'd seemed rather cowed before, but now sounded nearly vicious. "Always trying to make yourself better than everyone else, aren't you, Adam?"

"Oh, no," Charlene groaned and shot out a hand to grasp Adam's wrist. "Let it go."

He shook her off and then stepped far enough away that she couldn't reach him from her spot in the wheel-chair. "Oh, if it isn't little Billy Baby." Adam gave an appraising glance over Billy and wrinkled his nose. "Time hasn't done you any favors, has it? You were tubby in high school, but now you've become nothing more than a beach ball."

"Why, you—" Billy closed the distance, grabbed Adam by the bow tie, and jerked him forward.

"Knock it off!" I raised my voice enough that not only did it startle Billy into releasing Adam, but every conversation in the bookshop died instantly, leaving only the soft instrumental jazz version of Christmas carols. Even the chatter above in the bakery seemed to dim. Though it had only happened infrequently during my times as a professor, I'd broken up more than one fight between hotheads in my classroom. I wedged between them, nudging Adam away slightly to give me room. "I don't know what there is between you two, but clearly you've got a history. This isn't the time or the place for it."

"I don't need your defense. I can handle him myself. I have a million times before." Billy started to push past me.

I slapped a hand on his chest and pushed him away slightly. "I'm not coming to your defense. I'm telling you to *knock it off.*"

Adam chuckled behind me. "She told you."

Still keeping my hand on Billy's chest, I whirled toward Adam. "And you too. You're both middle-aged men and you're acting like twelve-year-old idiots."

Someone clapped, and I looked over to see Sheila lowering her hands. "Where have you been all our lives? If you'd been around growing up, maybe my brother wouldn't be such a prat."

Connie grinned from her spot behind her mother's wheelchair

Sheila released her belly and tried to nudge her way

between Connie and the wheelchair. "Here, Mom, let's get—"

Connie clamped her hands over the wheelchair and shot her sister a glare. "I've got her."

"Billy!" Another shout rang through the stillness of the bookshop. Anna stood in the middle of the steps and pointed toward her feet. "Get over here. Now!"

There was a loud clatter of claws as Watson hurried around the corner of the bakery, dashed down the steps, and made a beeline toward me. He came to a stop at my feet, looked up at the men on either side of me, and growled.

"Billy!" Anna nearly shrieked that time and pointed once more.

"Better do what your mommy says," Adam taunted in a singsong voice.

"Are you kidding me?" I whirled on Adam before Billy had the chance. "Get out of my shop." I nearly whipped around to command the same thing from Billy, but my friendship with his parents stopped me. Although if he said one more word, I'd kick him out as well. Adam opened his mouth to protest, but I cut him off, pointing to the door. "Out. Or I'm calling the police." That really would top off the night, having to call Susan Green to come to the rescue. She'd gloat about that for years.

At the staircase, Anna stomped her foot, causing Watson to growl louder, and after a moment, I felt Billy retreat.

Adam watched him go and then turned his gaze to me with a sniff. "Trust me, lady. I don't want to hang out in this flea-ridden establishment a second longer than I have to. And don't bother asking, you don't deserve to have my novels in here."

It took me having to remind myself that I was a woman

of nearly forty to keep from giving a childlike retort as he turned and headed toward the door.

As Connie started to turn her mother's wheelchair to follow, Charlene cast me a pained expression. "I'm sorry."

Glinda touched my arm. "I'm sorry as well. I should've thought about the Hansons being here, though I didn't know Billy was visiting his family as well." She sighed. "With the two of them in town for the season, it promises to be a very eventful solstice." She began to follow the Sweitzer family but turned back, her face cheerful as if nothing had happened. "Oh, I almost forgot. Deliveries arrive tomorrow. Your *Beauty and the Beast* snow globe should be in. Make sure to bring Watson when you come!"

Sure enough, like clockwork according to all the other store-owners, the tourists arrived the following day. It seemed a tradition that as soon as school was out for the winter holidays, Estes Park was a favorite family Christmas destination. Even though the entire town had been at the Cozy Corgi mere hours before, they all came back to the scene of the crime to have their morning coffees and pastries and revel in the drama that had happened in the bookshop.

Between the gossipy locals and the newly arrived tourists, the morning was a whirlwind. Ben and I barely had time to say five words to each other between helping customers with book sales. I'd been right to triple my order of children's books; they were flying off the shelves. As, interestingly, were romances set in beach locations. Apparently many readers wanted to spend the holidays surrounded by mountains and snow while dreaming of crystal blue waters and palm trees.

Christmas cheer was high. The Cozy Corgi, once again, was filled with all the holiday smells and sounds. People laughed and relaxed, and an easy vibe settled over the bookshop and bakery. Even so, it took all my effort to hide my Scrooge-like attitude. One minute I was angry at Adam and

Billy for causing such a scene, and the next, I found myself rather humiliated. Which, in and of itself, was also frustrating. I'd simply wanted the Christmas party to reflect how happy I was in Estes Park, to celebrate the physical embodiment of my dream while being surrounded by friends and family. I supposed I should be thankful there hadn't been a dead body in the middle of the event. That would've been truer to form, but it still felt like wherever Winifred Page went, drama or scandal was sure to follow.

Watson seemed to share my mood. Granted, he didn't need any encouragement or permission to be grumpy and evasive, but he took full advantage. He allowed a tourist to scratch between his ears here and there, but for the majority of the day, he abandoned his typical favorite napping spot in the sunshine pouring through the front windows, and sheltered in the mystery room, which was my favorite spot. For a few heart-stopping moments, I couldn't find him and feared he'd somehow wandered away, which wasn't like him at all, but then I had a good laugh when I discovered him wedged underneath the antique sofa in front of the mystery room's river rock fireplace.

I got on my hands and knees to peer underneath. "How in the world did you even fit under there? There's just enough room for a Chihuahua, and goodness knows, you're not as svelte as one of those." At my words, I became aware of the belt I'd cinched over the waist of my broomstick skirt gouging into my stomach. "And that's not a judgment. It's one of the ways that proves we're soulmates, you and I. But you don't see me crawling into tight spaces, do you?"

Watson blinked and let out a huff. He didn't even pretend to budge.

"Are you stuck or being stubborn? You can stay under there if you like. I don't blame you. After all the people last night, it's a little overwhelming in here today." I narrowed my eyes at him. "Actually, maybe you have the right idea. Is there room under there for two?"

"I don't think you need to take such drastic measures, Fred." From my kneeling position, I looked over to see Katie. She leaned her shoulder against the mantel of the fireplace, her arms crossed and a smirk over her face. "Can I coax you out by offering to make you a dirty chai?"

As if I was a Pavlov experiment, my stomach instantly growled at the mention of my favorite addiction. "In all fairness, I'm not actually under the sofa quite yet."

"Maybe not, but from the looks of things, I arrived just in time." She squatted enough to peer under the edge of the sofa, the spirals of her brown curls dragging on the hardwood floor. "And what about you, Your Highness? Would you come out for a treat?"

Watson's eyes widened, and he wriggled, but he stayed where he was.

"Wow, if he's refusing, things are more dire than I realized. I've never seen him turn down a treat." Katie straightened and offered her hand to help me up.

"Thank you. I think I ate one too many slices of your sweet potato pie last night." I took her hand, stood with a groan, and brushed the dog hair off my spruce-blue broomstick skirt. "I'll take you up on the offer of a dirty chai. Maybe a double shot of caffeine will get me back in the Christmas mood."

"I'll make you that dirty chai, but I've got something else to get you in the Christmas mood."

I cocked an eyebrow. "More pie?"

"No, better." She shook her head. "Well... not better than pie, but different." She tilted her chin slightly as if gesturing upstairs. "I already spoke to Nick and Ben.

They're going to watch the store the rest of the day. You and I are escaping."

My heart leaped nearly to a ridiculous level, which only proved how desperately I needed to get away. "We are?"

"We are!" Katie propped her hands on her hips in a pose worthy of Wonder Woman, although her sweatshirt's design of a cat sticking an angel mouse on top of a Christmas tree ruined the effect. "We're getting massages."

"We are?" I couldn't remember the last time I'd had a massage. "Is it massage day in the crystal room at Chakras?"

Katie chuckled. "It is, actually, but that's not what I have in mind. I love your sisters and their shop, but I was thinking a little more lavish. We have an appointment in two hours at the spa of Pinecone Manor."

"We do?"

"We do!" Katie chuckled again. "It sounds like we're on repeat. But yes, we do. We'll be finished in enough time to head to your house and start dinner before Leo comes over this evening."

"Katie, that's too much. I've seen the prices at the spa. They—"

"Consider it an early Christmas present." Katie moved toward the front door. "I know we technically don't need to head out yet, but we're going to."

"We shouldn't leave Ben and Nick. Especially right now—"

"They handled the shop alone during the height of summer season." She cut me off with a stern expression. "No more arguing. You need this. We both need this. It's been a hard few weeks. I should've thought of this earlier. Probably should've got one for Leo as well."

She was right. It *had* been a hard few weeks. A little guilt tried to arrive at the thought of escape, but I pushed it away. "All right, let's do it." I grabbed her hand. "Katie, thank you!"

"You're welcome." She shrugged. "And you don't really need to thank me. I'm getting a massage too."

"Okay! Let's do it!" I turned back to the sofa and patted my thigh. "Come on, Watson. We can escape!"

Katie and I waited, but there was no movement from the sofa.

I patted my thigh again.

Watson whimpered.

I bent, peering under once more.

Watson's eyes pleaded with me, wide and panicked.

Laughing, I straightened and moved to the arm of the sofa closest to the fireplace. "Katie, would you mind lifting the other end of this? It seems Watson has eaten one too many of your all-natural dog treat bones."

The massages were utter bliss. And though Pinecone Manor and the spa were decked out for the holiday and had a good three times the number of Christmas trees as the Cozy Corgi, they thankfully didn't play any carols during the treatment. There were no tourists, no arguments, no conversations of deception or failed relationships. After the ninety minutes was over, I felt like me again. As Katie and I drove back toward my house, with snow drifting gently down, some of the Christmas spirit returned as well.

We were about to turn off the main road that led through a new subdivision and then wound back to my little cabin in the woods, when Katie pointed at the wide meadow at the base of the mountains. "Hold on. I've heard of this, but I've never witnessed it."

I slowed my Mini Cooper to see what she'd noticed and

didn't require any clarification. "You haven't seen this? Well, consider it my Christmas present to you." I pulled the car over to the side of the road and shifted into Park.

Under the snowcapped mountains that glowed gold with the beginning of sunset, a large group of robe-covered people cavorted over the meadow, each holding a broomstick between their legs.

"That looks extremely awkward. I think if I tried that, I'd fall and break my arm within three minutes." Katie leaned farther across me to get a better view. "You know, I'm all for letting your freak flag fly and not worrying about what anyone else says about you, but that doesn't look like fun at all. Especially when it's supposed to give the impression of flying."

"I have to give them credit for true Harry Potter fandom, though. That's dedication to Quidditch." I couldn't disagree with Katie, though. Sure enough, as we watched, one of the broomstick galloping people tripped and a large ball fell from their hand. "If they're really into it, maybe it does feel like playing a sport flying on broomsticks."

"It looked a lot more fun in the movies." I shot Katie a quick glare, and she raised her hands. "I know, I know, the books are better than the movies. I'm just saying..."

Before I could reply, a large purple-robed man swooped over—or as close to swooped as he could get running around with the broom between his legs—and snagged the ball. "I think that's Mark Green. We're a little too far away to make out his face, but he's the biggest one out there."

"I bet you're right. So strange that Susan's brother does stuff like this." Katie nudged me with her elbow. "And see, we're not the only ones playing hooky. Mark clearly left Glinda to man Alakazam by herself while he pretends to be Harry Potter."

As we watched, he cavorted across the snow-covered meadow, weaving through broomstick-riding opponents, and tossed the ball through one of three hoops at the opposite end. Even from this distance, we could hear his whoop of celebration.

"You know... it's kinda sweet."

Katie was right. For as gruff and abrasive as Mark Green was, I found his willingness to play rather endearing, and I had to admire someone for doing what so many others would make fun of simply because they enjoyed it.

I smacked the steering wheel suddenly, causing Katie to flinch. "Sorry." I cast her an apologetic glance. "Seeing Mark reminded me. Glinda told me last night a Christmas present I ordered came in. I was supposed to drop by to pick it up this afternoon."

Katie shook her head. "No way. Get it tomorrow. We're not going back downtown for anyone or anything." She pointed out the windshield. "Now, onward to tacos!"

What little bit of Ebenezer Scrooge remained after the massage vanished while Katie, Leo, and I ate dinner in my little kitchen. The three of us worked together throwing together a meal of tacos and chili rellenos. Watson also seemed to catch the Christmas spirit, as he pranced between the three of us while we worked. Of course, there was no way to know if it was actual Christmas magic affecting him or simply being near his adored Leo and constantly gobbling up any scraps of food that happened to fall from our hands.

After dinner, we retired to the living room and gathered around the fireplace. Though we were all stuffed, we tore into another of Katie's fresh-baked sweet potato pies.

"I don't know if I like the filling or the homemade whipped cream better, Katie, my dear." Leo arched his back on the sofa as he patted his stomach before shoveling in another forkful of pie. "Either way, having a friend like you is going to make me as big as a house."

"Shut up!" Katie swatted at him. "If I didn't love you so much, I'd absolutely hate you. You eat just as much as I do, and yet you're all muscle with a thirty-two-inch waist. It's not fair."

Leo scooped up another forkful of pie and held it out to her, laughter filling his voice. "Here, this will make you feel better."

She swatted him again, but only managed to cause the morsel to fling across the room. Watson sprang from his curled-up napping spot as if he were a greyhound who'd just heard the buzzer and made short work of the bit of sweet potato pie. Turning, he looked at the three of us expectantly, licking his chops.

I couldn't blame him, I'd already finished my piece and was considering a second. "In Leo's defense, he does spend each and every day wandering around the national park. You spend every working hour saturated in butter and sugar, and I spend each spare moment curled up with my nose in a book."

"There is that..." Katie scowled. "I still say it's not fair."

Leo simply shrugged. "*I say* take your vengeance by making me even more pastries. See if you can conquer my metabolism." He finished the final bite and then stood. "Speaking of, I'm going to get another piece. Either of you want one?"

It was my turn to glare, but I thrust my plate at him. "Yes, you evil tempter."

"I hate you." Katie shoved hers toward him as well.

"And I'd like twice as much whipped cream on this one, please."

Once we'd settled back again with our second pieces of pie, conversation turned to the events of the night before.

"I can't believe I missed the show." Leo had changed places to sit beside Watson on the floor, balancing his plate on his lap as he stroked Watson's side with his free hand. "Sounded like quite the display."

"It was. Although brief, it was also rather revolting to see two grown men act in such a stupid, juvenile manner." Somehow talking about it with Katie and Leo didn't have the depressing effect the event had inspired all day. "I think the worst part was how embarrassed both of their families seemed."

"Maybe if they'd had you around when they were growing up, they would've turned out better." Katie grinned at me before addressing Leo. "I didn't see it happen, but you should've heard Fred. I was in the bakery, and even I straightened at the sound of her voice. It reminded me of being a kid when the teacher had finally reached her limit."

"That's exactly what it felt like."

"I would've liked to have seen that." Leo seemed to consider. "Maybe you should go on some of the tours I give at the national park. Every once in a while we get some participants who think it's their job to heckle."

I shuddered. "No, thank you. I'd enjoy working with the animals, I think, but not sure about giving tours. It's one thing to fill people in on what books I think they'd like—it's another trying to instill passion about the environment. I would imagine that's pretty frustrating."

"Can be. But there's not been a single case of poaching since..." He blushed and seemed to jump over the thought. "Granted, I know there will be poaching again, it's the nature of the beast, but maybe things will be better, or at least much less frequent."

An awkward silence fell, and when Katie spoke again, her words sounded a little formal. "Are you regretting getting promoted, Leo? Your hours are less consistent, and you didn't get Christmas off."

"I love it. I'm finally in a position to make some changes, to make a difference." He shrugged. "I actually have Christmas Eve and Day off, but not long enough to go home. It's the first time in years that I've not been home for Christmas."

"That part's sad." My gaze flitted to the Christmas tree sparkling in front of the living room window, then back to Leo. "Is your family upset?"

"Yeah. Mom is. But..." He shrugged again. "In the long run, it's probably good. She and my siblings need to..." His words trailed off as his blush deepened.

The silence returned, and once again after a few awkward moments, Katie broke it. "Well, I for one am glad you're here this year. You should join me with Winifred's family. Last Christmas was wonderful." She glared at me meaningfully. "Shouldn't he, Fred?"

The past couple of weeks, Katie had prompted several times that I should try to take things past the friendship level with Leo. She'd take it right to the edge of pressuring and then back off. She was convinced there was much more between Leo and me than friendship. Maybe she was right. Even if she was, I wasn't even close to being ready.

"No. I don't want to intrude," Leo said, and I couldn't tell if he sounded disappointed or not.

"We'd love to have you, Leo." Though I meant it, I wasn't sure if it sounded in my voice. "Really."

He shook his head. "Thank you. But even though I'm

not scheduled, I'm sure I'll need to be in the park. It's going to take months, if not years, to figure out all the damage Etta did. Not to mention attempting to determine if there were other rangers who Branson—" He shook his head. "Sorry. I don't need to bring him up. Not tonight."

Again my gaze flitted to the Christmas tree, then toward the fireplace, and then settled where Katie was curled into the edge of the couch. Only a few weeks before, I'd sat in that very spot as Branson asked me to leave Estes and join him. Where we'd said our goodbyes. There was still a twinge of loss, but greater than that, by far, was the endless self-flagellation that kept circling around in my mind. Poring over all the signs and hints that were oh so clear in hindsight.

"Okay! Enough of this!" Katie slapped her thighs and stood. "Branson has affected us enough. We're here, we're alive, and we're all wonderful people who are well fed and need to enjoy the moment." She looked back and forth between Leo and me in expectation.

Leo and I just stared.

"Well, come on. Get up!" She motioned for us to stand.

Leo did, looking at her questioningly. "What exactly are we standing for?"

"Come on, Fred. You heard me." Instead of letting me answer, she grabbed my hand and pulled me up.

I felt a wary smile form at the twinkle in her eyes. "Why do I get the feeling I should be worried?"

"Because you should be." She chuckled, crossed the room, and dug in her purse. "I was prepared for this, just in case things took a serious turn." She rumbled around in it for a few moments and then yanked out a fuzzy red-and-white Santa hat and thrust it toward Leo. "Here. I know chances are small that Watson will allow this to happen, but if anyone can convince him to do it, it's you. Work your magic."

He took the hat. "All right... but if I lose a finger, I expect you to cover my medical bills."

"Good luck with that, since every spare dime I had went into purchasing all the baking equipment for the bakery." She turned to me. "Get your keys, Fred. We're going caroling."

"Caroling?" I gaped at her. "As in going door-to-door singing?"

She struck her Wonder Woman pose again. "Yep! And don't give me that face. If grown adults can run around the field on broomsticks pretending they're wizards flying a mile in the air, *we* can go Christmas caroling." She rubbed her hands together gleefully. "And I know just where to start."

Within half an hour, the three of us were bundled in jackets, scarves, and the three matching Santa hats Katie had produced from her purse of shame. Katie rang the doorbell and hurried back to my side. Leo was on the other, and at our feet, a very grumpy corgi glared up at us with a Santa hat strapped to his head. He could've very easily yanked it off but was clearly showing his love of Leo in the purest way he knew how, even if he wasn't happy about it.

"Okay, you two"—fog emanated from Katie as she spoke—"I don't care if we're not on key, but you'd both better sing. I am not doing a solo!" As the door cracked open, she launched into the first lines of "Silent Night."

My Uncle Percival stuck his head out, and his eyes widened.

Katie paused in her singing to hiss, "I said sing, you idiots." And then launched into the next line.

Leo joined her, and then, giving into the peer pressure,

so did I.

Percival leaned back into the house and hollered to his husband, "Gary! Get out here! Winifred has lost her mind!"

Within moments, Gary joined him, and they stood side by side on their front porch, arms wrapped around each other with ridiculous grins over their faces as we finished a truly horrendous version of "Silent Night." They clapped uproariously as the final note faded.

"That was wonderful, kids! Simply wonderful!" Gary beamed at us.

Percival guffawed. "Are you kidding? It was atrocious. Which made it the best Christmas gift I might have had in years." He turned to Gary again, giving him a quick shove into the house. "Hurry up, go get our jackets and hats. I want my boysenberry fur coat and fuchsia scarf. And *don't* wear that army-green atrocity you call a hat." After shaking his finger at his husband, he turned back to us. "All righty then, here's the plan. Winifred, first, we're going to go pick up your mom and Barry, and then we're heading straight to Ethel Beaker's house." He clapped his hands. "Actually, no, we're going to save her for last. Make sure that she'll be asleep by the time we show up. Show that snooty woman what she gets for inserting herself into the top slot of the town council, acting as if she's better than anyone else." His eyes grew wider as he clapped his hands even louder. "Oh, oh, and we'll sing 'Santa Baby' in the sultriest way possible." He pointed down at Watson. "That includes you, mister." Suddenly, with a gasp, Percival threw his hands in the air and rushed back into the house without another word.

The three of us exchanged looks.

Percival's muffled voice drifted back to us from inside the house. "Gary! Where did I put that glitter bomb?"

Katie grinned at me. "*Best* idea, ever!"

FIVE

Though Watson and I went to sleep well past our bedtime, thanks to the impromptu Christmas caroling extravaganza, I woke up early the next day with all traces of Ebenezer Scrooge thoroughly vanquished. I looked through the pink flamingo-patterned tie-dyed curtains of the window above the kitchen sink to a softly lit dawn filled with freshly fallen snow and actually said out loud, "What a gorgeous Christmassy day it is outside," *before* my first drop of caffeine.

From his spot on the kitchen floor, Watson peered skeptically up at me with his stuffed yellow duck gripped firmly in his mouth.

I couldn't blame him for not trusting my mood. I wasn't exactly a monster before my first cup of joe, but I most definitely wasn't Little Miss Sunshine either. I patted his nub-tailed corgi butt as I set down his breakfast. "Well, it is! Hurry and eat. Let's go to the bakery and surprise Katie and Nick with our early arrival. I think it would be a good day for sweet potato pie for breakfast." I paused on my way out of the kitchen as my stomach rumbled, considering. "All right, maybe a ham-and-cheese croissant for breakfast, something with some protein, *followed* by a slice of sweet potato pie."

Watson ignored my plan as he scarfed down his bowl of cold baked chicken.

I'd just pulled my volcanic-orange Mini Cooper into my typical parking spot, affixed Watson's leash, and started to head to the Cozy Corgi, when I remembered the *Beauty and the Beast* snow globe waiting to be picked up. Even reliving the small fortune I was spending on Christmas presents couldn't dampen my mood, nor could the cold. I pulled my mustard-hued scarf tighter as Watson and I headed down the block. "A brisk walk will do us good. I doubt Alakazam is open yet, but we might as well check. Chances are we'll have another busy day with tourists."

Though Watson trotted along at my side, I felt, more than heard, his growl at the word *tourist*.

"None of that. It's time for Christmas cheer. Plus, you don't want to get yourself stuck under the sofa again." I grinned down at him. "If you do, I'm taking a picture and posting it on our Instagram page."

Most of the store windows we passed were dark due to the early hour, but a few showed signs of life as shop owners flicked on their Christmas decorations.

Watson and I were at the base of the wooden steps that led up to the small offshoot of shops that held Alakazam when Glinda rounded the corner from the other side of the waterwheel. "Well, aren't you two up early today." She smiled kindly, closed the distance, and though she cast a glance at Watson, she gave my arm a quick pat. "I *am* sorry about the drama at your shop the other night. I know I'm not responsible, but I do feel bad as it was my suggestion to bring the whole Sweitzer family."

"You're right, it's not your responsibility at all. There's

no reason to be sorry." I peered over her shoulder at her silver wings that matched the soft gray and pinks of her gossamer gown. "I figured you put those on once you got into the shop?"

She cocked her head. "Put what on, dear?" Instead of waiting for a reply, she led the way up the steps to the front door of Alakazam. She already had her keys in her hand, and paused as she lifted the small ring. "Oh. Goodness, the door's already unlocked." She sighed, rolled her eyes, and gave me an indulgent look. "I forgot. Last evening was Mark's monthly game night."

"Yes, Katie and I saw him playing."

Glinda cocked her head again. "You did? You were here last night?"

I felt like we were on two different pages, or maybe two entirely different books. "No. We saw him playing Quidditch."

She laughed. "Oh, yes. That too. But that's every week. I meant after. He has a board game night with three of his buddies here once a month." She pushed open the door and walked in but continued talking to me over her shoulder. "The boys typically drink to excess, and Mark often forgets to lock up, if he leaves at all. They have a good time. It's all in—" Glinda turned from me and halted. "Oh…"

Watson came to a stop at her feet and growled. Though Glinda was in front of me, she was small enough that I could see over her head. The magic shop wasn't destroyed, but a few shelves had been turned over and quite a bit of merchandise lay over the counter and floor. A glance at the cash register showed that its drawer hung open.

"We've been robbed." Glinda's wisp of a hand rose to the base of her throat and trembled. "Who would do this?"

My gaze flicked over the mess, and on second inspection

I noticed cash strewn among the debris over the countertop. A robber wouldn't have left cold hard cash.

Then I felt it. Not because Watson continued to growl, I could simply feel it. Maybe *feel it* wasn't the right phrase, I wasn't sure. Perhaps there was a smell, a taste to the air—who knew, but it was familiar.

Shortening Watson's leash, I stepped around Glinda, and he and I headed carefully to the end of the counter. I didn't scream, gasp, or flinch. I'd already known what we'd find.

A man lay sprawled on the floor. Though he was on his stomach and none of his limbs were at odd angles, it was clear he wasn't sleeping or passed out from a night of too much drinking. A small pool of drying blood had spread under his head, not much really, but there were streaks and footprints leading from his body to the back door of the shop. Strangely, there were also a few handprints. Hearing the rustle of Glinda's dress behind me, I turned and held up a hand. "Hold on, you don't need to see this."

She didn't listen and hurried forward but came to a stop beside Watson and me. Her other hand joined the first at the base of her throat but instead of screaming, she let out a long sigh of relief. "Thank the light, it's not Mark."

I hadn't even attempted to put a name to the body, but it would only make sense that it would be Mark Green. It clearly wasn't. Mark was a mountain of a man, while this body was small, barely larger than Glinda. Keeping Watson's leash held tight so he didn't get any closer to the blood and disrupt the scene, I leaned forward at an angle, trying to get a better look at the man's face. Though I couldn't see a wound, his face was bruised and swollen. "I think it's Adam. Adam Sweitzer."

That time, Glinda did gasp. "Adam!" She leaned

forward as well. "He doesn't look like..." She covered her mouth, clearly recognizing him.

About a foot away from Adam's abused face was one of the large snow globes, its glass shattered and its glittering silver snow spread over the floor. The gold-and-bronze image of Ebenezer Scrooge lay faceup.

Before I could inspect anything else, Glinda sucked in another breath and tore off toward the back, following the bloody footprints.

"Glinda, wait. We can't disrupt the scene. We need to call the—"

"Mark! Mark!" She ignored me, rushed to the back door, threw it open, and darted in.

Giving in to the impulse, I followed, Watson scurrying along at my side.

Glinda kept yelling Mark's name, and when we entered the surprisingly large back room, I found her shaking Mark's body where it sprawled over the sofa.

Mark had more blood on him than Adam. On his feet, hands, smeared over his shirt. There were even smears over a dark gray sheet that hung over something large and rectangular at the opposite end of the sofa.

"Mark. Oh... Mark." As Glinda continued to shake him, she began to cry.

I started to go to her, pull her away, wrap her in a hug, whatever I needed to do to both comfort her and secure the scene as much as possible.

Mark groaned, stopping me in my tracks. His large hand lifted and attempted to swat Glinda away. "Stop. The. Yelling." Another groan. "Headache."

At that, Glinda cried harder, ignored his protests, and displayed a surprising amount of strength by pulling his head to her chest in a fierce embrace.

I looked from Mark, followed the bloody prints from the back room to Adam's body. It appeared as if game night hadn't been such a good time after all.

Not knowing what else to do, I retrieved my cell phone and called the police station. When dispatch answered, I asked to be put through to Officer Brent Jackson. I wasn't leaving it up to chance that Susan Green would be the one to respond.

Despite my best effort, five minutes later, that was exactly who barged through the front door. Susan barely cast me a glare, gave a slightly longer one to Adam's body, and then hurried to where Mark and Glinda were huddled together on the sofa in the back room. The bloody sheet had been pulled away from the rectangular contraption, revealing the rabbit pen. Mandrake... Drake... was now curled up on Mark's lap.

Brent shrugged as he walked in a few seconds later. "Sorry, Susan was already in and..." Another shrug. "Well, you know Susan. Not like I could blame her in this case."

No, I couldn't either.

Brent gave more than a passing glance at Adam. Confusion flitted over his face as he winced. "Wow. He went through the wringer." He looked toward Ebenezer Scrooge. "I don't think that's the murder weapon. It wouldn't leave bruises like that."

He had a point, I could see what he meant. "Maybe so, but we haven't turned him over yet. Those snow globes are pretty heavy. It could have been—"

"I bet you just love this, don't you?"

I whirled at the angry voice and found Susan returning

from the back room and heading my way. Watson growled threateningly, and I pulled him closer.

Susan ignored him, focusing all her fury on me. "Why are you even here? I bet you've been wanting to find something like this for months. Just to make our lives miserable." She moved so quickly, I thought she was going to collide with me, shove me into the wall. She was the same height and roughly the same weight as me, but where I was curvy, Susan was all muscle, so she easily could have. She stopped less than a foot away. "He didn't do this. Don't you dare say my brother did this. He wouldn't." Her voice faltered. "Couldn't."

I had no idea what to say, so I said nothing.

Not getting a fight, after a few seconds, Susan finally looked toward Adam's body. If I wasn't mistaken, I saw doubt in her eyes, fear. It hardened instantly when she met my gaze again. "Mark didn't do this to that waste of—" She stopped herself with a shake of her head. "He didn't."

"Susan..." From behind, Officer Jackson placed a hand on her shoulder.

She shrugged him off with a hiss.

Though Brent was mild-mannered, he stood his ground. His voice remained kind but firm. "Why don't you step outside? I'll handle this."

She straightened and puffed out her chest. "Why? So *you* can arrest my brother?"

"I haven't even spoken to Mark yet. We don't know what he's going to say happened." Again, Brent didn't shy away.

Susan gestured toward the bloody footprints. "Really? Is there anything he can say that would satisfy?"

Brent didn't answer at first, seemed to be considering his options, and finally sighed. "It's a conflict of interest.

You know that. I know that. It's not going to look good on the station if—"

She laughed, wildly. "Are you kidding? After all the department has been through, you think *this* is going to even be a blip on the radar of shame? Get a grip." She shot out a hand and shoved Brent aside.

"Susan!" This time he barked out her name. "Don't do something I'll have to report."

She froze, turned slowly, and killed him with her glare. "Try me." She trembled in rage, flicked her pale blue gaze at me, then back at Brent. "I'm the best officer we have. And I know how to do my job. I always have." She stepped closer and shoved Brent once more. "If my brother needs to be taken in, *I'll* be the one to do it." She paused long enough to see how he was going to react. When he didn't, she glared at me again. "You and your fleabag get out of here. The last thing I need is some busybody taking enjoyment out of this."

"Fred's a witness." Brent didn't leave any room for argument in his tone. "We need to get her statement."

It looked like Susan was going to argue or shove him again. After a few heartbeats, she glared at me once more. "You disgust me." With that, she whirled and disappeared into the back room.

Brent cast me an apologetic shrug. "Sorry. She's just... Sorry."

I smiled at him and squeezed his shoulder. Brent was a good, good man, and a decent police officer. He'd gotten severely hurt in the line of duty in his attempt to save Katie and my lives. "You have nothing to be sorry about. And... I don't blame her. Not for this." And I didn't. I couldn't imagine the fear she was experiencing. The scary part was that I also couldn't imagine what she was going to do.

A little over ten minutes later, Officer Jackson had recorded my full statement. He'd just suggested that Watson and I should leave when Mark Green entered the main part of the shop, Susan following on his heels. She kept her gaze firmly focused ahead. It wasn't until they passed that I realized Mark's hands were cuffed behind his back.

SIX

"I've become that old woman who goes to bed by eight in the evening." I glanced at the clock on the mantel that sat between a wooden carving of Watson and a photo of the two of us dressed in roaring-twenties garb. "It's almost ten minutes after, so maybe that helps a bit."

Watson didn't bother to lift his head from where he napped beside the fire. He simply issued a long, relaxed groan.

"In my defense, we went to bed late last night and were up early this morning." Who knew why I was trying to rationalize being so bone-tired that I'd reread the second page of Agatha Christie's *The Adventure of the Christmas Pudding* at least five times and still had no idea what it said. Any day that started with discovering a dead body ought to provide a freebie for going to bed early.

Mentally waving the white flag of surrender, I closed the book and began to stand just as there was a knock at the front door.

Startled, Watson let out a solitary bark, hopped up, and pranced across the room.

My heart leapt, when for half a second I thought it must be Branson coming to visit me late at night; it wouldn't be the first time. He'd either tell me to keep my nose out of a case or offer me clues in order to help me solve one. A flicker of disappointment flashed and died before I took my first step. Those days were over. None of them had been what I thought they were anyway.

By the time I reached the door, I didn't bother checking the peephole before opening. From Watson's frantically joyful dance, there were only three possibilities of who was on the other side. Two, actually, as I couldn't imagine Ben Pacheco arriving on my doorstep unannounced.

The porch light lit up Leo Lopez's face, revealing that my primary guess of my stepfather, Barry, coming to check on me had been wrong. "Hey."

He smiled. "Hey." His gaze flicked to my nightgown. "Sorry. You're headed to bed, aren't you? I should've called first."

"No, I might be almost a decade older than you, but I'm not that old woman who goes to bed at eight at night." I stood aside. "Come on in."

Leo entered, giving me just enough room to shut the door as he knelt and greeted Watson. "Either way, I should've called first."

Ridiculously, I felt guilty for my white lie. "I'm glad you came by. I actually was headed to bed, so you're keeping me from becoming that old woman who goes to bed this early."

"From the day you've had, you deserve it."

"I was trying to convince myself of that very thing." I gestured toward the kitchen. "Can I get you anything? Water, hot tea? Food?" Another pain as I remembered the times Branson and I had sat at my seafoam-green kitchen table having tomato soup and grilled cheeses.

"No. I didn't come to be entertained." Leo gave Watson

a final scratch and stood, his honey-brown eyes meeting mine and holding. "I just came to check on you."

"Why? What's wrong?"

He grinned. "You found another dead body this morning. Unless something else happened, isn't that reason enough?"

"Hardly my first one. And you texted around noon making sure I was okay then."

Leo blinked and seemed to struggle for something to say. "You're right. I just... thought..." He nodded back to the door. "Sorry. You're heading to bed. I won't bother you." Something like embarrassment, or maybe hurt, flitted across his features.

"Wait." I reached out and stopped him. "I'm the one who's sorry. I'm not handling this well. I'm just a little thrown off." I decided to be bluntly honest. Which was my normal, and something Leo, as one of my dearest friends, was used to. "Every once in a while Branson would come by late at night and we'd talk about cases, as you know, or"—I laughed—"he'd tell me to mind my own business. When you knocked..." I shrugged. "Déjà vu, I guess."

Another flicker of hurt, and then his expression softened. "Sorry. You probably hoped..."

A million thoughts and sensations flashed in slow motion in that moment. The first time I'd met Leo as Watson and I entered the national park—hardly any time after I first met Branson. All the occasions he and Katie and I had gone to dinner or hung out at my house. The countless moments Leo and I had talked about clues around poachers and murderers. The times I'd wondered about whether he and Katie had more than friendship, or if he and the new park ranger had more than friendship. How Katie insisted

Leo only had eyes for me and that she knew I had feelings for him as well.

You want more from me than just friendship, don't you? The words nearly spilled out of my mouth. Nearly.

The problem was, I knew the answer. It scared me to death, but I knew the answer. And I couldn't go there.

"Do you want me to go? I didn't mean to trigger any memories or cause you pain." Again he motioned toward the door. "You had enough today, whether you're used to finding dead bodies by this point or not. I just left the park and simply came to check on you. Sorry."

I was tired, and not simply from the events of the day, but of... everything. My eyes burned, and tears threatened, which only indicated how truly exhausted I was. In an act very un-Winifred-Page-like, I shot out my hand to grip his, afraid he'd turn away. Words wouldn't come, at least I couldn't trust myself to form them, but I managed to shake my head.

Leo's eyes widened, and he glanced down at our hands. He smoothed his thumb over the back of my hand gently, tentatively. After a bit, he pulled it back and smiled tenderly. "You relax. I'll make us some tea. Got any of Katie's pie left from the other night?"

"A piece."

"We'll split it." He headed to the kitchen, Watson trailing like a shadow.

I watched him go for a heartbeat and then did as he said, though I chose the sofa instead of the armchair where I'd been before. Instead of trying to think and figure anything out, I simply let myself relax to the sounds drifting in from the kitchen as they mingled with the pop and crackle of the fire. As I watched, snow drifted slowly on the other side of the window framing the twinkling lights of the Christmas tree.

Leo soon brought in a tray with two plates, each with a thin slice of sweet potato pie, two steaming cups of hot tea, and one of Watson's favorite treats. He placed it between us on the couch cushions and sat. Without saying a word, he handed Watson his treat, smiled after him as he curled up once more by the fire, then handed me a slice of pie. "I bet you were slammed at the Cozy Corgi today. Lots of gossip and tourists."

Just like that, we moved on. Part of me wanted to resist what had occurred by the front door. Frazzled, exhausted, and on edge wasn't the time to make that leap, or even decide if there was a leap to make.

Before he arrived, discussing the long day at the shop after finding a body would've sounded like torture. But it felt familiar, comforting, distracting, and I settled into our routine. "We were. Everyone wanted to hear it again and again. Of course, they all had their own versions that they'd heard as well." I shook my head. "Maybe one of these days I'll get used to how different it is living in such a little town. Kansas City isn't the most sprawling metropolis, but it was easy to simply disappear when you wanted to. Not like here."

"You've revealed enough secrets in Estes so far that we know plenty of people managed to disappear here as well. Or at least partially." He took a bite of pie and paused long enough to chew and swallow. "Get any clues today in all that gossip?"

"Clues?"

Leo cocked a brow. "Aren't you looking for clues?"

I shook my head. "No. The arrest has already been made."

He chuckled. "Right, because that always stopped you before."

He had a point. "It seems pretty cut and dried. Mark was covered in Adam's blood. It was clear enough that his own sister arrested him."

Leo winced. "I gotta say, I'm impressed with Susan for that. It couldn't have been easy."

"No. Not at all." I'd had similar thoughts several times throughout the day. I took a bite of my slice of pie, savored it, and then bluntness took hold of me once more. "Do you think I'm a fool?"

He flinched. "What?"

"Branson." The words tumbled from me. "Was I simply blind and stupid? Susan hated his guts, that was obvious. But it was also clear she wasn't the least bit surprised when it was revealed he was a dirty cop. And you... How many times did you complain that he and Briggs wouldn't take your concerns about poaching seriously?"

Leo reached across the tray and put his hand over mine. "Fred, we've talked about this. A ton. Nobody saw this coming."

We had talked about it—he, Katie, and I—several times since all had been revealed. But this was different somehow, with just the two of us. "You really didn't know, didn't suspect?"

He shook his head. "I didn't. The thought never entered my mind." He pulled his hand back and shrugged. "Honestly, from my own experiences, I never had police be that receptive to me or to my family. About things that had absolutely nothing to do with poaching. It just felt normal." He smiled apologetically. "I know it's different for you, being a detective's daughter and all, but for a lot of us, police weren't always the friendly helpful heroes that they're supposed to be."

"I can see that." I'd heard several people say such sentiments, both personally and on the news. "But with Branson, specifically, you didn't like him."

He chuckled. "We didn't care for each other, no. But I don't really think it had anything to do with me being a park ranger and him being a cop, dirty or otherwise."

"Because of me?" I'd wondered that many times in the past, but saying it out loud sounded so arrogant.

As he laughed, it didn't seem that Leo felt that way. "I'm sure that didn't help. We were both aware of how the other felt. But no. Even without you in the picture, something about who he was, and who I am, was never going to mesh." He hurried on as if fearing he was making a mistake. "It doesn't mean you should have had the same experience of him that I did. Things were different with you two. Whatever Branson Wexler was, *whoever* Branson Wexler actually is, I believe he truly cared about you and that you were always safe with him. Well... he proved as much, I suppose." His smile faltered. "Cared about you so much that it's the only reason I'm alive right now. The only reason he spared me."

Though Katie, Leo, and I had talked about everything countless times over the past many weeks, it had all been filtered through our Scooby Gang ways. Full of speculation and theories. Leo and I hadn't sat down one-on-one since barely surviving the ordeal together, not like this. "Is it bothering you?"

"Bothering me?"

"You know..." I shrugged. "We both looked down the barrel of a gun. Are you having nightmares? PTSD?"

"It wasn't my first brush with nearly being killed, Fred."

He didn't sweep it away as if it was nothing, but neither did he make it sound all that life altering.

"It wasn't? You mean you've had close calls as a park ranger, or... almost being shot?" He most definitely had never mentioned that.

"I'm not having nightmares, no PTSD." His expression hardened for a moment. "Although I do keep replaying it, trying to find different ways I could've stopped him. Got us out of there without nearly dying."

"Yeah, me too."

His brown eyes flashed up at me with concern. "Are you having nightmares? Are you struggling? When the three of us talked about it, you seemed mostly okay."

"I am, surprisingly." I laughed, but it was a bitter sound. "And more angry than afraid. Angry that I was too stupid to see. Angry that he made me feel that way."

"Fred..." He reached for me again but stopped short when there was another knock at the door.

Once more, Watson barked and hopped up, but that time as he rushed toward the door, the barking and growling didn't cease.

Leo and I exchanged glances. "Safe to say you weren't expecting someone?"

"Not hardly."

Another knock.

As one, Leo and I put our plates back on the tray and stood before heading to the door.

That time, I did look through the peephole and couldn't believe my eyes. "It's Susan."

Susan's eyes widened when she saw Leo, and then her gaze flicked to me. "You move on quickly, don't you?" Before I could respond, she glanced back at Leo, who'd knelt to soothe Watson's growl. "Sorry."

Her apology to him threw me off nearly as much as her accusation. Probably more so. I was used to her hatred of me, but seeing Officer Green even the slightest bit deferential was akin to spotting a fabled unicorn. No sooner had that thought passed than I was proven wrong as her jibe found its mark. I had thought of Leo over the past many weeks, considered the possibility of him being more than just a friend. Nowhere in there had I given even a moment's consideration to what others would say. But Susan had nailed it. If anything happened between the two of us, it would look like I traded one man for the other, and that Leo was second choice, a consolation prize. That I'd been stringing both men along the entire time.

It was another thought I shoved away. The fact that it even entered my mind proved, once more, how tired I was. Since when did I care what people thought? Furthermore, I had been drawn to Leo since the very first day I'd met him.

And I'd tried to push him away for just as long. I hadn't come to Estes Park to have a relationship. Just the opposite.

Branson had never stopped pursuing me, despite my best efforts.

Leo had built a friendship.

"Are you experiencing indigestion right now?"

I flinched at Susan's question. "What?"

Her eyes narrowed, brows knitting in concern. "You look pained." She surprised me again by laughing. "Although, to be fair, if *you* showed up on *my* doorstep, I'd look pained as well."

"No, I'm fine. Thank you. It's just been a long..." I didn't finish the thought. No matter how long the day I'd had, I was certain Susan's had been much longer. "You've dropped by here before. That time was to chew me out. Is this a replay?"

"No." Susan dipped her head in another deferential motion, her brown hair, normally fixed tight in a short pony-tail at the nape of her neck, fell forward around her face, softening her. She was out of uniform, wearing jeans, a sweater, and a jacket. "I'm here because I need—" She glanced at Leo again.

"Do you want privacy?" When Susan nodded to Leo's question, he gave a final rub to Watson's flank and stood to face me. "You all right if I take off, or would you rather me hang around?"

It was strange watching him and Susan. Even with that little interaction, I saw a different side of her than I normally had witnessed. Like the two of them were friends, or something friend-adjacent.

"We'll be fine." I wished Susan was gone, or in another room, so Leo and I could say goodbye without an audience, though no sooner had the wish formed than I was glad it couldn't come true. I wasn't sure what that goodbye would've looked like. This way, I didn't need to figure it out. I gave him a quick hug. "Thanks for checking on me. Talk later?"

"Of course." His embrace didn't linger even a second longer than it normally would've, and his smile was his normal kind, gentle smile.

There I went looking for things, for signs.

Stupid. There weren't any signs needed. He made things perfectly clear. He had from the very beginning. *I* was the one who'd been jumbled up, not Leo.

Susan and I stared awkwardly at the closed door after Leo left. Watson had quit growling, but he plopped like a fluffy sentinel at my feet to glare at our intruder.

I expected her to jump into her normal round of accusation and insult. When she didn't, I was thrown more off-kilter than I already was. "What do you need from me, Susan?"

"I... wanted to ask..." She angled from me, looking around the room, her gaze landing here and there—on the Christmas tree, the fireplace, partially eaten pies. The tray of dessert seemed to capture her attention, and she cocked her head and studied it before finally looking back at me. "You really weren't with Branson, were you?"

There we went again, her litany of taunts and accusations of Branson and I a mile long, and I didn't have the energy. Here I thought I'd noticed something different in her. "Can we skip this part? I'm exhausted. I know that you are too. Can you just tell me what you need, or accuse me of whatever it is you want to accuse me of, and go?"

"Oh, for... You're so frustrating." She shook her head and let out a long puff of air, resembling a bull getting ready to charge. She pointed toward the sofa, toward the pies. "Can we sit?"

I opened my mouth to say no. To ask her to leave. I didn't have it in me to be verbally accosted, or even to engage in back-and-forth jibes. Then I noticed the slump of her shoulders. "Sure. Why not?" I gestured toward the couch, then Watson and I followed behind.

Susan sat where Leo had, and I resumed my original spot. Watson didn't return to the fire but sat at my feet, still not growling but never taking his wary eyes off Susan.

Again Susan studied what remained of the divided slice of pie before meeting my eyes again. Then she nodded, a firm, hard motion. We studied each other for several moments, and then she straightened, her chin jutting forward, and though she wasn't in uniform, she was once again Officer Green. "I need your help."

I could have been bowled over with a feather. Of all the things she might have said, that would've been my last guess. "You do?"

"I do." From the tightness of her lips as she spoke, it was clear whatever was happening between us, this was still the furthest thing from what she wanted to do. "Mark didn't kill Adam Sweitzer. And I need you to help prove that."

When there seemed to be no punch line coming, I leaned forward slightly. "Seriously?"

She rolled her eyes in annoyance, and it was such a Susan gesture that it was almost comforting. "If you're trying to get me to beg, I'm taking you and your little dog out right now and burying you both in the forest. I'll claim that crooked ex-boyfriend of yours came and did you in."

Despite myself, and how close to reality her accusation nearly had been, I laughed.

Susan's lips twitched. "I'm not kidding."

I laughed again but got a hold of myself rather quickly. "Fine. No begging. That's not what I wanted anyway. Why do you need my help? If Mark says he didn't kill Adam, and you believe him, surely you can prove it."

"That's just it." She let out a heavy sigh. "Mark isn't sure if he killed Adam or not."

"What?" Surely that statement had to have a punch line.

Again she rolled her eyes and anger filled her tone. "The moron was drunk. Drunker than I've seen him in ages. He doesn't remember a thing. Claims to have no idea how he got covered in the other moron's blood."

"Seriously?"

"Good grief, Fred, can you quit asking that!" she snapped, and then grabbed the plate of what remained of Leo's pie. "I'm going to eat this."

"Help yourself." I replayed the scene from that morning. Adam's body, Mark sprawled on the couch in the back room, blood everywhere. I hadn't been sugarcoating it to Leo; it really had seemed cut and dried. "Why are you so..." I lifted a hand. "Don't bite my head off, but... why are you so sure Mark didn't do it? If he was so drunk he couldn't remember what happened that night, he might've been so drunk that his anger at something got the best of him."

She spoke with her mouth full. "Because I know him. I know everything about him. I know all his good qualities and all of his bad—which vastly outnumber the good." She took another bite and groaned. "I hate that your annoying best friend is such a good baker." She chewed a couple of times and then continued. "Mark is an idiot. Always has been. He's a middle-age man who dresses up like a wizard and jumps around with a broom between his legs. He's a grown-up man who has board game night every month.

He's constantly leaving his wife for some new woman who turns his head and then comes crawling back when it all goes down the toilet. And she's an idiot for constantly taking him back. He loves his children, but he's a lackadaisical father at best, not nearly what those wonderful kids need. He's got his head in the clouds one hundred percent of the time. His best friend is an old woman who swears she's a fairy. He's got a temper the size of Texas, and to top it off, thanks to him, I now have a stupid rabbit in my house that's been squealing all evening. If I hadn't come here, I probably would've wrung its neck and had rabbit stew."

"You need to cover Drake's cage at night. Then he'll quit screaming."

She scowled. "Number one, that was not the important part, and number two, why in the world do you know that?"

I shrugged. "One of them mentioned it the other day. I don't remember if it was Glinda or Mark. But that's why Mark named him Drake... It's short for Mandrake. It's the plant in the Harry Potter books that screams when you pull it out of the dirt."

Susan lifted her hand and began to rub her temples. "I'm surrounded by freaks."

I managed to suppress a chuckle. "I'm surprised you have Drake. I would have assumed Glinda would be taking care of him."

"Yes, you would think." Susan sneered. "But Glinda lives at Aspen Grove, and that snooty retirement home won't allow them to have animals. And Mark's wife is allergic." She seemed to catch herself. "And for crying out loud, I'm not here because of that fleabag rabbit. Although if what you said is accurate, you just saved its worthless life. Can you focus on what's important, please?"

"Right." I took a second to regroup. "Well... from what

you said, you listed a whole bunch of reasons why Mark might be the killer. You have yet to give one to indicate why he isn't."

"Because he just isn't. That's the reason." She threw up her hands. "My big brother is a moron, an idiot, a horrible husband, a pathetic father, and not that great of a brother, truth be told, but the one thing he isn't, is a murderer." Anger gave way to disgust. "And if I needed any more proof that he deserves the craptastic brother of the year award, here it is—that he's put me in a situation where I have to come to you, of all people, and ask for help."

From the fiery passion in Susan's tone, I had no doubt she believed what she was saying, but that didn't mean she was correct. "Even if all that's true, why do you need me?"

Her lip curled. "Really? Your Highness requires flattery?"

It was my turn to roll my eyes. "No. I don't. But from day one, you've continued to give me a litany of reasons why I need to keep my nose out of it. And while we're on the topic, you've not been any less condescending, patronizing, and arrogant than Branson was about it. The only difference is you were consistent. Until now." I snorted a laugh. "Although, actually, even though you're asking for help, you're still somehow managing to be condescending, patronizing, and arrogant."

Once more her lips twitched, but she didn't address all of that. "I need you because you can do things that I can't. You can be your gossipy, busybody self and drive everyone crazy with your annoying questions and not have a warrant. People will talk to you because you don't have the badge. And..." Her expression soured. "Though I can't imagine why, it seems a lot of people in town find you likable. The same can't be said for myself."

I considered and studied her. "Are you sure your gut is telling you he's innocent? Or do you think it's more likely you just want him to be?"

"If I had to place money on a suspect, I'd say Billy Hanson." She practically snarled. "But he has an alibi."

I jolted at the mention of Anna and Carl's son. Though it made sense, considering their fight. "What's his alibi?"

She rolled her eyes. "He was with his annoying parents. Anna claims her precious baby boy was up all night with food poisoning."

Relief tried to trickle in, but didn't quite settle.

Susan launched in again. "Either way, I have no uncertainty at all. None. Mark didn't do this." She left no room for doubt. She looked like she was getting ready to stand. "But I'm not going to beg. If you don't want to do it because you don't like me, fine. I don't blame you. You're hardly my favorite person in the world either. If you're not going to do it out of loyalty to your parents, if it's some quest of the Barry Adams family to keep the Greens down, then whatever. I think it would be enough that you all won't allow Mark to purchase the store from you and give him the freedom to not pay rent. But if you require him to be behind bars, then there's nothing I can say to convince you."

"The freedom to not pay—" I barely cut off my exasperated words in time. I'd forgotten that Susan didn't know the specifics of exactly how much rent Mark Green had been paying my stepfather for the use of the Alakazam location. Either way, it didn't change the facts. "Surely you can hear how insane you sound with those accusations of my family?"

"He's tried to buy the building for years, Fred, and Barry won't budge, won't even consider selling the shop to Mark. How many properties does your hippie-dippy stepfather need? How much money does—" Susan's voice had started to rise, and she broke off abruptly and shook her head. "Not the point." She stood then, towering over me, causing Watson to growl once more, and she looked down into my eyes. "Are you going to help or not?"

I didn't even have to consider. "Of course I will."

There was a flicker of surprise, and then she nodded. "Great. Be at the station tomorrow afternoon, around four. I'll clear it for you to interview Mark first, get his side of it, even though the moron doesn't remember anything." She snagged the remaining edge of the sweet potato pie on my plate, stuffed it in her mouth, and stomped out of my house.

"My sister has lost her ever-loving mind." Mark Green tapped the metal table bolted to the floor in the interview room of the Estes Park police station as he glowered at me, and sent a glare toward the one-way window from where we both assumed Susan observed us, despite her claim of giving us privacy. "First she arrests me, then comes by my cell on an endless loop yelling about how stupid I am, and then tops it off by getting *you* involved."

I searched for something to do with my hands. I'd left Watson at the Cozy Corgi to hang out with Katie and Nick, and chugged the dirty chai Katie had made for me on my drive to the police station. I wished I'd milked it a little longer, to have the warm cup to hold. Better yet, I should've asked her for two of them one for the drive and one to make this new method of torture more bearable. "She's trying to help prove that you didn't kill anyone. To get you out of jail."

"Seeing as Susan was the one to put on the handcuffs, she has a funny way of showing it." He sent another glare at the window before gifting me with the same expression. "And of all people. Barry Adams's daughter. If it was up to you, the key to my cell would be thrown away."

Seeing Mark in his prison jumpsuit altered my perception of him. Without the wizard robes, he was just a big, lumbering bear. I hadn't been aware that his dressing up had so greatly altered my impression of him, but he seemed more approachable, more human, maybe. And strangely, less likable. Without his costume, the only excuse for his unpleasant disposition was the man himself. "Do you have someone else that you'd like to talk to? Someone you think could help clear this up for you? Maybe your lawyer?"

"Nah, Gerald came and talked to me yesterday. He says it looks pretty bad." The drumming of Mark's fingers lessened. "He didn't have any new ideas this morning either, but he'll fight for me."

It was only thanks to the second shot of espresso Katie had poured into my dirty chai that enabled me to keep from groaning. "Gerald Jackson is your lawyer?"

"Don't even think of saying anything bad about him. I know you think you're so much better than everyone" It seemed Mark had caught my thoughts of Gerald without me having to groan. "He's a great lawyer and my friend. And a whole lot smarter than you."

Of course Gerald was Mark's lawyer, *of course*! From what I'd seen of Gerald Jackson, he wouldn't be able to get someone off murder charges even if they had been in a coma at the time of the crime. "Mark, if you don't want me to look into it, I won't. I'm only doing this as a favor to Susan because she believes you're innocent, but if you're going to fight against me, then I won't waste any of our time."

He leaned forward. "And why *you,* exactly? She despises you, and our families hate each other."

I glanced toward the window that time. I'd been told on other occasions when I'd been in this room that it was soundproof, but I wasn't certain. Furthermore, by that point, I didn't care if Susan overheard her brother's secret. I turned back to Mark and matched his position, leaning toward him with a glare of my own. "I don't know what you're getting at, or why you play this game with Susan, but I *do* know what goes on between you and my stepfather and mother regarding your rent."

Mark's eyes widened before narrowing to slits once more. "Really, they're complaining about rent to you? The rent wouldn't be an issue if you all would just sell me the store."

I leaned closer and hissed. "You've not paid rent for over four years, Mark. What do you have to find fault with exactly?"

"Are you kidding? Have you ever tried to get air-head Barry and daffy Phyllis to repair something, fix a lock, or answer any number of inquiries without having to harass them for weeks on end?"

I bristled at the name-calling despite knowing that this part of his accusation was true. Both Mom and Barry could be a little bit forgetful and spacey. I truly had wanted to help Susan, if nothing else to make a gesture of good faith. But I had my limits.

Standing, I pressed both my fists into the table as I leaned over him. "Play this however you want. Barry and my mother have kept your secret from the rest of your family. They don't want to embarrass you in front of your wife or your sister or your children. I don't either. But one more name-calling or accusation of my family, and I will not continue offering you respect you haven't earned. And as far as this"—I gestured around the room and then at his jumpsuit—"if it doesn't bother you, why should it bother me? From what Susan said, you're not even sure that you're innocent." Without waiting for a reply, I turned on my booted heels and headed toward the door.

My hand was on the knob when Mark spoke up, his voice quiet. "I have a bruise on my elbow and on my hip."

"What?" Though I turned back toward him, I kept my hand where it was, ready to leave.

"Bruises." Mark lifted his left arm and pulled down the sleeve revealing a bruise on the elbow and then gestured toward his left hip though it was under the table. "I'm not sure, but I think I fell. I remember Drake screaming, the sound hurting my head. I remember getting up, feeling sick, but..." He closed his eyes, and his voice grew even softer, as if trying to picture it all. "I might've gone out to the shop, to the restroom to throw up or something. I don't know. I think I remember falling, I think..." His eyes opened once more—the pale blue hue matched his sister's. "Must've slipped in Adam's blood. Fallen. Then covered Drake's cage to shut him up and passed out again. It's the only thing I can think of."

"You don't recall seeing Adam's body?"

"I just said what I remembered, didn't I?" he bit at me, but when I turned to go once more, he adjusted his tone. "Sorry. I'm sorry. Don't leave."

I wasn't sure if he changed because he thought I might help clear his name or whether he was worried I'd tell that he'd been playing the victim, unjustifiably, to the rest of his family while casting mine as villains. Either way, I rejoined him at the table. "Why would Adam be in your shop in the middle the night?"

When he rolled his eyes, I prepared to stand again, but as he spoke, I got the sense the gesture wasn't meant toward me. "He barged in on game night. I don't even know how he knew it was going on, but the four of us had barely sat down to play Lords of Waterdeep when Adam started pounding on the door of the shop. When Gerald answered the door, Adam barged right in, came into the back room, and acted like he was just one of the guys, as if everything was okay again."

There was very little of that statement I understood, but one part caught my attention. "Gerald was there? Your lawyer?"

"Of course." Mark looked at me as if that should have been obvious. "He's there every game night. Gerald, me, Angus, and Rocky. We were all there."

I sorted through that for a second, then listed the names off on my fingers. "Your game night buddies are Gerald Jackson, your lawyer."

Mark nodded. "I just said yes to that, didn't I?"

I kept going, too flabbergasted to worry about his tone. "Angus Witt who owns Knit Witt?"

"There's only one Angus in town, isn't there?" Mark jumped in before I could finish. "And Rocky Castle, the same one who owns Rocky Road Tours, if you need it spelled out to you. Geesh, lady, it's like you just moved to town last week."

Again, I didn't give his jibe a second thought. If there'd ever been a grouping of people I wouldn't want to be a part of, Mark had just offered it up on a silver platter. Rocky Castle made my skin crawl. I had zero respect for Gerald Jackson, though no hostility. And Mark himself was the epitome of unpleasant. The only one I had no feelings about was Angus. It was an odd grouping. Mark, and judging from my impression Rocky, were both in their forties, the other two men at least two or three decades older. "The four of you get together once a month and play board games in the back of your shop?"

Mark glared. "How in the world is this so hard to understand? And how have you taken claim to solving murders if you can't even grasp the concept of game night?"

"I understand the concept of game night. My parents and uncles play spades once a..." I shook my head, I didn't need to defend myself to Mark or explain anything. But much to my own dismay, the curiosity bug had bitten me. It was such a weird group and such a strange circumstance that I wanted to explore it. I thought back to what Glinda had said about the game night and double-checked. "If what I understand is correct, on these game nights you often sleep in the back room of Alakazam."

Another eye roll. "Yeah. There's a lot of drinking on those nights, and Sharon doesn't like me to come home drunk. She's about as much fun as the whole forest of sticks in the mud."

I ignored the commentary on his wife. "If there were three other people there, you should have plenty of witnesses to confirm you didn't murder anyone."

"Didn't you just hear me? There's a lot of drinking at game night. Rocky and I were totally gone. Even more than normal because after Adam, the backstabbing traitor, left we really tore it up because of how infuriating he was."

I didn't know which part of that sentence to tackle first but decided to stick with the witness angles since we were already headed down that road. "Okay, so you and Rocky were drinking heavily, what about Gerald and Angus, were they as well?"

"Not beers." Mark made a sour face. "They always drink Gerald's kombucha. Nasty stuff."

"So they weren't drunk?"

He shook his head. "No, but they don't remember. I just said, they were drinking Gerald's kombucha."

His circular logic made me wonder if he thought we were still in the middle of game night and was intentionally being evasive and talking in riddles. I switched tactics. "Why don't you fill me in on what happened that night, just tell me the story. You said you and Rocky started to drink more heavily after Adam left. So he arrived and then left again?"

Mark opened his mouth, and I could read his thoughts through his expression and knew I was about to get told I was stupid.

I cut him to the chase. "Don't bite my head off. I realize how that question sounded, but you're not making any sense. So keep your insults to yourself and just tell me the story."

At my hard tone, he sat a little straighter. "You and Sharon should hang out. You both have a nasty attitude."

This was why they say curiosity killed the cat. "Get on with it, Mark."

Though he scowled again, he did as I asked. "Like I said, the guys and I were having game night. We were playing Lords of Waterdeep." Mark shrugged one shoulder. "It's Angus's favorite game. I don't love it. It's an offshoot of Dungeons & Dragons, but... not really. Not near as good as the real thing, but we humor him a couple of times a year and play it anyway. It's a lot more fun than when Rocky insists we play the stupid Bigfoot—"

"Mark." I adopted the tone I'd used when I was a college professor. "This'll be a lot easier if you don't go down bunny trails." Even as the words left my lips, I thought of the screaming Mandrake but pushed onward before Mark could comment. "I don't need to know what games you played. Just run me through the events of what happened and how Adam took part."

The irritation in Mark's tone increased, but he did as I asked. "As I said before, we were in the middle of playing, and Adam starts pounding on the door. Gerald answers, and Adam barges in and makes himself right at home, acting like no time has passed. Slapping me on the back, teasing Rocky about an old girl he'd dated ages and ages ago. Bragging about all he's accomplished, all the adventures he's gone on, all the great things he's done, when the whole room knew he was full of it. Just as obnoxious as he was in high school. I don't know why we put up with him then."

"You went to high school with Adam?" I made a guess. "Rocky as well?"

"Yep. The three of us were pretty tight back in the day. Adam was my best friend, until... he wasn't."

"Why?" Caught up now, I leaned forward again. "What happened?"

"In high school?"

I nodded.

"I thought you wanted me to tell you what happened at game night." He crossed his arms over his barrel chest.

"Fine." I'd come back the high school incident. Chances were things would go smoother if Mark didn't jump around. "You were saying Adam came into game night and was acting like no time had passed, and that was annoying you and Rocky."

"It would annoy *anyone*. Adam's a..." Mark seemed to search for a term, then his eyes widened and he leaned forward again. "I forgot. You said you read Harry Potter, right?"

I nodded.

"That's the best way to describe Adam, then. He's like Gilderoy Lockhart."

For the first time ever, I felt like I was on the same page

with Mark Green, and I put that together with a few other descriptors he'd given of Adam. "You mean he's constantly one-upping on the story or bragging about great and marvelous things he's done and accomplished, when either they were someone else's accomplishments or completely fictional?"

The smile that crossed Mark's face gave a glimpse into the boy and younger man he'd been. He relaxed. "Exactly." He reached out and tapped the table in front of me. "You nailed it. That's exactly what Adam was like."

Judging from the few minutes in his presence at the Cozy Corgi during the Christmas party, the description fit. "Okay, thank you. That makes sense. So what happened then?"

His expression darkened instantly. "Adam jumped in on game night, like he'd been invited. He dug in his backpack and pulled out Krampus Dimension." Though anger still filled his tone, the more he spoke, I could make out a tremble of awe. "The cover art on that box... man... totally righteous. Like for real. The board, the game pieces, the artwork on the cards, supreme. Totally, totally supreme." His tone shifted once more, leaving nothing but excitement. "See the point of the whole thing is, you got these four players, right? It's a cooperative game. You all have your own powers or skills, working together to beat the game itself. The four of you are trapped in this Nightmare Christmas dimension, and Krampus, he's this half goat, half demon Christmas character. Everywhere you turn, there is a trap or a monster or a—"

"Mark..." On impulse I started to reach out to touch his arm and then instantly pulled my hand back. "Focus, remember. Tell me what happened. I don't need to know how to play the game."

"Fine." His nostrils flared, and it appeared like it took effort to keep from biting my head off, but he succeeded. "Adam announced that the game he was setting up was the prototype, that Krampus Dimension is slated to go into production by next Christmas, but it's going to be a huge money-making success. So of course, I totally lost it, started screaming at him. And Rocky, he had my back. Because..." He shrugged the same solitary shoulder. "Well, he's Rocky. He's my man. He didn't necessarily have a dog in this fight, but he had my back. Gerald and Angus didn't understand why I was so mad until later, but they had my back as well. We kicked that loser out, locked the door behind him, and that was that. Although I was so furious, we didn't even return to playing games. Just drinking and raging about what a traitor Adam was." Mark looked me dead in the eye. "Adam got what he deserved." Venom dripped from Mark's statement, leaving no doubt he meant every syllable.

"But... you didn't kill him?"

"How could I? He wasn't there." Fear flitted over his face as he sank back into the chair, and confusion filled his tone. "At least I didn't see him again until Susan had me handcuffed and we walked past his body."

"You don't remember him coming back after the four of you kicked him out?"

He shook his head.

"Do you remember the other three leaving?"

Another headshake. "I passed out at some point. Rocky did as well... before me, but Glinda said he wasn't there when the two of you came in the next morning."

I was certain Susan would've already talked to the other three members of the game night, and if she'd been able to poke any holes in their stories she would've. I'd ask her about it either way. She hadn't given me any details, said it would be better if I got it straight from Mark himself so her anger at him didn't influence my impressions.

It sounded as if there were four suspects, including Mark. Though, from what I'd seen from Gerald and Angus, I couldn't imagine either of the elderly men beating someone a couple of decades younger to the point that they resembled Adam's bruised and injured face. I could easily picture it from Mark, both due to his size and strength and the anger still roaring over a day later, even after Adam was already dead. I could also see Rocky doing it, but that could simply be because he gave me the creeps.

While there were more suspects than I'd originally thought, listening to Mark talk about Adam only made him sound guiltier. "You said you all started playing this new game, the prototype of Krampus..."

"Krampus Dimensions."

"Right." It sounded like the worst Christmas game I'd ever heard of, though I could see it being popular. I didn't understand why anyone would want to take the Christmas holiday and turn it into something dark, but plenty of people liked that sort of thing. I even had a few books about the legend of Krampus in stock in the Cozy Corgi. "So... what happened during the game that made you so angry? Did Adam cheat?"

Mark snorted derisively. "To say the least." He cocked his head, his voice returning to annoyed mockery. "But I thought you didn't want me to tell you about the game."

Dear Lord. "Fine. What about the game?"

"It's brilliant." Excitement came back instantly, and he sat up straighter. "And brutal. You've gotta be a master at strategy to be able to beat it. Everywhere you turn, the game is ready for you. It took my freshman, sophomore, and junior year to map out all the pitfalls and twists and turns. I wasn't satisfied until it was so difficult that I was only able to beat it one out of ten times."

Surely I was misunderstanding something. "You're saying that *you* designed the game?"

"Yeah." He sounded as if that too was obvious. "It's my game. Though I didn't have the stupid Krampus Christmas angle. Mine was Asylum of Insanity. But it's the same game. Identical. Just a different setting and different characters. It felt familiar when we got started, and by the fourth round, it was blatantly obvious. Rocky didn't recognize it at first, so I reminded him of it after Adam left." His fists clenched. "I shouldn't be surprised. Adam was just like he was back in high school. Stealing everything from everybody, making sure the stories he told were bigger and better than everyone else's to make himself feel better."

"How would Adam have stolen it from you?"

"He played the test versions with me back in the day. He didn't come up with a *single* idea." Mark laughed darkly. "Well... that's not true. He had a billion ideas, each of them worse than the one before." His lip curled as he nearly snarled. "That thief took my game, gave it some stupid Krampus theme, and is going to make over fifteen million dollars on it."

"Fifteen million?" I nearly choked.

Mark jammed his finger onto the table. "Exactly. That money should be mine. It was my game."

I had no idea board game developers were paid so well. I took a few moments to consider, replaying the story as I studied him. "You told Susan all of this?"

"Yeah." He folded his arms once more. "She doesn't remember the game, but I never let her join in on any of that stuff when we were kids. She hated anything that took an ounce of imagination or had anything to do with fantasy.

She was always reading some stupid crime or mystery novel or doing her homework. Always a brownnoser." He jammed the table again. "But unlike Adam, Susan never cheats and never lies. She's earned everything she's gotten. Even if she is a pain about it."

Susan grew up reading mystery novels? Of all the things Mark had said, that nearly threw me off the most. I shoved it aside, as it was also the most unimportant of the things Mark had said.

It was no wonder Susan was desperate enough to ask for help from me. Every detail Mark disclosed only made it worse for himself. "You truly have no recollection of Adam coming back to Alakazam? You remember falling, but you don't remember any other physical interaction with him?"

"That's what I said, didn't I?" He cocked a brow. "Are you going to start asking all the same questions again?"

I stood. "No. I'm not. But if you think of something else, tell Susan, okay?"

"I don't need you to tell me what to say to my sister." The retort almost seemed automatic as he flinched and adjusted his tone instantly. "Sorry. So... you're going to clear my name?"

"I don't know." Once more I headed across the room and took the door handle before looking back at Mark. "But I'll find out who killed Adam Sweitzer."

After talking to her brother, comparing notes with Susan was almost relaxing. She wasn't pleasant, but neither was she particularly taunting or aggressive. Nor, unfortunately, was she overly helpful. Though it was clear Mark had told us the exact same story. I'd been correct in my theory that Susan had already spoken to the other members of Mark's game night, but she hadn't gotten anything of use from any of them either. Despite chances being high I'd have the same experience, that was where I would start, doubling back over Susan's tracks.

If there was any way around it, I would've chosen a different path. The idea of talking to Rocky Castle and Gerald Jackson was just this side of torture. So I'd start with Angus Witt, put the other two off as long as I could manage.

After returning to the bookshop I continued to mull things over and realized, with some surprise, that I believed Mark's story. My gut said he was being honest. Granted, he hadn't given all that much to lie about, but still... I had the sense that he told me everything exactly as he remembered. Even so, it was easy to see why Susan had felt that she had no choice but to arrest her own brother. He'd clearly hated

Adam Sweitzer, was covered in Adam's blood, and by his own admission, couldn't honestly say he hadn't killed him.

Mark's defense of Susan stuck with me as well. That she was a good police officer, that she'd been a smart and studious child. Her actions around Adam's death seemed to prove that. And... she'd enjoyed mystery novels. That went a long way in my book.

After sending Ben home, he'd done enough at the bookshop on his own, I took care of the remaining customers then locked up for the evening. As Watson and I drove by Habanero's, I did a double take. A large school-bus-shaped vehicle, completely covered in dirty white fur, sat in the parking lot of the Mexican restaurant.

Even as I tried to talk myself out of it, my hands seemed to move of their own accord and angled the wheel of my Mini Cooper so it pulled off Elkhorn Avenue, circled around into the parking lot, and came to a stop beside the atrocious eyesore. Though I hadn't seen this particular fur-covered bus before, there was only one person the contraption could belong to.

While I got out of the car and headed into the restaurant, I listed the reasons I should stick to the original plan. I was tired, despite the ridiculous amounts of caffeine I'd had. It was time to go home, to recoup. I had talked to both Mark and Susan Green only a couple hours before, and while I didn't have a violent temper, my average-length fuse had already been significantly shortened, considering the hour of the day. Still, I wasn't a corgi mama for nothing—Watson could be the most stubborn little thing alive, just like me.

Marcus Gonzales was in midlecture to the girl at the hostess stand when Watson and I walked in. The owner of Habanero's did a double take of his own, not pausing in his diatribe before looking back at me, eyes wide with hope. "Miss Winifred and Watson! There's been a murder!"

I paused, a hitch in my step, before continuing. "Yes. I'm surprised you haven't heard of it. It was yesterday morning. You must've really been slammed with tourists to have not heard." Although, that didn't make sense. Even the tourists were talking about it.

His expression fell. "Oh. At the magic shop?"

I nodded.

"So..." He looked around, twisting so he could peer into the different brightly painted rooms of his restaurant. "Not one here, then?"

I couldn't help but laugh as we joined the two at the hostess stand. "Marcus, don't you think you might've heard if someone had been killed in your restaurant?"

Marcus shrugged. "You're the one who is constantly stumbling onto bodies, not me." His eyes twinkled. "Want to take a quick walk around? Maybe you'll find one." He winked down at Watson. "I'll even let you tour the kitchen, just don't call the health inspector."

I had the sense he was only partially kidding. Luckily Watson didn't correlate the word kitchen with food, or he'd have started begging. "You need to quit hoping that your restaurant's going to be the scene of a murder. It's not a *good* thing."

"But it's exciting." He rubbed his hands together. "And a moneymaker. If Glinda opened Alakazam today, I guarantee you it would be their most profitable day of the year."

"Still, that would mean someone needs to die. Someone that you know."

"Goodness. I don't want that. Of course I don't want that." A little of the sparkle died. "That's not what I'm wishing at all, but... you keep discovering bodies, so"—he shrugged—"*somebody* has to die, somewhere, might as well be here. Just not family or anything like that. Maybe a tourist or an employee we haven't had so long." His gaze flicked to the hostess, who'd paled. He patted her shoulder. "Not you, Anya. I wasn't meaning you. Although... it would be nice if you could start getting the table numbers correct." He grinned back at me. "If you're not here for murder, then you must desire dinner. Can Anya get you a table?"

"No, sorry." I offered Anya an apologetic smile. "I'm looking for someone. I saw their—" A loud laugh burst from the bar area, and I glanced over Marcus's and Anya's shoulders. "Never mind. Target spotted." Rocky Castle was even larger than Mark Green, and with his massive, bright ginger hair and beard, he stood out like a beacon.

Marcus followed the gesture, his voice dipping to an excited whisper. "*Rocky* murdered someone?" He looked back at me, a huge smile over his face. "That doesn't surprise me."

"No. Rocky didn't kill anyone. I just want to—" That wasn't even close to true. "—*need* to speak to him."

Marcus cocked an eyebrow but said no more.

I started to walk past them and into the bar, but paused —might as well have something pleasurable come out of this. "You know, actually, would you mind placing an order for a dozen of your breakfast burritos? I'll swing by and pick them up in the morning? With the green chili on the side?" Katie was always feeding me. It would be a good day to bring in something special for her and the boys. "Oh, and maybe a baked chicken breast for Watson."

"You got it." Marcus grinned, then turned back to Anya. "For to-go orders, you don't put a table number at all. That'll only mess things up."

I left them to it and continued into the bar, but paused

once more as I noticed a new picture framed on the wall. Marcus had a huge collection of signed photographs of celebrities who'd eaten at Habanero's. In the midst of them, was a picture of me and my entire family that Marcus had taken on a recent visit. Hopefully, he never got his wish of having a murder at his restaurant.

Rocky had a huge margarita in his hand as he left the bar and walked toward a large table. When he noticed Watson and me, his sky-blue eyes ignited with a fire that reminded me why I hadn't wanted this conversation. At least one of the reasons why.

"Well... the beautiful woman with a man's name. It's been too long."

"Hi, Rocky." I was pleased to discover that even if my voice didn't sound pleasant, I'd achieved neutral. "I saw your vehicle outside. Or at least, figured it was yours."

Watson plopped down a foot or so behind me.

Rocky cast Watson a dismissive glance before leering my way. "Don't you love it?" He straightened and puffed up to an even bigger degree, seeming to fill the room. "It's my first year doing it. I don't know why I didn't think of it before. After Bigfoot hunting season was over, I was getting ready to put the Bigfoot-mobile up, and then was struck with sheer genius, if I do say so myself. I took the brown fur off, put white fur on, and... presto changeo, we now have abominable snowman tours." He used his margarita to gesture to the table he'd been headed toward. "As you can see, it's a hit."

Judging from the twenty or so people at the table, he was right. Proof that tourists would pay for anything. When I looked back at him, Rocky was taking a gulp from his margarita. "You're on a tour, right now?"

He nodded. "Sure I am. Throw in a meal, and you can

charge more. Granted, if they'd just come here and paid themselves, it would cost them less, but I offer them an experience." He took another chug.

I cocked an eyebrow meaningfully at the bowl-sized glass.

"Oh? This?" Rocky spared the margarita a glance before leering at me once more. "Don't worry. I had them make a virgin version. Safety first." He winked and gave what I supposed was meant to be a Boy Scout salute. An unconvincing one.

"While I hate to interrupt when you're... working, could I have a couple minutes of your time?"

"Sure." He took a step forward. "May I get you a drink? Yours can be just as virgin as mine." Another wink.

Yep... just as slimy as I remembered.

"Say yes. Come on." Though I was certain repulsion covered my face, Rocky seemed nonplussed. "I've told you, woman. You and me would make a strapping hoard of redheaded boys."

Chances were low my stomach would quit revolting in time to partake in any of the breakfast burritos. I took a step back from him, crossing my arms. Watson scooted back as well. "Rocky, what's my name?"

His mouth opened, and he paused. After second, he shrugged. "You got some guy name. Don't remember, but that's okay. We don't need to use names." His brows creased, and he glanced to my feet. "I do remember your rude fat hamster. Winston."

It was nearly enough to make me spin on my heels and leave. But... if I did that, I'd just have to hunt him down another time. Might as well get it over with. "Watson, actually, but it's not important. I wanted to ask you about game night. Adam's murder. I just got done talking to Mark, and he mentioned that you were there."

Instant anger flared, and I took another step back before I realized it wasn't directed at me.

"Leave it to Adam. That waste of space couldn't even get himself killed without causing problems for old friends." Rocky closed the distance between us again, but I stayed where I was. "Mark didn't hurt Adam. And if he did, Adam deserved it. Which... Adam did deserve it."

Feeling like I was showing exceptional restraint, I bypassed that Rocky had basically argued against his own point. "Mark claims he doesn't remember much of the night. He can't recall Adam coming back into Alakazam."

"*Claims?*" That time Rocky's anger did seem focused on me. "Are you trying to say Mark is lying?"

Still I didn't move away. "Do you remember?"

"Sure I remember. We had game night. Adam shows up uninvited. Jumps in like he thinks we're still friends, and then proceeds to make us play this game that..." He rolled his eyes. "The cards are cool, the art was pretty decent, almost as good as the Bigfoot Chasers game, but way too much reading. Annoying. Point of the game is to have fun, not feel like you're reading a book. Who wants to read a book? Talk about wasting time." He scratched his beard. "Oh, right. You sell books, don't ya?" His hand continued to scratch, moving up his face until he was digging into the heavy tangles of his hair. "Well, that's okay. Just because you sell them doesn't mean you have to read them. You're kind of like a drug dealer."

I didn't attempt to follow that logic, but had a nagging suspicion I would try to figure it out later. "What happened after the game, Rocky?"

"Mark told you I'm sure. It's a little insulting you're

coming to me, trying to prove he's lying to you." Again the anger was focused on me.

A growl emanated from beside my feet, but using every ounce of will I had, I made my voice pleasant, as if I was speaking to a child. "I'm trying to help your friend, Rocky. Susan asked me to help prove her brother isn't a murderer. I'm talking to *you* in the hope that you'll help me do that."

"Susan..." He rolled his eyes. "Fine." He finally stopped scratching and took another drink before continuing. "Mark realized that Adam stole his game he'd made way back in the day. Stole it and was going to be a billionaire because of it. So we kicked him out. We didn't lay a finger on him. Should've." The hand that had just been scratching closed into a fist. "We really should've. Wish we had while we'd had the chance."

I eyed his large fist, his large body, and remembered Adam's bruised and puffy face. It would've taken nothing for Rocky, or Mark for that matter, to inflict such damage on the smaller man. From what I'd seen from Rocky, it seemed his anger was close to the surface even when he was sober. I imagined he didn't make a very pretty picture when he was drunk. "Do you remember Adam coming back?"

"Nah. He didn't come back." Rocky took a drink, and his fist relaxed. "I was hoping we'd start playing Bigfoot Chasers, even started setting it up, but Mark was too angry. So we just blew off steam and drank until we passed out." Another shrug. "Just game night."

"Do you remember leaving the magic shop?"

He scowled in obvious insult. "Of course I do. I woke up after a bit. Angus and Gerald had already gone, which is normal. Mark was snoring away. Remember it as clear as mud. I can hold *my* liquor."

I nearly asked him if he meant he could remember as

clear as glass, but at that moment he chugged the rest of his margarita as if proving his point.

"When I drove home, Mark was by himself. Asleep. If Sharon didn't wear the pants in the family, then Mark could've gone home."

Basically the same version as Mark. "Do you remember locking up when you left?"

"I don't know." He shrugged. "Who cares? Not like it's a big..." Rocky's eyes narrowed once more and his tone became dangerous. "Now listen here, if you're insinuating that I did something to that rat, you and I are going to have problems. I didn't touch him. And if I did, Adam deserved it, which... He deserved it. But..." Confusion battled with his look of fury. "I didn't."

"Then who did?" Knowing it wasn't the smart thing to do but unable to let Rocky think he could intimidate me, I moved closer to Rocky, straightening my shoulders and lifting my chin. "If you didn't kill Adam, and neither did Mark, but both of you think he deserved it, then who did? Who killed Adam, Rocky?"

To my surprise, he took a step back. "Why would I know? What business is it of yours?"

I ignored the question; we'd already traveled down that road. "Who's your guess?"

That brought a new expression to Rocky's face, and he tilted his head, seeming to consider. After several moments, long enough that I'd given up on an answer, Rocky gave a definitive nod. "Sharon."

I was so thrown off, it took me a second to remember who Sharon was. "Mark's wife?"

Rocky nodded. "Good a bet as any."

I hadn't had a list of suspects, outside of the four members of the board game club and food-poisoned Billy

Hanson—as much as I didn't want to put Anna and Carl's son on the list—but even if I had, Sharon never would have been on it. From what I knew of their relationship, if Mark's wife was going to kill someone in the magic shop, it seemed like it would be Mark himself. "Why would Sharon kill Adam? You think she knew about all the money her family was missing out on because Adam stole the game from Mark?"

He scrunched up his nose. "How would she even know that? We didn't find it out until that very night?"

Exactly. "Then why?"

He shrugged again. "To set up Mark, obviously. Get him put away. Get the insurance money or something."

"What insurance money?"

Rocky looked at me as if the answer was blatantly obvious. "The insurance you have if your spouse dies or gets put in jail for murder or something." As I debated the worth of informing him that type of insurance didn't exist, he took another angle. "Maybe not even for the money. Probably just to get him out of her hair. Or to prove a point. She's an awful woman. Always bossing Mark around. Bet she snuck in and killed Adam just to set Mark up." He started scratching his beard once more. "I miss that girl Mark was seeing a while back, the one who worked in your shop." He paused in his scratching long enough to snap his fingers. "What was her name again?"

"Sammy." She hadn't worked for me, but for Katie. Nick had taken her place.

Rocky pointed at me. "Right, Sammy. Now *that* chick was chill. Talked too much, but she could cook. Much better choice than Sharon. Wish Sammy was back. Too bad she moved."

Sammy had been murdered, but I had no desire to

refresh Rocky's memory, or anything else. Clearly, talking to him was pointless. He had corroborated Mark's story, so unless they'd planned it together, at least that much was true. Although, they easily could've planned it together. One of them on their own could have taken down Adam with one hand tied behind their back, but the two of them together could have done it in a heartbeat, drunk or sober. And the idea of Sharon made absolutely no sense.

"Well, I've taken enough of your time. Thank you. I'll let you get back to your... abominable snowman tour." *There* was a sentence I never thought I'd say.

"You can join. Good day for it. You can even bring that fat hamster." He grinned. "I'll keep you warm."

"I'll pass." I couldn't bring myself to say thank you.

With a final shrug, Rocky started to take another drink, then glared at the glass when he discovered it was empty. Instead of heading to the table of tourists, he turned back toward the bar. Before I got two steps away, he spoke up again. "He might've just killed himself."

I looked back at him. "Adam? You think Adam might've killed himself?"

He considered for half a second. "Why not? He deserved it. Bet he knew it."

I just shook my head and walked away. On the one hand, such a suggestion would imply Rocky hadn't laid a hand on Adam or seen his body. No one in their right mind would insinuate that Adam had inflicted those wounds and bruises on himself. But... with Rocky, I wasn't willing to place a bet on anything regarding mental capacity for logic or being in his right mind.

I dug out my cell on the way to the Mini Cooper.

Susan answered on the second ring. "You already

figured it out?" The raw hope in her voice surprised and cut at me.

"No. I just finished talking to Rocky. He didn't have any new information." I unlocked the car and stood aside so Watson could hop in and get to the passenger seat.

"Then why are you calling?" Her dashed hope turned to irritation.

"Do you know about Rocky's new business venture?"

More irritation, though I couldn't blame her. "Good grief, yes. His stupid snow monster tour thing."

"He's at Habanero's right now with a whole bunch of tourists, getting ready to take one of those tours. He's starting on what I believe is at least his second mammoth margarita. You might want to send an officer to do a sobriety check before a fuzzy busload of tourists flying off the side of a mountain puts a screeching halt to Estes Park's Christmas season."

"Fine. I will." She sighed in exasperation. "Thanks."

At the sound of sincerity in her voice, I pulled the cell away from my ear and looked at it as if I'd accidentally called another dimension, then put it back. "You're welcome."

I started to hang up when Susan's tone shifted yet again. "You truly weren't with him. With Branson." It didn't sound like a question.

"Susan." I couldn't keep the sigh to myself, maybe I didn't even try. "This isn't why I called and I just got done talking with Rocky"—*and you and your brother earlier*—"do we have to do this?"

"Just answer me, okay?" She somehow made her growl sound plaintive.

It was none of her business. I knew that, and chances were, *she* knew that. But at the same time, what did it matter? Realizing I'd been standing there with the door open, I finally slid behind the wheel. "No, I wasn't, like I told you many times before." I pushed on before she could object like she always did to my claims of not being Branson's girlfriend. "Yes, we went on several dates. Maybe we were dating. I never quite figured out what label to stick on us. Either way it never clicked. Or... *we* never really clicked. Something wasn't right."

She spoke slowly, almost carefully. "And you truly didn't know he was crooked?"

"No. I most definitely didn't." I didn't attempt to keep the bite out of my voice. "Did you?"

"No." Susan's tone softened to a confessional timbre I'd never heard from her and was willing to bet wouldn't have been there if we'd been speaking face-to-face. "I feel like an idiot. I knew something was off with the chief, but I never would've guessed... I knew he wasn't by the book, but I didn't think about him being criminal. They were just both so entitled, arrogant, and condescending. But that's a dime a dozen when you are a woman surrounded by male police officers a hundred to one. Still... I should've..."

I sat there, completely stunned, not turning on the car, and stared off into the deepening darkness over the surrounding mountains. I couldn't believe she and I were actually having this conversation. Though I never thought we would, it felt overdue.

Watson glared at me from the passenger seat, clearly wanting an explanation as to why we were still sitting in the parking lot.

"Why am I even telling you this? I shouldn't—"

"I've been having those exact same feelings, those exact same thoughts." The words tumbled forth, and I surprised myself by not wanting her to hang up. Somehow, though

Susan hadn't had even a hint of a romance with Branson, it felt like she could understand how I felt in a way no one else could. "Well... not about being surrounded by policemen, but that I should have known. It all seems rather obvious now. Branson's nights away. Why he was gung ho for me looking into one case and then demanding I keep my nose out of it on the next." A laugh escaped, and once more tears threatened, though this time those were more of a strange relief. "Although, those I just chalked up to him being a man, at least *that* kind of man. It reminded me of my ex-husband, though not as severe."

She sounded awestruck. "That's why you pushed him away?"

"Largely. Yes. In the sense that we just weren't... right."

Something in her tone hardened. "Are you heartbroken?"

I flinched. No one had asked me that. I hadn't even asked myself. I started to shake my head and gave myself a few moments to consider even if she couldn't see me. Was I? I had a sense of loss, of regret. There were times I missed him. But was I heartbroken? I sat a little straighter in the seat when my gut settled on the truth, causing Watson to glance over at me. "No. I'm not."

"Good." I could practically see Susan nod her head in a declarative nod from the other side of the phone. "Good." She cleared her throat. "Thanks for telling me about Rocky. I'll head to Habanero's now."

"How can something wrapped in tinfoil taste this delicious?" Katie dunked the second of her hand-sized burritos into the Styrofoam carton of green chili and groaned as she took a huge bite.

I had to take a second before responding, as I'd just stuffed my mouth with my own massive bite. "You're the master of pastries, but Marcus is the king of breakfast burritos. Although I bet you could take him, if you tried."

She shook her head, sending her curls whirling, and spoke with her mouth full. "Not gonna happen. Why bother when perfection has already been achieved?"

We ate in silence for a bit, each lost in the peace of comfort food as we ate by the bakery windows that looked out over Elkhorn Avenue. The snow had stopped, and the downtown was covered in a thick layer of the white fluffy stuff, glittering in the late-morning sun. Below, though the sidewalks were already shoveled, the bundled-up tourists slipped and slid as they shopped for Christmas gifts and souvenirs.

Katie and I had insisted the twins eat their share of the burritos first and they were now manning the bookshop and bakery, giving Katie and me a break. After eating his chicken breast, Watson had followed Ben downstairs, but as I started in on my third and final burrito, he rounded the corner of the stairs and weaved his way through the feet of the customers, pausing here and there to grumpily accept a stroke or pat on the head. Finally reaching our table, he plopped at my feet and gave me an expectant stare.

"Really? The chicken breast wasn't enough?" I too offered him a pat on the head.

"In all fairness, we've just pigged out on three burritos apiece." Katie popped the last bite of hers into her mouth and once again barely chewed before speaking. "Watson kinda did get shafted."

"You make a valid observation." Gingerly I pulled out a large chunk of potato that had a piece of egg clinging to it and tossed it Watson's way. "You can thank your Auntie Katie for this."

Looking like an overweight seal, Watson shot his head upward without moving the rest of his body and swallowed the morsel whole.

"That's right." Katie licked her fingers on one hand as she bent down to scratch Watson's rump with her other. "You should start hero-worshiping me like you do Ben, Barry, and Leo. Heaven knows I provide more food than those three combined."

Watson shifted slightly as he raised one of his puppy eyebrows and gave a pitiful whimper.

Katie raised her hands. "Sorry, buddy. Mine's all gone."

Unimpressed, he refocused on me.

"You're impossible." I dug out another bit, tossed it his way, and shoved what remained of my burrito into my mouth.

Katie giggled. "I swear the two of you are like an old married couple."

That time I was the one speaking with my mouth full. "I'd say you're right on the money with that. Though Watson most definitely wears the pants in the family, it's the best relationship I've ever had. By far." Something about my own words made me wince.

"Ahh, the love of a dog. Completely unconditional." Katie sighed, then giggled again. "As long as there's food, in any case."

"It's like you've met Watson before." That time I raised my empty hands to him, offering proof. "Mines all gone too, little man."

He scowled, sniffed the air, then ducked under my chair and curled up for a nap.

I refocused out the window again, looking down the rows of shops. If Ben had things under control in the bookshop, which he always did, I needed to go to Knit Witt and talk to Angus. At least it was guaranteed to be much less painful than the day before talking to Mark or Rocky. Actually, between the two, the conversation with Mark was nearly a pleasure compared to Rocky. Then it hit me why my statement had rubbed me wrong. *Wearing the pants in the family.* That's how Rocky had described, with much disdain, Sharon's role in her and Mark's marriage. I started to lean toward Katie, then paused long enough to glance around, making sure no one was close enough to overhear, at least none of the locals, then turned back. "I'm no closer to figuring out who killed Adam, but you'll never guess who Rocky suspects is the murderer."

"Number one, Susan came to you *the night before last*, so the fact that you expect to be even a step closer to figuring it out after barely more than a day into this thing is ludicrous. Cut yourself a break." As her brown eyes gleamed in anticipation, Katie matched my position, and the admonition left her tone. "And since we're talking about Rocky Castle, I'll say..." She tapped her chin in mock consideration. "A yeti killed Adam. No... not a yeti, an abominable snowman."

I snorted out a laugh.

Smirking, Katie's gaze tracked a large group of tourists who carried a tray of baked goods to a nearby table, then refocused on me. "Who does he suspect?"

The eye roll I gave that time was not in affection. "His first guess is Sharon, Mark's wife."

Katie's brows creased, and she cocked her head. "*Mark's* wife? Why would Sharon kill Adam? From everything I've heard about their marriage, it sounds like if she was going to kill anyone it would be Mark. And she took him back just a matter of days after Sammy's funeral."

Again I was reminded that I lived in a small town, one where everybody knew everything about everyone. "Rocky didn't have a reason, other than that Sharon's a woman who doesn't seem to know her place and doesn't appreciate her husband returning home sloppy drunk to her and their children. My words, not his, but that was the gist."

"Well, when you put it like that, she does sound unreasonable. Just the kind of person who would randomly kill someone else who has no involvement with her family." Katie's brows smoothed out. "Although... if we go with that theory, I suppose it's possible that Sharon got so tired of the drunken game nights that she snuck in and decided to put an end to all the drama that is Mark. It was late at night, dark. Maybe she killed Adam by mistake."

I dismissed the idea instantly. "You should've seen Adam's face. That wasn't a solitary moment of fury in the dark. Even if she was mistaken, *and* able to hurt someone so badly, she would've realized Adam wasn't her husband.

Even in the dark, I don't see how anyone could mix the two up even for a second. Mark is at least twice the size Adam was."

She considered for a moment, then nodded her agreement. "All right... what was Rocky's second guess?"

"Adam himself."

Katie reared back. "What? How was Adam supposed to manage that?"

"Exactly. Rocky said Adam deserved it. And that Adam knew it, so somehow it must make sense that Adam couldn't take being such a horrible specimen of humanity and beat himself up until he intentionally killed himself in the middle of someone else's shop."

"That makes less sense than the abominable snowman showing up in Estes Park."

I laughed again. "Best argument I've ever heard for the abominable snowman."

She sighed. "So, basically, Rocky wasn't any help at all."

"Unsurprisingly, no. Although, his version of events matched Mark's story perfectly."

Katie shrugged. "So... unless they got their stories straight ahead of time, which would be fairly simple, that clears Mark."

I shook my head. "No, not hardly. Rocky said Adam was nowhere in sight when he left Alakazam. Either way, we're still left with the fact that at some point, Adam shows up again at the magic shop for some reason and gets murdered."

"Right, by Mark's wife or at his own hand."

"Or a yeti."

"Or Billy." All humor left Katie's eyes. "I mean, he and Adam got into it the night before Adam was—"

"I know." My heart had leaped at the suggestion, or

filled with dread, more accurately. "I've been wondering. Actually, I've being trying not to wonder about him. He's Carl and Anna's son. That would wreck them."

"I know, I almost didn't suggest him." She winced. "Maybe... maybe that's too obvious. Surely he wouldn't be so reckless... so... stupid that he'd kill Adam right after the entire town saw their argument."

"Right..." I sighed. "Because *no* murder ever happened because someone was too angry to think straight."

Before Katie could respond, Watson popped up suddenly, startling me as he bumped into the bottom of my chair and darted out. Following his motion, I discovered Ben walking toward us. "Hey, sorry to bother you, but we're packed downstairs, and the Sweitzer family is here to see you, Fred."

"The Sweitzer—" The name clicked a moment later and drove Billy Hanson from my mind. "Oh, of course. I'll be right down. Or are they on their way up?"

Ben knelt, rubbing Watson's flanks, though he continued to address me and Katie. "No, Mrs. Sweitzer is in a wheelchair, so she can't make it up."

Katie groaned. "They mentioned that during inspection. We were approved because we were grandfathered in and there's access to the main floor. But it was suggested we install an elevator as the stairway is too steep to turn part of it into a ramp. How embarrassing. I should go down and apologize."

Taking one of his hands off Watson, Ben reached up and patted Katie's arm in his typical sweet fashion. "I don't think they're worried about it. At least not right now."

Katie flushed. "No, of course they're not. Not right now." She looked over at me. "It's not really something we can afford, but how would you feel about installing an elevator? We could put it in the back storeroom, though that wouldn't be ideal; it connects it to the back of the kitchen."

"I think we'll figure out how to afford it." Finances weren't an issue for me as I received a sizable settlement when I'd been betrayed by my publishing house's business partner and ex-best friend, but not enough that I could easily fork out whatever *that* price tag was without it stinging. Still, it was a necessity, one that we shouldn't have waited a year to realize. "But that's a consideration for another day. Like Ben said, I doubt they're too worried about access to a bakery after just losing a brother and son."

"I better get back down there. We really are packed." Ben stood. "I asked them to wait in the mystery room, you might have a little more privacy there."

"Thanks, Ben. You're a dream."

He waved me off and headed toward the stairs, Watson trotting along beside him, casting a *Well, aren't you coming?* glare over his shoulder.

I glanced at Katie. "It's actually getting pretty busy up here too. You want to stay up here with Nick and I'll fill you in later?"

"Sure. I'm too embarrassed to show my face to them anyway right now."

"You're a dream too, Katie Pizzolato." As Ben had done only moments before, I patted her arm. "We'll figure it out."

To my surprise, instead of staying with Ben, Watson accompanied me as I joined the Sweitzer family in the mystery room. Connie had parked Charlene's wheelchair on the other side of the antique lamp and leaned against the handlebars while Sheila sat on the sofa, on the same level as their mother.

Charlene's eyes were puffy and bloodshot and glistened with tears.

Though Connie and Sheila both appeared solemn, they showed no signs of crying.

I glanced at the open end of the sofa, underneath the antique purple portobello lampshade, but wasn't sure of the correct protocol. I ended up standing awkwardly a few feet in front of Charlene. "Hi, sorry to keep you waiting, and I'm so very, very sorry for your loss."

"Thank you, dear." A tear escaped and ran down Charlene's cheek. "It's been quite a shock."

"I can't even imagine." I felt like I should kneel down to be on Charlene's level, reach out to her knee, stroke her hand, something. But I'd only met the woman once, and the gesture seemed both inadequate and too formal.

Coming to the rescue, Watson plopped at the base of the wheelchair and laid his head on Charlene's foot on the footrest.

Charlene smiled down at him. "Sweet dog."

I glanced around the shop, suddenly aware I didn't hear the screaming of children, then looked toward Sheila. "Are your kids here? If so, they can help themselves to whatever they want in the bakery. I can get you three something as well."

As she spoke, Sheila rubbed both hands over her extended belly. "Oh no, the boys are with their father at home. Thankfully."

"And we don't need anything to eat. People are being wonderful and bringing a whole smorgasbord worth of food to the house." Charlene held up a tray of beautifully decorated Christmas cookies shaped like ornaments and snowmen I hadn't notice she'd been holding in her lap. "Maybe it's silly, considering you have a bakery upstairs, but we brought you these."

"I bake when I'm upset." Connie offered a partial smile

from behind her mother. "Like Mom said, probably silly to bring them here. I'm sure they don't compare."

"Are you kidding? They're absolutely beautiful." I accepted the tray. From below, Watson followed the movement of the food, probably hoping for a crumb, but then returned his head to Charlene's foot. "Katie's going to be impressed."

A blush rose to Connie's cheeks.

"Connie always was the creative one in the family. I used to decorate with her, until"—Sheila rubbed her belly again—"things got busy."

"We just wanted to say thank you." Charlene wiped at her eyes and looked up at me. "So much."

"For what? There's no reason to thank me."

Charlene's voice grew stronger. "Yes, there is. Glinda told me that you're looking into Adam's death. I can't tell you what that means. That you'd take the time for a family you don't know to..." Her voice broke, but she shook her head and pressed on. "I know your reputation. You'll figure this horrible thing out. You'll find justice for my son."

Considering I'd discovered Adam's body a little more than two days before, I once more had no idea what the correct protocol was. "Well... thank you, for... the cookies. I hope I can help."

"I know you can." Another tear made its way down Charlene's cheek. "This whole thing is bad enough. Not seeing Adam for years and then..." She shook her head and continued on once more. "But Mark being accused just makes it so much worse. They were such good friends years ago. And poor Glinda. She..."

"We just popped by Alakazam to drop off a tray of cookies for Glinda as well." Sheila jumped in when her mother seemed unable to speak anymore. "She's not handling it very well."

"Still had on her ridiculous wings, though, didn't she?" Connie rolled her eyes.

Her mother shushed her. "That's just Glinda's way. Part of her charm."

Though Connie rolled her eyes again, she didn't contradict.

I shouldn't have been surprised that the magic shop was open so soon. Susan would've cleared it as quickly as possible. Though I didn't know Mark all that well, I could easily see him demanding that it be open. Going with Marcus's logic, which I figured was accurate, it would probably be the busiest day Alakazam ever had.

"Any leads yet?" For the first time, emotion sounded in Sheila's voice.

Charlene looked up at me hopefully, then appeared crestfallen when I shook my head.

"No. I've only spoken to Mark and Rocky. But I'll do my best to figure it out." It was my first time making such a promise to a victim's family, and it added heavier weight somehow, a new dimension that settled over my shoulders.

"Sounds like you already talked to the killer, then." Connie's whisper was barely audible over the background of Christmas music and chatter of tourists.

"Stop it!" Charlene's voice was sharp, and she twisted so quickly to glare up at her daughter that the motion looked painful. "We talked about this. Mark is innocent. He would never do that to his old friend. He's a good boy. Glinda adores him."

"Mom, get a grip. You have to face reality. You never really knew Adam; it turns out none of us did. And the same is true for Mark. The two of them haven't been friends in ages."

"That doesn't matter. Even though Adam disappeared for years at a time, that doesn't mean friendship dies." Charlene nearly sounded desperate.

"You're only convinced of that because you trust Glinda so much." Connie's tone wasn't harsh but was firm, certain. "Mark has proven what kind of person he is time and time again, hasn't he? Constantly cheating on his wife and abandoning his family, then coming back with his tail between his legs. Spends all his time playing dress-up and taking care of that screeching bunny and that stupid store, instead of—"

Charlene slumped back around but shook her head. "You've never given that store a chance. And Mark is just... different. He didn't kill your brother. He wouldn't."

"Yes, he would." Connie's voice hardened then. "Who knows what the two of them fought about that night. Knowing Adam, he probably tried to buy that stupid shop, and Mark lost his mind out of fear of losing that nasty little place."

"Connie." Sheila removed one of her hands from her belly and reached toward her sister. "Stop it. I know you're upset, we all are, but this isn't helping. If Glinda believes Mark, then..." She shrugged. "And there's no reason to start bashing the store. You know how important it is to Glinda and how important Glinda is to Mom. You never even set foot in it until today. Hardly the best time to get a good feel. The few times I've been in, it's actually fairly charming."

Though Connie rolled her eyes for the third time at that, she softened her tone and patted her mom's shoulder. "Sorry, Mom. Sheila's right. I'm just upset."

"It's okay, dear." Charlene turned back around, but less

drastically than before, and offered her a smile. "Maybe we should do more cookies when we get home."

Connie returned the smile with a little chuckle. "Maybe I should." It faded when she looked back at me. "I'm not trying to distress my mother, but she and Glinda are wrong about Mark. He was not Adam's friend, hasn't been for a very, very long time. Not even close."

I nearly told her she was right, that she was the only one of her family to get the measure of Mark Green. Confirm that less than twenty-four hours before, I'd heard him say how much he hated her brother. For once, I managed to keep my tongue in check and my foot out of my mouth. There was no reason to add to the conflict. It was only natural that the grieving family would search for responsible parties. Seeing the three women hurting, disagreeing, and in such need of a resolution only heightened my determination to figure it out, whatever the answer. Whether Connie was right or not. I started to say just that, to make a promise, when Sheila issued a quiet scream.

Watson sprang up and shuffled backward as if attempting escape.

"Oh no, I'm so sorry!" Sheila used one hand on the arm of the sofa to push herself up, revealing a huge wet spot over the fabric. "My water just broke."

"There's never a dull moment around here, is there?" With her face a couple of inches from the glass, Katie watched the ambulance turn on its flashing lights and siren before zooming down Elkhorn Avenue.

The small crowd gathered around the windows of the Cozy Corgi dispersed once the ambulance disappeared. "I did picture a little bit more of a quiet life when I envisioned opening a bookshop in a tiny mountain town." Talk about an understatement. Never in a million years would I have imagined the constant drama my life had become.

Katie nudged me. "Oh, come on, like you'd have it any other way."

I had to admit, it was rather fun. "Maybe a little less murder."

She cocked her eyebrow but didn't disagree. "This particular event wasn't murder, however. There's nothing for you to solve. Just a life entering the world. Or... starting to in any case."

"Yeah..." I shuddered, thinking of Sheila. "Five kids. Five! I can't even imagine."

Katie gave a little shudder of her own but remained positive. "It is rather lovely for the Sweitzers. I know they'll continue to grieve over Adam's death, but having a new baby will surely ease some of their pain."

"That's a good way to look at it. And I bet you're right." I hoped so, especially for Charlene's sake. She had three children, and soon-to-be five grandchildren. I couldn't imagine that either. But losing one had to be one of the hardest things in the world. Hopefully a granddaughter would bring a new joy, and I planned on giving her closure to her son's murder if at all possible. At the thought, I turned back to Katie. "If you're all right with it, I'm going to return to my original plan and head over to Knit Witt to talk to Angus, see what he remembers of game night."

"Of course." Katie glanced upward. "I'd like to go with you, I'm curious, but with all these people, I imagine we're going to have a rush in the bakery. I should help Nick get things going again."

Ben approached at that moment, Watson by his side. "Maybe this is a silly question, but..." A blush darkened his cheeks. "Is there a certain way to... ah... clean up the mystery room?"

"Clean up the—" I straightened with a laugh. "Oh my goodness, how did I forget that? Can't quite leave the mystery room in such a state, can we?" I considered for a moment and looked to Katie. "You know, I don't actually have the answer to that question. Is there a certain way we should clean... that?"

She shrugged. "How should I know?"

"Seriously?" I gaped at her. "There's never been a topic, no matter how random or bizarre that's come up that you've not been able to rattle off a whole bunch of obscure related facts."

Katie grimaced. "Well, I don't know this one, nor do I want to." She started walking as she pointed upstairs. "Did I mention that I think Nick needs help in the bakery? In fact, I'm pretty sure I hear him calling for me."

"Coward!" I called after her, chuckling. "And I'm not buying it, I've used that excuse myself."

She just waved and kept going.

I turned to Ben. "Looks like it's up to you and me."

He gestured across the store. "I think I hear some kids calling in the children's book section. I should probably help." When my mouth fell open, he just laughed. "Just kidding."

Within twenty minutes, Ben and I had the mystery room cleaned up, no thanks to Watson who'd trotted over to doze in the sunshine. We ultimately carried the sofa to the storage room, feeling that it was unsanitary to leave it out in the middle of the shop. Once things were settled, I woke Watson from his nap, and we walked out into the bright crisp winter day and headed over to Knit Witt.

I'd only been in the knitting store a handful of times, and on each occasion, I had left with the desire to become an artsy, craftsy person. Knit Witt wasn't what I envisioned most hobbyist shops looking like, not that I'd been in any yarn or knitting stores before. But if I'd envisioned one, I would've assumed the place would resemble a grandmother's house. Doilies here and there, a rather homey, cluttered vibe, probably with porcelain plates sporting hand-painted cats hung on the walls. Knit Witt was nothing like that. It was modern and sleek. The floors and ceiling were a matching deep, shiny mahogany, the walls soft steel blue. All the shelving and counters were more of a honey-hued oak, but equally as shiny. Glass and brushed steel covered the remaining surfaces. In and of itself, it would've felt cold, but every single surface was a riot of color, but not in tangled piles or clusters. I couldn't imagine how much time Angus had spent organizing, but every section was its own gradient of the rainbow. Each spool of yarn only a slightly different hue than the one beside it. It made it all so tempting.

If I'd been delusional enough to think I had the patience to give knitting a try, one look at the price tags would've swept any such notion away. There was one small section of yarn that was reasonably priced, but the rest was astronomical, going up to over three hundred dollars for one single bunch.

As Watson and I entered, Angus was behind the counter, talking to a customer who had his back to us. Angus looked around him and smiled. "Welcome to..." His greeting faded as recognition sparked, but his smile didn't waver. "I figured you two would be in today."

The customer at the counter turned and also broke into a smile. "Winifred and..." A line formed between Gerald Jackson's brows, and he shook his head. "Sidekick."

"Watson." Angus came to the rescue.

"Right. Watson." Gerald nodded his agreement, then looked toward me. "Watson?"

I nodded. "Yes. Watson." I halted for a heartbeat at the sight of Gerald Jackson. I supposed I should be grateful, killing two birds with one stone, but if I had known Gerald was there, I would've mentally prepared to deal with the man. He wasn't evil or mean or anything like that, just rather insufferably unenlightened, and an entrenched member of the good old boys club. I also found him to be an incompetent lawyer. Other than that, I'm sure he was a great guy. At least the men in my family thought so. I glanced around the shop as I approached them, using the distraction to buy myself some time.

"I see you're all decked out for..." The words fell away as I took in the change in the store. It was smooth and sleek, just like before but every space was covered with Christmas decorations, all of them knitted, crocheted, and... done with other mediums involving yarn and string that I had no name for. If Bushy Evergreens Workshop was the equivalent of Santa's toy lab, Knit Witt had become Mrs. Claus's domain.

I turned in a circle as I reached the center of the shop. Snowflakes, ranging from the size of my thumbnail to a couple of feet across, hung from the ceiling, each crafted from white yarn with flecks of metallic silver threaded throughout. On the far end of the store encompassing an entire corner was a winter woodland scene, complete with a couple of pine trees with snow on the branches, a deer with a red-and-white scarf around its neck, and a raccoon donning a Santa hat. At different places on the floor were clusters of presents, lights glistening from within. And every single thing was made of yarn and was utterly beautiful.

Watson seemed just as captivated as I felt, as he pattered over to a life-size fox with a ring of holly around its neck and sniffed.

The thing was so realistic, despite the clear woven pattern of the variegated orange yarn, it was all I could do to keep from petting its head as I joined Watson. Instead, I noticed a price tag hanging from its ear. Turning it over, I nearly choked. The craftsmanship and quality was unlike anything I'd ever seen nor could imagine coming from a spool of yarn, but neither could I imagine paying the thousands of dollars required to purchase it.

"That particular piece took me over two months to

craft." Though Angus spoke softly, pride was clearly evident in his words.

I turned, gaping at the thin old man. "You *made* this?"

He simply smiled. "I made everything you see in here. It relaxes me."

I'd already been astounded by the woven Christmas wonderland I'd wandered into, but being aware Angus was the artist made it even more astounding. Though I hadn't had the thought, I supposed I assumed he'd ordered them from somewhere to sell. "They're... spectacular. Unlike anything I've ever seen." From Watson's continual sniffing around the fox, he seemed to agree, as if trying to determine if the animal was real or not. "They should be in a museum."

"I *do* have a few pieces in a couple of art museums." Again there was that quiet pride.

I continued to gape. "I don't know what to say. I'm completely blown away."

"It's just a hobby. One that I started at my grandmother's knee when I was little. Anyone who gets to be my age and has done the skill their entire life should be a master at it by this point." Angus waved me off. "But I'm certain you're not here for yarn or decorations. And it looks like luck is on your side, as I imagine Gerald is on your list as well."

By that point, I was used to people assuming that I was looking into any murder that happened in Estes Park, but his easy, matter-of-fact acceptance of it surprised me.

Apparently, Gerald felt similar to me as he looked from Angus to me, blinking rapidly. "What? You're looking into Adam Sweitzer's death?"

"I am. Yes." I headed toward the counter, jerked to a

halt when Watson's leash came to an end, then paused as he finally abandoned his inspection of the fox.

"Now listen here, young lady. *I* am representing Mark, and I can promise you I have it well under control." Gerald sounded more offended than patronizing. "I can't believe he would ask you to look into it, or... are you simply taking it upon yourself?"

"Susan... err... Officer Green actually asked me to look into it." I stopped a few inches from the counter.

Gerald blushed. "Of course she did. She's let me know many times what she thinks of me."

One more thing outside of mystery novels that Susan and I apparently agreed upon.

"Come now, Gerald." Angus gave his friend a steely stare. "Miss Page has more than proved her intelligence and skill at solving murders. As Mark's representative, you should be glad to have her on your side."

Gerald made a sour face and appeared to require considerable effort to smooth it over. "I suppose you're right. Whatever it takes to clear Mark's name." He looked back at me. "Though I *do* have this under control."

"I'm certain you do." I wasn't sure if my white lie was audible or not. From the humor that lit in Angus's green eyes, I was willing to bet he'd caught it.

Proving that it had gone over Gerald's head, he nodded. "Thank you. I do."

Eyes still twinkling, Angus smiled at me. "Go ahead, my dear. Ask your questions." Before I could, he looked down at Watson. "Sorry to say I don't have any treats to offer your friend. How rude of me."

At Watson's favorite word, his ears poked up, and he gave a little hop.

"Oh..." Angus winced. "Sorry. It seems he knows that word."

"To say the least." I laughed and paused long enough to bend and stroke Watson's back, releasing a cloud of fur. "You've had plenty of those this morning, buddy. No more for you."

Watson looked at me curiously, then at Angus, who shook his head. Watson looked back at me once more, his eyes full of accusation.

"I know, you've got it rough." I gave him another stroke and straightened. "Sorry about the dog hair, I'd say it would help your fox look more lifelike, but it doesn't need any help in that area."

He waved me off again. "Don't give it a second thought. I have a very effective vacuum cleaner." Angus refocused on me but didn't wait for a question. "I'm sure you already know that Gerald and I were at the game night, and that's why you're here. But I'm afraid we don't have any more details than what we already shared with Susan. We were there when Adam arrived and when he was kicked out. We left together before he returned, whenever that might have been."

I didn't see any need to inform him that Susan hadn't told me what either of them had said, or explain that she felt it best for me to get it all firsthand. "Do you mind running through it again? I spoke to Mark and Rocky, and it seems that most of the night is a blur, thanks to all the beer."

Angus chuckled. "Game nights are rather indulgent. Makes an old man feel like he's in his prime again. Though I refrain from beer. I much prefer wine, but not over board games."

"Oh." I must've misunderstood something. "I was under

the impression that the entire group gets a little inebriated, and that things were a little blurry for all four of you."

"They were blurry. Very." Gerald looked at me as if I was daft. "Angus and I don't drink beer. We have my kombucha."

I thought I deserved a prize for not rolling my eyes. "Right, I remember. You make your own kombucha." I deserved a second prize for not reminding him that he'd left my stepfather in jail without legal representation because he'd driven all the way to Glen Haven because of said kombucha.

"Well then, I think it's understandable that Angus and I don't remember much more than the boys do." Gerald shrugged. "I'm afraid you're wasting your time, little lady."

I bristled, but thought I kept from showing it. "I'm sorry, but I'm not following. If the two of you weren't partaking in the alcohol, why are the evening's events not clear?"

Angus came to the rescue. "Gerald crafts his kombucha with cannabis-infused tea."

"Cannabis infused..." I flinched and looked back and forth between the two men. "Oh. *Oh*! Marijuana."

"It's legal to partake in Estes," Gerald rushed ahead. "You just can't buy or sell it within the city limits. I promise you, everything is on the up-and-up. I purchased it quite legally from Green Munchies in Lyons."

I flinched more violently at that. In addition to Branson's betrayal a few weeks before, I'd also learned that he'd been responsible for the murder of the manager of that particular dispensary.

Angus reached across the counter and patted my arm. "Are you doing okay with everything, Fred?"

His question threw me off, and I gaped at him. "Excuse me?"

He patted my arm again, and his voice remained gentle and caring. "The Green Munchies, the poaching, discovering the man you were dating was a dirty cop and a murderer? I can't imagine what you've been feeling."

I blinked. "What? How did you...?" I shook my head. That answer was obvious. Everyone knew. The whole town of Estes Park had known all about Branson within a matter of hours. It wasn't like our attempt at a relationship had been secret either. But still, Angus and I had barely said three sentences to each other.

"I'm friends with your stepfather, dear." He gave a paternal smile as he pulled his hand away. "Barry may not be your blood, but when you hurt, he hurts."

"Oh." I knew that much was true, and it wasn't like Barry was betraying any confidence. "You know, I'm still struggling to come to... Branson and I weren't..." Completely flustered, I began to ramble, then shook my head again. "I'm sorry if this sounds rude, but I really would rather not discuss it. Can we just..." I took a second to try to figure out if I could even continue.

At a weight plopping on my foot, I glanced down to see Watson looking up at me, with no admonition in his eyes for not providing a treat .

Feeling slightly more grounded at the contact, I pressed on. If I didn't do it now I'd simply have to revisit it all later. Might as well get it over with. "So, though blurry, you both remember Adam leaving the game night?"

"I wouldn't call it leaving." Gerald smirked. "Kicked out and leaving are two different things. Although it was kind of a pity. The game sounded fun. A little creepy for Christmas, but..." He shrugged and didn't finish the thought.

"Sorry if I overstepped, Fred." Angus drew my attention back to him. "But please know, if you ever need to talk, or clear your head, you've got friendly ears willing to listen and not judge. We knitters are good at that sort of thing. I know you have plenty of friends and support, but... if you need it."

I was oddly touched, considering the offer came from someone who was little more than a stranger. But kind nonetheless. "Thank you." The inner dialogue began to spin in my head and gripped at my chest, the sense of loss warring with feeling foolish for being so completely deceived. I shoved it all aside as best I could. "Back to that night..." I cleared my throat. "Even though things are a little blurry—as we were saying due to your kombucha—you remember Adam getting thrown out?"

Gerald sighed as if frustrated that we'd already been through that, but Angus remained gentle. "Yes. I do. We played a few rounds of the Krampus game, when Mark realized that it was a ripoff of something he'd created long ago. He and Adam started to argue." He made an exasperated sound. "And Rocky, of course, as he's never met a conflict he didn't want to take part in. But I can promise you there was nothing murderous about it. Just the typical combustion of alcohol and ego. Yelling, accusations, that sort of thing. I think the final straw was when Adam told Mark he was going to buy the store out from under him with the money he got from the game. It was already going downhill quickly, but that was the end of it."

"Adam said he was going to buy the store?" And there I thought I wasn't going to hear anything new. "Mark didn't mention that. Neither did Rocky."

Gerald gave a puzzled look at Angus. "You know I don't recall that, but I did have a couple of bottles of kombucha on the drive over, so I had a head start." His eyes widened as if he hadn't meant to give that admission, and he didn't meet my gaze.

I didn't give it a second thought and addressed Angus. "You're sure he said that?"

"I believe so. Yes." Angus nodded slowly. "But it's an empty threat. Barry would never sell the shop from under Mark's feet, even though it would be a financial benefit."

I flinched again in surprise and studied Angus.

"Yes, I know about Mark's inability to pay the rent." He shook a thumb at Gerald. "We both do—friends of Barry, remember?"

Gerald's chest puffed slightly. "But we can keep our mouths shut. A person doesn't betray a friend's confidence. Nor rub it in the face of another friend."

"I'm not surprised the boys didn't mention it. Everything happened quickly right at the end, and as you know, they were more than a little drunk. I doubt either of them remember the finer details." His eyes narrowed as he considered. "Actually, now that I say that, I'm not entirely certain I shared that with Susan. I think I forgot it myself until now."

"That's pretty big. That would most definitely make Mark upset." To say the least.

"You know..." Angus sighed. "I think I did tell Susan. Sorry. Blurry truly does describe that evening, but I do think I told her. That doesn't exactly help clear Mark, does it?" He chuckled. "Not something Susan would want to focus on." Angus rushed ahead. "Nor should she. I don't know what happened, but no part of me believes that Mark killed Adam Sweitzer. No matter how angry he was."

"I don't remember that at all." Gerald shook his head and blinked as if trying to bring it all back. "I remember the fighting, arguing rather, it was loud and chaotic. But I'm not saying Adam didn't threaten to buy Mark's shop. I had another couple of bottles of kombucha after he left to help me calm down." He chuckled again. "The boys had more than a couple of bottles of beer. Mark told us all about the game he'd designed in high school and how Adam must've ripped it off, but even then he didn't make any threatening comments."

"Do you remember leaving Alakazam? About what time it was?" Maybe Gerald and Angus had left and Rocky shortly after them, and then Adam had turned around and come back, to make more threats about taking Mark's magic shop away. Perhaps it was just Gerald and Angus's friendship that made them unable to envision Mark being capable of murder, but I could. Especially if he thought his store was at risk.

"I don't remember the time. Do you?" Angus glanced at Gerald and shook his head before continuing. "The two of us left together, I remember coming back here because Gerald suddenly needed the restroom."

"Angus!" Gerald snapped at Angus and looked shocked before turning to me. "When you get to be my age, when it hits, it hits. It can't be helped."

"Really, Gerald, no reason to be vulgar," Angus admonished his friend before appearing to drift back to the memories of that night. "We went our own ways directly after that." He refocused on me once more, then his eyes widened. "Oh! We ran into Anna and Carl's boy... Billy. He could confirm the time I bet."

I froze. "Billy Hanson? Where did you run into him?"

Angus gestured toward the window. "Right out front. Just as we were leaving." He narrowed his eyes at me again. "Why do you look surprised at that? Like I said, we told Susan. I just happened to think of Billy again because you asked about the time. He might be able to tell you. Though I'm not sure why it matters. Adam wasn't back and was nowhere to be seen."

For a while after moving to Estes Park I tried to avoid Carl and Anna Hanson. Their personalities were... intense, as was their love of gossip. It was that love of gossip that continued to bring us into constant contact, both by their snoopy ways and because they were great sources of information, even if not completely reliable. However, as time passed, they became friends, and while they were still best in small doses, I loved them.

It was that love, that sense of friendship and loyalty, that kept my psyche shoving the likelihood of Billy Hanson being Adam's killer from my mind.

I couldn't put it off any longer, shouldn't have put it off as long as I had. Still, Cabin and Hearth should've been my first stop after leaving Mark Green the day before.

Watson practically pranced as we entered the luxury home furnishings store. The Hansons might not hold deity status as Barry, Leo, and Ben, but they were a constant source of his favorite treats.

I wished I felt a little of his excitement. As the door closed behind us, I realized my mistake. We'd bee-lined it from Knit Witt, but I should've taken a moment to pull myself together, put on a game face.

From behind the counter, Anna stiffened, her eyes going wide when she saw me. She didn't break into an excited smile and twitter the way she normally would, and her gaze didn't even flick down to Watson. A few heartbeats too late she managed a plastered-on smile before she raised her voice loud enough to be heard in the back. "Carl! Fred's here. Come say hi." It seemed Anna required some time to get her game face on as well.

As Watson and I approached, I realized something I'd overlooked, or maybe my brain had refused to let me notice. Anytime there was drama, ranging from murder or some salacious tidbit of gossip, Anna and Carl were among the first to rush over to the Cozy Corgi to either get details or share their own. But I hadn't seen them since the night of the Christmas party.

They'd not rushed over to have me retell discovering the body or give their theories.

My heart sank.

Though Watson often amazed me at how attune to my emotions he was, he didn't seem to pick up on the heavy tension in the air. He continued his prance to the counter, peered up expectantly, then gave a little hop. When Anna didn't so much as look down at him, Watson whimpered and glanced at me over his shoulder as if I were to blame.

Carl hurried from the back, his face flushed, and little Styrofoam kernels drifted from his beard and over his round belly like snow. He'd probably been unboxing a new delivery of merchandise. "Fred, darling, wonderful to see you." His smile too was less than sincere, and instead of meeting my eyes, he kept his gaze firmly trained on Anna.

She took point. "What brings you in on this lovely day? Doing some Christmas shopping?" She gestured around the store, her attention landing on a hall tree made from a rather stunning piece of driftwood and brass hooks. Ropes of lighted garland swirled down its length. "Your mother was in here the other day. I noticed her eye was on that."

For a second I almost considered buying it, just in way of a preemptive apology, though I was certain this price tag would also be rather stunning—it turned out designer log furniture came at designer prices. "It is lovely. But..." *Just get it over with. Rip off the Band-Aid.* "I'm not here to shop. I was hoping to speak to—"

Watson whimpered again, this time high and mournful.

Anna jumped and looked down in surprise, as if she truly hadn't noticed Watson with me "Oh. Goodness." She fluttered her hand over her gingham-covered bosom. "Scared me to death." For the first time a genuine smile flickered across her face. "Watson, my sweet dear."

He whimpered again but finished it with a huff that was both plaintive and demanding.

"Well, of course! I'm so sorry. You need your treat!" She threw up her hands, whirled around, and with a rustle of skirts, she hurried through the store and disappeared into the back.

In shock, I watched her go. I had never, not once, seen Anna get the dog treats herself from the back room. Each and every time, she'd demanded Carl retrieve them, hand the treat to her, and she, in turn, would offer it to Watson.

When I turned back around, Carl met my gaze, surprise evident in his eyes as well. He forced a grin. "Very Christmassy weather we're having, isn't it? All the... snow."

"Yes." I searched for something to say, finding it hard to look at him, and glanced around the shop again. "It's looking very Christmassy in here as well. It's always beautiful in your shop, but with all the lights and decorations, the smell of cloves and cinnamon, it really makes a person feel like they're at their grandmother's house. Their... fancy, mountainy grandmother's house." I was rambling. "And with your white, fluffy beard, and you and Anna being so"— I felt my eyes bulge as I nearly said *short and round like Mr. and Mrs. Claus*—"um... jovial, it really makes it feel like Christmas."

"That's kind, thank you." Carl shuffled back and forth and began drumming his fingers on the countertop. His gaze flicked toward the back.

Watson whimpered again, straining at his leash.

A clatter sounded from the back room.

"I... ah... rearranged." His brows furrowed. "Anna must be having a hard time finding the dog treats."

Watson whimpered once more at his favorite word.

"It's okay. I hate for you to have to bother. As you can tell, Watson's not close to starving." I should just get it over with, not wait for Anna, and ask Carl directly. But how? *It is very Christmassy in here. Is the music a streaming service or a Christmas CD? By the way, you're acting a little strange. Do you suspect your son killed Adam Sweitzer as well?*

There was another clatter.

"You know..." Carl pointed toward the sound. "I think it might require some"—he took a few steps away—"assistance." He turned and hurried off.

Watson looked back at me in clear distress.

I leaned forward to hiss at him, "Can you please focus on what matters?"

He scowled, plopped down once more, and returned to staring toward the back.

Good grief, I was losing my mind.

There were no more clatters, but Anna and Carl's unintelligible, frantic whispers drifted to the main room.

I didn't need any further confirmation that Anna and Carl feared Billy had killed Adam.

"Sorry, Fred!" Anna's raised voice cut through the harpsichord version of "Little Drummer Boy," but she didn't peer into the shop. "We're still looking for the dog treats. Carl must've put them somewhere obscure; you know how he is."

"It's okay. Watson really will be fine."

"Nonsense!" Anna called back, but before she could add anything else, the front door chimed as another customer entered. Her voice grew louder. "Welcome to Cabin and Hearth! Merry Christmas! Be with you shortly!" Though her panic was still audible, I thought I caught a hint of relief.

I felt it myself. At least with a customer present, we'd have to put the conversation off for a few more minutes. "Sorry, I have them looking for something in the back. I'm sure they'll be right out with—" My words fell away as I turned to assure the tourist only to find Billy Hanson staring at me.

"Hiya." Billy halted, seemed to search for something to say, then smiled. "I grew up here, but now that I'm used to the California weather, I don't know how you all do it. I'm freezing." Despite the snow, it truly didn't feel that cold, but Billy was bundled up in so many layers he almost looked like a red-and-green beach ball.

"I'm from Kansas City, so though we didn't have mountains, the winters are much harsher in the Ozarks. Once the ice moves in, it tends to stick for weeks." I shrugged. "Here, the snow comes and melts pretty quickly. You could have a blizzard one day and a balmy fifty degrees the next." *Seriously? Now, I was talking to my newly elevated prime suspect about the weather?*

Watson gave another tug of his leash, added another pitiful whimper, and drew Billy's attention. "Your dog, right?"

"Yes. Your parents are getting him a snack." I glanced over my shoulder—still no sign of Anna or Carl—then gave myself a mental shake. Hemming and hawing and beating around the bush wasn't going to help anything. It was only going to draw out the inevitable. Steeling myself, I refocused on Billy. "You look like you're feeling better. Glad you're not still sick."

"Sick?" Billy cocked his head, and then his eyes widened. "Oh... right... sick." He started to unzip his coat. "The other night you mean. Yes... thank you. It was a nasty bug. But it must've only been one of those twenty-four-hour flu things. I'm all better."

"Food poisoning." Anna rushed back in and shot Billy a glare. "I thought I heard your voice. Food poisoning, remember?" She gave me a crazed smile. "It was awful. Absolutely awful. Probably the worst case of food poisoning I've ever seen. I just can't imagine what..." A shot of darkness entered Anna's eyes, an expression I'd never seen from her, and her tone dipped. "You know, I hate to say it, but the only thing I can come up with was Katie's sweet potato pie or the empanadas. I'm not sure which. Billy ate more than his share. It must've been that."

I blanched, surprised that she would go there. "I don't think that would've been the cause. No one else has complained about being sick."

She shrugged. "Well... something got to him." All timidness and nerves seemed to disappear, and the hardness in her eyes came into her tone. "Billy, go help your father in the back."

Billy was sliding off his jacket but had to pause to

remove his gloves before freeing his arms. "Mom, I helped you both enough yesterday. I'm here on vacation. Not to work. This is why I don't come home very often. You always put me right to—"

"Billy!" Anna barked, causing Watson, who'd been bouncing on his front paws in anticipation, to take a few steps back. She pointed behind her. "Help your father. The sooner we get everything done, the better. Your sisters will be here before we know it. And I want everything finished so we can enjoy being with Tiny Tim for his first Christmas."

With his gloves off, Billy was finally able to remove his jacket, and he jerked free of it as if it had been attempting to strangle him. "I wish you would quit calling him that. It's the stupidest name. You know that—"

"Billy!" That time the mix of fury and fear in her voice was undeniable, and if I had any doubts left to what Anna and Carl believed about their son, they faded. "Enough."

Billy ducked his head as if he was an embarrassed teenager instead of a man in his forties and cast me a humiliated glance before tossing his jacket over his shoulder and beginning to trudge away.

The flick of his jacket caught my attention and all my fears were realized. I didn't give myself a moment to reconsider. "Billy?"

He looked back at me, and Anna stiffened.

"What happened to your knuckles?" From where he gripped his jacket, his knuckles showed deep purplish black with bruises and a couple of scrapes.

"Nothing." He started to shove his hands back into his gloves.

"Billy is a boxer." Anna blurted the statement and then blinked as if she'd just baffled herself. "I mean... he's taking a boxing class, to lose weight. He's a little tubby." She patted her own belly.

"Mom!" Billy went completely red.

"Here we go! Here we go!" Carl hurried from the back room, a large all-natural dog bone in each hand. Completely forgetting protocol, he bypassed Anna as the middleman and shoved one of the treats at Watson.

Watson snagged it like a ravenous shark before starting to wander off to find a place in private to eat as he normally did. But he glared back at me from the end of his leash and then gave up. In pure desperation he crashed down right where he was and made short work of the treat.

Carl gave me the other bone. "Here you go, Fred, take one to go. Sorry to have kept you waiting. I know you've got things to do."

Not moving, I looked back and forth between the three of them, irritation warring with pity and hurt for my friends. They were doing such a horrid job of attempting to cover it up and made it all so much worse, so much more desperate. "Guys, come on. Obviously—"

"Fred!" Anna had both warning and pleading in her tone. "Don't. Please."

She nearly broke my heart, but it couldn't be helped. "I'm sorry." Maybe it was cowardice, but I looked away from her, unable to get through it if I was looking into my friend's eyes. Instead I focused on Billy. "Where were you when Adam Sweitzer was murdered? You told Officer Green, or someone did, that you had food poisoning. Clearly you didn't. And your knuckles are all bruised and cut up."

"Adam was killed with a snow globe." Carl moved to stand beside his son, but there was no warning in his voice, just unconvincing hope.

I never took my eyes off Billy. "That's not true, is it?" Technically I wasn't certain if it was true or not. I hadn't heard a final cause of death. I pushed forward anyway. "I saw Adam's body. What I'm seeing on your knuckles matches what I saw on his face."

Anna made a sound reminiscent of Watson's whimper. "No. No, he didn't do this. He didn't." I didn't think she was speaking to me.

"There's no use pretending, obviously none of this is true." I forced myself to look Anna and Carl in the eyes once more. "You both know that. It's obvious. And I know it's hard, but if your son..." I returned focus back to him. "If *Billy* did this, then an innocent man is in jail for a murder he didn't commit."

Billy snorted and rolled his eyes. "Are you kidding? You think Mark is innocent? Or Adam, for that matter? They're utter scum. Both of them."

"Billy, stop," Anna barked again, and Carl grabbed for his son's arm as if to hold him back from speaking.

It didn't work. "Adam deserved what he got. And Mark deserves whatever's coming his way." For the first time, Billy truly met my eyes, and the hardness in his own washed away any resemblance to his parents. "But I didn't kill him. Kinda wish I had. But I didn't."

For the first time since I entered Cabin and Hearth, it felt like I was hearing the truth. Anna began to cry, but I didn't look toward her. "Then where were you, Billy? You weren't home with food poisoning or flu or anything else. If you didn't kill Adam, who did?"

"Don't know." He shrugged. "But if it's someone other than Mark, let me know so I can give them a high-five."

"Billy!" Anna and Carl reprimanded together, both sounding appalled.

I ignored them again. "Where were you really?"

Billy jutted up his chin, and glanced toward Anna, some of his bravado wavering, but then it was back as he looked me full in the face. "I was with Delilah Johnson."

"Delilah!" Anna practically shrieked. "You were with *that* woman? I have told you to stay away from her since high school. She's nothing but a—" Anna stopped short, the internal debate showing clearly across her face. Finally she straightened and jutted her own chin as she looked at me. "You heard Billy. He was with that harlot." Her lower lip trembled, but her voice didn't waver. "It's time for you to go, Fred. You got your answer." She glanced down at Watson, who was sitting at attention between us, looking back and forth in clear confusion. Her lip trembled again, but she held fast. "I think you should leave."

As I left Cabin and Hearth, I gazed longingly across the street at the Cozy Corgi. It was even more charming than usual. It's tall and narrow log cabin façade, covered in fresh snow, practically screamed an invitation to all those wanting to curl up with a good book by the fire, while enjoying a warm steaming mug of dirty chai and a buttery almond croissant. Okay, maybe that particular recipe was what I saw in the shop, but its cozy charm wasn't simply because I was biased.

Then I remembered the mystery room's antique sofa was now out of commission, and even if it wasn't, the store was filled with Christmas shoppers. I could hardly curl up by the fire and read while Watson napped as I wished I could.

Besides, the worst was over with, and... it had been even worse than I'd feared. The look in Carl's and Anna's eyes, especially Anna's, as if I was betraying her, threatening her child. And as far as Billy himself? He seemed even guiltier than I'd imagined. Might as well check his alibi and get it over and done with.

Turning from the Cozy Corgi, Watson and I headed down the block. I was tempted to dart into Paws, get lost in the chaotic noise of the pet shop, its two crazed corgis, and my friend Paulie, but again, it would simply be putting off the inevitable.

I paused as I reached Old Tyme Photography and considered my reaction. Billy had an alibi, so he said. So why did I have such a sinking feeling in my gut?

It didn't take more than a heartbeat to figure out. Because the idea of Billy Hanson with Delilah Johnson was more laughable than the "I either had food poisoning or a twenty-four-hour flu bug" excuse. It wasn't even a looks issue, though as far as that went, Delilah was a ten on that particular scale while Billy was... well... *not* a ten. There was something about Billy that seemed as if he were nothing more than an overgrown child, and I couldn't see that turning Delilah's head.

The second we entered the little photography studio filled with tintype photos on the walls and racks of various outfits ranging from cowboy to flapper girls to old-time prison stripes, Watson gave a ridiculously happy bark.

I looked down at him in surprise. He seemed to like Delilah Johnson more than most, but not to the point that he displayed any overt excitement in her presence. I thought maybe he'd suddenly caught a whiff of the extra dog treat Carl had given me that I'd stuffed in my pocket. As he rushed to the end of his leash, I saw the reason and the picture fell into place, kinda.

Leo leaned against the counter talking to Delilah. My breath caught at the sight of them together. I couldn't see Delilah Johnson with Billy Hanson, but it didn't take any imagination at all to see what a perfect pairing she was with Leo Lopez. He stood in his green park ranger uniform—tall, dark, muscular, a leather jacket flung over his arm. Delilah, ever the reincarnation of a pinup girl, wore what looked like a Native American fringed buckskin that had been dyed the deep Christmas evergreen under a skimpy fur halter with a fur-lined hood. With her waves of fiery hair falling around her shoulders, she swept away any notion of Christmas being wholesome or cozy.

All of that came to me in a flash as they both turned the instant Watson barked.

Leo's eyes widened slightly in surprise, but a smile spread over his face as he saw me, and then he dropped to his knee in his typical greeting to Watson.

I released his leash, and Watson ran into Leo's arms.

Though I had mixed emotions about the woman, as Delilah operated her personal life in a way I couldn't respect, the two of us had grown friendly. She too smiled at me, but it faltered. Her eyes narrowed in a knowing glint, and the smile returned, but instead of welcome it showed a little wicked. She dropped her hand and rested it on Leo's shoulder as he patted Watson, while keeping her gaze on me. "Don't worry. I'm not corrupting our Boy Scout. He's merely dropping off my phone. I left it at Nadiya's house last night. We had a little Pink Panther's get-together."

I didn't want to think about whatever occurred at those meetings. Nor did I want to look too deeply into why my breath had caught at the sight of the two of them. Though even as Leo ruffled Watson's fur, eliciting a torrent of dog hair, I could still feel the sensation of his thumb running over the back of my hand as it had two nights before.

"I just got off shift. I saw Nadiya in passing, and she gave me the cell phone." His casual tone indicated either Leo hadn't noticed the exchange between Delilah and myself or he was jumping over it. "I was planning to come see you and Katie after I left here." He chuckled and refocused on Watson. "And you too, little man. You too."

I commanded my feet to move. To my surprise, they carried me across the store, and I joined the two of them at the counter. I then forced my tongue to work as well and demanded it sound nonchalant. "What did last night's Pink Panther meeting entail?" Better to think of that.

Delilah clucked her tongue and shook her finger. "Oh no, you've turned me down twice. You don't get to know what we Pink Panthers do if you're not one of us. But you have a standing invitation, so you can change that anytime."

I merely smiled, at least I hoped that was the expression I gave. It both flattered and threw me off to be invited into her small, exclusive girls' club.

Not giving me a chance to respond, not that I was sure what to say, she stage-whispered to Leo, "We baked Christmas cookies while we watched *The Family Stone*." Her deep blue eyes flashed at me. "Scandalous, I know." She gave a throaty laugh. "Although, Nadiya and Brit did overindulge in pumpkin spice Kahlúa."

Leo joined in on the laughter, finally giving an extra-long rub to Watson before standing. "Nadiya mentioned that. Said she barely dragged herself out of bed thirty minutes before her shift. I think Brit is still sleeping."

"Pumpkin spice is dangerous. But delicious." Though her tone remained friendly and teasing, Delilah's gaze went to a place that was much more dangerous than pumpkin spice ever thought of being as she glanced between Leo, Watson, and me. "I don't have any customers at the moment. Why don't the three of you get into some of my new Christmas line?" She gestured toward the racks of clothes. "Last time, Fred, I put you and Watson in roaring twenties, which I do think is most definitely your era, but you could pull off Victorian as well. And Leo..." She shrugged. "Well, look at him. He could pull off anything.

Watson would look utterly dashing in a top hat." She clapped her hands, growing genuinely excited. "Oh! And I have an adorable pair of steampunk aviator goggles. They're child-size, but I bet they'd work for him."

I couldn't keep from glaring at her. What was she doing, trying to arrange a photo with Watson and me and Leo?

"That's a great idea." Once more, I wasn't sure if Leo missed the tension or was remaining intentionally oblivious. "We should have Katie join."

Relief filled me as Delilah looked annoyed at being thwarted, so I added to the mix. "That's a great idea. Maybe the twins as well."

She rolled her eyes. "Oh, sure, why not simply do a photo of the entire town?"

I barely caught the look Leo shot at Delilah, one that clearly told her to *knock it off*, before his casual expression was back in place.

So he wasn't oblivious. And the familiarity he displayed toward Delilah and that expression suggested the two of them were close. But Delilah appeared to be trying to push the two of us together. So maybe they weren't *that* kind of close. Perhaps he'd even been talking to her about—

I stopped my thoughts right there, mentally giving myself the biggest, most painful kick in the shins. I didn't need to be thinking of anything like that.

Even if I was.

I motioned over my shoulder. "Watson and I need to be getting back. We've been gone from the Cozy Corgi for a while, but I just finished talking to the Hansons, and your name came up, Delilah."

"It's always business with you, isn't it? I do admire that about you, Fred, but I still think you should join the Pink Panthers. We all need to lighten up from time to time.

And *not* by getting lost in some book. Though there's a time and place for that as well." Delilah walked around the counter and took Leo's place by kneeling in front of Watson. He allowed her to pet him as she cooed, but his attention remained on Leo. Finally, Delilah sighed but continued to stroke Watson as she looked back up at me. "I suppose you're here about the other night? Adam's death?"

I nodded.

She rolled her eyes again, though I didn't get the impression it was directed at me. "Let me guess... Billy used me as an alibi?"

Leo shot her a surprised look.

A few of the things I truly liked about Delilah Johnson was that she was quick, smart, and blunt. All traits I valued and respected. "If that's your guess, then I take it that it's true, you were with him."

"Sure, for all of five seconds." She started to stand but then paused and pressed a quick kiss to the top of Watson's head. "I'm going to let you go now, otherwise I'm afraid I'll start ripping out your fur without meaning to. Besides, you only have eyes for Leo anyway. Not that I blame you." She finished standing, and her fingers curled into fists as she looked at me. "What'd he say? And just because whatever you pass on might be the reason I turn around and murder him, don't let that cause you to sugarcoat it."

It seemed my impression that Delilah wouldn't look at Billy twice was dead-on. "He didn't say much. Just that he was with you."

"*With* me?" She cocked a perfectly shaped eyebrow.

"Those were his exact words. '*I was with Delilah Johnson.*' Nothing more, nothing less."

She took a deep breath, seemed to consider. "Okay

then. I'm not promising there won't be bloodshed, but it's not an inevitability."

Leo and I exchanged glances, but I refocused on Delilah. "Care to elaborate?"

"Oh..." She threw up a hand in exasperation. "There's not much more to elaborate on. I was with Billy, and he was with me. For all of two minutes in the back alley, a little more than the five seconds I said earlier. I was throwing a cowboy hat one of the tourists had ruined into the dumpster, and there was Billy, pacing and muttering to himself. Nearly scared me to death. It wasn't all that late, but it was dark."

Again Leo and I exchanged glances, and he took point that time. "Billy was in the alley behind the shops? That's a little odd."

She snickered. "Billy is more than a little odd. Those terms are completely interchangeable, although I guess you didn't grow up with him." She glanced at me. "Either of you. But trust me." She moved both of her hands as if weighing a scale. "Billy Hanson, odd as crickets on pizza, same thing." She laughed again at my grimace but kept going. "But it's not all that odd when you stop to think about it. His parents own the shop just a couple of stores down. We all share the back alley, and they use the same dumpster that I do."

That was a good insight. I supposed it did make sense, or at least explain why he might be in the alley. "Did you catch what he was muttering?"

"I shouldn't have said muttering. He was practically raging. Although I don't think he saw me at first either. The alley was quiet, I was throwing away the hat and all of a sudden he started going off, but it was too jumbled to catch."

"So no idea why he was angry?"

"No, but that's nothing new. He's always had an anger problem." Her annoyed expression shifted to something darker. "Hadn't seen him in years, but he's the same old Billy Hanson he always was. Barely saw me and two seconds later he's asking me on a date, or insinuating that I should take him home with me. Different day... different year..." She snorted, somehow even managing to make that alluring. "Different *decade*, for that matter, *or two*, but same old Billy."

I decided to use one of Delilah's and my similarities and be blunt. "You've known Billy a long time. Do you think he's capable of murder?"

She began to shake her head, then seemed to consider. "I started to say no, as I don't think he has the spine for that, but maybe. Honestly, I can see it more from Mark, but if you're looking into Adam's death, then clearly you don't think it's him."

"I'm not sure, but I'm checking some things out."

Before I could figure out which angle to take next, Leo broke in. "You went to school with them, right? You're all about the same age, you, Billy, Mark, Adam, and Rocky?"

"Yes." She shimmied just a touch, a playful grin over her lips. "But unlike them, I'm aging like a fine wine."

Leo winked at her, but somehow managed to make it more friendly than flirtatious. "It sounds like the dynamic between them goes back a long time. What were they like?"

"Oh, Lord, where to start?" Delilah bugged out her eyes and leaned against the counter. She was quiet for several moments.

As we waited, Leo sank back to the floor and began stroking Watson again. It took all of a second and a half for Watson to roll over and demand belly rubs.

When Delilah spoke, though Leo was the one who'd asked the question, she addressed me. "This will probably sound strange, coming from me, but I hope you don't judge me on what I'm about to say. Most of the time I don't give a flying flip about what anyone thinks of me, but I don't like to judge people based on looks or their social standing, and that's what I'm about to do. There are plenty of rumors about me, and most of them are true, but I am *not* an elitist snob."

"I know that." I hoped she saw the sincerity in my eyes. It was one of the things I did like about Delilah, one of the things that had surprised me. Even in her small clique of cool girls, they weren't all of the gorgeous pinup-girl variety. And if that was the qualification, I never would have been invited in either.

She gave a sharp nod and then launched in. "Mark, Rocky, and Adam were the losers of the school. We're talking freaks-and-geeks sort of thing, but with less personality." Delilah issued an exasperated sigh. "I mean, really, Mark's a grown man who dresses like a wizard and runs around in broad daylight pretending to fly on a broomstick. That's totally freaks-and-geeks stuff, right? But it's also interesting. You have to admire a person who is willing to simply do whatever they want to do. But... somehow, Mark makes it boring. Don't get me started on Rocky's fuzzy van tours. That's what they were like in high school too. They did everything weird and different, but made it snoozeville. Adam was the same, though it felt like he simply followed the other two."

I didn't entirely agree with her. I actually found Mark's idiosyncrasies rather interesting and part of the reason I didn't want to picture him being the murderer. I couldn't give Rocky Castle any such leeway.

Delilah continued, and started to sound as if she were a million miles away, which considering we were talking about events over twenty-some years in the past, I supposed she was. "There was one exception. Billy. He was even lower on the rung than the other three. Though that was only partially true. To the rest of the school, all four of them were equal, but as Mark, Rocky, and Adam were bullied constantly, they took their frustrations out on Billy. He was quite literally the lowest man on the totem pole."

"Really?"

Delilah and I both jumped a little at Leo's interruption. She was in the past, and I was traveling right along with her.

"Sorry." Leo offered an apologetic smile before addressing Delilah. "I'm just surprised that if Billy was the way you described him that he'd have the nerve to pursue you back then. Or now, for that matter."

"Well... that was my own fault. They say no good deed goes unpunished, and I'm living proof. It was around Christmas. I remember because—" Delilah flinched and focused on me. "Did I hear that Adam was killed with a snow globe of Ebenezer Scrooge, or am I making that up?"

"I don't know if that's what ultimately killed him, but it appears that he was hit with one. At least the Ebenezer Scrooge snow globe was broken and close to his body."

Her beautiful face paled. She took a breath and let it out slowly. "Maybe it really wasn't Mark."

"Why?" Leo and I piped up in unison, causing Watson to grunt in surprise, but he didn't attempt to get away from the never-ending belly rub.

Delilah didn't smile or smirk at the scene, but remained serious, and her voice grew quieter as she spoke. "The one interesting thing Billy did was theater. During our junior year, he was Tiny Tim in the school's production of *A*

Christmas Carol. One Friday afternoon I stayed for chemistry club and hung around after everyone else had left. I don't even remember why now. Maybe I needed to use the restroom. I might've left something in my locker..." Her forehead furrowed in concentration. "Maybe the latter, not that it matters. Either way, no one was there, and I was walking down the hallway and heard a pounding. I followed it to a locker a few rows away and opened it. Mark, Rocky, and Adam had wrapped Billy in the chains they used for the play, the ones worn by that first ghost... the ghost of..." She snapped her fingers.

"No, he wasn't one of the ghosts of Christmas. It was Jacob Marley, the ghost of Jacob Marley, Scrooge's old business partner, who was in chains."

She grinned at me. "See, you make being a book geek cool." Her smile faltered quickly. "Anyway, they'd wrapped him up in those chains from the play and stuffed him in the locker and left him there. I don't think he'd been there very long, but if I hadn't wandered by..." She shrugged, and what little remembered pity remained vanished from her expression. "From then on, Billy took me releasing him as a sign that I had feelings for him, or that we were destined to be together, or who knows what. Whatever the case, he was persistent and demanding enough, and entitled about it—I must've wished I'd left him trapped in that locker a million times over the next year."

Silence fell at the end of the story, except for Watson's contented grunts. Finally Leo spoke what we were all thinking. "So... Billy would have a justifiable vendetta against Adam."

"And it would explain their argument at the Cozy Corgi the other night as well." No wonder things had exploded so quickly.

"And he used"—Delilah shook her head—"*the killer* used the Ebenezer Scrooge snow globe."

"Exactly." Another thought hit me. "If we're right, if Billy truly does have a vendetta, then there are still two more people to enact revenge upon before it's paid in full."

FOURTEEN

"I'm nervous." From my spot behind the Mini Cooper's steering wheel, I glanced over at Watson, who sat at alert in the passenger seat, intently watching the view shift as we drove higher into the mountains.

He didn't bother to look my way.

"Apparently you're not experiencing any nerves, but you may want to. It's not like the two of you are very good friends."

Still, Watson refused to give in to my warnings, instead focusing on the narrow passage through the towering rocks several yards in front of us.

It had been a while since I'd driven up Saint Vrain Avenue, and I'd forgotten how beautiful it was, especially in the soft light of dusk, with the full moon and the first clusters of stars glistening off the snow. Pushing past my nerves, maybe because of Watson's rapt attention, I was sidetracked as well by the walls of rock. The sharp cliffs towered fifty or more feet above the car—I wasn't sure why someone had thought it was the best place to construct a road through the spine of stone, but the end result was breathtaking, like passing through a gate to another world. Though the scenery didn't change on the other side, I couldn't help but feel the sensation I was leaving the relative safety of the Estes Valley below and entering into someone else's domain.

Perhaps I was just being dramatic. Then I remembered whose house we were going to, and decided I wasn't.

As the road wound, I decided we were entering the Snow Queen's territory, with the snow-laden pines and spruce trees. The massive groves of leafless aspen trees covering the dips and cracks over the landscape, enclosed on all sides by rugged peaks.

I spared Watson another glance. Somehow I didn't think he quite lived up to Aslan's effect on the Snow Queen, but then again, perhaps I was selling him short.

Even as the thought flitted through my mind, Watson, rather rudely, let out a large, dramatic yawn before giving a solitary spin and curling up into a napping ball.

Nope, not Aslan.

When we passed Fish Creek Road on the left, a flash of memories threatened to overwhelm me as the wooden sign with a white key and the carved words *Baldpate Inn* came into view. I strained to see through the trees down the gravel road and could just make out the tip of the roofline of the old hotel. There was a soup and salad bar that my grandmother had loved to eat at. When my parents would bring me to Estes as a kid, we would always eat there at least once. I'd forgotten the name, hadn't even recognized it when Barry mentioned Percival and Gary hoped to have their anniversary party there.

Lily Lake sat on the other side, a sleek covering of ice, further indicating we were in Snow Queen territory. Another minute or so, and I saw the turnoff on the left to Serenity Lane and snorted out a laugh.

Watson shook his head at my rude noise.

"Of course the Snow Queen would live on Serenity Lane, of all places."

He didn't seem impressed with my literary comparisons.

"You know what, sourpuss? It will serve you right if she turns you into stone." We drove down the winding road a little farther until a cabin, only a little smaller than my own, came into view. I checked the address in the text I'd received, thinking I must've taken a wrong turn.

The house was the Christmas version of Hansel and Gretel's candy cottage, with its snow-laden peaked roof and fluffy smoke billowing from the river rock chimney. Red-and-white candy cane lights framed the perimeter of the front porch—*candy cane lights!* And in addition to the inviting glow from the windows, a sparkling Christmas tree could be seen inside.

This had to be a joke. I'd anticipated if not the Snow Queen's castle, at least walking into the Grinch's lair.

After parking the car, Watson accompanied me up to the door of what was certainly going to be answered by an old grandmother who'd tell me the house I was looking for was a couple of bends farther up the road.

After only a few moments wait after my knock, Susan Green, her hair loose once more, and wearing a thick cream-colored sweater and sky-blue flannel pajama bottoms instead of her police uniform, opened the door, gave me a grimace of a smile, then scowled down at Watson. "Great. Looks like I'll be trying to clean up dog hair for the next month." She stood aside and made room. We both hesitated, Watson apparently getting on board with my trepidation. Susan gave an inpatient gesture. "Hurry up. Are you trying to make my heating bill go through the roof?"

"Sorry." I stepped in, Watson following me. At first

glance, the inside of the cabin was just as charming as the outside. "Is your home under renovation? Are you renting this one?"

She shut the door, then looked at me as if I was insane. "What?"

"This is *your* house?" I couldn't keep the incredulity out of my tone.

Her eyes narrowed. "Of course this is my house. Quit being weird." She pointed to the sofa in front of a roaring fireplace. "Have a seat. I'll get some drinks. Do you want water or beer?"

"Uhm. Water?" Susan cocked her eyebrow at my response, and I tried for humor and pointed at Watson. "He'd love a beer, though."

"Didn't I just say quit being weird?" With a huff, she turned and disappeared into the kitchen.

"Maybe traveling through those rock towers really did bring us to a different dimension," I whispered to Watson, who stared up at me wide-eyed.

Instead of going to the couch, a bookshelf that filled the entirety of one of the small walls caught my attention and drew me like a moth to a flame. I read the spines of the books like another person would sneak into the bathroom and paw through their host's medicine cabinet.

Mark hadn't been lying. Susan truly had grown up reading mystery novels. An entire shelf was filled with old editions of Nancy Drew and the Boxcar Children. Thankfully, the nostalgia stopped there. I didn't think I could handle much more. The rest of the shelves were filled with series by JD Robb, John Grisham, Michael Creighton, Dona Leon, and Sue Grafton. Three entire shelves were filled with nothing but Stephen King and Dean Koontz.

The very bottom shelf held DVD box sets instead of

books. *The Love Boat*, *I Love Lucy*, *Mork and Mindy*, *Gilligan's Island*, *Bewitched*, *The Golden Girls*, and *The Brady Bunch*. The last one nearly made my head spin. I'd forgotten Susan's love of classic television.

"You just can't keep yourself from snooping, can you?"

I turned to find Susan entering the living room, a glass of ice water in one hand, beer in the other. I gestured back toward the bookcase but was unable to find the right words.

"Yes, I'm literate. I know you would've placed money otherwise." Susan thrust the water into my hand. "And quit looking at me like that. We're not long-lost sisters because I read."

I most definitely had no delusions that we were long-lost sisters, but I did feel like I was standing in front of a stranger. I never would've guessed Susan was such an avid reader. Nor would I have envisioned a home like this. It was very similar to my own. I thought back, trying to remember if Susan had made derogatory comments about my house the first time she'd been inside it. I thought she had, but maybe I was wrong.

"Good grief, woman, pull it together. I didn't invite you here so we can bond. I simply wanted to brainstorm the case, and I needed to be in my own home. It's been a long few days." She gestured toward the couch again. "Sit."

I'd been surprised enough over getting Susan's text telling me to come to her house so we could talk and compare notes. I most definitely hadn't expected any of this. At least she still sounded like herself. I never would've thought I'd be relieved by her cantankerous demeanor. Finally obeying her directive, I followed her across the living room and took my place on the opposite side of the couch, Watson at my feet.

"Does"—she gave Watson another scowl—"*he* need something to drink?"

"No, thank you. He's okay." I sipped my water, more for something to do than out of any thirst.

Susan took a swig from her beer and pointed at me with the bottle. "Well... come on. This isn't a social visit. And I'm not making you dinner, so don't get the idea that you're hanging around. Fill me in."

Her familiar brittleness truly was grounding. "Well, as you know, it's only been a couple of days, but I was able to talk to quite a few people and received a surprising amount of information."

After another swig of beer, she had to swallow before speaking. Susan let her eye roll give me a preview of her thoughts. "I get it. The whole town gets it. You're the most brilliant Nancy Drew who ever existed."

Irritation sparked. "I wasn't saying that. I wasn't bragging. I was—" I shook my head. Us bickering wouldn't solve anything. Although with her, it was somehow settling, normal. "You asked me to help, so obviously you have enough faith in me to think that I can. Quit biting my head off."

"Then hurry up." Though the words were abrupt, her tone had softened. "Speaking of the people you talked to, I swung by Habanero's. Let's just say that Rocky didn't get to do his tour yesterday." Her pale blue eyes twinkled in humor. "And you're not exactly his favorite person at the moment."

So she had followed through. And maybe, together, we'd helped avoid a tragedy. "I'm all right with that. He's not my favorite person ever."

"I suppose that shows you have at least some taste in men. Your track record hasn't been the best." As I was about to bite her head off, she pivoted. "You were bragging about finding a surprising amount of information, so fill me in."

I decided to let the jabs go and get to the point. Susan's little house might be as inviting as my own, but that was only on the surface. She wasn't the only one who'd had a long day. I was ready to turn my brain off and get carried away in front of my own fireplace. "My main suspect is Billy Hanson." Saying the words almost felt like a confession.

It seemed Susan thought so as well as her brows rose and her voice lilted in surprise. "Really? You're looking at Carl and Anna's son? I thought they were in your inner circle."

"They are." Even as guilt nibbled at me, my determination settled. "The truth is the truth and facts are facts. I'll go wherever they lead, regardless. And I'm not saying it is Billy, but... it doesn't look good."

She studied me with narrowed eyes, similar to the expression she'd bestowed on me at my house, though she held it longer, and remained silent.

It lasted so long I began to feel uncomfortable. "What? You're staring." I dropped my freehand over the edge of the couch and stroked Watson's head.

She still didn't answer for a second, and when she did, her voice was gruff and her tone matter-of-fact. "I don't like you. I know that's not news. I find you annoying and entitled. But..." She gave an irritated shake of her head. "I had you pegged wrong. You're not going to look the other way or tell yourself lies simply because you care about someone. You don't play games, do you?"

"No. I don't." I tilted my chin. "I don't like you either." I wasn't entirely sure that was true anymore.

"Good. I would hope not." The hint of a smile that

played at the corner of her lips told me she wasn't entirely sure that was true either. "So break it down for me. Why Billy?"

I launched in. "What do you know about his relationship with your brother, Rocky, and Adam when they were in high school?"

"You're not interviewing me, Fred." Annoyance flickered. "But I don't know much. Mark graduated high school when I was in seventh grade. It's not like we had the same friends, and I wasn't one of those little sisters who followed him all around, trying to have his attention or be accepted by his buddies."

That fit with how I saw Susan, though I knew she was thoroughly devoted to and loved her brother, even if she saw him as a fool. "From what I gather, when I talked to Delilah—"

"*Delilah?*" Susan threw back her head and gave an exhausted sigh. "Seriously? Delilah?"

"Yes, Delilah." I straightened. "Deal with it. Anyway, when I talked to Delilah, she filled me in on their high school experience. It sounds like Mark, Rocky, and Adam were a pretty tight group, and on the lower rung of the high school hierarchy. Everyone picked on them. They, in turn, picked on Billy. The incident Delilah described happened during the production of *A Christmas Carol*. They wrapped Billy in the chains used from the play and stuffed him in a locker. Delilah found him and got him out."

All disgusted humor fled from Susan's face, and she was all cop as she stared at me with cold eyes. "*A Christmas Carol?*"

I nodded.

"The Ebenezer Scrooge snow globe." It wasn't a question, just a statement.

Even so, I nodded again. "There's not been enough time to get results back from the autopsy?" I asked anyway. "Was that what killed Adam?"

To my surprise, Susan didn't snap at me for asking a question. "It's not conclusive yet, obviously. However, it seems like it was probably a combination. Adam, as you saw, was beaten pretty severely. There was a lot of trauma, enough that he would've been left with a concussion, though there's no way to know at this point if it was severe enough to kill him. But if it was finished off with a blow with the world's heaviest snow globe, that impact might've been the final straw. Either way, it was definitely used in his assault." Her nostrils flared as she took in a breath. "That seems like a pretty big link between Billy and Adam. If so, then Billy might have designs on Rocky and my brother."

I couldn't help but be impressed. She'd jumped to that conclusion nearly instantly.

Apparently my thoughts showed over my face, and she rolled her eyes again. "You really did think I was an idiot, didn't you? That connection is hardly a giant leap of logic."

I didn't deny it. "You thought I was as well."

"No, I didn't." She surprised me by shaking her head. "But I did think your end goal was exactly what you achieved—wrapping Branson around your little finger." She held up her hand as I started to argue. "I was wrong, we've already crossed that bridge. So, keep going. Did you find anything else?"

Letting it go, I pushed on again, that time truly feeling like I was betraying Carl and Anna. "Billy wasn't sick with food poisoning, and he wasn't home with his parents. That was a lie."

Susan's eyes widened as she waited for me to continue. Before I could tell her about Angus and Gerald seeing Billy outside of Alakazam, a horrid scream cut through the house, causing me to jump and Watson to let out a startled bark.

Without even a flinch, Susan sprang to her feet and headed into the other room. "I swear, I'll kill the nasty little rabbit. It keeps pulling the sheet right off its cage and then starts that bellowing. Could get four lucky rabbits feet out of the deal. In fact, I could even..." Her words faded away as she left the room.

I exchanged a look with Watson as a curse wafted back in, and then a moment or so later, the excruciating sound died away.

Susan stomped back in. "I hate that thing."

I couldn't imagine hating any animal, but a few startling times of hearing that might convince me otherwise. "That was intense."

Susan just glared and plopped back down. "What's going to be intense is when I serve my idiot brother rabbit stew while he's behind bars." She let out an angry breath and seemed to focus. "Okay. Where were we before that demonic rodent tempted me with murder?"

"Um..." It took me a second to recall. "Oh right! Billy and Delilah."

Susan grimaced but motioned for me to continue.

"Billy claimed Delilah was his alibi, that he was with her. He didn't want his parents to know, and Anna most definitely didn't approve. But... preferable to murder and all."

She snorted. "Well that makes sense. Although I can only imagine how many men could claim Delilah as their alibi, and every one of them be a hundred percent true."

I started to rise to Delilah's defense, much to my own surprise, then admitted that I'd had the exact same thought, so I let it go. "In addition, Angus and Gerald ran into Billy after they left Alakazam and Delilah said that she saw Billy for just a few minutes in the back alley behind the shops that night when she was throwing something away. Said that he was upset and that he tried to hit on her. I'm not sure which interaction came first though." Before Susan could make a smart comment about that, I kept going. "Turns out, Billy has pursued Delilah since high school, since she freed him from the locker, and has been rather incapable of respecting her saying no."

At the look of disgust over her face, I expected another sneer or derogatory comment about Delilah, but Susan surprised me again. "Well, that's gross. And from what I've seen from Billy, doesn't surprise me that much. The hairs on the back of my neck stand up every time he's around, which, thankfully, isn't very often." She shuddered, then leveled her gaze back on me. "Anything else?"

"A few details here and there, but that's the main gist." I put my free hand back in my lap as Watson settled down on the floor to nap out of reach. "What about you? What have you uncovered?"

She gave me an exasperated sigh. "That's why I asked you to look into this. Because you can hopefully remain unbiased around my brother, can find out things that I can't, and because *unlike me*, you seem to have no problem abandoning your job to snoop around. I have a town full of tourists, we're short a police chief, and a sergeant, and I'm checking over my shoulder every couple of seconds because I'm not sure how many other officers and members of my team are rotten, dirty cops. I didn't spend my day interrogating people about Mark. I did that the day before and I had other priorities today."

It was almost irritating how much I was starting to like the woman. I had flashes of it before, surprisingly, from time to time in between our bickering over the last year, but my respect for her was growing immensely. "That makes sense. And I have to say, I admire that."

"Well, thank you. Now I can continue with my job since I have Winifred Page's approval." There was another smirk, but she didn't ease up. "Who are you harassing tomorrow? What's your next step?"

"Next step?" I looked at her in surprise. "I figured you'd take Billy in for questioning."

"Just because I asked for your help, doesn't mean I need your input into my job." Though her tone was harsh, it left no room for doubt. "I will question Billy, *and* his parents again, clearly. They lied to me during an investigation. However, before I do that, I want as many details as I can acquire. Just because they lied, just because he has a history with my brother and Adam, doesn't mean that Billy did this. Although it sounds that way." It looked like she was debating whether to continue for a moment, so I sat quietly and waited. Finally, she did, and it sounded like she was taking me into her confidence. "Honestly? If this was any other case, I'd bring Billy in right now. But this is *my* brother. And the Estes Park police are in the middle of the biggest scandal I can imagine. I'm not sure if we're in the middle or at the end of it, but either way..." She shrugged. "With Mark being my brother, everything has to be perfect. There cannot be even a hint of favoritism or corruption. I know that my brother is not a killer, so I have to have faith that we will prove that. In the meantime, it's his own stupid fault for being his own stupid self that he's in a cell. He can stay there as long as he needs to as far as I'm concerned—as long as the end result is the truth. And... if we somehow find proof that I'm wrong... which I'm not... but if I am, then he'll stay in a cage."

Yes, my respect for Susan Green was most definitely growing. "Okay then. That makes sense. As far as who to talk to tomorrow, I don't know yet. I think maybe I'll keep pursuing the high school angle. Especially if there's a chance that Billy has a vendetta against Rocky and your brother as well. I'd like to talk to the Sweitzer family about it, but hate to bother them when they're grieving and busy with Sheila's delivery."

"Sounds like a plan. Not the best one I've ever heard, but it's something." Susan took another swig of beer and then glanced toward the door meaningfully before looking back at me. "Is there anything else?"

"No, I don't suppose."

"Great." She stood. "Well then, you'd best be on your way. I haven't had dinner yet, and if you're waiting for me to bring out tea and cookies, you've got the wrong house."

Even with her annoying tone, I nearly laughed. When I stood, Watson woke and joined me as I crossed the room. On impulse I paused as I was even with the bookcase and gestured toward it. "I noticed you like mystery novels. Have you ever read any of Sherlock Holmes? That was always my dad's and my favorite. They're very—"

"Oh no." Susan shook her head and finished walking to the door and held it open, a gust of winter wind rushing in. "We don't do that, you and me. We're not friends. We don't do book talk. I appreciate your help, we'll check in tomorrow, but for now, you and your fleabag need to hightail it home."

I waited until Watson and I turned off Serenity Lane and back onto Saint Vrain Avenue before whispering to Watson as if Susan could hear us, "You know, I think she's starting to like us."

My phone buzzed when I was about three steps from entering the Cozy Corgi the next morning.

Come to Victorian Antlers the moment you get downtown. It's an emergency.

I stared at Percival's text as Watson turned back to me with a whine from where he waited to enter the bookshop. Figuring it was more efficient, I tapped Percival's name and held the cell to my ear.

It rang through to voicemail. I glared at my phone as I complained to Watson. "He *just* texted me. *Literally.* I know he's there."

Watson simply whined again and pawed at the door.

I supposed that's what I got for complaining to a corgi. Figuring it was easier to give in, I rerouted us down the street. "Come on. If I have to walk through the snow, so do you. Knowing Percival, he is probably staging an intervention to force me to use more than mascara and lip gloss. Although if he is, he better watch out. I've not even had my first dirty chai from Katie this morning."

Watson still offered no commentary and sulked behind me, moving as slowly as humanly possible or... corgily possible, I supposed. And good grief, I was still carrying on a conversation with my dog like a crazy person as we walked down the main street of Estes Park.

I succeeded in offering no more commentary or complaint to Watson as we finished the two blocks to my uncles' antique shop.

Watson whimpered again, this time in genuine discomfort, as we walked in to Judy Garland's version of "Have Yourself a Merry Little Christmas" blaring over the speakers.

Both of my uncles were waiting for me, standing in the center of the shop, surrounded by various antique furniture covered in an assortment of Christmas decorations and lights. Percival wore his boysenberry-colored fur coat as if they had just walked in, and Gary had his arms crossed and an irritated look on his face. He spoke first. "Sorry, Fred. This wasn't my idea. But you know how your uncle is. I told him you'd think there'd been another murder."

"Oh, pish!" Percival gave his husband a little shove, causing the mistletoe attached to the spring of the headband he wore to jiggle. "Fred knows me better than that. If there'd been a murder, the text would've been *much* more dramatic."

I raised my voice to compete with Judy. "I figured it was a makeup emergency. But I came anyway."

"See? Fred's no dunce." He gave me the once-over as he swept toward me. "However, if I'd been aware of this outfit and face, *that* would've been the purpose of my text. The fact that you thought so proves that you're aware of the problem."

"No, I just know you." I smirked

"The least you could do is a smoky cat-eye." He scowled at my face. "And I do mean the *least*. You were doing so good for a while. But it's Christmas, darling niece, there's glitter, sparkle, and jewel tones to be had. And don't get me started on your ever-expected broomstick skirt in *mustard*."

"If the reason you called me down was to critique my appearance, Watson and I can head back." The statement probably would've been more effective if I wasn't close to laughing. Trying to fix my appearance was just one more way Percival communicated his love and affection.

"No, there's an actual emergency. It's good that you came. And you too, I suppose." He bent toward Watson, who issued a fang-baring growl and scooted backward. Percival shot up and placed his hands on his hips. "Well, I never. I thought we were past this."

"You did the same thing to him last year," Gary called out from behind. "Watson hates that stupid mistletoe bobbing like a detached third eye above your head." He leaned so he could see around Percival to cock an eyebrow my direction. "Yet another entire year I have failed to find wherever he hides that piece of junk and throw it away."

Percival gave a matching expression. "If I didn't wear it, my loving husband would never kiss me."

"Oh, shut up!" A smile played on Gary's lips and he waved me onward. "It's *not* an actual emergency, but we do need your input."

Percival slid his arm through mine and pulled me along so we followed Gary behind the counter. I released Watson's leash as we walked so he wasn't subjected to the terrifying mistletoe and could go explore at will.

To my surprise, Percival turned down Judy without me having to make a request and then pulled a huge book out from underneath the table and slapped it down on the counter. "Truth be told, you're lucky we're asking for your input at all, as you can't be trusted." He gestured once more toward my mustard-hued skirt.

Only then did I realize it was a book of fabric. There had to be a couple of hundred samples in it. "I'm confused. You're making me an outfit?"

Though Percival just grinned, Gary pointed behind me from the way we'd just come. "We asked Nick to help us bring that down this morning. I'm surprised you didn't see him as he headed back to the bakery. You had to have just missed him."

"Bring what...?" I saw before I completed the thought. The mystery room's antique couch sat behind a large armoire and looked as though it had been attacked. All the fabric was gone and most of the stuffing had been pulled out. "What happened to it?"

"What happened to it is that lady attempted to give birth on a piece of furniture that's over a hundred and twenty years old." Percival *tsked* as he flipped through the book of samples. "Luckily, for Gary anyway, it doesn't need to be refinished, just reupholstered."

"I *did* help Nick carry it down." Gary gave me a knowing look. "Percival was feeling too delicate this morning."

"I'm older than you, so stop with the judgment. Plus, might as well use those ex-football-player muscles for something useful. You can't *just* be pretty. Besides, since I'll be the one doing the upholstery, I technically will be doing more heavy lifting than you." Percival waved me closer. "Now, take a look at these. You have three choices. Gary and I are thinking gold."

I blanched. "Gold? You want to reupholster the sofa in gold?" I didn't bother looking at Percival; the man was wearing boysenberry. Of course *he* thought it should be gold. To my surprise, Gary nodded his enthusiastic agreement.

Percival pushed on. "Here's the first one."

I looked down and blanched again. "Are those… sequins?"

"Absolutely." Percival gave them a loving stroke. "But not the ones that are so popular right now that they change colors when you rub the opposite direction. So passé."

"I kind of like them." Gary shrugged.

"What do you know? You threw around a pigskin and then ran back and forth down a field never actually going anywhere. We're not seeking your advice on sequin elegance." Without bothering to look at Gary, Percival refocused on me. "From your expression, I take it that option is a no?"

I pointed at him. "You're not a dunce either."

Nonplussed, he flipped to another offering. "All right then, option two."

This one was even worse. It was a solid gold velvet with crimson roses embroidered in tiny little clusters. I couldn't even form words.

"Okay, looking like a no on option two as well." Percival *tsked* again, more dramatically that time. "For a woman afraid of makeup and fashion, you're awfully opinionated. Here's your third and final choice."

"You know, just because you sold me the piece of furniture doesn't mean you get carte blanche on its upholstery." I didn't bother looking at the third sample. Instead I glared at my uncle. "It is my bookshop after all, you know."

Instead of arguing, he tapped the fabric.

I started to shake my head no before I even looked down, but then I froze for a second. I cocked my head and leaned closer. After another moment, I ran my hands over the fabric. It looked like a woven tapestry but felt softer. The particular golden hue was what might be expected if gold and mustard had a baby—a sort of deep dusty amber. Flecks of plum and cobalt fibers swirled here and there among the strands. It looked rich, sophisticated, and yet inviting. Something about it reminded me of a dragonfly. "It's... lovely." I hadn't thought the mystery room could be more beautiful, but I could picture it there underneath the purple portobello lamp, the muted sheen of the fabric gleaming slightly in the light of the fireplace. It was perfect, not something I would've ever picked myself, but perfect. I looked up at Percival. "You chose the other two horrible ones on purpose so I'd be more open to this one, didn't you?"

Percival tapped the end of his nose. "You're a detective's daughter."

I laughed but couldn't help feeling excited about the change. "Well played, you two, I have to admit. But still, it's hardly an emergency. I am looking into a murder, after all."

Percival rolled his eyes. "Darling, you're *always* looking into a murder. They can't *all* be emergencies." He refocused on the fabric and ran his long willowy fingers lovingly over the subtle pattern. "And since you arrived here expediently, I can get this going today while Gary deals with tourists and will have it ready for you in a snap. We can't have the Cozy Corgi looking subpar for all the Christmas visitors, can we?"

Watson trotted up and sat at my feet, apparently having had his fill of exploring. He looked up at me longingly.

"I know that face. Someone's ready for a t-r-e-a-t, and honestly, he's not the only one. I haven't hit the minimum intake of caffeine quite yet." I smiled at Percival and Gary in turn. "I can't say I appreciate your tactics, but I do appreciate you doing this. It's very kind, and as ever, your taste is both exotic and timeless."

"Wow, you managed to say that with a straight face to a man with mistletoe bobbing above his head." Gary winked at me. "Impressive."

"On a less important note than perfect reupholstering, we got a call from Carl and Anna last night." Percival's expression turned serious. "They fear you suspect Billy of killing Adam."

"He's definitely a possibility. It didn't help that they lied to Susan, and to me, for that matter."

"Don't judge them too harshly. Billy is their child, no matter how old he is." Percival was unusually grave.

"Even if he didn't inherit either their charm or kindness." Gary scrunched up his face. "I haven't had too many interactions with Billy, but while I hate to say it, he never struck me as overly kind. But that doesn't make him a murderer."

"No... it doesn't. But it sounds like he had reasons to be angry at Adam, and a couple of others as well." Fear bubbled up in the presence of my uncles, and I confessed what I wouldn't have to Susan the night before. "It makes sense that he did it, but I don't feel it in my gut. Then again, I don't feel it in my gut about Mark either. But that doesn't mean anything. Not right now." I was surprised to feel tears burn behind my eyes, and I blinked them away. "I didn't feel it in my gut about Branson either, and look how bamboozled I was."

Percival came to me instantly and wrapped his arm around my shoulder, Watson only scooted a little bit away. "He bamboozled all of us, Fred. You can't start questioning yourself because you're not psychic."

Gary closed in on the other side, wrapping me in their combined embrace. "Furthermore, your gut *did* know. Everyone was pressuring you to be with Branson. We've all heard what some of the people in town were saying about you when you rejected him. Still, you stayed strong. Maybe you couldn't put your finger on why, maybe you didn't know there was anything wrong, but..." He squeezed just a little tighter. "You knew it wasn't right. Maybe part of you knew that *he* wasn't right."

I nodded, afraid if I attempted words my voice would crack.

"Exactly so." Percival agreed and kissed the top of my head before releasing me. "Don't you worry about having a gut feeling around Adam's murder. You'll figure it out one way or another. Your gut isn't the only brilliant thing about you, Winifred Wendy Page." He tapped my head. "You're no dunce."

Before either the tourists began arriving in full swing or I'd decided who to talk to first that day regarding Adam Sweitzer—but *after* I was feeling more human having had a small bucket worth of Katie's dirty chais—Anna and Carl came into the Cozy Corgi.

Watson perked up instantly and scampered toward them, prancing at Anna's feet.

I took it as a good sign when she handed him his favorite dog bone treat and patted him on the head.

Watson allowed the affection as a form of thank-you and then took off, and the pair of them continued toward Ben and me at the counter.

I angled toward Ben and lowered my voice. "Do you mind hanging out in the bakery for a little bit? We could use a little privacy."

"Of course not." He smiled at me. "I'll ask Katie to have another dirty chai ready for when it's over."

"No wonder Watson adores you." I patted his hand, sent him off, and turned to face the Hansons. "Hi." It was all I could think to say. It felt like there should be something else—an apology, an explanation, a defense—but *hi* was all I had.

Both of them looked exhausted. Carl pushed up his glasses, drawing my attention to his puffy and bloodshot eyes.

Anna took point. "We came to apologize."

I flinched. "Apologize? To me? Whatever for?" If anything, I'd figured they'd come to demand an apology from me.

"We know you, Fred. And we love you." Anna reached across the counter, grasped my hand between both of hers, and held on. "I shouldn't have been unkind to you yesterday, shouldn't have kicked you out of the shop."

I started to object, but Carl broke in. "We also know our son. *And* we love him too." He took a shaky breath and straightened his shoulders and lifted his chin, making a more stalwart expression than I'd ever seen from the typically browbeaten Carl. "We know his weaknesses. They're many. I'm not going to list them here because... well, he's our son and we love him. But... we can't believe he would murder anyone."

It struck me that he didn't say they knew he *didn't* murder anyone. It was a small distinction, but an important one.

Anna bounced back in as she squeezed my hand once more. "And because we know you, we know that you won't stop until you find the truth, so we have to believe that means you'll prove Billy didn't kill that Sweitzer boy. Even if you have to look into Billy to prove it. We have faith in you."

That time when my eyes stung, I didn't attempt to hold back the tear that rolled down my cheek, though I did wipe it away with the back of my free hand. "Anna, Carl... I don't know what to say..." I suddenly felt the need to confess. "I told Susan the details I discovered yesterday. She may have to bring Billy in for questioning."

Anna, too, straightened her shoulders. "Like I said, we know you'll discover the truth even if you have to look into Billy to prove it." She held my gaze, letting me see both strength and desperation. "Keep looking. *Prove* it."

I only managed to nod.

"Thank you." She gave a third squeeze, then released my hand and forced a smile. "As an act of good faith, and of friendship, we wanted to invite you to join us at the hospital tonight. Carl and I are dressing up like Mr. and Mrs. Claus and visiting some of the patients, bring a little good cheer." She gave a self-conscious laugh. "In full disclosure, it's a little self-serving as Billy has agreed to be one of our elves, so you get to see him in a more positive light. We can all go to dinner or something after, and you can ask anything you need."

I most definitely hadn't expected that. "Well... I..." I'd seen them dressed as Mr. and Mrs. Claus last year. They were more convincing than any other I'd seen in person or in movies. They were enough to make a grown-up truly believe. But something felt off. "I thought you did that on Christmas Eve."

"We do." Carl nodded. "But that's only the children's ward. We bring them presents, the whole shebang. But the hospital picks another night where we go to other patients, the adults and such, try to bring a little Christmas cheer, but we don't bring presents or expect them to believe that we're actually Santa and his wife." His gaze held the same strength and desperation I'd seen in Anna's. "Please join us. Come get a different impression of Billy."

It wasn't how I'd planned on spending the evening, but I didn't see how I could say no. And though it might be tilted to a more positive light than normal, it would give me a chance to observe Billy. "Okay, I'll be there. Thank you."

Relief flooded Anna's face. "Good, good. I'm glad. We'll arrive at seven thirty." Her eyes lit up in the first shot of typical Anna happiness I'd seen. "And bring Watson. Maybe he'll wear his little scarf."

SIXTEEN

"It's for people who don't feel good. It'll make them smile." I gave a second attempt at looping the scarf around Watson's neck only to have him twist out of the way and take guard against the inside paneling of the Mini Cooper's passenger door. "I got special permission for you to be here, though there are a few places you can't go. You don't want to be responsible for ruining sick people's Christmas, do you?"

Watson's admonishing look clearly stated *Guilt? Really? You know I'm only persuaded by food. Amateur...*

Maybe if I took a note out of Percival's playbook... Pretending to give up, I dropped the scarf and reached into the narrow backseat and then pulled the Santa hat from under a jacket. "Okay then, how about this?"

Watson's eyes went wide and then glared communication of some other choice thoughts.

"I don't think you're old enough to think things like that." I held the hat out to him so he could sniff, as if that would make a difference. "Come on, you let Leo put it on you."

He perked up instantly and looked around in excitement.

"Sorry, buddy. Leo's not here at the moment."

Not believing me, Watson did a full circle, scanning the hospital parking lot.

Knowing it made me an utterly horrible, horrible corgi mama, I took advantage of his distraction and successfully looped the scarf around his neck.

He turned back to me with a look of utter betrayal.

I offered him the hat. "It would be cuter as a set."

From the look he gave that time, I figured it was good that we were so close to medical assistance.

"Fine. Fine." I tossed the Santa hat into the back. "The scarf will suffice. And you look dashing." I attempted to kiss the little pink spot on his nose, but he evaded. Feeling a little guilty taking away his free will, I snagged the Santa hat once more, pulled my hair through the strap and affixed the hat like a headband. Sure enough, the reflection in the rearview mirror contradicted my uncle's statement that I wasn't a dunce.

With a smirk, Watson allowed me to attach his leash.

We were running a little late, so Anna and Carl had started without us. I texted Anna to let her know Watson and I had arrived, and we walked into the hospital. There was no one on duty behind the welcome desk, though judging from the steaming cup of hot chocolate beside the computer, it appeared they'd recently stepped away. Knowing it could be a few minutes before I got an answering text from Anna, I decided not to wait. The hospital wasn't that big. It shouldn't be too difficult to track down Mr. and Mrs. Claus.

No one wandered down the corridor, and all of the doors on either side of the hallway were shut. The sound of Watson's nails and my boots clicking and clomping on the linoleum floor echoed. As we rounded the corner, we discovered Charlene Sweitzer sitting in her wheelchair, gazing into a large window, one of her hands pressed to the glass. She didn't look at us as we approached.

The reason why was obvious as I paused at her side. The window looked into the nursery. There were ten tiny little plastic cribs in the softly lit room, three of which were occupied by sleeping newborns. Above each bed hung large plastic Christmas bulbs, varying in bright, cheerful colors. A nurse fiddled at the far side of the room with her back toward us.

Unable to see, Watson plopped down at my feet, just far enough away to let me know I was not forgiven for his humiliation.

"Is"—I tried to remember what name Sheila had said she was naming the baby—"your granddaughter in there?"

Charlene flinched and looked over at me in surprise. "Oh!" Confusion seemed to cloud her eyes before she glanced down at Watson. "Fred. Goodness, I'm sorry. I was lost in my own universe." She looked like she'd been crying.

"Sorry to startle you. I figured you heard us coming. Though I can't blame you for being distracted." I glanced back at the babies. "Is she in there?" I suddenly realized I hadn't heard any news about the Sweitzer baby being born all day. A trickle of fear entered.

Charlene tapped the window soundlessly. "Tiffany. She's the one closest."

Relief flooded, and I looked at the tiny bundle wrapped in yellow. Her little face red and wrinkled, barely visible between the top of the blanket and the cap pulled over her head and ears. "She's beautiful." I never found newborns especially adorable, but I knew it was what a person was supposed to say. And I figured all new life was beautiful, even if Tiffany did resemble an old man.

"She really is." Charlene's tone was wistful and sad.

Though I supposed that made sense. I peered around the hallway, surprised to find Charlene on her own. "Is Sheila okay?"

Charlene kept her eyes on her granddaughter as she nodded. "Yes. Though it was a harder birth than we expected, especially considering Tiffany is the fifth child, but the doctors warned us there was a chance things might not go smoothly, considering Sheila's almost thirty-seven, which seems so young in every other way. But everything ended up perfectly, thank God. Mother and daughter are completely healthy." She chuckled softly. "I think Sheila plans on milking it, not that I blame her, by seeing if she can stay in the hospital another couple of days. That way Brian can take care of the four boys on his own. He's a good father."

I couldn't even fathom it. Just the few minutes the four boys had been in the Cozy Corgi had made me need a nap. The idea of adding another one to the mix would make me run for the hills. "You have a lovely family." Look at that, finally learning how to keep my foot out of my mouth.

Charlene nodded but gave a little squeak and when I looked down, I saw a tear rolling down her cheek.

As he had before, Watson drew near and rested his head on Charlene's foot.

She peered over, and a trembling smile appeared. "Oh, he's got a little scarf." Charlene looked at me and seemed to notice my hat for the first time. "And you're dressed up too. You look... lovely."

I knew what that meant. Not that it mattered.

She clutched my hand, instantly growing tense. "Have you discovered anything about who hurt my boy?"

"Um..." I wished we could go back to talking about babies. It was one thing to speculate with others, throw around theories and try to piece clues together, but that didn't feel appropriate with the victim's mother. "I... did talk to several people yesterday, and did quite a bit of research on the computer today while I was at the bookshop."

I'd picked apart Adam Sweitzer's online life, trying to get a better idea of him, see if there were some angles I was missing. The only things I found confirmed what Mark Green had said. Adam was pompous, self-centered, and unlikable. That was just from the things he posted about himself. Most of the things he boasted about were too outlandish to be real. I had found proof about his claims around the board game. Though it looked like the deal he'd struck would earn him thousands instead of the millions he'd claimed.

That seemed a safer angle to focus on with Charlene, to avoid what I'd heard from Billy, Rocky, and Delilah. "Do you know what happens to the money from the board game Adam designed? I was thinking maybe that might provide a clue." That angle wasn't necessarily true. If he'd been slated to earn millions, then it most definitely could have been motive, but I didn't think many people would kill for thousands of dollars. Plus, from the look of Adam, he'd been killed in anger, not for cash.

"No." Charlene sighed. "I've no doubt this makes me sound horrible, but I wasn't sure if there even was a game." She hurried on, clarifying. "I mean, I saw it, but I wasn't certain if there was a contract or if Adam was... fantasizing. He was so excited, so very, very excited. I hadn't seen him like that in years. It even kept me from feeling hurt too badly when he chose to go to his friends instead of watching *It's a Wonderful Life* with me. I watch it every year." Another tear fell. "Adam would go years between visits anyway, so he hadn't seen them in a long time. But... he seemed genuinely excited to show his old friends, hoping they'd be happy for him. I wouldn't begrudge him not watching some old movie with his old mother. Not when he had success to share with his friends." Her eyes widened, and she clutched my hand again. "The game! Did you find out about the game? Is that why you're asking? It was real? He really sold it?"

The questions came so hot and fast that I could barely jump in. "I did find it. And it was real."

A relieved smile crossed her face, and though her grasp held firm on one of my hands, her other rose to her chest. "That's wonderful. I'm so glad he wasn't fibbing this time." Her expression changed again. "So that's why you're asking? Is that why he died? Someone murdered him because he was going to be a millionaire?"

I considered lying, or at least pretending that I didn't know. She'd seemed so relieved at what appeared to be a rare act of honesty. But I figured that would only hurt more later. "Adam was... misinformed about that part. He did sell the rights to the game, but he wasn't going to make millions. I found an announcement of the game on the manufacturer's website, on their upcoming page. And when I looked into the company itself, what they pay game creators, it was a wide range, so I'm not sure what they offered Adam, but... it's not millions."

Her sigh of disappointment so clearly had absolutely nothing to do with the amount of money. "Well, at least he was partially honest, *and* I'm happy he could finally experience some genuine success, even if right at the end." Her smile returned. "No wonder he was so excited to show his friends. He was almost like a little kid rushing around the house before he went to the game night. And that's nice too. The last memory of him will be of him happy."

Unsure what to say once more, I simply squeezed her hand.

Charlene smiled down at Watson, who was still resting on her foot, and then refocused through the window to stare at Tiffany, but when she spoke, her words revealed she was still in that night. "Life is strange, hard. I think back to a million different things in Adam's life and wonder what I did wrong. If I should've been more lenient here or more strict there. Did I encourage too much, not enough?" Before I could attempt to figure out an answer, she kept going. "Even the night he died. I keep replaying it over and over. Not that I could've stopped it, but I was so rude to Connie for not waking me up at my favorite part of the movie. I snapped at her. What if I'd snapped at Adam and it was the last thing I'd ever said to him?" She sighed and shook her head.

Watson gave a matching sigh, which was more than I could figure out in way of response.

"You know that part, pretty early on, when Jimmy Stewart and Donna Reed are at the dance and the floor opens up and everyone falls into the pool?" A far-off look came into her eyes and a smile flitted on her lips. "Wouldn't that be wonderful? I remember watching that as a child, dreaming of going to a big dance like that one day. A fancy place that had a pool, falling in while wearing a beautiful dress."

"There you are. I knew you'd be here." Glinda arrived by our side, as if out of the ether, her silvery fairy wings attached. She put a hand on Charlene's shoulder, cast her a soft smile, then gave a similar expression to Watson and me. "Don't you two look festive. Utterly charming." She motioned to the window. "I see you've met our new girl here. Our little solstice miracle."

"She's lovely." And as I looked at her again, seeing Tiffany through her grandmother's eyes, she was. Lovely and perfect.

Still keeping one hand on Charlene's shoulder, Glinda placed her other over where Charlene and I still held on to each other. I hadn't even been aware we'd not let go. "I saw Mark today. Susan finally let me. He seemed hopeful, because of you."

"Really?" I couldn't keep the surprise out of my tone. "That wasn't really the impression I got from him."

Glinda chuckled indulgently. "Well, he is who he is."

Charlene looked at me again as well. "I have to thank you once more. Glinda loves Mark as if he were her own. Just like I love Adam. So glad you can save one of our boys."

"Mom!"

The three of us flinched, our hands separating as we turned toward the voice. Watson jumped up as well.

Connie rounded the corner, her face full of strain. "I've been looking everywhere for you. You just wandered off!"

"I'm sorry, dear." Charlene glanced toward the nursery before looking back at Connie. "I just wanted a few minutes alone with our girl."

"You should've told me. I was scared to death. And Sheila woke up asking where you were. She doesn't need that strain right now." Connie tucked a graying strand of hair behind her ear as her gaze flitted over Glinda and landed on me. "Oh, hi, Fred. Sorry, wasn't trying to be rude. I was just in the middle of heart palpitations." She looked back at her mother. "I hate when you scare me like that."

Charlene reached out a hand and patted Connie's. "I

know, baby. I wasn't thinking. I'm sorry. Thanks for taking such good care of me and loving your old mom so much."

Glinda cast a reproving expression at Connie. "She was *only* gone a few minutes, and really, where else would she be except with the wee one?"

From Connie's expression, it looked like she was about to bite back, but we were interrupted once more by the sound of bells as Mr. and Mrs. Claus arrived from the opposite corner.

Watson instantly hid under my skirt.

"There you are! I've been texting you." Though Anna smiled, it didn't quite reach her eyes.

I patted the pocket of my skirt and found nothing. "Oh, my goodness. I'm so sorry. I must've slipped it into my purse."

"Quite all right, dear." Carl sounded like himself, but just a touch deeper. He truly did have the Santa Claus effect. Though I'd seen them the year before, I'd forgotten just how realistic they were with the rich red velvet of their outfits lined in thick white fur covering their short round bodies.

"You two look perfect." They really did. Though, unsurprisingly, they didn't seem as cheerful as I recalled them appearing last year.

Anna reached up, motioning toward my Santa hat but only touched my hair instead. "You dressed up as well. You even wore an outfit that's not earth-toned."

"That's Katie's doing." I laughed and motioned down at my emerald-green blouse and the candy-red broomstick skirt covered in a reindeer pattern. "She demanded I get a couple of Christmas outfits that *she* picked out, of course."

"Well, it suits you." Anna lowered her hand from my hair, pausing to pluck corgi fur from my shoulder, though I was constantly covered, so I don't know why she bothered. "Watson didn't come?"

Adding insult to injury of my betrayal with the scarf, I lifted my skirt, revealing his hiding place. With a grunt, he emerged.

Anna clapped her hands. "Oh good, he wore his little scarf." She gave him a quick tickle under his chin. "I'll bring you an extra treat tomorrow!"

Watson didn't even perk up at his favorite word, as if he knew nothing so wonderful could come in the middle of his humiliation.

Carl stood on tiptoe so he could look through the window over Anna's shoulder. "Charlene, is that little Tiffany? She's beautiful!"

As if noticing the room of babies for the first time, Anna cooed. "Oh, she really is!" She turned in excitement toward Charlene. "She just has to meet Tiny Tim when he gets in town. He's not even a year old yet, so there's not that much age difference between them. Maybe they'll be soul mates meeting as babies."

Connie flinched and was unable to hide her disgusted expression before I saw it.

I nearly laughed. I couldn't blame her. The idea of soul mate babies was a little... well... I didn't know what the right word was, but... something.

For the next five minutes, we were swept away in talks of newborns and Christmas, no one even coming close to bringing up the elephant in the room of the conflict between Billy and Adam the night before the murder.

When we finally parted, Watson and I tagged along with Mr. and Mrs. Claus. Anna paused before we entered the first room, her expression grave. "Billy decided not to come tonight. Apparently, he isn't feeling well." She offered an apologetic grimace. "For real this time. I'm sorry you won't get to see him in a better light. But I do appreciate you coming."

"Did he know I was going to be here?" The question was out of my lips before I considered its implication.

"Yes. He did." Though Anna winced, Carl was direct. "Like we told you, Billy... well... we know he's not perfect. He likes to take the easy way out, avoid conflict, unless he's the one causing it, and is rather lazy. But he's not a murderer. I hope you don't take this as a sign that he is."

"No. Of course I don't." I wasn't sure if that was true or not, but I smiled at them nonetheless. "Either way, thank you for inviting me to this tonight. It's nice to do something good. You're both so important to me."

Both of their smiles were genuine and then, as one, transitioned from something sweet yet rather sad to full-on Mr. and Mrs. Claus joyful, as Carl opened the door to the hospital room and burst out with the best *"Ho, ho, ho"* I'd ever heard.

Though we weren't on the children's ward, Watson was just as big a hit with the adults we visited. Though he'd started the evening in the height of grumpiness, he played his role in pure Watson fashion. Maybe one day I'd stop being surprised when he seemed to be aware of people needing him. He didn't prance, dance, or pretend to be Santa's little helper. He was himself after all, but he never pulled away when a sick hand reached out to pet him, never grimaced when receiving a kiss on his nose, and brought a peaceful smile to every single face he encountered.

We were leaving the final room, the four of us heading toward the parking lot together, when Anna checked her cell and issued a startled cry. She passed it to Carl whose expression fell as he read.

They exchanged glances, and then he handed it to me. "You might as well see this now."

It was from Billy.

Mom, sorry to do this, but I can't be here right now. It was a mistake to come this year. Sorry for the drama. Sorry to leave you without saying goodbye. Please tell the rest of the family Merry Christmas and that I'll see them later. By the way, I took a few hundred from your sock drawer. You can count it as a Christmas present. You don't need to get me anything else. Love, Billy

"Oh, poor Anna and Carl. And here they thought they'd have the whole family together for Christmas." Katie both looked and sounded genuinely empathetic, but it didn't stop her from taking a large bite of her breakfast quiche and groaning. "Dear Lord, I hate to brag, but..." She tapped her fork on the plate.

Leo snorted out a laugh and gestured to his own plate, which was empty, save for a couple of crumbs of crust. "I second that emotion." His tone grew a bit more serious. "And I do feel bad for Anna and Carl, but the way it sounds, I bet they're pretty used to Billy. At least they'll have their daughters and grandkid here."

The morning rush had slowed, so as Nick and Ben managed the bookshop and bakery, Katie, Leo, and I sat by the window. Snow swirled so thick the street below was barely visible.

"Well, I still feel bad for them. Even if they are used to Billy." Katie took another bite of quiche and groaned again.

"You're really proud of yourself this morning, aren't you? Not that you don't have reason." I tore off a piece of the edge of my crust and tossed it to Watson, who sat by the end of the table looking back and forth between his three humans, searching for the weak link. "The second-breakfast thing may not be good on the waistline, but I think it might be my favorite tradition we have, at least when time allows."

"I've been thinking about that." Katie had started to take another bite but paused with a fork halfway through the quiche. "We should call this brunch. We have breakfast before the shop opens and then *brunch* afterward. It sounds less indulgent if we call it a different meal as opposed to having seconds. And..." She shrugged. "If we just *happen* to have lunch as well"—another shrug—"and that's the third meal, not seconds on brunch."

Leo patted his nonexistent belly. "I don't know how you two do it. Or you." He winked down at Watson. "Thankfully I'm leading a snowshoe hike in the park this afternoon. And this is my *first* breakfast!"

"Yes, but you had *two* pieces of quiche. Katie and I only had one." I winked at him, then felt my face blush.

"Exactly." Katie nodded and lifted one hand at a time. "One for breakfast and one for brunch. We've had two meals, while you, dear Leo, were just a pig. A pig with an annoying metabolism."

He grinned. "I stand, or sit rather, corrected." He nudged Katie with his shoulder and turned to me. "So back to Billy. Are you seeing him running as some sort of confession?"

I sighed, set my fork down, and interlocked my fingers. "It depends on which moment you ask me. Around two this morning, the answer would've been yes, and then again around five. Then somewhere around four, my sleep-rattled brain decided it was Mark after all—can you really be that drunk that you slip and slide in your dead ex-friend's blood and not remember?"

Katie grimaced.

"Sorry. But you see what I mean?" I shook my head, irritated at myself for being so wishy-washy. "Then while I was showering, I decided *Rocky* could be responsible. Avenging Mark or some such nonsense. I don't know. It's a toss-up on who is the most capable of murder."

"Even a toss-up on who had it coming." Katie's eyes widened as if surprised by her own words. "Sorry. I'm not saying they deserve it, but..." She grimaced again.

"No, I'm not saying they deserve it either. Nobody deserves to be murdered." I glanced out the window and was just able to make out Cabin and Hearth across the street through the snow, picturing the Hansons from the night before. Anna's fearful and heartbroken face. "I think that's what is throwing me off, or at least the aspect directly related to this particular murder, not with all the craziness that went down a few weeks ago." I refocused on Katie and Leo, shoving thoughts of Branson away. "Everything we know about these guys, everything we're hearing about from their friends and family, they're all pretty miserable people. Mark, Rocky, and Billy. To my surprise, Mark is the most likable of the three, but even he can't seem to get his act together. They're all selfish, irresponsible, rude, and manipulative. It could be any of them."

"You just described Adam as well."

Katie and I both looked at Leo.

He shrugged. "I don't want to speak ill of the dead, but I heard how he behaved at the Cozy Corgi Christmas party. It sounds like he disappears for years at a time, even though his mom isn't in the best of health, even though he had four nephews who might've needed an uncle."

"Leo's right." Katie turned to me as if laying out pieces of evidence. "You said yourself that Mark compared him to that Gilderoy Lockhart character from Harry Potter, constantly bragging or taking credit for things that he had nothing to do with, and that's how his *friend* described him."

Watson had been continuing his impression of "corgi attends tennis match" as he looked back and forth between us while we spoke. Finally giving up, he collapsed with a sigh and rested his head over his tiny front legs.

I grinned down at him but didn't give in to the guilt trip, staying focused on the matter at hand. "So basically, we have four guys who are grown-up versions of their teenage selves, in the worst ways possible."

"Boys behaving badly."

I pointed to Katie. "Exactly. And here's another thing they all have in common..." This had been a realization I'd had in the shower, though I hadn't added the victim to the list until that very moment. "All four of their families make constant excuses for them and rescue them from their bad behavior. Even Mark. Even though his wife leaves him, she keeps taking him back. Even though his sister is fully aware of all of his downfalls, Susan fights for him. The only one I don't know about in terms of family is Rocky, but either way he's got his friends, and I'm willing to bet Gerald Jackson and Angus Witt, as the older members of their little crew, in some ways fill that role. They condone all the bad behavior, and in some ways take part."

Katie's eyes widened again. "What if it's them? What if it's Gerald or Angus, or both of them? They're taking their substitute father role seriously, Adam shows up, presents the game he's stolen, taking credit for it, and is bragging about getting paid millions, so the *fathers* of the group dole out the punishment."

I started to object, then cut myself short. It was an interesting thought. In many ways, had just as much merit as anything else. But still. "Angus seems a little too... kind, I guess, to kill someone. And Gerald"—I rolled my eyes —"well, he's Gerald."

"If one of them was the killer, wouldn't the murder weapon either be a knitting needle or a kombucha bottle?" Leo chuckled.

"I still say they're options. You don't get much more powerful than family, in good and bad ways. That family doesn't always have to be blood." Katie shoved Leo back with her shoulder. "And you're ridiculous. Knitting needles and kombucha bottles? Not quite the same as an Ebenezer Scrooge snow globe."

I sat up a little straighter. "I'm glad you said that. Glinda called during the morning rush asking if I still wanted to pick up the snow globe I ordered for Christina. The last time I went down there to get it was when we discovered Adam, and obviously I didn't think about it then."

"Glinda!" Katie's eyes widened once more. "Maybe *she's* responsible. She takes on the parental role much more than Angus and Gerald. I could see her killing for Mark."

Honestly, I could too.

Leo seemed skeptical. "Well if it was her, wouldn't the murder weapon be a wand?"

Katie swatted at him. "She's a fairy, not a witch."

He simply shrugged. "Okay then, the murder weapon would've been pixie dust, so the point remains the same."

Watson wandered around Alakazam while I tried to calm my heart palpitations from signing the credit card receipt. One of the customers milling about the magic shop had just finished getting their future predicted by the coin-operated fortuneteller. Watson scowled up at the mechanical woman and seemed dubious of her intentions. When the light stopped flashing and she returned to her frozen state, he sniffed before trotting away to investigate the scents around Mandrake's cage.

For his part, the white bunny followed Watson's journey around the perimeter, trying desperately to peer over and make friends. The little guy was unbelievably adorable. I couldn't quite reconcile such a sweet, fuzzy thing issuing the horrific noises I'd heard at Susan's the other night. As if feeling my attention, his large black gaze locked onto mine. For just a moment, I thought he was about to scream, then Watson moved, pulling the bunny's attention away.

Unsettled, I turned back to Glinda who was bagging up the world's most expensive snow globe. "I thought Susan was taking care of Drake. She got tired of him?" Susan most definitely was not an animal kind of person. Although, I'd heard that she had a pet snake, but I hadn't noticed one when I'd been at her house the other night.

"Oh no." Glinda smiled and then reconsidered. "Actually, yes, she's sick to death of him, I'm sure. But though I know I'm not Susan's favorite person in the world, she has a heart of gold, that one." The older fairy's eyes grew misty. "It's been hard being here alone. I'm so used to having Mark around. It's just been me and the tourists the past couple of days. Then I go home, and I'm alone again. I have friends at the retirement community, but..." She shook her head as if shutting herself up. "Anyway, I asked Susan if she would mind bringing Drake by on her way to work so I would have some company, someone who knows me. It's very kind of her. And I know it takes extra time out of her day as she has to come back and pick him up before I go home. Thank goodness she has a truck, that makes it easier."

"That is kind of her. I'm glad she does that for you." Just went to show that people could surprise you. Although the more of the finer details I learned about Susan Green, the softer a heart I realized she had. Maybe it was gold as Glinda claimed, or maybe not. But it wasn't chiseled out of stone like I'd believed for so long.

Glinda slid the bag toward me on the counter, then looked over at the bunny before issuing a tinkling laugh. "Look at those two." Watson had propped himself up, the nails of his front paws latched onto the wires of the rabbit cage for balance, and he and Drake stood there sniffing noses. "They've made friends. How sweet. It's lovely to have friends."

Katie's theory tickled in the back of my mind. Glinda sounded so lonely without Mark. There was no doubt she saw herself in the mother role to him. What mother wouldn't kill for their child? Especially when that child was her main source of relationships. Although, that wasn't necessarily true. "You and the Sweitzers are close, aren't you?"

A couple of customers headed toward the door and drew Glinda's attention. "Thanks for coming in! Have a magical holiday!"

"Thank you! Um... Merry Christmas." The wife waved over her shoulder to Glinda before she and the husband walked out to the sound of the chiming of bells.

"Sorry about that." Glinda refocused on me. "And, yes. Charlene and I have been like sisters since we were children. I was a little... different, shall we say... back then as well. Charlene was one of the few who was always kind." She'd caught my implication instantly but didn't seem offended by it. "Don't you worry about me. I have more than a bunny in my life. Charlene and her family are very good to me. They have me over for the kids' birthday parties, to go out to dinner, sometimes Charlene, Connie, and I go to the movies. The Sunday matinees are discounted."

From the other side of the store, Drake hopped, kicking up a few cedar chips, causing Watson to sneeze. He pranced around and then popped back up to see what the bunny was doing next.

Glinda giggled. "Adorable."

"Maybe Charlene could come help you out at the shop until Mark is..." I nearly said free but wasn't exactly sure that's how this would end.

If Glinda noticed my hesitation, she didn't let on. "Oh no, Connie stays close to Charlene. And unfortunately, Connie can't stand Mark. She's never even come into the magic shop, at least until the other day. But Connie is the most devoted daughter I've ever seen. Charlene first got sick when the two oldest kids were in high school, and even then, Connie devoted herself to taking care of her mother." She chuckled. "Kind of like me with Mark, although he's not sick. Still... I don't trust anyone else to take care of him the way I do." She breathed out an exhausted sigh and gave me a knowing look. "Families are a funny thing, aren't they? So much conflict, yet so much love. Just like what we were saying about Susan. I know Mark drives her absolutely batty, and she barely darkens the door to the magic shop any more than Connie, but at the end of the day, there's nothing she wouldn't do for her brother."

"Yes, that's the thing about most families, my own included. We're all so different in a lot of ways, but very devoted to each other." There we were, and I'd come full circle since second breakfast, or brunch, as Katie had labeled it. I slid the bag off the counter and was once more caught off guard by how heavy the snow globe was. "I should really get back to the bookshop."

I started to pat my thigh and call Watson over, but Glinda shot out a hand and gripped my arm as she lowered her voice. "Hold on one moment. There's another reason I wanted you to come by this morning besides picking up your order." She glanced at a teenager who'd been milling about but seemed to be heading toward the door. "I'd like some privacy, though."

"Okay. Of course." I set the bagged snow globe on the floor.

Glinda folded her hands on the countertop and watched the teenager, her gaze traveling everywhere he went. After a few seconds, he became aware of her staring and glanced over warily. Glinda simply smiled. He smiled back. She continued to stare, somehow keeping it from feeling suspicious or invasive.

In less than a minute, he headed to the door, gave Glinda a friendly wave, and left.

I turned to her. "Wow. That was..." *Strange and awkward.* "You really do have magic."

"Yes, I do." She grinned and then motioned toward the door with her birdlike hand. "Fred, would you mind being a sweetheart and locking the door so we're not interrupted for a couple of minutes?"

I obliged instantly, though as I offered my back to her, Katie's theory returned. However, I managed to turn the deadbolt without getting clocked on the head.

By the time I got back to the counter, Glinda's face paled, and though we were alone, she still whispered. "I have a theory, and I feel simply horrible about even suggesting what I'm about to say."

"About who murdered Adam?" I supposed that was a stupid question, but if she had a thought that could clear Mark's name, I was surprised she'd held on to it.

She nodded solemnly. "Sharon." She let out a shaky breath as if uttering that solitary name cost her greatly.

"Mark's wife?" Déjà vu washed over me, reminding me of my conversation with Rocky and his similar accusation. "Why?"

She unfolded her hands and laid one of them on top of mine. "I know Mark has his weaknesses. I do. He and Sharon have been together since they were little more than children themselves, but he has a wandering eye, though she doesn't make marriage easy. And he leaves a lot to be desired in terms of being a good father to those kids, though he's not abusive in the slightest. He's not easy. I know that. I love him as if he were my own, but I am aware of his faults. Every wizard has their shadows."

And we circled back yet again. This particular revolution was making me the dizziest of all. Endless excuses for four men who didn't deserve any. "So... you think Sharon killed *Adam* because Mark isn't a good husband?" That logic still made no more sense than when Rocky had suggested it.

"Yes. At least partly." She swallowed, and though we were alone, glanced around the store. Her gaze lingered on the rabbit who seemed to be taunting Watson by dipping his head just low enough to be out of sight and then popping back out once more. She studied Drake for so long, I wondered if she feared that he would tattle on her. Finally she looked back at me. "I know what you're thinking. Why would Sharon kill Adam? Why not, if her husband is a target, just kill Mark?"

I nodded.

"That would be too obvious, too direct." Again she glanced around, but didn't hesitate very long. "Sharon doesn't need Mark dead, just out of the way. If she framed him for murder, he goes to jail, and no one would ever suspect her. Why would they?"

I did my best to consider it. When brainstorming, there were no bad ideas. Although, that felt like one. Then again, being a detective's daughter, I'd heard of more than one murder that had been committed for reasons that made much less sense than the one Glinda presented.

I didn't really expect an answer, but thought I'd play it out. "If that's true, then how did Mark get covered in Adam's blood?"

Glinda didn't hesitate, clearly she'd thought it through. "That's sort of what made me think of it. Well, not so much Mark being covered in the blood, as that part makes sense to me." Again she took on that reproachful yet indulgent tone I'd heard so much over the past several days. "The boy drinks too much. He does. He needs to get ahold on it, but he hasn't yet. He thinks he went to the bathroom and slipped and was simply too drunk to remember it. And that very well may be the case. However..." She straightened and glanced over at Drake and Watson. "It's the blood on the covering of Drake's cage. Mark loves that bunny, dotes on him. I can't see him forgetting to cover Drake up." She looked back at me meaningfully. "His screams at night truly are unnerving. Mark wouldn't forget. I think after Sharon killed Adam, she pulled the sheet off Drake's cage so that he'd start screaming, wake Mark up, and force him to stumble around in a drunken stupor. *Maybe* even led him through it. If Mark was drunk on the couch, it would have been impossible for her to drag him up on her own. Getting Drake to scream would've been the easiest way to do it, and then she led him through the blood."

That seemed like a lot of variables, but I supposed it could be one explanation. Instead of replying to Glinda, I looked over at the rabbit cage. Watson had given up and had returned to sniffing around the perimeter. Drake was still peering through the bars, but was now looking at Glinda and me. I'd never heard a rabbit scream before hearing Drake at Susan's. I doubted very many people had. Most probably weren't even aware that was something rabbits did. But as cute as the little white ball of fluff was, with the creepy way he was staring, I readied myself for him to do it again.

Drake looked away, hopped over to a carrot-shaped salt lick hanging from a string and began to gnaw.

As if it was creating a high-pitched noise I couldn't hear, Watson glanced up at the bottom of the cage in annoyance and padded over to me, clearly ready to go.

"Fred, are you okay?"

I felt when Glinda touched my arm, and I nodded, but something about the bunny had me transfixed.

Then one tiny little puzzle piece fell into place with the sound, or at least the remembered sound, of a bunny scream. A few seconds later, several more pieces clicked together.

Finally, I turned to Glinda. "I'm not completely certain, but I think I can get Mark out in time for Christmas."

EIGHTEEN

"Hi, sorry to come by unannounced in the middle of the day. I hope you don't mind." I clutched the lapels of my jacket closer in a way that shoved the mustard-hued scarf farther up my neck, acting as if I were colder than I truly was—with the nerves and adrenaline racing through my veins, I could have melted an avalanche. "Do you mind if Watson and I come in?"

"Of course not." The confusion remained in Connie's eyes, but she offered a friendly smile and stood aside. After we entered, she stuck her head out the door observing the snowstorm. "It's rather beautiful. I've been so busy helping Mom with exercises that I've barely done more than glance at the window all day. Still, I know she was hoping to go see Tiffany, but it doesn't seem safe to take the risk."

The last part seemed more to herself than to me, but I responded anyway. "Are Sheila and the baby going home today?"

"Tomorrow. Although I think Sheila is going to try to stay as long as possible." Connie shut the door and turned back to us. "Is everything okay?"

"Yes, at least I think so." I unwound my scarf and began taking off my jacket without being asked to stay. "I wanted to talk to you and your mom. I think I know who killed your brother."

Her eyes went wide. "Really? So... it *wasn't* Mark?"

I considered being evasive until we were with her mom but changed my mind. "No. It wasn't Mark. It was Billy."

Relief washed over her, and Connie fluttered her hand at her chest. "Oh! Thank God. Mom will be so relieved. On top of everything, she was worried sick how much that would hurt Glinda."

"Connie!" Charlene's exhausted voice sounded from another room. "Who is it?"

Instead of answering, Connie focused on me. "Mom's in the living room, watching a Christmas movie. I have to use them as rewards for when she completes her exercises. I swear, if it weren't for me she'd sit in that wheelchair and watch movies twenty-four seven and would have withered away decades ago." She smiled indulgently. "Why don't you come in and tell her about Billy yourself. It will be hard for her to hear, but I know she'll be relieved about Mark, and having closure will help."

"That's why I came personally." Making myself at home, I placed my jacket and scarf on a little bench by the door. Watson looked back and forth between Connie and me expectantly.

"Can I get you anything? Water or hot tea?" Connie glanced at Watson. "Does your dog need anything? Milk?"

"No, we're fine. But thank you." I motioned toward the doorway where I thought Charlene's voice had come from. "I don't want to take too much of your time, plus I left Katie and the twins all by themselves at the Cozy Corgi. I need to hurry back." Right... because they weren't used to managing things perfectly well without me.

"Oh, of course." Connie led the way to a large living

room where Charlene sat in her wheelchair, parked next to a large leather couch, a black-and-white movie playing on the huge flat-screen television.

"Fred!" She smiled welcomingly, but appeared even more drained than the night before. When her gaze dipped toward my feet, she bent slightly, lowering her hand. "Oh, and sweet Watson."

Without missing a beat, Watson headed her way. I dropped his leash so he could go to her. He lifted his head just enough so her fingertips brushed his fur, and then, as the other times, lay down and rested his head over one of her feet.

Charlene sighed, clearly soothed by Watson's presence, then looked at me. "So nice of you to visit. Are you simply stopping by to say hello, or...?" Strain showed at the corner of her lips. "Do you have news?"

"Fred has uncovered that Billy Hanson killed Adam." Connie blurted it out on her way to her mother, then knelt by the wheelchair to grasp Charlene's hand. Watson had to scoot over to avoid having one of his hind legs pinched under her knee. "You don't have to stress about Mark anymore, or Glinda."

Charlene sagged. "That's wonderful. I think that would've ruined Glinda." She sucked in a sharp breath. "Oh, but poor Anna and Carl. They must be devastated."

The woman's kindness was nearly overwhelming. Her son had been murdered only a few days before and she was concerned about the other people who would be affected.

It seemed Connie was thinking similarly, but took a different approach. "Don't worry about them, Mom. It's okay to focus on you. That's how you get through your grief. Don't worry, I'll be here every step of the way. We'll work through it together."

Charlene nodded, then stretched out her trembling hand to pat the arm of the sofa. "Come sit, Fred. "

"She can't stay, Mom. Fred's got the bookshop to run, remember?" Connie glanced toward the television. "Plus, we need to do more exercises. Gotta get your blood flowing."

As she spoke, I walked around the three of them and sat on the sofa, closest to Charlene. "What movie are you watching?"

Connie flinched and gave me a puzzled look, not that I could blame her, considering I'd told her we couldn't stay very long.

Charlene brightened. *The Shop Around the Corner*. It's with Jimmy Stewart. I adore Jimmy Stewart. Have you seen it?"

"I haven't. I grew up watching *White Christmas* with my family every year."

"I've tried to talk Mom out of watching it this year." Connie scowled at the screen. "Jimmy Stewart's boss attempts suicide. *Some* Christmas movie. Besides, we've had enough death."

"But he doesn't die." Charlene leaned forward slightly, her voice earnest. "That's the beauty of Jimmy. He chose movies that demonstrate the struggle and the pain of living, but by the end, always shows the beauty of life, strength. Even when it's not perfect."

"Just like in *It's a Wonderful Life*, right?" I waited until Charlene looked my way and nodded. "It's been a while since I've seen it."

Connie groaned. "See, another dark one. In that movie it's *Jimmy Stewart's* character who contemplates suicide. Completely depressing."

"Well, I'm going to watch it again this year since I slept

through it the other night. It will be a good reminder." Charlene's voice hitched, and she refocused on Connie. "Not that I blame you, dear. It's not your fault I slept through it. I'm sorry I sniped at you. I know you just wanted me to have my rest."

"I understand how that is." I gave Connie a sympathetic smile. "Every time I try to watch a movie with my mother, she falls asleep before the opening credits have even finished. It's always a movie that *she* picks, and of course it's never one that I enjoy. So I'm stuck there watching a movie I detest while she snores." I almost wished my mom could hear the lie. She would've gotten a kick at such a mental picture.

"Oh no." Charlene shook her head. "I woke up somewhere in the middle, right when Jimmy goes to Mr. Martini's house, but it's nothing but a cemetery. Connie wasn't here, not that I can blame her. I don't expect her to sit and watch a movie she hates while I sleep. Truth be told I was lost to dreamland before that scene even moved on to the next." Brows furrowed, she refocused on Connie. "I don't snore, do I?"

"No, Mom. You don't." Connie shifted uncomfortably, let go of her mother's hand and stood, her knees cracking, and looked my way. "Well, again, thank you so much for looking into Adam's murder. For letting us know what you found out. It means so much that he'll have justice."

Charlene's countenance fell instantly. As if she'd been swept away by Jimmy Stewart and was plunged back into the icy waters of reality. Even so, she nodded and smiled at me again. "Yes, thank you dear." She bent down to stroke Watson, who once more lifted his head slightly to meet her touch. "I hate to lose you so soon, sweet boy."

I didn't even make an attempt to get up. "I'm going to go

by Alakazam next, let Glinda know. Would you like to come with me, Charlene? I know how close the two of you are."

"No. She needs to stay here." Charlene had started to nod, but Connie spoke over her. "And we need to turn off the TV and get some more exercises done."

"Probably smart." I gave an approving nod, before leaning forward as if telling a secret. "Besides, I don't enjoy going in there. I think Watson's allergic to that rabbit, and the last time I was in, it screamed something horrible. Scared me to death."

"Tell me about it." Connie rolled her eyes, looking utterly disgusted. "Although it makes sense that Mark Green would have a rabbit that screams." She cast her mother a warning glance. "I know, you can find good in everyone, but it's not there with him. That rabbit is just further proof. I've never heard such a horrible sound in my life."

My heart sped up. "Totally agree. I was trying to explain it to Katie, what it sounded like, but I just couldn't quite figure out how. It wasn't exactly high-pitched like when elks bugle, but..." I furrowed my brows in what I hoped was convincing concentration. "How would you describe it exactly?"

Connie shuddered. "Like pigs squealing combined with cats screeching. It makes chills run down your spine."

"Yes. That's it exactly." I pointed at her as if she hit the nail on the head. "So bizarre that it only does it at night. I asked Glinda about it, and she said she thinks Drake is magical. That he screams to scare away evil spirits that lurk in shadows."

Charlene looked at me from the corner of her eye as if I were crazy. Maybe I'd gone too over the top with what

Glinda might claim. Though I couldn't imagine that statement came even close.

Connie didn't notice and gave a derisive snort. "Of course she does. I swear working in that horrible place has rattled her brain. There is no reason to ever step foot in there."

"I have to say, I agree with you. Even Watson acts differently when we're in the magic shop." I didn't look down at him, afraid he'd be glaring at me for roping him into the lie. "You're smart, Connie. Glinda said you've only been in Alakazam the other day when you were there with your mom and Sheila."

"And it was more than enough proof for me that I was right. Part of the reason I don't let Mom go down there." Connie gave her mother a knowing look. "See, even Fred agrees with me."

"What I don't understand"—I spoke before Charlene had the chance—"is how you've heard the rabbit scream if you've only been to the magic store once. Mandrake only screams at night." I cocked my head and channeled my best innocent tone. "Wasn't your one visit there during the day?"

"Yes, we were..." Connie's words trailed off as she straightened. "I must've..."

A look of dawning horror played over Charlene's face.

I pressed on, afraid to give even a second's leeway. "Maybe you heard Mandrake screaming the other night while your mom was sleeping through *It's a Wonderful Life*. Perhaps it was screaming at the exact moment of the pool scene—you know, where the floor opens up and everyone falls into the water in their pretty dresses. It's your mom's favorite part."

Shaking her head, Connie took a step back.

Watson stood, either understanding more English than

I ever imagined or simply picking up on the immediate shift in the room's energy. He left Charlene's feet and moved slightly to stand guard in front of me.

"Connie?" Charlene looked back and forth between her daughter and me. "What's going on?" She didn't wait for an answer and shocked me by catching on quicker than I ever would've imagined as her stare returned to Connie. "What did you do?"

Connie sent me a glare filled with hate, but when she looked back at her mother, a tear slid down her cheek. "I wasn't trying to kill him."

"What?" Charlene trembled more violently, but leaned forward, her voice rising. "What? You? You..."

"I didn't mean to." Connie took another step back as she shook her head.

I could sense her getting ready to turn and run, and I wished I'd filled Susan in on the plan. Had her waiting outside. But... I hadn't been sure. So many things didn't make sense, but as I'd stared at the rabbit taunting Watson from his cage, it clicked. It didn't really make sense, but it clicked, and when it did, for the first time since discovering Adam's body, I got that little tingling in my gut.

If only I had trusted it enough to tell Susan.

"If you weren't going to kill Adam, then why did you go to the magic shop?" I gambled and infused my voice with aggression, hoping that if I confronted her, she'd get angry and not run. Though I wasn't sure what I was going to do after that. "Why would you leave your mom sleeping alone in the house, without help if she needed it, to go downtown when you knew Adam was with others playing board games?"

"I knew Mom was safe. I wasn't going to be gone that long," Connie bit at me before turning beseechingly toward her mother. "I wasn't. I really wasn't. I'd never leave you, you know that. I was just so... so mad. Furious."

"Why?" Tears were streaming down Charlene's face. "Why Connie?"

Connie's upper lip curved and the pleading left her voice, leaving only disgust. "Because I know what he does, every time he comes into town. Every time he writes you letters. That's why I quit giving them to you. Every single one he would ask you for money. And I knew you. You've never been able to tell him no. After Adam left for his stupid game night and you fell asleep I checked your money bag. And sure enough, there was over two hundred dollars missing, Mom. Two hundred! You gave that waste of space hard-earned money."

Charlene blinked as if she was struggling to understand the language. When she spoke, her words were barely more than a whisper. "You killed your brother for two hundred dollars?"

"No!" Connie screamed. "Of course I didn't kill him for money. I didn't mean to kill him at all! I saw that the money was gone and went to confront Adam. Tell him to get out of our town and leave our lives again and to stop bothering to come back. That was it, that's all I was going to do. I was surprised to find him there. It was late enough I figured he'd be at the bar drinking your money away."

Charlene sat with her hand over her lips. "Over money?"

"No!" Connie screamed louder, enough to make Watson growl, but she didn't notice. "Aren't you listening? Not over money, over him using you. Using us. Over you giving him everything he ever asked for and acting like he deserves it. Practically being over the moon every time he comes home or calls, even though he doesn't show up for years or keep up contact unless he needs something. *I* stayed home with *you*, Mom!" Connie sounded half crazed as she leaned in toward her mother so quickly I thought she was about to strike. Before I could move, she stopped herself. "I stayed home to take care of you. I never went to college, never got married, never had children of my own. I helped finish raising Sheila after Adam left. He got to leave, Mom. Sheila got to have a family. At least she helps... even with four... five kids, she still helps, but not Adam."

A little anger filtered into Charlene's features. "I've begged you to find your own life. How many times have I tried to move in with Glinda at the retirement—"

"I would *never* do that to you! I would *never* leave you alone like that." Still Connie screamed.

I slipped my fingers into Watson's collar, just in case.

"And I didn't mean to kill him. I'm not sorry he's dead, but I didn't mean to kill him." Connie jerked as if hearing her own words, and finished with a whimper, "I really didn't."

"You beat him, Connie." I kept my gaze trained on her, knowing the words I said would hurt Charlene, but I didn't see another way. "Adam was beaten black-and-blue. That wasn't an accident."

"I didn't do that." Connie whipped toward me with a hiss, then back at her mom. "I didn't." Tears fell faster now, and panic grew in her voice, replacing the anger. "I walked into the magic shop, the door was unlocked, and that stupid rabbit was screaming. *Screaming*! But there was Adam. In the dark, robbing the place." She whipped her hand toward her mom. "*That's* the kind of man he was, Mom! Robbing his friend's store." Connie looked at me again. "I couldn't believe it. I stood there for a few moments, utterly speech-less. He just kept rifling through things, took the money out of the cash register and laid it on the counter. I thought nothing he could do would surprise me. But he did. I wouldn't have guessed he could sink so low."

"So you beat him with a snow globe?" I decided to push again, try to get her to confess to all of it.

"You're not listening!" she screamed at me then. "I didn't beat him. He picked up that stupid snow globe himself, studied it for a second and then laughed and set it down. Who knows why. I guess he decided it wasn't worth bothering with. Then he started going through other things. I was so angry. After manipulating our mother out of two hundred dollars he goes and robs a store. *Robs a store!*" Again she sneered. Her voice dropped suddenly, became quiet and distant as if seeing the scene herself all over again. "I marched straight toward him, grabbed that stupid snow globe, and hit him on the back of the head." She raised a trembling hand as if she too was going to cover her mouth, but she paused above her heart. "I hit him."

"No..." Charlene groaned. "No, baby. You didn't. You didn't."

Connie cast a pain-filled look at her mother and glared back at me. "I *didn't* beat him. I didn't mean to kill him. I only hit him once. Just once. Then he dropped. I didn't even know he was dead until..." She backed away again, shaking her head. "I didn't realize. I was just so shocked at myself that I turned and ran. I swear I didn't know. I didn't." Another shake of her head and she bolted, rushing back the way we had come in.

Growling, Watson tried to pursue, but I held tight to his collar.

"Connie, no!" Charlene yelled, pushed up off the arms of her chair into a standing position. "Connie!" She tried to go after her daughter but stumbled on the footrest of the wheelchair, and she fell with a cry.

Connie glanced over her shoulder and paused at the sight of her mother on the floor. She looked toward the front door once, then at her mother. She whimpered and rushed back to kneel at her mother's side.

Charlene twisted and clutched her chest, struggling for breath.

"She's having a heart attack! I think she's... she's..." Connie whipped her gaze up to me and screamed again. "Call for help. Now!"

NINETEEN

I studied the empty space as I reshelved books in the mystery room—one of the customers had brought ten books up to the counter wanting my opinion on each, then went in an entirely different direction and bought a cookbook instead. Almost enough to make me wonder if I should be in sales. Without the sofa, I'd moved the purple portobello lamp beside the fireplace. The little room looked bigger, more spacious. It was probably a good thing, allowing more foot traffic. The Cozy Corgi was especially busy, with only a few more shopping days until Christmas, all the tourists, and of course all those wanting the latest gossip about the Sweitzers. Even so, I was ready to have the sofa back. I preferred the homier, cozier feel. *Especially* in the mystery room. That was part of the draw of mystery novels. They offered a puzzle, the thrill of twists and turns and surprises. But even more than that, was the comfort of answers being uncovered, justice being served, and the good guys winning. That deserved a charming spot by the fire to read.

"Fred."

When I jumped at my name combined with the tap on my shoulder, I realized just how lost I'd been to my thoughts. I turned to see Ben.

"Hey, I know you're busy, but do you mind if I take a break for a few minutes..." He gestured back to his identical twin standing a few feet away. "Nick already asked Katie, and she said she's fine in the bakery on her own for a little while."

Before I could answer, Watson came up and pressed his head to Ben's shin and received a hearty side scratch for his efforts.

I nearly asked where they were going, and if they could wait, considering how busy we were. But the twins never asked for anything, and they'd manned the store on their own constantly while I was out snooping, sometimes with Katie at my side. "Of course. You guys deserve a break. Let me just—" I twisted, shoving the final two books back into place, then dusted off my hands. "Perfect." I followed them back into the main room and stopped at the front desk.

Watson continued on with them as they wove side by side through tourists and other customers toward the front door.

Ben looked down at Watson and then back at me. "He can come with us, if you don't mind."

"Of course." I gave the three of them a little wave, pleased to see that Watson appeared to look back at me requesting permission as well instead of just hightailing it out with one of his favorite people.

As they walked out the door, Anna and Carl came in, followed by three adults. Anna held a rather large baby in her arms as she hurried toward me. "Fred!" She closed the distance with surprising speed and rounded the corner of the counter and pulled me into a hug with her free arm. We'd spoken on the phone the night before, but hadn't seen each other. "Fred, I—" Her words seemed strangled by thick emotion as she held me close.

The baby grunted.

"Let the rest of us have a chance, dear." I traded one Hanson hug for another as Carl took Anna's place. "We knew we could count on you." His voice was as thick as he whispered by my ear.

When at last the embraces ended, I searched both of their gazes. "Are you okay? I know the past few days have been exhausting for you and painful. Is Billy coming back now that his name is clear?"

The two of them exchanged glances, and then Anna looked around the crowded shop to see if anyone was listening in. Though there were people close to us, she must have decided it didn't matter if they overheard her. "Well... that's part of why we came over, besides wanting to thank you. Billy is cleared of murder. When he finally called us back after we told him, he..." She shook her head, her voice trailing off again.

"He confessed." Carl's face was somber. He seemed to swell with just a touch of pride. "And that's thanks to you as well. Because of you searching for the truth, you gave Billy that strength to be honest. I can't say the last time that we've seen that from our son."

"That's good. I'm glad he..." I cocked my head, waiting for it to make sense, but it didn't. "I'm sorry, I'm confused. What did he confess?"

"Oh." Anna's eyes widened in surprise. "We talked to him this morning. And then called Officer Green. I figured she spoke to you." She shifted the baby to her other arm.

I shook my head. I hadn't heard from Susan since the day before when she'd arrived at the Sweitzer house, right behind the ambulance.

That time Anna did lower her voice as she leaned

forward. "Billy got into a fight with Adam, right before he ran into that Delilah woman, apparently."

"From the way it sounds, it wasn't really a fight." Some of the pride left Carl's expression. "From the way Billy described it, though he says it's a little blurry as he'd been drinking, he beat Adam pretty severely."

The rest of the puzzle finally clicked into place. Adam's face. Billy's knuckles. "Wait a minute, you said you called Officer Green. You told her that?"

They nodded as one, but it was Carl who responded. "Billy may not have killed Adam Sweitzer, but what he did wasn't okay, not in the slightest. And..." Once more he exchanged looks with Anna. "While we swore to you we knew he hadn't killed that boy, we weren't entirely sure. It's made us look at the kind of man we raised. We've got to quit shielding him. Otherwise we'll lose him for good. So if there are consequences for what he did to Adam, then he'll have to face them."

Anna sniffed, wiped a tear from her eyes, but nodded her agreement. After a second, she cleared her throat, lifted her chin, and brightened. "We also wanted you to meet this handsome fellow." She held the chubby baby out toward me, and unlike the newborn, he was Gerber-baby adorable head to toe. "This is Tiny..." Her words trailed off once more, and she shook her head. "I mean, this is Timothy."

Carl chimed in, explaining, "Billy also told us what happened between him and the other boys in high school. The bullying, what happened during the *Christmas Carol* play. No more Tiny Tim. It seemed it was one of the taunts Adam threw at Billy the other night. One shove too far. Anyway..." He waved back toward the other people who had come in with them, who'd been standing several feet away. "This is the rest of our family."

As if becoming herself once more, Anna barged in, pointing at each of the women. "This is our oldest girl, Sarah, and this is Betsy. She's Tiny... er... *Timothy's* mother." She started to turn back to me, then as an afterthought, gave a dismissive wave toward the man. "Oh, and that's Betsy's husband, Timothy's father." I nearly laughed, she was most definitely herself again. I'd forgotten that she wasn't overly fond of her daughter's husband. Before I had a chance to shake their hands, Anna began looking around at my feet. "And where's the star of the show?" Without looking back, she swatted at Carl with her free hand. "Pass me the treat. Poor little Watson is probably thinking I forgot all about him."

Though she was abrupt, I was rather relieved to have Anna back to normal. "Watson's out at the moment. He went on a little adventure with the twins. They walked out as you were coming in."

"What? I didn't notice." Pure offense crossed her face. "And he didn't even try to get my attention."

The front door of the Cozy Corgi opened in that moment, drawing all our attention. For a second, from the cluster of people, it looked like a parade was coming through. Then the picture came into focus.

Percival, in his boysenberry fur and his bobbing mistletoe headband, entered with a flourish and threw his arms wide. "Special delivery!"

The entire bookshop stilled and turned to watch the show.

Behind Percival, with the Pacheco twins carrying either side, the newly reupholstered antique sofa entered the bookshop. Watson trotted happily mere inches behind Ben's feet.

Gary made up the end of the little parade, holding a

huge rectangular package but still managed to close the door behind them.

Beside me, Anna let out an appreciative gasp. "Oh, it's lovely."

"Keep following me, boys!" Percival waved his hand and continued his march toward the mystery room, casting me a wink. "Thanks for letting me borrow your handsome, strapping young men, dear niece of mine. I'll consider it payment for a quick turnaround."

The twins blushed in unison at Percival's words as they passed, and Gary rolled his eyes.

Though I instantly felt better at having it back in the shop, my heart sank as I looked at the sofa. It was too much. Too gold. Too... too much. Percival was going to kill me when I asked him to redo it.

The twins had to twist and turn the sofa to get it through the mystery room door. Watson attempted to help by prancing in and out between Ben's feet, but only made the situation worse.

I debated telling them to not even set it down. Just rip the Band-Aid off and get the awkward conversation with my uncle over with. Before I worked up the nerve, however, it was too late. They plopped it back into place, and Percival pointed to the lamp. "All right, one of you muscly young things move that for me please. We might as well take advantage of the view while we've got you."

His cheeks growing ever more scarlet, Nick silently retrieved the lamp and put it back exactly where it had been before.

"Marvelous!" Percival yanked on one of the tasseled pulls, turning it on, causing the soft dusty purple fabric of the ornate shade to glow. Then he stepped back.

I froze, confused for a moment. Some metamorphosis

happened. The couch was still too gold. Still too much with its muted swirls of purple and blue threaded through it, but... I took another step back, getting the full picture of it—the lamp, the glowing hardwood floors, the river rock fireplace, the surrounding shelves of books, the snow falling lightly outside the window. "It's..."

"Fabulous perfection, I know, darling." Percival swooped over and kissed me on the cheek.

Though I couldn't explain it, Percival was right. The room was even more wonderful than it had been before. And somehow, even with the touch of glam, even more cozy and inviting. "Thank you, I... don't even know what to say."

Gary placed the package on the floor in front of the sofa. "One more thing. An early Christmas present for you." He glanced down at Watson. "Although it's actually kind of for *you*."

"Well..." Percival gave me a little shove. "Don't just stand there, open it."

Feeling self-conscious, surrounded by so many family and friends, not to mention all the tourists, I walked to the package, knelt down, and began to open it.

Watson came over to inspect but didn't assist in peeling back the paper.

When I finally got it open, Gary came over and pulled the item out as Percival removed the box, making room, and he set it on the floor. "It's an ottoman."

"We found it months ago. It's a matching set to your sofa." Percival motioned between the carved legs of the sofa and the identically carved legs of the large square ottoman. "Gary has been refinishing it, and took a few inches off the legs, which killed me to do to such an antique, but..." He gestured dismissively toward Watson. "His Royal Queen Highness the Corgi is worth it."

The overstuffed ottoman was covered in the same fabric as the sofa but only a few inches off the ground, almost too low for a footrest, but the perfect size for Watson's little legs to manage to hop up. "You made it into a bed." I ran my fingertips over the fabric, once more marveling at how soft it was, considering its tapestry-like appearance. "It's wonderful."

Watson sniffed around, his nub of a tail holding perfectly still during his inspection.

Ben came over to assist, knelt down, and patted the top of the elaborate ottoman. "Hop up, buddy. It's for you."

Watson cocked one of his corgi eyebrows.

"See." Percival cast Gary a glare. "I told you it was a waste of time. That dog has no taste." He gestured toward the much-hated bobbing mistletoe. "Which, we already knew."

Ben patted the ottoman again. "Come on. Try it."

I patted it as well, and though he still looked skeptical, Watson hopped up. He took a few slow, cursory spins, sniffing every inch, then finally lay down in a ball.

"See," Gary retorted as he elbowed Percival. "*I* told *you*. He loves it."

Watson let out a contented sigh then stood once more and stretched, that time waving his nubbed tail in the air and then after a loud yawn, jumped down, trotted out of the mystery room, wove between the feet of customers, and curled up once again, this time in the muted sunshine pouring through the front windows.

Percival elbowed Gary back. "When are you going to learn to trust me? I know a diva when I see one." A grin crossed Percival's face as he watched Watson. "At least he has one redeeming quality."

· · ·

The rest of the day was lost in the torrent of customers and tourists. There was barely a moment to think. After Katie, the twins, and I put everything to rights, I told the others to go on. I was tired enough that I should head home, but I wanted to enjoy the new and improved mystery room. I turned off all the overhead lights but left on the Christmas trees and the softly lit garland. The sofa was even more beautiful under the glowing light of the portobello and in the flickering flames of the fire.

As soon as everyone else had left, proving he was the diva my uncle claimed, Watson hopped up on his new ottoman and fell asleep.

Though I wasn't sure if it was a demented notion or not, I'd already decided halfway through the day that I was going to read *A Christmas Carol* that evening. I'd even laid it at the end of the sofa after the customers had left. I'd just sat down, but before I could sigh or even pick up the book, there was a knock at the door.

Watson lifted his head, but only for a moment, before drifting back off to sleep.

I recognized Susan Green on the other side of the door from the lights of the Christmas trees and opened to her instantly. "Hi. Come on in."

She did, wordlessly, and I shut the door behind her. Susan was in her uniform, short hair pulled back in its usual fashion of the tight ponytail at her nape.

"Everything okay?"

She wrinkled her nose in a way that made it look like she'd just tasted something sour. "We... need to talk."

Uh-oh... "Okay." I debated for a split second. My plan had been to break in the new sofa by curling up with the book and enjoying the fire, my bookshop, and the Christmas trees. Was I willing to give that first experience to Susan instead? I realized I was and motioned toward the mystery room. "Sounds rather serious. Why don't we go sit?"

"Wow, someone went fancy." Susan's eyes widened, and she gave a little snort when she entered the mystery room. "And as if your furball didn't already think he was ruler of the world, now he has his own throne."

I started to be offended, then really looked at how Watson appeared as he lay, watching us, on his softly glistening ottoman. His throne... That's exactly what it was. Leave it to Percival. "Next Christmas I plan on getting him a crown."

"You would." Susan's tone held just the hint of a tease.

I sat on one end of the sofa, Susan on the other, Watson's throne between us at our feet. Though I could feel her nerves, I couldn't tell if what Susan had to say was going to be harsh or not. I figured it was best to simply get it over with. "What's going on? Is there a new development with Connie? Or with Billy? I spoke to Anna and Carl earlier today. They told me about what happened."

She waved it off. "No. Nothing about that. That's all pretty cut and dried now that it's been explained. I'm not sure what that will mean for Connie. From the way it looks, the hit she gave Adam on any other day wouldn't have killed him, but after the trauma from Billy, it was one impact too many. She'll still be charged with murder, but probably to a lesser degree. And as far as Billy..." She shrugged. "Thankfully, that's not my job. That's up to a jury and a judge. The only thing I had to do was find the facts." Her pale blue gaze flicked toward me. "And you. You're... good at finding facts."

It sounded like the words cost her, it was more of a compliment than I'd ever dreamed of hearing from Susan Green, and it left me speechless.

"I want to thank you. You helped clear my brother's

name." Susan rolled her eyes. "And you got that horrid bunny out of my house."

Though it took effort, that time I found words. I couldn't believe this was happening. "You're welcome. Glad I could help."

"I still don't like you," Susan rushed on, finally sounding more like herself.

It was almost a relief, and I laughed. "That's okay. I still don't like you either."

"You're one of the most annoying people I've ever met. You and your dog." She grinned, and again, surprised me. "But I do respect you. Enough to admit that I was wrong. I'd already said as much, but you've confirmed that the past few days. I think I can see you clearly now that Branson's gone, finally."

"I've actually been thinking the same of you." I had the impulse to reach across the sofa to touch her, but it was easily squashed. "I can't imagine what it was like in your position, being under Chief Briggs and Branson. Feeling like something was off, and yet having them—"

"No." She shook her head sharply. "That's not why I'm here. I don't want to do that. We both know what happened, and apparently we are *both* intelligent individuals. That doesn't mean we need to hash through it."

As ever, the woman could make me bristle, and I tried to keep the annoyance out of my tone, though I doubted I succeeded. "Okay then. You just came to say thank you. You're welcome. I'm glad your brother's free."

Then her face really soured, and she stared off into the fire. "That's the other reason I'm here. I owe you..." She swallowed, and it was clear it was taking every ounce of her willpower to force herself to say what came next. "I owe you an apology. Mark told Sharon and me today about... about..."

I flinched in surprise. I'd spoken to my stepfather and mother the night before, after I'd explained what really happened at Alakazam. I asked Barry to quit covering for Mark. Told him I couldn't handle more people making excuses for grown men behaving badly. I knew how much he hated confrontation, how soft-hearted he was, so I hadn't figured anything would change. Apparently he'd had a visit with Mark after all.

When Susan didn't speak again, I finished for her. "He told you he hadn't been paying rent to Barry for the past however many years?"

She nodded and flashed me another quick glance. "That doesn't mean your folks aren't the most annoying people I've met either. As landlords, they're forgetful, irritating..." She shook her head. "Not the point." She started to look back at the fire but then returned to me again. "It appears I've been wrong about your family too. I should've known better than to believe Mark, but... well, anyway... it was kind of Barry to not kick Mark out of the shop."

Though I hadn't spoken to Barry since the night before, I knew him well enough to be certain of what I said next. "He still won't. He's not going to do that to a father of four. Mark, and Glinda, for that matter, aren't in danger."

"I know." One corner of her lip curled slightly. "That stepfather of yours is annoying, a trait the two of you share, but he's kind. Something else the two of you share, apparently." She straightened. "But the rent is going to be paid."

"Susan..." That time I did reach across the couch and touched her. To my surprise she didn't pull away. "You don't need to do that. I know you love your brother, but this is *his* battle. If anything, the past few days have driven home that not much is accomplished when good people make excuses and rescue the lazy or dishonest people in their lives over and over again."

She barked out a laugh. "Oh, honey. I know we don't like each other very much, but I thought you knew me better than that. I'm *not* paying my brother's rent." She laughed again, and though her eyes were hard, they shone with a bit of glee. "*Oh, no.* Sharon's putting her foot down, finally. So am I. And God help us, so is Glinda. We're talking to a lawyer and will see if we can get any money from that stupid game Mark invented. Even a few thousand will help. It will go to the shop, and then any extra money that Mark has will go to supporting his family. That man spends a fortune on his own collection of memorabilia, costumes, and conferences. That ends now if he wants one bit of contact with any member of his family." She smiled. "He might be a waste of space, but I do know him. He'll come around. He's selfish, selfish, selfish. But deep down there, he loves his family."

I hoped she was right.

Susan shook her head and rolled her eyes again. "Good grief, I didn't mean to get into all of that. *That's* absolutely none of your business. But..." She softened once more. "I've been angry at your family for holding my brother back for years. And in one way, Barry has, but in the exact same way that Sharon and I have done as well, and Glinda, so I can't fault Barry any more than the rest of us. So... I just wanted to say... well, just wanted to apologize."

"Thank you." True to form, I decided to push the limit just a little further. "While we're having this heart-to-heart, I do have a question for you."

She cocked an eyebrow in way of response.

"Just out of curiosity, the next time I stumble on a dead body, are you going to tell me to keep my nose out of it?"

Her other brow rose. "You're planning on discovering another dead body? One would think you enjoy these murders."

I ignored that aspect and went for the jugular—even though it was manipulative, it was also true. "I'm just saying. Branson always went back and forth, one minute telling me how much he admired my investigating skills, then the next telling me to keep my nose out of it and mind my own business. I simply want to know what to expect from you."

She considered for a moment. "I'll repeat what I've already said to you. I find you annoying, condescending, pompous, arrogant, and often a brownnosing know-it-all. But—" She held up a finger as I started to object. "I respect you. I respect your intelligence, the integrity you display, and your search for the truth."

I waited a few seconds, but it appeared she was done. "Thank you, I think, but that didn't quite answer my question."

She smirked. "Well, that's interesting, isn't it?" She stood and dusted off her uniform pants even though there was nothing on them. "I think we're done here. I'll leave you and your fur factory to enjoy your thrones. I've got a house with no screaming bunny to get to." She stalked away, then waved over her shoulder. "Have a Merry Christmas, Fred. You and your fleabag."

The plastic elf bopped and swayed in time to "Grandma Got Run Over by a Reindeer" from his place beside the porcelain village spread out under the Christmas tree. Watson sat a few feet away glowering at it. I could practically hear him wondering if he could be quick enough to take a leap and rip the elf's head off before he got into trouble.

"Barry Adams, if you pinch that stupid thing's ear one more time, chestnuts won't be the only thing roasted on an open fire." Percival stretched out his long legs in the recliner beside my parents' Christmas tree. He cast a Watson-like look at the elf. "It's bad enough it sings and dances, but its fashion taste is beyond ludicrous. Nobody sane pairs tie-dye with fur."

"Your sister says differently. And she's *quite* sane." Barry gave Mom a squeeze, pulling her into the overstuffed jacket she'd given him that morning for Christmas. Though its tie-dyed pattern of red, green, and gold *did* seem at odds with its luxurious fur-lined hood.

"No. That wasn't a commentary on Phyllis. Notice that she's dressed sensibly—maybe too many crystal necklaces, but other than that, tasteful and elegant." Percival winked at my mother. "She simply demonstrated excellent gift giving. She knew the limits to your mental capacities when she married you. For crying out loud, we just had a Christmas feast where you pigged out on a ham roast that contained no pig. I'm pretty sure I heard the Christmas angels weeping when you cut into that thing. My sister simply bought you the appropriate gift *for you*." He gestured toward Barry as he wrinkled his nose. "Fur-lined tie-dye." He cast a quick glance at Gary, who was helping my sisters' husbands bring in dessert from the kitchen. "Quick, lover of mine, bring me enough wine that I can erase the fact the words *fur-lined tie-dye* ever left my lips, and enough to drown out that screeching elf."

Mom sighed indulgently. "It sounds like someone's in the mood to pontificate this afternoon."

Percival cast her a scowl as well, and Katie giggled.

As Gary, Noah, and Jonah passed out plates of sweet potato pie, Katie followed behind with the big bowl of her homemade whipped cream and dolloped each piece fresh. "I know some people like a little, and some people like a lot, just tell me when you have enough."

"Careful, Barry." Percival angled in the armchair to see around Katie. "I saw her slipping actual meat into the whipped cream."

"Katie, darling, please know that I love you because of *you* and that you're family by choice always and forever, no matter what," Mom piped up before another round of playful bickering could begin. "You don't need to do anything to earn that, but having our Christmas desserts be so much better with you around is certainly a wonderful bonus."

Beaming, Katie plopped an extra mountainous dollop of whipped cream on Mom's plate. "I'm glad you think so.

And I absolutely love the ring you made for me." The red stone glistened from Katie's finger.

"Garnet can help the flow of creativity." Mom smiled sweetly, but her tone had just a hint of teasing. "It's really self-serving. Any little bit I can assist to your marvelous baking creations helps us all."

"If that's the case, you should try on Fred's boots. We put on so many crystals, they're practically made for Wonder Woman. You bake like an Olympian god." Zelda motioned toward the crystal-and-precious-stone-encrusted cowboy boots that sat between the Christmas tree and the fireplace. "I'm so glad you like them, Fred. They looked really spectacular on you."

"They really do." Zelda's twin, Verona chimed in. "And I must say, in the months since we've made them, I'd forgotten how beautiful they are. Especially as they're twinkling by the fire."

"I love them. They're the most beautiful and glamorous cowboy boots I've ever owned." They were also the heaviest. My stepsisters had made them for me as a thank-you gift several months before, and I figured Christmas was the perfect day to wear them. I'd go straight to my parents, I wouldn't have to walk very far before I could take them off, and no one in town would see me.

"Imagine how beautiful they would be if you paired them with a skirt that wasn't the hue of baby poo."

"Oh, hush." Gary popped a forkful of his sweet potato pie into Percival's mouth before he could keep going.

That elicited another giggle from Katie. "Thank you! I even helped Fred get a couple different Christmas outfits, but she showed up today in mustard and pea green, again!"

Percival did quick work of the bite of sweet potato pie

and cocked an eyebrow toward Katie's sweater. "Is that a felt representation of the Nativity?"

Katie nodded enthusiastically. "Yes, but they're all mallards." She pointed to the center of the manger. "Baby Jesus is an egg."

"Well... *that's* not sacrilegious at all." Percival cast a side-mutter to Gary before addressing Katie. "I'm glad I'm not alone in trying to elevate Fred's fashion taste."

I sat on the floor next to Watson, warmed by the spicy aromatics of sweet potato pie, slipping Watson crumbs of crust, and simply enjoyed watching my family bicker, eat, and be together beside the Christmas tree and the fire.

Since wrapping things up with Adam's murder, the last several days leading up to Christmas had been a whirlwind at the shop. I hadn't realized how much I needed to do nothing but sit and be surrounded by those I loved with no other expectation than to be one of them. After a little while, Watson let out a dramatically large yawn, rolled over so that his back was pressed against my thigh, not-so-subtly demanding belly rubs, and fell asleep.

Once dessert had been devoured, my nephews and nieces ran off to play with their newly opened Christmas presents, or, more likely, check in with their friends on their cell phones, while we adults, and Watson, languished in the contented state brought on by warmth and too much food.

After a while, I realized Verona was speaking to me. I had been lulled into such a peaceful place that I was nearly asleep. "I'm sorry, what did you say?"

"I was just saying that I feel bad about how much you spent on the kids this year." Verona pointed to the four snow globes that sat on the other side of the Christmas tree. I'd decided to make things completely even, so I'd bought a snow globe for my older nephew and niece as well. "Zelda and I went into the magic shop a couple of days ago, hoping to get a few little stocking stuffers, and happened to look at the snow globes. I nearly fainted at the price tag."

"They are very nice." Zelda jumped in as if she feared I'd be offended. "I'm sure the kids will love them. They're… quite a keepsake."

All four of the kids had done an excellent job of offering heartfelt smiles and genuine thanks when they opened the snow globes. It was also clearly obvious the reactions had been rehearsed. By that point, I was certain they'd come to expect having to force gratitude anytime their aunt gave them anything.

I cast a reproachful glance at the four snow globes before refocusing on my step-sisters. "It's a long story on those things. It all kind of happened by accident."

"Next year why don't we make sure to have the kids write out a list for you in advance, like you've suggested."

"That's a great idea." Verona nodded in agreement at Zelda's plan. "And we'll put a price limit on it. With those four snow globes, you practically could've paid for the first semester of college."

Percival studied the snow globes, blinking thoughtfully. "Anyone else find it a little morbid that our resident Nancy Drew gave the children in our family the most recent murder weapons?"

The whole room went silent, and then Katie burst out laughing. A few heartbeats passed and everyone else joined in.

Once more, I glared at the snow globes. "I can't believe I didn't even consider that. And what a perfect excuse that would've been to have returned them."

Katie laughed even harder.

When the laughter softened, Barry spoke up. "I visited Glinda at Aspen Grove yesterday."

"Really? You're looking at retirement communities?" Percival leaned forward, not missing a beat. "Betting you'd age a lot slower if you ate some meat like the rest of us."

Mom chuckled, and Barry rolled his eyes before he continued, looking at me. "Charlene moved in with Glinda and seemed quite pleased with the new living arrangement. I know she's sad and hurting about Adam and Connie, but reading between the lines, her life is going to be better. I think in many ways she was a prisoner in her own home."

I'd wondered about that from the few things Glinda had implied about Connie's controlling nature around her mother. "And she's still feeling okay, healthwise?"

Barry nodded. "As far as heart attacks go, it was a small one. I guarantee now that her life is so much less stressful, and more enjoyable, for that matter, she should be completely fine. In fact, I bet she's enjoying that new grand-daughter of hers at this very moment."

To my surprise, there weren't very many people at Hidden Valley. There were only a couple of other families enjoying the old ski slopes turned sledding hills. The sun was setting and the day was getting colder, so maybe we'd missed the Christmas rush. With the snow falling, I couldn't even see very many tracks.

Though the kids had complained, not wanting to leave their electronics, their laughter cut cheerfully through the late-afternoon air. True to form, Watson was unpredictable. On some days, he'd test one paw in the snow and pull it back as if he were too delicate to ever consider letting the cold white stuff touch his fur, then others, he would bury his nose like a ground squirrel and tunnel through the depths, playing like a puppy. At the moment, the latter of his personalities prevailed, and I marveled at how nimble my short, overly 'fluffy' corgi could be as he leapt and twisted in midair while he chased the sleds and wallowed in the deep drifts of snow.

Katie, also true to form, had brought a picnic basket and was serving homemade hot chocolate and huge homemade cinnamon rolls she'd stuck in the oven while we'd hung out around the Christmas tree.

Once more, a sense of peace and gratitude washed over me. What a wonderful life I was living. Even though there'd been so much recent change, so much confusion. I was surrounded by family, friends I loved with my whole being, my fuzzy sidekick and partner in crime, and all encompassed by the most beautiful, mountainous scenery in the world.

"Well, well, look what the cat dragged in." Percival's voice cut through my reverie and got my attention. I did a double take when I noticed who he was pulling behind him.

Leo gave a little wave.

I straightened. "Hey!"

"Hey." Leo glanced out at the sledders. "Looks like fun. We talked about it, but we never got out here, did we?"

"I believe we went caroling instead." I was suddenly nervous. Which was irritating. Leo was my friend; there was no reason to be nervous.

Releasing Leo, Percival shoved a thermos of hot chocolate into my hands. "Here, this is for you two to share. Katie made it extra-large. And..." From one of the deep pockets of his boysenberry fur, he pulled out the atrocious headband with the mistletoe bobbing from a spring and shoved it on my head beside my earmuffs. "I think this would look adorable on you." He cocked an eyebrow. "Don't argue with your elders. You won't listen to my fashion advice, which is holding you back in this world, so give me this." He gave me a quick kiss on the cheek and then turned and walked away, swatting Leo's backside as he headed toward the others. "You kids be good. Remember, we're all watching." I was willing to bet the maniacal quality to his following laughter was intentional.

Leo stood, shifting foot to foot. "I hope you don't mind that I joined you. Katie and Percival took turns calling me all afternoon, telling me to come."

"Mind? Why would I mind?" It seemed he was nervous as well, which only increased my own sensation. "I told you to join us for family Christmas. I meant it."

"I know you did. But... I don't want to intrude. Not on family things." He stuffed his gloved hands into his pockets.

"Katie was with us. She was last year too."

"Yeah, but she truly is your family by this point."

"So are you." It stung that he thought he meant less to me, to any of us, than Katie.

"I know. But... it's different." Before he gave me a chance to consider that, he switched topics on a dime. "How'd the snow globes go over?"

"About as well as could be expected when you give your nephews and nieces overpriced murder weapons." I barked out a laugh, and from over his shoulder, I noticed Watson perk up at the noise. Realizing who was there, he began to bound over, a frantic smile across his muzzle.

"Murder weapon?" Leo's honey-brown eyes widened, and he grinned. "Oh my goodness, how did I not even think of that?"

"That's what I said!"

Before any other conversation happened, Watson crashed into Leo in a cloud of snow and fur.

"Buddy!" Instantly more at ease, Leo knelt and greeted his little worshiper. "Merry Christmas, little man." The two of them continued on in a ridiculous level of cuteness until Watson finally calmed to the place where he could contentedly sit by Leo's feet.

I searched for something to say, nervous again. "So... what did you do for your Christmas?"

"I called my family. It's been a while since I've missed Christmas with them." He hurried on as if he was afraid it sounded like he was complaining. "And then I went on the longest, most beautiful Christmas hike in the world. It was stunning, peaceful and serene. It reminded me how lucky I am, and how thankful I should be, to live here in such a wonderful place"—his eyes met mine and held—"filled with such wonderful people."

Part of me wanted to look away, but I couldn't. Or... maybe actually didn't *want* to. "I was literally just thinking that as I watched everyone sledding. I have so much more than I ever thought I would." Maybe it was because the snow had picked up, giving the illusion of privacy as the others blurred and dimmed in the distance, or maybe it was just those honey-brown eyes. "You're part of that. A big, big part of that. With everything that's going on, it's made me question... well... everything. Including who I can trust. Who isn't what they claim to be." I motioned toward my family frolicking behind the curtain of snow. "I don't have to do that with any of them or"—still I couldn't look away —"with you."

Leo took a step closer, and Watson scooted up to stay beside him. He didn't say anything for a few moments, then to my surprise pulled off his right glove and lifted his warm hand to my face, running his thumb over my cheek. He remained silent, though I thought I saw words flicker behind his eyes, emotions, possibly declarations. After a bit, his gaze flicked up above my head and a grin spread over his handsome face. "You're under the mistletoe."

I laughed, more a self-conscious thing than pure laughter. "Yes, Percival's not the king of subtlety, or queen as he would put it." I tilted the extra-large thermos of hot chocolate between us. "Nor Katie for that matter."

"No. They're not. And I kind of adore them for it." Reaching up, leaving the skin of my cheek cold from his touch, he bopped the mistletoe.

I could feel it wobbling above my head, and at our feet, Watson growled.

Leo chuckled, bopped it again, and was rewarded with yet another growl. Then he returned his gaze to mine. He took a breath, then let it out nervously and glanced behind, toward the sledders, where Percival and Katie were probably squinting their eyes trying to see us through the snow, and then he looked back.

For a second, just a second, I thought...

Instead he smiled softly and stroked my cheek once more before lowering his hand. "Merry Christmas, Fred."

My heart leaped, as did my nerves. But somewhere, in my gut, a puzzle piece clicked into place.

Katie's Quiche recipe provided by:

2716 Welton St Denver, CO 80205
(720) 708-3026

Click the links for more Rolling Pin deliciousness:

RollingPinBakeshop.com

Rolling Pin Facebook Page

KATIE'S QUICHE

Ingredient:
 1 1/3 Cup heavy cream
 3 eggs
 2 egg yolks
 2 Tbs flour
 salt and white pepper to taste
 small pinch of nutmeg

Directions
 1. Combine all ingredients well
 2. Pour with desired filling ingredients into par-baked shell (empty pie shell baked until almost done)
 3. Bake in preheated 350° oven for 45-60 minutes or until egg filling is set.

Filling ingredient options:
 *Crumbled bacon and Gruyère cheese (Quiche Lorraine)

*Cooked asparagus and shredded swiss cheese

*Roasted vegetables (red, orange and yellow peppers, zucchini, summer squash and red onions cut and roasted with olive oil and Herbes de Provence)

*Or any flavors you desire, you too can be as daring as Pastor Davis.

KATIE'S GARLIC INFUSED ARTISAN BREAD

First Step:

    Garlic

    3 ounces garlic cloves, coated in olive oil and roasted in 350 degree oven until tender. Set aside.

Second Step:

    1 ounce active dry yeast

    20 ounces (2 1/2 cups) warm water

    Place yeast and water in mixing bowl to activate the yeast.

Third Step:

    Add-

    2 pounds 11 ounces bread flour

    10 ounces warm water

    1 ounce salt

    2 ounces olive oil

    With dough hook, knead on low speed for 10 to 20 minutes.

    Add roasted garlic after about 10 minutes.

Fourth Step:

Place in greased bowl, cover loosely with plastic wrap, and put in a warm place.

After dough doubles in size, punch down and turn out onto flour-covered surface.

Fifth Step:

Cut into 5 - 1 pound pieces.

Roll each piece with both hands to form a ball. Place on baking parchment-lined sheet pans dusted with flour and cover with plastic wrap for 30 to 45 minutes.

Sixth Step:

Remove plastic wrap and let sit for another 10 to 15 minutes.

Seventh Step:

When ready to put in oven, dust top of each round loaf with flour, and with very sharp knife, score the top of each loaf.

Bake in 400 degree oven for 15 to 20 minutes or until dark golden brown. Should have a hollow sound when tapped.

KATIE'S SWEET POTATO PIE

Sweet Potato Filling

Ingredients:

  1 sweet potato (boil 40-50 minutes. Immerse in cold water to remove skin)

  4 ounces butter (1 stick), softened

  1 C sugar

  ½ C milk

  2 whole eggs

  ½ tsp nutmeg

  ½ tsp cinnamon

  1 tsp vanilla extract

  Pinch of salt

Directions:

  1. Preheat oven to 350°

2. After boiling and peeling sweet potato, mash with a fork. Some chunks will be okay.
3. Mix sweet potato, butter and sugar in mixing bowl with whisk attachment until combined.
4. Add milk, eggs, nutmeg, cinnamon, vanilla, and salt. Mix until thoroughly combined.
5. Pour into prepared pie shell (recipe below). Place on a baking sheet and bake for 55-60 minutes, until there is slight movement when you jiggle the pie.
6. Let cool. Slice and serve with whipped cream.

Pie dough for one 10" deep dish pie

Ingredients:
   1 ¼ C all-purpose flour
   4 ounces (1 stick) butter, chilled
   ¼ C ice water
   Pinch salt
   1 tsp white vinegar

Directions:

1. Cut cold butter into cubes about ¼" square.
2. Place flour in bowl and add butter. Using just your fingertips, coat all butter pieces with flour and work it in until the butter pieces are about the size of small peas.
3. Add salt, ice water and vinegar and just mix until not crumbly. It's okay if there is some wayward flour in the bowl.

4. Place entire mix on plastic wrap and wrap up, flatten slightly and place in refrigerator for about 30-45 minutes.

5. Take dough out of refrigerator, unwrap and place on floured surface.

6. With a rolling pin, start rolling out pie dough. Turning ¼ turn after each roll until the dough is about an eighth of an inch thick.

7. With a 10" deep dish pie pan next to you, fold pie dough circle in half and half again and place in pie pan and unfold and place evenly within the pie pan. DO NOT STRETCH THE DOUGH!

8. Trim edges and make any kind of decorative edge on pie dough that you wish.

9. Now the pie dough is ready for filling

AUTHOR NOTE

Dear Reader:

Thank you so much for reading the third collection of the Cozy Corgi Cozy Mystery series. If you enjoyed Fred and Watson's adventures, I would greatly appreciate a review on Amazon and Goodreads. You can review the collection, each book individually, or, even more wonderfully, both! Please drop me a note on Facebook or on my website (MildredAbbott.com) whenever you'd like. I'd love to hear from you. If you're interested in receiving advanced reader copies of upcoming installments, please join Mildred Abbott's Cozy Mystery Club on Facebook.

    I also wanted to mention the elephant in the room... or the over-sugared corgi, as it were. Watson's personality is based around one of my own corgis, Alastair. He's the sweetest little guy in the world, and, like Watson, is a bit of a grump. Also, like Watson (and every other corgi to grace the world with their presence), he lives for food. In the Cozy Corgi series, I'm giving Alastair the life of his dreams through Watson. Just like I don't spend my weekends solving murders, neither does he spend his days snacking on scones and unending dog treats. But in the books? Well, we both get to live out our fantasies. If you are a corgi parent, you already know your little angel shouldn't truly have free rein of the pastry case, but you can read them snippets of Watson's life for a pleasant bedtime fantasy.

Much love, Mildred

PS: I'd also love it if you signed up for my newsletter. That way you'll never miss a new release. You won't hear from me more than once a month, nobody needs that many newsletters!

Newsletter link: Mildred Abbott Newsletter Signup

ACKNOWLEDGMENTS

A special thanks to Agatha Frost, who gave her blessing and her wisdom. If you haven't already, you simply MUST read Agatha's Peridale Cafe Cozy Mystery series. They are absolute perfection.

The biggest and most heartfelt gratitude to Katie Pizzolato, for her belief in my writing career and being the inspiration for the character of the same name in this series. Thanks to you, Katie, our beloved baker, has completely stolen both mine and Fred's heart!

Desi, I couldn't imagine an adventure without you by my side. A.J. Corza, you have given me the corgi covers of my dreams. A huge, huge thank you to all of the lovely souls who proofread the ARC versions and helped me look somewhat literate (in completely random order): Melissa Brus, Cinnamon, Ron Perry, Rob Andresen-Tenace, Anita Ford, TL Travis, Victoria Smiser, Lucy Campbell, Sue Paulsen, Bernadette Ould, Lisa Jackson, Kelly Miller, Gloria Lakritz, and Reg Franchi. Thank you all, so very, very much!

A further and special thanks to some of my dear readers and friends who support my passion: Andrea Johnson,

Fiona Wilson, Katie Pizzolato, Maggie Johnson, Marcia Gleason, Rob Andresen- Tenace, Robert Winter, Jason R., Victoria Smiser, Kristi Browning, and those of you who wanted to remain anonymous. You make a huge, huge difference in my life and in my ability to continue to write. I'm humbled and grateful beyond belief! So much love to you all!

ALSO BY MILDRED ABBOTT

-the Cozy Corgi Cozy Mystery Series-

Cruel Candy

Traitorous Toys

Bickering Birds

Savage Sourdough

Scornful Scones

Chaotic Corgis

Quarrelsome Quartz

Wicked Wildlife

Malevolent Magic

Killer Keys (Coming Jan. 2019)

———

-Cordelia's Casserole Caravan-

New series beginning Spring 2019

Printed in Poland
by Amazon Fulfillment
Poland Sp. z o.o., Wrocław

54517101R00432